HAROLD

THE LAST OF THE SAXON KINGS

HAROLD

THE LAST OF THE SAXON KINGS

BY

EDWARD BULWER LYTTON

WILDSIDE PRESS

Dedicatory Epistle

TO THE

RIGHT HON. C. T. D'EYNCOURT, M.P.

I DEDICATE to you, my dear friend, a work principally composed under your hospitable roof, and to the materials of which your library, rich in the authorities I most needed, largely contributed.

The idea of founding an historical romance on an event so important and so national as the Norman Invasion, I had long entertained, and the chronicles of that time had long been familiar to me. But it is an old habit of mine to linger over the plan and subject of a work for years, perhaps, before the work has in truth advanced a sentence; "busying myself," as old Burton saith, "with this playing labour, — *otiosaque diligentia ut vitarem torporem feriandi.*"

The main consideration which long withheld me from the task was in my sense of the unfamiliarity of the ordinary reader with the characters, events, and, so to speak, with the very physiognomy of a period *ante Agamemnona*, — before the brilliant age of matured chivalry, which has given to song and romance the deeds of the later knighthood, and the glorious frenzy of the Crusades. The Norman Conquest was our Trojan War, — an epoch beyond which our learning seldom induces our imagination to ascend.

In venturing on ground so new to fiction, I saw before me the option of apparent pedantry, in the obtrusion of such research as might carry the reader along with the Author, fairly and truly into the real records of the time ; or of throwing aside pretensions to accuracy altogether, and so rest contented to turn history into flagrant romance, rather than pursue my own conception of extracting its natural romance from the actual history. Finally, not without some encouragement from you (whereof take your due share of blame !), I decided to hazard the attempt, and to adopt that mode of treatment which, if making larger demand on the attention of the reader, seemed the more complimentary to his judgment.

The age itself, once duly examined, is full of those elements which should awaken interest, and appeal to the imagination. Not untruly has Sismondi said, that " the eleventh century has a right to be considered a great age. It was a period of life and of creation ; all that there was of noble, heroic, and vigorous in the Middle Ages commenced at that epoch." [1] But to us Englishmen in especial, besides the more animated interest in that spirit of adventure, enterprise, and improvement of which the Norman chivalry was the noblest type, there is an interest more touching and deep in those last glimpses of the old Saxon monarchy which open upon us in the mournful pages of our chroniclers.

I have sought in this work less to portray mere manners, which modern researches have rendered familiar to ordinary students in our history, than to bring forward the great characters, so carelessly dismissed in the long and loose record of centuries ; to show more clearly the motives and policy of the agents in an event the most memorable in Europe ; and to convey a definite, if general, notion of

---

[1] Sismondi, History of France, vol. iv. p. 484.

the human beings whose brains schemed and whose hearts beat in that realm of shadows which lies behind the Norman Conquest.

> " Spes hominum cæcos, morbos, votumque labores,
> Et passim toto volitantes æthere curas." [1]

I have thus been faithful to the leading historical incidents in the grand tragedy of Harold, and as careful as contradictory evidences will permit, both as to accuracy in the delineation of character, and correctness in that chronological chain of dates without which there can be no historical philosophy, — that is, no tangible link between the cause and the effect. The fictitious part of my narrative is, as in " Rienzi " and the " Last of the Barons," confined chiefly to the private life, with its domain of incident and passion, which is the legitimate *appanage* of novelist or poet. The love-story of Harold and Edith is told differently from the well-known legend, which implies a less pure connection. But the whole legend respecting the *Edeva faira* (Edith the fair) whose name meets us in the " Domesday " roll, rests upon very slight authority considering its popular acceptance ; [2] and the reasons for my alterations will be sufficiently obvious in a work intended not only for general perusal, but which on many accounts,

---

[1] " Men's blinded hopes, diseases, toil, and prayer,
And wingèd troubles peopling daily air."

[2] Merely upon the obscure Manuscript of the Waltham Monastery ; yet, such is the ignorance of popular criticism that I have been as much attacked for the license I have taken with the *legendary* connection between Harold and Edith as if that connection were a proven and authenticated fact ! Again, the pure attachment to which in the romance the loves of Edith and Harold are confined has been alleged to be a sort of moral anachronism, — a sentiment wholly modern ; whereas, on the contrary, an attachment so pure was infinitely more common in that day than in this, and made one of the most striking characteristics of the eleventh century, indeed of all the earlier ages, in the Christian era, most subjected to monastic influences.

I hope, may be entrusted fearlessly to the young; while those alterations are in strict accordance with the spirit of the time, and tend to illustrate one of its most marked peculiarities.

More apology is perhaps due for the liberal use to which I have applied the superstitions of the age. But with the age itself those superstitions are so interwoven,—they meet us so constantly, whether in the pages of our own chroniclers or the records of the kindred Scandinavians,— they are so intruded into the very laws, so blended with the very life, of our Saxon forefathers, that without employing them in somewhat of the same credulous spirit with which they were originally conceived, no vivid impression of the people they influenced can be conveyed. Not without truth has an Italian writer remarked, " that he who would depict philosophically an unphilosophical age should remember that, to be familiar with children, one must sometimes think and feel as a child."

Yet it has not been my main endeavour to make these ghostly agencies conducive to the ordinary poetical purposes of terror; and if that effect be at all created by them, it will be, I apprehend, rather subsidiary to the more historical sources of interest than in itself a leading or popular characteristic of the work. My object, indeed, in the introduction of the Danish Vala especially, has been perhaps as much addressed to the reason as to the fancy, in showing what large, if dim, remains of the ancient "heathenesse" still kept their ground on the Saxon soil, contending with and contrasting the monkish superstitions by which they were ultimately replaced. Hilda is not in history; but without the romantic impersonation of that which Hilda represents, the history of the time would be imperfectly understood.

In the character of Harold, while I have carefully ex-

amined and weighed the scanty evidences of its distinguish-
ing attributes which are yet preserved to us, — and, in
spite of no unnatural partiality, have not concealed what
appear to me its deficiencies, and still less the great error
of the life it illustrates, — I have attempted somewhat and
slightly to shadow out the ideal of the pure Saxon character, such as it was then, with its large qualities undeveloped, but marked already by patient endurance, love of
justice, and freedom, — the manly sense of duty rather than
the chivalric sentiment of honour, — and that indestructi-
ble element of practical purpose and courageous will which,
defying all conquest and steadfast in all peril, was ordained
to achieve so vast an influence over the destinies of the
world.

To the Norman Duke I believe I have been as lenient as
justice will permit, though it is as impossible to deny his
craft as to dispute his genius ; and so far as the scope of
my work would allow, I trust that I have indicated fairly
the grand characteristics of his countrymen, more truly
chivalric than their lord. It has happened, unfortunately
for that illustrious race of men, that they have seemed to
us, in England, represented by the Anglo-Norman kings.
The fierce and plotting William, the vain and worthless
Rufus, the cold-blooded and relentless Henry, are no ade-
quate representatives of the far nobler Norman vavasours,
whom even the English Chronicler admits to have been
" kind masters," and to whom, in spite of their kings, the
after liberties of England were so largely indebted. But
this work closes on the Field of Hastings ; and in that noble
struggle for national independence the sympathies of every
true son of the land, even if tracing his lineage back to
the Norman victor, must be on the side of the patriot
Harold.

In the notes, which I have thought necessary aids to the

better comprehension of these volumes, my only wish has been to convey to the general reader such illustrative information as may familiarize him more easily with the subject-matter of the book, or refresh his memory on incidental details not without a national interest. In the mere references to authorities I do not pretend to arrogate to a fiction the proper character of a history ; the references are chiefly used either where wishing pointedly to distinguish from invention what was borrowed from a chronicle, or, when differing from some popular historian to whom the reader might be likely to refer, it seemed well to state the authority upon which the difference was founded.[1]

In fact, my main object has been one that compelled me to admit graver matter than is common in romance, but which I would fain hope may be saved from the charge of dulness by some national sympathy between author and reader ; my object is attained, and attained only, if, in closing the last page of this work, the reader shall find that, in spite of the fictitious materials admitted, he has formed a clearer and more intimate acquaintance with a time heroic though remote, and characters which ought to have a household interest to Englishmen, than the succinct accounts of the mere historian could possibly afford him.

Thus, my dear D'Eyncourt, under cover of an address to yourself, have I made to the Public those explanations which authors in general (and I not the least so) are often over-anxious to render.

This task done, my thoughts naturally fly back to the associations I connected with your name when I placed it at the head of this epistle. Again I seem to find myself

---

[1] Notes less immediately necessary to the context, or too long not to interfere with the current of the narrative, are thrown to the end of the work.

under your friendly roof; again to greet my provident host, entering that Gothic chamber in which I had been permitted to establish my unsocial study, heralding the advent of majestic folios, and heaping libraries round the unworthy work. Again, pausing from my labour, I look through that castle casement and beyond that feudal moat, over the broad landscapes, which, if I err not, took their name from the proud brother of the Conqueror himself; or when in those winter nights the grim old tapestry waved in the dim recesses, I hear again the Saxon thegn winding his horn at the turret door, and demanding admittance to the halls from which the prelate of Bayeux had so unrighteously expelled him,[1] — what marvel that I lived in the times of which I wrote, Saxon with the Saxon, Norman with the Norman, — that I entered into no gossip less venerable than that current at the court of the Confessor, or startled my fellow-guests (when I deigned to meet them) with the last news which Harold's spies had brought over from the camp at St. Valery? With all those folios, giants of the gone world, rising around me daily, more and more, higher and higher, — Ossa upon Pelion, — on chair and table, hearth and floor; invasive as Normans, indomitable as Saxons, and tall as the tallest Danes (ruthless host, I behold them still!), — with all those disburied spectres rampant in the chamber, all the armour rusting in thy galleries, all those mutilated statues of early English kings (including Saint Edward himself) niched into thy gray, ivied walls, — say in thy conscience, O host (if indeed that conscience be not wholly callous!), shall I ever return to the nineteenth century again?

But far beyond these recent associations of a single

---

[1] There is a legend attached to my friend's house, that on certain nights in the year Eric the Saxon winds his horn at the door, and *in forma spectri* serves his notice of ejectment.

winter (for which Heaven assoil thee!) goes the memory of a friendship of many winters, and proof to the storms of all. Often have I come for advice to your wisdom, and sympathy to your heart, bearing back with me in all such seasons new increase to that pleasurable gratitude which is, perhaps, the rarest nor the least happy sentiment that experience leaves to man. Some differences, it may be, — whether on those public questions which we see every day alienating friendships that should have been beyond the reach of laws and kings, or on the more scholastic controversies which as keenly interest the minds of educated men, — may at times deny to us the *idem velle, atque idem nolle;* but the *firma amicitia* needs not those common links; the sunshine does not leave the wave for the slight ripple which the casual stone brings a moment to the surface.

Accept, in this dedication of a work which has lain so long on my mind, and been endeared to me from many causes, the token of an affection for you and yours strong as the ties of kindred, and lasting as the belief in truth.

E. B. L.

PREFACE TO THE THIRD EDITION.

THE author of an able and learned article on Mabillon[1] in the "Edinburgh Review" has accurately described my aim in this work; although, with that generous courtesy which characterizes the true scholar, in referring to the labours of a contemporary, he has overrated my success. It was indeed my aim "to solve the problem how to produce the greatest amount of dramatic effect at the least expense of historical truth," — I borrow the words of the Reviewer, since none other could so tersely express my design, or so clearly account for the leading characteristics in its conduct and completion.

There are two ways of employing the materials of History in the service of Romance: the one consists in lending to ideal personages and to an imaginary fable the additional interest to be derived from historical groupings; the other, in extracting the main interest of romantic narrative from History itself. Those who adopt the former mode are at liberty to exclude all that does not contribute to theatrical effect or picturesque composition; their fidelity to the period they select is towards the manners and costume, not towards the precise order of events, the moral causes from which the events proceeded, and the physical agencies by which they were influenced and controlled. The plan thus adopted is unquestionably the more popular and attractive, and, being favoured by the most illustrious

[1] The Edinburgh Review, No. CLXXIX., January, 1849. Art. I., "Correspondance inédite de Mabillon et de Montfaucon, avec l'Italie." Par M. Valéry, Paris, 1848.

writers of historical romance, there is presumptive reason
for supposing it to be also that which is the more agreeable
to the art of fiction.

But he who wishes to avoid the ground preoccupied by
others, and claim in the world of literature some spot, however humble, which he may " plough with his own heifer,"
will seek to establish himself not where the land is the
most fertile, but where it is the least enclosed. So, when
I first turned my attention to Historical Romance, my
main aim was to avoid as much as possible those fairer
portions of the soil that had been appropriated by the first
discoverers. The great author of " Ivanhoe," and those
among whom, abroad and át home, his mantle was divided,
had employed History to aid Romance ; I contented myself with the humbler task to employ Romance in the aid
of History, — to extract from authentic but neglected
chronicles, and the unfrequented storehouse of Archæology,
the incidents and details that enliven the dry narrative of
facts to which the general historian is confined, — construct
my plot from the actual events themselves, and place the
staple of such interest as I could create in reciting the
struggles and delineating the characters of those who had
been the living actors in the real drama. For the main
materials of the three Historical Romances I have composed, I consulted the original authorities of the time with
a care as scrupulous as if intending to write, not a fiction,
but a history. And having formed the best judgment I
could of the events and characters of the age, I adhered
faithfully to what, as an Historian, I should have held to
be the true course and true causes of the great political
events, and the essential attributes of the principal agents.
Solely in that inward life which not only as apart from the
more public and historical, but which as almost wholly
unknown, becomes the fair domain of the poet, did I claim

the legitimate privileges of fiction; and even here I employed the agency of the passions only so far as they served to illustrate what I believed to be the genuine natures of the beings who had actually lived, and to restore the warmth of the human heart to the images recalled from the grave.

Thus, even had I the gifts of my most illustrious predecessors, I should be precluded the use of many of the more brilliant. I shut myself out from the wider scope permitted to their fancy, and denied myself the license to choose or select materials, alter dates, vary causes and effects according to the convenience of that more imperial fiction which invents the Probable where it discards the Real. The mode I have adopted has perhaps only this merit, that it is my own, — mine by discovery and mine by labour. And if I can raise not the spirits that obeyed the great master of Romance, nor gain the key to the fairyland that opened to his spell, at least I have not rifled the tomb of the wizard to steal my art from the book that lies clasped on his breast.

In treating of an age with which the general reader is so unfamiliar as that preceding the Norman Conquest, it is impossible to avoid (especially in the earlier portions of my tale) those explanations of the very character of the time which would have been unnecessary if I had only sought in History the picturesque accompaniments to Romance. I have to do more than present an amusing picture of national manners, — detail the dress, and describe the banquet. According to the plan I adopt, I have to make the reader acquainted with the imperfect fusion of races in Saxon England, familiarize him with the contests of parties and the ambition of chiefs, show him the strength and the weakness of a kindly but ignorant church; of a brave but turbulent aristocracy; of a people partially free, and naturally energetic, but disunited by successive immigrations, and having lost much of the proud jealousies of national liberty by submission to the preceding conquests of the Dane ; acquiescent in the sway of foreign kings, and with that bulwark against invasion which an hereditary order of aristocracy usually erects loosened to its very foundations by the copious admixture of foreign nobles.   I have to present to the reader, here the imbecile priestcraft of the illiterate monk, there the dark superstition that still consulted the deities of the North by runes on the elm-bark and adjurations of the dead.   And in contrast to these pictures of a decrepit monarchy and a fated race, I have to bring forcibly before the reader the vigorous attributes of the coming conquerors, — the stern will and deep guile of the Norman chief, the comparative knowledge of the rising Norman Church, the nascent spirit of chivalry in the Norman vavasours ; a spirit destined to emancipate the very people it contributed to enslave, associated, as it imperfectly was, with the sense of freedom : disdainful, it is true, of the villein, but proudly curbing, though into feudal limits, the domination of the liege.   In a word, I must place fully before the reader, if I would be faithful to the plan of my work, the political and moral features of the age, as well as its lighter and livelier attributes, and so lead him to perceive, when he has closed the book, why England was conquered, and how England survived the Conquest.

In accomplishing this task, I inevitably incur the objections which the task itself raises up, — objections to the labour it has cost, to the information which the labour was undertaken in order to bestow ; objections to passages which seem to interrupt the narrative, but which in reality prepare for the incidents it embraces, or explain the position of the persons whose characters it illustrates, whose fate it involves ; objections to the reference to authorities, where a fact might be disputed or mistaken for fiction ; objections to the use of Saxon words, for which no accurate synonyms could be exchanged ; objections, in short, to the colouring, conduct, and composition of the whole work ; objections to all that separate it from the common crowd of Romances, and stamp on it, for good or for bad, a character peculiarly its own. Objections of this kind I cannot remove, though I have carefully weighed them all. And with regard to the objection most important to story-teller and novel-reader, namely, the dryness of some of the earlier portions, though I have thrice gone over those passages, with the stern determination to inflict summary justice upon every unnecessary line, I must own to my regret that I have found but little which it was possible to omit without rendering the after narrative obscure, and without injuring whatever of more stirring interest the story, as it opens, may afford to the general reader of Romance.

As to the Saxon words used, an explanation of all those that can be presumed unintelligible to a person of ordinary education is given either in the text or a foot-note. Such archaisms are much less numerous than certain critics would fain represent them to be ; and they have rarely indeed been admitted where other words could have been employed without a glaring anachronism or a tedious periphrase. Would it indeed be possible, for instance, to convey a notion of the customs and manners of our Saxon forefathers without employing words so mixed up with their daily usages and modes of thinking as " weregeld " and " niddering "? Would any words from the modern vocabulary suggest the same idea, or embody the same meaning ?

One critic good-humouredly exclaims : " We have a full

attendance of thegns and cnehts, but we should have liked much better our old friends and approved good masters thanes and knights." Nothing could be more apposite for my justification than the instances here quoted in censure; nothing could more plainly vindicate the necessity of employing the Saxon words. For I should sadly indeed have misled the reader if I had used the word "knight" in an age when knights were wholly unknown to the Anglo-Saxon; and "cneht" no more means what we understand by "knight," than a templar in modern phrase means a man in chain mail vowed to celibacy and the redemption of the Holy Sepulchre from the hands of the Mussulman. While, since thegn and thane are both archaisms, I prefer the former,—not only for the same reason that induces Sir Francis Palgrave to prefer it, namely, because it is the more etymologically correct, but because we take from our neighbours the Scotch not only the word "thane" but the sense in which we apply it; and that sense is not the same that we ought to attach to the various and complicated notions of nobility which the Anglo-Saxon comprehended in the title of "thegn." It has been peremptorily said by more than one writer in periodicals, that I have overrated the erudition of William in permitting him to know Latin; nay, to have read the Comments of Cæsar at the age of eight. Where these gentlemen find the authorities to confute my statement, I know not; all I know is, that in the statement I have followed the original authorities usually deemed the best. And I content myself with referring the disputants to a work not so difficult to procure as, and certainly more pleasant to read than, the old Chronicles. In Miss Strickland's "Lives of the Queens of England" (Matilda of Flanders) the same statement is made, and no doubt upon the same authorities.

More surprised should I be (if modern criticism had not

taught me in all matters of assumption the *nil admirari*)
to find it alleged that I have overstated, not only the learning of the Norman Duke, but that which flourished in Normandy under his reign ; for I should have thought that
the fact of the learning which sprung up in the most thriving period of that principality, the rapidity of its growth,
the benefits it derived from Lanfranc, the encouragement
it received from William, had been phenomena too remarkable in the annals of the age and in the history of literature
to have met with an incredulity which the most moderate
amount of information would have sufficed to dispel. Not
to refer such sceptics to graver authorities, historical and
ecclesiastical, in order to justify my representations of that
learning which under William the Bastard made the schools
of Normandy the popular academies of Europe, a page or
two in a book so accessible as Villemain's "Tableau du
Moyen Age" will perhaps suffice to convince them of
the hastiness of their censure and the error of their
impressions.

It is stated in the "Athenæum," and, I believe, by a
writer whose authority on the merits of opera singers I am
far from contesting, but of whose competence to instruct
the world in any other department of human industry or
knowledge I am less persuaded, that I am much mistaken
when I represent not merely the clergy, but the young
soldiers and courtiers of the reign of the Confessor, as well
acquainted with the literature of Greece and Rome.

The remark, to say the least of it, is disingenuous. I
have done no such thing. This general animadversion
is only justified by a reference to the pedantry of the
Norman Mallet de Graville; and it is expressly stated in
the text that Mallet de Graville was originally intended for
the Church, and that it was the peculiarity of his literary
information, rare in a soldier, — but for which his earlier

studies for the ecclesiastical calling readily account, at a time when the Norman convent of Bec was already so famous for the erudition of its teachers and the number of its scholars, — that attracted towards him the notice of Lanfranc, and founded his fortunes. Pedantry is made one of his characteristics, — as it generally was the characteristic of any man with some pretensions to scholarship, in the earlier ages; and if he indulges in a classical allusion, whether in taunting a courtier or conversing with a " Saxon from the wealds of Kent," it is no more out of keeping with the pedantry ascribed to him than it is unnatural in Dominie Sampson to rail at Meg Merrilies in Latin, or James the First to examine a young courtier in the same unfamiliar language. Nor should the critic in question, when inviting his readers to condemn me for making Mallet de Graville quote Horace, have omitted to state that De Graville expressly laments that he had never read, nor could even procure, a copy of the Roman poet, — judging only of the merits of Horace by an extract in some monk‑ish author, who was equally likely to have picked up his quotation second-hand.

So, when a reference is made either by Graville, or by any one else in the Romance, to Homeric fables and per‑sonages, a critic who had gone through the ordinary edu‑cation of an English gentleman would never thereby have assumed that the person so referring had read the poems of Homer themselves, — he would have known that Ho‑meric fables or personages, though not the Homeric poems, were made familiar, by quaint travesties,[1] even to the most illiterate audience of the Gothic age. It was scarcely more necessary to know Homer then than now, in order to have

---

[1] And long before the date of the travesty known to us, and most popular among our mediæval ancestors, it might be shown that some rude notion of Homer's fables and personages had crept into the North.

heard of Ulysses. The writer in the "Athenæum" is acquainted with Homeric personages, but who on earth would ever presume to assert that he is acquainted with Homer?

Some doubt has been thrown upon my accuracy in ascribing to the Anglo-Saxons the enjoyments of certain luxuries (gold and silver plate, the use of glass, etc.) which were extremely rare in an age much more recent. There is no ground for that doubt; nor is there a single article of such luxury named in the text, for the mention of which I have not ample authority.

I have indeed devoted to this work a degree of research which, if unusual to Romance, I cannot consider superfluous when illustrating an age so remote, and events unparalleled in their influence over the destinies of England. Nor am I without the hope that what the Romance-reader at first regards as a defect, he may ultimately acknowledge as a merit; forgiving me that strain on his attention by which alone I could leave distinct in his memory the action and the actors in that solemn tragedy which closed on the Field of Hastings, over the corpse of the last Saxon King.

LIST OF ILLUSTRATIONS.

HAROLD,

THE LAST OF THE SAXON KINGS.

———•———

BOOK I.

THE NORMAN VISITOR, THE SAXON KING, AND THE DANISH PROPHETESS.

————

CHAPTER I.

MERRY was the month of May in the year of our Lord 1052. Few were the boys, and few the lasses, who overslept themselves on the first of that buxom month. Long ere the dawn the crowds had sought mead and woodland, to cut poles and wreathe flowers. Many a mead then lay fair and green beyond the village of Charing, and behind the isle of Thorney, amidst the brakes and briers of which were then rising fast and fair the Hall and Abbey of Westminster; many a wood lay dark in the starlight, along the higher ground that sloped from the dank Strand, with its numerous canals or dikes, and on either side of the great road into Kent. Flutes and horns sounded far and near through the green places, and laughter and song, and the crash of breaking boughs.

As the dawn came gray up the east, arch and blooming faces bowed down to bathe in the May dew. Patient oxen stood dozing by the hedgerows, all fragrant with blossoms, till the gay spoilers of the May came forth from the woods with lusty poles, followed by girls with laps full of flowers, which they had caught asleep. The poles were pranked with nosegays, and a chaplet was hung round the horns of every ox. Then towards daybreak the processions streamed back into the city through all its gates; boys with their May-gads (peeled willow-wands twined with cowslips) going before; and clear through the lively din of the horns and flutes, and amidst the moving grove of branches, choral voices, singing some early Saxon stave, precursor of the later song, — .

"We have brought the summer home."

Often in the good old days before the monk-king reigned, kings and ealdermen had thus gone forth a maying; but these merriments, savouring of heathenesse, that good prince misliked. Nevertheless the song was as blithe, and the boughs were as green, as if king and ealderman had walked in the train.

On the great Kent road the fairest meads for the cowslip and the greenest woods for the bough surrounded a large building that once had belonged to some voluptuous Roman, now all defaced and despoiled; but the boys and the lasses shunned those demesnes; and even in their mirth, as they passed homeward along the road, and saw near the ruined walls and timbered outbuildings gray Druid stones (that spoke of an age before either Saxon or Roman invader) gleaming through the dawn, the song was hushed, the very youngest crossed themselves; and the elder, in solemn whispers, suggested the precaution of changing the song into a psalm. For in that old building dwelt Hilda, of famous and dark repute, — Hilda, who, despite all law and canon, was still believed to practise the dismal arts of the Wicca and Morthwyrtha (the witch and worshipper of the dead). But once out of sight of those fearful precincts, the psalm was forgotten; and again broke, loud, clear, and silvery, the joyous chorus.

So, entering London about sunrise, doors and windows were duly wreathed with garlands; and every village in the suburbs had its May-pole, which stood in its place all the year. On that happy day labour rested; ceorl and theowe had alike a holiday to dance and tumble round the May-pole; and thus, on the first of May, Youth and Mirth and Music "brought the summer home."

The next day you might still see where the buxom bands had been; you might track their way by fallen flowers and green leaves, and the deep ruts made by oxen (yoked often in teams from twenty to forty, in the wains that carried home the poles); and fair and frequent throughout the land, from any eminence, you might behold the hamlet swards still crowned with the May trees, and the air still seemed fragrant with their garlands.

It is on that second day of May, 1052, that my story opens, at the house of Hilda, the reputed Morthwyrtha. It stood upon a gentle and verdant height; and even through all the barbarous mutilation it had undergone from barbarian hands, enough was left strikingly to contrast the ordinary abodes of the Saxon.

The remains of Roman art were indeed still numerous throughout England, but it happened rarely that the Saxon had chosen his home amidst the villas of those noble and primal conquerors. Our first forefathers were more inclined to destroy than to adapt.

By what chance this building became an exception to the ordinary rule, it is now impossible to conjecture, but from a very remote period it had sheltered successive races of Teuton lords.

The changes wrought in the edifice were mournful and grotesque. What was now the hall had evidently been the atrium; the round shield, with its pointed boss, the spear, sword, and small curved sæx of the early Teuton, were suspended from the columns on which once had been wreathed the flowers; in the centre of the floor, where fragments of the old mosaic still glistened from the hard-pressed paving of clay and lime, what now was the fireplace had been the impluvium, and the smoke went sullenly through the aperture in the roof, made of old to receive the rains of heaven. Around the hall were still left the old cubicula, or dormitories,— small, high, and lighted but from the doors,— which now served for the sleeping-rooms of the humbler guest or the household servant; while at the farther end of the hall, the wide space between the columns, which had once given

ample vista from graceful awnings into tablinum and virida-
rium, was filled up with rude rubble and Roman bricks,
leaving but a low, round, arched door, that still led into the
tablinum. But that tablinum, formerly the gayest state-
room of the Roman lord, was now filled with various lumber,
piles of fagots, and farming utensils. On either side of
this desecrated apartment stretched, to the right, the old
lararium, stripped of its ancient images of ancestor and
god; to the left, what had been the gynœcium, or women's
apartment.

One side of the ancient peristyle, which was of vast extent,
was now converted into stabling, sties for swine, and stalls
for oxen. On the other side was constructed a Christian
chapel, made of rough oak planks, fastened by plates at the
top, and with a roof of thatched reeds. The columns and
wall at the extreme end of the peristyle were a mass of ruins,
through the gigantic rents of which loomed a grassy hillock,
its sides partially covered with clumps of furze. On this
hillock were the mutilated remains of an ancient Druidical
crommel, in the centre of which (near a funeral mound, or
barrow, with the bautastean, or gravestone, of some early
Saxon chief at one end) had been sacrilegiously placed an
altar to Thor, as was apparent both from the shape, from a
rude, half-obliterated, sculptured relief of the god, with his
lifted hammer, and a few Runic letters. Amidst the temple
of the Briton the Saxon had reared the shrine of his triumphant war-god.

Now still, amidst the ruins of that extreme side of the
peristyle which opened to this hillock were left, first, an
ancient Roman fountain, that now served to water the swine,
and next, a small sacellum, or fane to Bacchus (as relief and
frieze, yet spared, betokened). Thus the eye, at one survey,
beheld the shrines of four creeds, — the Druid, mystical and
symbolical; the Roman, sensual, but humane; the Teutonic,
ruthless and destroying; and, latest risen and surviving all,
though as yet with but little of its gentler influence over the
deeds of men, the edifice of the Faith of Peace.

Across the peristyle theowes and swineherds passed to and

fro; in the atrium men of a higher class, half armed, were, some drinking, some at dice, some playing with huge hounds, or caressing the hawks that stood grave and solemn on their perches.

The lararium was deserted. The gynœcium was still, as in the Roman time, the favoured apartment of the female portion of the household, and indeed bore the same name;[1] and with the group there assembled we have now to do.

The appliances of the chamber showed the rank and wealth of the owner. At that period the domestic luxury of the rich was infinitely greater than has been generally supposed. The industry of the women decorated wall and furniture with needlework and hangings; and as a thegn forfeited his rank if he lost his lands, so the higher orders of an aristocracy rather of wealth than birth had usually a certain portion of superfluous riches, which served to flow towards the bazaars of the East and the nearer markets of Flanders and Saracenic Spain.

In this room the walls were draped with silken hangings richly embroidered. The single window was glazed with a dull gray glass.[2] On a beaufet were ranged horns tipped with silver, and a few vessels of pure gold. A small circular table in the centre was supported by symbolical monsters quaintly carved. At one side of the wall, on a long settle, some half-a-dozen handmaids were employed in spinning; remote from them, and near the window, sat a woman advanced in years, and of a mien and aspect singularly majestic. Upon a small tripod before her was a Runic manuscript, and an inkstand

---

[1] "The apartment in which the Anglo-Saxon women lived, was called Gynecium." — FOSBROOKE, vol. ii. p. 570.

[2] Glass, introduced about the time of Bede, was more common then in the houses of the wealthy, whether for vessels or windows, than in the much later age of the gorgeous Plantagenets. Alfred, in one of his poems, introduces glass as a familiar illustration, —

> So oft the mild sea
> With south wind
> As gray glass clear
> Becomes grimly troubled.
>
> SHARON TURNER.

of elegant form, with a silver graphium, or pen. At her feet
reclined a girl somewhat about the age of sixteen, her long
hair parted across her forehead and falling far down her
shoulders.   Her dress was a linen under-tunic, with long
sleeves, rising high to the throat, and without one of the
modern artificial restraints of the shape; the simple belt sufficed to show the slender proportions and delicate outline of
the wearer.   The colour of the dress was of the purest white,
but its hems or borders were richly embroidered.   This girl's
beauty was something marvellous.   In a land proverbial for
fair women, it had already obtained her the name of "the
fair."   In that beauty were blended, not as yet without a
struggle for mastery, the two expressions seldom united in
one countenance, the soft and the noble.   Indeed in the whole
aspect there was the evidence of some internal struggle; the
intelligence was not yet complete; the soul and heart were
not yet united; and Edith the Christian maid dwelt in the
home of Hilda the heathen prophetess.   The girl's blue eyes,
rendered dark by the shade of their long lashes, were fixed
intently upon the stern and troubled countenance which was
bent upon her own, but bent with that abstract gaze which
shows that the soul is absent from the sight.   So sat Hilda,
and so reclined her grandchild Edith.

   "Grandam," said the girl, in a low voice and after a long
pause; and the sound of her voice so startled the handmaids
that every spindle stopped for a moment, and then plied with
renewed activity, — "Grandam, what troubles you?   Are you
not thinking of the great earl and his fair sons, now outlawed
far over the wide seas?"

As the girl spoke, Hilda started slightly, like one awakened
from a dream; and when Edith had concluded her question,
she rose slowly to the height of a statue, unbowed by her
years, and towering far above even the ordinary standard of
men; and turning from the child, her eye fell upon the row
of silent maids, each at her rapid, noiseless, stealthy work.
"Ho!" said she, her cold and haughty eye gleaming as she
spoke; "yesterday they brought home the summer, to-day
ye aid to bring home the winter.   Weave well, heed well

warf and woof; Skulda[1] is amongst ye, and her pale fingers guide the web!"

The maidens lifted not their eyes, though in every cheek the colour paled at the words of the mistress. The spindles revolved, the thread shot, and again there was silence more freezing than before.

"Askest thou," said Hilda at length, passing to the child, as if the question so long addressed to her ear had only just reached her mind, — "askest thou if I thought of the earl and his fair sons? Yea, I heard the smith welding arms on the anvil, and the hammer of the shipwright shaping strong ribs for the horses of the sea. Ere the reaper has bound his sheaves, Earl Godwin will scare the Normans in the halls of the monk-king, as the hawk scares the brood in the dovecot. Weave well, heed well warf and woof, nimble maidens! Strong be the texture, for biting is the worm."

"What weave they, then, good grandmother?" asked the girl, with wonder and awe in her soft mild eyes.

"The winding-sheet of the great!"

Hilda's lips closed; but her eyes, yet brighter than before, gazed upon space, and her pale hand seemed tracing letters, like runes, in the air. Then slowly she turned, and looked forth through the dull window. "Give me my coverchief and my staff," said she, quickly.

Every one of the handmaids, blithe for excuse to quit a task which seemed recently commenced and was certainly not endeared to them by the knowledge of its purpose communicated to them by the lady, rose to obey.

Unheeding the hands that vied with each other, Hilda took the hood, and drew it partially over her brow. Leaning lightly on a long staff, the head of which formed a raven, carved from some wood stained black, she passed into the hall, and thence through the desecrated tablinum, into the mighty court formed by the shattered peristyle; there she stopped, mused a moment, and called on Edith. The girl was soon by her side.

"Come with me. There is a face you shall see but twice

[1] Skulda, the Norna, or Fate, that presided over the future.

in life, — this day — " And Hilda paused, and the rigid and almost colossal beauty of her countenance softened.

"And when again, my grandmother?"

"Child, put thy warm hand in mine. So! the vision darkens from me. When again, saidst thou, Edith? Alas, I know not."

While thus speaking, Hilda passed slowly by the Roman fountain and the heathen fane, and ascended the little hillock. There, on the opposite side of the summit, backed by the Druid crommel and the Teuton altar, she seated herself deliberately on the sward.

A few daisies, primroses, and cowslips grew around; these Edith began to pluck, — singing, as she wove, a simple song, that, not more by the dialect than the sentiment, betrayed its origin in the ballad of the Norse,[1] which had in its more careless composition a character quite distinct from the artificial poetry of the Saxons. The song may be thus imperfectly rendered: —

"Merrily the throstle sings
  Amid the merry May;
The throstle sings but to my ear, —
  My heart is far away!

"Blithely bloometh mead and bank,
  And blithely buds the tree;
And hark! they bring the summer home;
  It has no home with me!

"They have outlawed *him*, — my Summer!
  An outlaw far away!
The birds may sing, the flowers may bloom, —
  Oh, give me back my May!"

As she came to the last line, her soft low voice seemed to awaken a chorus of sprightly horns and trumpets, and certain

---

[1] The historians of our literature have not done justice to the great influence which the poetry of the Danes has had upon our early national muse. I have little doubt but that to that source may be traced the minstrelsy of our borders and the Scottish Lowlands, while even in the central counties the example and exertions of Canute must have had considerable effect on the taste and spirit of our Scots. That great prince afforded the amplest encouragement to Scandinavian poetry, and Olaus names eight Danish poets who flourished at his court.

other wind instruments peculiar to the music of that day. The hillock bordered the high-road to London, which then wound through wastes of forest land; and now emerging from the trees to the left appeared a goodly company. First came two riders abreast, each holding a banner. On the one was depicted the cross and five martlets, the device of Edward, afterwards surnamed the Confessor; on the other, a plain broad cross with a deep border round it, and the streamer shaped into sharp points.

The first was familiar to Edith, who dropped her garland to gaze on the approaching pageant; the last was strange to her. She had been accustomed to see the banner of the great Earl Godwin by the side of the Saxon king; and she said almost indignantly, —

"Who dares, sweet grandam, to place banner or pennon where Earl Godwin's ought to float?"

"Peace!" said Hilda, "peace, and look!"

Immediately behind the standard-bearers came two figures, strangely dissimilar indeed in mien, in years, in bearing; each bore on his left wrist a hawk. The one was mounted on a milk-white palfrey, with housings inlaid with gold and uncut jewels. Though not really old, for he was much on this side of sixty, both his countenance and carriage evinced age. His complexion indeed was extremely fair, and his cheeks ruddy; but the visage was long and deeply furrowed, and from beneath a bonnet not dissimilar to those in use among the Scotch, streamed hair long and white as snow, mingling with a large and forked beard. White seemed his chosen colour. White was the upper tunic, clasped on his shoulder with a broad ouche, or brooch; white the woollen leggings fitted to somewhat emaciated limbs; and white the mantle, though broidered with a broad hem of gold and purple. The fashion of his dress was that which well became a noble person, but it suited ill the somewhat frail and graceless figure of the rider. Nevertheless, as Edith saw him, she rose, with an expression of deep reverence on her countenance, and saying, "It is our lord the king," advanced some steps down the hillock, and there stood, her arms folded on her breast, and quite forgetful, in her innocence and youth, that she had left the house without the cloak and coverchief which were deemed indispensable to the fitting appearance of maid and matron when they were seen abroad.

"Fair sir, and brother mine," said the deep voice of the younger rider, in the Romance or Norman tongue, "I have heard that the small people of whom my neighbours the Bretons tell us much, abound greatly in this fair land of yours; and if I were not by the side of one whom no creature unassoilzied and unbaptized dare approach, by sweet Saint Valery I should say yonder stands one of those same *gentilles fées!*"

King Edward's eye followed the direction of his companion's outstretched hand, and his quiet brow slightly contracted as he beheld the young form of Edith standing motionless a few yards before him, with the warm May wind lifting and playing with her long golden locks. He checked his palfrey, and murmured some Latin words which the knight beside him recognized as a prayer, and to which, doffing his cap, he added an Amen, in a tone of such unctuous gravity that the royal saint rewarded him with a faint approving smile, and an affectionate "Bene, bene, Piosissime."

Then inclining his palfrey's head towards the knoll, he motioned to the girl to approach him. Edith, with a heightened colour, obeyed, and came to the roadside. The standard-bearers halted, as did the king and his comrade; the procession behind halted, — thirty knights, two bishops, eight abbots, all on fiery steeds and in Norman garb, squires and attendants on foot, — a long and pompous retinue, — they halted all. Only a stray hound or two broke from the rest, and wandered into the forest land with heads trailing.

"Edith, my child," said Edward, still in Norman-French, for he spoke his own language with hesitation, and the Romance tongue, which had long been familiar to the higher classes in England, had since his accession become the only language in use at court, and as such every one of 'Eorlkind' was supposed to speak it, — "Edith, my child, thou hast not forgotten my lessons, I trow; thou singest the hymns

I gave thee, and neglectest not to wear the relic round thy neck."

The girl hung her head, and spoke not.

"How comes it then," continued the king, with a voice to which he in vain endeavoured to impart an accent of severity, "how comes it, O little one, that thou, whose thoughts should be lifted already above this carnal world, and eager for the service of Mary the chaste and blessed, standest, thus hoodless and alone on the waysides, a mark for the eyes of men? Go to, it is nought."

Thus reproved, and in presence of so large and brilliant a company, the girl's colour went and came, her breast heaved high; but with an effort beyond her age she checked her tears, and said meekly, — "My grandmother, Hilda, bade me come with her, and I came."

"Hilda!" said the king, backing his palfrey with apparent perturbation; "but Hilda is not with thee, — I see her not."

As he spoke, Hilda rose; and so suddenly did her tall form appear on the brow of the hill that it seemed as if she had emerged from the earth. With a light and rapid stride she gained the side of her grandchild; and after a slight and haughty reverence, said, —

"Hilda is here; what wants Edward the King with his servant Hilda?"

"Nought, nought," said the king, hastily, and something like fear passed over his placid countenance; "save, indeed," he added with a reluctant tone, as of that of a man who obeys his conscience against his inclination, "that I would pray thee to keep this child pure to threshold and altar, as is meet for one whom our Lady the Virgin in due time will elect to her service."

"Not so, son of Ethelred, son of Woden; the last descendant of Penda should live, not to glide a ghost amidst cloisters, but to rock children for war in their father's shield. Few men are there yet like the men of old; and while the foot of the foreigner is on the Saxon soil no branch of the stem of Woden should be nipped in the leaf."

"*Per la resplendar Dé,*[1] bold dame," cried the knight by the side of Edward, while a lurid flush passed over his cheek of bronze, "but thou art too glib of tongue for a subject, and pratest overmuch of Woden, the Paynim, for the lips of a Christian matron."

Hilda met the flashing eye of the knight with a brow of lofty scorn, on which still a certain terror was visible.

"Child," she said, putting her hand upon Edith's fair locks, "this is the man thou shalt see but twice in thy life; look up, and mark well!"

Edith instinctively raised her eyes, and, once fixed upon the knight, they seemed chained as by a spell. His vest, of a cramoisay so dark that it seemed black beside the snowy garb of the Confessor, was edged by a deep band of embroidered gold; leaving perfectly bare his firm, full throat, — firm and full as a column of granite, — a short jacket or manteline of fur, pendent from the shoulders, left developed in all its breadth a breast that seemed meet to stay the march of an army; and on the left arm, curved to support the falcon, the vast muscles rose, round and gnarled, through the close sleeve.

In height he was really but little above the stature of many of those present;[2] nevertheless, so did his port, his air, the nobility of his large proportions, fill the eye that he seemed to tower immeasurably above the rest.

His countenance was yet more remarkable than his form; still in the prime of youth, he seemed at the first glance younger, at the second older, than he was. At the first glance younger; for his face was perfectly shaven, without even the mustache which the Saxon courtier, in imitating the Norman, still declined to surrender; and the smooth visage and bare throat sufficed in themselves to give the air of youth to that dominant and imperious presence. His small skull-cap left unconcealed his forehead, shaded with short thick hair, uncurled, but black and glossy as the wings of a raven. It was on that forehead that time had set its trace; it was knit into

1 " By the splendour of God."
2 See Note A at the end of this volume.

a frown over the eyebrows; lines deep as furrows crossed its broad but not elevated expanse. That frown spoke of hasty ire and the habit of stern command; those furrows spoke of deep thought and plotting scheme: the one betrayed but temper and circumstance; the other, more noble, spoke of the character and the intellect. The face was square, and the regard lion-like; the mouth — small, and even beautiful in outline — had a sinister expression in its exceeding firmness; and the jaw, vast, solid, as if bound in iron, showed obstinate, ruthless, determined will, — such a jaw as belongs to the tiger amongst beasts, and the conqueror amongst men; such as it is seen in the effigies of Cæsar, of Cortes, of Napoleon.

That presence was well calculated to command the admiration of women, not less than the awe of men. But no admiration mingled with the terror that seized the girl as she gazed long and wistfully upon the knight. The fascination of the serpent on the bird held her mute and frozen. Never was that face forgotten; often in after-life it haunted her in the noonday, it frowned upon her dreams.

"Fair child," said the knight, fatigued at length by the obstinacy of the gaze, while that smile peculiar to those who have commanded men relaxed his brow, and restored the native beauty to his lip, — "fair child, learn not from thy peevish grandam so uncourteous a lesson as hate of the foreigner. As thou growest into womanhood, know that Norman knight is sworn slave to lady fair;" and doffing his cap, he took from it an uncut jewel set in Byzantine filigree work. "Hold out thy lap, my child; and when thou hearest the foreigner scoffed, set this bauble in thy locks, and think kindly of William Count of the Normans."[1]

He dropped the jewel on the ground as he spoke; for Edith,

---

[1] It is noticeable that the Norman dukes did not call themselves Counts or Dukes of Normandy, but of the Normans; and the first Anglo-Norman kings, till Richard the First, styled themselves Kings of the English, not of England. In both Saxon and Norman chronicles William usually bears the title of Count (*Comes*); but in this tale he will be generally called Duke, as a title more familiar to us.

shrinking and unsoftened towards him, held no lap to receive it; and Hilda, to whom Edward had been speaking in a low voice, advanced to the spot and struck the jewel with her staff under the hoofs of the king's palfrey.

"Son of Emma, the Norman woman, who sent thy youth into exile, trample on the gifts of thy Norman kinsman; and if, as men say, thou art of such gifted holiness that Heaven grants thy hand the power to heal, and thy voice the power to curse, heal thy country, and curse the stranger!"

She extended her right arm to William as she spoke; and such was the dignity of her passion, and such its force, that an awe fell upon all. Then dropping her hood over her face, she slowly turned away, regained the summit of the knoll, and stood erect beside the altar of the Northern god, her face invisible through the hood drawn completely over it, and her form motionless as a statue.

"Ride on!" said Edward, crossing himself.

"Now, by the bones of Saint Valery," said William, after a pause, in which his dark keen eye noted the gloom upon the king's gentle face, "it moves much my simple wonder how even presence so saintly can hear without wrath words so unleal and foul. Gramercy, and the proudest dame in Normandy (and I take her to be wife to my stoutest baron, William Fitzosborne) had spoken thus to me —"

"Thou wouldst have done as I, my brother," interrupted Edward, — "prayed to our Lord to pardon her, and rode on pitying."

William's lip quivered with ire, yet he curbed the reply that sprang to it, and he looked, with affection genuinely more akin to admiration than scorn, upon his fellow-prince. For, fierce and relentless as the duke's deeds were, his faith was notably sincere; and while this made, indeed, the prince's chief attraction to the pious Edward, so, on the other hand, this bowed the duke in a kind of involuntary and superstitious homage to the man who sought to square deeds to faith. It is ever the case with stern and stormy spirits, that the meek ones which contrast them steal strangely into their affections. This principle of human nature can alone account for the enthusiastic devotion which the mild sufferings of the Saviour awoke in the fiercest exterminators of the North. In proportion, often, to the warrior's ferocity, was his love to that Divine model, at whose sufferings he wept, to whose tomb he wandered barefoot, and whose example of compassionate forgiveness he would have thought himself the basest of men to follow!

"Now, by my halidame, I honour and love thee, Edward," cried the duke, with a heartiness more frank than was usual to him; "and were I thy subject, woe to man or woman that wagged tongue to wound thee by a breath! But who and what is this same Hilda? — one of thy kith and kin? Surely not less than kingly blood runs so bold?"

"William, *bien aimé*,"[1] said the king, "it is true that Hilda, whom the saints assoil, is of kingly blood, though not of our kingly line. It is feared," added Edward, in a timid whisper, as he cast a hurried glance around him, "that this unhappy woman has ever been more addicted to the rites of her pagan ancestors than to those of Holy Church; and men do say that she hath thus acquired from fiend or charm secrets devoutly to be eschewed by the righteous. Nathless, let us rather hope that her mind is somewhat distraught with her misfortunes."

The king sighed, and the duke sighed too, but the duke's sigh spoke impatience. He swept behind him a stern and withering look towards the proud figure of Hilda, still seen through the glades, and said in a sinister voice, —

"Of kingly blood; but this witch of Woden hath no sons or kinsmen, I trust, who pretend to the throne of the Saxon?"

"She is sibbe to Githa, wife of Godwin," answered the king, "and that is her most perilous connection; for the banished earl, as thou knowest, did not pretend to fill the throne, but he was content with nought less than governing our people."

---

[1] The few expressions borrowed occasionally from the Romance tongue, to give individuality to the speaker, will generally be translated into modern French; for the same reason as Saxon is rendered into modern English, namely, that the words may be intelligible to the reader.

The king then proceeded to sketch an outline of the history of Hilda; but his narrative was so deformed both by his superstitions and prejudices, and his imperfect information in all the leading events and characters in his own kingdom, that we will venture to take upon ourselves his task; and while the train ride on through glade and mead, we will briefly narrate, from our own special sources of knowledge, the chronicle of Hilda, the Scandinavian Vala.

———◆———

CHAPTER II.

A MAGNIFICENT race of men were those war sons of the old North, whom our popular histories, so superficial in their accounts of this age, include in the common name of the "Danes." They replunged into barbarism the nations over which they swept, but from that barbarism they reproduced the noblest elements of civilization. Swede, Norwegian, and Dane, differing in some minor points when closely examined, had yet one common character viewed at a distance. They had the same prodigious energy, the same passion for freedom, individual and civil, the same splendid errors in the thirst for fame and the "point of honour;" and above all, as a main cause of civilization, they were wonderfully pliant and malleable in their admixtures wi h the peoples they overran. This is their true distinction fr m the stubborn Celt, who refuses to mingle and disdains to improve.

Frankes, the archbishop, baptized Rolf-ganger;[1] and within a little more than a century afterwards, the descendants of those terrible heathens, who had spared neither priest nor altar, were the most redoubtable defenders of the Christian Church; their old language forgotten (save by a few in the town of Bayeux), their ancestral names[2] (save among a few

---

[1] Roman de Rou, part i. v. 1914.

[2] The reason why the Normans lost their old names is to be found in their conversion to Christianity. They were baptized; and Franks, as their god-

of the noblest) changed into French titles, and little else but the indomitable valour of the Scandinavian remained unaltered amongst the arts and manners of the Frankish-Norman.

In like manner their kindred tribes, who had poured into Saxon England to ravage and lay desolate, had no sooner obtained from Alfred the Great permanent homes than they became perhaps the most powerful, and in a short time not the least patriotic, part of the Anglo-Saxon population.[1] At the time our story opens, these Northmen, under the common name of Danes, were peaceably settled in no less than fifteen[2] counties in England; their nobles abounded in towns and cities beyond the boundaries of those counties which bore the distinct appellation of Danelagh. They were numerous in London, in the precincts of which they had their own burial-place, to the chief municipal court of which they gave their own appellation, — the Hustings.[3] Their power in the national assembly of the Witan had decided the choice of kings.

fathers, gave them new appellations. Thus, Charles the Simple insists that Rolf-ganger shall change his law (creed) and his name, and Rolf or Rou is christened Robert. A few of those who retained Scandinavian names at the time of the Conquest will be cited hereafter.

[1] Thus in 991, about a century after the first settlement, the Danes of East Anglia gave the only efficient resistance to the host of the Vikings under Justin and Gurthmund ; and Brithnoth, celebrated by the Saxon poet as a Saxon *par excellence,* the heroic defender of his native soil, was, in all probability, of Danish descent. Mr. Laing, in his preface to his translation of the "Heimskringla," truly observes, "that the rebellions against William the Conqueror and his successors appear to have been almost always raised, or mainly supported, in the counties of recent Danish descent, not in those peopled by the old Anglo-Saxon race."

The portion of Mercia consisting of the burghs of Lancaster, Lincoln, Nottingham, Stamford, and Derby became a Danish State in A. D. 877 ; East Anglia, consisting of Cambridge, Suffolk, Norfolk, and the Isle of Ely, in A. D. 879–80; and the vast territory of Northumbria, extending all north the Humber, into all that part of Scotland south of the Frith, in A. D. 876. (See Palgrave's Commonwealth.) But besides their more allotted settlements, the Danes were interspersed as landowners all over England.

[2] Namely, Essex, Middlesex, Suffolk, Norfolk, Herts, Cambridgeshire, Hants, Lincoln, Notts, Derby, Northampton, Leicestershire, Bucks, Beds, and the vast territory called Northumbria.— Brompton Chronicle.

[3] Palgrave's History of England, p. 315.

Thus, with some differences of law and dialect, these once turbulent invaders had amalgamated amicably with the native race.[1] And to this day the gentry, traders, and farmers of more than one third of England, and in those counties most confessed to be in the van of improvement, descend from Saxon mothers, indeed, but from Viking fathers. There was in reality little difference in race between the Norman knight of the time of Henry I. and the Saxon franklin of Norfolk and York. Both on the mother's side would most probably have been Saxon, both on the father's would have traced to the Scandinavian.

But though this character of adaptability was general, exceptions in some points were necessarily found; and these were obstinate in proportion to the adherence to the old pagan faith or the sincere conversion to Christianity. The Norwegian chronicles, and passages in our own history, show how false and hollow was the assumed Christianity of many of these fierce Odin-worshippers. They willingly enough accepted the outward sign of baptism, but the holy water changed little of the inner man. Even Harold, the son of Canute, scarce seventeen years before the date we have now entered, being unable to obtain from the Archbishop of Canterbury, who had espoused the cause of his brother Hardicanute, the consecrating benediction, lived and reigned as one "who had abjured Christianity." [2]

The priests, especially on the Scandinavian continent, were often forced to compound with their grim converts, by indulgence to certain habits, such as indiscriminate polygamy. To eat horse-flesh in honour of Odin, and to marry wives *ad libitum*, were the main stipulations of the neophytes; and the puzzled monks, often driven to a choice, yielded the point

---

[1] The laws collected by Edward the Confessor, and in later times so often and so fondly referred to, contained many introduced by the Danes, which had grown popular with the Saxon people. Much which we ascribe to the Norman Conqueror pre-existed in the Anglo-Danish, and may be found both in Normandy and parts of Scandinavia to this day. See Hakewell's Treatise on the Antiquity of Laws in this Island, in Hearne's Curious Discourses.

[2] Palgrave's History of England, p. 322.

of the wives, but stood firm on the graver article of the horse-flesh.

With their new religion, very imperfectly understood even when genuinely received, they retained all that host of heathen superstition which knits itself with the most obstinate instincts in the human breast. Not many years before the reign of the Confessor, the laws of the great Canute against witchcraft and charms, the worship of stones, fountains, runes by ash and elm, and the incantations that do homage to the dead, were obviously rather intended to apply to the recent Danish converts than to the Anglo-Saxons, already subjugated for centuries, body and soul, to the domination of the Christian monks.

Hilda, a daughter of the royalty of Denmark, and cousin to Githa (niece to Canute, whom that king had bestowed in second spousals upon Godwin), had come over to England with a fierce Jarl, her husband, a year after Canute's accession to the throne, — both converted nominally, both secretly believers in Thor and Odin.

Hilda's husband had fallen in one of the actions in the Northern seas, between Canute and Saint Olave, King of Norway (that saint himself, by the by, a most ruthless persecutor of his forefathers' faith, and a most unqualified practical asserter of his heathen privilege to extend his domestic affections beyond the severe pale which should have confined them to a single wife. His natural son Magnus then sat on the Danish throne). The Jarl died as he had wished to die, the last man on board his ship, with the soothing conviction that the Valkyrs would bear him to Valhalla.

Hilda was left with an only daughter, whom Canute bestowed on Ethelwolf, a Saxon earl of large domains, and tracing his descent from Penda, that old King of Mercia who refused to be converted, but said so discreetly that he had no objection to his neighbours being Christians, if they would practise that peace and forgiveness which the monks told him were the elements of the faith.

Ethelwolf fell under the displeasure of Hardicanute, perhaps because he was more Saxon than Danish; and though that savage king did not dare openly to arraign him before the Witan, he gave secret orders by which he was butchered on his own hearthstone, in the arms of his wife, who died shortly afterwards of grief and terror. The only orphan of this unhapy pair, Edith, was thus consigned to the charge of Hilda.

It was a necessary and invaluable characteristic of that "adaptability" which distinguished the Danes, that they transferred to the land in which they settled all the love they had borne to that of their ancestors; and so far as attachment to soil was concerned, Hilda had grown no less in heart an Englishwoman than if she had been born and reared amidst the glades and knolls from which the smoke of her hearth rose through the old Roman compluvium.

But in all else she was a Dane, — Dane in her creed and her habits, — Dane in her intense and brooding imagination; in the poetry that filled her soul, peopled the air with spectres, and covered the leaves of the trees with charms. Living in austere seclusion after the death of her lord, to whom she had borne a Scandinavian woman's devoted but heroic love, — sorrowing, indeed, for his death, but rejoicing that he fell amidst the feast of ravens, — her mind settled more and more, year by year and day by day, upon those visions of the unknown world which in every faith conjure up the companions of solitude and grief.

Witchcraft in the Scandinavian North assumed many forms, and was connected by many degrees. There was the old and withered hag, on whom, in our later mediæval ages, the character was mainly bestowed; there was the terrific witch-wife, or wolf-witch, who seems wholly apart from human birth and attributes, like the weird sisters of Macbeth, — creatures who entered the house at night and seized warriors to devour them, who might be seen gliding over the sea with the carcass of the wolf dripping blood from their giant jaws; and there was the more serene, classical, and awful vala, or sibyl, who, honoured by chiefs and revered by nations, foretold the future, and advised the deeds of heroes. Of these last, the Norse chronicles tell us much. They were often of rank and wealth;

they were accompanied by trains of handmaids and servants; kings led them (when their counsel was sought) to the place of honour in the hall, and their heads were sacred, as those of ministers to the gods.

This last state in the grisly realm of the Wig-lær (wizard-lore) was the one naturally appertaining to the high rank and the soul, lofty though blind and perverted, of the daughter of warrior-kings. All practice of the art to which now for long years she had devoted herself that touched upon the humble destinies of the vulgar, the child of Odin[1] haughtily disdained. Her reveries were upon the fate of kings and kingdoms; she aspired to save or to rear the dynasties which should rule the races yet unborn. In youth proud and ambitious, — common faults with her countrywomen, — on her entrance into the darker world she carried with her the prejudices and passions that she had known in that coloured by the external sun.

All her human affections were centred in her grandchild Edith, the last of a race royal on either side. Her researches into the future had assured her that the life and death of this fair child were entwined with the fates of a king, and the same oracles had intimated a mysterious and inseparable connection between her own shattered house and the flourishing one of Earl Godwin, the spouse of her kinswoman Githa; so that with this great family she was as intimately bound by the links of superstition as by the ties of blood. The eldest born of Godwin, Sweyn, had been at first especially her care and her favourite; and he, of more poetic temperament than his brothers, had willingly submitted to her influence. But of all the brethren, as will be seen hereafter, the career of Sweyn had been most noxious and ill-omened; and at that moment, while the rest of the house carried with it into exile the deep and indignant sympathy of England, no man said of Sweyn, "God bless him!"

But as the second son, Harold, had grown from childhood

---

[1] The name of this god is spelled *Odin*, when referred to as the object of Scandinavian worship; *Woden*, when applied directly to the deity of the Saxons.

into youth, Hilda had singled him out with a preference even
more marked than that she had bestowed upon Sweyn. The
stars and the runes assured her of his future greatness, and
the qualities and talents of the young earl had, at the very
onset of his career, confirmed the accuracy of their predic·
tions. Her interest in Harold became the more intense,
partly because whenever she consulted the future for the lot
of her grandchild Edith, she invariably found it associated
with the fate of Harold; partly because all her arts had failed
to penetrate beyond a certain point in their joint destinies,
and left her mind agitated and perplexed between hope and
terror. As yet, however, she had wholly failed in gaining
any ascendancy over the young earl's vigorous and healthful
mind; and though before his exile he came more often than
any of Godwin's sons to the old Roman house, he had smiled
with proud incredulity at her vague prophecies, and rejected
all her offers of aid from invisible agencies with the calm
reply, —

"The brave man wants no charms to encourage him to his
duty, and the good man scorns all warnings that would deter
him from fulfilling it."

Indeed, though Hilda's magic was not of the malevolent
kind, and sought the source of its oracles not in fiends, but
gods (at least the gods in whom she believed), it was noticeable that all over whom her influence had prevailed had come
to miserable and untimely ends, — not alone her husband and
her son-in-law (both of whom had been as wax to her counsel), but such other chiefs as rank or ambition permitted to
appeal to her lore. Nevertheless, such was the ascendancy
she had gained over the popular mind that it would have
been dangerous in the highest degree to put into execution
against her the laws condemnatory of witchcraft. In her all
the more powerful Danish families reverenced and would
have protected the blood of their ancient kings, and the
widow of one of their most renowned heroes. Hospitable,
liberal, and beneficent to the poor, and an easy mistress over
numerous ceorls, while the vulgar dreaded, they would yet
have defended her. Proofs of her art it would have been

hard to establish; hosts of compurgators to attest her inno·
cence would have sprung up. Even if subjected to the ordeal,
her gold could easily have bribed the priests with whom the
power of evading its dangers rested. And with that worldly
wisdom which persons of genius in their wildest chimeras
rarely lack, she had already freed herself from the chance of
active persecution from the Church by ample donations to all
the neighbouring monasteries.

Hilda, in fine, was a woman of sublime desires and extraordinary gifts, — terrible, indeed, but as the passive agent of
the Fates she invoked, and rather commanding for herself a
certain troubled admiration and mysterious pity; no fiend-
hag, beyond humanity in malice and in power, but essentially human, even when aspiring most to the secrets of a
god. Assuming, for the moment, that by the aid of intense
imagination persons of a peculiar idiosyncrasy of nerves and
temperament might attain to such dim affinities with a world
beyond our ordinary senses, as forbid entire rejection of the
magnetism and magic of old times, it was on no foul and
mephitic pool, overhung with the poisonous nightshade and
excluded from the beams of heaven, but on the living stream
on which the star trembled, and beside whose banks the green
herbage waved, that the demon shadows fell dark and dread.

Thus safe and thus awful lived Hilda; and under her care,
a rose beneath the funeral cedar, bloomed her grandchild
Edith, goddaughter of the Lady of England.

It was the anxious wish, both of Edward and his virgin
wife, pious as himself, to save this orphan from the contami-
nation of a house more than suspected of heathen faith, and
give to her youth the refuge of the convent. But this, without her guardian's consent or her own expressed will, could
not be legally done; and Edith as yet had expressed no desire
to disobey her grandmother, who treated the idea of the convent with lofty scorn.

This beautiful child grew up under the influence, as it were,
of two contending creeds; all her notions on both were necessarily confused and vague. But her heart was so genuinely
mild, simple, tender, and devoted — there was in her so much

of the inborn excellence of the sex — that in every impulse of
that heart struggled for clearer light and for purer air the
unquiet soul.   In manner, in thought, and in person as yet
almost an infant, deep in her heart lay yet one woman's secret,
known scarcely to herself, but which taught her, more power-
fully than Hilda's proud and scoffing tongue, to shudder at
the thought of the barren cloister and the eternal vow.

CHAPTER III.

WHILE King Edward was narrating to the Norman duke all
that he knew, and all that he knew not, of Hilda's history
and secret arts, the road wound through lands as wild and
wold-like as if the metropolis of England lay a hundred miles
distant.   Even to this day patches of such land in the neighbourhood of Norwood may betray what the country was in the
old times, — when a mighty forest, "abounding with wild
beasts" ("the bull and the boar"), skirted the suburbs of
London, and afforded pastime to king and thegn.   For the
Norman kings have been maligned by the popular notion that
assigns to them *all* the odium of the forest laws.   Harsh and
severe were those laws in the reign of the Anglo-Saxon; as
harsh and severe, perhaps, against the ceorl and the poor man
as in the days of Rufus, though more mild unquestionably to
the nobles.   To all beneath the rank of abbot and thegn the
king's woods were made, even by the mild Confessor, as
sacred as the groves of the Druids; and no less penalty than
that of life was incurred by the low-born huntsman who violated their recesses.[1]

Edward's only mundane passion was the chase, and a day
rarely passed but that after Mass he went forth with hawk or
hound; so that though the regular season for hawking did not
commence till October, he had ever on his wrist some young
falcon to essay, or some old favourite to exercise.   And now,

[1] See Note B.

just as William was beginning to grow weary of his good cousin's prolix recitals, the hounds suddenly gave tongue, and from a sedge-grown pool by the wayside, with solemn wing and harsh boom, rose a bittern.

"Holy Saint Peter!" exclaimed the saint-king, spurring his palfrey, and loosing his famous Peregrine falcon.[1] William was not slow in following that animated example; and the whole company rode at half speed across the rough forest land, straining their eyes upon the soaring quarry, and the large wheels of the falcons. Riding thus, with his eyes in the air, Edward was nearly pitched over his palfrey's head, as the animal stopped suddenly, checked by a high gate, set deep in a half-embattled wall of brick and rubble. Upon this gate sat, quite unmoved and apathetic, a tall ceorl, or labourer; while behind it was a gazing curious group of men of the same rank, clad in those blue tunics of which our peasant's smock is the successor, and leaning on scythes and flails. Sour and ominous were the looks they bent upon that Norman cavalcade. The men were at least as well clad as those of the same condition are now; and their robust limbs and ruddy cheeks showed no lack of the fare that supports labour. Indeed, the working-man of that day, if not one of the absolute theowes, or slaves, was, physically speaking, better off, perhaps, than he has ever since been in England, more especially if he appertained to some wealthy thegn of pure Saxon lineage, whose very title of lord came to him in his quality of dispenser of bread;[2] and those men had been ceorls under Harold, son of Godwin, now banished from the land.

"Open the gate, open quick, my merry men," said the gentle Edward (speaking in Saxon, though with a strong foreign accent), after he had recovered his seat, murmured a benediction, and crossed himself three times. The men stirred not.

---

[1] The Peregrine hawk built on the rocks of Llandudno, and this breed was celebrated even to the days of Elizabeth Burleigh thanks one of the Mostyns for a cast of hawks from Llandudno.

[2] *Hlaf*, loaf; *Hlaford*, lord, giver of bread; *Hleafdian*, lady, server of bread. — VERSTEGAN.

"No horse tramps the seeds we have sown for Harold the Earl to reap," said the ceorl, doggedly, still seated on the gate; and the group behind him gave a shout of applause.

Moved more than ever he had been known to be before, Edward spurred his steed up to the boor, and lifted his hand. At that signal twenty swords flashed in the air behind, as the Norman nobles spurred to the place. Putting back with one hand his fierce attendants, Edward shook the other at the Saxon. "Knave, knave," he cried, "I would hurt you, if I could!"

There was something in these words, fated to drift down into history, at once ludicrous and touching. The Normans saw them only in the former light, and turned aside to conceal their laughter; the Saxon felt them in the latter and truer sense, and stood rebuked. That great king, whom he now recognized, with all those drawn swords at his back, could not do him hurt; that king had not the heart to hurt him. The ceorl sprang from the gate, and opened it, bending low.

"Ride first, Count William, my cousin," said the king, calmly.

The Saxon ceorl's eyes glared as he heard the Norman's name uttered in the Norman tongue; but he kept open the gate, and the train passed through, Edward lingering last. Then said the king, in a low voice, —

"Bold man, thou spokest of Harold the Earl and his harvests; knowest thou not that his lands have passed from him, and that he is outlawed, and his harvests are not for the scythes of his ceorls to reap?"

"May it please you, dread Lord and King," replied the Saxon, simply, "these lands that were Harold the Earl's are now Clapa's, the sixhændman's."

"How is that?" quoth Edward, hastily; "we gave them neither to sixhændman nor to Saxon. All the lands of Harold hereabout were divided amongst sacred abbots and noble chevaliers, — Normans all."

"Fulke the Norman had these fair fields, yon orchards and tynen. Fulke sold them to Clapa, the earl's sixhændman; and what in mancusses and pence Clapa lacked of the price, we, the ceorls of the earl, made up from our own earnings in the earl's noble service. And this very day, in token thereof, have we quaffed the bedden-ale.[1] Wherefore, please God and our Lady, we hold these lands part and parcel with Clapa; and when Earl Harold comes again, as come he will, here at least he will have his own."

Edward, who, despite a singular simplicity of character which at times seemed to border on imbecility, was by no means wanting in penetration when his attention was fairly roused, changed countenance at this proof of rough and homely affection on the part of these men to his banished earl and brother-in-law. He mused a little while in grave thought, and then said kindly, —

"Well, man, I think not the worse of you for loyal love to your thegn, but there are those who would do so; and I advise you, brotherlike, that ears and nose are in peril if thou talkest thus indiscreetly."

"Steel to steel, and hand to hand," said the Saxon, bluntly, touching the long knife in his leathern belt; "and he who sets gripe on Sexwolf, son of Elfhelm, shall pay his weregeld twice over."

"Forewarned, foolish man, thou art forewarned. Peace!" said the king; and shaking his head, he rode on to join the Normans, who now in a broad field where the corn sprang green, and which they seemed to delight in wantonly trampling as they curveted their steeds to and fro, watched the movements of the bittern and the pursuit of the two falcons.

"A wager, Lord King!" said a prelate, whose strong family likeness to William proclaimed him to be the duke's bold and haughty brother Odo,[2] Bishop of Bayeux, — "a wager. My steed to your palfrey that the duke's falcon first fixes the bittern."

---

[1] When any man was set up in his estate by the contributions of his friends, those friends were bid to a feast, and the ale so drunk was called the bedden-ale, from *bedden*, to pray, or to bid. See Brand's Popular Antiquities.

[2] Herleve (Arlotta), William's mother, married Herluin de Conteville, after the death of Duke Robert, and had by him two sons, — Robert, Count of Mortain, and Odo, Bishop of Bayeux. — *Ord. Vital.* lib. vii.

"Holy father," answered Edward, in that slight change of voice which alone showed his displeasure, "these wagers all savour of heathenesse, and our canons forbid them to mone [1] and priest.   Go to, it is nought."

The bishop, who brooked no rebuke even from his terrible brother, knit his brows, and was about to make no gentle rejoinder, when William, whose profound craft or sagacity was always at watch lest his followers should displease the king, interposed, and taking the word out of the prelate's mouth, said, —

"Thou reprovest us well, Sir and King; we Normans are too inclined to such levities.   And see, your falcon is first in pride of place.   By the bones of Saint Valery, how nobly he towers!   See him cover the bittern, see him rest on the wing! Down he swoops!   Gallant bird!"

"With his heart split in two on the bittern's bill," said the bishop; and down, rolling one over the other, fell bittern and hawk, while William's Norway falcon, smaller of size than the king's, descended rapidly, and hovered over the two. Both were dead.

"I accept the omen," muttered the gazing duke; "let the natives destroy each other!"   He placed his whistle to his lips, and his falcon flew back to his wrist.

"Now home," said King Edward.

———◆———

CHAPTER IV.

THE royal party entered London by the great bridge which divided Southwark from the capital; and we must pause to gaze a moment on the animated scene which the immemorial thoroughfare presented.

The whole suburb before entering Southwark was rich in orchards and gardens, lying round the detached houses of the

[1] Monk.

wealthier merchants and citizens. Approaching the river-side, to the left, the eye might see the two circular spaces set apart, the one for bear, the other for bull-baiting. To the right, upon a green mound of waste, within sight of the populous bridge, the gleemen were exercising their art. Here one dexterous juggler threw three balls and three knives alternately in the air, catching them one by one as they fell.[1] There another was gravely leading a great bear to dance on its hind legs, while his coadjutor kept time with a sort of flute or flageolet. The lazy bystanders, in great concourse, stared and laughed; but the laugh was hushed at the tramp of the Norman steeds; and the famous count by the king's side, as with a smiling lip but observant eye he rode along, drew all attention from the bear.

On now approaching that bridge which not many years before had been the scene of terrible contest between the invading Danes and Ethelred's ally, Olave of Norway,[2] you might still see, though neglected and already in decay, the double fortifications that had wisely guarded that vista into the city. On both sides of the bridge, which was of wood, were forts, partly of timber, partly of stone, and breastworks, and by the forts a little chapel. The bridge, broad enough to admit two vehicles abreast,[3] was crowded with passengers, and lively with stalls and booths. Here was the favourite spot of the popular ballad-singer.[4] Here, too, might be seen

---

[1] Strutt's Horda.

[2] There is an animated description of this "Battle of London Bridge," which gave ample theme to the Scandinavian scalds, in Snorro Sturleson : —

> London Bridge is broken down ;
> Gold is won and bright renown ;
> Shields resounding,
> War-horns sounding,
> Hildur shouting in the din,
> Arrows singing,
> Mail-coats ringing,
> Odin makes our Olaf win.
>
> LAING's *Heimskringla*, vol. ii. p. 10.

[3] Sharon Turner.

[4] Hawkins, vol. ii p. 94.

the swarthy Saracen, with wares from Spain and Afric.[1]
Here the German merchant from the Steel-yard swept along
on his way to his suburban home. Here, on some holy office,
went quick the muffled monk. Here the city gallant paused
to laugh with the country girl, her basket full of May-boughs
and cowslips. In short, all bespoke that activity, whether in
business or pastime, which was destined to render that city
the mart of the world, and which had already knit the trade
of the Anglo-Saxon to the remoter corners of commercial
Europe. The deep dark eye of William dwelt admiringly
on the bustling groups, on the broad river, and the forest of
masts which rose by the indented marge near Belin's gate.[2]
And he to whom, whatever his faults, or rather crimes, to the
unfortunate people he not only oppressed but deceived, London at least may yet be grateful, not only for chartered
franchise,[3] but for advancing, in one short vigorous reign,
her commerce and wealth beyond what centuries of Anglo-
Saxon domination, with its inherent feebleness, had effected,
exclaimed aloud, —

"By rood and Mass, O dear king, thy lot hath fallen on a
goodly heritage."

[1] Doomsday makes mention of the Moors, and the Germans (the Emperor's
merchants) that were sojourners or settlers in London. The Saracens at that
time were among the great merchants of the world; Marseilles, Arles, Avig-
non, Montpellier, Toulouse, were the wonted *étapes* of their active traders.
What civilizers, what teachers they were, — those same Saracens! How much
in arms and in arts we owe them! Fathers of the Provençal poetry, they, far
more than even the Scandinavian scalds, have influenced the literature of
Christian Europe. The most ancient chronicle of the Cid was written in
Arabic, a little before the Cid's death, by two of his pages, who were Mus-
sulmans. The medical science of the Moors for six centuries enlightened Europe, and their metaphysics were adopted in nearly all the Christian
universities.

[2] Billingsgate. See Note C.

[3] London received a charter from William at the instigation of the Norman
Bishop of London; but it probably only confirmed the previous municipal
constitution, since it says briefly, "I grant you all to be as law-worthy as ye
were in the days of King Edward." The rapid increase, however, of the
commercial prosperity and political importance of London after the Conquest
is attested in many chronicles, and becomes strikingly evident even on the
surface of history.

"Hem!" said Edward, lazily; "thou knowest not how troublesome these Saxons are. And while thou speakest, lo, in yon shattered walls, built first, they say, by Alfred of holy memory, are the evidences of the Danes. Bethink thee how often they have sailed up this river. How know I but what the next year the raven flag may stream over these waters? Magnus of Denmark hath already claimed my crown as heir to the royalties of Canute, and" (here Edward hesitated) "Godwin and Harold, whom alone of my thegns Dane and Northman fear, are far away."

"Miss not them, Edward, my cousin," cried the duke, in haste. "Send for me if danger threat thee. Ships enow await thy hest in my new port of Cherbourg. And I tell thee this for thy comfort, that were I king of the English and lord of this river, the citizens of London might sleep from vespers to prime without fear of the Dane. Never again should the raven flag be seen by this bridge! Never, I swear, by the Splendour Divine."

Not without purpose spoke William thus stoutly; and he turned on the king those glittering eyes (*micantes oculos*) which the chroniclers have praised and noted; for it was his hope and his aim in this visit, that his cousin Edward should formally promise him that goodly heritage of England. But the king made no rejoinder, and they now neared the end of the bridge.

"What old ruin looms yonder?"[1] asked William, hiding his disappointment at Edward's silence; "it seemeth the remains of some stately keape, which, by its fashion, I should pronounce Roman."

"Ay!" said Edward, "it is said to have been built by

---

[1] There seems good reason for believing that a keep did stand where the Tower stands, before the Conquest, and that William's edifice spared some of its remains. In the very interesting letter from John Bayford relating to the city of London (Leland's Collectanea, lviii.), the writer, a thorough master of his subject, states that "the Romans made a public military way, that of Watling Street, from the Tower to Ludgate, in a straight line, at the end of which they built stations or citadels, one of which was where the White Tower now stands." Bayford adds that "when the White Tower was fitted up for the reception of records, there remained many Saxon inscriptions."

the Romans; and one of the old Lombard freemasons employed on my new palace of Westminster giveth that,
and some others in my domain, the name of the Juillet
Tower."

"Those Romans were our masters in all things gallant and
wise," said William; "and I predict that, some day or other,
on that site a King of England will re-erect palace and tower.
And yon castle towards the west?"

"Is the Tower Palatine, where our predecessors have lodged,
and ourself sometimes; but the sweet loneliness of Thorney
Isle pleaseth me more now."

Thus talking, they entered London, a rude, dark city, built
mainly of timbered houses; streets narrow and winding; windows rarely glazed, but protected chiefly by linen blinds;
vistas opening, however, at times into broad spaces, round
the various convents, where green trees grew up behind low
palisades. Tall roods and holy images, to which we owe the
names of existing thoroughfares (Rood-lane and Lady-lane [1]),
where the ways crossed, attracted the curious and detained the
pious. Spires there were not then; but blunt, cone-headed
turrets, pyramidal, denoting the Houses of God, rose often
from the low, thatched, and reeded roofs. But every now and
then a scholar's, if not an ordinary, eye could behold the
relics of Roman splendour, — traces of that elder city, which
now lies buried under our thoroughfares, and of which, year
by year, are dug up the stately skeletons.

Along the Thames still rose, though much mutilated, the
wall of Constantine. [2] Round the humble and barbarous
Church of St. Paul's (wherein lay the dust of Sebba, that
king of the East Saxons who quitted his throne for the sake
of Christ, and of Edward's feeble and luckless father, Ethelred) might be seen, still gigantic in decay, the ruins of the
vast temple of Diana. [3] Many a church and many a convent
pierced their mingled brick and timber work with Roman capital and shaft. Still by the tower, to which was afterwards
given the Saracen name of Barbican, were the wrecks of **the**

---

[1] Rude-lane; Lad-lane. —BAYFORD.
[2] Fitzsepthen.   [3] Camden.

Roman station, where cohorts watched night and day, in case of fire within or foe without.[1]

In a niche near the Aldersgate stood the headless statue of Fortitude, which monks and pilgrims deemed some unknown saint in the old time, and halted to honour. And in the midst of Bishopsgate Street sat on his desecrated throne a mangled Jupiter, his eagle at his feet. Many a half-converted Dane there lingered, and mistook the Thunderer and the bird for Odin and his hawk. By Leod-gate (the People's gate)[2] still too were seen the arches of one of those mighty aqueducts which the Roman learned from the Etrurian. And close by the Steel-yard, occupied by "the Emperor's cheap men" (the German merchants), stood, almost entire, the Roman temple, extant in the time of Geoffrey of Monmouth. Without the walls the old Roman vineyards[3] still put forth their green leaves and crude clusters in the plains of East Smithfield, in the fields of St. Giles's, and on the site where now stands Hatton Garden. Still massere[4] and cheapmen chaffered and bargained, at booth and stall, in Mart-lane, where the Romans had bartered before them. With every encroachment on new soil, within the walls and without, urn, vase, weapon, human bones, were shovelled out, and lay disregarded amidst heaps of rubbish.

Not on such evidences of the past civilization looked the practical eye of the Norman Count, — not on things, but on men, looked he; and as silently he rode on from street to street, out of those men, stalwart and tall, busy, active, toiling, the Man-Ruler saw the civilization that was to come.

So, gravely through the small city, and over the bridge that spanned the little river of the Fleet, rode the train along the Strand. To the left, smooth sands; to the right, fair pastures below green holts, thinly studded with houses; over numerous cuts and inlets running into the river, rode they on. The hour and the season were those in which youth enjoyed its

---

[1] Bayford, Leland's Collectanea, p. lviii.
[2] Ludgate (Leod-gate). — VERSTEGAN.
[3] See Note D.
[4] Merchant, mercer.

holiday, and gay groups resorted to the then[1] fashionable haunts of the Fountain of Holywell, "streaming forth among glistening pebbles."

So they gained at length the village of Charing, which Edward had lately bestowed on his Abbey of Westminster, and which was now filled with workmen, native and foreign, employed on that edifice and the contiguous palace. Here they loitered awhile at the Mews[2] (where the hawks were kept), passed by the rude palace of stone and rubble, appropriated to the tributary kings of Scotland,[3] — a gift from Edgar to Kenneth, — and finally, reaching the inlet of the river, which, winding round the Isle of Thorney (now Westminster), separated the rising church, abbey, and palace of the saint-king from the mainland, dismounted, and were ferried across[4] the narrow stream to the broad space round the royal residence.

CHAPTER V.

THE new palace of Edward the Confessor, the palace of Westminster, opened its gates to receive the Saxon King and the Norman Duke, remounting on the margin of the isle, and now riding side by side. And as the duke glanced from brows, habitually knit, first over the pile, stately though not yet completed, with its long rows of round arched windows, cased by indented fringes and fræt (tooth) work, its sweep of solid columns with circling cloisters, and its ponderous towers of simple grandeur; then over the groups of courtiers, with

---

[1] Fitzstephen.

[2] *Meuse.* Apparently rather a hawk hospital, from *Muta* (Camden). Du Fresne, in his Glossary, says, *Muta* is in French *Le Meue,* and a disease to which the hawk was subject on changing its feathers.

[3] Scotland-yard. — STRYPE.

[4] The first bridge that connected Thorney Isle with the mainland is said to have been built by Matilda, wife of Henry I.

close vests and short mantles and beardless cheeks, that filled
up the wide space, to gaze in homage on the renowned guest,
his heart swelled within him, and checking his rein, he drew
near to his brother of Bayeux, and whispered, —

"Is not this already the court of the Norman? Behold
yon nobles and earls, how they mimic our garb! Behold the
very stones in yon gate, how they range themselves, as if
carved by the hand of the Norman mason! Verily and
indeed, brother, the shadow of the rising sun rests already
on these halls."

"Had England no people," said the bishop, "England were
yours already. But saw you not, as we rode along, the lowering brows, and heard you not the angry murmurs? The villeins are many, and their hate is strong."

"Strong is the roan I bestride," said the duke; "but a bold
rider curbs it with the steel of the bit, and guides it with the
goad of the heel."

And now, as they neared the gate, a band of minstrels in
the pay of the Norman touched their instruments, and woke
their song, — the household song of the Norman, — the battle
hymn of Roland, the Paladin of Charles the Great. At the
first word of the song the Norman knights and youths, pro-
fusely scattered amongst the Normanized Saxons, caught up
the lay, and with sparkling eyes and choral voices they welcomed the mighty duke into the palace of the last meek successor of Woden.

By the porch of the inner court the duke flung himself from
his saddle, and held the stirrup for Edward to dismount. The
king placed his hand gently on his guest's broad shoulder, and
having somewhat slowly reached the ground, embraced and
kissed him in the sight of the gorgeous assemblage; then led
him by the hand towards the fair chamber which was set apart
for the duke, and so left him to his attendants.

William, lost in thought, suffered himself to be disrobed in
silence; but when Fitzosborne, his favourite confidant and
haughtiest baron, who yet deemed himself but honoured by
personal attendance on his chief, conducted him towards the
bath, which adjoined the chamber, he drew back, and wrap-

ping round him more closely the gown of fur that had been thrown over his shoulders, he muttered low, "Nay, if there be on me yet one speck of English dust, let it rest there, — seizin, Fitzosborne, seizin of the English land." Then, waving his hand, he dismissed all his attendants except Fitzosborne and Rolf, Earl of Hereford,[1] nephew to Edward, but French on the father's side, and thoroughly in the duke's councils. Twice the duke paced the chamber without vouchsafing a word to either, then paused by the round window that overlooked the Thames. The scene was fair; the sun, towards its decline, glittered on numerous small pleasure-boats, which shot to and fro between Westminster and London, or towards the opposite shores of Lambeth. His eye sought eagerly, along the curves of the river, the gray remains of the fabled Tower of Julius, and the walls, gates, and turrets that rose by the stream, or above the dense mass of silent roofs; then it strained hard to descry the tops of the more distant masts of that infant navy, fostered under Alfred the far-seeing, for the future civilization of wastes unknown, and the empire of seas untracked.

The duke breathed hard, and opened and closed the hand which he stretched forth into space as if to grasp the city he beheld. "Rolf," said he, abruptly, "thou knowest, no doubt, the wealth of the London traders, one and all; for, *foi de Guillaume*, my *gentil chevalier*, thou art a true Norman, and scentest the smell of gold as a hound the boar!"

Rolf smiled, as if pleased with a compliment which simpler men might have deemed, at the best, equivocal, and replied, —

"It is true, my liege; and, gramercy, the air of England sharpens the scent; for in this villein and motley country, made up of all races, — Saxon and Fin, Dane and Fleming, Pict and Walloon, — it is not as with us, where the brave man and the pure descent are held chief in honour. Here gold and land are, in truth, name and lordship; even their popular name for their national assembly of the Witan is

---

[1] We give him that title, which this Norman noble generally bears in the Chronicles, though Palgrave observes that he is rather to be styled Earl of the Magesetan (the Welch Marches).

'The Wealthy.'[1] He who is but a ceorl to-day, let him be rich, and he may be earl to-morrow, marry in king's blood, and rule armies under a gonfanon statelier than a king's; while he whose fathers were ealdermen and princes, if by force or by fraud, by waste or by largess, he become poor, falls at once into contempt and out of his state, — sinks into a class they call ' six-hundred men,' in their barbarous tongue, and his children will probably sink still lower, into ceorls. Wherefore gold is the thing here most coveted; and, by Saint Michael, the sin is infectious."

William listened to the speech with close attention.

"Good," said he, rubbing slowly the palm of his right hand over the back of the left; "a land all compact with the power of one race, a race of conquering men, as our fathers were, whom nought but cowardice or treason can degrade, — such a land, O Rolf of Hereford, it were hard indeed to subjugate or decoy or tame — "

"So has my lord the duke found the Bretons; and so also do I find the Welch upon my marches of Hereford."

"But," continued William, not heeding the interruption, "where wealth is more than blood and race, chiefs may be bribed or menaced; and the multitude — by 'r Lady, the multitude are the same in all lands, mighty under valiant and faithful leaders, powerless as sheep without them. But to my question, my gentle Rolf; this London must be rich?"[2]

"Rich enow," answered Rolf, "to coin into armed men that should stretch from Rouen to Flanders on the one hand, and Paris on the other."

"In the veins of Matilda, whom thou wooest for wife," said Fitzosborne, abruptly, "flows the blood of Charlemagne. God grant his empire to the children she shall bear thee!"

The duke bowed his head, and kissed a relic suspended from his throat. Further sign of approval of his counsellor's words he gave not, but after a pause, he said, —

[1] Eadigan. — SHARON TURNER, vol. i. p. 274.

[2] The comparative wealth of London was indeed considerable. When, in 1018, all the rest of England was taxed to an amount considered stupendous, namely, 71,000 Saxon pounds, London contributed 11,000 pounds besides.

"When I depart, Rolf, thou wendest back to thy marches. These Welch are brave and fierce, and shape work enow for thy hands."

"Ay, by my halidame! poor sleep by the side of the beehive you have stricken down."

"Marry, then," said William, "let the Welch prey on Saxon, Saxon on Welch; let neither win too easily. Remember our omens to-day, Welch hawk and Saxon bittern, and over their corpses, Duke William's Norway falcon! Now dress we for the complin [1] and the banquet."

[1] The second vespers.

BOOK II.

ANFRANC THE SCHOLAR.

CHAPTER I.

FOUR meals a day, nor those sparing, were not deemed too extravagant an interpretation of the daily bread for which the Saxon prayed. Four meals a day, from earl to ceorl! "Happy times!" may sigh the descendant of the last, if he read these pages. Partly so they were for the ceorl, but not in all things; for never sweet is the food, and never gladdening is the drink, of servitude. Inebriety, the vice of the warlike nations of the North, had not, perhaps, been the pre-eminent excess of the earlier Saxons, while yet the active and fiery Britons, and the subsequent petty wars between the kings of the Heptarchy, enforced on hardy warriors the safety of temperance; but the example of the Danes had been fatal. Those giants of the sea, like all who pass from great vicissitudes of toil and repose, from the tempest to the haven, snatched with full hands every pleasure in their reach. With much that tended permanently to elevate the character of the Saxon, they imparted much for a time to degrade it. The Anglian learned to feast to repletion, and drink to delirium; but such were not the vices of the court of the Confessor. Brought up from his youth in the cloister-camp of the Normans, what he loved in their manners was the abstemious sobriety and the ceremonial religion which distinguished those sons of the Scandinavian from all other kindred tribes.

The Norman position in France, indeed, in much resembled that of the Spartan in Greece. He had forced a settlement with scanty numbers in the midst of a subjugated and sullen population, surrounded by jealous and formidable foes. Hence sobriety was a condition of his being, and the policy of the chief lent a willing ear to the lessons of the preacher. Like the Spartan, every Norman of pure race was free and noble; and this consciousness inspired not only that remarkable dignity of mien which Spartan and Norman alike possessed, but also that fastidious self-respect which would have revolted from exhibiting a spectacle of debasement to inferiors. And, lastly, as the paucity of their original numbers, the perils that beset, and the good fortune that attended them, served to render the Spartans the most religious of all the Greeks in their dependence on the Divine aid; so, perhaps, to the same causes may be traced the proverbial piety of the ceremonial Normans. They carried into their new creed something of feudal loyalty to their spiritual protectors; did homage to the Virgin for the lands that she vouchsafed to bestow, and recognized in Saint Michael the chief who conducted their armies.

After hearing the complin vespers in the temporary chapel fitted up in that unfinished abbey of Westminster, which occupied the site of the temple of Apollo,[1] the king and his guests repaired to their evening meal in the great hall of the palace. Below the dais were ranged three long tables for the knights in William's train, and that flower of the Saxon nobility who, fond, like all youth, of change and imitation, thronged the court of their Normanized saint, and scorned the rude patriotism of their fathers. But hearts truly English were not there. Yea, many of Godwin's noblest foes sighed for the English-hearted earl, banished by Norman guile on behalf of English law.

At the oval table on the dais the guests were select and chosen. At the right hand of the king sat William; at the left Odo of Bayeux. Over these three stretched a canopy of cloth of gold; the chairs on which each sat were of metal, richly gilded over, and the arms carved in elaborate ara-

---

[1] Camden. A church was built out of the ruins of that temple by Sibert, King of the East Saxons; and Canute favoured much the small monastery attached to it (originally established by Dunstan for twelve Benedictines), on account of its Abbot Wulnoth, whose society pleased him. The old palace of Canute, in Thorney Isle, had been destroyed by fire.

besques. At this table too was the king's nephew, the Earl
of Hereford, and, in right of kinsmanship to the duke, the
Norman's beloved baron and grand seneschal, William Fitzosborne, who, though in Normandy even he sat not at the
duke's table, was, as related to his lord, invited by Edward
to his own. No other guests were admitted to this board; so
that, save Edward, all were Norman. The dishes were of
gold and silver, the cups inlaid with jewels. Before each
guest was a knife with hilt adorned by precious stones, and
a napkin fringed with silver. The meats were not placed on
the table, but served upon small spits, and between every
course a basin of perfumed water was borne round by high-
born pages. No dame graced the festival; for she who should
have presided — she, matchless for beauty without pride, piety
without asceticism, and learning without pedantry, — she, the
pale rose of England, loved daughter of Godwin, and loathed
wife of Edward, — had shared in the fall of her kindred, and
had been sent by the meek king or his fierce counsellors to an
abbey in Hampshire, with the taunt that it was not meet that
the child and sister should enjoy state and pomp, while the
sire and brethren ate the bread of the stranger in banishment
and disgrace.

But, hungry as were the guests, it was not the custom of
that holy court to fall to without due religious ceremonial.
The rage for psalm-singing was then at its height in England;
psalmody had excluded almost every other description of vocal
music; and it is even said that great festivals on certain occasions were preluded by no less an effort of lungs and memory
than the entire songs bequeathed to us by King David! This
day, however, Hugoline, Edward's Norman chamberlain, had
been pleased to abridge the length of the prolix grace, and the
company were let off, to Edward's surprise and displeasure,
with the curt and unseemly preparation of only nine psalms
and one special hymn in honour of some obscure saint to
whom the day was dedicated. This performed, the guests
resumed their seats, Edward murmuring an apology to William for the strange omission of his chamberlain, and saying
thrice to himself, "Naught, naught, — very naught."

The mirth languished at the royal table, despite some gay efforts from Rolf and some hollow attempts at light-hearted cheerfulness from the great duke, whose eyes, wandering down the table, were endeavouring to distinguish Saxon from Norman, and count how many of the first might already be reckoned in the train of his friends. But at the long tables below, as the feast thickened, and ale, mead, pigment, morat, and wine circled round, the tongue of the Saxon was loosed, and the Norman knight lost somewhat of his superb gravity. It was just as what a Danish poet called the "sun of the night" (in other words, the fierce warmth of the wine) had attained its meridian glow, that some slight disturbance at the doors of the hall, without which waited a dense crowd of the poor on whom the fragments of the feast were afterwards to be bestowed, was followed by the entrance of two strangers, for whom the officers appointed to marshal the entertainment made room at the foot of one of the tables. Both these new comers were clad with extreme plainness, — one in a dress, though not quite monastic, that of an ecclesiastic of low degree; the other in a long gray mantle and loose gonna, the train of which last was tucked into a broad leathern belt, leaving bare the leggings, which showed limbs of great bulk and sinew, and which were stained by the dust and mire of travel. The first mentioned was slight and small of person; the last was of the height and port of the sons of Anak. The countenance of neither could be perceived, for both had let fall the hood, worn by civilians as by priests out of doors, more than half-way over their faces.

A murmur of great surprise, disdain, and resentment at the intrusion of strangers so attired circulated round the neighbourhood in which they had been placed, checked for a moment by a certain air of respect which the officer had shown towards both, but especially the taller; but breaking out with greater vivacity from the faint restraint, as the tall man unceremoniously stretched across the board, drew towards himself an immense flagon, which (agreeably to the custom of arranging the feast in "messes" of four) had been specially appropriated to Ulf the Dane, Godrith the Saxon, and two young Norman knights akin to the puissant Lord of Grant-mesnil, and having offered it to his comrade, who shook his head, drained it with a gusto that seemed to bespeak him at least no Norman, and wiped his lips boorishly with the sleeve of his huge arm.

"Dainty sir," said one of those Norman knights, William Mallet, of the House of Mallet de Graville,[1] as he moved as far from the gigantic intruder as the space on the settle would permit, "forgive the observation that you have damaged my mantle, you have grazed my foot, and you have drunk my wine. And vouchsafe, if it so please you, the face of the man who hath done this triple wrong to William Mallet de Graville."

A kind of laugh — for laugh absolute it was not — rattled under the cowl of the tall stranger, as he drew it still closer over his face, with a hand that might have spanned the breast of his interrogator; and he made a gesture as if he did not understand the question addressed to him.

Therewith the Norman knight, bending with demure courtesy across the board to Godrith the Saxon, said, —

"*Pardex*,[2] but this fair guest and seigneur seemeth to me, noble Godree (whose name I fear my lips do but rudely enounce), of Saxon line and language; our Romance tongue he knoweth not. Pray you, is it the Saxon custom to enter a king's hall so garbed, and drink a knight's wine so mutely?"

Godrith, a young Saxon of considerable rank, but one of the most sedulous of the imitators of the foreign fashions, coloured high at the irony in the knight's speech, and turning rudely to the huge guest, who was now causing immense fragments of pasty to vanish under the cavernous cowl, he said in his native tongue, though with a lisp as if unfamiliar to him, —

"If thou beest Saxon, shame us not with thy ceorlish man-

---

[1] See note to Pluquet's Roman de Rou, p. 285. **N. B.** Whenever the "Roman de Rou" is quoted in these pages, it is from the excellent edition of M. Pluquet.

[2] *Pardex* or *Pardé*, corresponding to the modern French expletive, *pardie.*

ners; crave pardon of this Norman thegn, who will doubtless yield it to thee in pity. Uncover thy face, and — "

Here the Saxon's rebuke was interrupted; for one of the servitors just then approaching Godrith's side with a spit, elegantly caparisoned with some score of plump larks, the unmannerly giant stretched out his arm within an inch of the Saxon's startled nose, and possessed himself of larks, broche, and all. He drew off two, which he placed on his friend's platter, despite all dissuasive gesticulations, and deposited the rest upon his own. The young banqueters gazed upon the spectacle in wrath too full for words.

At last spoke Mallet de Graville, with an envious eye upon the larks, — for though a Norman was not gluttonous, he was epicurean, —

"Certes, and *foi de chevalier!* a man must go into strange parts if he wish to see monsters; but we are fortunate people " (and he turned to his Norman friend, Aymer, Quen[1] or Count, D'Evreux), "that we have discovered Polyphemus without going so far as Ulysses; " and pointing to the hooded giant, he quoted, appropriately enough, —

"Monstrum horrendum, informe, ingens, cui lumen ademptum."

The giant continued to devour his larks as complacently as the ogre to whom he was likened might have devoured the Greeks in his cave. But his fellow-intruder seemed agitated by the sound of the Latin; he lifted up his head suddenly, and showed lips glistening with white even teeth, and curved into an approving smile, while he said, —

"Bene, mi fili! bene, lepidissime, poetæ verba, in militis ore, non indecora sonant." [2]

The young Norman stared at the speaker, and replied, in the same tone of grave affectation, —

"Courteous sir! the approbation of an ecclesiastic so eminent as I take you to be, from the modesty with which

---

[1] *Quen,* or rather *Quens;* synonymous with *Count* in the Norman Chronicles. Earl Godwin is strangely styled by Wace *Quens Gwine.*

[2] " Good, good, pleasant son ! the words of the poet sound gracefully on the lips of the knight."

you conceal your greatness, cannot fail to draw upon me the envy of my English friends; who are accustomed to swear *in verba magistri,* only for *verba* they learnedly substitute *vina.*"

"You are pleasant, Sire Mallet," said Godrith, reddening; "but I know well that Latin is only fit for monks and shavelings; and little enow even *they* have to boast of."

The Norman's lip curled in disdain. "Latin! — Oh, Godree, *bien aimé!* Latin is the tongue of Cæsars and senators, *fortes* conquerors and *preux* chevaliers. Knowest thou not that Duke William the Dauntless at eight years old had the Comments of Julius Cæsar by heart, and that it is his saying, that ' a king without letters is a crowned ass '?[1] When the king is an ass, asinine are his subjects. Wherefore go to school, speak respectfully of thy betters, the monks and shavelings, who with us are often brave captains and sage councillors, and learn that a full head makes a weighty hand."

"Thy name, young knight?" said the ecclesiastic, in Norman French, though with a slight foreign accent.

"I can give it thee," said the giant, speaking aloud for the first time, in the same language, and in a rough voice, which a quick ear might have detected as disguised; "I can describe to thee name, birth, and quality. By name, this youth is Guillaume Mallet, sometimes styled De Graville, because our Norman *gentilhommes,* forsooth, must always now have a ' de ' tacked to their names; nevertheless he hath no other right to the seigneurie of Graville, which appertains to the head of his House, than may be conferred by an old tower on one corner of the demesnes so designated, with lands that would feed one horse and two villeins, — if they were not in pawn to a Jew for moneys to buy velvet mantelines and a chain of gold. By birth, he comes from Mallet,[2] a bold Norwegian in the fleet of Rou the Sea-king; his mother was a Frank woman, from whom he inherits his best possessions, — videlicet, a shrewd wit and a railing tongue. His qualities are

---

[1] A sentiment variously assigned to William and to his son Henry the Beau Clerc.

[2] Mallet is a genuine Scandinavian name to this day.

abstinence, for he eateth nowhere save at the cost of another; some Latin, for he was meant for a monk, because he seemed too slight of frame for a warrior; some courage, for in spite of his frame he slew three Burgundians with his own hand; and Duke William, among other foolish acts, spoilt a friar *sans tache*, by making a knight *sans terre;* and for the rest — "

"And for the rest," interrupted the Sire de Graville, turning white with wrath, but speaking in a low, repressed voice, "were it not that Duke William sat yonder, thou shouldst have six inches of cold steel in thy huge carcass to digest thy stolen dinner, and silence thy unmannerly tongue — "

"For the rest," continued the giant, indifferently, and as if he had not heard the interruption, — "for the rest, he only resembles Achilles in being *impiger iracundus.* Big men can quote Latin as well as little ones, Messire Mallet the *beau clerc!* "

Mallet's hand was on his dagger, and his eye dilated like that of the panther before he springs; but fortunately at that moment the deep, sonorous voice of William, accustomed to send its sounds down the ranks of an army, rolled clear through the assemblage, though pitched little above its ordinary key, —

"Fair is your feast, and bright your wine, Sir King and brother mine! But I miss here what king and knight hold as the salt of the feast and the perfume to the wine, — the lay of the minstrel. Beshrew me, but both Saxon and Norman are of kindred stock, and love to hear in hall and bower the deeds of their northern fathers. Crave I therefore from your glee-men, or harpers, some song of the olden time! "

A murmur of applause went through the Norman part of the assembly. The Saxons looked up; and some of the more practised courtiers sighed wearily, for they knew well what ditties alone were in favour with the saintly Edward.

The low voice of the king in reply was not heard, but those habituated to read his countenance in its very faint varieties of expression might have seen that it conveyed reproof; and its purport soon became practically known, when a lugubrious prelude was heard from a quarter of the hall in which sat certain ghost-like musicians in white robes, — white as winding-sheets; and forthwith a dolorous and dirgelike voice chanted a long and most tedious recital of the miracles and martyrdom of some early saint. So monotonous was the chant that its effect soon became visible in a general drowsiness. And when Edward, who alone listened with attentive delight, turned towards the close to gather sympathizing admiration from his distinguished guests, he saw his nephew yawning as if his jaw were dislocated; the Bishop of Bayeux, with his well-ringed fingers interlaced and resting on his stomach, fast asleep; Fitzosborne's half-shaven head balancing to and fro with many an uneasy start; and William, wide awake indeed, but with eyes fixed on vacant space, and his soul far away from the gridiron to which (all other saints be praised!) the saint of the ballad had at last happily arrived.

"A comforting and salutary recital, Count William," said the king.

The duke started from his revery, and bowed his head; then said rather abruptly, "Is not yon blazon that of King Alfred?"

"Yea. Wherefore?"

"Hem! Matilda of Flanders is in direct descent from Alfred; it is a name and a line the Saxons yet honour!"

"Surely, yes; Alfred was a great man, and reformed the Psalmster," replied Edward.

The dirge ceased, but so benumbing had been its effect that the torpor it created did not subside with the cause. There was a dead and funereal silence throughout the spacious hall, when suddenly, loudly, mightily, as the blast of the trumpet upon the hush of the grave, rose a single voice. All started, all turned, all looked to one direction; and they saw that the great voice pealed from the farthest end of the hall. From under his gown the gigantic stranger had drawn a small three-stringed instrument, somewhat resembling the modern lute, and thus he sang: —

THE BALLAD OF ROU.[1]

I.

From Blois to Senlis, wave by wave, rolled on the Norman flood,
And Frank on Frank went drifting down the weltering tide of blood;
There was not left in all the land a castle wall to fire,
And not a wife but wailed a lord, a child but mourned a sire.
To Charles the king the mitred monks, the mailéd barons flew,
While, shaking earth, behind them strode the thunder march of **Rou.**

II.

"O King," then cried those barons bold, "in vain are mace and mail,
We fall before the Norman axe, as corn before the hail."
"And vainly," cried the pious monks, "by Mary's shrine we kneel,
For prayers, like arrows, glance aside, against the Norman steel."
The barons groaned, the shavelings wept, while near and nearer drew,
As death-birds round their scented feast, the raven flags of Rou.

III.

Then said King Charles, "Where thousands fail, what king can stand alone ?
The strength of kings is in the men that gather round the throne.
When war dismays my barons bold, 't is time for war to cease;
When Heaven forsakes my pious monks, the will of Heaven is peace.
Go forth, my monks, with Mass and rood the Norman camp unto,
And to the fold, with shepherd crook, entice this grisly Rou.

IV.

"I'll give him all the ocean coast, from Michael Mount to Eure,
And Gille, my child, shall be his bride, to bind him fast and sure.
Let him but kiss the Christian cross, and sheathe the heathen sword,
And hold the lands I cannot keep, a fief from Charles his lord."
Forth went the pastors of the Church, the Shepherd's work to do,
And wrap the golden fleece around the tiger loins of Rou.

V.

Psalm-chanting came the shaven monks within the camp of dread;
Amidst his warriors, Norman Rou stood taller by the head.
Out spoke the Frank archbishop then, a priest devout and sage:
"When peace and plenty wait thy word, what need of war and rage ?
Why waste a land as fair as aught beneath the arch of blue,
Which might be thine to sow and reap ? Thus saith the king to Rou:

---

[1] *Rou,*— the name given by the French to Rollo, or Rolf-ganger, the founder of the Norman settlement.

vi.

" ' I 'll give thee all the ocean coast, from Michael Mount to Eure,
And Gille, my fairest child, as bride, to bind thee fast and sure,
If thou but kneel to Christ our God, and sheathe thy paynim sword,
And hold thy land, the Church's son, a fief from Charles thy lord.' "
The Norman on his warriors looked, to counsel they withdrew.
The saints took pity on the Franks, and moved the soul of Rou.

VII.

So back he strode, and thus he spoke to that archbishop meek :
" I take the land thy king bestows from Eure to Michael peak ;
I take the maid, or foul or fair, a bargain with the coast,
And for thy creed, a sea-king's gods are those that give the most.
So hie thee back, and tell thy chief to make his proffer true
And he shall find a docile son, and ye a saint in Rou."

VIII.

So o'er the border stream of Epte came Rou the Norman, where,
Begirt with barons, sat the king, enthroned at Green St. Clair ;
He placed his hand in Charles's hand, — loud shouted all the throng;
But tears were in King Charles's eyes, — the grip of Rou was strong
" Now kiss the foot," the bishop said, "that homage still is due ; "
Then dark the frown and stern the smile of that grim convert, Rou.

IX.

He takes the foot, as if the foot to slavish lips to bring.
The Normans scowl ; he tilts the throne, and backwards falls the king.
Loud laugh the joyous Norman men, pale stare the Franks aghast ;
And Rou lifts up his head as from the wind springs up the mast :
" I said I would adore a God, but not a mortal too ;
The foot that fled before a foe let cowards kiss ! " said Rou.

No words can express the excitement which this rough
minstrelsy, marred as it is by our poor translation from the
Romance-tongue in which it was chanted, produced amongst
the Norman guests, — less perhaps, indeed, the song itself
than the recognition of the minstrel; and as he closed, from
more than a hundred voices came the loud murmur, only subdued from a shout by the royal presence, "Taillefer, our
Norman Taillefer!"

"By our joint saint, Peter, my cousin the king," exclaimed
William, after a frank, cordial laugh, "well I wot, no tongue

less free than my warrior minstrel's could have so shocked
our ears. Excuse his bold theme, for the sake of his bold
heart, I pray thee; and since I know well" (here the duke's
face grew grave and anxious) "that nought save urgent and
weighty news from my stormy realm could have brought over
this rhyming petrel, permit the officer behind me to lead hither
a bird, I fear, of omen as well as of song."

"Whatever pleases thee, pleases me," said Edward, dryly;
and he gave the order to the attendant. In a few moments,
up the space in the hall, between either table, came the large
stride of the famous minstrel, preceded by the officer, and
followed by the ecclesiastic. The hoods of both were now
thrown back, and discovered countenances in strange contrast,
but each equally worthy of the attention it provoked. The
face of the minstrel was open and sunny as the day; and that
of the priest, dark and close as night. Thick curls of deep
auburn (the most common colour for the locks of the Norman)
wreathed in careless disorder round Taillefer's massive, unwrinkled brow. His eye, of light hazel, was bold and joyous;
mirth, though sarcastic and sly, mantled round his lips. His
whole presence was at once engaging and heroic.

On the other hand the priest's cheek was dark and sallow;
his features singularly delicate and refined; his forehead high,
but somewhat narrow, and crossed with lines of thought; his
mien composed, modest, but not without calm self-confidence.
Amongst that assembly of soldiers, noiseless, self-collected,
and conscious of his surpassing power over swords and mail,
moved the SCHOLAR.

William's keen eye rested on the priest with some surprise,
not unmixed with pride and ire; but first addressing Taillefer,
who now gained the foot of the dais, he said, with a familiarity almost fond, —

"Now, by 'r Lady, if thou bringest not ill news, thy gay
face, man, is pleasanter to mine eyes than thy rough song to
my ears. Kneel, Taillefer, kneel to King Edward, and with
more address, rogue, than our unlucky countryman to King
Charles."

But Edward, as ill liking the form of the giant as the

subject of his lay, said, pushing back his seat as far as he could, —

"Nay, nay, we excuse thee, we excuse thee, tall man." Nevertheless the minstrel still knelt; and so, with a look of profound humility, did the priest. Then both slowly rose, and at a sign from the duke, passed to the other side of the table, standing behind Fitzosborne's chair.

"Clerk," said William, eying deliberately the sallow face of the ecclesiastic, "I know thee of old; and if the Church have sent me an envoy, *per la resplendar Dé,* it should have sent me at least an abbot."

"*Hein, hein!*" said Taillefer, bluntly, "vex not my *bon camarade,* Count of the Normans. Gramercy, thou wilt welcome him, peradventure, better than me; for the singer tells but of discord, and the sage may restore the harmony."

"Ha!" said the duke; and the frown fell so dark over his eyes that the last seemed only visible by two sparks of fire. "I guess, my proud Vavasours are mutinous. Retire, thou and thy comrade. Await me in my chamber. The feast shall not flag in London because the wind blows a gale in Rouen."

The two envoys, since so they seemed, bowed in silence and withdrew.

"Nought of ill-tidings, I trust," said Edward, who had not listened to the whispered communications that had passed between the duke and his subjects. "No schism in thy Church? The clerk seemed a peaceful man, and a humble."

"An there were schism in my Church," said the fiery duke, "my brother of Bayeux would settle it by arguments as close as the gap between cord and throttle."

"Ah! thou art, doubtless, well read in the canons, holy Odo!" said the king, turning to the bishop with more respect than he had yet evinced towards that gentle prelate.

"Canons? Yes, Seigneur, I draw them up myself for my flock conformably with such interpretations of the Roman Church as suit best with the Norman realm: and woe to deacon, monk, or abbot who chooses to misconstrue them."[1]

[1] Pious severity to the heterodox was a Norman virtue. William of Poic-tiers says of William: "One knows with what zeal he pursued and exter-

The bishop looked so truculent and menacing, while his fancy thus conjured up the possibility of heretical dissent, that Edward shrank from him as he had done from Taillefer; and in a few minutes after, on exchange of signals between himself and the duke, who, impatient to escape, was too stately to testify that desire, the retirement of the royal party broke up the banquet; save, indeed, that a few of the elder Saxons and more incorrigible Danes still steadily kept their seats, and were finally dislodged from their later settlements on the stone floors, to find themselves at dawn carefully propped in a row against the outer walls of the palace, with their patient attendants, holding links, and gazing on their masters with stolid envy, if not of the repose, at least of the drugs that had caused it.

CHAPTER II.

"AND now," said William, reclining on a long and narrow couch, with raised carved work all round it like a box (the approved fashion of a bed in those days), "now, Sire Taillefer, thy news."

There were then in the duke's chamber the Count Fitzosborne, Lord of Breteuil, surnamed "the Proud Spirit," who with great dignity was holding before the brazier the ample tunic of linen (called *dormitorium* in the Latin of that time, and night-rail in the Saxon tongue) in which his lord was to robe his formidable limbs for repose;[1] Taillefer, who stood erect before the duke as a Roman sentry at his post; and the

minated those who thought differently;" that is, on transubstantiation. But the wise Norman, while flattering the tastes of the Roman Pontiff in such matters, took special care to preserve the independence of his Church from any undue dictation.

[1] A few generations later this comfortable and decent fashion of night-gear was abandoned; and our forefathers, Saxon and Norman, went to bed *in puris naturalibus* like the Laplanders.

ecclesiastic, a little apart, with arms gathered under his gown, and his bright dark eyes fixed on the ground.

"High and puissant, my liege," then said Taillefer, gravely, and with a shade of sympathy on his large face, "my news is such as is best told briefly: Bunaz, Count d'Eu and descendant of Richard Sanspeur, hath raised the standard of revolt."

"Go on," said the duke, clenching his hand.

"Henry, King of the French, is treating with the rebel, and stirring up mutiny in thy realm, and pretenders to thy throne."

"Ha!" said the duke, and his lip quivered; "this is not all."

"No, my liege! and the worst is to come. Thy uncle Mauger, knowing that thy heart is bent on thy speedy nuptials with the high and noble damsel Matilda of Flanders, has broken out again in thine absence, — is preaching against thee in hall and from pulpit. He declares that such espousals are incestuous, both as within the forbidden degrees, and inasmuch as Adele, the lady's mother, was betrothed to thine uncle Richard; and Mauger menaces excommunication if my liege pursues his suit![1] So troubled is the realm that I, waiting not for debate in council, and fearing sinister ambassage if I did so, took ship from thy port of Cherbourg, and have not flagged rein, and scarce broken bread, till I could say to the heir of Rolf the Founder, 'Save thy realm from the men of mail, and thy bride from the knaves in serge.'"

"Ho, ho!" cried William; then bursting forth in full wrath, as he sprang from the couch: "Hearest thou this, Lord Seneschal? Seven years, the probation of the patriarch, have I wooed and waited; and lo, in the seventh does a proud

---

[1] Most of the chroniclers merely state the parentage within the forbidden degrees as the obstacle to William's marriage with Matilda; but the betrothal, or rather nuptials, of her mother Adele with Richard III. (though never consummated) appears to have been the true canonical objection. (See note to Wace, p. 27.) Nevertheless, Matilda's mother, Adele, stood in the relation of aunt to William, as widow of his father's elder brother, — "an affinity," as is observed by a writer in the "Archæologia," "quite near enough to account for, if not to justify, the interference of the Church." — *Arch.* vol. **xxxii. p. 109.**

priest say to me, ' Wrench the love from thy heart-strings! '
Excommunicate *me*, — ME, — William, the son of Robert the
Devil! Ha, by God's splendour, Mauger shall live to wish
the father stood, in the foul fiend's true likeness, by his side,
rather than brave the bent brow of the son! "

"Dread my lord," said Fitzosborne, desisting from his
employ, and rising to his feet, "thou knowest that I am
thy true friend and leal knight; thou knowest how I have
aided thee in this marriage with the lady of Flanders, and
how gravely I think that what pleases thy fancy will guard
thy realm; but rather than brave the order of the Church and
the ban of the Pope, I would see thee wed to the poorest
virgin in Normandy."

William, who had been pacing the room like an enraged
lion in his den, halted in amaze at this bold speech.

"This from thee, William Fitzosborne! — from thee! I
tell thee that if all the priests in Christendom and all the
barons in France stood between me and my bride, I would
hew my way through the midst. Foes invade my realm, —
let them; princes conspire against me, — I smile in scorn;
subjects mutiny, — this strong hand can punish, or this large
heart can forgive. All these are the dangers which he who
governs men should prepare to meet; but man has a right to
his love, as the stag to his hind, and he who wrongs me here
is foe and traitor to me, not as Norman duke, but as human
being. Look to it, — thou and thy proud barons, look to it! "

"Proud may thy barons be," said Fitzosborne, reddening,
and with a brow that quailed not before his lord's; "for they
are the sons of those who carved out the realm of the Norman,
and owned in Rou but the feudal chief of free warriors. Vassals are not villeins; and that which we hold our duty, whether
to Church or chief,—that, Duke William, thy proud barons will
doubtless do; nor less, believe me, for threats which, braved
in discharge of duty and defence of freedom, we hold as air."

The duke gazed on his haughty subject with an eye in
which a meaner spirit might have seen its doom. The veins
in his broad temples swelled like cords, and a light foam
gathered round his quivering lips. But fiery and fearless as

William was, not less was he sagacious and profound. In that one man he saw the representative of that superb and matchless chivalry, that race of races, those men of men, in whom the brave acknowledge the highest example of valiant deeds, and the free the manliest assertion of noble thoughts,[1] since the day when the last Athenian covered his head with his mantle and mutely died; and far from being the most stubborn against his will, it was to Fitzosborne's paramount influence with the council that he had often owed their submission to his wishes and their contributions to his wars. In the very tempest of his wrath he felt that the blow he longed to strike on that bold head would shiver his ducal throne to the dust. He felt, too, that awful indeed was that power of the Church which could thus turn against him the heart of his truest knight; and he began (for with all his outward frankness his temper was suspicious) to wrong the great-souled noble by the thought that he might already be won over by the enemies whom Mauger had arrayed against his nuptials. Therefore, with one of those rare and mighty efforts of that dissimulation which debased his character but achieved his fortunes, he cleared his brow of its dark cloud, and said in a low voice, that was not without its pathos, —

"Had an angel from heaven forewarned me that William Fitzosborne would speak thus to his kinsman and brother in arms, in the hour of need and the agony of passion, I would have disbelieved him. Let it pass —"

But ere the last word was out of his lips, Fitzosborne had

---

[1] It might be easy to show, were this the place, that though the Saxons never lost their love of liberty, yet that the victories which gradually regained the liberty from the gripe of the Anglo-Norman kings were achieved by the Anglo-Norman aristocracy. And even to this day the few rare descendants of that race (whatever their political faction) will generally exhibit that impatience of despotic influence and that disdain of corruption which characterize the homely bonders of Norway, in whom we may still recognize the sturdy likeness of their fathers; while it is also remarkable that the modern inhabitants of those portions of the kingdom originally peopled by their kindred Danes are, irrespective of mere party divisions, noted for their intolerance of all oppression, and their resolute independence of character; to wit, Yorkshire, Norfolk, Cumberland, and large districts in the Scottish Lowlands

fallen on his knees before the duke, and clasping his hand, exclaimed, while the tears rolled down his swarthy cheek, —

"Pardon, pardon, my liege! When thou speakest thus, my heart melts. What thou willest, that will I! Church or Pope, no matter. Send me to Flanders; I will bring back thy bride."

The slight smile that curved William's lip showed that he was scarce worthy of that sublime weakness in his friend; but he cordially pressed the hand that grasped his own, and said, "Rise; thus should brother speak to brother." Then — for his wrath was only concealed, not stifled, and yearned for its vent — his eye fell upon the delicate and thoughtful face of the priest, who had watched this short and stormy conference in profound silence, despite Taïllefer's whispers to him to interrupt the dispute. "So, priest," he said, "I remember me that when Mauger before let loose his rebellious tongue, thou didst lend thy pedant learning to eke out his brainless treason. Methought that I then banished thee my realm?"

"Not so, Count and Seigneur," answered the ecclesiastic, with a grave but arch smile on his lip; "let me remind thee that to speed me back to my native land thou didst graciously send me a horse halting on three legs and all lame on the fourth. Thus mounted, I met thee on my road. I saluted thee; so did the beast, for his head well-nigh touched the ground. Whereon I did ask thee, in a Latin play of words, to give me at least a quadruped, not a tripod, for my journey.[1] Gracious, even in ire, and with relenting laugh, was thine answer. My liege, thy words implied banishment, thy laughter pardon. So I stayed."

Despite his wrath, William could scarce repress a smile; but recollecting himself, he replied more gravely, —

"Peace with this levity, priest. Doubtless thou art the envoy from this scrupulous Mauger, or some other of my gentle clergy; and thou comest, as doubtless, with soft words and whining homilies. It is in vain. I hold the Church in

---

[1] *Ex pervetusto codice,* MS. Chron. Bec. in Vit. Lanfranc, quoted in the "Archæologia," vol. xxxii. p. 109. The joke, which is very poor, seems to have turned upon *pede* and *quadrupede*; it is a little altered in the text.

holy reverence; the pontiff knows it. But Matilda of Flanders I have wooed; and Matilda of Flanders shall sit by my side in the halls of Rouen, or on the deck of my war-ship, till it anchors on a land worthy to yield a new domain to the son of the Sea-king."

"In the halls of Rouen, and it may be on the throne of England, shall Matilda reign by the side of William," said the priest, in a clear, low, and emphatic voice; "and it was to tell my lord the duke that I repent me of my first unconsidered obeisance to Mauger as my spiritual superior; that since then I have myself examined canon and precedent; and though the letter of the law be against thy spousals, it comes precisely under the category of those alliances to which the Fathers of the Church accord dispensation; — it is to tell thee this, that I, plain Doctor of Laws and priest of Pavia, have crossed the seas."

"Ha, Rou! Ha, Rou!" cried Taillefer, with his usual bluffness, and laughing with great glee, "why wouldst thou not listen to me, Monseigneur?"

"If thou deceivest me not," said William, in surprise, "and thou canst make good thy words, no prelate in Neustria, save Odo of Bayeux, shall lift his head high as thine." And here William, deeply versed in the science of men, bent his eyes keenly upon the unchanging and earnest face of the speaker. "Ah!" he burst out, as if satisfied with the survey, "and my mind tells me that thou speakest not thus boldly and calmly without ground sufficient. Man, I like thee. Thy name? I forget it."

"Lanfranc of Pavia, please you, my lord; called sometimes 'Lanfranc the Scholar' in thy cloister of Bec. Nor misdeem me that I, humble, unmitred priest, should be thus bold. In birth I am noble, and my kindred stand near to the grace of our ghostly pontiff; to the pontiff I myself am not unknown. Did I desire honours, in Italy I might seek them; it is not so. I crave no guerdon for the service I proffer; none but this, — leisure and books in the Convent of Bec."

"Sit down, — nay, sit, man," said William, greatly interested, but still suspicious. "One riddle only I ask thee to solve, before I give thee all my trust, and place my very heart in thy hands. Why, if thou desirest not rewards, shouldst thou thus care to serve me, — thou, a foreigner?"

A light, brilliant and calm, shone in the eyes of the scholar, and a blush spread over his pale cheeks.

"My Lord Prince, I will answer in plain words. But first permit *me* to be the questioner."

The priest turned towards Fitzosborne, who had seated himself on a stool at William's feet, and leaning his chin on his hand, listened to the ecclesiastic, not more with devotion to his calling than wonder at the influence one so obscure was irresistibly gaining over his own martial spirit and William's iron craft.

"Lovest thou not, William Lord of Breteuil, — lovest thou not fame for the sake of fame?"

"*Sur mon âme,* yes!" said the baron.

"And thou, Taillefer the minstrel, lovest thou not song for the sake of song?"

"For song alone," replied the mighty minstrel. "More gold in one ringing rhyme than in all the coffers of Christendom."

"And marvellest thou, reader of men's hearts," said the scholar, turning once more to William, "that the student loves knowledge for the sake of knowledge? Born of high race, poor in purse, and slight of thews, betimes I found wealth in books, and drew strength from lore. I heard of the Count of Rouen and the Normans, as a prince of small domain, with a measureless spirit, a lover of letters, and a captain in war. I came to thy duchy; I noted its subjects and its prince, and the words of Themistocles rang in my ear: ' I cannot play the lute, but I can make a small State great.' I felt an interest in thy strenuous and troubled career. I believe that knowledge, to spread amongst the nations, must first find a nursery in the brain of kings; and I saw in the deed-doer the agent of the thinker. In those espousals, on which with untiring obstinacy thy heart is set, I might sympathize with thee, perchance" (here a melancholy smile flitted over the student's pale lips), — "perchance even as a lover. Priest though I be now, and dead to human love, once I loved, and I know what it is to strive in hope and to waste in despair. But my sym-pathy, I own, was more given to the prince than to the lover. It was natural that I, priest and foreigner, should obey at first the orders of Mauger, archprelate and spiritual chief, and the more so as the law was with him; but when I resolved to stay despite thy sentence which banished me, I resolved to aid thee; for if with Mauger was the dead law, with thee was the living cause of man. Duke William, on thy nuptials with Matilda of Flanders rests thy duchy, — rest, perchance, the mightier sceptres that are yet to come. Thy title disputed, thy principality new and unestablished, thou, above all men, must link thy new race with the ancient line of kings and kaisers. Matilda is the descendant of Charlemagne and Alfred. Thy realm is insecure as long as France under-mines it with plots, and threatens it with arms. Marry the daughter of Baldwin, — and thy wife is the niece of Henry of France, — thine enemy becomes thy kinsman, and must per-force be thine ally. This is not all: it were strange, looking round this disordered royalty of England, — a childless king, who loves thee better than his own blood; a divided nobility, already adopting the fashions of the stranger, and accus-tomed to shift their faith from Saxon to Dane, and Dane to Saxon; a people that has respect indeed for brave chiefs, but seeing new men rise daily from new houses, has no reverence for ancient lines and hereditary names; with a vast mass of villeins or slaves that have no interest in the land or its rulers, — strange, seeing all this, if thy day-dreams have not also beheld a Norman sovereign on the throne of Saxon England. And thy marriage with the descendant of the best and most beloved prince that ever ruled these realms, if it does not give thee a title to the land, may help to conciliate its affections, and to fix thy posterity in the halls of their mother's kin. Have I said eno' to prove why, for the sake of nations, it were wise for the pontiff to stretch the harsh girths of the law; why I might be enabled to prove to the Court of Rome the policy of conciliating the love and strengthening the hands of the Norman Count, who may so become the main prop of

Christendom? Yea, have I said eno' to prove that the humble
clerk can look on mundane matters with the eye of a man
who can make small States great?"

William remained speechless, his hot blood thrilled with a
half-superstitious awe; so thoroughly had this obscure Lombard divined, detailed, all the intricate meshes of that policy
with which he himself had interwoven his pertinacious affection for the Flemish princess, that it seemed to him as if he
listened to the echo of his own heart, or heard from a sooth-
sayer the voice of his most secret thoughts.

The priest continued: "Wherefore, thus considering, I said
to myself, 'Now has the time come, Lanfranc the Lombard,
to prove to thee whether thy self-boastings have been a vain
deceit, or whether in this age of iron and amidst this lust
of gold thou, the penniless and the feeble, canst make knowledge and wit of more avail to the destinies of kings than
armed men and filled treasuries.' I believe in that power. I
am ready for the test. Pause, judge from what the Lord of
Breteuil hath said to thee what will be the defection of thy
lords if the Pope confirm the threatened excommunication of
thine uncle. Thine armies will rot from thee; thy treasures
will be like dry leaves in thy coffers; the Duke of Bretagne
will claim thy duchy as the legitimate heir of thy forefathers;
the Duke of Burgundy will league with the King of France,
and march on thy faithless legions under the banner of the
Church. The handwriting is on the walls, and thy sceptre
and thy crown will pass away."

William set his teeth firmly, and breathed hard.

"But send me to Rome, thy delegate, and the thunder of
Mauger shall fall powerless. Marry Matilda, bring her to thy
halls, place her on thy throne, laugh to scorn the interdict of
thy traitor uncle, and rest assured that the Pope shall send
thee his dispensation to thy spousals, and his benison on thy
marriage-bed. And when this be done, Duke William, give
me not abbacies and prelacies; multiply books, and stablish
schools, and bid thy servant found the royalty of knowledge,
as thou shalt found the sovereignty of war."

The duke, transported from himself, leaped up and embraced the priest with his vast arms; he kissed his cheeks, he kissed his forehead, as, in those days, king kissed king with "the kiss of peace."

"Lanfranc of Pavia," he cried, "whether thou succeed or fail, thou hast my love and gratitude evermore. As thou speakest, would I have spoken, had I been born, framed, and reared as thou. And verily, when I hear thee, I blush for the boasts of my barbarous pride, that no man can wield my mace or bend my bow. Poor is the strength of body, — a web of law can entangle it, and a word from a priest's mouth can palsy. But thou! — let me look at thee."

William gazed on the pale face; from head to foot he scanned the delicate, slender form, and then, turning away, he said to Fitzosborne, —

"Thou, whose mailed hand hath felled a war-steed, art thou not ashamed of thyself? The day is coming, I see it afar, when these slight men shall set their feet upon our corselets."

He paused as if in thought, again paced the room, and stopped before the crucifix, and image of the Virgin, which stood in a niche near the bed-head.

"Right, noble prince," said the priest's low voice, "pause there for a solution to all enigmas; there view the symbol of all-enduring power; there learn its ends below, comprehend the account it must yield above. To your thoughts and your prayers we leave you."

He took the stalwart arm of Taillefer, as he spoke, and with a grave obeisance to Fitzosborne, left the chamber.

CHAPTER III.

The next morning, William was long closeted alone with Lanfranc, — that man, among the most remarkable of his age, of whom it was said, that "to comprehend the extent of his

talents, one must be Herodian in grammar, Aristotle in dialectics, Cicero in rhetoric, Augustine and Jerome in Scriptural
lore," [1] — and ere the noon the duke's gallant and princely
train were ordered to be in readiness for return home.

The crowd in the broad space, and the citizens from their
boats in the river, gazed on the knights and steeds of that
gorgeous company, already drawn up and awaiting without
the open gates the sound of the trumpets that should announce
the duke's departure. Before the hall-door in the inner court
were his own men; the snow-white steed of Odo, the alezan
of Fitzosborne, and, to the marvel of all, a small palfrey
plainly caparisoned. What did that palfrey amid those
steeds? The steeds themselves seemed to chafe at the
companionship; the duke's charger pricked up his ears and
snorted; the Lord of Breteuil's alezan kicked out, as the
poor nag humbly drew near to make acquaintance; and the
prelate's white barb, with red vicious eye, and ears laid
down, ran fiercely at the low-bred intruder, with difficulty
reined in by the squires, who shared the beast's amaze and
resentment.

Meanwhile the duke thoughtfully took his way to Edward's
apartments. In the anteroom were many monks and many
knights; but conspicuous amongst them all was a tall and
stately veteran, leaning on a great two-handed sword, and
whose dress and fashion of beard were those of the last generation, the men who had fought with Canute the Great or
Edmund Ironsides. So grand was the old man's aspect, and
so did he contrast in appearance the narrow garb and shaven
chins of those around, that the duke was roused from his
revery at the sight, and marvelling why one, evidently a chief
of high rank, had neither graced the banquet in his honour
nor been presented to his notice, he turned to the Earl of
Hereford, who approached him with gay salutation, and
inquired the name and title of the bearded man in the loose
flowing robe.

"Know you not, in truth?" said the lively earl, in some
wonder. "In him you see the great rival of Godwin. He is

[1] Ord. Vital. See note on Lanfranc, at the end of the volume.

the hero of the Danes, as Godwin is of the Saxons, a true son of Odin, Siward, Earl of the Northumbrians."[1]

"Notre Dame be my aid, — his fame hath oft filled my ears, and I should have lost the most welcome sight in merrie England had I not now beheld him."

Therewith the duke approached courteously, and doffing the cap he had hitherto retained, he greeted the old hero with those compliments which the Norman had already learned in the courts of the Frank.

The stout earl received them coldly, and replying in Danish to William's Romance-tongue, he said, —

"Pardon, Count of the Normans, if these old lips cling to their old words. Both of us, methinks, date our lineage from the lands of the Norse. Suffer Siward to speak the language the sea-kings spoke. The old oak is not to be transplanted, and the old man keeps the ground where his youth took root."

The duke, who with some difficulty comprehended the general meaning of Siward's speech, bit his lip, but replied courteously, —

"The youths of all nations may learn from renowned age. Much doth it shame me that I cannot commune with thee in the ancestral tongue; but the angels at least know the language of the Norman Christian, and I pray them and the saints for a calm end to thy brave career."

"Pray not to angel or saint for Siward, son of Beorn," said the old man, hastily; "let me not have a cow's death, but a warrior's, — die in my mail of proof, axe in hand, and helm

---

[1] Siward was almost a giant (*pene gigas statura*). There are some curious anecdotes of this hero, immortalized by Shakspeare, in the "Brompton Chronicle." His grandfather is said to have been a bear, who fell in love with a Danish lady; and his father, Beorn, retained some of the traces of the parental physiognomy in a pair of pointed ears. The origin of this fable seems evident. His grandfather was a Berserker; for whether that name be derived, as is more generally supposed, from *bare-sark*, or rather from *bear-sark*, — that is, whether this grisly specimen of the Viking genus fought in his shirt or his bearskin, — the name equally lends itself to those mystifications from which half the old legends, whether of Greece or Norway, are derived.

on head. And such may be my death, if Edward the King reads my rede and grants my prayer."

"I have influence with the king," said William; "name thy wish, that I may back it."

"The fiend forfend," said the grim earl, "that a foreign prince should sway England's King, or that thegn and earl should ask other backing than leal service and just cause. If Edward be the saint men call him, he will loose me on the hell-wolf without other cry than his own conscience."

The duke turned inquiringly to Rolf, who, thus appealed to, said, —

"Siward urges my uncle to espouse the cause of Malcolm of Cumbria against the bloody tyrant Macbeth; and but for the disputes with the traitor Godwin, the king had long since turned his arms to Scotland."

"Call not traitors, young man," said the earl, in high disdain, "those who with all their faults and crimes have placed thy kinsman on the throne of Canute."

"Hush, Rolf!" said the duke, observing the fierce young Norman about to reply hastily. "But methought, though my knowledge of English troubles is but scant, that Siward was the sworn foe to Godwin?"

"Foe to him in his power, friend to him in his wrongs," answered Siward. "And if England needs defenders when I and Godwin are in our shrouds, there is but one man worthy of the days of old, and his name is Harold, the outlaw."

William's face changed remarkably, despite all his dissimulation; and with a slight inclination of his head, he strode on, moody and irritated.

"This Harold! this Harold!" he muttered to himself, "all brave men speak to me of this Harold! Even my Norman knights name him with reluctant reverence, and even his foes do him honour; verily his shadow is cast from exile over all the land."

Thus murmuring, he passed the throng with less than his wonted affable grace, and pushing back the officers who wished to precede him, entered, without ceremony, Edward's private chamber.

The king was alone, but talking loudly to himself, gesticulating vehemently, and altogether so changed from his ordinary placid apathy of mien that William drew back in alarm
and awe. Often had he heard indirectly that of late years
Edward was said to see visions, and be rapt from himself into
the world of spirit and shadow; and such, he now doubted
not, was the strange paroxysm of which he was made the
witness. Edward's eyes were fixed on him, but evidently
without recognizing his presence; the king's hands were outstretched, and he cried aloud in a voice of sharp anguish, —

"*Sanguelac, Sanguelac!* — the Lake of Blood! The waves
spread, the waves redden! Mother of mercy, where is the
ark, where the Ararat? Fly, fly, — this way, this — " and he
caught convulsive hold of William's arm. "No! there the
corpses are piled, — high and higher; there the horse of the
Apocalypse tramples the dead in their gore."

In great horror, William took the king, now gasping on his
breast, in his arms, and laid him on his bed, beneath its canopy of state, all blazoned with the martlets and cross of his
insignia. Slowly Edward came to himself, with heavy sighs;
and when at length he sat up and looked round, it was with
evident unconsciousness of what had passed across his haggard and wandering spirit, for he said, with his usual drowsy
calmness, —

"Thanks, Guillaume, *bien aimé*, for rousing me from un-
seasoned sleep. How fares it with thee?"

"Nay, how with thee, dear friend and king? Thy dreams
have been troubled."

"Not so; I slept so heavily, methinks I could not have
dreamed at all. But thou art clad as for a journey, — spur
on thy heel, staff in thy hand!"

"Long since, O dear host, I sent Odo to tell thee of the ill
news from Normandy that compelled me to depart."

"I remember, — I remember me now," said Edward, passing
his pale womanly fingers over his forehead. "The heathen
rage against thee. Ah! my poor brother, a crown is an awful
head-gear. While yet time, why not both seek some quiet
convent, and put away these earthly cares?"

William smiled and shook his head. "Nay, holy Edward, from all I have seen of convents, it is a dream to think that the monk's serge hides a calmer breast than the warrior's mail or the king's ermine. Now give me thy benison, for I go."

He knelt as he spoke; and Edward bent his hands over his head, and blessed him. Then, taking from his own neck a collar of zimmes (jewels and uncut gems), of great price, the king threw it over the broad throat bent before him, and rising, clapped his hands. A small door opened, giving a glimpse of the oratory within, and a monk appeared.

"Father, have my behests been fulfilled? Hath Hugoline, my treasurer, dispensed the gifts that I spoke of ?"

"Verily, yes; vault, coffer, and garde-robe, stall and meuse, are well-nigh drained," answered the monk, with a sour look at the Norman, whose native avarice gleamed in his dark eyes as he heard the answer.

"Thy train go not hence empty-handed," said Edward, fondly. "Thy father's halls sheltered the exile, and the exile forgets not the sole pleasure of a king, — the power to requite. We may never meet again, William; age creeps over me, and who will succeed to my thorny throne?"

William longed to answer, — to tell the hope that consumed him, — to remind his cousin of the vague promise in their youth, that the Norman Count should succeed to that "thorny throne;" but the presence of the Saxon monk repelled him, nor was there in Edward's uneasy look much to allure him on.

"But peace," continued the king, "be between thine and mine, as between thee and me!"

"Amen," said the duke, "and I leave thee at least free from the proud rebels who so long disturbed thy reign. This House of Godwin, — thou wilt not again let it tower above thy palace?"

"Nay, the future is with God and his saints," answered Edward, feebly. "But Godwin is old, older than I, and bowed by many storms."

"Ay, his sons are more to be dreaded and kept aloof, — mostly Harold!"

"Harold, — he was ever obedient, he alone of his kith; truly my soul mourns for Harold," said the king, sighing.

"The serpent's egg hatches but the serpent. Keep thy heel on it," said William, sternly.

"Thou speakest well," said the irresolute prince, who never seemed three days or three minutes together in the same mind. "Harold is in Ireland, — there let him rest; better for all."

"For all," said the duke; "so the saints keep thee, O royal saint!"

He kissed the king's hand, and strode away to the hall where Odo, Fitzosborne, and the priest Lanfranc awaited him; and so that day, half-way towards the fair town of Dover, rode Duke William, and by the side of his roan barb ambled the priest's palfrey.

Behind came his gallant train, and with tumbrils and sumpter-mules laden with baggage, and enriched by Edward's gifts; while Welch hawks, and steeds of great price from the pastures of Surrey and the plains of Cambridge and York, attested no less acceptably than zimme and golden chain and broidered robe the munificence of the grateful king.[1]

As they journeyed on, and the fame of the duke's coming was sent abroad by the bodes, or messengers, despatched to prepare the towns through which he was to pass for an arrival sooner than expected, the more high-born youths of England, especially those of the party counter to that of the banished Godwin, came round the ways to gaze upon that famous chief who from the age of fifteen had wielded the most redoubtable sword of Christendom. And those youths wore the Norman garb; and in the towns Norman counts held his stirrup to dismount, and Norman hosts spread the fastidious board; and when, at the eve of the next day, William saw the pennon of one of his own favourite chiefs waving in the van of armed men that sallied forth from the towers of Dover (the key of the coast), he turned to the Lombard, still by his side, and said, —

"Is not England part of Normandy already?"

And the Lombard answered: "The fruit is well-nigh ripe,

[1] Wace.

and the first breeze will shake it to thy feet. Put not out thy hand too soon. Let the wind do its work."

And the duke made reply: "As thou thinkest, so think I; and there is but one wind in the halls of heaven that can waft the fruit to the feet of another."

"And that?" asked the Lombard.

"Is the wind that blows from the shores of Ireland, when it fills the sails of Harold, son of Godwin."

"Thou fearest that man, and why?" asked the Lombard, with interest.

And the duke answered: "Because in the breast of Harold beats the heart of England."

BOOK III.

THE HOUSE OF GODWIN.

CHAPTER I.

AND all went to the desire of Duke William the Norman. With one hand he curbed his proud vassals, and drove back his fierce foes; with the other he led to the altar Matilda, the maid of Flanders; and all happened as Lanfranc had foretold. William's most formidable enemy, the King of France, ceased to conspire against his new kinsman; and the neighbouring princes said, "The Bastard hath become one of us, since he placed by his side the descendant of Charlemagne." And Mauger, Archbishop of Rouen, excommunicated the duke and his bride, and the ban fell idle; for Lanfranc sent from Rome the Pope's dispensation and blessing,[1] conditionally only that bride and bridegroom founded each a church. And Mauger was summoned before the synod, and accused of unclerical crimes; and they deposed him from his state, and took from him abbacies and sees. And England every day waxed more and more Norman; and Edward grew more feeble and infirm, and there seemed not a barrier between the Norman Duke and the English throne, when suddenly the wind blew in the halls of heaven, and filled the sails of Harold the Earl.

And his ships came to the mouth of the Severn; and the people of Somerset and Devon, a mixed and mainly a Celtic race, who bore small love to the Saxons, drew together against him, and he put them to flight.[2]

Meanwhile Godwin and his sons, Sweyn, Tostig, and Gurth, who had taken refuge in that very Flanders from which Wil-

---

[1] See Note E, (foot-note on the date of William's marriage).
[2] Anglo-Saxon Chronicle.

liam the Duke had won his bride, — for Tostig had wed, previously, the sister of Matilda, the rose of Flanders; and Count
Baldwin had for his sons-in-law both Tostig and William, —
meanwhile, I say, these, not holpen by the Count Baldwin,
but helping themselves, lay at Bruges, ready to join Harold
the Earl.   And Edward, advised of this from the anxious
Norman, caused forty ships[1] to be equipped, and put them
under command of Rolf, Earl of Hereford.   The ships lay at
Sandwich in wait for Godwin.   But the old earl got from
them, and landed quietly on the southern coast; and the fort
of Hastings opened to his coming with a shout from its armed
men.

All the boatmen, all the mariners, far and near, thronged to
him, with sail and with shield, with sword and with oar.
All Kent (the foster-mother of the Saxons) sent forth the cry,
"Life or death with Earl Godwin."[2]   Fast over the length
and breadth of the land, went the bodes[3] and riders of the
earl; and hosts, with one voice, answered the cry of the children of Horsa, "Life or death with Earl Godwin."   And the
ships of King Edward, in dismay, turned flag and prow to
London, and the fleet of Harold sailed on.   So the old earl
met his young son on the deck of a war-ship that had once
borne the Raven of the Dane.

Swelled and gathering sailed the armament of the English
men.   Slow up the Thames it sailed, and on either shore
marched tumultuous the swarming multitudes.   And King
Edward sent after more help, but it came up very late.   So
the fleet of the earl nearly faced the Julliet Keape of London,
and abode at Southwark till the flood-tide came up.   When
he had mustered his host, then came the flood-tide.[4]

---

[1] Some writers say fifty.   [2] Hovenden.
[3] Messengers.   [4] Anglo-Saxon Chronicle.

CHAPTER II.

KING EDWARD sat, not on his throne, but on a chair of state, in the presence-chamber of his palace of Westminster; his diadem, with the three zimmes shaped into a triple trefoil[1] on his brow, his sceptre in his right hand. His royal robe, tight to the throat, with a broad band of gold, flowed to his feet; and at the fold gathered round the left knee, where now the kings of England wear the badge of Saint George, was embroidered a simple cross.[2] In that chamber met the thegns and proceres of his realm; but not they alone. No national Witan there assembled, but a council of war, composed at least one third part of Normans, — counts, knights, prelates, and abbots of high degree.

And King Edward looked a king! The habitual lethargic meekness had vanished from his face, and the large crown threw a shadow, like a frown, over his brow. His spirit seemed to have risen from the weight it took from the sluggish blood of his father, Ethelred the Unready, and to have re-mounted to the brighter and earlier source of ancestral heroes. Worthy in that hour, he seemed to boast the blood, and wield the sceptre of Athelstan and Alfred.[3]

Thus spoke the king: "Right worthy and beloved, my ealdermen, earls, and thegns of England; noble and familiar, my friends and guests, counts and chevaliers of Normandy, my mother's land; and you, our spiritual chiefs, above all ties of birth and country, Christendom your common appanage, and from Heaven your seignories and fiefs, — hear the words of Edward, the King of England under grace of the Most High. The rebels are in our river; open yonder lattice, and you will see the piled shields glittering from their barks,

---

[1] Or fleur-de-lis, which seems to have been a common form of ornament with the Saxon kings.

[2] Bayeux tapestry.   [3] See note F.

and hear the hum of their hosts. Not a bow has yet been drawn, not a sword left its sheath; yet on the opposite side of the river are our fleets of forty sail, — along the Strand, between our palace and the gates of London, are arrayed our armies. And this pause, because Godwin the traitor hath demanded truce and his nuncius waits without. Are ye willing that we should hear the message; or would ye rather that we dismiss the messenger unheard, and pass at once, to rank and to sail, the war-cry of a Christian king, ' Holy Crosse and our Lady!' "

The king ceased, his left hand grasping firm the leopard head carved on his throne, and his sceptre untrembling in his lifted hand.

A murmur of " Notre Dame, Notre Dame," the war-cry of the Normans, was heard amongst the stranger-knights of the audience; but haughty and arrogant as those strangers were, no one presumed to take precedence, in England's danger, of men English born.

Slowly then rose Alred, Bishop of Winchester, the worthiest prelate in all the land.[1]

" Kingly son," said the bishop, " evil is the strife between men of the same blood and lineage, nor justified but by extremes, which have not yet been made clear to us. And ill would it sound throughout England were it said that the king's council gave, perchance, his city of London to sword and fire, and rent his land in twain, when a word in season might have disbanded yon armies, and given to your throne a submissive subject, where now you are menaced by a formidable rebel. Wherefore, I say, admit the nuncius."

Scarcely had Alred resumed his seat, before Robert the Norman, prelate of Canterbury, started up, — a man, it was said, of worldly learning, — and exclaimed, —

---

[1] The " York Chronicle," written by an Englishman, Stubbs, gives this eminent person an excellent character as peacemaker. " He could make the warmest friends of foes the most hostile, — " " de inimicissimis, amicissimos faceret." This gentle priest had yet the courage to curse the Norman Conqueror in the midst of his barons. That scene is not within the range of this work, but it is very strikingly told in the " Chronicle."

"To admit the messenger is to approve the treason. I do beseech the king to consult only his own royal heart and royal honour. Reflect, — each moment of delay swells the rebel hosts, strengthens their cause; of each moment they avail themselves to allure to their side the misguided citizens. Delay but proves our own weakness; a king's name is a tower of strength, but only when fortified by a king's authority. Give the signal for — *war* I call it not, — no — for chastisement and justice."

"As speaks my brother of Canterbury, speak I," said William, Bishop of London, another Norman.

But then there rose up a form at whose rising all murmurs were hushed. Gray and vast, as some image of a gone and mightier age, towered over all, Siward, the son of Beorn, the great Earl of Northumbria.

"We have nought to do with the Normans. Were they on the river, and our countrymen, Dane or Saxon, alone in this hall, small doubt of the king's choice, and niddering were the man who spoke of peace; but when Norman advises the dwellers of England to go forth and slay each other, no sword of mine shall be drawn at his hest. Who shall say that Siward of the Strong Arm, the grandson of the Berserker, ever turned from a foe? The foe, son of Ethelred, sits in these halls; I fight thy battles when I say Nay to the Norman! Brothers-in-arms of the kindred race and common tongue, Dane and Saxon long intermingled, proud alike of Canute the glorious and Alfred the wise, ye will hear the man whom Godwin, our countryman, sends to us; he at least will speak our tongue, and he knows our laws. If the demand he delivers be just, such as a king should grant, and our Witan should hear, woe to him who refuses; if unjust be the demand, shame to him who accedes. Warrior sends to warrior, countryman to countryman; hear we as countrymen, and judge as warriors. I have said."

The utmost excitement and agitation followed the speech of Siward, — unanimous applause from the Saxons, even those who in times of peace were most under the Norman contagion; but no words can paint the wrath and scorn of the Normans.

They spoke loud, and many at a time; the greatest disorder prevailed. But the majority being English, there could be no doubt as to the decision; and Edward, to whom the emergence gave both a dignity and presence of mind rare to him, resolved to terminate the dispute at once. He stretched forth his sceptre, and motioning to his chamberlain, bade him introduce the nuncius.[1]

A blank disappointment, not unmixed with apprehensive terror, succeeded the turbulent excitement of the Normans; for well they knew that the consequences, if not condition, of negotiations would be their own downfall and banishment at the least, — happy, it might be, to escape massacre at the hands of the exasperated multitude.

The door at the end of the room opened, and the nuncius appeared. He was a sturdy, broad-shouldered man, of middle age, and in the long loose garb originally national with the Saxon, though then little in vogue; his beard thick and fair, his eyes gray and calm, — a chief of Kent, where all the prejudices of his race were strongest, and whose yeomanry claimed in war the hereditary right to be placed in the front of battle.

He made his manly but deferential salutation to the august council as he approached; and pausing midway between the throne and door, he fell on his knees without thought of shame, for the king to whom he knelt was the descendant of Woden and the heir of Hengist. At a sign and a brief word from the king, still on his knees, Vebba the Kentman spoke: —

"To Edward, son of Ethelred, his most gracious king and lord, Godwin, son of Wolnoth, sends faithful and humble greeting, by Vebba, the thegn-born. He prays the king to hear him in kindness, and judge of him with mercy. Not against the king comes he hither with ships and arms; but against those only who would stand between the king's heart and the subject's, — those who have divided a house against itself, and parted son and father, man and wife."

---

[1] Heralds, though probably the word is Saxon, were not then known in the modern acceptation of the word. The name given to the messenger, or envoy, who fulfilled that office was bode, or nuncius. See Note G.

At those last words Edward's sceptre trembled in his hand, and his face grew almost stern.

"Of the king Godwin but prays, with all submiss and earnest prayer, to reverse. the unrighteous outlawry against him and his; to restore him and his sons their just possessions and well-won honours; and, more than all, to replace them where they have sought by loving service not unworthily to stand, in the grace of their born lord, and in the van of those who would uphold the laws and liberties of England. This done, the ships sail back to their haven, the thegn seeks his homestead, and the ceorl returns to the plough; for with Godwin are no strangers, and his force is but the love of his countrymen."

"Hast thou said?" quoth the king.

"I have said."

"Retire, and await our answer."

The Thegn of Kent was then led back into an anteroom, in which, armed from head to heel in ring-mail, were several Normans whose youth or station did not admit them into the council, but still of no mean interest in the discussion, from the lands and possessions they had already contrived to gripe out of the demesnes of the exiles; burning for battle and eager for the word. Amongst these was Mallet de Graville.

The Norman valour of this young knight was, as we have seen, guided by Norman intelligence; and he had not disdained, since William's departure, to study the tongue of the country in which he hoped to exchange his mortgaged tower on the Seine for some fair barony on the Humber or the Thames.

While the rest of his proud countrymen stood aloof, with eyes of silent scorn, from the homely nuncius, Mallet approached him with courteous bearing, and said in Saxon, —

"May I crave to know the issue of thy message from the reb — that is, from the doughty earl?"

"I wait to learn it," said Vebba, bluffly.

"They heard thee throughout, then?"

"Throughout."

"Friendly sir," said the Sire de Graville, seeking to subdue the tone of irony habitual to him, and acquired, perhaps, from his maternal ancestry, the Franks, — "friendly and peace-making sir, dare I so far venture to intrude on the secrets of thy mission as to ask if Godwin demands, among other reasonable items, the head of thy humble servant, — not by name indeed, for my name is as yet unknown to him, — but as one of the unhappy class called Normans?"

"Had Earl Godwin," returned the nuncius, "thought fit to treat for peace by asking vengeance, he would have chosen another spokesman. The earl asks but his own; and thy head is not, I trow, a part of his goods and chattels."

"That is comforting," said Mallet. "Marry, I thank thee, Sir Saxon; and thou speakest like a brave man and an honest. And if we fall to blows, as I suspect we shall, I should deem it a favour of our Lady the Virgin if she send thee across my way. Next to a fair friend I love a bold foe."

Vebba smiled, for he liked the sentiment; and the tone and air of the young knight pleased his rough mind, despite his prejudices against the stranger.

Encouraged by the smile, Mallet seated himself on the corner of the long table that skirted the room, and with a debonnair gesture invited Vebba to do the same; then looking at him gravely, he resumed, —

"So frank and courteous thou art, Sir Envoy, that I yet intrude on thee my ignorant and curious questions."

"Speak out, Norman."

"How comes it, then, that you English so love this Earl Godwin? Still more, why think you it right and proper that King Edward should love him too? It is a question I have often asked, and to which I am not likely in these halls to get answer satisfactorily. If I know aught of your troublous history, this same earl has changed sides oft eno', — first for the Saxon, then for Canute the Dane; Canute dies, and your friend takes up arms for the Saxon again. He yields to the advice of your Witan, and sides with Hardicanute and Harold, the Danes; a letter, nathless, is written as from Emma, the mother to the young Saxon princes, Edward and Alfred, inviting them over to England and promising aid; the saints protect Edward, who continues to say *aves* in Normandy; Alfred comes over, Earl Godwin meets him, and, unless belied, does him homage, and swears to him faith. Nay, listen yet. This Godwin, whom ye love so, then leads Alfred and his train into the ville of Guildford, I think ye call it, — fair quarters enow. At the dead of the night rush in King Harold's men, seize prince and follower, six hundred men in all; the next morning, saving only every tenth man, they are tortured and put to death. The prince is borne off to London, and shortly afterwards his eyes are torn out in the Islet of Ely, and he dies of the anguish! That ye should love Earl Godwin withal may be strange, but yet possible. But is it possible, *cher* envoy, for the king to love the man who thus betrayed his brother to the shambles?"

"All this is a Norman fable," said the Thegn of Kent, with a disturbed visage; "and Godwin cleared himself on oath of all share in the foul murder of Alfred."

"The oath, I have heard, was backed," said the knight, dryly, "by a present to Hardicanute, who after the death of King Harold resolved to avenge the black butchery, — a present, I say, of a gilt ship, manned by fourscore warriors with gold-hilted swords and gilt helms. But let this pass."

"Let it pass," echoed Vebba, with a sigh. "Bloody were those times, and unholy their secrets."

"Yet answer me still, why love you Earl Godwin? He hath changed sides from party to party, and in each change won lordships and lands. He is ambitious and grasping, ye all allow; for the ballads sung in your streets liken him to the thorn and the bramble, at which the sheep leaves his wool. He is haughty and overbearing. Tell me, O Saxon, frank Saxon, why you love Godwin the Earl? Fain would I know; for, please the saints (and you and your earl so permitting), I mean to live and die in this merrie England; and it would be pleasant to learn that I have but to do as Earl Godwin, in order to win love from the English."

The stout Vebba looked perplexed; but after stroking his beard thoughtfully, he answered thus, —

"Though of Kent, and therefore in his earldom, I am not one of Godwin's especial party; for that reason was I chosen his bode. Those who are under him doubtless love a chief liberal to give and strong to protect. The old age of a great leader gathers reverence, as an oak gathers moss. But to me, and those like me, living peaceful at home, shunning courts, and tempting not broils, Godwin the *man* is not dear, — it is Godwin the *thing*."

"Though I do my best to know your language," said the knight, "ye have phrases that might puzzle King Solomon. What meanest thou by ' Godwin the thing '?"

"That which to us Godwin only seems to uphold. We love justice; whatever his offences, Godwin was banished unjustly. We love our laws; Godwin was dishonoured by maintaining them. We love England, and are devoured by strangers; Godwin's cause is England's, and — Stranger, forgive me for not concluding."

Then examining the young Norman with a look of rough compassion, he laid his large hand upon the knight's shoulder and whispered, —

"Take my advice, and fly."

"Fly!" said De Graville, reddening. "Is it to fly, think you, that I have put on my mail and girded my sword?"

"Vain, — vain! Wasps are fierce, but the swarm is doomed when the straw is kindled. I tell you this, — fly in time, and you are safe; but let the king be so misguided as to count on arms, and strive against yon multitude, and verily before nightfall not one Norman will be found alive within ten miles of the city. Look to it, youth! Perhaps thou hast a mother, — let her not mourn a son!"

Before the Norman could shape into Saxon sufficiently polite and courtly his profound and indignant disdain of the counsel, his sense of the impertinence with which his shoulder had been profaned, and his mother's son had been warned, the nuncius was again summoned into the presence-chamber. Nor did he return into the anteroom, but conducted forthwith

from the council — his brief answer received — to the stairs
of the palace, he reached the boat in which he had come, and
was rowed back to the ship that held the earl and his sons.

Now, this was the manœuvre of Godwin's array. His
vessels, having passed London Bridge, had rested awhile on
the banks of the southward suburb (Suth-weorde), — since
called Southwark, — and the king's ships lay to the north;
but the fleet of the earl's, after a brief halt, veered majestically round, and coming close to the palace of Westminster,
inclined northward, as if to hem the king's ships. Meanwhile the land forces drew up close to the Strand, almost
within bow-shot of the king's troops, that kept the ground
inland; thus Vebba saw before him, so near as scarcely to be
distinguished from each other, on the river the rival fleets,
on the shore the rival armaments.

High above all the vessels towered the majestic bark, or
æsca, that had borne Harold from the Irish shores. Its fashion was that of the ancient sea-kings, to one of whom it had
belonged. Its curved and mighty prow, richly gilded, stood
out far above the waves, — the prow the head of the sea-
snake, the stern its spire; head and spire alike glittering in
the sun.

The boat drew up to the lofty side of the vessel, a ladder
was lowered, the nuncius ascended lightly and stood on deck.
At the farther end grouped the sailors, few in number, and at
respectful distance from the earl and his sons.

Godwin himself was but half armed. His head was bare,
nor had he other weapon of offence than the gilt battle-axe of
the Danes, — weapon as much of office as of war; but his
broad breast was covered with the ring mail of the time.
His stature was lower than that of any of his sons; nor did
his form exhibit greater physical strength than that of a man
well shaped, robust, and deep of chest, who still preserved in
age the pith and sinew of mature manhood. Neither, indeed,
did legend or fame ascribe to that eminent personage those
romantic achievements, those feats of purely animal prowess,
which distinguished his rival, Siward. Brave he was, but
brave as a leader; those faculties in which he appears to have

excelled all his contemporaries were more analogous to the
requisites of success in civilized times than those which won
renown of old.   And perhaps England was the only country
then in Europe which could have given to those faculties their
fitting career.   He possessed essentially the arts of party; he
knew how to deal with vast masses of mankind; he could
carry along with his interests the fervid heart of the multitude; he had in the highest degree that gift, useless in most
other lands, — in all lands where popular assemblies do not
exist, — the gift of popular eloquence.   Ages elapsed, after
the Norman conquest, ere eloquence again became a power in
England.[1]

But like all men renowned for eloquence, he went with the
popular feeling of his times; he embodied its passions, its
prejudices, but also that keen sense of self-interest which is
the invariable characteristic of a multitude.   He *was* the sense
of the commonalty carried to its highest degree.   Whatever
the faults, it may be the crimes, of a career singularly prosperous and splendid, amidst events the darkest and most terrible, — shining with a steady light across the thunder-clouds,
— he was never accused of cruelty or outrage to the mass of
the people.   English, emphatically, the English deemed him;
and this not the less that in his youth he had sided with
Canute, and owed his fortunes to that king: for so intermixed were Danes and Saxons in England, that the agreement
which had given to Canute one half the kingdom had been
received with general applause; and the earlier severities of
that great prince had been so redeemed in his later years by
wisdom and mildness — so, even in the worst period of his
reign, relieved by extraordinary personal affability, and so
lost now in men's memories by pride in his power and fame
— that Canute had left behind him a beloved and honoured
name,[2] and Godwin was the more esteemed as the chosen

---

[1] When the chronicler praises the gift of speech, he unconsciously proves
the existence of constitutional freedom.

[2] Recent Danish historians have in vain endeavoured to detract from the
reputation of Canute as an *English* monarch.   The Danes are, doubtless, the
best authorities for his character in Denmark.   But our own English authori-

counsellor of that popular prince. At his death Godwin was known to have wished, and even armed, for the restoration of the Saxon line; and only yielded to the determination of the Witan, no doubt acted upon by the popular opinion. Of one dark crime he was suspected, and, despite his oath to the contrary, and the formal acquittal of the national council, doubt of his guilt rested then, as it rests still, upon his name; namely, the perfidious surrender of Alfred, Edward's murdered brother.

But time had passed over the dismal tragedy; and there was an instinctive and prophetic feeling throughout the English nation that with the House of Godwin was identified the cause of the English people. Everything in this man's aspect served to plead in his favour. His ample brows were calm with benignity and thought; his large dark blue eyes were serene and mild, though their expression, when examined, was close and inscrutable. His mien was singularly noble, but wholly without formality or affected state; and though haughtiness and arrogance were largely attributed to him, they could be found only in his deeds, not manner, — plain, familiar, kindly to all men, his heart seemed as open to the service of his countrymen as his hospitable door to their wants.

Behind him stood the stateliest group of sons that ever filled with pride a father's eye, — each strikingly distinguished from the other, all remarkable for beauty of countenance and strength of frame.

Sweyn, the eldest,[1] had the dark hues of his mother the

---

ties are sufficiently decisive as to the personal popularity of Canute in this country, and the affection entertained for his laws.

[1] Some of our historians erroneously represent Harold as the eldest son. But Florence, the best authority we have, in the silence of the "Saxon Chronicle," as well as Knyghton, distinctly states Sweyn to be the eldest; Harold was the second, and Tostig was the third. Sweyn's seniority seems corroborated by the greater importance of his earldom. The Norman chroniclers, in their spite to Harold, wish to make him junior to Tostig, for the reasons evident at the close of this work. And the Norwegian chronicler, Snorro Sturleson, says that Harold was the youngest of all the sons; so little was really known, or cared to be accurately known, of that great House which so nearly founded a new dynasty of English kings.

Dane.   A wild and mournful majesty sat upon features
aquiline and regular, but wasted by grief or passion; raven
locks, glossy even in neglect, fell half over eyes hollow in
their sockets, but bright, though with troubled fire.   Over
his shoulder he bore his mighty axe.   His form, spare, but
of immense power, was sheathed in mail, and he leaned on
his great pointed Danish shield.   At his feet sat his young
son Haco,— a boy with a countenance preternaturally thoughtful for his years, which were yet those of childhood.

Next to him stood the most dreaded and ruthless of the
sons of Godwin, — he, fated to become to the Saxon what
Julian was to the Goth.   With his arms folded on his breast,
stood Tostig; his face was beautiful as a Greek's, in all save
the forehead, which was low and lowering.   Sleek and trim
were his bright chestnut locks; and his arms were damascened
with silver, for he was one who loved the pomp and luxury
of war.

Wolnoth, the mother's favourite, seemed yet in the first
flower of youth; but he alone of all the sons had something
irresolute and effeminate in his aspect and bearing.   His
form, though tall, had not yet come to its full height and
strength; and as if the weight of mail were unusual to him,
he leaned with both hands upon the wood of his long spear.
Leofwine, who stood next to Wolnoth, contrasted him notably; his sunny locks wreathed carelessly over a white un-
clouded brow, and the silken hair on the upper lip quivered
over arch lips, smiling, even in that serious hour.

At Godwin's right hand, but not immediately near him,
stood the last of the group, Gurth and Harold.   Gurth had
passed his arm over the shoulder of his brother, and, not
watching the nuncius while he spoke, watched only the effect
his words produced on the face of Harold; for Gurth loved
Harold as Jonathan loved David.   And Harold was the only
one of the group not armed; and had a veteran skilled in war
been asked who of that group was born to lead armed men, he
would have pointed to the man unarmed.

"So what says the king?" asked Earl Godwin.

"This: he refuses to restore thee and thy sons, or to hear

thee, till thou hast disbanded thine army, dismissed thy ships, and consented to clear thyself and thy House before the Witanagemot."

A fierce laugh broke from Tostig; Sweyn's mournful brow grew darker; Leofwine placed his right hand on his ateghar; Wolnoth rose erect; Gurth kept his eyes on Harold, and Harold's face was unmoved.

"The king received thee in his council of war," said Godwin, thoughtfully, "and doubtless the Normans were there. Who were the Englishmen most of mark?"

"Siward of Northumbria, thy foe."

"My sons," said the earl, turning to his children, and breathing loud as if a load were off his heart, "there will be no need of axe or armour to-day. Harold alone was wise;" and he pointed to the linen tunic of the son thus cited.

"What mean you, Sir Father?" said Tostig, imperiously. "Think you to —"

"Peace, son, peace!" said Godwin, without asperity, but with conscious command. "Return, brave and dear friend," he said to Vebba, "find out Siward the Earl; tell him that I, Godwin, his foe in the old time, place honour and life in his hands, and what he counsels that will we do. Go."

The Kent man nodded, and regained his boat. Then spoke Harold, —

"Father, yonder are the forces of Edward; as yet without leaders, since the chiefs must still be in the halls of the king. Some fiery Norman amongst them may provoke an encounter; and this city of London is not won, as it behooves us to win it, if one drop of English blood dye the sword of one English man. Wherefore, with your leave, I will take boat, and land; and unless I have lost in my absence all right lere in the hearts of our countrymen, at the first shout from our troops which proclaims that Harold, son of Godwin, is on the soil of our fathers, half yon array of spears and helms pass at once to our side."

"And if not, my vain brother?" said Tostig, gnawing his lip with envy.

"And if not, I will ride alone into the midst of them, and ask what Englishmen are there who will aim shaft or spear at this breast, never mailed against England!"

Godwin placed his hand on Harold's head, and the tears came to those close cold eyes.

"Thou knowest by nature what I have learned by art. Go, and prosper. Be it as thou wilt."

"He takes thy post, Sweyn, — thou art the elder," said Tostig to the wild form by his side.

"There is guilt on my soul, and woe in my heart," answered Sweyn, moodily. "Shall Esau lose his birthright, and Cain retain it?" So saying, he withdrew, and, reclining against the stern of the vessel, leaned his face upon the edge of his shield.

Harold watched him with deep compassion in his eyes, passed to his side with a quick step, pressed his hand, and whispered, "Peace to the past, O my brother!"

The boy Haco, who had noiselessly followed his father, lifted his sombre, serious looks to Harold as he thus spoke; and when Harold turned away, he said to Sweyn timidly, "*He*, at least, is ever good to thee and to me."

"And thou, when I am no more, shalt cling to him as thy father, Haco," answered Sweyn, tenderly smoothing back the child's dark locks.

The boy shivered; and bending his head, murmured to himself: "When thou art no more! No more? Has the Vala doomed *him* too, — father and son, both?"

Meanwhile Harold had entered the boat lowered from the sides of the æsca to receive him; and Gurth, looking appealingly to his father and seeing no sign of dissent, sprang down after the young earl, and seated himself by his side.

Godwin followed the boat with musing eyes.

"Small need," said he, aloud, but to himself, "to believe in soothsayers, or to credit Hilda the saga, when she prophesied, ere we left our shores, that Harold — " He stopped short, for Tostig's wrathful exclamation broke on his revery.

"Father, Father! My blood surges in my ears, and boils in my heart, when I hear thee name the prophecies of Hilda in favour of thy darling. Dissension and strife in our House

have they wrought already; and if the feuds between Harold
and me have sown gray in thy locks, thank thyself when,
flushed with vain soothsayings for thy favoured Harold, thou
saidst, in the hour of our first childish broil, ' Strive not with
Harold; for his brothers will be his men.' "

"Falsify the prediction," said Godwin, calmly; "wise men
may always make their own future, and seize their own fates.
Prudence, patience, labour, valour, — these are the stars that
rule the career of mortals."

Tostig made no answer; for the splash of oars was near,
and two ships, containing the principal chiefs that had joined
Godwin's cause, came alongside the Runic æsca to hear the
result of the message sent to the king. Tostig sprang to the
vessel's side, and exclaimed, —

"The king, girt by his false counsellors, will hear us not;
and arms must decide between us."

"Hold, hold, malignant, unhappy boy!" cried Godwin,
between his grinded teeth, as a shout of indignant yet joyous ferocity broke from the crowded ships thus hailed. "The
curse of all time be on him who draws the first native blood
in sight of the altars and hearths of London! Hear me, thou
with the vulture's blood-lust, and the peacock's vain joy in the
gaudy plume! Hear me, Tostig, and tremble. If but by one
word thou widen the breach between me and the king, outlaw
thou enterest England, outlaw shalt thou depart, — for earldom and broad lands, choose the bread of the stranger and the
weregeld of the wolf!"

The young Saxon, haughty as he was, quailed at his father's
thrilling voice, bowed his head, and retreated sullenly. Godwin sprang on the deck of the nearest vessel, and all the passions that Tostig had aroused he exerted his eloquence to
appease.

In the midst of his arguments there rose from the ranks on
the Strand the shout of "Harold! Harold the Earl! Harold
and Holy Crosse!" And Godwin, turning his eye to the
king's ranks, saw them agitated, swayed, and moving; till
suddenly from the very heart of the hostile array, came, as
by irresistible impulse, the cry, —

"Harold, our Harold! All hail, the good earl!"

While this chanced without, within the palace Edward
had quitted the presence-chamber, and was closeted with
Stigand the bishop. This prelate had the more influence
with Edward, inasmuch as, though Saxon, he was held to
be no enemy to the Normans, and had indeed on a former
occasion been deposed from his bishopric on the charge of too
great an attachment to the Norman queen-mother Emma.[1]
Never in his whole life had Edward been so stubborn as on
this occasion. For here, more than his realm was concerned,
— he was threatened in the peace of his household and the
comfort of his tepid friendships. With the recall of his
powerful father-in-law, he foresaw the necessary reintrusion
of his wife upon the charm of his chaste solitude. His
favourite Normans would be banished, he should be surrounded with faces he abhorred. All the representations
of Stigand fell upon a stern and unyielding spirit, when
Siward entered the king's closet.

"Sir, my King," said the great son of Beorn, "I yielded to
your kingly will in the council, that, before we listened to
Godwin, he should disband his men, and submit to the judgment of the Witan. The earl hath sent to me to say that he
will put honour and life in my keeping, and abide by my
counsel; and I have answered as became the man who will
never snare a foe or betray a trust."

"How hast thou answered?" asked the king.

"That he abide by the laws of England, as Dane and Saxon
agreed to abide in the days of Canute; that he and his sons
shall make no claim for land or lordship, but submit all to
the Witan."

"Good," said the king; "and the Witan will condemn
him now, as it would have condemned when he shunned to
meet it."

---

[1] Anglo-Saxon Chronicle, A. D. 1043. "Stigand was deposed from his
bishopric, and all that he possessed was seized into the king's hands, because he
was received to his mother's counsel, and she went just as he advised her,
as people thought." The saintly Confessor dealt with his bishops as sum-
marily as Henry VIII. could have done after his quarrel with the Pope.

"And the Witan *now*," returned the earl, emphatically, "will be free and fair and just."

"And meanwhile the troops —"

"Will wait on either side; and if reason fail, then the sword," said Siward.

"This I will not hear," exclaimed Edward; when the tramp of many feet thundered along the passage. The door was flung open, and several captains, Norman as well as Saxon, of the king's troops rushed in, wild, rude, and tumultuous.

"The troops desert! Half the ranks have thrown down their arms at the very name of Harold!" exclaimed the Earl of Hereford. "Curses on the knaves!"

"And the lithsmen of London," cried a Saxon thegn, "are all on his side, and marching already through the gates."

"Pause yet," whispered Stigand; "and who shall say, this hour to-morrow, if Edward or Godwin reign on the throne of Alfred?"

His stern heart moved by the distress of his king, and not the less for the unwonted firmness which Edward displayed, Siward here approached, knelt, and took the king's hand.

"Siward can give no niddering counsel to his king; to save the blood of his subjects is never a king's disgrace. Yield thou to mercy, Godwin to the law!"

"Oh for the cowl and cell!" exclaimed the prince, wringing his hands. "Oh, Norman home, why did I leave thee?"

He took the cross from his breast, contemplated it fixedly, prayed silently but with fervour, and his face again became tranquil.

"Go," he said, flinging himself on his seat in the exhaustion that follows passion, — "go, Siward, go, Stigand, deal with things mundane as ye will."

The bishop, satisfied with this reluctant acquiescence, seized Siward by the arm and withdrew him from the closet. The captains remained a few moments behind, — the Saxons silently gazing on the king; the Normans whispering each other in great doubt and trouble, and darting looks of the bitterest scorn at their feeble benefactor. Then, as with one

accord, these last rushed along the corridor, gained the hall
where their countrymen yet assembled, and exclaimed, —

"*À toute bride! Franc étrier!* All is lost but life! God
for the first man, — knife and cord for the last!"

Then, as the cry of fire or as the first crash of an earthquake
dissolves all union, and reduces all emotion into one thought
of self-saving, the whole conclave, crowding pell-mell on each
other, bustled, jostled, clamoured to the door, — happy he who
could find horse, palfrey, even monk's mule! This way, that
way, fled those lordly Normans, those martial abbots, those
mitred bishops, — some singly, some in pairs, some by tens, and
some by scores, but all prudently shunning association with
those chiefs whom they had most courted the day before, and
who they now knew would be the main mark for revenge, —
save only two, who yet, from that awe of the spiritual power
which characterized the Norman, who was already half monk,
half soldier (Crusader and Templar before Crusades were yet
preached, or the Templars yet dreamed of), even in that hour
of selfish panic rallied round them the prowest chivalry of
their countrymen, namely, the Bishop of London and the
Archbishop of Canterbury. Both these dignitaries, armed
cap-à-pie, and spear in hand, headed the flight; and good service that day, both as guide and champion, did Mallet de
Graville. He led them in a circuit behind both armies; but
being intercepted by a new body, coming from the pastures of
Hertfordshire to the help of Godwin, he was compelled to
take the bold and desperate resort of entering the city gates.
These were wide open, — whether to admit the Saxon earls,
or vomit forth their allies, the Londoners. Through these,
up the narrow streets, riding three abreast, dashed the slaughtering fugitives; worthy in flight of their national renown,
they trampled down every obstacle. Bodies of men drew up
against them at every angle, with the Saxon cry of "Out!
out!" "Down with the outland men!" Through each, spear
pierced, and sword clove, the way. Red with gore was the
spear of the prelate of London; broken to the hilt was the
sword militant in the terrible hand of the Archbishop of Canterbury. So on they rode, so on they slaughtered, — gained

the Eastern Gate, and passed with but two of their number lost.

The fields once gained, for better precaution they separated. Some few, not quite ignorant of the Saxon tongue, doffed their mail, and crept through forest and fell towards the seashore; others retained steed and arms, but shunned equally the high-roads. The two prelates were among the last; they gained in safety Ness, in Essex, threw themselves into an open, crazy fishing-boat, committed themselves to the waves, and half drowned and half famished, drifted over the Channel to the French shores. Of the rest of the courtly foreigners, some took refuge in the forts yet held by their countrymen; some lay concealed in creeks and caves till they could find or steal boats for their passage. And thus, in the year of our Lord 1052, occurred the notable dispersion and ignominious flight of the counts and vavasours of great William the Duke!

CHAPTER III.

THE Witanagemot was assembled in the great hall of Westminster in all its imperial pomp.

It was on his throne that the king sat now, and it was the sword that was in his right hand. Some seated below, and some standing beside, the throne, were the officers of the Basileus[1] of Britain. There were to be seen camararius and pincerna, chamberlain and cupbearer, disc thegn and hors thegn,[2] the thegn of the dishes and the thegn of the stud, with many more, whose state offices may not impossibly have been borrowed from the ceremonial pomp of the Byzantine court; for Edgar, King of England, had in the old time styled himself the Heir of Constantine. Next to these sat the clerks

---

[1] The title of Basileus was retained by our kings so late as the time of John, who styled himself "Totius Insulæ Britannicæ Basileus." — AGARD, *On the antiquity of Shires in England, ap. Hearne, Cur. Disc.*

[2] Sharon Turner.

of the chapel, with the king's confessor at their head. Officers were they of higher note than their name bespeaks, and wielders, in the trust of the Great Seal, of a power unknown of old, and now obnoxious to the Saxon. For tedious is the suit which lingers for the king's writ and the king's seal; and from those clerks shall arise hereafter a thing of torture and of might, which shall grind out the hearts of men, and be called CHANCERY! [1]

Below the scribes a space was left on the floor, and farther down sat the chiefs of the Witan. Of these, first in order, both from their spiritual rank and their vast temporal possessions, sat the lords of the Church; the chairs of the prelates of London and Canterbury were void. But still goodly was the array of Saxon mitres, with the harsh, hungry, but intelligent face of Stigand, — Stigand, the stout and the covetous; and the benign but firm features of Alred, true priest and true patriot, distinguished amidst all. Around each prelate, as stars round a sun, were his own special priestly retainers, selected from his diocese. Farther still down tne hall are the great civil lords and vice-king vassals of the "Lord-Paramount." Vacant the chair of the King of the Scots, for Siward hath not yet had his wish; Macbeth is in his fastnesses, or listening to the weird sisters in the wold; and Malcolm is a fugitive in the halls of the Northumbrian earl. Vacant the chair of the hero Gryffyth, son of Llewelyn, the dread of the marches, Prince of Gwyned, whose arms has subjugated all Cymry. But there are the lesser sub-kings of Wales, true to the immemorial schisms amongst themselves which destroyed the realm of Ambrosius and rendered vain the arm of Arthur. With their torques of gold, and wild eyes, and hair cut round ears and brow, [2] they stare on the scene.

[1] See the Introduction to Palgrave's History of the Anglo-Saxons, from which this description of the Witan is borrowed so largely that I am left without other apology for the plagiarism than the frank confession that if I could have found in others, or conceived from my own resources, a description half as graphic and half as accurate, I would only have plagiarized to half the extent I have done.

[2] Girald. Gambrensis.

On the same bench with these sub-kings, distinguished from them by height of stature, and calm collectedness of mien, no less than by their caps of maintenance and furred robes, are those props of strong thrones and terrors of weak, — the earls to whom shires and counties fall, as hyde and carricate to the lesser thegns. But three of these were then present, and all three the foes of Godwin, — Siward, Earl of Northumbria; Leofric of Mercia (that Leofric whose wife Godiva yet lives in ballad and song); and Rolf, Earl of Hereford and Worcestershire, who, strong in his claim of "king's blood," left not the court with his Norman friends. And on the same benches, though a little apart, are the lesser earls, and that higher order of thegns, called king's thegns.

Not far from these sat the chosen citizens from the free burgh of London, already of great weight in the senate,[1] sufficing often to turn its counsels; all friends were they of the English earl and his house. In the same division of the hall were found the bulk and true popular part of the meeting, — popular indeed, as representing not the people, but the things the people most prized, — valour and wealth; the thegn landowners, called in the old deeds the "Ministers." They sat with swords by their side, all of varying birth, fortune, and connection, whether with king, earl, or ceorl; for in the different districts of the old Heptarchy, the qualification varied, — high in East Anglia, low in Wessex, — so that what was wealth in the one shire was poverty in the other. There sat, half a yeoman, the Saxon thegn of Berkshire or Dorset, proud of his five hydes of land; there, half an ealderman, the Danish thegn of Norfolk or Ely, discontented with his forty; some were there in right of smaller offices under the crown; some traders, and sons of traders, for having crossed the high seas three times at their own risk; some could boast the blood of Offa and Egbert; and some traced but three generations back to neat-herd and ploughman; and

---

[1] Palgrave omits, I presume accidentally, these members of the Witan; but it is clear from the "Anglo-Saxon Chronicle" that the London "lithsmen" were represented in the great national Witans, and helped to decide the election even of kings.

some were Saxons and some were Danes: and some from the
western shires were by origin Britons, though little cognizant
of their race.   Farther down still, at the extreme end of the
hall, crowding by the open doors, filling up the space without,
were the ceorls themselves, a vast and not powerless body; in
these high courts (distinct from the shire gemots, or local
senates) never called upon to vote or to speak or to act, or
even to sign names to the doom, but only to shout, "Yea,
yea," when the proceres pronounced their sentence.   Yet not
powerless were they, but rather to the Witan what public
opinion is to the Witan's successor, our modern parliament:
they *were* opinion!   And according to their numbers and
their sentiments, easily known and boldly murmured, often
and often must that august court of basileus and prelate,
vassal-king and mighty earl, have shaped the council and
adjudged the doom.

And the forms of the meeting had been duly said and done;
and the king had spoken words, no doubt wary and peaceful,
gracious and exhortatory; but those words — for his voice
that day was weak — travelled not beyond the small circle
of his clerks and his officers; and a murmur buzzed through
the hall, when Earl Godwin stood on the floor with his six
sons at his back; and you might have heard the hum of the
gnat that vexed the smooth cheek of Earl Rolf, or the click
of the spider from the web on the vaulted roof, the moment
before Earl Godwin spoke.

"If," said he, with the modest look and downcast eye of
practised eloquence, — "if I rejoice once more to breathe the
air of England, in whose service, often perhaps with faulty
deeds, but at all times with honest thoughts, I have, both in
war and council, devoted so much of my life that little now
remains but (should you, my king, and you, prelates, proceres,
and ministers, so vouchsafe) to look round and select that
spot of my native soil which shall receive my bones; if I
rejoice to stand once more in that assembly which has often
listened to my voice when our common country was in peril,
— who here will blame that joy?   Who among my foes, if
foes now I have, will not respect the old man's gladness?

Who amongst you, earls and thegns, would not grieve, if his
duty bade him say to the gray-haired exile, ' In this English
air you shall not breathe your last sigh, on this English soil
you shall not find a grave!' Who amongst you would not
grieve to say it?" Suddenly he drew up his head and faced
his audience. "Who amongst you hath the courage and the
heart to say it? Yes, I rejoice that I am at last in an assembly fit to judge my cause and pronounce my innocence. For
what offence was I outlawed? For what offence were I, and
the six sons I have given to my land, to bear the wolf's penalty, and be chased and slain as the wild beasts? Hear me,
and answer!

"Eustace, Count of Boulogne, returning to his domains from
a visit to our lord the king, entered the town of Dover in mail
and on his war-steed; his train did the same. Unknowing
our laws and customs (for I desire to press light upon all old
grievances, and will impute ill designs to none), these foreigners invade by force the private dwellings of citizens, and
there select their quarters. Ye all know that this was the
strongest violation of Saxon right; ye know that the meanest
ceorl hath the proverb on his lip, ' Every man's house is his
castle.' One of the townsmen, acting on this belief, — which
I have yet to learn was a false one, — expelled from his
threshold a retainer of the French earl's. The stranger
drew his sword and wounded him; blows followed, — the
stranger fell by the arm he had provoked. The news arrives
to Earl Eustace; he and his kinsmen spur to the spot; they
murder the Englishman on his hearthstone — "

Here a groan, half stifled and wrathful, broke from the
ceorls at the end of the hall. Godwin held up his hand in
rebuke of the interruption, and resumed: —

"This deed done, the outlanders rode through the streets
with their drawn swords; they butchered those who came in
their way; they trampled even children under their horses'
feet. The burghers armed. I thank the Divine Father, who
gave me for my countrymen those gallant burghers! They
fought, as we English know how to fight; they slew some
nineteen or score of these mailed intruders; they chased them

from the town. Earl Eustace fled fast. Earl Eustace, we know, is a wise man; small rest took he, little bread broke he, till he pulled rein at the gate of Gloucester, where my lord the king then held court. He made his complaint. My lord the king, naturally hearing but one side, thought the burghers in the wrong; and scandalized that such high persons of his own kith should be so aggrieved, he sent for me, in whose government the burgh of Dover is, and bade me chastise, by military execution, those who had attacked the foreign count. I appeal to the great earls whom I see before me, — to you, illustrious Leofric; to you, renowned Siward, — what value would ye set on your earldoms, if ye had not the heart and the power to see right done to the dwellers therein?

"What was the course I proposed? Instead of martial execution, which would involve the whole burgh in one sentence, I submitted that the reeve and gerefas of the burgh should be cited to appear before the king, and account for the broil. My lord, though ever most clement and loving to his good people, either unhappily moved against me or overswayed by the foreigners, was counselled to reject this mode of doing justice, which our laws, as settled under Edgar and Canute, enjoin. And because I would not, — and I say in the presence of all, because I, Godwin, son of Wolnoth, *durst* not, if I would, have entered the free burgh of Dover with mail on my back and the doomsman at my right hand, these outlanders induced my lord the king to summon me to attend in person (as for a sin of my own) the council of the Witan, convened at Gloucester, thên filled with the foreigners, not, as I humbly opined, to do justice to me and my folk of Dover, but to secure to this Count of Boulogne a triumph over English liberties, and sanction his scorn for the value of English lives.

"I hesitated, and was menaced with outlawry; I armed in self-defence, and in defence of the laws of England; I armed, that men might not be murdered on their hearthstones, nor children trampled under the hoofs of a stranger's war-steed. My lord the king gathered his troops round ' the cross and the martlets.' Yon noble earls, Siward and Leofric, came to that

standard, as (knowing not then my cause) was their duty to
the Basileus of Britain. But when they knew my cause, and
saw *with* me the dwellers of the land, *against* me the outland
aliens, they righteously interposed. An armistice was concluded; I agreed to refer all matters to a Witan held where it
is held this day. My troops were disbanded; but the foreigners induced my lord not only to retain his own, but to
issue his Herr-bann for the gathering of hosts far and near,
even allies beyond the seas. When I looked to London for
the peaceful Witan, what saw I? The largest armament that
had been collected in this reign, — that armament headed by
Norman knights. Was this the meeting where justice could
be done mine and me? Nevertheless, what was my offer?
That I and my six sons would attend, provided the usual
sureties, agreeable to our laws, from which only thieves[1] are
excluded, were given that we should come and go life-free
and safe. Twice this offer was made, twice refused; and so I
and my sons were banished. We went; we have returned!"

"And in arms," murmured Earl Rolf, son-in-law to that
Count Eustace of Boulogne whose violence had been temperately and truly narrated.[2]

"And in arms," repeated Godwin; "true: in arms against
the foreigners who had thus poisoned the ear of our gracious
king, — in arms, Earl Rolf; and at the first clash of those
arms, Franks and foreigners have fled. We have no need of
arms now. We are amongst our countrymen, and no Frenchman interposes between us and the ever gentle, ever generous
nature of our born king.

"Peers and proceres, chiefs of this Witan, perhaps the
largest ever yet assembled in man's memory, it is for you
to decide whether I and mine, or the foreign fugitives, caused
the dissensions in these realms; whether our banishment was
just or not; whether in our return we have abused the power
we possessed. Ministers, on those swords by your sides there

[1] By Athelstan's law, every man was to have peace going to and from the
Witan, unless he was a thief. — WILKINS, p. 137.

[2] Goda, Edward's sister, married, first, Rolf's father, Count of Mantes;
secondly, the Count of Boulogne.

is not one drop of blood! At all events, in submitting to you our fate, we submit to our own laws and our own race. I am here to clear myself, on my oath, of deed and thought of treason. There are amongst my peers, as king's thegns, those who will attest the same on my behalf, and prove the facts I have stated, if they are not sufficiently notorious. As for my sons, no crime can be alleged against them, unless it be a crime to have in their veins that blood which flows in mine, — blood which they have learned from me to shed in defence of that beloved land to which they now ask to be recalled."

The earl ceased and receded behind his children, having artfully, by his very abstinence from the more heated eloquence imputed to him often as a fault and a wile, produced a powerful effect upon an audience already prepared for his acquittal.

But now as, from the sons, Sweyn the eldest stepped forth, with a wandering eye and uncertain foot, there was a movement like a shudder amongst the large majority of the audience, and a murmur of hate or of horror.

The young earl marked the sensation his presence produced, and stopped short. His breath came thick; he raised his right hand, but spoke not. His voice died on his lips; his eyes roved wildly round with a haggard stare more imploring than defying. Then rose, in his episcopal stole, Alred the bishop, and his clear sweet voice trembled as he spoke.

"Comes Sweyn, son of Godwin, here, to prove his innocence of treason against the king? If so, let him hold his peace; for if the Witan acquit Godwin, son of Wolnoth, of that charge, the acquittal includes his House. But in the name of the holy Church here represented by its fathers, will Sweyn say, and fasten his word by oath, that he is guiltless of treason to the King of Kings, guiltless of sacrilege that my lips shrink to name? Alas that the duty falls on me, — for I loved thee once, and love thy kindred now. But I am God's servant before all things — " The prelate paused, and gathering up new energy, added in unfaltering accents: "I charge thee here, Sweyn the outlaw, that, moved by the fiend, thou didst bear off from God's house and violate a daughter of the Church, — Algive, Abbess of Leominster!"

"And I," cried Siward, rising to the full height of his stature, — "I, in the presence of these proceres, whose proudest title is *milites*, or warriors, — I charge Sweyn, son of Godwin, that not in open field and hand to hand, but by felony and guile, he wrought the foul and abhorrent murder of his cousin Beorn the Earl!"

At these two charges from men so eminent, the effect upon the audience was startling. While those not influenced by Godwin raised their eyes, sparkling with wrath and scorn, upon the wasted yet still noble face of the eldest born, even those most zealous on behalf of that popular House evinced no sympathy for its heir. Some looked down abashed and mournful; some regarded the accused with a cold, unpitying gaze. Only perhaps among the ceorls, at the end of the hall, might be seen some compassion on anxious faces; for before those deeds of crime had been bruited abroad, none among the sons of Godwin more blithe of mien and bold of hand, more honoured and beloved, than Sweyn the outlaw. But the hush that succeeded the charges was appalling in its depth. Godwin himself shaded his face with his mantle, and only those close by could see that his breast heaved and his limbs trembled. The brothers had shrunk from the side of the accused, outlawed even amongst his kin, — all save Harold, who, strong in his blameless name and beloved repute, advanced three strides amidst the silence, and standing by his brother's side, lifted his commanding brow above the seated judges, but he did not speak.

Then said Sweyn the Earl, strengthened by such solitary companionship in that hostile assemblage, —

"I might answer that for these charges in the past, for deeds alleged as done eight long years ago, I have the king's grace and the inlaw's right; and that in the Witans over which I as earl presided, no man was twice judged for the same offence. That I hold to be the law, in the great councils as the small."

"It is, it is!" exclaimed Godwin; his paternal feelings

conquering his prudence and his decorous dignity. "Hold to it, my son!"

"I hold to it not," resumed the young earl, casting a haughty glance over the somewhat blank and disappointed faces of his foes, "for my law is *here*," — and he smote his heart, — "and that condemns me not once alone, but evermore! Alred, O holy father, at whose knees I once confessed my every sin, I blame thee not that thou first, in the Witan, liftest thy voice against me, though thou knowest that I loved Algive from youth upward; she, with her heart yet mine, was given in the last year of Hardicanute, when might was right, to the Church. I met her again, flushed with my victories over the Walloon kings, with power in my hand and passion in my veins. Deadly was my sin! But what asked I? That vows compelled should be annulled, — that the love of my youth might yet be the wife of my manhood. Pardon, that I knew not then how eternal are the bonds ye of the Church have woven round those of whom, if ye fail of saints, ye may at least make martyrs!"

He paused, and his lip curled, and his eye shot wild fire, — for in that moment his mother's blood was high within him, and he looked and thought, perhaps, as some heathen Dane; but the flash of the former man was momentary, and humbly smiting his breast, he murmured: "Avaunt, Satan! Yea, deadly was my sin! And the sin was mine alone; Algive, if stained, was blameless; she escaped — and — and died!

"The king was wroth; and first to strive against my pardon was Harold my brother, who now alone in my penitence stands by my side. He strove manfully and openly; I blamed *him* not. But Beorn, my cousin, desired my earldom, and he strove against me wilily and in secret, — to my face kind, behind my back despiteful. I detected his falsehood, and meant to detain, but not to slay him. He lay bound in my ship; he reviled and he taunted me in the hour of my gloom, and when the blood of the sea-kings flowed in fire through my veins. And I lifted my axe in ire, and my men lifted theirs; and so — and so — Again I say, deadly was my sin!

"Think not that I seek now to make less my guilt, as I

sought when I deemed that life was yet long, and **power was
yet sweet.** Since then I have known worldly evil and worldly
good,— the storm and the shine of life. I have swept the seas,
a sea-king; I have battled with the Dane in his native land;
I have almost grasped in my right hand, as I grasped in my
dreams, the crown of my kinsman Canute. Again, I have
been a fugitive and an exile; again, I have been inlawed, and
earl of all the lands from Isis to the Wye.[1] And whether in
state or in penury, whether in war or in peace, I have seen
the pale face of the nun betrayed, and the gory wounds of the
murdered man. Wherefore I come not here to plead for a
pardon, which would console me not, but formally to dissever
my kinsmen's cause from mine, which alone sullies and de-
grades it. I come here to say that, coveting not your
acquittal, fearing not your judgment, I pronounce mine own
doom. Cap of noble and axe of warrior I lay aside forever.
Barefooted and alone, I go hence to the Holy Sepulchre; there
to assoil my soul, and implore that grace which cannot come
from man! Harold, step forth in the place of Sweyn the
first-born! And ye prelates and peers, milites and ministers,
proceed to adjudge the living! To you, and to England, he
who now quits you is the dead!"

He gathered his robe of state over his breast, as a monk
his gown, and looking neither to right nor to left, passed
slowly down the hall, through the crowd, which made way
for him in awe and silence; and it seemed to the assembly as
if a cloud had gone from the face of day.

And Godwin still stood with his face covered by his robe.

And Harold anxiously watched the faces of the assembly,
and saw no relenting.

And Gurth crept to Harold's side.

And the gay Leofwine looked sad.

And the young Wolnoth turned pale, and trembled.

And the fierce Tostig played with his golden chain.

And one low sob was heard; and it came from the breast of
Alred the meek accuser, — God's firm but gentle priest.

[1] More correctly of Oxford, Somerset, Berkshire, Gloucester, and Hereford

CHAPTER IV.

THIS memorable trial ended, as the reader will have fore-
seen, in the formal renewal of Sweyn's outlawry, and the
formal restitution of the Earl Godwin and his other sons to
their lands and honours, with declarations imputing all the
blame of the late dissensions to the foreign favourites, and
sentence of banishment against them, except only, by way of
a bitter mockery, some varlets of low degree, such as Humphrey Cock's-foot, and Richard, son of Scrob.[1]

The return to power of this able and vigorous family was
attended with an instantaneous effect upon the long-relaxed
strings of the imperial government. Macbeth heard, and
trembled in his moors; Gryffyth of Wales lit the fire-beacon
on moel and craig. Earl Rolf was banished, but merely as a
nominal concession to public opinion. His kinship to Edward
sufficed to restore him soon, not only to England, but to the
lordship of the Marches; and thither was he sent, with ade-
quate force, against the Welch, who had half-repossessed themselves of the borders they harried. Saxon prelates and abbots
replaced the Norman fugitives; and all were contented with
the revolution, save the king, — for the king lost his Norman
friends, and regained his English wife.

In conformity with the usages of the times, hostages of the
loyalty and faith of Godwin were required and conceded.
They were selected from his own family; and the choice
fell on Wolnoth, his son, and Haco, the son of Sweyn. As,

---

[1] Yet how little safe it is for the great to despise the low-born. This very
Richard, son of Scrob, more euphoniously styled by the Normans Richard
Fitz-Scrob, settled in Herefordshire (he was probably among the retainers of
Earl Rolf), and on William's landing became the chief and most active sup-
porter of the invader in those districts. The sentence of banishment seems
to have been mainly confined to the foreigners about the court, — for it is
clear that many Norman landowners and priests were still left scattered
throughout the country.

when nearly all England may be said to have repassed to the hands of Godwin, it would have been an idle precaution to consign these hostages to the keeping of Edward, it was settled, after some discussion, that they should be placed in the court of the Norman Duke until such time as the king, satisfied with the good faith of the family, should authorize their recall. Fatal hostage, fatal ward and host!

It was some days after this national crisis, and order and peace were again established in city and land, forest and shire, when, at the setting of the sun, Hilda stood alone by the altar-stone of Thor.

The orb was sinking red and lurid, amidst long cloud-wracks of vermeil and purple, and not one human form was seen in the landscape, save that tall and majestic figure by the Runic shrine and the Druid crommell. She was leaning both hands on her wand, — or seid-staff, as it was called in the language of Scandinavian superstition, — and bending slightly forward as in the attitude of listening or expectation. Long before any form appeared on the road below she seemed to be aware of coming footsteps, and probably her habits of life had sharpened her senses; for she smiled, muttered to herself, "Ere it sets!" and changing her posture, leaned her arm on the altar, and rested her face upon her hand.

At length two figures came up the road; they neared the hill; they saw her, and slowly ascended the knoll. The one was dressed in the serge of a pilgrim; and his cowl, thrown back, showed the face where human beauty and human power lay ravaged and ruined by human passions. He upon whom the pilgrim lightly leaned was attired simply, without the brooch or bracelet common to the thegns of high degree; yet his port was that of majesty, and his brow that of mild command. A greater contrast could not be conceived than that between these two men, yet united by a family likeness; for the countenance of the last described was, though sorrowful at that moment, and indeed habitually not without a certain melancholy, wonderfully imposing from its calm and sweetness. There no devouring passions had left the cloud or ploughed the line, but all the smooth loveliness of youth

took dignity from the conscious resolve of man. The long
hair, of a fair brown, with a slight tinge of gold, as the last
sunbeams shot through its luxuriance, was parted from the
temples, and fell in large waves half-way to the shoulder.
The eyebrows, darker in hue, arched and finely traced; the
straight features, not less manly than the Norman, but less
strongly marked; the cheek, hardy with exercise and exposure, yet still retaining somewhat of youthful bloom under the
pale bronze of its sunburned surface; the form tall, not gigantic, and vigorous rather from perfect proportion and athletic
habits than from breadth and bulk,— were all singularly characteristic of the Saxon beauty in its highest and purest type.
But what chiefly distinguished this personage was that peculiar dignity, so simple, so sedate, which no pomp seems to
dazzle, no danger to disturb; and which perhaps arises from
a strong sense of self-dependence, and is connected with self-
respect, — a dignity common to the Indian and the Arab, and
rare except in that state of society in which each man is a
power in himself. The Latin tragic poet touches close upon
that sentiment in the fine lines, —

> " Rex est qui metuit nihil ;
> Hoc regnum sibi quisque dat." [1]

So stood the brothers, Sweyn the outlaw and Harold the
Earl, before the reputed prophetess. She looked on both
with a steady eye, which gradually softened almost into tenderness as it finally rested upon the pilgrim.

"And is it thus," she said at last, "that I see the first-born
of Godwin the Fortunate, for whom so often I have tasked
the thunder and watched the setting sun, for whom my runes
have been graven on the bark of the elm, and the Scin-læca [2]
been called in pale splendour from the graves of the dead?"

"Hilda," said Sweyn, "not now will I accuse thee of the
seeds thou hast sown; the harvest is gathered, and the sickle

---

[1] " He is a king who fears nothing ; that kingdom every man gives to himself." — SENECA, *Thyest.* Act ii.

[2] Literally, a shining corpse ; a species of apparition invoked by the witch
or wizard. See Sharon Turner on the Superstitions of the Anglo-Saxons, b. ii.
c. 14.

is broken. Abjure thy dark Galdra,[1] and turn as I to the sole light in the future, which shines from the tomb of the Son Divine."

The prophetess bowed her head and replied: —

"Belief cometh as the wind. Can the tree say to the wind, ' Rest thou on my boughs!' or Man to Belief, ' Fold thy wings on my heart!' Go where thy soul can find comfort, for thy life hath passed from its uses on earth. And when I would read thy fate, the runes are as blanks, and the wave sleeps unstirred on the fountain. Go where the Fylgia,[2] whom Alfader gives to each at his birth, leads thee. Thou didst desire love that seemed shut from thee, and I predicted that thy love should awake from the charnel in which the creed that succeeds to the faith of our sires inters life in its bloom. And thou didst covet the fame of the Jarl and the Viking, and I blessed thine axe to thy hand, and wove the sail for thy masts. So long as man knows *desire,* can Hilda have power over his doom; but when the heart lies in ashes, I raise but a corpse, that at the hush of the charm falls again into its grave. Yet come to me nearer, O Sweyn, whose cradle I rocked to the chant of my rhyme."

The outlaw turned aside his face, and obeyed.

She sighed as she took his passive hand in her own, and examined the lines on the palm. Then, as if by an involuntary impulse of fondness and pity, she put aside his cowl and kissed his brow.

"Thy skein is spun, and happier than the many who scorn, and the few who lament thee, thou shalt win where they lose. The steel shall not smite thee, the storm shall forbear thee, the goal that thou yearnest for thy steps shall attain. Night hallows the ruin, and peace to the shattered wrecks of the brave!"

The outlaw heard as if unmoved; but when he turned to Harold, who covered his face with his hand, but could not restrain the tears that flowed through the clasped fingers, a moisture came into his own wild, bright eyes, and he said, —

[1] Magic.
[2] Tutelary divinity. See Note H.

"Now, my brother, farewell, for no farther step shalt thou
wend with me."

Harold started, opened his arms, and the outlaw fell upon
his breast.

No sound was heard save a single sob, and so close was
breast to breast that you could not say from whose heart it
came.   Then the outlaw wrenched himself from the embrace,
and murmured, —

"And Haco, — my son, — motherless, fatherless, — hostage
in the land of the stranger!   Thou wilt remember, — thou
wilt shield him; thou be to him mother, father, in the days
to come!   So may the saints bless thee!"   With these words
he sprang down the hillock.

Harold bounded after him; but Sweyn, halting, said mournfully, "Is this thy promise?   Am I so lost that faith should
be broken even with thy father's son?"

At that touching rebuke Harold paused, and the outlaw
passed his way alone.   As the last glimpse of his figure vanished at the turn of the road, whence on the 2d of May, the
Norman Duke and the Saxon King had emerged side by side,
the short twilight closed abruptly, and up from the far forest-
land rose the moon.

Harold stood rooted to the spot, and still gazing on the
space, when the Vala laid her hand on his arm.

"Behold, as the moon rises on the troubled gloaming, so
rises the fate of Harold, as yon brief, human shadow, halting
between light and darkness, passes away to-night.   Thou art
now the first-born of a House that unites the hopes of the
Saxon with the fortunes of the Dane."

"Thinkest thou," said Harold, with a stern composure,
"that I can have joy and triumph in a brother's exile and
woe?"

"Not now, and not yet, will the voice of thy true nature be
heard; but the warmth of the sun brings the thunder, and the
glory of fortune wakes the storm of the soul."

"Kinswoman," said Harold, with a slight curl of his lip,
"by me at least have thy prophecies ever passed as the sough
of the air; neither in horror nor with faith do I think of thy

incantations and charms; and I smile alike at the exorcism of the shaveling and the spells of the Saga. I have asked thee not to bless mine axe, nor weave my sail. No runic rhyme is on the sword-blade of Harold. I leave my fortunes to the chance of mine own cool brain and strong arm. Vala, between thee and me there is no bond."

The prophetess smiled loftily. "And what thinkest thou, O self-dependent! — what thinkest thou is the fate which thy brain and thine arm shall win?"

"The fate they have won already, — I see no Beyond, — the fate of a man sworn to guard his country, love justice, and do right."

The moon shone full on the heroic face of the young earl as he spoke; and on its surface there seemed nought to belie the noble words. Yet the prophetess, gazing earnestly on that fair countenance, said, in a whisper that, despite a reason singularly sceptical for the age in which it had been cultured, thrilled to the Saxon's heart, —

"Under that calm eye sleeps the soul of thy sire, and beneath that brow, so haught and so pure, works the genius that crowned the kings of the North in the lineage of thy mother the Dane."

"Peace!" said Harold, almost fiercely; then, as if ashamed of the weakness of his momentary irritation, he added, with a faint smile, "Let us not talk of these matters while my heart is still sad and away from the thoughts of the world, with my brother the lonely outlaw. Night is on us, and the ways are yet unsafe; for the king's troops, disbanded in haste, were made up of many who turn to robbers in peace. Alone, and unarmed, save my ateghar, I would crave a night's rest under thy roof; and " — he hesitated, and a slight blush came over his cheek — "and I would fain see if your grandchild is as fair as when I last looked on her blue eyes, that then wept for Harold ere he went into exile."

"Her tears are not at her command, nor her smiles," said the Vala, solemnly; "her tears flow from the fount of thy sorrows, and her smiles are the beams from thy joys. For know, O Harold! that Edith is thine earthly Fylgia; thy fate

and her fate are as one. And vainly as man would escape
from his shadow, would soul wrench itself from the soul that
Skulda hath. linked to his doom."

Harold made no reply; but his step, habitually slow, grew
more quick and light, and this time his reason found no fault
with the oracles of the Vala.

———◆———

CHAPTER V.

As Hilda entered the hall, the various idlers accustomed to
feed at her cost were about retiring, — some to their homes
in the vicinity; some, appertaining to the household, to the
dormitories in the old Roman villa.

It was not the habit of the Saxon noble, as it was of the
Norman, to put hospitality to profit, by regarding his guests
in the light of armed retainers. Liberal as the Briton, the
cheer of the board and the shelter of the roof were afforded
with a hand equally unselfish and indiscriminate; and the
doors of the more wealthy and munificent might be almost
literally said to stand open from morn to eve.

As Harold followed the Vala across the vast atrium, his face
was recognized, and a shout of enthusiastic welcome greeted
the popular earl. The only voices that did not swell that cry
were those of three monks from a neighbouring convent, who
chose to wink at the supposed practices of the Morthwyrtha,[1]
from the affection they bore to her ale and mead, and the
gratitude they felt for her ample gifts to their convent.

"One of the wicked House, brother," whispered the monk.

"Yea; mockers and scorners are Godwin and his lewd
sons," answered the monk.

And all three sighed and scowled, as the door closed on the
hostess and her stately guest.

Two tall and not ungraceful lamps lighted the same chamber
in which Hilda was first presented to the reader. The hand-

[1] Worshipper of the dead.

maids were still at their spindles, and the white web nimbly shot as the mistress entered. She paused, and her brow knit, as she eyed the work.

"But three parts done?" she said; "weave fast, and weave strong."

Harold, not heeding the maids or their task, gazed inquiringly round; and from a nook near the window Edith sprang forward with a joyous cry, and a face all glowing with delight, — sprang forward as if to the arms of a brother; but within a step or so of that noble guest, she stopped short, and her eyes fell to the ground.

Harold held his breath in admiring silence. The child he had loved from her cradle stood before him as a woman. Even since we last saw her, in the interval between the spring and the autumn, the year had ripened the youth of the maiden, as it had mellowed the fruits of the earth; and her cheek was rosy with the celestial blush, and her form rounded to the nameless grace, which say that infancy is no more.

He advanced and took her hand, but for the first time in his life in their greetings he neither gave nor received the kiss.

"You are no child now, Edith," said he, involuntarily; "but still set apart, I pray you, some remains of the old childish love for Harold."

Edith's charming lips smiled softly; she raised her eyes to his, and their innocent fondness spoke through happy tears.

But few words passed in the short interval between Harold's entrance and his retirement to the chamber prepared for him in haste. Hilda herself led him to a rude ladder which admitted to a room above, evidently added, by some Saxon lord, to the old Roman pile. The ladder showed the precau· tion of one accustomed to sleep in the midst of peril; for by a kind of windlass in the room, it could be drawn up at the inmate's will, and, so drawn, left below a dark and deep chasm, delving down to the foundations of the house. Nevertheless the room itself had all the luxury of the time; the bedstead was quaintly carved, and of some rare wood; a trophy of arms — though very ancient, sedulously polished — hung on the wall. There were the small round shield and spear of the earlier Saxon, with his vizorless helm; and the short curved knife, or sæx,[1] from which some antiquarians deem that the Saxish men take their renowned name.

Edith, following Hilda, proffered to the guest, on a salver of gold, spiced wines and confections; while Hilda, silently and unperceived, waved her seid-staff over the bed, and rested her pale hand on the pillow.

"Nay, sweet cousin," said Harold, smiling, "this is not one of the fashions of old, but rather, methinks, borrowed from the Frankish manners in the court of King Edward."

"Not so, Harold," answered Hilda, quickly turning; "such was ever the ceremony due to Saxon king, when he slept in a subject's house, ere our kinsmen the Danes introduced that unroyal wassail, which left subject and king unable to hold or to quaff cup, when the board was left for the bed."

"Thou rebukest, O Hilda, too tauntingly the pride of Godwin's house, when thou givest to his homely son the ceremonial of a king; but, so served, I envy not kings, fair Edith."

He took the cup, raised it to his lips; and when he placed it on the small table by his side, the women had left the chamber, and he was alone. He stood for some minutes absorbed in revery, and his soliloquy ran somewhat thus: —

"Why said the Vala that Edith's fate was inwoven with mine? And why did I believe and bless the Vala, when she so said? Can Edith ever be my wife? The monk-king designs her for the cloister. Woe, and well-a-day! Sweyn, Sweyn, let thy doom forewarn me! And if I stand up in my place and say, ' Give age and grief to the cloister, youth and delight to man's hearth,' what will answer the monks? ' Edith cannot be thy wife, son of Godwin, for faint and scarce traced

---

[1] It is a disputed question whether the sæx of the earliest Saxon invaders was a long or short curved weapon, — nay, whether it was curved or straight; but the author sides with those who contend that it was a short, crooked weapon, easily concealed by a cloak, and similar to those depicted on the banner of the East Saxons.

though your affinity of blood, ye are within the banned degrees of the Church. Edith may be wife to another, if thou wilt, — barren spouse of the Church, or mother of children who lisp not Harold's name as their father.' Out on these priests with their mummeries, and out on their war upon human hearts!"

His fair brow grew stern and fierce as the Norman Duke's in his ire; and had you seen him at that moment you would have seen the true brother of Sweyn. He broke from his thoughts with the strong effort of a man habituated to self-control, and advanced to the narrow window, opened the lattice, and looked out.

The moon was in all her splendour. The long deep shadows of the breathless forest checkered the silvery whiteness of open sward and intervening glade. Ghostly arose on the knoll before him the gray columns of the mystic Druid; dark and indistinct the bloody altar of the Warrior god. But there his eye was arrested; for whatever is least distinct and defined in a landscape has the charm that is the strongest; and while he gazed, he thought that a pale phosphoric light broke from the mound with the bautastein, that rose by the Teuton altar. He *thought*, for he was not sure that it was not some cheat of the fancy. Gazing still, in the centre of that light, there appeared to gleam forth for one moment a form of superhuman height. It was the form of a man, that seemed clad in arms like those on the wall, leaning on a spear, whose point was lost behind the shafts of the crommell. And the face grew in that moment distinct from the light which shimmered around it, — a face large as some early god's, but stamped with unutterable and solemn woe. He drew back a step, passed his hand over his eyes, and looked again. Light and figure alike had vanished; nought was seen save the gray columns and the dim fane. The earl's lip curved in derision of his weakness. He closed the lattice, undressed, knelt for a moment or so by the bedside; and his prayer was brief and simple, nor accompanied with the crossings and signs customary in his age. He rose, extinguished the lamp, and threw himself on the bed.

The moon, thus relieved of the lamplight, came clear and bright through the room, shone on the trophied arms, and fell upon Harold's face, casting its brightness on the pillow on which the Vala had breathed her charm. And Harold slept, — slept long, — his face calm, his breathing regular; but ere the moon sunk and the dawn rose, the features were dark and troubled, the breath came by gasps, the brow was knit, and the teeth clenched.

BOOK IV.

THE HEATHEN ALTAR AND THE SAXON CHURCH.

CHAPTER I.

WHILE Harold sleeps, let us here pause to survey for the first time the greatness of that House to which Sweyn's exile had left him the heir. The fortunes of Godwin had been those which no man not eminently versed in the science of his kind can achieve. Though the fable which some modern historians of great name have repeated and detailed, as to his early condition as the son of a cow-herd, is utterly groundless,[1] and he belonged to a House all-powerful at the time of his youth, he was unquestionably the builder of his own greatness. That he should rise so high in the early part of his career was less remarkable than that he should have so long continued the possessor of a power and state in reality more than regal.

But, as has been before implied, Godwin's civil capacities were more prominent than his warlike; and this it is which invests him with that peculiar interest which attracts us to those who knit our modern intelligence with the past. In that dim world before the Norman deluge, we are startled to recognize the gifts that ordinarily distinguish a man of peace in a civilized age.

His father, Wolnoth, had been "Childe"[2] of the South Saxons, or thegn of Sussex, a nephew of Edric Streone, Earl

------

[1] See Note I.

[2] Saxon Chronicle, Florence Wigorn. Sir F. Palgrave says that the title of Childe is equivalent to that of Atheling. With that remarkable appreciation of evidence which generally makes him so invaluable as a judicial authority

of Mercia, the unprincipled but able minister of Ethelred, who betrayed his master to Canute, by whom, according to most authorities, he was righteously, though not very legally, slain as a reward for the treason.

"I promised," said the Dane King, "to set thy head higher than other men's, and I keep my word." The trunkless head was set on the gates of London.

Wolnoth had quarrelled with his uncle Brightric, Edric's brother, and before the arrival of Canute had betaken himself to the piracy of a sea-chief, seduced twenty of the king's ships, plundered the southern coasts, burned the royal navy, and then his history disappears from the chronicles; but immediately afterwards the great Danish army, called Thurkell's Host, invaded the coast, and kept their chief station on the Thames. Their victorious arms soon placed the country almost at their command. The traitor Edric joined them with a power of more than ten thousand men; and it is probable enough that the ships of Wolnoth had before this time melted amicably into the armament of the Danes. If this, which seems the most likely conjecture, be received, Godwin, then a mere youth, would naturally have commenced his career in the cause of Canute; and as the son of a formidable chief of thegn's rank, and even as kinsman to Edric, who, whatever his crimes, must have retained a party it was wise to conciliate, Godwin's favour with Canute, whose policy would lead him to show marked distinction to any able Saxon follower, ceases to be surprising.

The son of Wolnoth accompanied Canute in his military expedition to the Scandinavian continent; and here a signal victory, planned by Godwin, and executed solely by himself and the Saxon band under his command, without aid from Canute's Danes, made the most memorable military exploit of his life, and confirmed his rising fortunes.

Edric, though he is said to have been low born, had married

where accounts are contradictory, Sir F. Palgrave discards with silent contempt the absurd romance of Godwin's station of herdsman, to which, upon such very fallacious and flimsy authorities, Thierry and Sharon Turner have been betrayed into lending their distinguished names.

the sister of King Ethelred; and as Godwin advanced in fame, Canute did not disdain to bestow his own sister in marriage on the eloquent favourite, who probably kept no small portion of the Saxon population to their allegiance. On the death of this, his first wife, who bore him but one son [1] (who died by accident), he found a second spouse in the same royal House; and the mother of his six living sons and two daughters was the niece of his king, and sister of Sweyn, who subsequently filled the throne of Denmark. After the death of Canute, the Saxon's predilections in favour of the Saxon line became apparent; but it was either his policy or his principles always to defer to the popular will as expressed in the national council; and on the preference given by the Witan to Harold the son of Canute over the heirs of Ethelred, he yielded his own inclinations. The great power of the Danes, and the amicable fusion of their race with the Saxon which had now taken place, are apparent in this decision; for not only did Earl Leofric, of Mercia, though himself a Saxon (as well as the Earl of Northumbria, with the thegns north of the Thames), declare for Harold the Dane, but the citizens of London were of the same party; and Godwin represented little more than the feeling of his own principality of Wessex.

From that time Godwin, however, became identified with the English cause; and even many who believed him guilty of some share in the murder, or at least the betrayal, of Alfred, Edward's brother, sought excuses in the disgust with which Godwin had regarded the foreign retinue that Alfred had brought with him, as if to owe his throne [2] to Norman swords rather than to English hearts.

Hardicanute, who succeeded Harold, whose memory he

---

[1] This first wife, Thyra, was of very unpopular repute with the Saxons She was accused of sending young English persons as slaves into Denmark, and is said to have been killed by lightning.

[2] It is just, however, to Godwin to say that there is no *proof* of his share in this barbarous transaction; the presumptions, on the contrary, are in his favour, but the authorities are too contradictory, and the whole event too obscure, to enable us unhesitatingly to confirm the acquittal he received in his own age and from his own national tribunal.

abhorred, whose corpse he disinterred and flung into a fen,[1] had been chosen by the unanimous council both of English and Danish thegns; and despite Hardicanute's first vehement accusations of Godwin, the earl still remained throughout that reign as powerful as in the two preceding it. When Hardicanute dropped down dead at a marriage banquet, it was Godwin who placed Edward upon the throne; and that great earl must either have been conscious of his innocence of the murder of Edward's brother, or assured of his own irresponsible power, when he said to the prince who knelt at his feet, and, fearful of the difficulties in his way, implored the earl to aid his abdication of the throne and return to Normandy, —

"You are the son of Ethelred, grandson of Edgar. Reign, — it is your duty; better to live in glory than die in exile. You are of mature years, and having known sorrow and need, can better feel for your people. Rely on me, and there will be none of the difficulties you dread; whom I favour, England favours."

And shortly afterwards, in the national assembly, Godwin won Edward his throne. "Powerful in speech, powerful in bringing over people to what he desired, some yielded to his words, some to bribes."[2] Verily, Godwin was a man to have risen as high, had he lived later!

So Edward reigned, and agreeably, it is said, with previous stipulations, married the daughter of his king-maker. Beautiful as Edith the Queen was in mind and in person, Edward apparently loved her not. She dwelt in his palace, his wife only in name.

Tostig (as we have seen) had married the daughter of Baldwin, Count of Flanders, sister to Matilda, wife to the Norman Duke; and thus the House of Godwin was triply allied to princely lineage, — the Danish, the Saxon, the Flemish. And Tostig might have said, as in his heart William the Norman said, "My children shall descend from Charlemagne and Alfred."

Godwin's life, though thus outwardly brilliant, was too incessantly passed in public affairs and politic schemes to

---

[1] Anglo-Saxon Chronicle.　　[2] William of Malmesbury.

allow the worldly man much leisure to watch over the nurture and rearing of the bold spirits of his sons. Githa his wife, the Dane, a woman with a haughty but noble spirit, imperfect education, and some of the wild and lawless blood derived from her race of heathen sea-kings, was more fitted to stir their ambition and inflame their fancies than curb their tempers and mould their hearts.

We have seen the career of Sweyn; but Sweyn was an angel of light compared to his brother Tostig. He who *can* be penitent has ever something lofty in his original nature; but Tostig was remorseless as the tiger, as treacherous and as fierce. With less intellectual capacities than any of his brothers, he had more personal ambition than all put together. A kind of effeminate vanity, not uncommon with daring natures (for the bravest races and the bravest soldiers are usually the vainest; the desire to shine is as visible in the fop as in the hero), made him restless both for command and notoriety. "May I ever be in the mouths of men," was his favourite prayer. Like his maternal ancestry, the Danes, he curled his long hair, and went as a bridegroom to the feast of the ravens.

Two only of that House had studied the Humane Letters, which were no longer disregarded by the princes of the Continent; they were the sweet sister, the eldest of the family, fading fast in her loveless home, and Harold.

But Harold's mind, — in which what we call common-sense was carried to genius, — a mind singularly practical and sagacious, like his father's, cared little for theological learning and priestly legend, — for all that poesy of religion in which the Woman was wafted from the sorrows of earth.

Godwin himself was no favourite of the Church, and had seen too much of the abuses of the Saxon priesthood (perhaps, with few exceptions, the most corrupt and illiterate in all Europe, which is saying much) to instil into his children that reverence for the spiritual authority which existed abroad; and the enlightenment which in him was experience in life, was in Harold, betimes, the result of study and reflection. The few books of the classical world then within reach of the student opened to the young Saxon views of human duties

and human responsibilities utterly distinct from the unmean-
ing ceremonials and fleshly mortifications in which even the
higher theology of that day placed the elements of virtue.
He smiled in scorn when some Dane, whose life had been
passed in the alternate drunkenness of wine and of blood,
thought he had opened the gates of heaven by bequeathing
lands gained by a robber's sword, to pamper the lazy sloth of
some fifty monks. If those monks had presumed to question
his own actions, his disdain would have been mixed with
simple wonder that men so besotted in ignorance, and who
could not construe the Latin of the very prayers they pat-
tered, should presume to be the judges of educated men. It
is possible (for his nature was earnest) that a pure and enlightened clergy, — that even a clergy, though defective in
life, zealous in duty and cultivated in mind, — such a clergy
as Alfred sought to found, and as Lanfranc endeavoured, not
without some success, to teach — would have bowed his strong
sense to that grand and subtle truth which dwells in spiritual
authority; but as it was, he stood aloof from the rude superstition of his age, and early in life made himself the arbiter
of his own conscience. Reducing his religion to the simplest
elements of our creed, he found rather in the books of heathen
authors than in the lives of the saints, his notions of the larger
morality which relates to the citizen and the man. The love
of country, the sense of justice, fortitude in adverse and temperance in prosperous fortune, became portions of his very
mind. Unlike his father, he played no actor's part in those
qualities which had won him the popular heart. He was
gentle and affable; above all, he was fair-dealing and just,
not because it was politic to *seem*, but his nature to *be*, so.

Nevertheless, Harold's character, beautiful and sublime in
many respects as it was, had its strong leaven of human im-
perfection in that very self-dependence which was born of his
reason and his pride. In resting so solely on man's percep-
tions of the right, he lost one attribute of the true hero, —
faith. We do not mean that word in the religious sense
alone, but in the more comprehensive. He did not rely on
the Celestial Something pervading all Nature, never seen,

only felt when duly courted, stronger and lovelier than what eye could behold and mere reason could embrace. Believing, it is true, in God, he lost those fine links that unite God to man's secret heart, and which are woven alike from the simplicity of the child and the wisdom of the poet. To use a modern illustration, his large mind was a "cupola lighted from below."

His bravery, though inflexible as the fiercest sea-king's when need arose for its exercise, was not his prominent characteristic. He despised the brute valour of Tostig; his bravery was a necessary part of a firm and balanced manhood, — the bravery of Hector, not Achilles. Constitutionally averse to bloodshed, he could seem timid where daring only gratified a wanton vanity or aimed at a selfish object. On the other hand, if *duty* demanded daring, no danger could deter, no policy warp him, — he could seem rash, he could even seem merciless. In the what *ought* to be he understood a *must* be.

And it was natural to this peculiar yet thoroughly English temperament to be, in action, rather steadfast and patient than quick and ready. Placed in perils familiar to him, nothing could exceed his vigour and address; but if taken unawares, and before his judgment could come to his aid, he was liable to be surprised into error. Large minds are rarely quick, unless they have been corrupted into unnatural vigilance by the necessities of suspicion; but a nature more thoroughly unsuspecting, more frank, trustful, and genuinely loyal than that young earl's, it was impossible to conceive. All these attributes considered, we have the key to much of Harold's character and conduct in the later events of his fated and tragic life.

But with this temperament, so manly and simple, we are not to suppose that Harold, while rejecting the superstitions of one class, was so far beyond his time as to reject those of another. No son of fortune, no man placing himself and the world in antagonism, can ever escape from some belief in the Invisible. Cæsar could ridicule and profane the mystic rites of Roman mythology, but he must still believe in his *fortune,* as in a god; and Harold, in his very studies, seeing the freest and boldest minds of antiquity subjected to influences akin to those of his Saxon forefathers, felt less shame in yielding to *them*, vain as they might be, than in monkish impostures so easily detected. Though hitherto he had rejected all direct appeal to the magic devices of Hilda, the sound of her dark sayings, heard in childhood, still vibrated on his soul as man. Belief in omens, in days lucky or unlucky, in the stars, was universal in every class of the Saxon. Harold had his own fortunate day, the day of his nativity, the 14th of October. All enterprises undertaken on that day had hitherto been successful. He believed in the virtue of that day, as Cromwell believed in his 3d of September. For the rest, we have described him as he was in that part of his career in which he is now presented. Whether altered by fate and circumstances, time will show. As yet, no selfish ambition leagued with the natural desire of youth and intellect, for their fair share of fame and power. His patriotism, fed by the example of Greek and Roman worthies, was genuine, pure, and ardent; he could have stood in the pass with Leonidas, or leaped into the gulf with Curtius.

CHAPTER II.

AT dawn Harold woke from uneasy and broken slumbers; and his eyes fell upon the face of Hilda, large, and fair, and unutterably calm, as the face of Egyptian sphinx.

"Have thy dreams been prophetic, son of Godwin?" said the Vala.

"Our Lord forfend," replied the earl, with unusual devoutness.

"Tell them, and let me read the rede; sense dwells in the voices of the night."

Harold mused, and after a short pause he said: "Methinks, Hilda, I can myself explain how those dreams came to haunt me."

Then raising himself on his elbow, he continued, while he fixed his clear penetrating eyes upon his hostess, —

"Tell me frankly, Hilda, didst thou not cause some light to shine on yonder knoll, by the mound and stone, within the temple of the Druids?"

But if Harold had suspected himself to be the dupe of some imposture, the thought vanished when he saw the look of keen interest, even of awe, which Hilda's face instantly assumed.

"Didst thou see a light, son of Godwin, by the altar of Thor, and over the bautastein of the mighty dead, — a flame, lambent and livid, like moonbeams collected over snow?"

"So seemed to me the light."

"No human hand ever kindled that flame, which announces the presence of the Dead," said Hilda, with a tremulous voice; "though seldom, uncompelled by the seid and the rune, does the spectre itself warn the eyes of the living."

"What shape, or what shadow of shape, does that spectre assume?"

"It rises in the midst of the flame, pale as the mist on the mountain, and vast as the giants of old; with the sæx and the spear and the shield of the sons of Woden. Thou hast seen the Scin-læca," continued Hilda, looking full on the face of the earl.

"If thou deceivest me not," began Harold, doubting still.

"Deceive thee! Not to save the crown of the Saxon dare I mock the might of the dead! Knowest thou not — or hath thy vain lore stood in place of the lore of thy fathers — that where a hero of old is buried, his treasures lie in his grave; that over that grave is at times seen at night the flame that thou sawest, and the dead in his image of air? Oft seen in the days that are gone, when the dead and the living had one faith, were one race; now never marked, but for portent and prophecy and doom, — glory or woe to the eyes that see! On yon knoll Æsc (the first-born of Cerdic, that Father-King of the Saxons, has his grave where the mound rises green, and the stone gleams wan by the altar of Thor. He smote the Britons in their temple, and he fell smiting. They buried him in his arms, and with the treasures his right hand had won. Fate hangs on the House of Cerdic or the realm of the Saxon, when Woden calls the læca of his son from the grave."

Hilda, much troubled, bent her face over her clasped hands, and rocking to and fro, muttered some runes unintelligible to the ear of her listener. Then she turned to him commandingly, and said, —

"Thy dreams now, indeed, are oracles, more true than living Vala could charm with the wand and the rune; unfold them."

Thus adjured, Harold resumed: —

"Methought, then, that I was on a broad, level plain, in the noon of day; all was clear to my eye, and glad to my heart. I was alone, and went on my way rejoicing. Suddenly the earth opened under my feet, and I fell deep, fathom-deep, — deep as if to that central pit which our heathen sires called Niffelheim, the Home of Vapour, the hell of the dead who die without glory. Stunned by the fall, I lay long, locked as in a dream in the midst of a dream. When I opened my eyes, behold, I was girt round with dead men's bones; and the bones moved round me, undulating, as the dry leaves that wirble round in the winds of the winter. And from the midst of them peered a trunkless skull, and on the skull was a mitre, and from the yawning jaws a voice came hissing, as a serpent's hiss, ' Harold, the scorner, thou art ours!' Then, as from the buzz of an army, came voices multitudinous, ' Thou art ours!' I sought to rise, and behold my limbs were bound, and the gyves were fine and frail, as the web of the gossamer, and they weighed on me like chains of iron. And I felt an anguish of soul that no words can speak, — an anguish both of horror and shame; and my manhood seemed to ooze from me, and I was weak as a child new born. Then suddenly there rushed forth a freezing wind, as from an air of ice, and the bones from their whirl stood still, and the buzz ceased, and the mitred skull grinned on me still and voiceless; and serpents darted their arrowy tongues from the eyeless sockets. And, lo, before me stood (O Hilda, I see it now!) the form of the spectre that had risen from yonder knoll. With his spear and sæx and his shield, he stood before me; and his face, though pale as that of one long dead, was stern as the face of a warrior in the van of armed men. He stretched his hand, and he smote his sæx on his shield, and the clang sounded hollow; the gyves broke at the clash. I sprang to my feet, and I stood side by side with the phantom, dauntless. Then, suddenly, the mitre on the skull changed to a helm; and where the skull had grinned, trunkless and harmless, stood a shape like War, made incarnate, — a Thing above giants, with its crest to the stars and its form an eclipse between the sun and the day. The earth changed to ocean, and the ocean was blood, and the ocean seemed deep as the seas where the whales sport in the North; but the surge rose not to the knee of that measureless image. And the ravens came round it from all parts of the heaven, and the vultures with dead eyes and dull scream. And all the bones, before scattered and shapeless, sprung to life and to form, — some monks and some warriors; and there was a hoot, and a hiss, and a roar, and the storm of arms. And a broad pennon rose out of the sea of blood, and from the clouds came a pale hand, and it wrote on the pennon, 'Harold, the Accursed!' Then said the stern shape by my side, 'Harold, fearest thou the dead men's bones?' and its voice was as a trumpet that gives strength to the craven, and I answered, 'Niddering, indeed, were Harold, to fear the bones of the dead!'

"As I spoke, as if hell had burst loose, came a gibber of scorn; and all vanished at once, save the ocean of blood. Slowly came from the north, over the sea, a bird like a raven, save that it was blood-red, like the ocean; and there came from the south, swimming towards me, a lion. And I looked to the spectre; and the pride of war had gone from its face, which was so sad that methought I forgot raven and lion, and wept to see it. Then the spectre took me in its vast arms, and its breath froze my veins, and it kissed my brow and my lips, and said gently and fondly, as my mother in some childish sickness, 'Harold, my best beloved, mourn not. Thou hast all which the sons of Woden dreamed in their dreams of

Valhalla!' Thus saying, the form receded slowly, slowly, still gazing on me with its sad eyes. I stretched forth my hand to detain it, and in my grasp was a shadowy sceptre. And, lo! round me, as if from the earth, sprang up thegns and chiefs, in their armour; and a board was spread, and a wassail was blithe around me. So my heart felt cheered and light, and in my hand was still the sceptre. And we feasted long and merrily; but over the feast flapped the wings of the blood-red raven, and over the blood-red sea beyond swam the lion, near and near. And in the heavens there were two stars, — one pale and steadfast, the other rushing and luminous; and a shadowy hand pointed from the cloud to the pale star, and a voice said, ' Lo, Harold! the star that shone on thy birth.' And another hand pointed to the luminous star, and another voice said, ' Lo, the star that shone on the birth of the victor.' Then, lo! the bright star grew fiercer and larger; and rolling on with a hissing sound, as when iron is dipped into water, it rushed over the disc of the mournful planet, and the whole heavens seemed on fire. So methought the dream faded away, and in fading I heard a full swell of music, as the swell of an anthem in an aisle; a music like that which but once in my life I heard, — when I stood in the train of Edward, in the halls of Winchester, the day they crowned him king."

Harold ceased; and the Vala slowly lifted her head from her bosom, and surveyed him in profound silence, and with a gaze that seemed vacant and meaningless.

"Why dost thou look on me thus, and why art thou so silent?" asked the earl.

"The cloud is on my sight, and the burden is on my soul, and I cannot read thy rede," murmured the Vala. "But morn, the ghost-chaser, that waketh life the action, charms into slumber life the thought. As the stars pale at the rising of the sun, so fade the lights of the soul when the buds revive in the dews, and the lark sings to the day. In thy dream lies thy future, as the wing of the moth in the web of the changing worm; but whether for weal or for woe, thou shalt burst through thy mesh, and spread thy plumes in the air. Of myself I know not. Await the hour when Skulda shall pass into the soul of her servant, and thy fate shall rush from my lips as the rush of the waters from the heart of the cave."

"I am content to abide," said Harold, with his wonted smile, so calm and so lofty; "but I cannot promise thee that I shall heed thy rede or obey thy warning, when my reason hath awoke, as while I speak it awakens, from the fumes of the fancy and the mists of the night."

The Vala sighed heavily, but made no answer.

CHAPTER III.

GITHA, Earl Godwin's wife, sat in her chamber, and her heart was sad. In the room was one of her sons, the one dearer to her than all, — Wolnoth, her darling. For the rest of her sons were stalwart and strong of frame, and in their infancy she had known not a mother's fears. But Wolnoth had come into the world before his time, and sharp had been the travail of the mother, and long between life and death the struggle of the new-born babe. And his cradle had been rocked with a trembling knee, and his pillow been bathed with hot tears. Frail had been his childhood, — a thing that hung on her care; and now, as the boy grew, blooming and strong, into youth, the mother felt that she had given life twice to her child. Therefore was he more dear to her than the rest; and therefore, as she gazed upon him now, fair and smiling and hopeful, she mourned for him more than for Sweyn, the outcast and criminal, on his pilgrimage of woe to the waters of Jordan and the tomb of our Lord. For Wolnoth, selected as the hostage for the faith of his House, was to be sent from her arms to the court of William the Norman. And the youth smiled and was gay, choosing vestment and mantle, and ateghars of gold, that he might be flaunting and brave in the halls of knighthood and beauty, — the school of the proudest chivalry of the Christian world. Too young and too thoughtless to share the wise hate of his elders for the manners and forms of the foreigners, their gayety and splendour, as his boyhood had seen them, relieving the gloom of the cloister court, and contrasting the spleen and the rudeness of the Saxon temperament, had dazzled his fancy and half Normanized his mind. A proud and happy boy was he, to go as hostage for the faith and representative of the rank of his mighty kinsmen, and step into manhood in the eyes of the dames of Rouen.

By Wolnoth's side stood his young sister, Thyra, a mere infant; and her innocent sympathy with her brother's pleasure in gaud and toy saddened Githa yet more.

"Oh, my son!" said the troubled mother, "why, of all my children, have they chosen thee? Harold is wise against danger, and Tostig is fierce against foes, and Gurth is too loving to wake hate in the sternest, and from the mirth of sunny Leofwine sorrow glints aside, as the shaft from the sheen of a shield. But thou, thou, O beloved! — cursed be the king that chose thee, and cruel was the father that forgot the light of the mother's eyes!"

"Tut, mother the dearest," said Wolnoth, pausing from the contemplation of a silk robe, all covered with broidered peacocks, which had been sent him as a gift from his sister the queen, and wrought with her own fair hands; for a notable needle-woman, despite her sage lere, was the wife of the saint-king, as sorrowful women mostly are, — "tut! the bird must leave the nest when the wings are fledged. Harold the eagle, Tostig the kite, Gurth the ring-dove, and Leofwine the stare. See, my wings are the richest of all, Mother; and bright is the sun in which thy peacock shall spread his pranked plumes."

Then, observing that his liveliness provoked no smile from his mother, he approached, and said more seriously, —

"Bethink thee, Mother mine. No other choice was left to king or to father. Harold and Tostig and Leofwine have their lordships and offices. Their posts are fixed, and they stand as the columns of our House. And Gurth is so young,

and so Saxish, and so the shadow of Harold, that his hate to
the Norman is a byword already among our youths; for hate
is the more marked in a temper of love, as the blue of this
border seems black against the white of the woof. But *I*—
the good king knows that I shall be welcome; for the Norman
knights love Wolnoth, and I have spent hours by the knees of
Montgommeri and Grantmesnil, listening to the feats of Rolf-
ganger, and playing with their gold chains of knighthood.
And the stout count himself shall knight me, and I shall come
back with the spurs of gold which thy ancestors, the brave
kings of Norway and Daneland, wore ere knighthood was
known. Come, kiss me, my mother, and come see the brave
falcons Harold has sent me, — true Welch!"

Githa rested her face on her son's shoulder, and her tears
blinded her. The door opened gently, and Harold entered;
and with the earl, a pale dark-haired boy, Haco, the son of
Sweyn.

But Githa, absorbed in her darling Wolnoth, scarce saw the
grandchild reared afar from her knees, and hurried at once to
Harold. In his presence she felt comfort and safety; for
Wolnoth leaned on her heart, and her heart leaned on Harold.

"Oh, son, son!" she cried, "firmest of hand, surest of
faith, and wisest of brain in the House of Godwin, tell me
that he yonder, he thy young brother, risks no danger in the
halls of the Normans!"

"Not more than in these, Mother," answered Harold,
soothing her with caressing lip and gentle tone. "Fierce
and ruthless, men say, is William the Duke against foes with
their swords in their hands, but debonnair and mild to the
gentle,[1] frank host and kind lord. And these Normans have
a code of their own, more grave than all morals, more binding than even their fanatic religion. Thou knowest it well,
Mother, for it comes from thy race of the North; and this
code of *honour*, they call it, makes Wolnoth's head as sacred
as the relics of a saint set in zimmes. Ask only, my brother,
when thou comest in sight of the Norman Duke, ask only ' the

---

[1] So Robert of Gloucester says pithily of William, "Kyng Wylliam was to
mild men debonnere ynou." — HEARNE, vol. ii. p. 309.

kiss of peace;' and, that kiss on thy brow, thou wilt sleep more safe than if all the banners of England waved over thy couch." [1]

"But how long shall the exile be?" asked Githa, comforted. Harold's brow fell.

"Mother, not even to cheer thee will I deceive. The time of the hostageship rests with the king and the duke. As long as the one affects fear from the race of Godwin, as long as the other feigns care for such priests or such knights as were not banished from the realm, being not courtiers, but scattered wide and far in convent and homestead, so long will Wolnoth and Haco be guests in the Norman halls."

Githa wrung her hands.

"But comfort, my mother! Wolnoth is young, his eye is keen, and his spirit prompt and quick. He will mark these Norman captains; he will learn their strength and their weakness, their manner of war; and he will come back, not as Edward the King came, a lover of things un-Saxon, but able to warn and to guide us against the plots of the camp-court, which threatens more, year by year, the peace of the world. And he will see there arts we may worthily borrow, — not the cut of a tunic, and the fold of a gonna, but the arts of men who found States and build nations. William the Duke is splendid and wise; merchants tell us how crafts thrive under his iron hand, and war-men say that his forts are constructed with skill and his battle-schemes planned as the mason plans keystone and arch, with weight portioned out to the prop, and the force of the hand made tenfold by the science of the brain. So that the boy will return to us a man round and complete, a teacher of graybeards, and the sage of his kin; fit for earldom and rule, fit for glory and England. Grieve not, daughter of the Dane kings, that thy son, the

---

[1] This kiss of peace was held singularly sacred by the Normans, and all the more knightly races of the continent. Even the craftiest dissimulator, designing fraud and stratagem and murder to a foe, would not, to gain his ends, betray the pledge of the kiss of peace. When Henry II. consented to meet Becket after his return from Rome, and promised to remedy all of which his prelate complained, he struck prophetic dismay into Becket's heart by evading the kiss of peace.

best loved, hath nobler school and wider field than his brothers."

This appeal touched the proud heart of the niece of Canute the Great, and she almost forgot the grief of her love in the hope of her ambition.

She dried her tears and smiled upon Wolnoth, and already, in the dreams of a mother's vanity, saw him great as Godwin in council, and prosperous as Harold in the field. Nor, half Norman as he was, did the young man seem insensible of the manly and elevated patriotism of his brother's hinted lessons, though he felt they implied reproof. He came to the earl, whose arm was round his mother, and said with a frank heartiness not usual to a nature somewhat frivolous and irresolute, —

"Harold, thy tongue could kindle stones into men, and warm those men into Saxons. Thy Wolnoth shall not hang his head with shame when he comes back to our merrie land with shaven locks and spurs of gold. For if thou doubtest his race from his look, thou shalt put thy right hand on his heart, and feel England beat there in every pulse."

"Brave words, and well spoken!" cried the earl; and he placed his hand on the boy's head as in benison.

Till then Haco had stood apart, conversing with the infant Thyra, whom his dark, mournful face awed and yet touched, for she nestled close to him, and put her little hand in his; but now, inspired no less than his cousin by Harold's noble speech, he came proudly forward by Wolnoth's side, and said, —

"I, too, am English, and I have the name of Englishman to redeem."

Ere Harold could reply, Githa exclaimed, —

"Leave there thy right hand on my child's head, and say simply: 'By my troth and my plight, if the duke detain Wolnoth, son of Githa, against just plea, and king's assent to his return, I, Harold, will, failing letter and nuncius, cross the seas, to restore the child to the mother.'"

Harold hesitated.

A sharp cry of reproach that went to his heart broke from Githa's lips.

"Ah! cold and self-heeding, wilt thou send him to bear a peril from which thou shrinkest thyself?"

"By my troth and my plight, then,", said the earl, "if, fair time elapsed, peace in England, without plea of justice, and against my king's fiat, Duke William of Normandy detain the hostages, — thy son and this dear boy, more sacred and more dear to me for his father's woes, — I will cross the seas, to restore the child to the mother, the fatherless to his fatherland. So help me, all-seeing One, Amen and Amen!"

———◆———

CHAPTER IV.

WE have seen, in an earlier part of this record, that Harold possessed, amongst his numerous and more stately possessions, a house not far from the old Roman dwelling-place of Hilda; and in this residence he now, save when with the king, made his chief abode. He gave, as the reasons for his selection, the charm it took in his eyes from that signal mark of affection which his ceorls had rendered him in purchasing the house and tilling the ground in his absence, and more especially the convenience of its vicinity to the new palace at Westminster; for, by Edward's special desire, while the other brothers repaired to their different domains, Harold remained near his royal person. To use the words of the great Norwegian chronicler, "Harold was always with the court itself, and nearest to the king in all service." "The king loved him very much, and kept him as his own son, for he had no children." [1] This attendance on Edward was naturally most close at the restoration to power of the earl's family. For Harold, mild and conciliating, was, like Alred, a great peacemaker, and Edward had never cause to complain of him, as he believed he had of the rest of that haughty House. But the true spell which made dear to Harold the rude building of

[1] Snorro Sturleson's Heimskringla, Laing's Translation, pp. 75-77.

timber, with its doors open all day to his lithsmen, when with
a light heart he escaped from the halls of Westminster, was
the fair face of Edith his neighbour. The impression which
this young girl had made upon Harold seemed to partake of
the strength of a fatality. For Harold had loved her before
the marvellous beauty of her womanhood began; and, occupied
from his earliest youth in grave and earnest affairs, his heart
had never been frittered away on the mean and frivolous
affections of the idle. Now, in that comparative leisure of
his stormy life, he was naturally most open to the influence
of a charm more potent than all the glamoury of Hilda.

The autumn sun shone through the golden glades of the
forest-land, when Edith sat alone, on the knoll that faced
forest-land and road, and watched afar.

And the birds sung cheerily, — but that was not the sound
for which Edith listened; and the squirrel darted from tree
to tree on the sward beyond, — but not to see the games of
the squirrel sat Edith by the grave of the Teuton. By and
by came the cry of the dogs, and the tall gre-hound [1] of Wales
emerged from the bosky dells. Then Edith's heart heaved,
and her eyes brightened. And now, with his hawk on his
wrist and his spear [2] in his hand, came, through the yellowing boughs, Harold the Earl.

And well may ye ween that his heart beat as loud and his eye
shone as bright as Edith's, when he saw who had watched for
his footsteps on the sepulchral knoll. Love, forgetful of the
presence of Death, — so has it ever been, so ever shall it be!
He hastened his stride, and bounded up the gentle hillock;
and his dogs, with a joyous bark, came round the knees of
Edith. Then Harold shook the bird from his wrist, and it
fell, with its light wing, on the altar-stone of Thor.

"Thou art late, but thou art welcome, Harold my kinsman," said Edith, simply, as she bent her face over the
hounds, whose gaunt heads she caressed.

---

[1] The gre-hound was so called from hunting the gre, or badger.

[2] The spear and the hawk were as the badges of Saxon nobility; and a
thegn was seldom seen abroad without the one on his left wrist, the other in
his right hand.

"Call me not kinsman," said Harold, shrinking, and with a dark cloud on his broad brow.

"And why, Harold?"

"Oh, Edith, why?" murmured Harold; and his thought added, "She knows not, poor child, that in that mockery of kinship the Church sets its ban on our bridals."

He turned, and chid his dogs fiercely as they gambolled in rough glee round their fair friend.

The hounds crouched at the feet of Edith; and Edith looked in mild wonder at the troubled face of the earl.

"Thine eyes rebuke me, Edith, more than my words the hounds!" said Harold, gently. "But there is quick blood in my veins; and the mind must be calm when it would control the humour. Calm was my mind, sweet Edith, in the old time, when thou wert an infant on my knee, and wreathing with these rude hands flower-chains for thy neck like the swan's down, I said, 'The flowers fade, but the chain lasts when love weaves it.'"

Edith again bent her face over the crouching hounds. Harold gazed on her with mournful fondness; and the bird still sung and the squirrel swung himself again from bough to bough. Edith spoke first.

"My godmother, thy sister, hath sent for me, Harold, and I am to go to the court to-morrow. Shalt thou be there?"

"Surely," said Harold, in an anxious voice, — "surely, I will be there! So my sister hath sent for thee. Wittest thou wherefore?"

Edith grew very pale, and her tone trembled as she answered: "Well-a-day, yes."

"It is as I feared, then!" exclaimed Harold, in great agitation; "and my sister, whom these monks have demented, leagues herself with the king against the law of the wide welkin and the grand religion of the human heart. Oh!" continued the earl, kindling into an enthusiasm rare to his even moods, but wrung as much from his broad sense as from his strong affection, "when I compare the Saxon of our land and day, all enervated and decrepit by priestly superstition, with his forefathers in the first Christian era, yielding to the

religion they adopted in its simple truths, but not to that
rot of social happiness and free manhood which this cold
and lifeless monachism, making virtue the absence of
human ties, spreads around, — which the great Bede,[1]
though himself a monk, vainly but bitterly denounced, —
yea, verily, when I see the Saxon already the theowe of the
priest, I shudder to ask how long he will be folk-free of the
tyrant."

He paused, breathed hard, and seizing almost sternly the
girl's trembling arm, he resumed between his set teeth: "So
they would have thee be a nun? Thou wilt not, thou durst
not, — thy heart would perjure thy vows!"

"Ah, Harold!" answered Edith, moved out of all bashful-
ness by his emotion and her own terror of the convent, and
answering, if with the love of a woman, still with all the
unconsciousness of a child; "better, oh, better the grate of the
body than that of the heart! In the grave I could still live
for those I love; behind the grate love itself must be dead.
Yes, thou pitiest me, Harold; thy sister, the queen, is gentle
and kind; I will fling myself at her feet, and say, ' Youth is
fond, and the world is fair; let me live my youth, and bless
God in the world that he saw was good!'"

"My own, own dear Edith!" exclaimed Harold, overjoyed,
"say this. Be firm; they cannot and they dare not force
thee! The law cannot wrench thee against thy will from the
ward of thy guardian Hilda; and where the law is, there
Harold at least is strong, — and there at least our kinship, if
my bane, is thy blessing."

"Why, Harold, sayest thou that our kinship is thy bane?
It is so sweet to me to whisper to myself, ' Harold is of thy
kith, though distant; and it is natural to thee to have pride
in his fame, and joy in his presence!' Why is that sweetness
to me, to thee so bitter?"

"Because," answered Harold, dropping the hand he had
clasped, and folding his arms in deep dejection, — "because
but for that I should say, ' Edith, I love thee more than a
brother; Edith, be Harold's wife!' And were I to say it,

[1] Bed. Epist. ad Egbert.

and were we to wed, all the priests of the Saxons would lift
up their hands in horror, and curse our nuptials, and I should
be the banned of that spectre the Church; and my House
would shake to its foundations; and my father, and my
brothers, and the thegns and the proceres, and the abbots
and prelates, whose aid makes our force, would gather round
me with threats and with prayers that I might put thee aside.
And mighty as I am now, so mighty once was Sweyn my
brother; and outlaw as Sweyn is now, might Harold be; and
outlaw if Harold were, what breast so broad as his could fill
up the gap left in the defence of England? And the passions
that I curb, as a rider his steed, might break their rein; and,
strong in justice, and child of Nature, I might come with
banner and mail against Church and House and Fatherland,
and the blood of my countrymen might be poured like water;
and therefore, slave to the lying thraldom he despises, Harold
dares not say to the maid of his love, ' Give me thy right
hand, and be my bride!'"

Edith had listened in bewilderment and despair, her eyes
fixed on his, and her face locked and rigid, as if turned to
stone. But when he had ceased, and, moving some steps
away, turned aside his manly countenance, that Edith might
not perceive its anguish, the noble and sublime spirit of that
sex which ever, when lowliest, most comprehends the lofty,
rose superior both to love and to grief; and rising, she advanced, and placing her slight hand on his stalwart shoulder,
she said, half in pity, half in reverence, —

" Never before, O Harold, did I feel so proud of thee; for
Edith could not love thee as she doth, and will till the grave
clasp her, if thou didst not love England more than Edith.
Harold, till this hour I was a child, and I knew not my own
heart; I look now into that heart, and I see that I am woman.
Harold, of the cloister I have now no fear; and all life does
not shrink, — no, it enlarges, and it soars into one desire, —
to be worthy to pray for thee!"

" Maid, maid!" exclaimed Harold, abruptly, and pale as
the dead, "do not say thou hast no fear of the cloister. I
adjure, I command thee, build not up between us that dismal

everlasting wall. While thou art free, Hope yet survives, — a phantom, haply, but Hope still."

"As thou wilt, I will," said Edith, humbly; "order my fate so as pleases thee the best."

Then, not daring to trust herself longer, for she felt the tears rushing to her eyes, she turned away hastily, and left him alone beside the altar-stone and the tomb.

CHAPTER V.

THE next day, as Harold was entering the palace of Westminster, with intent to seek the king's lady, his father met him in one of the corridors, and, taking him gravely by the hand, said, —

"My son, I have much on my mind regarding thee and our House; come with me."

"Nay," said the earl, "by your leave let it be later; for I have it on hand to see my sister, ere confessor or monk or schoolman claim her hours!"

"Not so, Harold," said the earl, briefly. "My daughter is now in her oratory, and we shall have time enow to treat of things mundane ere she is free to receive thee, and to preach to thee of things ghostly, the last miracle at St. Alban's, or the last dream of the king, who would be a great man and a stirring, if as restless when awake as he is in his sleep. Come."

Harold, in that filial obedience which belonged, as of course, to his antique cast of character, made no further effort to escape, but with a sigh followed Godwin into one of the contiguous chambers.

"Harold," then said Earl Godwin, after closing the door carefully, "thou must not let the king keep thee longer in dalliance and idleness; thine earldom needs thee without delay. Thou knowest that these East Angles, as we Saxons still call them, are in truth mostly Danes and Norsemen, — a people jealous and fierce and free, and more akin to the Normans than to the Saxons. My whole power in England hath been founded not less on my common birth with the freefolk of Wessex — Saxons like myself, and therefore easy for me, a Saxon, to conciliate and control — than on the hold I have ever sought to establish, whether by arms or by arts, over the Danes in the realm. And I tell and I warn thee, Harold, as the natural heir of my greatness, that he who cannot command the stout hearts of the Anglo-Danes will never maintain the race of Godwin in the post they have won in the vanguard of Saxon England."

"This I wot well, my father," answered Harold; "and I see with joy, that while those descendants of heroes and freemen are blended indissolubly with the meeker Saxon, their freer laws and hardier manners are gradually supplanting, or rather regenerating, our own."

Godwin smiled approvingly on his son, and then, his brow becoming serious, and the dark pupil of his blue eye dilating, he resumed : —

"This is well, my son; and hast thou thought also, that while thou art loitering in these galleries, amidst the ghosts of men in monk cowls, Siward is shadowing our House with his glory, and all north the Humber rings with his name? Hast thou thought that all Mercia is in the hands of Leofric our rival, and that Algar his son, who ruled Wessex in my absence, left there a name so beloved that had I stayed a year longer, the cry had been ' Algar,' not ' Godwin '? — for so is the multitude ever! Now aid me, Harold, for my soul is troubled, and I cannot work alone; and though I say nought to others, my heart received a death-blow when tears fell from its blood-springs on the brow of Sweyn, my first-born." The old man paused, and his lip quivered.

"Thou, thou alone, Harold, noble boy, thou alone didst stand by his side in the hall, — alone, alone; and I blessed thee in that hour over all the rest of my sons. Well, well! now to earth again. Aid me, Harold. I open to thee my web; complete the woof when this hand is cold. The new tree that stands alone in the plain is soon nipped by the winter; fenced round with the forest, its youth takes shelter from its fellows.[1] So is it with a house newly founded; it must win strength from the allies that it sets round its slender stem. What had been Godwin, son of Wolnoth, had he not married into the kingly House of great Canute? It is this that gives my sons now the right to the loyal love of the Danes. The throne passed from Canute and his race, and the Saxons again had their hour; and I gave, as Jephtha gave his daughter, my blooming Edith to the cold bed of the Saxon king. Had sons sprung from that union, the grandson of Godwin, royal alike from Saxon and Dane, would reign on the throne of the isle. Fate ordered otherwise, and the spider must weave web anew. Thy brother Tostig has added more splendour than solid strength to our line, in his marriage with the daughter of Baldwin the Count. The foreigner helps us little in England. Thou, O Harold, must bring new props to the House. I would rather see thee wed to the child of one of our great rivals than to the daughter of kaisar, or outland king. Siward hath no daughter undisposed of. Algar, son of Leofric, hath a daughter fair as the fairest; make her thy bride, that Algar may cease to be a foe. This alliance will render Mercia, in truth, subject to our principalities, since the stronger must quell the weaker. It doth more. Algar himself has married into the royalty of Wales.[2] Thou wilt win all those fierce tribes to thy side. Their forces will gain thee the marches, now held so feebly under Rolf the Norman, and in case of brief reverse or sharp danger, their mountains will give refuge from all foes. This day, greeting Algar, he told me he meditated bestowing his daughter on Gryffyth, the rebel under-king of North Wales. Therefore," continued the old earl, with a smile, "thou must speak in time, and win and woo in the same breath. No hard task, methinks, for Harold of the golden tongue."

[1] Tegner's Frithiof.

[2] Some of the chroniclers say that he married the daughter of Gryffyth, the king of North Wales; but Gryffyth certainly married Algar's daughter, and that double alliance could not have been permitted. It was probably, therefore, some more distant kinswoman of Gryffyth's that was united to Algar.

"Sir, and Father," replied the young earl, whom the long speech addressed to him had prepared for its close, and whose habitual self-control saved him from disclosing his emotion, "I thank you duteously for your care for my future, and hope to profit by your wisdom. I will ask the king's leave to go to my East Anglians, and hold there a folkmuth, administer justice, redress grievances, and make thegn and ceorl content with Harold their earl. But vain is peace in the realm if there is strife in the house; and Aldyth, the daughter of Algar, cannot be house-wife to me."

"Why?" asked the old earl, calmly, and surveying his son's face with those eyes so clear yet so unfathomable.

"Because, though I grant her fair, she pleases not my fancy, nor would give warmth to my hearth. Because, as thou knowest well, Algar and I have ever been opposed, both in camp and in council; and I am not the man who can sell my love, though I may stifle my anger. Earl Harold needs no bride to bring spearmen to his back at his need; and his lordships he will guard with the shield of a man, not the spindle of a woman."

"Said in spite and in error," replied the old earl, coolly. "Small pain had it given thee to forgive Algar old quarrels, and clasp his hand as a father-in-law, if thou hadst had for his daughter what the great are forbidden to regard save as a folly."

"Is love a folly, my father?

"Surely, yes," said the earl, with some sadness, — "surely, yes, for those who know that life is made up of business and care, spun out in long years, not counted by the joys of an hour, — surely, yes. Thinkest thou that I loved my first wife, the proud sister of Canute, or that Edith, thy sister, loved Edward, when he placed the crown on her head?"

"My father, in Edith, my sister, our House has sacrificed enow to selfish power."

"I grant it, to selfish power," answered the eloquent old man, "but not enow for England's safety. Look to it, Harold; thy years and thy fame and thy state place thee free from my control as a father, but not till thou sleepest in thy cerements art thou free from that father,—thy Land! Ponder it in thine own wise mind, —wiser already than that which speaks to it under the hood of gray hairs. Ponder it, and ask thyself if thy power, when I am dead, is not necessary to the weal of England; and if aught that thy schemes can suggest would so strengthen that power as to find in the heart of the kingdom a host of friends like the Mercians; or if there could be a trouble and a bar to thy greatness, a wall in thy path, or a thorn in thy side, like the hate or the jealousy of Algar, the son of Leofric?"

Thus addressed, Harold's face, before serene and calm, grew overcast; and he felt the force of his father's words when appealing to his reason, not to his affections. The old man saw the advantage he had gained, and prudently forbore to press it. Rising, he drew round him his sweeping gonna lined with furs; and only when he reached the door, he added, —

"The old see afar, —they stand on the height of experience, as a warder on the crown of a tower; and I tell thee, Harold, that if thou let slip this golden occasion, years hence, long and many, thou wilt rue the loss of the hour; and that unless Mercia, as the centre of the kingdom, be reconciled to thy power, thou wilt stand high indeed, —but on the shelf of a precipice. And if, as I suspect, thou lovest some other, who now clouds thy perception, and will then check thy ambition, thou wilt break her heart with thy desertion, or gnaw thine own with regret. For love dies in possession; ambition has no fruition, and so lives forever."

"That ambition is not mine, my father," exclaimed Harold, earnestly; "I have not thy love of power, glorious in thee, even in its extremes. I have not thy —"

"Seventy years!" interrupted the old man, concluding the sentence. "At seventy all men who have been great will speak as I do; yet all will have known love. Thou not ambitious, Harold? Thou knowest not thyself, nor knowest thou yet what ambition is. That which I see far before me as thy natural prize, I dare not, or I will not say. When time sets that prize within reach of thy spear's point, say then, 'I am not ambitious!' Ponder and decide."

And Harold pondered long, and decided not as Godwin could have wished. For he had not the seventy years of his father, and the prize lay yet in the womb of the mountains; though the dwarf and the gnome were already fashioning the ore to the shape of a crown.

CHAPTER VI.

WHILE Harold mused over his father's words, Edith, seated on a low stool beside the Lady of England, listened with earnest but mournful reverence to her royal namesake.

The queen's[1] closet opened, like the king's, on one hand to an oratory, on the other to a spacious anteroom; the lower part of the walls was covered with arras, leaving space for a niche that contained an image of the Virgin. Near the doorway to the oratory was the stoup, or aspersorium, for holy water; and in various cysts and crypts, in either room, were caskets containing the relics of saints. The purple light from the stained glass of a high narrow window, shaped in the Saxon arch, streamed rich and full over the queen's bended head like a glory, and tinged her pale cheek, as with a maiden blush; and she might have furnished a sweet model for early artist, in his dreams of Saint Mary the Mother, not when, young and blessed, she held the divine infant in her arms, but when sorrow had reached even the immaculate bosom, and the stone had been rolled over the Holy Sepulchre, — for beautiful the face still was, and mild beyond all words, but beyond all words, also, sad in its tender resignation.

And thus said the queen to her godchild: "Why dost thou hesitate and turn away? Thinkest thou, poor child, in thine

[1] The title of queen is employed in these pages, as one which our historians have unhesitatingly given to the consorts of our Saxon kings; but the usual and correct designation of Edward's royal wife in her own time would be Edith the Lady.

ignorance of life, that the world ever can give thee a bliss greater than the calm of the cloister? Pause, and ask thyself, young as thou art, if all the true happiness thou hast known is not bounded to hope. As long as thou hopest, thou art happy."

Edith sighed deeply, and moved her young head in involuntary acquiescence.

"And what is life to the nun, but hope? In that hope she knows not the present, she lives in the future; she hears ever singing the chorus of the angels, as Saint Dunstan heard them sing at the birth of Edgar.[1] That hope unfolds to her the heiligthum of the future. On earth her body, in heaven her soul!"

"And her heart, O Lady of England?" cried Edith, with a sharp pang.

The queen paused a moment, and laid her pale hand kindly on Edith's bosom.

"Not beating, child, as thine does now, with vain thoughts and worldly desires; but calm, calm as mine. It is in our power," resumed the queen, after a second pause, — "it is in our power to make the life within us all soul; so that the heart is not, or is felt not; so that grief and joy have no power over us; so that we look tranquil on the stormy earth, as yon image of the Virgin, whom we make our example, looks from the silent niche. Listen, my godchild and darling! I have known human state and human debasement. In these halls I woke Lady of England, and ere sunset my lord banished me, without one mark of honour, without one word of comfort, to the convent of Wherwell, — my father, my mother, my kin, all in exile; and my tears falling fast for them, but not on a husband's bosom."

"Ah, then, noble Edith," said the girl, colouring with anger at the remembered wrong for her queen, "ah, then, surely, at least, thy heart made itself heard."

"Heard, yea verily," said the queen, looking up, and pressing her hands; "heard, but the soul rebuked it. And the soul

[1] Ethel. De Gen. Reg. Ang.

said, ' Blessed are they that mourn; ' and I rejoiced at the new trial which brought me nearer to Him who chastens those He loves."

"But thy banished kin, — the valiant, the wise; they who placed thy lord on the throne?"

"Was it no comfort," answered the queen, simply, "to think that in the House of God my prayers for them would be more accepted than in the halls of kings? Yes, my child, I have known the world's honour and the world's disgrace, and I have schooled my heart to be calm in both."

"Ah, thou art above human strength, Queen and Saint," exclaimed Edith; "and I have heard it said of thee that as thou art now, thou wert from thine earliest years,[1] — ever the sweet, the calm, the holy, — ever less on earth than in heaven."

Something there was in the queen's eyes, as she raised them towards Edith at this burst of enthusiasm, that gave for a moment to a face otherwise so dissimilar the likeness to her father, — something, in that large pupil, of the impenetrable, unrevealing depth of a nature close and secret in self-control; and a more acute observer than Edith might long have been perplexed and haunted with that look, wondering if indeed, under the divine and spiritual composure, lurked the mystery of human passion.

"My child," said the queen, with the faintest smile upon her lips, and drawing Edith towards her, "there are moments when all that breathe the breath of life feel or have felt alike. In my vain youth I read, I mused, I pondered, but over worldly lore; and what men called the sanctity of virtue was perhaps but the silence of thought. Now I have put aside those early and childish dreams and shadows, remembering them not, save " (here the smile grew more pronounced) "to puzzle some poor schoolboy with the knots and riddles of the sharp grammarian.[2] But not to speak of myself have I sent for thee. Edith, again and again, solemnly and sincerely, I pray thee to obey the wish of my lord the king; and now, while yet in all the bloom of thought as of youth, while

---

[1] Ailred, De Vit. Edward Confess.   [2] Ingulfus.

thou hast no memory save the child's, enter on the Realm of Peace."

"I cannot, I dare not, I cannot, — ah, ask me not," said poor Edith, covering her face with her hands.

Those hands the queen gently withdrew; and looking steadfastly in the changeful and half-averted face, she said mournfully, —

"Is it so, my godchild? and is thy heart set on the hopes of earth, thy dreams on the love of man?"

"Nay," answered Edith, equivocating; "but I have promised not to take the veil."

"Promised to Hilda?"

"Hilda," exclaimed Edith, readily, "would never consent to it. Thou knowest her strong nature, her distaste to — to — "

"The laws of our holy Church. I do; and for that reason it is, mainly, that I join with the king in seeking to abstract thee from her influence. But it is not Hilda that thou hast promised?"

Edith hung her head.

"Is it to woman or to man?"

Before Edith could answer, the door from the anteroom opened gently but without the usual ceremony, and Harold entered. His quick, quiet eye embraced both forms, and curbed Edith's young impulse, which made her start from her seat and advance joyously towards him as a protector.

"Fair day to thee, my sister," said the earl, advancing; and pardon if I break thus rudely on thy leisure, for few are the moments when beggar and Benedictine leave thee free to receive thy brother."

"Dost thou reproach me, Harold?"

"No, Heaven forfend!" replied the earl, cordially, and with a look at once of pity and admiration; "for thou art one of the few, in this court of simulators, sincere and true; and it pleases thee to serve the Divine Power in thy way, as it pleases me to serve Him in mine."

"Thine, Harold?" said the queen, shaking her head, but with a look of some human pride and fondness in her fair face.

"Mine; as I learned it from thee when I was thy pupil, Edith, — when to those studies in which thou didst precede me, thou first didst lure me from sport and pastime, and from thee I learned to glow over the deeds of Greek and Roman, and say, 'They lived and died as men; like them may I live and die!'"

"Oh, true, — too true!" said the queen, with a sigh; "and I am to blame grievously that I did so pervert to earth a mind that might otherwise have learned holier examples. Nay, smile not with that haughty lip, my brother; for believe me, — yea, believe me, — there is more true valour in the life of one patient martyr than in the victories of Cæsar or even the defeat of Brutus."

"It may be so," replied the earl, "but out of the same oak we carve the spear and the cross; and those not worthy to hold the one may yet not guiltily wield the other. Each to his path of life, — and mine is chosen." Then, changing his voice, with some abruptness he said: "But what hast thou been saying to thy fair godchild, that her cheek is pale, and her eyelids seem so heavy? Edith, Edith, my sister, beware how thou shapest the lot of the martyr without the peace of the saint. Had Algive the nun been wedded to Sweyn our brother, Sweyn were not wending, barefooted and forlorn, to lay the wrecks of desolated life at the Holy Tomb."

"Harold, Harold!" faltered the queen, much struck with his words.

"But," the earl continued, — and something of the pathos which belongs to deep emotion vibrated in the eloquent voice, accustomed to command and persuade, — "we strip not the green leaves for our yule-hearths, we gather them up when dry and sear. Leave youth on the bough, — let the bird sing to it, let it play free in the airs of heaven. Smoke comes from the branch which, cut in the sap, is cast upon the fire, and regret from the heart which is severed from the world while the world is in its May."

The queen paced slowly, but in evident agitation, to and fro the room, and her hands clasped convulsively the rosary round her neck; then, after a pause of thought, she motioned to Edith, and pointing to the oratory, said with forced composure, —

"Enter there, and there kneel; commune with thyself, and be still. Ask for a sign from above, — pray for the grace within. Go; I would speak alone with Harold."

Edith crossed her arms on her bosom meekly, and passed into the oratory. The queen watched her for a few moments, tenderly, as the slight, child-like form bent before the sacred symbol. Then she closed the door gently, and coming with a quick step to Harold, said in a low but clear voice, —

"Dost thou love the maiden?"

"Sister," answered the earl, sadly, "I love her as a man should love woman, — more than my life, but less than the ends life lives for."

"Oh, world, world, world!" cried the queen, passionately, "not even to thine own objects art thou true. O world! O world! thou desirest happiness below, and at every turn, with every vanity, thou tramplest happiness under foot! Yes, yes; they said to me, ' For the sake of our greatness, thou shalt wed King Edward.' And I live in the eyes that loathe me — and — and — " The queen, as if conscience-stricken, paused aghast, kissed devoutly the relic suspended to her rosary, and continued, with such calmness that it seemed as if two women were blent in one, so startling was the contrast: "And I have had my reward, but not from the world! Even so, Harold the Earl, and Earl's son, thou lovest yon fair child, and she thee; and ye might be happy, if happiness were earth's end; but, though high-born, and of fair temporal possessions, she brings thee not lands broad enough for her dowry, nor troops of kindred to swell thy lithsmen, and she is not a markstone in thy march to ambition; and so thou lovest her as man loves woman, — ' less than the ends life lives for!' "

"Sister," said Harold, "thou speakest as I love to hear thee speak, — as my bright-eyed, rose-lipped sister spoke in the days of old; thou speakest as a woman with warm heart, and not as the mummy in the stiff cerements of priestly form; and if thou art with me, and thou wilt give me countenance, I will marry thy godchild, and save her alike from the dire superstitions of Hilda and the grave of the abhorrent convent."

"But my father, — my father!" cried the queen, "who ever bended that soul of steel?"

"It is not my father I fear; it is thee and thy monks. Forgettest thou that Edith and I are within the six banned degrees of the Church?"

"True, most true," said the queen, with a look of great terror; "I had forgotten. Avaunt, the very thought! Pray — fast — banish it — my poor, poor brother!" and she kissed his brow.

"So there fades the woman, and the mummy speaks again!" said Harold, bitterly. "Be it so; I bow to my doom. Well, there may be a time when Nature on the throne of England shall prevail over priestcraft; and, in guerdon for all my services, I will then ask a king who hath blood in his veins to win me the Pope's pardon and benison. Leave me that hope, my sister, and leave thy godchild on the shores of the living world."

The queen made no answer; and Harold, auguring ill from her silence, moved on and opened the door of the oratory. But the image that there met him — that figure still kneeling, those eyes, so earnest in the tears that streamed from them fast and unheeded, fixed on the holy rood — awed his step and checked his voice. Nor till the girl had risen, did he break silence; then he said gently, "My sister will press thee no more, Edith —"

"I say not that!" exclaimed the queen.

"Or if she doth, remember thy plighted promise under the wide cope of blue heaven, the old nor least holy temple of our common Father."

With these words he left the room.

CHAPTER VII.

HAROLD passed into the queen's antechamber. Here the attendance was small and select compared with the crowds which we shall see presently in the anteroom to the king's closet; for here came chiefly the more learned ecclesiastics, attracted instinctively by the queen's own mental culture, and few indeed were they at that day, perhaps the most illiterate known in England since the death of Alfred;[1] and here came not the tribe of impostors, and the relic-venders, whom the infantine simplicity and lavish waste of the Confessor attracted. Some four or five priests and monks, some lonely widow, some orphan child, humble worth, or unprotected sorrow, made the noiseless levee of the sweet, sad queen.

The groups turned, with patient eyes, towards the earl as he emerged from that chamber, which it was rare indeed to quit unconsoled, and marvelled at the flush in his cheek and the disquiet on his brow; but Harold was dear to the clients of his sister, — for, despite his supposed indifference to the mere priestly virtues (if virtues we call them) of the decrepit time, his intellect was respected by yon learned ecclesiastics; and his character, as the foe of all injustice, and the fosterer of all that were desolate, was known to yon pale-eyed widow and yon trembling orphan.

In the atmosphere of that quiet assembly the earl seemed to recover his kindly temperament, and he paused to address a friendly or a soothing word to each; so that when he vanished, the hearts there felt more light, and the silence, hushed before his entrance, was broken by many whispers in praise of the good earl.

[1] The clergy (says Malmesbury), contented with a very slight share of learning, could scarcely stammer out the words of the sacraments; and a person who understood grammar was an object of wonder and astonishment. Other authorities, likely to be impartial, speak quite as strongly as to the prevalent ignorance of the time.

Descending a staircase without the walls, — as even in royal halls the principal staircases were then, — Harold gained a wide court, in which loitered several house carles [1] and attendants, whether of the king or the visitors; and reaching the entrance of the palace, took his way towards the king's rooms, which lay near, and round what is now called "The Painted Chamber," then used as a bedroom by Edward on state occasions.

And now he entered the antechamber of his royal brother-in-law. Crowded it was, but rather seemed it the hall of a convent than the anteroom of a king. Monks, pilgrims, priests, met his eye in every nook; and not there did the earl pause to practise the arts of popular favour. Passing erect through the midst, he beckoned forth the officer in attendance at the extreme end, who, after an interchange of whispers, ushered him into the royal presence. The monks and the priests, gazing towards the door which had closed on his stately form, said to each other, —

"The king's Norman favourites at least honoured the Church."

"That is true," said an abbot; "and an it were not for two things, I should love the Norman better than the Saxon."

"What are they, my father?" asked an aspiring young monk.

"*Inprinis*," quoth the abbot, proud of the one Latin word he thought he knew, but that, as we see, was an error, "they cannot speak so as to be understood, and I fear me much they incline to mere carnal learning."

Here there was a sanctified groan.

"Count William himself spoke to me in Latin!" continued the abbot, raising his eyebrows.

"Did he? Wonderful!" exclaimed several voices. "And what did you answer, holy father?"

---

[1] House carles in the royal court were the body-guard, mostly, if not all, of Danish origin. They appear to have been first formed, or at least employed, in that capacity by Canute. With the great earls, the house carles probably exercised the same functions; but in the ordinary acceptation of the word in families of lower rank, house carle was a domestic servant.

"Marry," said the abbot, solemnly, "I replied, *Inprinis*."

"Good!" said the young monk, with a look of profound admiration.

"Whereat the good count looked puzzled, as I meant him to be, — a heinous fault, and one intolerant to the clergy, that love of profane tongues! And the next thing against your Norman is," added the abbot, with a sly wink, "that he is a close man, who loves not his stoup; now, I say that a priest never has more hold over a sinner than when he makes the sinner open his heart to him."

"That's clear!" said a fat priest, with a lubricate and shining nose.

"And how," pursued the abbot, triumphantly, "can a sinner open his heavy heart until you have given him something to lighten it? Oh, many and many a wretched man have I comforted spiritually over a flagon of stout ale; and many a good legacy to the Church hath come out of a friendly wassail between watchful shepherd and strayed sheep! But what hast thou there?" resumed the abbot, turning to a man, clad in the lay garb of a burgess of London, who had just entered the room, followed by a youth bearing what seemed a coffer, covered with a fine linen cloth.

"Holy father!" said the burgess, wiping his forehead, "it is a treasure so great that I trow Hugoline, the king's treasurer, will scowl at me for a year to come, for he likes to keep his own grip on the king's gold."

At this indiscreet observation the abbot, the monks, and all the priestly bystanders looked grim and gloomy; for each had his own special design upon the peace of poor Hugoline, the treasurer, and liked not to see him the prey of a layman.

"*Inprinis!*" quoth the abbot, puffing out the word with great scorn; "thinkest thou, son of Mammon, that our good king sets his pious heart on gewgaws, and gems, and such vanities? Thou shouldst take the goods to Count Baldwin of Flanders; or Tostig, the proud earl's proud son."

"Marry!" said the cheapman, with a smile; "my treasure will find small price with Baldwin the scoffer, and Tostig the vain! Nor need ye look at me so sternly, my fathers; but

rather vie with each other who shall win this wonder of won-
ders for his own convent. Know, in a word, that it is the
right thumb of Saint Jude, which a worthy man bought at
Rome for me, for three thousand pounds weight of silver; and
I ask but five hundred pounds over the purchase for my pains
and my fee." [1]

"Humph!" said the abbot.

"Humph!" said the aspiring young monk; the rest gathered wistfully round the linen cloth.

A fiery exclamation of wrath and disdain was here heard;
and all, turning, saw a tall, fierce-looking thegn, who had
found his way into that group, like a hawk in a rookery.

"Dost thou tell me, knave," quoth the thegn, in a dialect
that bespoke him a Dane by origin, with the broad burr still
retained in the North, — "dost thou tell me that the king will
waste his gold on such fooleries, while the fort built by
Canute at the flood of the Humber is all fallen into ruin,
without a man in steel jacket to keep watch on the war fleets
of Swede and Norwegian?"

"Worshipful minister," replied the cheapman, with some
slight irony in his tone, "these reverend fathers will tell
thee that the thumb of Saint Jude is far better aid against
Swede and Norwegian than forts of stone and jackets of steel;
nathless, if thou wantest jackets of steel, I have some to sell
at a fair price, of the last fashion, and helms with long nose-
pieces, as are worn by the Normans."

"The thumb of a withered old saint," cried the Dane, not
heeding the last words, "more defence at the mouth of the
Humber than crenellated castles and mailed men!"

"Surely, naught son," said the abbot, looking shocked, and
taking part with the cheapman. "Dost thou not remember
that in the pious and famous council of 1014 it was decreed to
put aside all weapons of flesh against thy heathen countrymen,
and depend alone on Saint Michael to fight for us? Thinkest
thou that the saint would ever suffer his holy thumb to fall

---

[1] This was cheap; for Agelnoth, Archbishop of Canterbury, gave the
Pope six thousand pounds weight of silver for the arm of Saint Augustine. — MALMESBURY.

into the hands of the Gentiles? Never! Go to, thou art not
fit to have conduct of the king's wars. Go to, and repent, my
son, or the king shall hear of it."

"Ah, wolf in sheep's clothing!" muttered the Dane, turning on his heel; "if thy monastery were but built on the other
side the Humber!"

The cheapman heard him, and smiled. While such the
scene in the anteroom, we follow Harold into the king's
presence.

On entering, he found there a man in the prime of life, and
though richly clad in embroidered gonna, and with gilt ateghar at his side, still with the loose robe, the long mustache,
and the skin of the throat and right hand punctured with
characters and devices which proved his adherence to the
fashions of the Saxon.[1] And Harold's eye sparkled, for in
this guest he recognized the father of Aldyth, Earl Algar, son
of Leofric. The two nobles exchanged grave salutations, and
each eyed the other wistfully.

The contrast between the two was striking. The Danish
race were men generally of larger frame and grander mould
than the Saxon;[2] and though in all else, as to exterior, Harold
was eminently Saxon, yet, in common with his brothers, he
took from the mother's side the lofty air and iron frame of
the old kings of the sea. But Algar, below the middle height,
though well set, was slight in comparison with Harold. His
strength was that which men often take rather from the nerve
than the muscle, — a strength that belongs to quick tempers
and restless energies. His light blue eye, singularly vivid
and glittering; his quivering lip, the veins swelling at each
emotion on the fair white temples; the long yellow hair,

[1] William of Malmesbury says that the English, at the time of the Conquest, loaded their arms with gold bracelets, and *adorned* their skins with
punctured designs, that is, a sort of tattooing. He says that they then wore
short garments, reaching to the midknee; but that was a Norman fashion,
and the loose robes assigned in the text to Algar were the old Saxon fashion,
which made but little distinction between the dress of women and that of men.

[2] And in England, to this day, the descendants of the Anglo-Danes, in
Cumberland and Yorkshire, are still a taller and bonier race than those of
the Anglo-Saxons, as in Surrey and Sussex.

bright as gold, and resisting, in its easy curls, all attempts to curb it into the smooth flow most in fashion; the nervous movements of the gesture; the somewhat sharp and hasty tones of the voice, — all opposed, as much as if the two men were of different races, the steady, deep eye of Harold; his composed mien, sweet and majestic; his decorous locks parted on the king-like front, with their large single curl where they touched the shoulder. Intelligence and will were apparent in both the men; but the intelligence of one was acute and rapid, that of the other profound and steadfast; the will of one broke in flashes of lightning, that of the other was calm as the summer sun at noon.

"Thou art welcome, Harold," said the king, with less than his usual listlessness, and with a look of relief as the earl approached him.

"Our good Algar comes to us with a suit well worthy consideration, though pressed somewhat hotly, and evincing too great a desire for goods worldly; contrasting in this his most laudable father our well-beloved Leofric, who spends his substance in endowing monasteries and dispensing alms; wherefor he shall receive a hundred-fold in the treasure-house above."

"A good interest, doubtless, my lord the king," said Algar, quickly, "but one that is not paid to his heirs; and the more need, if my father (whom I blame not for doing as he lists with his own) gives all he hath to the monks, — the more need, I say, to take care that his son shall be enabled to follow his example. As it is, most noble king, I fear me that Algar, son of Leofric, will have nothing to give. In brief, Earl Harold," continued Algar, turning to his fellow-thegn, — "in brief, thus stands the matter. When our lord the king was first graciously pleased to consent to rule in England, the two chiefs who most assured his throne were thy father and mine; often foes, they laid aside feud and jealousy for the sake of the Saxon line. Now, since then, thy father hath strung earldom to earldom, like links in a coat-mail. And, save Northumbria and Mercia, well-nigh all England falls to him and his sons; whereas my father remains what he was, and my father's son stands landless and pence-less. In thine absence the king was graciously pleased to bestow on me thy father's earldom; men say that I ruled it well. Thy father returns, and though" (here Algar's eyes shot fire, and his hand involuntarily rested on his ateghar) "I could have held it, methinks, by the strong hand, I gave it up at my father's prayer and the king's hest, with a free heart. Now, therefore, I come to my lord, and I ask, 'What lands and what lordships canst thou spare in broad England to Algar, once Earl of Wessex, and son to the Leofric whose hand smoothed the way to thy throne?' My lord the king is pleased to preach to me contempt of the world; thou dost not despise the world, Earl of the East Angles, — what sayest thou to the heir of Leofric?"

"That thy suit is just," answered Harold, calmly, "but urged with small reverence."

Earl Algar bounded like a stag that the arrow hath startled.

"It becomes thee, who hast backed thy suits with war-ships and mail, to talk of reverence, and rebuke one whose fathers reigned over earldoms,[1] when thine were, no doubt, ceorls at the plough. But for Edric Streone, the traitor and low-born, what had been Wolnoth, thy grandsire?"

So rude and home an assault in the presence of the king, who, though personally he loved Harold in his lukewarm way, yet, like all weak men, was not displeased to see the strong split their strength against each other, brought the blood into Harold's cheek; but he answered calmly, —

"We live in a land, son of Leofric, in which birth, though not disesteemed, gives of itself no power in council or camp.

---

[1] Very few of the greater Saxon nobles could pretend to a lengthened succession in their demesnes. The wars with the Danes, the many revolutions which threw new families uppermost, the confiscations and banishments, and the invariable rule of rejecting the heir, if not of mature years at his father's death, caused rapid changes of dynasty in the several earldoms. But the family of Leofric had just claims to a very rare antiquity in their Mercian lordship. Leofric was the sixth Earl of Chester and Coventry, in lineal descent from his namesake, Leofric the First; he extended the supremacy of his hereditary lordship over all Mercia. See Dugdale, Monast. vol. iii. p. 102; and Palgrave's Commonwealth, proofs and illustrations, p. 291.

We belong to a land where men are valued for what they are, not for what their dead ancestors might have been. So has it been for ages in Saxon England, where my fathers, through Godwin, as thou sayest, might have been ceorls; and so, I have heard, it is in the land of the martial Danes, where my fathers, through Githa, reigned on the thrones of the North."

"Thou dost well," said Algar, gnawing his lip, "to shelter thyself on the spindle side, but we Saxons of pure 'descent think little of your kings of the North, pirates and idolaters, and eaters of horseflesh; but enjoy what thou hast, and let Algar have his due."

"It is for the king, not his servant, to answer the prayer of Algar," said Harold, withdrawing to the farther end of the room.

Algar's eye followed him, and observing that the king was fast sinking into one of the fits of religious revery in which he sought to be inspired with a decision whenever his mind was perplexed, he moved with a light step to Harold, put his hand on his shoulder, and whispered, —

"We do ill to quarrel with each other, — I repent me of hot words, — enough. Thy father is a wise man, and sees far, — thy father would have us friends. Be it so. Hearken! My daughter Aldyth is esteemed not the least fair of the maidens in England; I will give her to thee as thy wife; and as thy morgen gift, thou shalt win for me from the king the earldom forfeited by thy brother Sweyn, now parcelled out amongst sub-earls and thegns, — easy enow to control. By the shrine of Saint Alban, dost thou hesitate, man?"

"No, not an instant!" said Harold, stung to the quick. "Not, couldst thou offer me all Mercia as her dower, would I wed the daughter of Algar; and bend my knee, as a son to a wife's father, to the man who despises my lineage, while he truckles to my power."

Algar's face grew convulsed with rage; but without saying a word to the earl, he strode back to Edward, who now with vacant eyes looked up from the rosary over which he had been bending, and said abruptly, —

"My lord the king, I have spoken as I think it becomes a man who knows his own claims, and believes in the gratitude of princes. Three days will I tarry in London for your gracious answer; on the fourth I depart. May the saints guard your throne, and bring around it its best defence, the thegnborn satraps whose fathers fought with Alfred and Athelstan. All went well with merrie England till the hoof of the Dane King broke the soil, and mushrooms sprung up where the oaktrees fell."

When the son of Leofric had left the chamber, the king rose wearily, and said in Norman French, to which language he always yearningly returned when with those who could speak it, —

"*Beau frère* and *bien aimé*, in what trifles must a king pass his life! and, all this while, matters grave and urgent demand me. Know that Eadmer the cheapman waits without, and hath brought me, dear and good man, the thumb of Saint Jude! What thought of delight! And this unmannerly son of strife, with his jay's voice and wolf's eyes, screaming at me for earldoms! — oh the folly of man! Naught, naught, very naught!"

"Sir and King," said Harold; "it ill becomes me to arraign your pious desires, but these relics are of vast cost; our coasts are ill defended, and the Dane yet lays claim to your kingdom. Three thousand pounds of silver and more does it need to repair even the old wall of London and Southweorc."

"Three thousand pounds!" cried the king; "thou art mad, Harold! I have scarce twice that sum in the treasury; and besides the thumb of Saint Jude, I daily expect the tooth of Saint Remigius, — the tooth of Saint Remigius!"

Harold sighed. "Vex not yourself, my lord, I will see to the defences of London. For, thanks to your grace, my revenues are large, while my wants are simple. I seek you now to pray your leave to visit my earldom. My lithsmen murmur at my absence; and grievances, many and sore, have arisen in my exile."

The king stared in terror; and his look was that of a child when about to be left in the dark.

"Nay, nay; I cannot spare thee, *beau frère*. Thou curbest all these stiff thegns, — thou leavest me time for the devout; moreover, thy father, thy father, — I will not be left to thy father! I love him not!"

"My father," said Harold, mournfully, "returns to his own earldom; and of all our House you will have but the mild face of your queen by your side!"

The king's lip writhed at that hinted rebuke or implied consolation.

"Edith the Queen," he said, after a slight pause, "is pious and good; and she hath never gainsaid my will, and she hath set before her as a model the chaste Susannah, as I, unworthy man, from youth upward, have walked in the pure steps of Joseph.[1] But," added the king, with a touch of human feeling in his voice, "canst thou not conceive, Harold, thou who art a warrior, what it would be to see ever before thee the face of thy deadliest foe, — the one against whom all thy struggles of life and death had turned into memories of hyssop and gall?"

"My sister!" exclaimed Harold, in indignant amaze, "my sister thy deadliest foe! She who never once murmured at neglect, disgrace, — she whose youth hath been consumed in prayers for thee and thy realm, — my sister! O King, I dream?"

"Thou dreamest not, carnal man," said the king, peevishly. "Dreams are the gifts of the saints, and are not granted to such as thou! Dost thou think that in the prime of my manhood I could have youth and beauty forced on my sight, and hear man's law and man's voice say, 'They are thine, and thine only,' and not feel that war was brought to my hearth, and a snare set on my bed, and that the fiend had set watch on my soul? Verily, I tell thee, man of battle, that thou hast known no strife as awful as mine, and achieved no victory as hard and as holy. And now, when my beard is silver, and the Adam of old is expelled at the precincts of death, — now thinkest thou that I can be reminded of the strife and temptation of yore without bitterness and shame;

---

[1] Ailred, De Vit Edward Confess.

when days were spent in fasting, and nights in fierce prayer, and in the face of woman I saw the devices of Satan?"

Edward coloured as he spoke, and his voice trembled with the accents of what seemed hate. Harold gazed on him mutely, and felt that at last he had won the secret that had ever perplexed him, and that in seeking to be above the humanity of love, the would-be saint had indeed turned love into the hues of hate, — a thought of anguish, and a memory of pain.

The king recovered himself in a few moments, and said with some dignity, —

"But God and his saints alone should know the secrets of the household. What I have said was wrung from me. Bury it in thy heart. Leave me, then, Harold, sith so it must be. Put thine earldom in order, attend to the monasteries and the poor, and return soon. As for Algar, what sayest thou?"

"I fear me," answered the large-souled Harold, with a victorious effort of justice over resentment, "that if you reject his suit you will drive him into some perilous extremes. Despite his rash and proud spirit, he is brave against foes, and beloved by the ceorls, who oft like best the frank and hasty spirit. Wherefore some power and lordship it were wise to give, without dispossessing others; and not more wise than due, for his father served you well."

"And hath endowed more houses of God than any earl in the kingdom. But Algar is no Leofric. We will consider your words and heed them. Bless you, *beau frère!* and send in the cheapman. The thumb of Saint Jude! What a gift to my new church of St. Peter! The thumb of Saint Jude! *Non nobis gloria! Sancta Maria!* The thumb of Saint Jude!"

BOOK V.

DEATH AND LOVE.

'————

CHAPTER I.

HAROLD, without waiting once more to see Edith, nor even taking leave of his father, repaired to Dunwich,[1] the capital of his earldom. In his absence the king wholly forgot Algar and his suit; and in the mean while the only lordships at his disposal, Stigand, the grasping bishop, got from him without an effort. In much wrath, Earl Algar, on the fourth day, assembling all the loose men-at-arms he could find around the metropolis, and at the head of a numerous disorderly band, took his way into Wales, with his young daughter Aldyth, to whom the crown of a Welch king was perhaps some comfort for the loss of the fair earl; though the rumour ran that she had long since lost her heart to her father's foe.

Edith, after a long homily from the king, returned to Hilda; nor did her godmother renew the subject of the convent. All she said on parting was, "Even in youth the silver cord may be loosened, and the golden bowl may be broken; and rather perhaps in youth than in age, when the heart has grown hard, wilt thou recall with a sigh my counsels."

Godwin had departed to Wales; all his sons were at their several lordships; Edward was left alone to his monks and relic-venders. And so months passed.

Now it was the custom with the old kings of England to hold state and wear their crowns thrice a year, — at Christmas, at Easter, and at Whitsuntide; and in those times their

---

[1] Dunwich, now swallowed up by the sea. Hostile element to the House of Godwin.

nobles came round them, and there was much feasting and great pomp.

So, in the Easter of the year of our Lord 1053, King Edward kept his court at Windshore;[1] and Earl Godwin and his sons, and many others of high degree, left their homes to do honour to the king. And Earl Godwin came first to his house in London, — near the Tower Palatine, in what is now called the Fleet; and Harold the Earl, and Tostig, and Leofwine, and Gurth were to meet him there, and go thence, with the full state of their sub-thegns, and cnehts, and housecarles, their falcons and their hounds, as become men of such rank, to the court of King Edward.

Earl Godwin sat with his wife, Githa, in a room out of the hall, which looked on the Thames, — awaiting Harold, who was expected to arrive ere nightfall. Gurth had ridden forth to met his brother, and Leofwine and Tostig had gone over to Southwark, to try their band-dogs on the great bear, which had been brought from the north a few days before, and was said to have hugged many good hounds to death, and a large train of thegns and house-carles had gone with them to see the sport; so that the old earl and his lady the Dane sat alone. And there was a cloud upon Earl Godwin's large forehead, and he sat by the fire, spreading his hands before it, and looking thoughtfully on the flame, as it broke through the smoke which burst out into the *cover*, or hole in the roof. And in that large house there were no less than three "covers," or rooms, wherein fires could be lit in the centre of the floor; and the rafters above were blackened with the smoke; and in those good old days, ere chimneys, if existing, were much in use, "poses and rheumatisms and catarrhs" were unknown, so wholesome and healthful was the smoke. Earl Godwin's favourite hound, old, like himself, lay at his feet dreaming, for it whined and was restless. And the earl's old hawk, with its feathers all stiff and sparse, perched on the dossel of the earl's chair; and the floor was pranked with rushes and sweet herbs, — the first of the spring; and Githa's feet were on her stool, and she leaned her proud face on the small hand which

[1] Windsor.

proved her descent from the Dane, and rocked herself to and fro, and thought of her son Wolnoth in the court of the Norman.

"Githa," at last said the earl, "thou hast been to me a good wife and a true, and thou hast borne me tall and bold sons, some of whom have caused us sorrow, and some joy; and in sorrow and in joy we have but drawn closer to each other. Yet when we wed thou wert in thy first youth, and the best part of my years was fled; and thou wert a Dane and I a Saxon; and thou a king's niece, and now a king's sister, and I but tracing two descents to thegn's rank."

Moved and marvelling at this touch of sentiment in the calm earl, in whom indeed such sentiment was rare, Githa roused herself from her musings, and said simply and anxiously, —

"I fear my lord is not well, that he speaks thus to Githa!"

The earl smiled faintly. "Thou art right with thy woman's wit, wife; and for the last few weeks, though I said it not to alarm thee, I have had strange noises in my ears, and a surge, as of blood, to the temples."

"O Godwin, dear spouse!" said Githa, tenderly, "and I was blind to the cause, but wondered why there was some change in thy manner! But I will go to Hilda to-morrow; she hath charms against all disease."

"Leave Hilda in peace, to give her charms to the young; age defies Wigh and Wicca. Now hearken to me. I feel that my thread is nigh spent; and, as Hilda would say, my Fylgia forewarns me that we are about to part. Silence, I say, and hear me. I have done proud things in my day; I have made kings and built thrones, and I stand higher in England than ever thegn or earl stood before. I would not, Githa, that the tree of my house, planted in the storm and watered with lavish blood, should wither away."

The old earl paused; and Githa said loftily, —

"Fear not that thy name will pass from the earth, or thy race from power. For fame has been wrought by thy hands, and sons have been born to thy embrace; and the boughs of the tree thou hast planted shall live in the sunlight when we, its roots, O my husband, are buried in the earth."

"Githa," replied the earl, "thou speakest as the daughter of kings and the mother of men; but listen to me, for my soul is heavy. Of these our sons, our first-born, alas! is a wanderer and outcast, — Sweyn, once the beautiful and brave; and Wolnoth, thy darling, is a guest in the court of the Norman, our foe. Of the rest, Gurth is so mild and so calm that I predict without fear that he will be a warrior of fame, for the mildest in hall are ever the boldest in field. But Gurth hath not the deep wit of these tangled times; and Leofwine is too light, and Tostig too fierce. So wife mine, of these our six sons, Harold alone, dauntless as Tostig, mild as Gurth, hath his father's thoughtful brain. And if the king remains as aloof as now from his royal kinsman, Edward the Atheling, who" — the earl hesitated and looked round — "who so near to the throne, when I am no more, as Harold, the joy of the ceorls, and the pride of the thegns? — he whose tongue never falters in the Witan, and whose arm never yet hath known defeat in the field?"

Githa's heart swelled, and her cheek grew flushed.

"But what I fear the most," resumed the earl, "is, not the enemy without, but the jealousy within. By the side of Harold stands Tostig, rapacious to grasp, but impotent to hold, able to ruin, strengthless to save."

"Nay, Godwin, my lord, thou wrongest our handsome son."

"Wife, wife," said the earl, stamping his foot, "hear me and obey me; for my words on earth may be few, and while thou gainsayest me the blood mounts to my brain, and my eyes see through a cloud."

"Forgive me, sweet lord," said Githa, humbly.

"Mickle and sore it repents me that in their youth I spared not the time from my worldly ambition to watch over the hearts of my sons; and thou wert too proud of the surface without to look well to the workings within, and what was once soft to the touch is now hard to the hammer. In the battle of life the arrows we neglect to pick up, Fate, our foe, will store in her quiver; we have armed her ourselves with the shafts,

—the more need to be ware with the shield. Wherefore, if thou survivest me, and if, as I forebode, dissension break out between Harold and Tostig, I charge thee, by memory of our love, and reverence for my grave, to deem wise and just all that Harold deems just and wise. For when Godwin is in the dust, his House lives alone in Harold. Heed me now, and heed ever. And so, while the day lasts, I will go forth into the marts and the guilds, and talk with the burgesses, and smile on their wives, and be, to the last, Godwin the smooth and the strong."

So saying, the old earl arose, and walked forth with a firm step; and his old hound sprang up, pricked its ears, and followed him; the blinded falcon turned its head towards the clapping door, but did not stir from the dossel.

Then Githa again leaned her cheek on her hand, and again rocked herself to and fro, gazing into the red flame of the fire, — red and fitful through the blue smoke, — and thought over her lord's words. It might be the third part of an hour after Godwin had left the house, when the door opened, and Githa, expecting the return of her sons, looked up eagerly; but it was Hilda, who stooped her head under the vault of the door; and behind Hilda came two of her maidens, bearing a small cyst, or chest. The Vala motioned to her attendants to lay the cyst at the feet of Githa; and, that done, with lowly salutation they left the room.

The superstitions of the Danes were strong in Githa; and she felt an indescribable awe when Hilda stood before her, the red light playing on the Vala's stern marble face, and contrasting robes of funereal black. But, with all her awe, Githa, who, not educated like her daughter Edith, had few feminine resources, loved the visits of her mysterious kinswoman. She loved to live her youth over again in discourse on the wild customs and dark rites of the Dane; and even her awe itself had the charm which the ghost tale has to the child, — for the illiterate are ever children. So, recovering her surprise and her first pause, she rose to welcome the Vala, and said, —

"Hail, Hilda, and thrice hail! The day has been warm,

and the way long; and ere thou takest food and wine, let me prepare for thee the bath for thy form, or the bath for thy feet, — for as sleep to the young, is the bath to the old."

Hilda shook her head.

"Bringer of sleep am I, and the baths I prepare are in the halls of Valhalla. Offer not to the Vala the bath for mortal weariness, and the wine and the food meet for human guests. Sit thee down, daughter of the Dane, and thank thy new gods for the past that hath been thine. Not ours is the present, and the future escapes from our dreams; but the past is ours ever, and all eternity cannot revoke a single joy that the moment hath known."

Then seating herself in Godwin's large chair, she leaned over her seid-staff, and was silent, as if absorbed in her thoughts.

"Githa," she said at last, "where is thy lord? I came to touch his hands and to look on his brow."

"He hath gone forth into the mart, and my sons are from home; and Harold comes hither, ere night, from his earldom."

A faint smile, as of triumph, broke over the lips of the Vala, and then as suddenly yielded to an expression of great sadness.

"Githa," she said slowly, "doubtless thou rememberest in thy young days to have seen or heard of the terrible hell-maid Belsta?"

"Ay, ay," answered Githa, shuddering; "I saw her once in gloomy weather, driving before her herds of dark gray cattle. Ay, ay; and my father beheld her ere his death, riding the air on a wolf, with a snake for a bridle. Why askest thou?"

"Is it not strange," said Hilda, evading the question, "that Belsta and Heidr and Hulla of old, the wolf-riders, the men-devourers, could win to the uttermost secrets of galdra, though applied only to purposes the direst and fellest to man, and that I, though ever in the future, I, though tasking the Nornas not to afflict a foe, but to shape the careers of those I love, — I find, indeed, my predictions fulfilled; but how often, alas! only in horror and doom!"

"How so, kinswoman, how so?" said Githa, awed, yet

charmed in the awe, and drawing her chair nearer to th⌐ mournful sorceress. "Didst thou not foretell our return in triumph from the unjust outlawry, and, lo, it hath come to pass; and hast thou not" (here Githa's proud face flushed) "foretold also that my stately Harold shall wear the diadem of a king?"

"Truly, the first came to pass," said Hilda; "but —" She paused, and her eye fell on the cyst; then breaking off she continued, speaking to herself rather than to Githa: "And Harold's dream, — what did that portend? The runes fail me, and the dead give no voice. And beyond one dim day, in which his betrothed shall clasp him with the arms of a bride, all is dark to my vision, — dark, dark. Speak not to me, Githa; for a burden, heavy as the stone on a grave, rests on a weary heart!"

A dead silence succeeded, till, pointing with her staff to the fire, the Vala said, —

"Lo, where the smoke and the flame contend! The smoke rises in dark gyres to the air, and escapes, to join the wrack of clouds. From the first to the last we trace its birth and its fall, from the heart of the fire to the descent in the rain; so is it with human reason, which is not the light but the smoke: it struggles but to darken us; it soars but to melt in the vapour and dew. Yet, lo, the flame burns in our hearth till the fuel fails, and goes at last, none know whither. But it lives in the air, though we see it not; it lurks in the stone, and waits the flash of the steel; it coils round the dry leaves and sear stalks, and a touch re-illumines it; it plays in the marsh, it collects in the heavens, it appalls us in the lightning, it gives warmth to the air, — life of our life, and element of all elements. Oh, Githa, the flame is the light of the soul, the element everlasting; and it liveth still, when it escapes from our view; it burneth in the shapes to which it passes; it vanishes, but is never extinct."

So saying, the Vala's lips again closed; and again both the women sat silent by the great fire, as it flared and flickered over the deep lines and high features of Githa, the earl's wife, and the calm, unwrinkled, solemn face of the melancholy Vala.

CHAPTER II.

WHILE these conferences took place in the House of Godwin, Harold, on his way to London, dismissed his train to precede him to his father's roof, and, striking across the country, rode fast and alone towards the old Roman abode of Hilda. Months had elapsed since he had seen or heard of Edith. News at that time, I need not say, was rare and scarce, and limited to public events, either transmitted by special nuncius or passing pilgrim, or borne from lip to lip by the talk of the scattered multitude. But even in his busy and anxious duties Harold had in vain sought to banish from his heart the image of that young girl, whose life he needed no Vala to predict to him was interwoven with the fibres of his own. The obstacles which, while he yielded to, he held unjust and tyrannical — obstacles allowed by his reluctant reason and his secret ambition, not sanctified by conscience — only inflamed the deep strength of the solitary passion his life had known; a passion that, dating from the very childhood of Edith, had, often unknown to himself, animated his desire of fame, and mingled with his visions of power. Nor, though hope was far and dim, was it extinct. The legitimate heir of Edward the Confessor was a prince living in the court of the emperor, of fair repute, and himself wedded; and Edward's health, always precarious, seemed to forbid any very prolonged existence to the reigning king. Therefore he thought that through the successor, whose throne would rest in safety upon Harold's support, he might easily obtain that dispensation from the Pope which he knew the present king would never ask, — a dispensation rarely indeed, if ever, accorded to any subject, and which therefore needed all a king's power to back it.

So in that hope, and fearful lest it should be quenched forever by Edith's adoption of the veil and the irrevocable vow, with a beating, disturbed, but joyful heart he rode over field and through forest to the old Roman house.

He emerged at length to the rear of the villa; and the sun, fast hastening to its decline, shone full upon the rude columns of the Druid temple. And there, as he had seen her before, when he had first spoken of love and its barriers, he beheld the young maiden.

He sprang from his horse, and leaving the well-trained animal loose to browse on the waste land, he ascended the knoll. He stole noiselessly behind Edith, and his foot stumbled against the gravestone of the dead Titan-Saxon of old. But the apparition, whether real or fancied, and the dream that had followed, had long passed from his memory; and no superstition was in the heart springing to the lips that cried "Edith" once again.

The girl started, looked round, and fell upon his breast.

It was some moments before she recovered consciousness, and then, withdrawing herself gently from his arms, she leaned for support against the Teuton altar.

She was much changed since Harold had seen her last, — her cheek had grown pale and thin, and her rounded form seemed wasted; and sharp grief, as he gazed, shot through the soul of Harold.

"Thou hast pined, thou hast suffered," said he, mournfully; "and I, who would shed my life's blood to take one from thy sorrows, or add to one of thy joys, have been afar, unable to comfort, perhaps only a cause of thy woe."

"No, Harold," said Edith, faintly, "never of woe; always of comfort, even in absence. I have been ill, and Hilda hath tried rune and charm all in vain. But I am better, now that spring hath come tardily forth, and I look on the fresh flowers, and hear the song of the birds."

But tears were in the sound of her voice, while she spoke.

"And they have not tormented thee again with the thoughts of the convent?"

"They, no; but my soul, yes. Oh, Harold, release me from my promise; for the time already hath come that thy sister foretold to me: the silver cord is loosened, and the golden bowl is broken, and I would fain take the wings of the dove, and be at peace."

"Is it so? Is there peace in the home where the thought of Harold becomes a sin?"

"Not sin then and there, Harold, not sin. Thy sister hailed the convent when she thought of prayer for those she loved."

"Prate not to me of my sister!" said Harold, through his set teeth. "It is but a mockery to talk of prayer for the heart that thou thyself rendest in twain. Where is Hilda? I would see her."

"She hath gone to thy father's house with a gift; and it was to watch for her return that I sat on the green knoll."

The earl then drew near and took her hand, and sat by her side, and they conversed long. But Harold saw with a fierce pang that Edith's heart was set upon the convent, and that even in his presence, and despite his soothing words, she was broken-spirited and despondent. It seemed as if her youth and life had gone from her, and the day had come in which she said, "There is no pleasure."

Never had he seen her thus; and deeply moved as well as keenly stung, he rose at length to depart. Her hand lay passive in his parting clasp, and a slight shiver went over her frame.

"Farewell, Edith; when I return from Windshore, I shall be at my old home yonder, and we shall meet again."

Edith's lips murmured inaudibly, and she bent her eyes to the ground.

Slowly Harold regained his steed; and as he rode on, he looked behind and waved oft his hand. But Edith sat motionless, her eyes still on the ground; and he saw not the tears that fell from them fast and burning, nor heard he the low voice that groaned amidst the heathen ruins, —

"Mary, sweet mother, shelter me from my own heart!"

The sun had set before Harold gained the long and spacious abode of his father. All around it lay the roofs and huts of the great earl's special tradesmen, for even his goldsmith was but his freed ceorl. The house itself stretched far from the

Thames inland, with several low courts built only of timber, rugged and shapeless, but filled with bold men, then the great furniture of a noble's halls.

Amidst the shouts of hundreds eager to hold his stirrup, the earl dismounted, passed the swarming hall, and entered the room, in which he found Hilda and Githa, and Godwin, who had preceded his entry but a few minutes.

In the beautiful reverence of son to father, which made one of the loveliest features of the Saxon character[1] (as the frequent want of it makes the most hateful of the Norman vices), the all-powerful Harold bowed his knee to the old earl, who placed his hand on his head in benediction, and then kissed him on the cheek and brow.

"Thy kiss, too, dear mother," said the younger earl; and Githa's embrace, if more cordial than her lord's, was not, perhaps, more fond.

"Greet Hilda, my son," said Godwin; "she hath brought me a gift, and she hath tarried to place it under thy special care. Thou alone must heed the treasure, and open the casket. But when and where, my kinswoman?"

"On the sixth day after thy coming to the king's hall," answered Hilda, not returning the smile with which Godwin spoke, — "on the sixth day, Harold, open the chest, and take out the robe which hath been spun in the house of Hilda for Godwin the Earl. And now, Godwin, I have clasped thine hand, and I have looked on thy brow, and my mission is done. and I must wend homeward."

"That shalt thou not, Hilda," said the hospitable earl; "the meanest wayfarer hath a right to bed and board in this house for a night and a day, and thou wilt not disgrace us by leaving our threshold, the bread unbroken, and the couch unpressed. Old friend, we were young together, and thy face is welcome to me as the memory of former days."

Hilda shook her head; and one of those rare, and for that reason most touching, expressions of tenderness of which the

---

[1] The chronicler, however, laments that the household ties, formerly so strong with the Anglo-Saxon, had been much weakened in the age prior to the Conquest.

calm and rigid character of her features, when in repose, seemed scarcely susceptible, softened her eye, and relaxed the firm lines of her lips.

"Son of Wolnoth," said she, gently, "not under thy roof-tree should lodge the raven of bode. Bread have I not broken since yestere'en, and sleep will be far from my eyes to-night. Fear not, for my people without are stout and armed; and for the rest there lives not the man whose arm can have power over Hilda."

She took Harold's hand as she spoke, and leading him forth, whispered in his ear, "I would have a word with thee ere we part." Then, reaching the threshold, she waved her hand thrice over the floor, and muttered in the Danish tongue a rude verse, which translated, ran somewhat thus: —

> " All free from the knot
>   Glide the thread of the skein,
> And rest to the labour,
>   And peace to the pain ! "

"It is a death-dirge," said Githa, with whitening lips; but she spoke inly, and neither husband nor son heard her words.

Hilda and Harold passed in silence through the hall; and the Vala's attendants, with spears and torches, rose from the settles, and went before to the outer court, where snorted impatiently her black palfrey.

Halting in the midst of the court, she said to Harold, in a low voice, —

"At sunset we part; at sunset we shall meet again. And behold, the star rises on the sunset; and the star, broader and brighter, shall rise on the sunset then! When thy hand draws the robe from the chest, think on Hilda, and know that at that hour she stands by the grave of the Saxon warrior, and that from the grave dawns the future. Farewell to thee!"

Harold longed to speak to her of Edith, but a strange awe at his heart chained his lips; so he stood silent by the great wooden gates of the rude house. The torches flamed round him, and Hilda's face seemed lurid in the glare. There he stood musing long after torch and ceorl had passed away; nor did he wake from his revery till Gurth, springing from his panting horse, passed his arm round the earl's shoulder, and cried, —

"How did I miss thee, my brother; and why didst thou forsake thy train?"

"I will tell thee anon. Gurth, has my father ailed? There is that in his face which I like not."

"He hath not complained of misease," said Gurth, startled; "but now thou speakest of it, his mood hath altered of late, and he hath wandered much alone, or only with the old hound and the old falcon."

Then Harold turned back, and his heart was full; and when he reached the house, his father was sitting in the hall on his chair of state; and Githa sat on his right hand, and a little below her sat Tostig and Leofwine, who had come in from the bear-hunt by the river-gate, and were talking loud and merrily; and thegns and cnehts sat all around, and there was wassail as Harold entered. But the earl looked only to his father, and he saw that his eyes were absent from the glee, and that he was bending his head over the old falcon, which sat on his wrist.

———◆———

CHAPTER III.

No subject of England, since the race of Cerdic sat on the throne, ever entered the court-yard of Windshore with such train and such state as Earl Godwin. Proud of that first occasion, since his return, to do homage to him with whose cause that of England against the stranger was bound, all truly English at heart amongst the thegns of the land swelled his retinue. Whether Saxon or Dane, those who alike loved the laws and the soil came from north and from south to the peaceful banner of the old earl. But most of these were of the past generation, for the rising race were still dazzled by the pomp of the Norman; and the fashion of English manners and the pride in English deeds had gone out of date with long locks and bearded chins. Nor there were the bishops and abbots and the lords of the Church, — for dear to them already the fame of the Norman piety, and they shared the distaste of their holy king to the strong sense and homely religion of Godwin, who founded no convents, and rode to war with no relics round his neck. But they with Godwin were the stout and the frank and the free, in whom rested the pith and marrow of English manhood; and they who were against him were the blind and willing and fated fathers of slaves unborn.

Not then the stately castle we now behold, which is of the masonry of a prouder race, nor on the same site, but two miles distant on the winding of the river shore (whence it took its name), a rude building, partly of timber and partly of Roman brick, adjoining a large monastery and surrounded by a small hamlet, constituted the palace of the saint-king.

So rode the earl and his four fair sons, all abreast, into the courtyard of Windshore.[1] Now when King Edward heard the tramp of the steeds and the hum of the multitudes, as he sat in his closet with his abbots and priests, all in still contemplation of the thumb of Saint Jude, the king asked, —

"What army, in the day of peace and the time of Easter, enters the gates of our palace?"

Then an abbot rose and looked out of the narrow window, and said with a groan, —

"Army thou mayst well call it, O King! and foes to us and to thee head the legions — "

"*Inprinis*," quoth our abbot the scholar; "thou speakest, I trow, of the wicked earl and his sons."

The king's face changed. "Come they," said he, "with so

---

[1] Some authorities state Winchester as the scene of these memorable festivities. Old Windsor Castle is supposed by Mr. Lysons to have occupied the site of a farm of Mr. Isherwood's surrounded by a moat, about two miles distant from New Windsor. He conjectures that it was still occasionally inhabited by the Norman kings till 1110. The ville surrounding it only contained ninety-five houses, paying gabel-tax, in the Norman survey.

large a train? This smells more of vaunt than of loyalty;
naught, — very naught."

"Alack!" said one of the conclave, "I fear me that the
men of Belial will work us harm; the heathen are mighty,
and —"

"Fear not," said Edward, with benign loftiness, observing
that his guests grew pale, and himself, though often weak to
childishness, and morally wavering and irresolute, still so far
king and gentleman that he knew no craven fear of the body,
— "fear not for me, my fathers; humble as I am, I am strong
in the faith of heaven and its angels."

The Churchmen looked at each other, sly yet abashed; it
was not precisely for the king that they feared.

Then spoke Alred, the good prelate and constant peacemaker, — fair column and lone one of the fast-crumbling
Saxon Church, —

"It is ill in you, brethren, to arraign the truth and good
meaning of those who honour your king; and in these days
that lord should ever be the most welcome who brings to the
halls of his king the largest number of hearts, stout and
leal."

"By your leave, brother Alred," said Stigand, who, though
from motives of policy he had aided those who besought the
king not to peril his crown by resisting the return of Godwin,
benefited too largely by the abuses of the Church to be sincerely espoused to the cause of the strong-minded earl, — "by
your leave, brother Alred, to every leal heart is a ravenous
mouth; and the treasures of the king are well-nigh drained
in feeding these hungry and welcomeless visitors. Durst I
counsel my lord, I would pray him, as a matter of policy, to
baffle this astute and proud earl. He would fain have the
king feast in public, that he might daunt him and the Church
with the array of his friends."

"I conceive thee, my father," said Edward, **with** more
quickness than habitual, and with the cunning, sharp though
guileless, that belongs to minds undeveloped, "I conceive
thee; it is good and most politic. This our orgulous earl
shall not have his triumph, and, so fresh from his exile,

brave his king with the mundane parade of his power. Our health is our excuse for our absence from the banquet; and, sooth to say, we marvel much why Easter should be held a fitting time for feasting and mirth. Wherefore, Hugoline, my chamberlain, advise the earl that to-day we keep fast till the sunset, when temperately, with eggs, bread, and fish, we will sustain Adam's nature. Pray him and his sons to attend us, — they alone be our guests." And with a sound that seemed a laugh, or the ghost of a laugh, low and chuckling, — for Edward had at moments an innocent humour which his monkish biographer disdained not to note,[1] — he flung himself back in his chair. The priests took the cue, and shook their sides heartily, as Hugoline left the room, not ill pleased, by the way, to escape an invitation to the eggs, bread, and fish.

Alred sighed, and said: "For the earl and his sons, this is honour; but the other earls and the thegns will miss at the banquet him whom they design but to honour, and — "

"I have said," interrupted Edward, dryly, and with a look of fatigue.

"And," observed another Churchman, with malice, "at least the young earls will be humbled, for they will not sit with the king and their father, as they would in the hall, and must serve my lord with napkin and wine."

"*Inprinis*," quoth our scholar the abbot, "that will be rare! I would I were by to see. But this Godwin is a man of treachery and wile, and my lord should beware of the fate of murdered Alfred, his brother!"

The king started, and pressed his hands to his eyes.

"How darest thou, Abbot of Fatchere," cried Alred, indignantly, "how darest thou revive grief without remedy, and slander without proof?"

"Without proof?" echoed Edward, in a hollow voice. "He who could murder, could well stoop to forswear! Without proof before man; but did he try the ordeals of God, — did his feet pass the ploughshare, did his hand grasp the seething iron? Verily, verily, thou didst wrong to name to me Alfred my brother! I shall see his sightless and gore·

---

[1] Ailred, De Vit. Edward Confess.

dropping sockets in the face of Godwin, this day, at my board."

The king rose in great disorder; and after pacing the room some moments, disregardful of the silent and scared looks of his Churchmen, waved his hand, in sign to them to depart. All took the hint at once, save Alred; but he, lingering the last, approached the king with dignity in his step and compassion in his eyes.

"Banish from thy breast, O King and son, thoughts unmeet, and of doubtful charity! All that man could know of Godwin's innocence or guilt — the suspicion of the vulgar, the acquittal of his peers — was known to thee before thou didst seek his aid for thy throne, and didst take his child for thy wife. Too late is it now to suspect; leave thy doubts to the solemn day which draws nigh to the old man, thy wife's father!"

"Ha!" said the king, seeming not to heed, or wilfully to misunderstand the prelate, — "ha! leave him to God, I will!"

He turned away impatiently; and the prelate reluctantly departed.

CHAPTER IV.

Tostig chafed mightily at the king's message, and on Harold's attempt to pacify him, grew so violent that nothing short of the cold stern command of his father, who carried with him that weight of authority never known but to those in whom wrath is still and passion noiseless, imposed sullen peace on his son's rugged nature. But the taunts heaped by Tostig upon Harold disquieted the old earl, and his brow was yet sad with prophetic care when he entered the royal apartments. He had been introduced into the king's presence but a moment before Hugoline led the way to the chamber of repast, and the greeting between king and earl had been brief and formal.

Under the canopy of state were placed but two chairs, for, the king and the queen's father; and the four sons — Harold, Tostig, Leofwine, and Gurth — stood behind. Such was the primitive custom of ancient Teutonic kings; and the feudal Norman monarchs only enforced, though with more pomp and more rigour, the ceremonial of the forest patriarchs, — youth to wait on age, and the ministers of the realm on those whom their policy had made chiefs in council and war.

The earl's mind, already embittered by the scene with his sons, was chafed yet more by the king's unloving coldness; for it is natural to man, however worldly, to feel affection for those he has served, and Godwin had won Edward his crown; nor, despite his warlike though bloodless return, could even monk or Norman, in counting up the old earl's crimes, say that he had ever failed in personal respect to the king he had made; nor over-great for subject, as the earl's power must be confessed, will historian now be found to say that it had not been well for Saxon England if Godwin had found more favour with his king, and monk and Norman less.[1]

So the old earl's stout heart was stung, and he looked from those deep, impenetrable eyes mournfully upon Edward's chilling brow.

And Harold, with whom all household ties were strong, but to whom his great father was especially dear, watched his face and saw that it was very flushed; but the practised courtier sought to rally his spirits, and to smile and jest.

From smile and jest, the king turned and asked for wine. Harold, starting, advanced with the goblet; as he did so, he stumbled with one foot, but lightly recovered himself with the other; and Tostig laughed scornfully at Harold's awkwardness.

The old earl observed both stumble and laugh, and will-

---

[1] "Is it astonishing," asked the people, referring to Edward's preference of the Normans, "that the author and support of Edward's reign should be indignant at seeing new men from a foreign nation raised above him, and yet never does he utter one harsh word to the man whom he himself created king?" — HAZLITT : *Thierry*, vol. i. p. 126.

This is the English account (*versus* the Norman). There can be little doubt that it is the true one.

ing to suggest a lesson to both his sons, said, laughing pleasantly, —

"Lo, Harold, how the left foot saves the right! — so one brother, thou seest, helps the other!"[1]

King Edward looked up suddenly. "And so, Godwin, also, had my brother Alfred helped me, hadst thou permitted."

The old earl, galled to the quick, gazed a moment on the king; and his cheek was purple, and his eyes seemed bloodshot.

"O Edward!" he exclaimed, "thou speakest to me hardly and unkindly of thy brother Alfred, and often hast thou thus more than hinted that I caused his death."

The king made no answer.

"May this crumb of bread choke me," said the earl, in great emotion, "if I am guilty of thy brother's blood!"[2]

But scarcely had the bread touched his lips, when his eyes fixed, — the long warning symptoms were fulfilled; and he fell to the ground, under the table, sudden and heavy, smitten by the stroke of apoplexy.

Harold and Gurth sprang forward; they drew their father from the ground. His face, still deep-red with streaks of purple, rested on Harold's breast; and the son, kneeling, called in anguish on his father. The ear was deaf.

Then said the king, rising, "It is the hand of God; remove him!" and he swept from the room, exulting.

CHAPTER V.

For five days and five nights did Godwin lie speechless,[3] and Harold watched over him night and day. And the leaches[4] would not bleed him, because the season was against

---

[1] Henry of Huntingdon, etc.

[2] Henry of Huntingdon; Brompton Chronicle, etc.

[3] Hoveden.

[4] The origin of the word *leach* (physician), which has puzzled some inquirers, is from *lich* or *leac*, a body. *Leich* is the old Saxon word for surgeon.

EARL GODWIN IN THE APOPLECTIC FIT WHICH CAUSED HIS DEATH.

It, in the increase of the moon and the tides; but they bathed his temples with wheat flour boiled in milk, according to a prescription which an angel in a dream[1] had advised to another patient; and they placed a plate of lead on his breast, marked with five crosses, saying a paternoster over each cross; together with other medical specifics in great esteem.[2] But, nevertheless, five days and five nights did Godwin lie speechless; and the leaches then feared that human skill was in vain.

The effect produced on the court, not more by the earl's death-stroke than the circumstances preceding it, was such as defies description. With Godwin's old comrades in arms it was simple and honest grief; but with all those under the influence of the priests, the event was regarded as a direct punishment from Heaven. The previous expression of the king, repeated by Edward to his monks, circulated from lip to lip, with sundry exaggerations as it travelled; and the superstition of the day had the more excuse, inasmuch as the speech of Godwin touched near upon the defiance of one of the most popular ordeals of the accused, — namely, that called the "corsned," in which a piece of bread was given to the supposed criminal: if he swallowed it with ease he was innocent; if it stuck in his throat, or choked him, nay, if he shook and turned pale, he was guilty. Godwin's words had appeared to invite the ordeal; God had heard, and stricken down the presumptuous perjurer!

Unconscious, happily, of these attempts to blacken the name of his dying father, Harold, towards the gray dawn succeeding the fifth night, thought that he heard Godwin stir in his bed; so he put aside the curtain, and bent over him. The old earl's eyes were wide open, and the red colour had gone from his cheeks, so that he was as pale as death.

"How fares it, dear father?" asked Harold.

Godwin smiled fondly, and tried to speak; but his voice died in a convulsive rattle. Lifting himself up, however, with an effort, he pressed tenderly the hand that clasped his

---

[1] Sharon Turner, vol. i. p. 472.   [2] Fosbrooke.

own, leaned his head on Harold's breast, and so gave up the ghost.

When Harold was at last aware that the struggle was over, he laid the gray head gently on the pillow; he closed the eyes, and kissed the lips, and knelt down and prayed. Then, seating himself at a little distance, he covered his face with his mantle.

At this time his brother Gurth, who had chiefly shared watch with Harold, — for Tostig, foreseeing his father's death, was busy soliciting thegn and earl to support his own claims to the earldom about to be vacant; and Leofwine had gone to London on the previous day to summon Githa, who was hourly expected, — Gurth, I say, entered the room on tiptoe, and seeing his brother's attitude, guessed that all was over. He passed on to the table, took up the lamp, and looked long on his father's face. That strange smile of the dead, common alike to innocent and guilty, had already settled on the serene lips; and that no less strange transformation from age to youth, when the wrinkles vanish, and the features come out clear and sharp from the hollows of care and years, had already begun. And the old man seemed sleeping in his prime.

So Gurth kissed the dead, as Harold had done before him, and came up and sat himself by his brother's feet, and rested his head on Harold's knee; nor would he speak till, appalled by the long silence of the earl, he drew away the mantle from his brother's face with a gentle hand, and the large tears were rolling down Harold's cheeks.

"Be soothed, my brother," said Gurth; "our father has lived for glory, his age was prosperous, and his years more than those which the Psalmist allots to man. Come and look on his face, Harold; its calm will comfort thee."

Harold obeyed the hand that led him like a child; in passing towards the bed, his eye fell upon the cyst which Hilda had given to the old earl, and a chill shot through his veins.

"Gurth," said he, "is not this the morning of the sixth day in which we have been at the king's court?"

"It is the morning of the sixth day."

Then Harold took forth the key which Hilda had given him, and unlocked the cyst, and there lay the white winding-sheet of the dead, and a scroll. Harold took the scroll, and bent over it, reading by the mingled light of the lamp and the dawn: —

"All hail, Harold, heir of Godwin the great, and Githa the king-born! Thou hast obeyed Hilda, and thou knowest now that Hilda's eyes read the future, and her lips speak the dark words of truth. Bow thy heart to the Vala, and mistrust the wisdom that sees only the things of the daylight. As the valour of the warrior and the song of the scald, so is the lore of the prophetess. It is not of the body; it is soul within soul. It marshals events and men, like the valour; it moulds the air into substance, like the song. Bow thy heart to the Vala. Flowers bloom over the grave of the dead; and the young plant soars high, when the king of the woodland lies low!"

CHAPTER VI.

THE sun rose, and the stairs and passages without were filled with the crowds that pressed to hear news of the earl's health. The doors stood open, and Gurth led in the multitude to look their last on the hero of council and camp, who had restored with strong hand and wise brain the race of Cerdic to the Saxon throne. Harold stood by the bed-head silent, and tears were shed and sobs were heard; and many a thegn who had before half believed in the guilt of Godwin as the murderer of Alfred, whispered in gasps to his neighbour, —

"There is no weregeld for manslaying on the head of him who smiles so in death on his old comrades in life!"

Last of all lingered Leofric, the great Earl of Mercia; and when the rest had departed, he took the pale hand, that lay heavy on the coverlid, in his own, and said, —

"Old foe, often stood we in Witan and field against each other; but few are the friends for whom Leofric would mourn as he mourns for thee. Peace to thy soul! Whatever its sins, England should judge thee mildly, for England beat in each pulse of thy heart, and with thy greatness was her own!"

Then Harold stole round the bed, and put his arms round Leofric's neck, and embraced him. The good old earl was touched, and he laid his tremulous hands on Harold's brown locks and blessed him.

"Harold," he said, "thou succeedest to thy father's power; let thy father's foes be thy friends. Wake from thy grief, for thy country now demands thee, — the honour of thy House, and the memory of the dead. Many even now plot against thee and thine. Seek the king, demand as thy right thy father's earldom, and Leofric will back thy claim in the Witan."

Harold pressed Leofric's hand, and raising it to his lips, replied: "Be our Houses at peace henceforth and forever."

Tostig's vanity indeed misled him, when he dreamed that any combination of Godwin's party could meditate supporting his claims against the popular Harold; nor less did the monks deceive themselves, when they supposed that with Godwin's death the power of his family would fall.

There was more than even the unanimity of the chiefs of the Witan in favour of Harold; there was that universal noiseless impression throughout all England, Danish and Saxon, that Harold was now the sole man on whom rested the State, — which, whenever it so favours one individual, is irresistible. Nor was Edward himself hostile to Harold, whom alone of that House, as we have before said, he esteemed and loved.

Harold was at once named Earl of Wessex; and relinquishing the earldom he held before, he did not hesitate as to the successor to be recommended in his place. Conquering all jealousy and dislike for Algar, he united the strength of his party in favour of the son of Leofric; and the election fell upon him. With all his hot errors, the claims of no other earl, whether from his own capacities or his father's services, were so strong; and his election probably saved the State from a great danger, in the results of that angry mood and that irritated ambition with which he had thrown himself into the arms of England's most valiant aggressor, Gryffyth, King of North Wales.

To outward appearance, by this election, the House of Leofric — uniting in father and son the two mighty districts of Mercia and the East Anglians — became more powerful than that of Godwin; for in that last House Harold was now the only possessor of one of the great earldoms, and Tostig and the other brothers had no other provision beyond the comparatively insignificant lordships they held before. But if Harold had ruled no earldom at all, he had still been immeasurably the first man in England, — so great was the confidence reposed in his valour and wisdom. He was of that height in himself that he needed no pedestal to stand on.

The successor of the first great founder of a House succeeds to more than his predecessor's power, if he but know how to wield and maintain it; for who makes his way to greatness without raising foes at every step, and who ever rose to power supreme without grave cause for blame? But Harold stood free from the enmities his father had provoked, and pure from the stains that slander or repute cast upon his father's name. The sun of the yesterday had shone through cloud; the sun of the day rose in a clear firmament. Even Tostig recognized the superiority of his brother; and after a strong struggle between baffled rage and covetous ambition, yielded to him as to a father. He felt that all Godwin's House was centred in Harold alone; and that only from his brother (despite his own daring valour, and despite his alliance with the blood of Charlemagne and Alfred, through the sister of Matilda, the Norman duchess) could his avarice of power be gratified.

"Depart to thy home, my brother," said Earl Harold to Tostig, "and grieve not that Algar is preferred to thee; for even had his claim been less urgent, ill would it have beseemed us to arrogate the lordships of all England as our dues. Rule thy lordship with wisdom; gain the love of thy lithsmen. High claims hast thou in our father's name, and moderation now will but strengthen thee in the season to come. Trust on Harold somewhat, on thyself more. Thou hast but to add temper and judgment to valour and zeal, to be worthy mate of the first earl in England. Over my father's corpse I embraced my father's foe. Between brother and brother shall there not be love, as the best bequest of the dead?"

"It shall not be my fault if there be not," answered Tostig, humbled though chafed; and he summoned his men and returned to his domains.

———◆———

CHAPTER VII.

Fair, broad, and calm set the sun over the western woodlands; and Hilda stood on the mound, and looked with undazzled eyes on the sinking orb. Beside her Edith reclined on the sward, and seemed with idle hand tracing characters in the air. The girl had grown paler still, since Harold last parted from her on the same spot; and the same listless and despondent apathy stamped her smileless lips and her bended head.

"See, child of my heart," said Hilda, addressing Edith, while she still gazed on the western luminary, "see, the sun goes down to the far deeps, where Rana and Ægir[1] watch over the worlds of the sea; but with morning he comes from the halls of the Asas, — the golden gates of the East, — and joy comes in his train. And yet thou thinkest, sad child, whose years have scarce passed into woman, that the sun, once set, never comes back to life. But even while we speak,

---

[1] _Ægir_, the Scandinavian god of the ocean. Not one of the Aser, or Asas (the celestial race), but sprung from the giants. _Ran_, or _Rana_, his wife, a more malignant character, who caused shipwrecks, and drew to herself, by a net, all that fell into the sea. The offspring of this marriage were nine daughters, who became the Billows, the Currents, and the Storms.

thy morning draws near, and the dunness of cloud takes the hues of the rose!"

Edith's hand paused from its vague employment, and fell droopingly on her knee. She turned with an unquiet and anxious eye to Hilda; and after looking some moments wistfully at the Vala, the colour rose to her cheek, and she said in a voice that had an accent half of anger, —

"Hilda, thou art cruel!"

"So is Fate!" answered the Vala. "But men call not Fate cruel when it smiles on their desires. Why callest thou Hilda cruel, when she reads in the setting sun the runes of thy coming joy?"

"There is no joy for me," returned Edith, plaintively; "and I have that on my heart," she added, with a sudden and almost fierce change of tone, "which at last I will dare to speak. I reproach thee, Hilda, that thou hast marred all my life, that thou hast duped me with dreams, and left me alone in despair."

"Speak on," said Hilda, calmly, as a nurse to a froward child.

"Hast thou not told me, from the first dawn of my wondering reason, that my life and lot were inwoven with — with (the word, mad and daring, must out) — with those of Harold the peerless? But for that, which my infancy took from thy lips as a law, I had never been so vain and so frantic! I had never watched each play of his face, and treasured each word from his lips; I had never made my life but a part of his life, — all my soul but the shadow of his sun. But for that, I had hailed the calm of the cloister; but for that, I had glided in peace to my grave. And now, — *now*, O Hilda —" Edith paused, and that break had more eloquence than any words she could command. "And," she resumed quickly, "thou knowest that these hopes were but dreams, — that the law ever stood between him and me, and that it was guilt to love him."

"I knew the law," answered Hilda; "but the law of fools is to the wise as the cobweb swung over the brake to the wing of the bird. Ye are sibbe to each other, some five times removed; and therefore an old man at Rome saith that ye ought not to wed. When the shavelings obey the old man at Rome, and put aside their own wives and frillas,[1] and abstain from the wine-cup and the chase and the brawl, I will stoop to hear of their laws, — with disrelish it may be, but without scorn.[2] It is no sin to love Harold; and no monk and no law shall prevent your union on the day appointed to bring ye together, form and heart."

"Hilda! Hilda! madden me not with joy," cried Edith, starting up in rapturous emotion, her young face dyed with blushes, and all her renovated beauty so celestial that Hilda herself was almost awed, as if by the vision of Freya, the northern Venus, charmed by a spell from the halls of Asgard.

"But that day is distant," renewed the Vala.

"What matters! what matters!" cried the pure child of Nature; "I ask but hope. Enough, — oh! enough, if we were but wedded on the borders of the grave!"

"Lo, then," said Hilda, "behold, the sun of thy life dawns again!"

As she spoke, the Vala stretched her arm; and through the intersticed columns of the fane, Edith saw the large shadow of a man cast over the still sward. Presently into the space of the circle came Harold, her beloved. His face was pale with grief yet recent; but, perhaps more than ever, dignity was in his step and command on his brow, for he felt that now alone with him rested the might of Saxon England. And what royal robe so invests with imperial majesty the form of a man as the grave sense of power responsible, in an earnest soul?

"Thou comest," said Hilda, "in the hour I predicted, — at the setting of the sun and the rising of the star."

---

[1] The Danish word for a lady, who, often with the wife's consent, was added to the domestic circle by the husband. The word is here used by Hilda in a general sense of reproach. Both marriage and concubinage were common amongst the Anglo-Saxon priesthood, despite the unheeded canons; and so, indeed, they were with the French clergy.

[2] Hilda, not only as a heathen, but as a Dane, would be no favourer of monks; they were unknown in Denmark at that time, and the Danes held them in odium. — *Ord. Vital.* lib. vii.

"Vala," said Harold, gloomily, "I will not oppose my sense to thy prophecies; for who shall judge of that power of which he knows not the elements, or despise the marvel of which he cannot detect the imposture? But leave me, I pray thee, to walk in the broad light of the common day. These hands are made to grapple with things palpable, and these eyes to measure the forms that front my way. In my youth I turned in despair or disgust from the subtleties of the schoolmen, which split upon hairs the brains of Lombard and Frank; in my busy and stirring manhood entangle me not in the meshes which confuse all my reason, and sicken my waking thoughts into dreams of awe. Mine be the straight path and the plain goal!"

The Vala gazed on him with an earnest look, that partook of admiration and yet more of gloom; but she spoke not, and Harold resumed, —

"Let the dead rest, Hilda, — proud names with glory on earth, and shadows escaped from our ken, submissive to mercy in heaven. A vast chasm have my steps overleaped since we met, O Hilda, sweet Edith, — a vast chasm, but a narrow grave." His voice faltered a moment, and again he renewed: "Thou weepest, Edith; ah, how thy tears console me! Hilda, hear me! I love thy grandchild, — loved her by irresistible instinct since her blue eyes first smiled on mine. I loved her in her childhood, as in her youth, — in the blossom as in the flower. And thy grandchild loves me. The laws of the Church proscribe our marriage, and therefore we parted; but I feel, and thine Edith feels, that the love remains as strong in absence: no other will be her wedded lord, no other my wedded wife. Therefore, with a heart made soft by sorrow, and, in my father's death, sole lord of my fate, I return, and say to thee in her presence, 'Suffer us to hope still!' The day may come when under some king less enthralled than Edward by formal Church laws, we may obtain from the Pope absolution for our nuptials, — a day, perhaps, far off; but we are both young, and love is strong and patient: we can wait."

"O Harold," exclaimed Edith, "we can wait!"

"Have I not told thee, son of Godwin," said the Vala, solemnly, "that Edith's skein of life was inwoven with thine? Dost thou deem that my charms have not explored the destiny of the last of my race? Know that it is in the decrees of the fates that ye are to be united, nevermore to be divided. Know that there shall come a day, though I can see not its morrow, and it lies dim and afar, which shall be the most glorious of thy life, and on which Edith and fame shall be thine, — the day of thy nativity, on which hitherto all things have prospered with thee. In vain against the stars preach the mone and the priest; what shall be, shall be. Wherefore take hope and joy, O Children of Time! And now, as I join your hands, I betroth your souls."

Rapture unalloyed and unprophetic, born of love deep and pure, shone in the eyes of Harold, as he clasped the hand of his promised bride. But an involuntary and mysterious shudder passed over Edith's frame, and she leaned close, close, for support upon Harold's breast; and as if by a vision, there rose distinct in her memory a stern brow, a form of power and terror, — the brow and the form of him who but once again in her waking life the Prophetess had told her she should behold. The vision passed away in the warm clasp of those protecting arms; and looking up into Harold's face, she there beheld the mighty and deep delight that transfused itself at once into her own soul.

Then Hilda, placing one hand over their heads, and raising the other towards heaven, all radiant with bursting stars, said in her deep and thrilling tones, —

"Attest the betrothal of these young hearts, O ye Powers that draw nature to nature by spells which no galdra can trace, and have wrought in the secrets of creation no mystery so perfect as love! Attest it, thou temple, thou altar! Attest it, O sun and O air! While the forms are divided, may the souls cling together, — sorrow with sorrow, and joy with joy. And when at length bride and bridegroom are one, O stars, may the trouble with which ye are charged have exhausted its burden; may no danger molest, and no malice disturb, but over the marriage-bed shine in peace, O ye stars!"

Up rose the moon. May's nightingale called its mate from the breathless boughs; and so Edith and Harold were betrothed by the grave of the son of Cerdic. And from the line of Cerdic had come, since Ethelbert, all the Saxon kings who with sword and with sceptre had reigned over Saxon England.

BOOK VI.

AMBITION.

CHAPTER I.

THERE was great rejoicing in England. King Edward had been induced to send Alred the prelate[1] to the court of the German Emperor, for his kinsman and namesake, Edward Atheling, the son of the great Ironsides. In his childhood this prince, with his brother Edmund, had been committed by Canute to the charge of his vassal, the King of Sweden; and it has been said (though without sufficient authority), that Canute's design was that they should be secretly made away with. The King of Sweden, however, forwarded the children to the court of Hungary; they were there honourably reared and received. Edmund died young, without issue. Edward married a daughter of the German Emperor, and during the commotions in England, and the successive reigns of Harold Harefoot, Hardicanute, and the Confessor, had remained forgotten in his exile, until now suddenly recalled to England as the heir presumptive of his childless namesake. He arrived with Agatha his wife, one infant son, Edgar, and two daughters, Margaret and Christina.

Great were the rejoicings. The vast crowd that had followed the royal visitors in their procession to the old London palace (not far from St. Paul's) in which they were lodged, yet swarmed through the streets, when two thegns who had personally accompanied the Atheling from Dover, and had just taken leave of him, now emerged from the palace, and with some difficulty made their way through the crowded streets.

[1] Chron. Knyghton.

The one in the dress and short hair imitated from the Norman, was our old friend Godrith, whom the reader may remember as the rebuker of Taillefer, and the friend of Mallet de Graville; the other, in a plain linen Saxon tunic, and the gonna worn on state occasions, to which he seemed unfamiliar, but with heavy gold bracelets on his arms, long haired and bearded, was Vebba, the Kentish thegn, who had served as nuncius from Godwin to Edward.

"Troth and faith!" said Vebba, wiping his brow, "this crowd is enow to make plain man stark wode. I would not live in London for all the gauds in the goldsmiths' shops, or all the treasures in King Edward's vaults. My tongue is as parched as a hay-field in the weyd-month.[1] Holy Mother be blessed! I see a cumen-hus [2] open; let us in and refresh ourselves with a horn of ale."

"Nay, friend," quoth Godrith, with a slight disdain, "such are not the resorts of men of our rank. Tarry yet awhile, till we arrive near the bridge by the river-side; there, indeed, you will find worthy company and dainty cheer."

"Well, well, I am at your hest, Godrith," said the Kent man, sighing; "my wife and my sons will be sure to ask me what sights I have seen, and I may as well know from thee the last tricks and ways of this hurly-burly town."

Godrith, who was master of all the fashions in the reign of our lord King Edward, smiled graciously, and the two proceeded in silence, only broken by the sturdy Kent man's exclamations, — now of anger when rudely jostled, now of wonder and delight when amidst the throng he caught sight of a gleeman, with his bear or monkey, who took advantage of some space near convent garden or Roman ruin to exhibit his craft, — till they gained a long low row of booths, most pleasantly situated to the left of this side London bridge, and which was appropriated to the celebrated cookshops, that even to the time of Fitzstephen retained their fame and their fashion.

Between the shops and the river was a space of grass worn brown and bare by the feet of the customers, with a few

---

[1] Meadow month, June.   [2] Tavern.

clipped trees with vines trained from one to the other in arcades, under cover of which were set tables and settles. The place was thickly crowded, and but for Godrith's popularity amongst the attendants, they might have found it difficult to obtain accommodation. However, a new table was soon brought forth, placed close by the cool margin of the water, and covered in a trice with tankards of hippocras, pigment, ale, and some Gascon as well as British wines; varieties of the delicious cake-bread for which England was then renowned; while viands strange to the honest eye and taste of the wealthy Kent man were served on spits.

"What bird is this?" said he, grumbling.

"Oh, enviable man, it is a Phrygian attagen [1] that thou art about to taste for the first time; and when thou hast recovered that delight, I commend to thee a Moorish compound, made of eggs and roes of carp from the old Southweorc stewponds, which the cooks here dress notably."

"Moorish! Holy Virgin!" cried Vebba, with his mouth full of the Phrygian attagen, "how came anything Moorish in our Christian island?"

Godrith laughed outright.

"Why, our cook here is Moorish; the best singers in London are Moors. Look yonder! see those grave, comely Saracens!"

"Comely, quotha, burned and black as a charred pine-pole!" grunted Vebba; "well, who are they?"

"Wealthy traders; thanks to whom, our pretty maids have risen high in the market." [2]

"More the shame," said the Kent man; "that selling of English youth to foreign masters, whether male or female, is a blot on the Saxon name."

"So saith Harold our Earl, and so preach the monks," returned Godrith. "But thou, my good friend, who art fond of all things that our ancestors did, and hast sneered more than once at my Norman robe and cropped hair, — *thou*

---

[1] Fitzstephen.

[2] William of Malmesbury speaks with just indignation of the Anglo-Saxon custom of selling female servants, either to public prostitution or foreign slavery.

shouldst not be the one to find fault with what our fathers have done since the days of Cerdic."

"Hem," said the Kent man, a little perplexed, "certainly old manners are the best, and I suppose there is some good reason for this practice, which I, who never trouble myself about matters that concern me not, do not see."

"Well, Vebba, and how likest thou the Atheling? He is of the old line," said Godrith.

Again the Kent man looked perplexed, and had recourse to the ale, which he preferred to all more delicate liquor, before he replied, —

"Why, he speaks English worse than King Edward; and as for his boy Edgar, the child can scarce speak English at all. And then their German carles and cnehts! An I had known what manner of folk they were, I had not spent my mancuses in running from my homestead to give them the welcome. But they told me that Harold the good Earl had made the king send for them; and whatever the earl counselled must, I thought, be wise, and to the weal of sweet England."

"That is true," said Godrith, with earnest emphasis; for, with all his affectation of Norman manners, he was thoroughly English at heart, and was now among the stanchest supporters of Harold, who had become no less the pattern and pride of the young nobles than the darling of the humbler population, — "that is true; and Harold showed us his noble English heart when he so urged the king to his own loss."

As Godrith thus spoke, nay, from the first mention of Harold's name, two men richly clad, but with their bonnets drawn far over their brows, and their long gonnas so worn as to hide their forms, who were seated at a table behind Godrith and had thus escaped his attention, had paused from their wine-cups, and they now listened with much earnestness to the conversation that followed.

"How to the earl's loss?" asked Vebba.

"Why, simple thegn," answered Godrith, "why, suppose that Edward had refused to acknowledge the Atheling as his heir, suppose the Atheling had remained in the German court, and our good king died suddenly, — who, thinkest thou, could succeed to the English throne?"

"Marry, I have never thought of that at all," said the Kent man, scratching his head.

"No, nor have the English generally; yet whom could we choose but Harold?"

A sudden start from one of the listeners was checked by the warning finger of the other; and the Kent man exclaimed, —

"Body o' me! But we have never chosen king (save the Danes) out of the line of Cerdic. These be new cranks, with a vengeance; we shall be choosing German or Saracen or Norman next!"

"Out of the line of Cerdic! But that line is gone, root and branch, save the Atheling, and he thou seest is more German than English. Again I say, failing the Atheling, whom could we choose but Harold, brother-in-law to the king; descended through Githa from the royalties of the Norse, the head of all armies under the Herr-ban, the chief who has never fought without victory, yet who has always preferred conciliation to conquest, — the first counsellor in the Witan, the first man in the realm, — who but Harold? Answer me, staring Vebba!"

"I take in thy words slowly," said the Kent man, shaking his head; "and after all, it matters little who is king, so he be a good one. Yes, I see now that the earl was a just and generous man when he made the king send for the Atheling. Drink-hæl! long life to them both!"

"Was-hæl," answered Godrith, draining his hippocras to Vebba's more potent ale. "Long life to them both! May Edward the Atheling reign, but Harold the Earl rule! Ah, then, indeed, we may sleep without fear of fierce Algar and still fiercer Gryffyth the Walloon, who now, it is true, are stilled for the moment, thanks to Harold, — but not more still than the smooth waters in Gwyned, that lie just above the rush of a torrent."

"So little news hear I," said Vebba, "and in Kent so little are we plagued with the troubles elsewhere (for there Harold governs us, and the hawks come not where the eagles hold eyry!) that I will thank thee to tell me something about our old earl for a year,[1] Algar the restless, and this Gryffyth the Welch King, so that I may seem a wise man when I go back to my homestead."

"Why, thou knowest at least that Algar and Harold were ever opposed in the Witan, and hot words thou hast heard pass between them!"

"Marry, yes! But Algar was as little match for Earl Harold in speech as in sword-play."

Now again one of the listeners started (but it was not the same as the one before), and muttered an angry exclamation.

"Yet is he a troublesome foe," said Godrith, who did not hear the sound Vebba had provoked, "and a thorn in the side both of the earl and of England; and sorrowful for both England and earl was it, that Harold refused to marry Aldyth, as it is said his father, wise Godwin, counselled and wished."

"Ah! but I have heard scops and harpers sing pretty songs that Harold loves Edith the Fair,— a wondrous proper maiden, they say!" .

"It is true; and for the sake of his love he played ill for his ambition."

"I like him the better for that," said the honest Kent man; "why does he not marry the girl at once? She hath broad lands, I know, for they run from the Sussex shore into Kent."

"But they are cousins five times removed, and the Church forbids the marriage; nevertheless Harold lives only for Edith; they have exchanged the true-lofa,[2] and it is whispered that Harold hopes the Atheling, when he comes to be king, will get him the Pope's dispensation. But to return to Algar; in a day most unlucky he gave his daughter to

---

[1] It will be remembered that Algar governed Wessex, which principality included Kent, during the year of Godwin's outlawry.

[2] *Trulofa*, from which comes our popular corruption, "true lover's knot;" *à veteri Danico* trulofa, that is, *fidem do*, to pledge faith. — HICKE : *Thesaur.*

"A knot, among the ancient northern nations, seems to have been the emblem of love, faith, and friendship." — BRANDE : *Pop. Antiq.*

Gryffyth, the most turbulent sub-king the land ever knew, who, it is said, will not be content till he has won all Wales for himself without homage or service, and the Marches to boot. Some letters between him and Earl Algar, to whom Harold had secured the earldom of the East Angles, were discovered; and in a Witan at Winchester thou wilt doubtless have heard (for thou didst not, I know, leave thy lands to attend it) that Algar [1] was outlawed."

"Oh, yes, these are stale tidings, — I heard thus much from a palmer, — and then Algar got ships from the Irish, sailed to north Wales, and beat Rolf, the Norman Earl, at Hereford. Oh, yes, I heard that; and" added the Kent man, laughing, "I was not sorry to hear that my old Earl Algar, since he is a good and true Saxon, beat the cowardly Norman, — more shame to the king for giving a Norman the ward of the Marches!"

"It was a sore defeat to the king and to England," said Godrith, gravely. "The great minster of Hereford built by King Athelstan was burned and sacked by the Welch, and the crown itself was in danger, when Harold came up at the head of the Fyrd. Hard is it to tell the distress and the marching and the camping and the travail, and destruction of men, and also of horses, which the English endured [2] till Harold came; and then luckily came also the good old Leofric, and Bishop Alred the peacemaker, and so strife was patched up, — Gryffyth swore oaths of faith to King Edward, and Algar was inlawed; and there for the nonce

---

[1] The "Saxon Chronicle" contradicts itself as to Algar's outlawry, stating in one passage that he was outlawed without any kind of guilt, and in another that he was outlawed as *swike*, or traitor, and that he made a confession of it before all the men there gathered. His treason, however, seems naturally occasioned by his close connection with Gryffyth, and proved by his share in that king's rebellion. Some of our historians have unfairly assumed that his outlawry was at Harold's instigation. Of this there is not only no proof, but one of the best authorities among the chroniclers says just the contrary, — that Harold did all he could to intercede for him; and it is certain that he was fairly tried and condemned by the Witan, and afterwards restored by the concurrent articles of agreement between Harold and Leofric Harold's policy with his own countrymen stands out very markedly prominent in the annals of the time; it was invariably that of conciliation.

[2] Saxon Chronicle, *verbatim*.

rests the matter now. But well I ween that Gryffyth will never keep troth with the English, and that no hand less strong than Harold's can keep in check a spirit as fiery as Algar's; therefore did I wish that Harold might be king."

"Well," quoth the honest Kent man, "I hope, nevertheless, that Algar will sow his wild oats, and leave the Walloons to grow the hemp for their own halters; for though he is not of the height of our Harold, he is a true Saxon, and we liked him well enow when he ruled us. And how is our earl's brother Tostig esteemed by the Northmen? It must be hard to please those who had Siward of the strong arm for their earl before."

"Why, at first, when (at Siward's death in the wars for young Malcolm) Harold secured to Tostig the Northumbrian earldom, Tostig went by his brother's counsel, and ruled well and won favour. Of late I hear that the Northmen murmur. Tostig is a man indeed dour and haughty."

After a few more questions and answers on the news of the day, Vebba rose and said, —

"Thanks for thy good fellowship; it is time for me now to be jogging homeward. I left my ceorls and horses on the other side the river, and must go after them. And now forgive me my bluntness, fellow-thegn, but ye young courtiers have plenty of need for your mancuses, and when a plain countryman like me comes sight-seeing, he ought to stand payment; wherefore," here he took from his belt a great leathern purse, — "wherefore, as these outlandish birds and heathenish puddings must be dear fare — "

"How!" said Godrith, reddening, "thinkest thou so meanly of us thegns of Middlesex as to deem we cannot entertain thus humbly a friend from a distance? Ye Kent men I know are rich, but keep your pennies to buy stuffs for your wife, my friend."

The Kent man, seeing he had displeased his companion, did not press his liberal offer, — put up his purse, and suffered Godrith to pay the reckoning. Then, as the two thegns shook hands, he said, —

"But I should like to have said a kind word or so to Earl Harold, — for he was too busy and too great for me to come across him in the old palace yonder. I have a mind to go back and look for him at his own house."

"You will not find him there," said Godrith, "for I know that as soon as he hath finished his conference with the Atheling, he will leave the city; and I shall be at his own favourite manse over the water at sunset, to take orders for repairing the forts and dikes on the Marches. You can tarry awhile and meet us; you know his old lodge in the forest land?"

"Nay, I must be back and at home ere night, for all things go wrong when the master is away. Yet, indeed, my good wife will scold me for not having shaken hands with the handsome earl."

"Thou shalt not come under that sad infliction," said the good-natured Godrith, who was pleased with the thegn's devotion to Harold, and who, knowing the great weight which Vebba (homely as he seemed) carried in his important county, was politically anxious that the earl should humour so sturdy a friend, — "thou shalt not sour thy wife's kiss, man. For look you, as you ride back you will pass by a large old house, with broken columns at the back."

"I have marked it well," said the thegn, "when I have gone that way, — with a heap of queer stones, on a little hillock, which they say the witches or the Britons heaped together."

"The same. When Harold leaves London, I trow well towards that house will his road wend; for there lives Edith the swan's-neck, with her awful grandam the Wicca. If thou art there a little after noon, depend on it thou wilt see Harold riding that way."

"Thank thee heartily, friend Godrith," said Vebba, taking his leave, "and forgive my bluntness if I laughed at thy cropped head, for I see thou art as good a Saxon as e'er a franklin of Kent, and so the saints keep thee."

Vebba then strode briskly over the bridge; and Godrith, animated by the wine he had drunk, turned gayly on his heel to look amongst the crowded tables for some chance friend with whom to while away an hour or so at the games of hazard then in vogue.

Scarce had he turned, when the two listeners, who, having paid their reckoning, had moved under shade of one of the arcades, dropped into a boat which they had summoned to the margin by a noiseless signal, and were rowed over the water. They preserved a silence which seemed thoughtful and gloomy until they reached the opposite shore; then one of them, pushing back his bonnet, showed the sharp and haughty features of Algar.

"Well, friend of Gryffyth," said he, with a bitter accent, "thou hearest that Earl Harold counts so little on the oaths of thy king that he intends to fortify the Marches against him; and thou hearest also that nought save a life as fragile as the reed which thy feet are trampling, stands between the throne of England and the only Englishman who could ever have humbled my son-in-law to swear oath of service to Edward."

"Shame upon that hour!" said the other, whose speech, as well as the gold collar round his neck and the peculiar fashion of his hair, betokened him to be Welch. "Little did I think that the great son of Llewellyn, whom our bards had set above Roderic Mawr, would ever have acknowledged the sovereignty of the Saxon over the hills of Cymry."

"Tut, Meredydd," answered Algar, "thou knowest well that no Cymrian ever deems himself dishonoured by breaking faith with the Saxon; and we shall yet see the lions of Gryffyth scaring the sheepfolds of Hereford."

"So be it," said Meredydd, fiercely; "and Harold shall give to his Atheling the Saxon land, shorn at least of the Cymrian kingdom."

"Meredydd," said Algar, with a seriousness that seemed almost solemn, "no Atheling will live to rule these realms! Thou knowest that I was one of the first to hail the news of his coming, — I hastened to Dover to meet him. Methought I saw death writ on his countenance, and I bribed the German leach who attends him to answer my questions; the Atheling knows it not, but he bears within him the seeds of a mortal complaint. Thou wottest well what cause I have to hate Earl Harold; and were I the only man to oppose his way to the throne, he should not ascend it but over my corpse. But when Godrith, his creature, spoke, I felt that he spoke the truth; and the Atheling dead, on no head but Harold's can fall the crown of Edward."

"Ha!" said the Cymrian chief, gloomily; "thinkest thou so indeed?"

"I think it not; I know it. And for that reason, Meredydd, we must wait not till he wields against us all the royalty of England. As yet, while Edward lives, there is hope; for the king loves to spend wealth on relics and priests, and is slow when the mancuses are wanted for fighting men. The king too, poor man! is not so ill-pleased at my outbursts as he would fain have it thought; he thinks, by pitting earl against earl, that he himself is the stronger.[1] While Edward lives, therefore, Harold's arm is half crippled; wherefore, Meredydd, ride thou, with good speed, back to King Gryffyth, and tell him all I have told thee. Tell him that our time to strike the blow and renew the war will be amidst the dismay and confusion that the Atheling's death will occasion. Tell him that if we can entangle Harold himself in the Welch defiles, it will go hard but what we shall find some arrow or dagger to pierce the heart of the invader. And were Harold but slain, who then would be king in England? The line of Cerdic gone, the House of Godwin lost in Earl Harold (for Tostig is hated in his own domain, Leofwine is too light, and Gurth is too saintly for such ambition), — who then, I say, can be king in England but Algar, the heir of the great Leofric? And I, as King of England, will set all Cymry free, and restore to the realm of Gryffyth the shires of Hereford and Worcester. Ride fast, O Meredydd, and heed well all I have said."

"Dost thou promise and swear that wert thou king of England, Cymry should be free from all service?"

"Free as air, free as under Arthur and Uther: I swear it.

[1] Hume.

And remember well how Harold addressed the Cymrian chiefs, when he accepted Gryffyth's oaths of service."

"Remember it, ay!" cried Meredydd, his face lighting up with intense ire and revenge. "The stern Saxon said, ' Heed well, ye chiefs of Cymry, and thou Gryffyth the King, that if again ye force, by ravage and rapine, by sacrilege and murder, the majesty of England to enter your borders, duty must be done. God grant that your Cymrian lion may leave us in peace; if not, it is mercy to human life that bids us cut the talons and draw the fangs.' "

"Harold, like all calm and mild men, ever says less than he means," returned Algar; "and were Harold king, small pretext would he need for cutting the talons and drawing the fangs."

"It is well," said Meredydd, with a fierce smile. "I will now go to my men who are lodged yonder; and it is better that thou shouldst not be seen with me."

"Right; so Saint David be with you, — and forget not a word of my message to Gryffyth my son-in-law."

"Not a word," returned Meredydd, as with a wave of his hand he moved towards a hostelry, to which, as kept by one of their own countrymen, the Welch habitually resorted in the visits to the capital which the various intrigues and dissensions in their unhappy land made frequent.

The chief's train, which consisted of ten men, all of high birth, were not drinking in the tavern, — for sorry customers to mine host were the abstemious Welch. Stretched on the grass under the trees of an orchard that backed the hostelry, and utterly indifferent to all the rejoicings that animated the population of Southwark and London, they were listening to a wild song of the old hero-days from one of their number; and round them grazed the rough shagged ponies which they had used for their journey. Meredydd, approaching, gazed round, and seeing no stranger was present, raised his hand to hush the song, and then addressed his countrymen briefly in Welch, — briefly, but with a passion that was evident in his flashing eyes and vehement gestures. The passion was contagious; they all sprang to their feet with a low but fierce cry, and in a few moments they had caught and saddled their diminutive palfreys, while one of the band, who seemed singled out by Meredydd, sallied forth alone from the orchard, and took his way, on foot, to the bridge. He did not tarry there long; at the sight of a single horseman, whom a shout of welcome on that swarming thoroughfare proclaimed to be Earl Harold, the Welchman turned, and with a fleet foot regained his companions.

Meanwhile Harold smilingly returned the greetings he received, cleared the bridge, passed the suburbs, and soon gained the wild forest-land that lay along the great Kentish road. He rode somewhat slowly, for he was evidently in deep thought; and he had arrived about half-way towards Hilda's house when he heard behind quick, pattering sounds, as of small unshod hoofs. He turned, and saw the Welchmen at the distance of some fifty yards. But at that moment there passed along the road in front several persons bustling into London to share in the festivities of the day. This seemed to disconcert the Welch in the rear, and after a few whispered words they left the high-road and entered the forest-land. Various groups from time to time continued to pass along the thoroughfare. But still ever through the glades Harold caught glimpses of the riders, — now distant, now near. Sometimes he heard the snort of their small horses, and saw a fierce eye glaring through the bushes; then, as at the sight or sound of approaching passengers, the riders wheeled and shot off through the brakes.

The earl's suspicions were aroused; for though he knew of no enemy to apprehend, and the extreme severity of the laws against robbers made the high-roads much safer in the latter days of the Saxon domination than they were for centuries under that of the subsequent dynasty, when Saxon thegns themselves had turned kings of the greenwood, the various insurrections in Edward's reign had necessarily thrown upon society many turbulent disbanded mercenaries.

Harold was unarmed, save the spear which even on occasions of state the Saxon noble rarely laid aside, and the ateghar in his belt; and seeing now that the road had become deserted, he set spurs to his horse, and was just in sight of the Druid temple, when a javelin whizzed close by his breast, and another transfixed his horse, which fell head-foremost to the ground.

The earl gained his feet in an instant, and that haste was needed to save his life; for while he rose ten swords flashed around him. The Welchmen had sprung from their palfreys as Harold's horse fell. Fortunately for him, only two of the party bore javelins (a weapon which the Welch wielded with deadly skill), and, those already wasted, they drew their short swords, which were probably imitated from the Romans, and rushed upon him in simultaneous onset. Versed in all the weapons of the time, with his right hand seeking by his spear to keep off the rush, with the ateghar in his left parrying the strokes aimed at him, the brave earl transfixed the first assailant, and sore wounded the next; but his tunic was dyed red with three gashes, and his sole chance of life was in the power yet left him to force his way through the ring. Dropping his spear, shifting his ateghar into the right hand, wrapping round his left arm his gonna as a shield, he sprang fiercely on the onslaught and on the flashing swords. Pierced to the heart fell one of his foes, — dashed to the earth another; from the hand of a third (dropping his own ateghar) he wrenched the sword. Loud rose Harold's cry for aid, and swiftly he strode towards the hillock, turning back and striking as he turned; and again fell a foe, and again new blood oozed through his own garb. At that moment his cry was echoed by a shriek so sharp and so piercing that it startled the assailants, it arrested the assault; and ere the unequal strife could be resumed, a woman was in the midst of the fray, a woman stood dauntless between the earl and his foes.

"Back, Edith! O God! Back, back!" cried the earl, recovering all his strength in the sole fear which that strife had yet stricken into his bold heart; and drawing Edith aside with his strong arm, he again confronted the assailants.

"Die!" cried, in the Cymrian tongue, the fiercest of the foes, whose sword had already twice drawn the earl's blood, — "die, that Cymry may be free!"

Meredydd sprang; with him sprang the survivors of his band; and by a sudden movement Edith had thrown herself on Harold's breast, leaving his right arm free, but sheltering his form with her own.

At that sight every sword rested still in air. These Cymrians, hesitating not at the murder of the man whose death seemed to their false virtue a sacrifice due to their hopes of freedom, were still the descendants of Heroes, and the children of noble Song, and their swords were harmless against a woman. The same pause which saved the life of Harold saved that of Meredydd; for the Cymrian's lifted sword had left his breast defenceless, and Harold, despite his wrath, and his fears for Edith, touched by that sudden forbearance, forbore himself the blow.

"Why· seek ye my life?" said he. "Whom in broad England hath Harold wronged?"

That speech broke the charm, revived the suspense of vengeance. With a sudden aim Meredydd smote at the head which Edith's embrace left unprotected. The sword shivered on the steel of that which parried the stroke; and the next moment, pierced to the heart, Meredydd fell to the earth, bathed in his gore. Even as he fell, aid was at hand. The ceorls in the Roman house had caught the alarm, and were hurrying down the knoll, with arms snatched in haste, while a loud whoop broke from the forest-land hard by; and a troop of horse, headed by Vebba, rushed through the bushes and brakes. Those of the Welch still surviving, no longer animated by their fiery chief, turned on the instant, and fled with that wonderful speed of foot which characterized their active race; calling, as they fled, to their Welch pygmy steeds, which, snorting loud and lashing out, came at once to the call. Seizing the nearest at hand, the fugitives sprang to selle, while the animals unchosen paused by the corpses of their former riders, neighing piteously and shaking their long manes. And then, after wheeling round and round the coming horsemen, with many a plunge and lash and savage cry, they darted after their companions, and disappeared amongst the bush wood. Some of the Kentish men gave chase to the fugitives, but in vain; for the nature of the ground favoured flight. Vebba and the rest, now joined by Hilda's lithsmen, gained the spot where Harold, bleeding fast, yet strove to keep his footing, and, forgetful of his own wounds, was joyfully assuring himself of Edith's safety. Vebba dismounted, and recognizing the earl, exclaimed, —

"Saints in heaven! are we in time? You bleed, you faint! Speak, Lord Harold! How fares it?"

"Blood enow yet left here for our merrie England!" said Harold, with a smile; but as he spoke, his head drooped, and he was borne senseless into the house of Hilda.

———◆———

CHAPTER II.

THE Vala met them at the threshold, and testified so little surprise at the sight of the bleeding and unconscious earl that Vebba, who had heard strange tales of Hilda's unlawful arts, half suspected that those wild-looking foes, with their uncanny diminutive horses, were imps conjured by her to punish a wooer to her grandchild, who had been perhaps too successful in the wooing. And fears so reasonable were not a little increased when Hilda, after leading the way up the steep ladder to the chamber in which Harold had dreamed his fearful dream, bade them all depart, and leave the wounded man to her care.

"Not so," said Vebba, bluffly. "A life like this is not to be left in the hands of woman or wicca. I shall go back to the great town, and summon the earl's own leach; and I beg thee to heed, meanwhile, that every head in this house shall answer for Harold's."

The great Vala and high-born Hleafdian, little accustomed to be accosted thus, turned round abruptly, with so stern an eye and so imperious a mien that even the stout Kent man felt abashed. She pointed to the door opening on the ladder, and said briefly, —

"Depart! Thy lord's life hath been saved already, and by woman. Depart!"

"Depart, and fear not for the earl, brave and true friend in need," said Edith, looking up from Harold's pale lips, over which she bent; and her sweet voice so touched the good thegn that, murmuring a blessing on her fair face, he turned and departed.

Hilda then proceeded, with a light and skilful hand, to examine the wounds of her patient. She opened the tunic, and washed away the blood from four gaping orifices on the breast and shoulders. And as she did so, Edith uttered a faint cry, and falling on her knees, bowed her head over the drooping hand, and kissed it with stifling emotions, of which perhaps grateful joy was the strongest; for over the heart of Harold was punctured, after the fashion of the Saxons, a device, — and that device was the knot of betrothal, and in the centre of the knot was graven the word "Edith."

—————•—————

CHAPTER III.

WHETHER owing to Hilda's runes or to the merely human arts which accompanied them, the earl's recovery was rapid, though the great loss of blood he had sustained left him awhile weak and exhausted; but perhaps he blessed the excuse which detained him still in the house of Hilda and under the eyes of Edith.

He dismissed the leach sent to him by Vebba, and confided, not without reason, to the Vala's skill; and how happily went his hours beneath the old Roman roof!

It was not without a superstition, more characterized, however, by tenderness than awe, that Harold learned that Edith had been undefinably impressed with a foreboding of danger to her betrothed, and all that morning she had watched his coming from the old legendary hill. Was it not in that watch that his good Fylgia had saved his life?

Indeed, there seemed a strange truth in Hilda's assertions that in the form of his betrothed his tutelary spirit lived and guarded, for smooth every step and bright every day in his career since their troth had been plighted. And gradually the sweet superstition had mingled with human passion to hallow and refine it. There was a purity and a depth in the love of these two, which, if not uncommon in women, is most rare in men.

Harold, in sober truth, had learned to look on Edith as on his better angel; and calming his strong manly heart in the hour of temptation, would have recoiled, as a sacrilege, from aught that could have sullied that image of celestial love. With a noble and sublime patience, of which perhaps only a character so thoroughly English in its habits of self-control and steadfast endurance could have been capable, he saw the months and the years glide away, and still contented himself with hope, — hope, the sole godlike joy that belongs to men!

As the opinion of an age influences even those who affect to despise it, so perhaps, this holy and unselfish passion was preserved and guarded by that peculiar veneration for purity which formed the characteristic fanaticism of the last days of the Anglo-Saxons, — when still, as Aldhelm had previously sung in Latin less barbarous than perhaps any priest in the reign of Edward could command, —

> " Virginitas castam servans sine crimine carnem
> Cætera virtutem vincit præconia laudi —
> Spiritus altithroni templum sibi vindicat almus ; " [1]

when, amidst a great dissoluteness of manners, alike common to Church and laity, the opposite virtues were, as is invariable in such epochs of society, carried by the few purer natures into heroic extremes. "And as gold, the adorner of the world,

---

[1] "The chaste who blameless keep unsullied fame,
Transcend all other worth, all other praise.
The Spirit, high enthroned, has made their hearts
His sacred temple."

Sharon Turner's Translation of Aldhelm, vol. iii. p. 366. It is curious to see how, even in Latin, the poet preserves the *alliterations* that characterized the Saxon muse.

springs from the sordid bosom of earth, so chastity, the image of gold, rose bright and unsullied from the clay of human desire." [1]

And Edith, though yet in the tenderest flush of beautiful youth, had, under the influence of that sanctifying and scarce earthly affection, perfected her full nature as woman. She had learned so to live in Harold's life, that — less, it seemed, by study than intuition — a knowledge graver than that which belonged to her sex and her time seemed to fall upon her soul, — fall as the sunlight falls on the blossoms, expanding their petals and brightening the glory of their hues.

Hitherto, living under the shade of Hilda's dreary creed, Edith, as we have seen, had been rather Christian by name and instinct than acquainted with the doctrines of the Gospel, or penetrated by its faith. But the soul of Harold lifted her own out of the Valley of the Shadow up to the Heavenly Hill; for the character of their love was so pre-eminently Christian, so by the circumstances that surrounded it, so by hope and self-denial, elevated out of the empire, not only of the senses, but even of that sentiment which springs from them, and which made the sole refined and poetic element of the heathen's love, that but for Christianity it would have withered and died. It required all the aliment of prayer; it needed that patient endurance which comes from the soul's consciousness of immortality; it could not have resisted earth, but from the forts and armies it won from heaven. Thus from Harold might Edith be said to have taken her very soul; and with the soul and through the soul woke the mind from the mists of childhood.

In the intense desire to be worthy the love of the foremost man of her land, — to be the companion of his mind as well as the mistress of his heart, — she had acquired, she knew not how, strange stores of thought and intelligence, and pure, gentle wisdom. In opening to her confidence his own high aims and projects, he himself was scarcely conscious how often he confided but to consult, — how often and how insensibly she coloured his reflections and shaped his designs.

---

[1] Slightly altered from Aldhelm.

Whatever was highest and purest, *that* Edith ever, as by instinct, beheld as the wisest. She grew to him like a second conscience, diviner than his own. Each therefore reflected virtue on the other, as planet illumines planet.

All these years of probation, then, which might have soured a love less holy, changed into weariness a love less intense, had only served to wed them more intimately soul to soul; and in that spotless union what happiness there was! what rapture in word and glance, and the slight, restrained caress of innocence, beyond all the transports love only human can bestow!

CHAPTER IV.

It was a bright, still summer noon, when Harold sat with Edith amidst the columns of the Druid temple, and in the shade which those vast and mournful relics of a faith departed cast along the sward. And there, conversing over the past and planning the future, they had sat long, when Hilda approached from the house, and entering the circle, leaned her arm upon the altar of the war-god, and gazing on Harold with a calm triumph in her aspect, said, —

"Did I not smile, son of Godwin, when, with thy short-sighted wisdom, thou didst think to guard thy land and secure thy love by urging the monk-king to send over the seas for the Atheling? Did I not tell thee, ' Thou dost right, for in obeying thy judgment thou art but the instrument of fate; and the coming of the Atheling shall speed thee nearer to the ends of thy life; but not from the Atheling shalt thou take the crown of thy love, and not by the Atheling shall the throne of Athelstan be filled '?"

"Alas," said Harold, rising in agitation, "let me not hear of mischance to that noble prince. He seemed sick and feeble when I parted from him; but joy is a great restorer, and the air of the native land gives quick health to the exile."

"Hark!" said Hilda, "you hear the passing bell for the soul of the son of Ironsides!"

The mournful knell, as she spoke, came dull from the roofs of the city afar, borne to their ears by the exceeding stillness of the atmosphere. Edith crossed herself and murmured a prayer, according to the custom of the age; then, raising her eyes to Harold, she murmured, as she clasped her hands, —

"Be not saddened, Harold; hope still."

"Hope!" repeated Hilda, rising proudly from her recumbent position, — "hope! In that knell from St. Paul's, dull indeed is thine ear, O Harold, if thou hearest not the joy-bells that inaugurate a future king!"

The earl started; his eyes shot fire; his breast heaved.

"Leave us, Edith," said Hilda, in a low voice; and after watching her grandchild's slow, reluctant steps descend the knoll, she turned to Harold, and leading him towards the gravestone of the Saxon chief, said, —

"Rememberest thou the spectre that rose from this mound? — rememberest thou the dream that followed it?"

"The spectre, or deceit of mine eye, I remember well," answered the earl; "the dream, not, — or only in confused and jarring fragments."

"I told thee then that I could not unriddle the dream by the light of the moment, and that the dead who slept below never appeared to men save for some portent of doom to the House of Cerdic. The portent is fulfilled; the Heir of Cerdic is no more. To whom appeared the great Scin-læca, but to him who shall lead a new race of kings to the Saxon throne?"

Harold breathed hard, and the colour mounted bright and glowing to his cheek and brow.

"I cannot gainsay thee, Vala. Unless, despite all conjecture, Edward should be spared to earth till the Atheling's infant son acquires the age when bearded men will acknowledge a chief,[1] I look round in England for the coming king, and all England reflects but mine own image."

[1] It is impossible to form any just view of the state of parties, and the position of Harold in the later portions of this work, unless the reader will

His head rose erect as he spoke; and already the brow seemed august, as if circled by the diadem of the Basileus.

"And if it be so," he added, "I accept that solemn trust, and England shall grow greater in my greatness."

"The flame breaks at last from the smouldering fuel," cried the Vala, "and the hour I so long foretold to thee hath come!"

Harold answered not, for high and kindling emotions deafened him to all but the voice of a grand ambition, and the awakening joy of a noble heart.

"And then — and then," he exclaimed, "I shall need no mediator between nature and monkcraft, — then, O Edith, the life thou hast saved will indeed be thine!" He paused; and it was a sign of the change that an ambition long repressed, but now rushing into the vent legitimately open to it, had already begun to work in the character hitherto so self-reliant, when he said in a low voice: "But that dream which hath so long lain locked, not lost, in my mind, — that dream of which I recall only vague remembrances of danger yet defiance, trouble yet triumph, — canst thou unriddle it, O Vala, into auguries of success?"

"Harold," answered Hilda, "thou didst hear at the close of thy dream the music of the hymns that are chanted at the crowning of a king, — and a crowned king shalt thou be; yet fearful foes shall assail thee, — foreshown in the shapes of a lion and raven, that came in menace over the blood-red sea. The two stars in the heaven betoken that the day of thy birth was also the birthday of a foe whose star is fatal to thine; and

bear constantly in mind the fact that from the earliest period minors were set aside as a matter of course, by the Saxon customs. Henry observes that in the whole history of the Heptarchy there is but one example of a minority, and that a short and unfortunate one: so in the later times the great Alfred takes the throne, to the exclusion of the infant son of his elder brother. Only under very peculiar circumstances, backed, as in the case of Edmund Ironsides, by precocious talents and manhood on the part of the minor, were there exceptions to the general laws of succession. The same rule obtained with the earldoms; the fame, power, and popularity of Siward could not transmit his Northumbrian earldom to his infant son Waltheof, so gloomily renowned in a subsequent reign.

they warn thee against a battle-field fought on the day when those stars shall meet. Farther than this the mystery of thy dream escapes from my lore. Wouldst thou learn thyself, from the phantom that sent the dream, stand by my side at the grave of the Saxon hero, and I will summon the Scin-læca to counsel the living. For what to the Vala the dead may deny, the soul of the brave on the brave may bestow!"

Harold listened with a serious and musing attention which his pride or his reason had never before accorded to the warnings of Hilda; but his sense was not yet fascinated by the voice of the charmer, and he answered with his wonted smile, so sweet yet so haughty, —

"A hand outstretched to a crown should be armed for the foe; and the eye that would guard the living should not be dimmed by the vapours that encircle the dead."

CHAPTER V.

BUT from that date changes, slight yet noticeable and important, were at work both in the conduct and character of the great earl.

Hitherto he had advanced on his career without calculation; and nature, not policy, had achieved his power. But henceforth he began thoughtfully to cement the foundations of his House, to extend the area, to strengthen the props. Policy now mingled with the justice that had made him esteemed, and the generosity that had won him love. Before, though by temper conciliatory, yet through honesty indifferent to the enmities he provoked in his adherence to what his conscience approved, he now laid himself out to propitiate all ancient feuds, soothe all jealousies, and convert foes into friends. He opened constant and friendly communication with his uncle Sweyn, King of Denmark; he availed himself sedulously of all the influence over the Anglo-Danes which his mother's birth made so facile. He strove also, and wisely, to conciliate the animosities which the Church had cherished against Godwin's House: he concealed his disdain of the monks and monkridden; he showed himself the Church's patron and friend; he endowed largely the convents, and especially one at Waltham, which had fallen into decay, though favourably known for the piety of its brotherhood. But if in this he played a part not natural to his opinions, Harold could not, even in simulation, administer to evil. The monasteries he favoured were those distinguished for purity of life, for benevolence to the poor, for bold denunciation of the excesses of the great. He had not, like the Norman, the grand design of creating in the priesthood a college of learning, a school of arts; such notions were unfamiliar in homely, unlettered England. And Harold, though for his time and his land no mean scholar, would have recoiled from favouring a learning always made subservient to Rome, — always at once haughty and scheming, and aspiring to complete domination over both the souls of men and the thrones of kings. But his aim was, out of the elements he found in the natural kindliness existing between Saxon priest and Saxon flock, to rear a modest, virtuous, homely clergy, not above tender sympathy with an ignorant population. He selected as examples for his monastery at Waltham, two low-born humble brothers, Osgood and Ailred, — the one known for the courage with which he had gone through the land, preaching to abbot and thegn the emancipation of the theowes, as the most meritorious act the safety of the soul could impose; the other, who, originally a clerk, had, according to the common custom of the Saxon clergy, contracted the bonds of marriage, and with some eloquence had vindicated that custom against the canons of Rome, and refused the offer of large endowments and thegn's rank to put away his wife. But on the death of that spouse he had adopted the cowl, and while still persisting in the lawfulness of marriage to the unmonastic clerks, had become famous for denouncing the open concubinage which desecrated the holy office and violated the solemn vows of many a proud prelate and abbot.

To these two men (both of whom refused the abbacy of
Waltham) Harold committed the charge of selecting the new
brotherhood established there; and the monks of Waltham
were honoured as saints throughout the neighbouring district,
and cited as examples to all the Church.

But though in themselves the new politic arts of Harold
seemed blameless enough, *arts* they were, and as such they
corrupted the genuine simplicity of his earlier nature. He
had conceived for the first time an ambition apart from that
of service to his country. It was no longer only to serve the
land, it was to serve it as its ruler, that animated his heart
and coloured his thoughts. Expediencies began to dim to his
conscience the healthful loveliness of Truth. And now too,
gradually, that empire which Hilda had gained over his
brother Sweyn began to sway this man, heretofore so strong
in his sturdy sense. The future became to him a dazzling
mystery, into which his conjectures plunged themselves more
and more. He had not yet stood in the Runic circle and
invoked the dead; but the spells were around his heart, and
in his own soul had grown up the familiar demon.

Still Edith reigned alone, if not in his thoughts at least in
his affections; and perhaps it was the hope of conquering all
obstacles to his marriage that mainly induced him to propitiate the Church, through whose agency the object he sought
must be attained; and still that hope gave the brightest lustre
to the distant crown. But he who admits Ambition to the
companionship of Love admits a giant that outstrides the
gentler footsteps of its comrade.

Harold's brow lost its benign calm. He became thoughtful and abstracted. He consulted Edith less; Hilda more.
Edith seemed to him now not wise enough to counsel. The
smile of his Fylgia, like the light of the star upon a stream,
lit the surface, but could not pierce to the deep.

Meanwhile, however, the policy of Harold throve and prospered. He had already arrived at that height that the least
effort to make power popular redoubled its extent. Gradually
all voices swelled the chorus in his praise; gradually men became familiar to the question, "If Edward dies before Edgar,

the grandson of Ironsides, is of age to succeed, where can we find a king like Harold?"

In the midst of this quiet but deepening sunshine of his fate, there burst a storm which seemed destined either to darken his day or to disperse every cloud from the horizon. Algar, the only possible rival to his power, the only opponent no arts could soften, — Algar, whose hereditary name endeared him to the Saxon laity, whose father's most powerful legacy was the love of the Saxon Church, whose martial and turbulent spirit had only the more elevated him in the esteem of the warlike Danes in East Anglia (the earldom in which he had succeeded Harold), by his father's death, lord of the great principality of Mercia, — availed himself of that new power to break out again into rebellion. Again he was outlawed, again he leagued with the fiery Gryffyth. All Wales was in revolt; the Marches were invaded and laid waste. Rolf, the feeble Earl of Hereford, died at this critical juncture, and the Normans and hirelings under him mutinied against other leaders; a fleet of vikings from Norway ravaged the western coasts, and sailing up the Menai, joined the ships of Gryffyth, and the whole empire seemed menaced with dissolution, when Edward issued his Herr-ban, and Harold at the head of the royal armies marched on the foe.

Dread and dangerous were those defiles of Wales; amidst them had been foiled or slaughtered all the warriors under Rolf the Norman; no Saxon armies had won laurels in the Cymrian's own mountain-home within the memory of man; nor had any Saxon ships borne the palm from the terrible vikings of Norway. Fail, Harold, and farewell the crown! — succeed, and thou hast on thy side the *ultimam rationem regum* (the last argument of kings), the heart of the army over which thou art chief.

CHAPTER VI.

It was one day in the height of summer that two horsemen
rode slowly, and conversing with each other in friendly wise,
notwithstanding an evident difference of rank and of nation,
through the lovely country which formed the Marches of
Wales. The younger of these men was unmistakably a Norman; his cap only partially covered the head, which was
shaven from the crown to the nape of the neck,[1] while in
front the hair, closely cropped, curled short and thick round
a haughty but intelligent brow. His dress fitted close to his
shape, and was worn without mantle; his leggings were curiously crossed in the fashion of a tartan, and on his heels were
spurs of gold. He was wholly unarmed; but behind him and
his companion, at a little distance, his war-horse, completely
caparisoned, was led by a single squire, mounted on a good
Norman steed; while six Saxon theowes, themselves on foot,
conducted three sumpter-mules, somewhat heavily laden, not
only with the armour of the Norman knight, but panniers
containing rich robes, wines, and provender. At a few paces
farther behind marched a troop, light-armed, in tough hides,
curiously tanned, with axes swung over their shoulders, and
bows in their hands.

The companion of the knight was as evidently a Saxon as
the knight was unequivocally a Norman. His square short
features, contrasting the oval visage and aquiline profile of
his close-shaven comrade, were half concealed beneath a bushy
beard and immense mustache. His tunic, also, was of hide,
and tightened at the waist, fell loose to his knee; while a kind
of cloak, fastened to the right shoulder by a large round
button or brooch, flowed behind and in front, but left both
arms free. His cap differed in shape from the Norman's,

---

[1] Bayeux tapestry.

being round and full at the sides, somewhat in shape like a turban. His bare, brawny throat was curiously punctured with sundry devices, and a verse from the Psalms.

His countenance, though without the high and haughty brow, and the acute, observant eye of his comrade, had a pride and intelligence of its own, — a pride somewhat sullen, and an intelligence somewhat slow.

"My good friend Sexwolf," quoth the Norman, in very tolerable Saxon, "I pray you not so to misesteem us. After all, we Normans are of your own race: our fathers spoke the same language as yours."

"That may be," said the Saxon, bluntly; "and so did the Danes, with little difference, when they burned our houses and cut our throats."

"Old tales those," replied the knight, "and I thank thee for the comparison; for the Danes, thou seest, are now settled amongst ye, peaceful subjects and quiet men, and in a few generations it will be hard to guess who comes from Saxon, who from Dane."

"We waste time, talking such matters," returned the Saxon, feeling himself instinctively no match in argument for his lettered companion; and seeing, with his native strong sense, that some ulterior object, though he guessed not what, lay hid in the conciliatory language of his companion; "nor do I believe, Master Mallet or Gravel, — forgive me if I miss of the right forms to address you, — that Norman will ever love Saxon, or Saxon Norman; so let us cut our words short. There stands the convent, at which you would like to rest and refresh yourself."

The Saxon pointed to a low, clumsy building of timber, forlorn and decayed, close by a rank marsh, over which swarmed gnats and all foul animalcules.

Mallet de Graville, for it was he, shrugged his shoulders, and said, with an air of pity and contempt, —

"I would, friend Sexwolf, that thou couldst but see the houses we build to God and his saints, in our Normandy, — fabrics of stately stone, on the fairest sites. Our Countess Matilda hath a notable taste for the masonry; and our workmen are the brethren of Lombardy, who know all the mysteries thereof."

"I pray thee, Dan-Norman," cried the Saxon, "not to put such ideas into the soft head of King Edward. We pay enow for the Church, though built but of timber; saints help us, indeed, if it were builded of stone!"

The Norman crossed himself, as if he had heard some signal impiety, and then said, —

"Thou lovest not Mother Church, worthy Sexwolf?"

"I was brought up," replied the sturdy Saxon, "to work and sweat hard; and I love not the lazy who devour my sub stance, and say, 'The saints gave it them.' Knowest thou not, Master Mallet, that one third of all the lands of England is in the hands of the priests?"

"Hem!" said the acute Norman, who with all his devotion could stoop to wring worldly advantage from each admission of his comrade, "then in this merrie England of thine thou hast still thy grievances and cause of complaint?"

"Yea, indeed, and I trow it," quoth the Saxon, even in that day a grumbler; "but I take it, the main difference between thee and me is, that I can say what mislikes me out like a man; and it would fare ill with thy limbs or thy life if thou wert as frank in the grim land of thy heretogh."

"Now, *Notre Dame* stop thy prating," said the Norman, in high disdain, while his brow frowned and his eye sparkled. "Strong judge and great captain as is William the Norman, his barons and knights hold their heads high in his presence, and not a grievance weighs on the heart that we give not out with the lip."

"So have I heard," said the Saxon, chuckling; "I have heard, indeed, that ye thegns, or great men, are free enow and plain-spoken; but what of the commons, — the sixhændmen and the ceorls, master Norman? Dare they speak as we speak of king and of law, of thegn and of captain?"

The Norman wisely curbed the scornful "No, indeed," that rushed to his lips, and said, all sweet and debonnair, —

"Each land hath its customs, dear Sexwolf: and if the Norman were king of England, he would take the laws as he finds them, and the ceorls would be as safe with William as Edward."

"The Norman king of England!" cried the Saxon, reddening to the tips of his great ears, "what dost thou babble of, stranger? The Norman! — how could that ever be?"

"Nay, I did but suggest — but suppose such a case," replied the knight, still smothering his wrath. "And why thinkest thou the conceit so outrageous? Thy king is childless; William is his next of kin, and dear to him as a brother; and if Edward did leave him the throne —"

"The throne is for no man to leave," almost roared the Saxon. "Thinkest thou the people of England are like cattle and sheep and chattels and theowes, to be left by will, as man fancies? The king's wish has its weight, no doubt; but the Witan hath its yea or its nay, and the Witan and Commons are seldom at issue thereon. Thy duke king of England! Marry! Ha! ha!"

"Brute!" muttered the knight to himself; then adding aloud, with his old tone of irony (now much habitually subdued by years and discretion), "Why takest thou so the part of the ceorls? — thou a captain, and well-nigh a thegn!"

"I was born a ceorl, and my father before me," returned Sexwolf, "and I feel with my class; though my grandson may rank with the thegns, and, for aught I know, with the earls."

The Sire de Graville involuntarily drew off from the Saxon's side, as if made suddenly aware that he had grossly demeaned himself in such unwitting familiarity with a ceorl and a ceorl's son; and he said, with a much more careless accent and lofty port than before, —

"Good man, thou wert a ceorl, and now thou leadest Earl Harold's men to the war! How is this? I do not quite comprehend it."

"How shouldst thou, poor Norman?" replied the Saxon, compassionately. "The tale is soon told. Know that when Harold our Earl was banished, and his lands taken, we his ceorls helped with his sixhændman, Clapa, to purchase his land, nigh by London, and the house wherein thou didst find me, of a stranger, thy countryman, to whom they were lawlessly given. And we tilled the land, we tended the herds, and we kept the house till the earl came back."

"Ye had moneys, then, moneys of your own, ye ceorls!" said the Norman, avariciously.

"How else could we buy our freedom? Every ceorl hath some hours to himself to employ to his profit, and can lay by for his own ends. These savings we gave up for our earl, and when the earl came back, he gave the sixhændman hides of land enow to make him a thegn; and he gave the ceorls who had holpen Clapa their freedom and broad shares of his boc-land, and most of them now hold their own ploughs and feed their own herds. But I loved the earl (having no wife) better than swine and glebe, and I prayed him to let me serve him in arms. And so I have risen, as with us ceorls can rise."

"I am answered," said Mallet de Graville, thoughtfully, and still somewhat perplexed. "But these theowes (they are slaves) never rise. It cannot matter to them whether shaven Norman or bearded Saxon sit on the throne?"

"Thou art right there," answered the Saxon; "it matters as little to them as it doth to thy thieves and felons, for many of them are felons and thieves, or the children of such; and most of those who are not, it is said, are not Saxons, but the barbarous folks whom the Saxons subdued. No, wretched things, and scarce men, they care nought for the land. Howbeit, even they are not without hope, for the Church takes their part; and that, at least, I for one think Church-worthy," added the Saxon, with a softened eye. "And every abbot is bound to set free three theowes on his lands, and few who own theowes die without freeing some by their will; so that the sons of theowes may be thegns, and thegns some of them are at this day."

"Marvels!" cried the Norman. "But surely they bear a stain and stigma, and their fellow-thegns flout them?"

"Not a whit, — why so? Land is land, money money. Little, I trow, care we what a man's father may have been, if the man himself hath his ten hides or more of good boc-land."

"Ye value land and the moneys," said the Norman; "so do we, but we value more name and birth."

"Ye are still in your leading-strings, Norman," replied the Saxon, waxing good-humoured in his contempt. "We have an old saying and a wise one, 'All come from Adam except Tib the ploughman: but when Tib grows rich, all call him 'dear brother.'"

"With such pestilent notions," quoth the Sire de Graville, no longer keeping temper, "I do not wonder that our fathers of Norway and Daneland beat ye so easily. The love for things ancient — creed, lineage, and name — is better steel against the stranger than your smiths ever welded."

Therewith, and not waiting for Sexwolf's reply, he clapped spurs to his palfrey, and soon entered the courtyard of the convent.

A monk of the order of Saint Benedict,[1] then most in favour, ushered the noble visitor into the cell of the abbot; who, after gazing at him a moment in wonder and delight, clasped him to his breast and kissed him heartily on brow and cheek.

"Ah, Guillaume," he exclaimed in the Norman tongue, "this is indeed a grace for which to sing *Jubilate*. Thou canst not guess how welcome is the face of a countryman in this horrible land of ill-cooking and exile."

"Talking of grace, my dear father, and food," said De Graville, loosening the cincture of the tight vest which gave him the shape of a wasp, — for even at that early period small waists were in vogue with the warlike fops of the French Continent, — "talking of grace, the sooner thou say'st it over some friendly refection, the more will the Latin sound unctuous and musical. I have journeyed since daybreak, and am now hungered and faint."

"Alack, alack!" cried the abbot, plaintively, "thou knowest little, my son, what hardships we endure in these parts, — how larded our larders, and how nefarious our fare. The flesh of swine salted — "

"The flesh of Beelzebub," cried Mallet de Graville, aghast.

[1] Indeed, apparently the only monastic order in England.

"But comfort thee, I have stores on my sumpter-mules, — *poulardes* and fishes, and other not despicable comestibles, and a few flasks of wine, not pressed, laud the saints! from the vines of this country: wherefore, wilt thou see to it, and instruct thy cooks how to season the cheer?"

"No cooks have I to trust to," replied the abbot, — "of cooking know they here as much as of Latin; nathless, I will go and do my best with the stewpans. Meanwhile thou wilt at least have rest and the bath. For the Saxons, even in their convents, are a clean race, and learned the bath from the Dane."

"That I have noted," said the knight, "for even at the smallest house at which I have lodged in my way from London, the host hath courteously offered me the bath, and the hostess linen curious and fragrant; and to say truth, the poor people are hospitable and kind, despite their uncouth hate of the foreigner; nor is their meat to be despised, plentiful and succulent; but, *pardex*, as thou sayest, little helped by the art of dressing. Wherefore, my father, I will while the time till the *poulardes* be roasted, and the fish broiled or stewed, by the ablutions thou profferest me. I shall tarry with thee some hours, for I have much to learn."

The abbot then led the Sire de Graville by the hand to the cell of honour and guestship, and having seen that the bath prepared was of warmth sufficient, — for both Norman and Saxon, hardy men as they seem to us from afar, so shuddered at the touch of cold water, that a bath of natural temperature, as well as a hard bed, was sometimes imposed as a penance, — the good father went his way, to examine the sumpter-mules, and admonish the much suffering and bewildered lay-brother who officiated as cook, and who, speaking neither Norman nor Latin, scarce made out one word in ten of his superior's elaborate exhortations.

Mallet's squire, with a change of raiment, and goodly coffers of soaps, unguents, and odours, took his way to the knight, — for a Norman of birth was accustomed to much personal attendance, and had all respect for the body; and it was nearly an hour before, in a long gown of fur, reshaven, dainty, and decked, the Sire de Graville bowed and sighed and prayed before the refection set out in the abbot's cell.

The two Normans, despite the sharp appetite of the layman, ate with great gravity and decorum, drawing forth the morsels served to them on spits with silent examination; seldom more than tasting, with looks of patient dissatisfaction, each of the comestibles; sipping rather than drinking, nibbling rather than devouring, washing their fingers in rose-water with nice care at the close, and waving them afterwards gracefully in the air, to allow the moisture somewhat to exhale before they wiped off the lingering dews with their napkins. Then they exchanged looks and sighed in concert, as if recalling the polished manners of Normandy, still retained in that desolate exile. And their temperate meal thus concluded, dishes, wines, and attendants vanished, and their talk commenced.

"How camest thou in England?" asked the abbot, abruptly.

"Sauf your reverence," answered De Graville, "not wholly for reasons different from those that bring thee hither. When, after the death of that truculent and orgulous Godwin, King Edward entreated Harold to let him have back some of his dear Norman favourites, thou, then little pleased with the plain fare and sharp discipline of the convent of Bec, didst pray Bishop William of London to accompany such train as Harold, moved by his poor king's supplication, was pleased to permit. The bishop consented, and thou wert enabled to change monk's cowl for abbot's mitre. In a word, ambition brought thee to England, and ambition brings me hither."

"Hem! and how? Mayst thou thrive better than I in this swine-sty!"

"You remember," renewed De Graville, "that Lanfranc the Lombard was pleased to take interest in my fortunes, then not the most flourishing, and after his return from Rome, with the Pope's dispensation for Count William's marriage with his cousin, he became William's most trusted adviser. Both William and Lanfranc were desirous to set an example of learning to our Latinless nobles, and therefore my scholarship found grace in their eyes. In brief, since then I have

prospered and thriven. I have fair lands by the Seine, free
from clutch of merchant and Jew. I have founded a convent,
and slain some hundreds of Breton marauders. Need I say
that I am in high favour? Now it so chanced that a cousin
of mine, Hugo de Magnaville, a brave lance and franc-rider,
chanced to murder his brother in a little domestic affray, and
being of conscience tender and nice, the deed preyed on him,
and he gave his lands to Odo of Bayeux, and set off·to Jerusalem. There, having prayed at the Tomb" (the knight
crossed himself), "he felt at once miraculously cheered and
relieved; but, journeying back, mishaps befell him. He was
made slave by some infidel, to one of whose wives he sought
to be gallant, *par amours*, and only escaped at last by setting
fire to paynim and prison. Now, by the aid of the Virgin, he
has got back to Rouen, and holds his own land again in fief
from proud Odo, as a knight of the bishop's. It so happened
that, passing homeward through Lycia, before these misfortunes befell him, he made friends with a fellow-pilgrim who
had just returned, like himself, from the Sepulchre, but not
lightened, like him, of the load of his crime. This poor
palmer lay broken-hearted and dying in the hut of an eremite,
where my cousin took shelter; and, learning that Hugo was
on his way to Normandy, he made himself known as Sweyn,
the once fair and proud Earl of England, eldest son to old
Godwin, and father to Haco, whom our count still holds as a
hostage. He besought Hugo to intercede with the count for
Haco's speedy release and return, if King Edward assented
thereto; and charged my cousin, moreover, with a letter to
Harold, his brother, which Hugo undertook to send over. By
good luck, it so chanced that through all his sore trials cousin
Hugo kept safe round his neck a leaden effigy of the Virgin.
The infidels disdained to rob him of lead, little dreaming the
worth which the sanctity gave to the metal. To the back of
the image Hugo fastened the letter; and so, though somewhat tattered and damaged, he had it still with him on
arriving in Rouen.

"Knowing, then, my grace with the count, and not, despite
absolution and pilgrimage, much wishing to trust himself in

the presence of William, who thinks gravely of fratricide, he prayed me to deliver the message, and ask leave to send to England the letter."

"It is a long tale," quoth the abbot.

"Patience, my father! I am nearly at the end. Nothing more in season could chance for my fortunes. Know that William has been long moody and anxious as to matters in England. The secret accounts he receives from the Bishop of London make him see that Edward's heart is much alienated from him, especially since the count has had daughters and sons; for, as thou knowest, William and Edward both took vows of chastity in youth,[1] and William got absolved from his, while Edward hath kept firm to the plight. Not long ere my cousin came back, William had heard that Edward had acknowledged his kinsman as natural heir to his throne. Grieved and troubled at this, William had said in my hearing, 'Would that amidst yon statues of steel there were some cool head and wise tongue I could trust with my interests in England! and would that I could devise fitting plea and excuse for an envoy to Harold the Earl!' Much had I mused over these words, and a light-hearted man was Mallet de Graville, when, with Sweyn's letter in hand, he went to Lanfranc the abbot, and said, 'Patron and father! thou knowest that I, almost alone of the Norman knights, have studied the Saxon language. And if the duke wants messenger and plea, here stands the messenger, and in his hand is the plea.' Then I told my tale. Lanfranc went at once to Duke William. By this time news of the Atheling's death had arrived, and things looked more bright to my liege. Duke William was pleased to summon me straightway, and give me his instructions. So over the sea I came alone, save a single squire, reached London, learned the king and his court were at Winchester (but with them I had little to do), and that Harold the Earl was at the head of his forces in Wales against Gryffyth the Lion King. The earl had sent in haste for a picked and chosen band of his own retainers, on his demesnes near the city. These I joined, and learning thy name at the

---

[1] See note to Robert of Gloucester, vol. ii. p. 372.

monastery at Gloucester, I stopped here to tell thee my news
and hear thine."

"Dear brother," said the abbot, looking enviously on the
knight, "would that, like thee, instead of entering the
Church, I had taken up arms! Alike once was our lot,
well born and penniless. Ah me! Thou art now as the
swan on the river, and I as the shell on the rock."

"But," quoth the knight, "though the canons, it is true,
forbid monks to knock people on the head, except in self-
preservation, thou knowest well that even in Normandy
(which, I take it, is the sacred college of all priestly lore
on this side the Alps) those canons are deemed too rigorous
for practice; and at all events, it is not forbidden thee to look
on the pastime with sword or mace by thy side in case of
need. Wherefore, remembering thee in times past, I little
counted on finding thee like a slug in thy cell; no, but
with mail on thy back, the canons clean forgotten, and helping
stout Harold to sliver and brain these turbulent Welchmen!"

"Ah me! ah me! No such good fortune!" sighed the tall
abbot. "Little, despite thy former sojourn in London and
thy lore of their tongue, knowest thou of these unmannerly
Saxons. Rarely indeed do abbot and prelate ride to the battle;[1] and were it not for a huge Danish monk, who took
refuge here to escape mutilation for robbery, and who mis-
takes the Virgin for a Valkyr, and Saint Peter for Thor, —
were it not, I say, that we now and then have a bout at sword-
play together, my arm would be quite out of practice."

"Cheer thee, old friend," said the knight, pityingly; "better
times may come yet. Meanwhile, now to affairs; for all I
hear strengthens all William has heard, that Harold the Earl
is the first man in England. Is it not so?"

"Truly, and without dispute."

---

[1] The Saxon priests were strictly forbidden to bear arms. — SPELM : *Concil.*
p. 238.

It is mentioned in the English Chronicles, as a very extraordinary circumstance, that a bishop of Hereford, who had been Harold's chaplain, did
actually take sword and shield against the Welch. Unluckily, this valiant
prelate was slain so soon that it was no encouraging example.

"Is he married, or celibate? For that is a question which even his own men seem to answer equivocally."

"Why, all the wandering minstrels have songs, I am told by those who comprehend this poor barbarous tongue, of the beauty of *Editha pulchra*, to whom it is said the earl is betrothed, or it may be worse. But he is certainly not married, for the dame is akin to him within the degrees of the Church."

"Hem, not married! that is well; and this Algar, or Elgar, — he is not now with the Welch, I hear."

"No; sore ill at Chester with wounds and much chafing, for he hath sense to see that his cause is lost. The Norwegian fleet have been scattered over the seas by the earl's ships, like birds in a storm. The rebel Saxons who joined Gryffyth under Algar have been so beaten that those who survive have deserted their chief, and Gryffyth himself is penned up in his last defiles, and cannot much longer resist the stout foe, who, by valorous Saint Michael, is truly a great captain. As soon as Gryffyth is subdued, Algar will be crushed in his retreat, like a bloated spider in his web; and then England will have rest, unless our liege, as thou hintest, set her to work again."

The Norman knight mused a few moments, before he said, —

"I understand, then, that there is no man in the land who is peer to Harold, — not, I suppose, Tostig his brother?"

"Not Tostig, surely, whom nought but Harold's repute keeps a day in his earldom. But of late — for he is brave and skilful in war — he hath done much to command the respect, though he cannot win back the love, of his fierce Northumbrians, for he hath holpen the earl gallantly in this invasion of Wales, both by sea and by land. But Tostig shines only from his brother's light; and if Gurth were more ambitious, Gurth alone could be Harold's rival."

The Norman, much satisfied with the information thus gleaned from the abbot, who, despite his ignorance of the Saxon tongue, was, like all his countrymen, acute and curious, now rose to depart. The abbot, detaining him a few moments, and looking at him wistfully, said in a low voice, —

"What thinkest thou are Count William's chances of England?"

"Good, if he have recourse to stratagem; sure, if he can win Harold."

"Yet, take my word, the English love not the Normans, and will fight stiffly."

"That I believe. But if fighting must be, I see that it will be the fight of a single battle, for there is neither fortress nor mountain to admit of long warfare. And look you, my friend, everything here is *worn out!* The royal line is extinct with Edward, save in a child, whom I hear no man name as a successor; the old nobility are gone, there is no reverence for old names; the Church is as decrepit in the spirit as thy lath monastery is decayed in its timbers; the martial spirit of the Saxon is half rotted away in the subjugation to a clergy, not brave and learned, but timid and ignorant; the desire for money eats up all manhood; the people have been accustomed to foreign monarchs under the Danes; and William, once victor, would have but to promise to retain the old laws and liberties, to establish himself as firmly as Canute. The Anglo-Danes might trouble him somewhat, but rebellion would become a weapon in the hands of a schemer like William. He would bristle all the land with castles and forts, and hold it as a camp. My poor friend, we shall live yet to exchange gratulations, — thou prelate of some fair English see, and I baron of broad English lands."

"I think thou art right," said the tall abbot, cheerily; "and marry, when the day comes, I will at least fight for the duke. Yea, thou art right," he continued, looking round the dilapidated walls of the cell; "all here is worn out, and nought can restore the realm, save the Norman William, or — "

"Or who?"

"Or the Saxon Harold. But thou goest to see him, — judge for thyself."

"I will do so, and heedfully," said the Sire de Graville; and embracing his friend, he renewed his journey.

CHAPTER VII.

MESSIRE MALLET DE GRAVILLE possessed in perfection that cunning astuteness which characterized the Normans, as it did all the old pirate races of the Baltic; and if, O reader, thou peradventure shouldst ever in this remote day have dealings with the tall men of Ebor or Yorkshire, there wilt thou yet find the old Dane-father's wit, — it may be to thy cost, — more especially if treating for those animals which the ancestors ate, and which the sons, without eating, still manage to fatten on.

But though the crafty knight did his best, during his progress from London into Wales, to extract from Sexwolf all such particulars respecting Harold and his brethren as he had reasons for wishing to learn, he found the stubborn sagacity or caution of the Saxon more than a match for him. Sexwolf had a dog's instinct in all that related to his master; and he felt, though he scarce knew why, that the Norman cloaked some design upon Harold in all the cross-questionings so carelessly ventured. And his stiff silence or bluff replies when Harold was mentioned contrasted much the unreserve of his talk when it turned upon the general topics of the day, or the peculiarities of Saxon manners.

By degrees, therefore, the knight, chafed and foiled, drew into himself; and seeing no further use could be made of the Saxon, suffered his own national scorn of villein companionship to replace his artificial urbanity. He therefore rode alone, and a little in advance of the rest, noticing with a soldier's eye the characteristics of the country, and marvelling, while he rejoiced, at the insignificance of the defences which, even on the Marches, guarded the English country from the Cymrian ravager.[1] In musings of no very auspi-

[1] See Note K.

cious and friendly nature towards the land he thus visited, the Norman, on the second day from that in which he had conversed with the abbot, found himself amongst the savage defiles of North Wales.

Pausing there in a narrow pass overhung with wild and desolate rocks, the knight deliberately summoned his squires, clad himself in his ring mail, and mounted his great *destrier*.

"Thou dost wrong, Norman," said Sexwolf, "thou fatiguest thyself in vain, — heavy arms here are needless. I have fought in this country before; and as for thy steed, thou wilt soon have to forsake it, and march on foot."

"Know, friend," retorted the knight, "that I come not here to learn the horn-book of war; and for the rest, know also, that a noble of Normandy parts with his life ere he forsakes his good steed."

"Ye outlanders and Frenchmen," said Sexwolf, showing the whole of his teeth through his forest of beard, "love boast and big talk; and, on my troth, thou mayest have thy belly full of them yet, for we are still in the track of Harold, and Harold never leaves behind him a foe. Thou art as safe here as if singing psalms in a convent."

"For thy jests, let them pass, courteous sir," said the Norman; "but I pray thee only not to call me Frenchman.[1] I impute it to thy ignorance in things comely and martial, and not to thy design to insult me. Though my own mother was French, learn that a Norman despises a Frank only less than he doth a Jew."

"Crave your grace," said the Saxon, "but I thought all ye outlanders were the same, rib and rib, sibbe and sibbe."

---

[1] The Normans and French detested each other: and it was the Norman who taught to the Saxon his own animosities against the Frank. A very eminent antiquary, indeed, De la Rue, considered that the Bayeux tapestry could not be the work of Matilda, or her age, because in it the Normans are called *French*. But that is a gross blunder on his part; for William, in his own charters, calls the Normans "Franci." Wace, in his "Roman de Rou," often styles the Normans "French;" and William of Poitiers, a contemporary of the Conqueror, gives them also in one passage the same name. Still, it is true that the Normans were generally very tenacious of their distinction from their gallant but hostile neighbours.

"Thou wilt know better one of these days. March on, master Sexwolf."

The pass gradually opened on a wide patch of rugged and herbless waste; and Sexwolf, riding up to the knight, directed his attention to a stone on which was inscribed the words, "Hic victor fuit Haroldus" (Here Harold conquered).

"In sight of a stone like that, no Walloon dare come," said the Saxon.

"A simple and classical trophy," remarked the Norman, complacently, "and saith much. I am glad to see thy lord knows the Latin."

"I say not that he knows Latin," replied the prudent Saxon, fearing that that could be no wholesome information on his lord's part which was of a kind to give gladness to the Norman. "Ride on while the road lets ye, — in God's name."

On the confines of Caernarvonshire the troop halted at a small village, round which had been newly dug a deep military trench, bristling with palisades; and within its confines might be seen — some reclined on the grass, some at dice, some drinking — many men, whose garbs of tanned hide, as well as a pennon waving from a little mound in the midst, bearing the tiger heads of Earl Harold's insignia, showed them to be Saxons.

"Here we shall learn," said Sexwolf, "what the earl is about, — and here, at present, ends my journey."

"Are these the earl's head-quarters then? — no castle, even of wood, — no wall, nought but ditch and palisades?" asked Mallet de Graville, in a tone between surprise and contempt.

"Norman," said Sexwolf, "the castle is there, though you see it not, and so are the walls. The castle is Harold's name, which no Walloon will dare to confront; and the walls are the heaps of the slain which lie in every valley around." So saying, he wound his horn, which was speedily answered, and led the way over a plank which admitted across the trench.

"Not even a drawbridge!" groaned the knight.

Sexwolf exchanged a few words with one who seemed the head of the small garrison, and then regaining the Norman, said, —

"The earl and his men have advanced into the mountainous regions of Snowdon; and there, it is said, the blood-lusting Gryffyth is at length driven to bay. Harold hath left orders that after as brief a refreshment as may be, I and my men, taking the guide he hath left for us, join him on foot. There may now be danger; for though Gryffyth himself may be pinned to his heights, he may have yet some friends in these parts to start up from crag and combe. The way on horse is impassable; wherefore, master Norman, as our quarrel is not thine nor thine our lord, I commend thee to halt here in peace and in safety, with the sick and the prisoners."

"It is a merry companionship, doubtless," said the Norman; "but one travels to learn, and I would fain see somewhat of thine uncivil skirmishings with these men of the mountains; wherefore, as I fear my poor mules are light of the provender, give me to eat and to drink. And then shalt thou see, should we come in sight of the enemy, if a Norman's big words are the sauce of small deeds."

"Well spoken, and better than I reckoned on," said Sexwolf, heartily.

While De Graville, alighting, sauntered about the village, the rest of the troop exchanged greetings with their countrymen. It was, even to the warrior's eye, a mournful scene. Here and there, heaps of ashes and ruin, — houses riddled and burned, — the small, humble church, untouched indeed by war, but looking desolate and forlorn, — with sheep grazing on large recent mounds thrown over the brave dead, who slept in the ancestral spot they had defended.

The air was fragrant with the spicy smells of the gale or bog myrtle; and the village lay sequestered in a scene wild indeed and savage, but prodigal of a stern beauty to which the Norman — poet by race, and scholar by culture — was not insensible. Seating himself on a rude stone, apart from all the warlike and murmuring groups, he looked forth on the dim and vast mountain peaks, and the rivulet that rushed below, intersecting the village, and lost amidst copses of mountain ash. From these more refined contemplations he was roused by Sexwolf, who with greater courtesy than was habitual to him accompanied the theowes who brought the knight a repast, consisting of cheese, and small pieces of seethed kid, with a large horn of very indifferent mead.

"The earl puts all his men on Welch diet," said the captain, apologetically; "for indeed, in this lengthy warfare, nought else is to be had!"

The knight curiously inspected the cheese, and bent earnestly over the kid.

"It sufficeth, good Sexwolf," said he, suppressing a natural sigh. "But instead of this honey-drink, which is more fit for bees than for men, get me a draught of fresh water: water is your only safe drink before fighting."

"Thou hast never drank ale, then!" said the Saxon; "but thy foreign tastes shall be heeded, strange man."

A little after noon the horns were sounded, and the troop prepared to depart. But the Norman observed that they had left behind all their horses; and his squire, approaching, informed him that Sexwolf had positively forbidden the knight's steed to be brought forth.

"Was it ever heard before," cried Sire Mallet de Graville, "that a Norman knight was expected to walk, and to walk against a foe too! Call hither the villein, — that is, the captain."

But Sexwolf himself here appeared, and to him De Graville addressed his indignant remonstrance. The Saxon stood firm, and to each argument replied simply, "It is the earl's orders;" and finally wound up with a bluff — "Go or let alone; stay here with thy horse, or march with us on thy feet."

"My horse is a gentleman," answered the knight, "and, as such, would be my more fitting companion. But as it is, I yield to compulsion, — I bid thee solemnly observe, by compulsion; so that it may never be said of William Mallet de Graville, that he walked, *bon gré*, to battle." With that he loosened his sword in the sheath, and still retaining his ring mail, fitting close as a shirt, strode on with the rest.

A Welch guide, subject to one of the under-kings (who was in allegiance to England, and animated, as many of those petty chiefs were, with a vindictive jealousy against the rival tribe of Gryffyth, far more intense than his dislike of the Saxon), led the way.

The road wound for some time along the course of the river Conway; Penmaen-mawr loomed before them. Not a human being came in sight, not a goat was seen on the distant ridges, not a sheep on the pastures. The solitude in the glare of the broad August sun was oppressive. Some houses they passed, — if buildings of rough stones, containing but a single room, can be called houses, — but they were deserted. Desolation preceded their way, for they were on the track of Harold the Victor. At length they passed the old Conovium, now Caer-hên, lying low near the river. There were still (not as we now scarcely discern them, after centuries of havoc) the mighty ruins of the Romans, — vast shattered walls, a tower half demolished, visible remnants of gigantic baths, and, proudly rising near the present ferry of Tal-y-Cafn, the fortress, almost unmutilated, of Castell-y-Bryn. On the castle waved the pennon of Harold. Many large flat-bottomed boats were moored to the river-side, and the whole place bristled with spears and javelins.

Much comforted, — for, though he disdained to murmur, and rather than forego his mail, would have died therein a martyr, Mallet de Graville was mightily wearied by the weight of his steel, — and hoping now to see Harold him-self, the knight sprang forward with a spasmodic effort at liveliness, and found himself in the midst of a group, among whom he recognized at a glance his old acquaintance, Godrith. Doffing his helm with its long nose-piece, he caught the thegn's hand, and exclaimed, —

"Well met, *ventre de Guillaume!* well met, O Godree the debonair! Thou rememberest Mallet de Graville, and in this unseemly guise, on foot, and with villeins, sweating under the eyes of plebeian Phœbus, thou beholdest that much-suffering man!"

"Welcome, indeed," returned Godrith, with some embar-rassment; "but how camest thou hither, and whom seekest thou?"

"Harold, thy count, man, — and I trust he is here."

"Not so, but not far distant, — at a place by the mouth of the river called Caer Gyffin.[1] Thou shalt take boat, and be there ere the sunset."

"Is a battle at hand? Yon churl disappointed and tricked me; he promised me danger, and not a soul have we met."

"Harold's besom sweeps clean," answered Godrith, smiling. "But thou art like, perhaps, to be in at the death. We have driven this Welch lion to bay at last, — he is ours, or grim Famine's. Look yonder!" and Godrith pointed to the heights of Penmaen-mawr. "Even at this distance you may yet descry something gray and dim against the sky."

"Deemest thou my eye so ill practised in siege as not to see towers? Tall and massive they are, though they seem here as airy as masts and as dwarfish as landmarks."

"On that hill-top and in those towers is Gryffyth, the Welch king, with the last of his force. He cannot escape us; our ships guard all the coasts of the shore; our troops, as here, surround every pass. Spies, night and day, keep watch. The Welch moels (or beacon-rocks) are manned by our warders; and were the Welch King to descend, signals would blaze from post to post, and gird him with fire and sword. From land to land, from hill to hill, from Hereford to Caerleon, from Caerleon to Milford, from Milford to Snowdon, through Snowdon to yonder fort, — built, they say, by the fiends or the giants, — through defile and through forest, over rock, through morass, we have pressed on his heels. Battle and foray alike have drawn the blood from his heart; and thou wilt have seen the drops yet red on the way, where the stone tells that Harold was victor."

"A brave man and true king, then, this Gryffyth," said the Norman, with some admiration; "but," he added in a colder tone, "I confess, for my own part, that though I pity the valiant man beaten, I honour the brave man who wins; and though I have seen but little of this rough land as yet, I can well judge from what I have seen, that no captain not of patience unwearied and skill most consummate could conquer a bold enemy in a country where every rock is a fort."

[1] The present town and castle of Conway.

"So I fear," answered Godrith, "that thy countryman Rolf
found; for the Welch beat him sadly, and the reason was
plain.   He insisted on using horses where no horses could
climb, and attiring men in full armour to fight against men
light and nimble as swallows, that skim the earth, then are
lost in the clouds.   Harold, more wise, turned our Saxons into
Welchmen, flying as they flew, climbing where they climbed;
it has been as a war of the birds.   And now there rests but the
eagle, in his last lonely eyry."

"Thy battles have improved thy eloquence much, Messire
Godree," said the Norman, condescendingly.   "Nevertheless,
I cannot but think a few light horse — "

"Could scale yon mountain-brow?" said Godrith, laughing,
and pointing to Penmaen-mawr.

The Norman looked and was silent, though he thought to
himself, "That Sexwolf was no such dolt, after all!"

BOOK VII.

THE WELCH KING.

CHAPTER I.

THE sun had just cast its last beams over the breadth of water into which Conway, or rather Cyn-wy, "the great river," emerges its winding waves. Not at that time existed the matchless castle which is now the monument of Edward Plantagenet and the boast of Wales. But besides all the beauty the spot took from Nature, it had even some claim from ancient art. A rude fortress rose above the stream of Gyffin, out of the wrecks of some greater Roman hold,[1] and vast ruins of a former town lay round it; while opposite the fort, on the huge and ragged promontory of Gogarth, might still be seen, forlorn and gray, the wrecks of the imperial city, destroyed ages before by lightning.

All these remains of a power and a pomp that Rome in vain had bequeathed to the Briton were full of pathetic and solemn interest, when blent with the thought that on yonder steep the brave prince of a race of heroes whose line transcended by ages all the other royalties of the North, awaited, amidst the ruins of man and in the stronghold which Nature yet gave, the hour of his doom.

But these were not the sentiments of the martial and observant Norman, with the fresh blood of a new race of conquerors.

"In this land," thought he, "far more even than in that of the Saxon, there are the ruins of old; and when the present

[1] See Camden's Britannia: "Caernarvonshire."

can neither maintain nor repair the past, its future is subjection or despair."

Agreeably to the peculiar usages of Saxon military skill, which seems to have placed all strength in dikes and ditches, as being perhaps the cheapest and readiest outworks, a new trench has been made round the fort on two sides, connecting it on the third and fourth with the streams of Gyffin and the Conway. But the boat was rowed up to the very walls; and the Norman, springing to land, was soon ushered into the presence of the earl.

Harold was seated before a rude table, and bending over a rough map of the great mountain of Penmaen; a lamp of iron stood beside the map, though the air was yet clear.

The earl rose, as De Graville, entering with the proud but easy grace habitual to his countrymen, said, in his best Saxon, —

"Hail to Earl Harold! William Mallet de Graville, the Norman, greets him, and brings him news from beyond the seas."

There was only one seat in that bare room, — the seat from which the earl had risen. He placed it with simple courtesy before his visitor, and leaning himself against the table, said in the Norman tongue, which he spoke fluently, —

"It is no slight thanks that I owe to the Sire de Graville that he hath undertaken voyage and journey on my behalf; but before you impart your news, I pray you to take rest and food."

"Rest will not be unwelcome; and food, if unrestricted to goats' cheese and kid-flesh, — luxuries new to my palate, — will not be untempting; but neither food nor rest can I take, noble Harold, before I excuse myself, as a foreigner, for thus somewhat infringing your laws by which we are banished, and acknowledging gratefully the courteous behaviour I have met from thy countrymen notwithstanding."

"Fair Sir," answered Harold, "pardon us if, jealous of our laws, we have seemed inhospitable to those who would meddle with them. But the Saxon is never more pleased than when the foreigner visits him only as the friend: to the many who settle amongst us for commerce — Fleming, Lombard, German, and Saracen — we proffer shelter and welcome; to the few who, like thee, Sir Norman, venture over the seas but to serve us, we give frank cheer and free hand."

Agreeably surprised at this gracious reception from the son of Godwin, the Norman pressed the hand extended to him, and then drew forth a small case, and related accurately and with feeling the meeting of his cousin with Sweyn, and Sweyn's dying charge.

The earl listened, with eyes bent on the ground, and face turned from the lamp; and when Mallet had concluded his recital, Harold said, with an emotion he struggled in vain to repress, —

"I thank you cordially, gentle Norman, for kindness kindly rendered! I — I — " The voice faltered. "Sweyn was very dear to me in his sorrows! We heard that he had died in Lycia, and grieved much and long. So, after he had thus spoken to your cousin, he — he — Alas! O Sweyn, my brother!"

"He died," said the Norman, soothingly, "but shriven and absolved; and my cousin says, calm and hopeful, as they die ever who have knelt at the Saviour's tomb!"

Harold bowed his head, and turned the case that held the letter again and again in his hand, but would not venture to open it. The knight himself, touched by a grief so simple and manly, rose with the delicate instinct that belongs to sympathy, and retired to the door, without which yet waited the officer who had conducted him.

Harold did not attempt to detain him, but followed him across the threshold, and briefly commanding the officer to attend to his guest as to himself, said, —

"With the morning, Sire de Graville, we shall meet again; I see that you are one to whom I need not excuse man's natural emotions."

"A noble presence!" muttered the knight, as he descended the stairs; "but he hath Norman, at least Norse, blood in his veins on the distaff side. — Fair Sir!" (this aloud to the officer) "any meat save the kid-flesh, I pray thee; and any drink save the mead!"

"Fear not, guest," said the officer; "for Tostig the Earl hath two ships in yon bay, and hath sent us supplies that would please Bishop William of London, for Tostig the Earl is a toothsome man."

"Commend me, then, to Tostig the Earl," said the knight; "he is an earl after my own heart."

CHAPTER II.

On re-entering the room, Harold drew the large bolt across the door, opened the case, and took forth the distained and tattered scroll: —

" When this comes to thee, Harold, the brother of thy childish days will sleep in the flesh, and be lost to men's judgment and earth's woe in the spirit. I have knelt at the Tomb; but no dove hath come forth from the cloud, — no stream of grace hath re-baptized the child of wrath! They tell me now — monk and priest tell me — that I have atoned all my sins ; that the dread weregeld is paid ; that I may enter the world of men with a spirit free from the load, and a name redeemed from the stain. Think so, O brother! Bid my father (if he still lives, the dear old man!) think so; tell Githa to think it; and oh, teach Haco, my son, to hold the belief as a truth! Harold, again I commend to thee my son ; be to him as a father ! My death surely releases him as a hostage. Let him not grow up in the court of the stranger, in the land of our foes. Let his feet, in his youth, climb the green holts of England ; let his eyes, ere sin dims them, drink the blue of her skies ! When this shall reach thee, thou in thy calm, effortless strength wilt be more great than Godwin our father. Power came to him with travail and through toil, the geld of craft and of force. Power is born to thee as strength to the strong man; it gathers around thee as thou movest ; it is not thine aim, it is thy nature, to be great. Shield my child with thy might ; lead him forth from the prison-house by thy serene right hand ! I ask not for lordships and earldoms, as the appanage of his father, — train him not to be rival to thee, — I ask but for freedom and English air ! So counting on thee, O Harold, I turn my face to the wall, and hush my wild heart to peace ! "

The scroll dropped noiseless from Harold's hand.

"Thus," said he, mournfully, "hath passed away less a life than a dream! Yet of Sweyn, in our childhood, was Godwin most proud; who so lovely in peace, and so terrible in wrath? My mother taught him the songs of the Baltic, and Hilda led his steps through the woodland with tales of hero and scald. Alone of our House, he had the gift of the Dane in the flow of fierce song, and for him things lifeless had being. Stately tree, from which all the birds of heaven sent their carol, where the falcon took roost, whence the mavis flew forth in its glee, — how art thou blasted and seared, bough and core! — smit by the lightning and consumed by the worm!"

He paused; and though none were by, he long shaded his brow with his hand.

"Now," thought he, as he rose, and slowly paced the chamber, "now to what lives yet on earth, — his son! Often hath my mother urged me in behalf of these hostages, and often have I sent to reclaim them. Smooth and false pretexts have met my own demand, and even the remonstrance of Edward himself. But, surely, now that William hath permitted this Norman to bring over the letter, he will assent to what it hath become a wrong and an insult to refuse; and Haco will return to his father's land, and Wolnoth to his mother's arms."

CHAPTER III.

MESSIRE MALLET DE GRAVILLE, as becomes a man bred up to arms, and snatching sleep with quick grasp whenever that blessing be his to command, no sooner laid his head on the pallet to which he had been consigned than his eyes closed, and his senses were deaf even to dreams. But at the dead of the midnight he was wakened by sounds that might have roused the Seven Sleepers, — shouts, cries, and yells, the blast of horns, the tramp of feet, and the more distant roar of hurrying multitudes. He leaped from his bed, and the whole chamber was filled with a lurid blood-red air. His first thought was that the fort was on fire. But springing upon the settle along the wall, and looking through the loophole of the tower, it seemed as if not the fort but the whole land was one flame, and through the glowing atmosphere he beheld all the ground, near and far, swarming with men. Hundreds were swimming the rivulet, clambering up dike mounds, rushing on the levelled spears of the defenders, breaking through line and palisade, pouring into the enclosures, — some in half-armour of helm and corselet, others in linen tunics, many almost naked. Loud, sharp shrieks of "Alleluia!"[1] blended with those of "Out! out! Holy crosse!"[2] He divined at once that the Welch were storming the Saxon hold. Short time indeed sufficed for that active knight to case himself in his mail; and, sword in hand, he burst through the door, cleared the stairs, and gained the hall below, which was filled with men arming in haste.

"Where is Harold?" he exclaimed.

"On the trenches already," answered Sexwolf, buckling his corselet of hide. "This Welch hell hath broke loose."

"And yon are their beacon-fires? Then the whole land is upon us!"

"Prate less," quoth Sexwolf; "those are the hills now held by the warders of Harold. Our spies gave them notice, and the watchfires prepared us ere the fiends came in sight, otherwise we had been lying here limbless or headless. Now, men, draw up, and march forth." •

---

[1] When (A. D. 220) the bishops Germanicus and Lupus headed the Britons against the Picts and Saxons, in Easter week, fresh from their baptism in the Alyn, Germanicus ordered them to attend to his war-cry, and repeat it; he gave "Alleluia." The hills so loudly re-echoed the cry, that the enemy caught panic, and fled with great slaughter. Maes-Garmon, in Flintshire, was the scene of the victory.

[2] The cry of the English at the onset of battle was "Holy Crosse, God Almighty;" afterwards in fight, "Ouct, ouct" (out, out). — HEARNE: *Disc. Antiquity of Motts.*

The latter cry probably originated in the habit of defending their standard and central posts with barricades and closed shields; and thus, idiomatically and vulgarly, signified "get out!"

"Hold! hold!" cried the pious knight, crossing himself, "is there no priest here to bless us? First a prayer and a psalm!"

"Prayer and psalm!" cried Sexwolf, astonished; "an thou hadst said ale and mead, I could have understood thee — Out! out! — Holyrood, Holyrood!"

"The godless paynims!" muttered the Norman, borne away with the crowd.

Once in the open space, the scene was terrific. Brief as had been the onslaught, the carnage was already unspeakable. By dint of sheer physical numbers, animated by a valour that seemed as the frenzy of madmen or the hunger of wolves, hosts of the Britons had crossed trench and stream, seizing with their hands the points of the spears opposed to them, bounding over the corpses of their countrymen, and with yells of wild joy rushing upon the close serried lines drawn up before the fort. The stream seemed literally to run gore; pierced by javelins and arrows, corpses floated and vanished, while numbers, undeterred by the havoc, leaped into the waves from the opposite banks. Like bears that surround the ship of a sea-king beneath the polar meteors or the midnight sun of the north, came the savage warriors through that glaring atmosphere.

Amidst all, two forms were pre-eminent. The one, tall and towering, stood by the trench, and behind a banner, that now drooped round the stave, now streamed wide and broad, stirred by the rush of men, — for the night in itself was breezeless. With a vast Danish axe wielded by both hands, stood this man, confronting hundreds, and at each stroke, rapid as the levin, fell a foe. All round him was a wall of his own, — the dead. But in the centre of the space, leading on a fresh troop of shouting Welchmen who had forced their way from another part, was a form which seemed charmed against arrow and spear. For the defensive arms of this chief were as slight as if worn but for ornament; a small corselet of gold covered only the centre of his breast, a gold collar of twisted wires circled his throat, and a gold bracelet adorned his bare arm, dropping gore, not his own, from the wrist to the elbow. He was small and slight-shaped, — below the common standard of men, — but he seemed as one made a giant by the sublime inspiration of war. He wore no helmet, merely a golden circlet; and his hair, of deep red (longer than was usual with the Welch), hung like the mane of a lion over his shoulders, tossing loose with each stride. His eyes glared like the tiger's at night, and he leaped on the spears with a bound. Lost a moment amidst hostile ranks, save by the swift glitter of his short sword, he made, amidst all, a path for himself and his followers, and emerged from the heart of the steel unscathed and loud-breathing; while round the line he had broken, wheeled and closed his wild men, striking, rushing, slaying, slain.

"*Pardex*, this is war worth the sharing," said the knight. "And now, worthy Sexwolf, thou shalt see if the Norman is the vaunter thou deemest him. *Dieu nous aide! Notre Dame!* — Take the foe in the rear." But turning round, he perceived that Sexwolf had already led his men towards the standard, which showed them where stood the earl, almost alone in his peril. The knight, thus left to himself, did not hesitate; a minute more, and he was in the midst of the Welch force, headed by the chief with the golden panoply. Secure in his ring mail against the light weapons of the Welch, the sweep of the Norman sword was as the scythe of Death. Right and left he smote through the throng which he took in the flank, and had almost gained the small phalanx of Saxons that lay firm in the midst, when the Cymrian chief's flashing eye was drawn to this new and strange foe, by the roar and the groan round the Norman's way; and with the half-naked breast against the shirt of mail, and the short Roman sword against the long Norman falchion, the Lion King of Wales fronted the knight.

Unequal as seems the encounter, so quick was the spring of the Briton, so pliant his arm, and so rapid his weapon, that that good knight (who rather from skill and valour than brute physical strength ranked amongst the prowest of William's band of martial brothers) would willingly have preferred to see before him Fitzosborne or Montgommeri, all clad in steel and armed with mace and lance, than parried those dazzling strokes, and fronted the angry majesty of that helmless brow. Already the strong rings of his mail had been twice pierced, and his blood trickled fast, while his great sword had but smitten the air in its sweeps at the foe; when the Saxon phalanx, taking advantage of the breach in the ring that girt them, caused by this diversion, and recognizing with fierce ire the gold torque and breastplate of the Welch King, made their desperate charge. Then for some minutes the *pêle mêle* was confused and indistinct, — blows blind and at random, — death coming no man knew whence or how; till discipline and steadfast order (which the Saxons kept, as by mechanism, through the discord) obstinately prevailed. The wedge forced its way; and, though reduced in numbers and sore wounded, the Saxon troop cleared the ring, and joined the main force drawn up by the fort, and guarded in the rear by its wall.

Meanwhile Harold, supported by the band under Sexwolf, had succeeded at length in repelling further reinforcements of the Welch at the more accessible part of the trenches; and casting now his practised eye over the field, he issued orders for some of the men to regain the fort, and open from the battlements and from every loophole the batteries of stone and javelin, which then (with the Saxons, unskilled in sieges) formed the main artillery of forts. These orders given, he planted Sexwolf and most of his band to keep watch round the trenches; and shading his eye with his hand, and looking towards the moon, all waning and dimmed in the watchfires, he said calmly, —

"Now patience fights for us. Ere the moon reaches yon hill-top, the troops at Aber and Caer-hên will be on the slopes of Penmaen, and cut off the retreat of the Walloons. Advance my flag to the thick of yon strife."

But as the earl, with his axe swung over his shoulder, and followed but by some half-score or more with his banner, strode on where the wild war was now mainly concentred, just midway between trench and fort, Gryffyth caught sight both of the banner and the earl, and left the press at the very moment when he had gained the greatest advantage, and when indeed, but for the Norman, who, wounded as he was, and unused to fight on foot, stood resolute in the van, the Saxons, wearied out by numbers and falling fast beneath the javelins, would have fled into their walls, and so sealed their fate, — for the Welch would have entered at their heels.

But it was the misfortune of the Welch heroes never to learn that war is a science; and instead of now centring all force on the point most weakened, the whole field vanished from the fierce eye of the Welch King, when he saw the banner and form of Harold.

The earl beheld the coming foe, wheeling round, as the hawk on the heron; halted, drew up his few men in a semi-circle, with their large shields as a rampart, and their levelled spears as a palisade; and before them all, as a tower, stood Harold with his axe. In a minute more he was surrounded; and through the rain of javelins that poured upon him, hissed and glittered the sword of Gryffyth. But Harold, more prac-tised than the Sire de Graville in the sword-play of the Welch, and unencumbered by other defensive armour (save only the helm, which was shaped like the Norman's) than his light coat of hide, opposed quickness to quickness, and suddenly dropping his axe, sprang upon his foe, and clasping him round with the left arm, with the right hand griped at his throat, —

"Yield and quarter! — yield, for thy life, son of Llewellyn!"

Strong was that embrace, and deathlike that gripe; yet, as the snake from the hand of the dervise, as a ghost from the grasp of the dreamer, the lithe Cymrian glided away, and the broken torque was all that remained in the clutch of Harold.

At this moment a mighty yell of despair broke from the Welch near the fort: stones and javelins rained upon them from the walls, and the fierce Norman was in the midst, with his sword drinking blood; but not for javelin, stone, and sword, shrank and shouted the Welchmen. On the other side of the trenches were marching against them their own coun-trymen, the rival tribes that helped the stranger to rend the

land; and far to the right were seen the spears of the Saxon
from Aber, and to the left was heard the shout of the forces
under Godrith from Caer-hên; and they who had sought the
leopard in his lair were now themselves the prey caught in
the toils. With new heart, as they beheld these reinforcements, the Saxons pressed on; tumult and flight and indiscriminate slaughter wrapped the field. The Welch rushed to
the stream and the trenches; and in the bustle and hullabaloo
Gryffyth was swept along, as a bull by a torrent. Still facing
the foe, now chiding, now smiting his own men, now rushing
alone on the pursuers, and halting their onslaught, he gained,
still unwounded, the stream, paused a moment, laughed loud,
and sprang into the wave. A hundred javelins hissed into
the sullen and bloody waters. "Hold!" cried Harold the
Earl, lifting his hand on high; "no dastard dart at the
brave!"

CHAPTER IV.

THE fugitive Britons, scarce one tenth of the number that
had first rushed to the attack, performed their flight with
the same Parthian rapidity that characterized the assault;
and escaping both Welch foe and Saxon, though the former
broke ground to pursue them, they regained the steeps of
Penmaen.

There was no further thought of slumber that night within
the walls. While the wounded were tended, and the dead
were cleared from the soil, Harold, with three of his chiefs,
and Mallet de Graville, whose feats rendered it more than
ungracious to refuse his request that he might assist in the
council, conferred upon the means of terminating the war
with the next day. Two of the thegns, their blood hot with
strife and revenge, proposed to scale the mountain with the
whole force the reinforcements had brought them, and put all
they found to the sword. The third, old and prudent, and
inured to Welch warfare, thought otherwise.

"None of us," said he, "know what is the true strength of the place which ye propose to storm. Not even one Welchman have we found who hath ever himself gained the summit, or examined the castle which is said to exist there." [1]

"Said!" echoed De Graville, who, relieved of his mail, and with his wounds bandaged, reclined on his furs on the floor. "Said, noble sir! Cannot our eyes perceive the towers?"

The old thegn shook his head. "At a distance and through mists stones loom large, and crags themselves take strange shapes. It may be castle, may be rock, may be old roofless temples of heathenesse that we see. But to repeat (and, as I am slow, I pray not again to be put out in my speech), none of us know what there exists of defence, man-made or Nature-built. Not even thy Welch spies, son of Godwin, have gained to the heights. In the midst lie the scouts of the Welch King, and those on the top can see the bird fly, the goat climb. Few of thy spies, indeed, have ever returned with life; their heads have been left at the foot of the hill, with the scroll in their lips, 'Dic ad inferos quid in superis novisti,'—Tell to the shades below what thou hast seen in the heights above."

"And the Walloons know Latin!" muttered the knight; "I respect them!"

The slow thegn frowned, stammered, and renewed,—

"One thing at least is clear,—that the rock is well-nigh insurmountable to those who know not the passes; that strict watch, baffling even Welch spies, is kept night and day; that the men on the summit are desperate and fierce; that our own troops are awed and terrified by the belief of the Welch that the spot is haunted and the towers fiend-founded. One single defeat may lose us two years of victory. Gryffyth may break from the eyry, regain what he hath lost, win back our Welch allies, ever faithless and hollow. Wherefore, I say, go on as we have begun. Beset all the country round; cut off all supplies, and let the foe rot by famine, or waste, as he hath done this night his strength by vain onslaught and sally."

---

[1] Certain high places in Wales, of which this might well be one, were held so sacred that even the dwellers in the immediate neighbourhood never presumed to approach them.

"Thy counsel is good," said Harold, "but there is yet something to add to it, which may shorten the strife, and gain the
end with less sacrifice of life. The defeat of to-night will
have humbled the spirits of the Welch; take them yet in the
hour of despair and disaster. I wish, therefore, to send to
their outposts a nuncius, with these terms: 'Life and pardon
to all who lay down arms and surrender.'"

"What, after such havoc and gore?" cried one of the
thegns.

"They defend their own soil," replied the earl, simply;
"had not we done the same?"

"But the rebel Gryffyth?" asked the old thegn, — "thou
canst not accept *him* again as crowned sub-king of Edward?"

"No," said the earl; "I propose to exempt Gryffyth alone
from the pardon, with promise, nathless, of life, if he give
himself up as prisoner; and count, without further condition,
on the king's mercy."

There was a prolonged silence. None spoke against the
earl's proposal, though the two younger thegns misliked it
much.

At last said the elder: "But hast thou thought who will
carry this message? Fierce and wild are yon blood-dogs; and
man must needs shrive soul and make will, if he go to their
kennel."

"I feel sure that my bode will be safe," answered Harold;
"for Gryffyth has all the pride of a king, and, sparing neither
man nor child in the onslaught, will respect what the Roman
taught his sires to respect, — envoy from chief to chief, as a
head scathless and sacred."

"Choose whom thou wilt, Harold," said one of the young
thegns, laughing, "but spare thy friends; and whomsoever
thou choosest, pay his widow the weregeld."

"Fair sirs," then said De Graville, "if ye think that I,
though a stranger, could serve you as nuncius, it would be a
pleasure to me to undertake this mission, — first, because,
being curious as concerns forts and castles, I would fain see
if mine eyes have deceived me in taking yon towers for a hold
of great might; secondly, because that same wild-cat of a king

must have a court rare to visit. And the only reflection that
withholds my pressing the offer as a personal suit is that
though I have some words of the Breton jargon at my tongue's
need, I cannot pretend to be a Tully in Welch; howbeit, since
it seems that one at least among them knows something of
Latin, I doubt not but that I shall get out my meaning!"

"Nay, as to that, Sire de Graville," said Harold, who seemed
well pleased with the knight's offer, "there shall be no hin-
drance or let, as I will make clear to you; and in spite of what
you have just heard, Gryffyth shall harm you not in limb or
in life. But, kindly and courteous sir, will your wounds
permit the journey, not long, but steep and laborious, and
only to be made on foot?"

"On foot!" said the knight, a little staggered. "*Pardex!*
well and truly, I did not count upon that!"

"Enough," said Harold, turning away in evident disappointment; "think of it no more."

"Nay, by your leave, what I have once said I stand to,"
returned the knight; "albeit you may as well cleave in two
one of those respectable centaurs of which we have read in
our youth, as part Norman and horse. I will forthwith go to
my chamber, and apparel myself becomingly, — not forget-
ting, in case of the worst, to wear my mail under my robe.
Vouchsafe me but an armourer, just to rivet up the rings
through which scratched so felinely the paw of that well-
appelled *Griffin*."

"I accept your offer frankly," said Harold; "and all shall
be prepared for you, as soon as you yourself will re-seek me
here."

The knight rose, and though somewhat stiff and smart-
ing with his wounds, left the room lightly, summoned his
armourer and squire, and having dressed with all the care
and pomp habitual to a Norman, his gold chain round his
neck, and his vest stiff with broidery, he re-entered the apartment of Harold.

The earl received him alone, and came up to him with a
cordial face. "I thank thee more, brave Norman, than I
ventured to say before my thegns, for I tell thee frankly, that

my intent and aim are to save the life of this brave king; and thou canst well understand that every Saxon amongst us must have his blood warmed by contest, and his eyes blind with national hate. You alone, as a stranger, see the valiant warrior and hunted prince, and as such you can feel for him the noble pity of manly foes."

"That is true," said De Graville, a little surprised, "though we Normans are at least as fierce as you Saxons, when we have once tasted blood; and I own nothing would please me better than to dress that catamaran in mail, put a spear in its claws, and a horse under its legs, and thus fight out my disgrace at being so clawed and mauled by its *griffes*. And though I respect a brave knight in distress, I can scarce extend my compassion to a thing that fights against all rule, martial and kingly."

The earl smiled gravely. "It is the mode in which his ancestors rushed on the spears of Cæsar. Pardon him."

"I pardon him, at your gracious request," quoth the knight, with a grand air, and waving his hands; "say on."

"You will proceed with a Welch monk — whom, though not of the faction of Gryffyth, all Welchmen respect — to the mouth of a frightful pass, skirting the river; the monk will bear aloft the holy rood in signal of peace. Arrived at that pass, you will doubtless be stopped. The monk here will be spokesman, and ask safe-conduct to Gryffyth to deliver my message; he will also bear certain tokens, which will no doubt win the way for you. Arrived before Gryffyth, the monk will accost him; mark and heed well his gestures, since thou wilt know not the Welch tongue he employs. And when he raises the rood, thou — in the mean while having artfully approached close to Gryffyth — wilt whisper in Saxon, which he well understands, and pressing the ring I now give thee into his hand, ' Obey, by this pledge; thou knowest Harold is true, and thy head is sold by thine own people.' If he asks more, thou knowest nought."

"So far this is as should be from chief to chief," said the Norman, touched, "and thus had Fitzosborne done to his foe. I thank thee for this mission, and the more that thou hast not asked me to note the strength of the bulwark, and number the men that may keep it."

Again Harold smiled. "Praise me not for this, noble Norman, — we plain Saxons have not your refinements. If ye are led to the summit, which I think ye will not be, the monk at least will have eyes to see and tongue to relate. But to thee I confide this much: I know already that Gryffyth's strongholds are not his walls and his towers, but the superstition of our men and the despair of his own. I could win those heights, as I have won heights as cloudcapped, but with fearful loss of my own troops, and the massacre of every foe. Both I would spare, if I may."

"Yet thou hast not shown such value for life in the solitudes I passed," said the knight, bluntly.

Harold turned pale, but said firmly: "Sire de Graville, a stern thing is duty, and resistless is its voice. These Welchmen, unless curbed to their mountains, eat into the strength of England, as the tide gnaws into a shore. Merciless were they in their ravages on our borders, and ghastly and torturing their fell revenge. But it is one thing to grapple with a foe fierce and strong, and another to smite when his power is gone, fang and talon. And when I see before me the fated king of a great race, and the last band of doomed heroes, too few and too feeble to make head against my arms, — when the land is already my own, and the sword is that of the deathsman, not of the warrior, — verily, Sir Norman, duty releases its iron tool, and man becomes man again."

"I go," said the Norman, inclining his head low as to his own great duke, and turning to the door; yet there he paused, and looking at the ring which he had placed on his finger, he said: "But one word more, if not indiscreet, — your answer may help argument, if argument be needed. What tale lies hid in this token?"

Harold coloured and paused a moment; then answered, —

"Simply this. Gryffyth's wife, the Lady Aldyth, a Saxon by birth, fell into my hands. We were storming Rhadlan, at the farther end of the isle; she was there. We war not against women; I feared the license of my own soldiers, and

I sent the lady to Gryffyth. Aldyth gave me this ring on parting; and I bade her tell Gryffyth that whenever, at the hour of his last peril and sorest need, I sent that ring back to him, he might hold it the pledge of his life."

"Is this lady, think you, in the stronghold with her lord?"

"I am not sure, but I fear yes," answered Harold.

"Yet one word: And if Gryffyth refuse, despite all warning?"

Harold's eyes drooped.

"If so, he dies; but not by the Saxon sword. God and our Lady speed you!"

CHAPTER V.

On the height called Pen-y-Dinas (or "Head of the City") forming one of the summits of Penmaen-mawr, and in the heart of that supposed fortress which no eye in the Saxon camp had surveyed,[1] reclined Gryffyth, the hunted king. Nor is it marvellous that at that day there should be disputes as to the nature and strength of the supposed bulwark, since in times the most recent and among antiquaries the most learned the greatest discrepancies exist, not only as to theoretical opinion, but plain matter of observation and simple measurement. The place, however, I need scarcely say, was not as we see it now, with its foundations of gigantic ruin, affording ample space for conjecture; yet even then, a wreck as of Titans, its date and purpose were lost in remote antiquity.

The central area (in which the Welch King now reclined) formed an oval barrow of loose stones; whether so left from the origin, or the relics of some vanished building, was unknown even to bard and diviner. Round this space were four strong circumvallations of loose stones, with a space about eighty yards between each; the walls themselves generally about eight feet wide, but of various height, as the stones had

[1] See Note L.

fallen by time and blast. Along these walls rose numerous and almost countless circular buildings, which might pass for towers, though only a few had been recently and rudely roofed in. To the whole of this quadruple enclosure there was but one narrow entrance, now left open as if in scorn of assault; and a winding narrow pass down the mountain, with innumerable curves, alone led to the single threshold. Far down the hill, walls again were visible; and the whole surface of the steep soil, more than half-way in the descent, was heaped with vast loose stones, as if the bones of a dead city. But beyond the innermost enclosure of the fort (if fort, or sacred enclosure, be the correcter name), rose, thick and frequent, other mementos of the Briton, — many crom-lechs, already shattered and shapeless; the ruins of stone houses; and high over all, those upraised, mighty amber piles, as at Stonehenge, once reared, if our dim learning be true, in honour to Bel, or Bál-Huan,[1] the idol of the sun. All, in short, showed that the name of the place, "the Head of the City," told its tale; all announced that there once the Celt had his home, and the gods of the Druid their worship. And musing amidst these skeletons of the past, lay the doomed son of Pen Dragon.

Beside him a kind of throne had been raised with stones, and over it was spread a tattered and faded velvet pall. On this throne sat Aldyth the Queen; and about the royal pair was still that mockery of a court which the jealous pride of the Celt king retained amidst all the horrors of carnage and famine. Most of the officers, indeed (originally in number twenty-four), whose duties attached them to the king and queen of the Cymry, were already feeding the crow or the worm. But still, with gaunt hawk on his wrist, the penhe-bogydd (grand falconer) stood at a distance; still, with beard sweeping his breast, and rod in hand, leaned against a pro-jecting shaft of the wall the noiseless gosdegwr, whose duty it was to command silence in the king's hall; and still the penbard bent over his bruised harp, which once had thrilled through the fair vaults of Caerleon and Rhadlan, in high

[1] See Note M.

praise of God, and the king, and the hero dead.   In the pomp
of gold dish and vessel[1] the board was spread on the stones
for the king and queen; and on the dish was the last fragment
of black bread, and in the vessel, full and clear, the water
from the spring that bubbled up everlastingly through the
bones of the dead city.

Beyond this innermost space, round a basin of rock, through
which the stream overflowed as from an artificial conduit, lay
the wounded and exhausted, crawling, turn by turn, to the
lips of the basin, and happy that the thirst of fever saved
them from the gnawing desire of food.   A wan and spectral
figure glided listlessly to and fro amidst those mangled and
parched and dying groups.   This personage in happier times
filled the office of physician to the court, and was placed
twelfth in rank amidst the chiefs of the household.   And for
cure of the "three deadly wounds," the cloven skull or the
gaping viscera or the broken limb (all three classed alike),
large should have been his fee.[2]   But feeless went he now
from man to man, with his red ointment and his muttered
charm; and those over whom he shook his lean face and
matted locks smiled ghastly at that sign that release and death
were near.   Within the enclosures either lay supine or stalked
restless the withered remains of the wild army.   A sheep and
a horse and a dog were yet left them all to share for the day's
meal.   And the fire of flickering and crackling brushwood
burned bright from a hollow amidst the loose stones; but the

---

[1] The Welch seem to have had a profusion of the precious metals, very
disproportioned to the scarcity of their coined money.   To say nothing of the
torques, bracelets, and even breastplates of gold, common with their numerous chiefs, their laws affix to offences penalties which attest the prevalent
waste both of gold and silver.   Thus an insult to a sub-king of Aberfraw is
atoned by a silver rod as thick as the king's little finger, which is in length to
reach from the ground to his mouth when sitting; and a gold cup, with a
cover as broad as the king's face, and the thickness of a ploughman's nail,
or the shell of a goose's egg.   I suspect that it was precisely because the
Welch coined little or no money, that the metals they possessed became thus
common in domestic use.   Gold would have been more rarely seen, even
amongst the Peruvians, had they coined it into money.

[2] Leges Wallicæ.

animals were yet unslain, and the dog crept by the fire, wink
ing at it with dim eyes.

But over the lower part of the wall nearest to the barrow,
leaned three men. The wall there was so broken that they
could gaze over it on that grotesque yet dismal court; and the
eyes of the three men, with a fierce and wolfish glare, were
bent on Gryffyth.

Three princes were they of the great old line; far as
Gryffyth they traced the fabulous honours of their race, to
Hu-Gadarn, and Prydain, and each thought it shame that
Gryffyth should be lord over him! Each had had throne and
court of his own; each his "white palace" of peeled willow
wands, — poor substitutes, O kings, for the palaces and towers
that the arts of Rome had bequeathed your fathers! And
each had been subjugated by the son of Llewellyn, when in
his day of might he re-united under his sole sway all the
multiform principalities of Wales, and regained for a moment's splendour the throne of Roderic the Great.

"Is it," said Owain, in a hollow whisper, "for yon man,
whom heaven hath deserted, who could not keep his very
torque from the gripe of the Saxon, that we are to die on
these hills, gnawing the flesh from our bones? Think ye
not the hour is come?"

"The hour will come, when the sheep and the horse and
the dog are devoured," replied Modred, "and when the whole
force, as one man, will cry to Gryffyth, '*Thou* a king! — give
us bread!'"

"It is well," said the third, an old man, leaning on a wand
of solid silver, while the mountain wind, sweeping between
the walls, played with the rags of his robe, — "it is well that
the night's sally, less of war than of hunger, was foiled even
of forage and food. Had the saints been with Gryffyth, who
had dared to keep faith with Tostig the Saxon?"

Owain laughed, — a laugh hollow and false.

"Art thou Cymrian, and talkest of faith with a Saxon?
Faith with the spoiler, the ravisher, and butcher? But a
Cymrian keeps faith with revenge; and Gryffyth's trunk
should be still crownless and headless, though Tostig had

never proffered the barter of safety and food. Hist! Gryffyth wakes from the black dream, and his eyes glow from under his hair."

And indeed at this moment the king raised himself on his elbow, and looked round with a haggard and fierce despair in his glittering eyes.

"Play to us, harper; sing some song of the deeds of old!"

The bard mournfully strove to sweep the harp; but the chords were broken, and the note came discordant and shrill as the sigh of a wailing fiend.

"O king!" said the bard, "the music hath left the harp."

"Ha!" murmured Gryffyth, "and Hope the earth! Bard, answer the son of Llewellyn. Oft in my halls hast thou sung the praise of the men that have been. In the halls of the race to come, will bards yet unborn sweep their harps to the deeds of thy king? Shall they tell of the days of Torques by Llyn-Afange, when the princes of Powys fled from his sword as the clouds from the blast of the wind? Shall they sing, as the Hirlas goes round, of his steeds of the sea, when no flag came in sight of his prows between the dark isle of the Druid [1] and the green pastures of Huerdan? [2] Or the towns that he fired, on the lands of the Saxon, when Rolf and the Northmen ran fast from his javelin and spear? Or say, Child of Truth, if all that is told of Gryffyth thy king shall be his woe and his shame?"

The bard swept his hand over his eyes, and answered, —

"Bards unborn shall sing of Gryffyth the son of Llewellyn; but the song shall not dwell on the pomp of his power, when twenty sub-kings knelt at his throne, and his beacon was lighted in the holds of the Norman and Saxon. Bards shall sing of the hero, who fought every inch of crag and morass in the front of his men; and on the heights of Penmaen-mawr, Fame recovers thy crown!"

"Then I have lived as my fathers in life, and shall live with their glory in death!" said Gryffyth; "and so the shadow hath passed from my soul." Then turning round, still propped upon his elbow, he fixed his proud eye upon Aldyth, and said gravely, —

[1] Mona, or Anglesea. [2] Ireland.

"Wife, pale is thy face, and gloomy thy brow; mournest thou the throne or the man?"

Aldyth cast on her wild lord a look of more terror than compassion, a look without the grief that is gentle, or the love that reveres, and answered, —

"What matter to thee my thoughts or my sufferings? The sword or the famine is the doom thou hast chosen. Listening to vain dreams from thy bard, or thine own pride as idle, thou disdainest life for us both: be it so; let us die!"

A strange blending of fondness and wrath troubled the pride on Gryffyth's features, uncouth and half savage as they were, but still noble and kingly.

"And what terror has death, if thou lovest me?" said he.

Aldyth shivered and turned aside. The unhappy king gazed hard on that face, which, despite sore trial and recent exposure to rough wind and weather, still retained the proverbial beauty of the Saxon women, — but beauty without the glow of the heart, as a landscape from which sunlight has vanished; and as he gazed, the colour went and came fitfully over his swarthy cheeks, whose hue contrasted the blue of his eye and the red tawny gold of his shaggy hair.

"Thou wouldst have me," he said at length, "send to Harold, thy countryman; thou wouldst have me, *me*, — rightful lord of all Britain, — beg for mercy and sue for life. Ah, traitress, and child of robber-sires, fair as Rowena art thou, but no Vortimer am I! Thou turnest in loathing from the lord whose marriage-gift was a crown; and the sleek form of thy Saxon Harold rises up through the clouds of the carnage."

All the fierce and dangerous jealousy of man's most human passion, when man loves and hates in a breath, trembled in the Cymrian's voice, and fired his troubled eye; for Aldyth's pale cheek blushed like the rose, but she folded her arms haughtily on her breast, and made no reply.

"No," said Gryffyth, grinding teeth white[1] and strong as those of a young hound, — "no, Harold in vain sent me the

---

[1] The Welch were then, and still are, remarkable for the beauty of their teeth. Giraldus Cambrensis observes, as something very extraordinary, that *they cleaned them.*

casket; the jewel was gone. In vain thy form returned to my side; thy heart was away with thy captor: and not to save my life (were I so base as to seek it), but to see once more the face of him to whom this cold hand, in whose veins no pulse answers my own, had been given, if thy House had consulted its daughter, wouldst thou have me crouch like a lashed dog at the feet of my foe! Oh, shame, shame, shame! Oh, worst perfidy of all! Oh, sharp — sharper than Saxon sword or serpent's tooth, is — is — "

Tears gushed to those fierce eyes, and the proud king dared not trust to his voice.

Aldyth rose coldly. "Slay me if thou wilt, — not insult me. I have said, ' Let us die! ' "

With these words, and vouchsafing no look on her lord, she moved away towards the largest tower or cell, in which the single and rude chamber it contained had been set apart for her.

Gryffyth's eye followed her, softening gradually as her form receded, till lost to his sight; and then that peculiar household love, which in uncultivated breasts often survives trust and esteem, rushed back on his rough heart, and weakened it, as woman only can weaken the strong to whom death is a thought of scorn.

He signed to his bard, who during the conference between wife and lord had retired to a distance, and said, with a writhing attempt to smile, —

"Was there truth, thinkest thou, in the legend that Guenever was false to King Arthur? "

"No," answered the bard, divining his lord's thought; "for Guenever survived not the king, and they were buried side by side in the Vale of Avallon."

"Thou art wise in the lore of the heart, and love hath been thy study from youth to gray hairs. Is it love, is it hate, that prefers death for the loved one to the thought of her life as another's? "

A look of the tenderest compassion passed over the bard's wan face, but vanished in reverence, as he bowed his head and answered, —

"O King, who shall say what note the wind calls from the harp, or what impulse love wakes in the soul, — now soft and now stern? But," he added, raising his form and with a dread calm on his brow, — "but the love of a king brooks no thought of dishonour; and she who hath laid her head on his breast should sleep in his grave."

"Thou wilt outlive me," said Gryffyth, abruptly. "This carn be my tomb!"

"And if so," said the bard, "thou shalt sleep not alone. In this carn what thou lovest best shall be buried by thy side; the bard shall raise his song over thy grave, and the bosses of shields shall be placed at intervals, as rises and falls the sound of song. Over the grave of *two* shall a new mound arise, and we will bid the mound speak to others in the far days to come. But distant yet be the hour when the mighty shall be laid low! and the tongue of thy bard may yet chant the rush of the lion from the toils and the spears. Hope still!"

Gryffyth, for answer, leaned on the harper's shoulder, and pointed silently to the sea, that lay, lake-like at the distance, dark, — studded with the Saxon fleet. Then turning, his hands stretched over the forms that hollow-eyed and ghost-like flitted between the walls, or lay dying, but mute, around the water-spring. His hand then dropped, and rested on the hilt of his sword.

At this moment there was a sudden commotion at the outer entrance of the wall; the crowd gathered to one spot, and there was a loud hum of voices. In a few moments one of the Welch scouts came into the enclosure, and the chiefs of the royal tribes followed him to the carn on which the king stood.

"Of what tellest thou?" said Gryffyth, resuming on the instant all the royalty of his bearing.

"At the mouth of the pass," said the scout, kneeling, "there are a monk bearing the holy rood, and a chief, unarmed. And the monk is Evan, the Cymrian, of Gwentland; and the chief, by his voice, seemeth not to be Saxon. The monk bade me give thee these tokens" (and the scout displayed the broken torque which the king had left in the grasp of Harold, together with a live falcon belled and blinded), "and bade me say thus to the king: 'Harold the Earl greets Gryffyth, son of Llewellyn, and sends him, in proof of good will, the richest prize he hath ever won from a foe, and a hawk from Llandudno, — that bird which chief and equal give to equal and chief. And he prays Gryffyth, son of Llewellyn, for the sake of his realm and his people, to grant hearing to his nuncius.' "

A murmur broke from the chiefs, — a murmur of joy and surprise from all, save the three conspirators, who interchanged anxious and fiery glances. Gryffyth's hand had already closed, while he uttered a cry that seemed of rapture, on the collar of gold, — for the loss of that collar had stung him, perhaps, more than the loss of the crown of all Wales; and his heart, so generous and large amidst all its rude passions, was touched by the speech and the tokens that honoured the fallen outlaw both as foe and as king. Yet in his face there was still seen a moody and proud struggle; he paused before he turned to the chiefs.

"What counsel ye, — ye strong in battle and wise in debate?" said he.

With one voice all, save the Fatal Three, exclaimed: "Hear the monk, O King!"

'Shall we dissuade?" whispered Modred to the old chief, his accomplice.

"No; for so doing, we shall offend all, and we must win all."

Then the bard stepped into the ring; and the ring was hushed, for wise is ever the counsel of him whose book is the human heart.

"Hear the Saxons," said he, briefly, and with an air of command when addressing others, which contrasted strongly his tender respect to the king, — "hear the Saxons, but not in these walls. Let no man from the foe see our strength or our weakness. We are still mighty and impregnable, while our dwelling is in the realm of the Unknown. Let the king and his officers of state and his chieftains of battle descend to the

pass; and behind, at the distance, let the spearmen range
from cliff to cliff, as a ladder of steel; so will their numbers
seem the greater."

"Thou speakest well," said the king.

Meanwhile the knight and the monk waited below at that
terrible pass,[1] which then lay between mountain and river,
and over which the precipices frowned, with a sense of horror
and weight. Looking up, the knight murmured, —

"With those stones and crags to roll down on a marching
army, the place well defies storm and assault; and a hundred
on the height would overmatch thousands below."

He then turned to address a few words, with all the far-
famed courtesy of Norman and Frank, to the Welch guards at
the outpost. They were picked men, — the strongest and best
armed and best fed of the group; but they shook their heads
and answered not, gazing at him fiercely, and showing their
white teeth, as dogs at a bear before they are loosened from
the band.

"They understand me not, poor languageless savages!"
said Mallet de Graville, turning to the monk, who stood by
with the lifted rood; "speak to them in their own jargon."

"Nay," said the Welch monk, who, though of a rival tribe
from South Wales and at the service of Harold, was esteemed
throughout the land for piety and learning; "they will not
open mouth till the king's orders come to receive or dismiss
us unheard."

"Dismiss us unheard!" repeated the punctilious Norman;
"even this poor barbarous king can scarcely be so strange to
all comely and gentle usage as to put such insult on Guillaume Mallet de Graville. But," added the knight, colouring,
"I forgot that he is not advised of my name and land; and,
indeed, sith thou art to be spokesman, I marvel why Harold
should have prayed my service at all, at the risk of subjecting
a Norman knight to affronts contumelious."

"Peradventure," replied Evan, — "peradventure thou hast
something to whisper apart to the king, which, as stranger

---

[1] I believe it was not till the last century that a good road took the place
of this pass.

and warrior, none will venture to question, but which from me, as countryman and priest, would excite the jealous suspicions of those around him."

"I conceive thee," said De Graville. "And see, spears are gleaming down the path; and *per pedes Domini*, yon chief with the mantle, and circlet of gold on his head, is the cat-king that so spitted and scratched in the *mêlée* last night."

"Heed well thy tongue," said Evan, alarmed; "no jests with the leader of men."

"Knowest thou, good monk, that a facete and most *gentil* Roman (if the saintly writer from whom I take the citation reports aright — for, alas! I know not where myself to purchase or to steal one copy of Horatius Flaccus) hath said, 'Dulce est desipere in loco.' It is sweet to jest, but not within reach of claws, whether of kaisars or cats."

Therewith the knight drew up his spare but stately figure, and arranging his robe with grace and dignity, awaited the coming chief.

Down the paths, one by one, came first the chiefs privileged by birth to attend the king; and each, as he reached the mouth of the pass, drew on the upper side, among the stones of the rough ground. Then a banner, tattered and torn, with the lion ensign that the Welch princes had substituted for the old national dragon, which the Saxons of Wessex had appropriated to themselves,[1] preceded the steps of the king. Behind him came his falconer and bard, and the rest of his scanty

---

[1] The Saxons of Wessex seem to have adopted the dragon for their ensign from an early period. It was probably for this reason that it was assumed by Edward Ironsides, as the hero of the Saxons; the principality of Wessex forming the most important portion of the pure Saxon race, while its founder was the ancestor of the imperial House of the Basileus of Britain. The dragon seems also to have been a Norman ensign. The lions or leopards, popularly assigned to the Conqueror, are certainly a later invention. There is no appearance of them on the banners and shields of the Norman army in the Bayeux tapestry. Armorial bearings were in use amongst the Welch, and even the Saxons, long before heraldry was reduced to a science by the Franks and Normans; and the dragon, which is supposed by many critics to be borrowed from the East, through the Saracens, certainly existed as an armorial ensign with the Cymrians before they could have had any obligation to the songs and legends of that people.

household. The king halted in the pass, a few steps from the Norman knight; and Mallet de Graville, though accustomed to the majestic mien of Duke William, and the practised state of the princes of France and Flanders, felt an involuntary thrill of admiration at the bearing of the great child of Nature with his foot on his father's soil.

Small and slight as was his stature, worn and ragged his mantle of state, there was that in the erect mien and steady eye of the Cymrian hero which showed one conscious of authority and potent in will; and the wave of his hand to the knight was the gesture of a prince on his throne. Nor, indeed, was that brave and ill-fated chief without some irregular gleams of mental cultivation which under happier auspices might have centred into steadfast light. Though the learning which had once existed in Wales (the last legacy of Rome) had long since expired in broil and blood, and youths no longer flocked to the colleges of Caerleon, and priests no longer adorned the casuistical theology of the age, Gryffyth himself, the son of a wise and famous father,[1] had received an education beyond the average of Saxon kings. But, intensely national, his mind had turned from all other literature to the legends and songs and chronicles of his land; and if he is the best scholar who best understands his own tongue and its treasures, Gryffyth was the most erudite prince of his age.

His natural talents, for war especially, were considerable; and judged fairly, — not as mated with an empty treasury, without other army than the capricious will of his subjects afforded, and amidst his bitterest foes in the jealous chiefs of his own country, against the disciplined force and comparative civilization of the Saxon, but as compared with all the other princes of Wales, in warfare, to which he was habituated, and in which chances were even, — the fallen son of Llewellyn had been the most renowned leader that Cymry had known since the death of the great Roderic.

---

[1] "In whose time the earth brought forth double, and there was neither beggar nor poor man from the North to the South Sea." — POWELL: *History of Wales*, p. 83.

GRYFFYTH, THE WELCH KING, HOLDING A PARLEY WITH THE
EMISSARIES OF HAROLD.

So there he stood; his attendants, ghastly with famine, drawn up on the unequal ground; above, on the heights, and rising from the stone crags, long lines of spears artfully placed; and, watching him with deathful eyes, somewhat in his rear, the Traitor Three.

"Speak, father or chief," said the Welch King in his native tongue; "what would Harold the Earl of Gryffyth the King?"

Then the monk took up the word and spoke.

"Health to Gryffyth-ap-Llewellyn, his chiefs, and his people! Thus saith Harold, King Edward's thegn: 'By land all the passes are watched; by sea all the waves are our own. Our swords rest in our sheaths; but famine marches each hour to gride and to slay. Instead of sure death from the hunger, take sure life from the foe. Free pardon to all, chiefs and people, and safe return to their homes, — save Gryffyth alone. Let him come forth, not as victim and outlaw, not with bent form and clasped hands, but as chief meeting chief, with his household of state. Harold will meet him, in honour, at the gates of the fort. Let Gryffyth submit to King Edward, and ride with Harold to the Court of the Basileus. Harold promises him life, and will plead for his pardon. And though the peace of this realm and the fortune of war forbid Harold to say, "Thou shalt yet be a king," yet thy crown, son of Llewellyn, shall at least be assured in the line of thy fathers, and the race of Cadwallader shall still reign in Cymry.'"

The monk paused, and hope and joy were in the faces of the famished chiefs; while two of the Traitor Three suddenly left their post, and sped to tell the message to the spearmen and multitudes above. Modred, the third conspirator, laid his hand on his hilt, and stole near to see the face of the king; the face of the king was dark and angry, as a midnight of storm.

Then, raising the cross on high, Evan resumed: —

"And I, though of the people of Gwentland, which the arms of Gryffyth have wasted, and whose prince fell beneath Gryffyth's sword on the hearth of his hall, — I, as God's servant, the brother of all I behold, and, as son of the soil, mourning over the slaughter of its latest defenders, — I, by

this symbol of love and command, which I raise to the heaven,
adjure thee, O King, to give ear to the mission of peace, — to
cast down the grim pride of earth; and instead of the crown
of a day, fix thy hopes on the crown everlasting. For much
shall be pardoned to thee in thine hour of pomp and of conquest, if now thou savest from doom and from death the last
lives over which thou art lord."

It was during this solemn appeal that the knight, marking
the sign announced to him and drawing close to Gryffyth,
pressed the ring into the king's hand, and whispered, —

"Obey by this pledge. Thou knowest Harold is true, and
thy head is sold by thine own people."

The king cast a haggard eye at the speaker, and then at the
ring, over which his hand closed with a convulsive spasm.
And at that dread instant the man prevailed over the king;
and far away from people and monk, from adjuration and
duty, fled his heart on the wings of the storm, — fled to the
cold wife he distrusted; and the pledge that should assure
him of life seemed as a love-token insulting his fall. Amidst
all the roar of roused passions, loudest of all was the hiss of
the jealous fiend.

As the monk ceased, the thrill of the audience was percepti-
ble, and a deep silence was followed by a general murmur, as
if to constrain the king.

Then the pride of the despot chief rose up to second the
wrath of the suspecting man. The red spot flushed the dark
cheek, and he tossed the neglected hair from his brow. He
made one stride towards the monk, and said, in a voice loud
and deep and slow, rolling far up the hill, —

"Monk, thou hast said; and now hear the reply of the son
of Llewellyn, the true heir of Roderic the Great, who from
the heights of Eryri saw all the lands of the Cymrian sleeping under the dragon of Uther. King was I born, and king
will I die. I will not ride by the side of the Saxon to the
feet of Edward, the son of the spoiler. I will not, to purchase base life, surrender the claim, vain before men and the
hour, but solemn before God and posterity, — the claim of my
line and my people. All Britain is ours, — all the island of

Pines. And the children of Hengist are traitors and rebels, not the heirs of Ambrosius and Uther. Say to Harold the Saxon, Ye have left us but the tomb of the Druid and the hills of the eagle; but freedom and royalty are ours, in life and in death, — not for you to demand them, not for us to betray. Nor fear ye, O my chiefs, few, but unmatched in glory and truth; fear not ye to perish by the hunger thus denounced as our doom, on these heights that command the fruits of our own fields! No, die we may, but not mute and revengeless. Go back, whispering warrior; go back, false son of Cymry, and tell Harold to look well to his walls and his trenches. We will vouchsafe him grace for his grace, — we will not take him by surprise nor under cloud of the night. With the gleam of our spears and the clash of our shields, we will come from the hill; and, famine-worn as he deems us, hold a feast in his walls which the eagles of Snowdon spread their pinions to share!"

"Rash man and unhappy!" cried the monk; "what curse drawest thou down on thy head? Wilt thou be the murderer of thy men, in strife unavailing and vain? Heaven holds thee guilty of all the blood thou shalt cause to be shed."

"Be dumb! Hush thy screech, lying raven!" exclaimed Gryffyth, his eyes darting fire and his slight form dilating. "Once, priest and monk went before us to inspire, not to daunt; and our cry, 'Alleluia!' was taught us by the saints of the Church, on the day when Saxons, fierce and many as Harold's, fell on the field of Maes-Garmon. No; the curse is on the head of the invader, not on those who defend hearth and altar. Yea, as the song to the bard, the CURSE leaps through my veins, and rushes forth from my lips. By the land they have ravaged; by the gore they have spilt; on these crags, our last refuge; below the carn on yon heights, where the dead stir to hear me, — I launch the curse of the wronged and the doomed on the children of Hengist! They in turn shall know the steel of the stranger, — their crown shall be shivered as glass, and their nobles be as slaves in the land; and the line of Hengist and Cerdic shall be razed from the roll of empire; and the ghosts of our fathers shall glide, appeased, over the grave of their nation. But we — WE, though weak in the body, in the soul shall be strong to the last! The ploughshare may pass over our cities, but the soil shall be trod by our steps, and our deeds keep our language alive in the songs of our bards. Nor, in the great Judgment Day, shall any race but the race of Cymry rise from their graves in this corner of earth, to answer for the sins of the brave!" [1]

So impressive the voice, so grand the brow, and sublime the wild gesture of the king, as he thus spoke, that not only the monk himself was awed; not only, though he understood not the words, did the Norman knight bow his head, as a child when the lightning he fears as by instinct flashes out from the cloud, — but even the sullen and wide-spreading discontent at work among most of the chiefs was arrested for a moment. But the spearmen and multitude above, excited by the tidings of safety to life, and worn out by repeated defeat, and the dread fear of famine, too remote to hear the king, were listening eagerly to the insidious addresses of the two stealthy conspirators, creeping from rank to rank; and already they began to sway and move, and sweep slowly down towards the king.

Recovering his surprise, the Norman again neared Gryffyth, and began to re-urge his mission of peace; but the chief waved him back sternly, and said aloud, though in Saxon, —

"No secrets can pass between Harold and me. This much alone take thou back as answer: I thank the earl, for myself,

---

[1] "During the military expeditions made in our days against South Wales, an old Welchman, at Pencadair, who had faithfully adhered to him (Henry II.), being desired to give his opinion about the royal army, and whether he thought that of the rebels would make resistance, and what he thought would be the final event of this war, replied: ' This nation, O King, may now, as in former times, be harassed, and in a great measure be weakened and destroyed by you and other powers ; and it will often prevail by its laudable exertions, but it can never be totally subdued by the wrath of man, unless the wrath of God shall concur. *Nor do I think that any other nation than this of Wales, or any other language (whatever may hereafter come to pass), shall in the day of severe examination before the Supreme Judge answer for this corner of the earth!* '" — HOARE : *Giraldus Cumbrensis*, vol. i. p. 361.

my queen, and my people. Noble have been his courtesies, as foe; as foe, I thank him, — as king, defy. The torque he hath returned to my hand, he shall see again ere the sun set. Messengers, ye are answered. Withdraw, and speed fast, that we may pass not your steps on the road."

The monk sighed, and cast a look of holy compassion over the circle; and a pleased man was he to see in the faces of most there, that the king was alone in his fierce defiance. Then lifting again the rood, he turned away, and with him went the Norman.

The retirement of the messengers was the signal for one burst of remonstrance from the chiefs, — the signal for the voice and the deeds of the Fatal Three. Down from the heights sprang and rushed the angry and turbulent multitudes; round the king came the bard and the falconer, and some faithful few.

The great uproar of many voices caused the monk and the knight to pause abruptly in their descent, and turn to look behind. They could see the crowd rushing down from the higher steeps; but on the spot itself which they had so lately left, the nature of the ground only permitted a confused view of spear-points, lifted swords, and heads crowned with shaggy locks, swaying to and fro.

"What means all this commotion?" asked the knight, with his hand on his sword.

"Hist!" said the monk, pale as ashes, and leaning for support upon the cross.

Suddenly, above the hubbub, was heard the voice of the king, in accents of menace and wrath, singularly distinct and clear; it was followed by a moment's silence, — a moment's silence, followed by the clatter of arms, a yell, and a howl, and the indescribable shock of men.

And suddenly again was heard a voice that seemed that of the king, but no longer distinct and clear; was it laugh? — was it groan?

All was hushed: the monk was on his knees in prayer; the knight's sword was bare in his hand. All was hushed, and the spears stood still in the air; when there was again a cry, as multitudinous but less savage than before. And the Welch came down the pass and down the crags.

The knight placed his back to a rock. "They have orders to murder us," he murmured; "but woe to the first who come within reach of my sword!"

Down swarmed the Welchmen, nearer and nearer; and in the midst of them three chiefs, — the Fatal Three. And the old chief bore in his hand a pole or spear, and on the top of that spear, trickling gore step by step, was the trunkless head of Gryffyth the King.

"This," said the old chief as he drew near, — "this is our answer to Harold the Earl. We will go with ye."

"Food! food!" cried the multitude.

And the three chiefs (one on either side the trunkless head that the third bore aloft) whispered, "We are avenged!"

BOOK VIII.

FATE.

CHAPTER I.

Some days after the tragical event with which the last chapter closed, the ships of the Saxons were assembled in the wide waters of Conway; and on the small fore-deck of the stateliest vessel stood Harold, bare-headed, before Aldyth, the widowed queen. For the faithful bard had fallen by the side of his lord; the dark promise was unfulfilled, and the mangled clay of the jealous Gryffyth slept *alone* in the narrow bed. A chair of state, with dossell and canopy, was set for the daughter of Algar; and behind, stood maidens of Wales, selected in haste for her attendants.

But Aldyth had not seated herself; and, side by side with her dead lord's great victor, thus she spoke: —

"Woe worth the day and the hour when Aldyth left the hall of her fathers and the land of her birth! Her robe of a queen has been rent and torn over an aching heart, and the air she has breathed has reeked as with blood. I go forth, widowed and homeless and lonely; but my feet shall press the soil of my sires, and my lips draw the breath which came sweet and pure to my childhood. And thou, O Harold, standest beside me, like the shape of my own youth; and the dreams of old come back at the sound of thy voice. Fare thee well, noble heart and true Saxon. Thou hast twice saved the child of thy foe, — first from shame, then from famine. Thou wouldst have saved my dread lord from open force and dark murder; but the saints were wroth, the blood of my kinsfolk, shed by his hand, called for vengeance, and the shrines he had pillaged and burned murmured doom from their desolate altars. Peace be with the dead, and peace with the living! I shall go back to my father and brethren; and if the fame and life of child and sister be dear to them, their swords will never more leave their sheaths against Harold. So thy hand, and God guard thee!"

Harold raised to his lips the hand which the queen extended to him; and to Aldyth now seemed restored the rare beauty of her youth, as pride and sorrow gave her the charm of emotion, which love and duty had failed to bestow.

"Life and health to thee, noble lady," said the earl. "Tell thy kindred from me, that for thy sake, and thy grandsire's, I would fain be their brother and friend; were they but united with me, all England were now safe against every foe and each peril. Thy daughter already awaits thee in the halls of Morcar; and when time has scarred the wounds of the past, may thy joys re-bloom in the face of thy child. Farewell, noble Aldyth!"

He dropped the hand he had held till then, turned slowly to the side of the vessel, and re-entered his boat. As he was rowed back to shore, the horn gave the signal for raising anchor; and the ship, righting itself, moved majestically through the midst of the fleet. But Aldyth still stood erect, and her eyes followed the boat that bore away the secret love of her youth.

As Harold reached the shore, Tostig and the Norman, who had been conversing amicably together on the beach, advanced towards the earl.

"Brother," said Tostig, smiling, "it were easy for thee to console the fair widow, and bring to our House all the force of East Anglia and Mercia." Harold's face slightly changed, but he made no answer.

"A marvellous fair dame," said the Norman, "notwithstanding her cheek be somewhat pinched, and the hue sun-burned; and I wonder not that the poor cat-king kept her so close to his side."

"Sir Norman," said the earl, hastening to change the subject, "the war is now over, and for long years Wales will ıeave our Marches in peace. This eve I propose to ride hence towards London, and we will converse by the way."

"Go you so soon?" cried the knight, surprised. "Shall you not take means utterly to subjugate this troublesome race, parcel out the lands among your thegns, to hold as martial fiefs at need, build towers and forts on the heights and at the river mouths? Where a site, like this, for some fair castle and vawmure? In a word, do you Saxons merely overrun, and neglect to hold what you win?"

"We fight in self-defence, not for conquest, Sir Norman. We have no skill in building castles; and I pray you not to hint to my thegns the conceit of dividing a land, as thieves would their plunder. King Gryffyth is dead, and his brothers will reign in his stead. England has guarded her realm, and chastised the aggressors. What need England do more? We are not like our first barbarous fathers, carving out homes with the scythe of their sæxes. The wave settles after the flood, and the races of men after lawless convulsions."

Tostig smiled, in disdain, at the knight, who mused a little over the strange words he had heard, and then silently followed the earl to the fort.

But when Harold gained his chamber, he found there an express, arrived in haste from Chester, with the news that Algar, the sole enemy and single rival of his power, was no more. Fever, occasioned by neglected wounds, had stretched him impotent on a bed of sickness, and his fierce passions had aided the march of disease; the restless and profitless race was run.

The first emotion which these tidings called forth was that of pain. The bold sympathize with the bold; and in great hearts there is always a certain friendship for a gallant foe. But recovering the shock of that first impression, Harold could not but feel that England was freed from its most dangerous subject, himself from the only obstacle apparent to the fulfilment of his luminous career.

"Now, then, to London," whispered the voice of his ambition. "Not a foe rests to trouble the peace of that empire which thy conquests, O Harold, have made more secure and

compact than ever yet has been the realm of the Saxon kings.
Thy way through the country that thou hast henceforth delivered from the fire and sword of the mountain ravager will be
one march of triumph, like a Roman's of old; and the voice
of the people will echo the hearts of the army; those hearts
are thine own. Verily Hilda is a prophetess; and when
Edward rests with the saints, from what English heart will
not burst the cry, ' LONG LIVE HAROLD THE KING '? "

CHAPTER II.

THE Norman rode by the side of Harold, in the rear of the
victorious armament. The ships sailed to their havens, and
Tostig departed to his northern earldom.

"And now," said Harold, "I am at leisure to thank thee,
brave Norman, for more than thine aid in council and war; at
leisure now to turn to the last prayer of Sweyn, and the often
shed tears of Githa my mother, for Wolnoth the exile. Thou
seest with thine own eyes that there is no longer pretext or plea
for thy count to detain these hostages. Thou shalt hear from
Edward himself that he no longer asks sureties for the faith of
the House of Godwin; and I cannot think that Duke William
would have suffered thee to bring me over this news from the
dead if he were not prepared to do justice to the living."

"Your speech, Earl of Wessex, goes near to the truth. But,
to speak plainly and frankly, I think William, my lord, hath
a keen desire to welcome in person a chief so illustrious as
Harold, and I guess that he keeps the hostages to make thee
come to claim them." The knight, as he spoke, smiled gayly;
but the cunning of the Norman gleamed in the quick glance
of his clear hazel eye.

"Fain must I feel pride at such wish, if you flatter me not,"
said Harold; "and I would gladly myself, now the land is in
peace, and my presence not needful, visit a court of such fame.
I hear high praise from cheapman and pilgrim of Count Wil-

liam's wise care for barter and trade, and might learn much
from the ports of the Seine that would profit the marts of the
Thames. Much, too, I hear of Count William's zeal to revive
the learning of the Church, aided by Lanfranc the Lombard;
much I hear of the pomp of his buildings, and the grace of his
court. All this would I cheerfully cross the ocean to see; but
all this would but sadden my heart if I returned without Haco
and Wolnoth."

"I dare not speak so as to plight faith for the duke," said
the Norman, who, though sharp to deceive, had that rein on
his conscience that it did not let him openly lie; "but this I
do know, that there are few things in his countdom which my
lord would not give to clasp the right hand of Harold, and
feel assured of his friendship."

Though wise and far-seeing, Harold was not suspicious, —
no Englishman, unless it were Edward himself, knew the
secret pretensions of William to the English throne; and he
answered simply, —

"It were well, indeed, both for Normandy and England,
both against foes and for trade, to be allied and well-liking.
I will think over your words, Sire de Graville; and it shall
not be my fault if old feuds be not forgotten, and those now
in thy court be the last hostages ever kept by the Norman
for the faith of the Saxon."

With that he turned the discourse; and the aspiring and
able envoy, exhilarated by the hope of a successful mission,
animated the way by remarks, alternately lively and shrewd,
which drew the brooding earl from those musings which had
now grown habitual to a mind once clear and open as the day.

Harold had not miscalculated the enthusiasm his victories
had excited. Where he passed, all the towns poured forth
their populations to see and to hail him; and on arriving at
the metropolis, the rejoicings in his honour seemed to equal
those which had greeted, at the accession of Edward, the
restoration of the line of Cerdic.

According to the barbarous custom of the age, the head of
the unfortunate sub-king and the prow of his special war-ship
had been sent to Edward as the trophies of conquest: but

Harold's uniform moderation respected the living.   The race
of Gryffyth[1] were re-established on the tributary throne of
that hero, in the persons of his brothers, Blethgent and Rig-
watle; "and they swore oaths," says the graphic old chronicler, "and delivered hostages to the king and the earl that
they would be faithful to him in all things, and be everywhere ready for him, by water and by land, and make such
renders from the land as had been done before to any other
king."

Not long after this, Mallet de Graville returned to Normandy, with gifts for William from King Edward, and special requests from that prince, as well as from the earl, to
restore the hostages. But Mallet's acuteness readily perceived
that in much Edward's mind had been alienated from William.   It was clear that the duke's marriage and the pledges
that had crowned the union were distasteful to the asceticism
of the saint-king; and with Godwin's death, and Tostig's
absence from the court, seemed to have expired all Edward's
bitterness towards that powerful family of which Harold was
now the head.   Still, as no subject out of the House of Cerdic
had ever yet been elected to the Saxon throne, there was no
apprehension on Mallet's mind that in Harold was the true
rival to William's cherished aspirations.   Though Edward
the Atheling was dead, his son Edgar lived, the natural heir
to the throne; and the Norman, whose liege had succeeded to
the duchy at the age of eight, was not sufficiently cognizant
of the invariable custom of the Anglo-Saxons to set aside,
whether for kingdoms or for earldoms, all claimants unfitted
for rule by their tender years.   He could indeed perceive that
the young Atheling's minority was in favour of his Norman
liege, and would render him but a weak defender of the realm,
and that there seemed no popular attachment to the infant
orphan of the Germanized exile: his name was never mentioned at the court, nor had Edward acknowledged him as
heir, — a circumstance which he interpreted auspiciously for
William.   Nevertheless, it was clear that both at court and

---

[1] Gryffyth left a son, Caradoc; but he was put aside, as a minor, according
to the Saxon customs.

among the people the Norman influence in England was at the lowest ebb; and that the only man who could restore it, and realize the cherished dreams of his grasping lord, was Harold the all-powerful.

CHAPTER III.

TRUSTING for the time to the success of Edward's urgent demand for the release of his kinsmen as well as his own, Harold was now detained at the court by all those arrears of business which had accumulated fast under the inert hands of the monk-king during the prolonged campaigns against the Welch; but he had leisure at least for frequent visits to the old Roman house; and those visits were not more grateful to his love than to the harder and more engrossing passion which divided his heart.

The nearer he grew to the dazzling object to the possession of which Fate seemed to have shaped all circumstances, the more he felt the charm of those mystic influences which his colder reason had disdained. He who is ambitious of things afar and uncertain passes at once into the Poet-Land of Imagination; to aspire and to imagine are yearnings twin-born.

When in his fresh youth and his calm lofty manhood, Harold saw action, how adventurous soever, limited to the barriers of noble duty; when he lived but for his country, all spread clear before his vision in the sunlight of day; but as the barriers receded, while the horizon extended, his eye left the Certain to rest on the Vague. As self, though still half concealed from his conscience, gradually assumed the wide space love of country had filled, the maze of delusion commenced: he was to shape fate out of circumstance, no longer defy fate through virtue; and thus Hilda became to him as a voice that answered the questions of his own restless heart. He needed encouragement from the Unknown to sanction his desires and confirm his ends. But Edith, rejoicing in the fair fame of her betrothed, and content in the pure rapture of beholding him again, reposed in the divine credulity of the happy hour. She marked not, in Harold's visits, that, on entrance, the earl's eye sought first the stern face of the Vala; she wondered not why those two conversed in whispers together, or stood so often at moonlight by the Runic grave. Alone, of all womankind, she felt that Harold loved her, — that that love had braved time, absence, change, and hope deferred; and she knew not that what love has most to dread in the wild heart of aspiring man is not persons, but things, — is not things, but their symbols.

So weeks and months rolled on, and Duke William returned no answer to the demands for his hostages; and Harold's heart smote him, that he neglected his brother's prayer and his mother's accusing tears.

Now Githa, since the death of her husband, had lived in seclusion and apart from town; and one day Harold was surprised by her unexpected arrival at the large timbered house in London, which had passed to his possession. As she abruptly entered the room in which he sat, he sprang forward to welcome and embrace her; but she waved him back with a grave and mournful gesture, and sinking on one knee, she said thus: —

"See, the mother is a suppliant to the son for the son. No, Harold, no, — I will not rise till thou hast heard me. For years, long and lonely, have I lingered and pined, — long years! Will my boy know his mother again? Thou hast said to me, 'Wait till the messenger returns.' I have waited. Thou hast said, 'This time the count cannot resist the demand of the king.' I bowed my head and submitted to thee as I had done to Godwin, my lord. And I have not till now claimed thy promise; for I allowed thy country, thy king, and thy fame to have claims more strong than a mother. Now I tarry no more; now no more will I be amused and deceived. Thine hours are thine own; free thy coming and thy going. Harold, I claim thine oath. Harold, I touch thy right hand. Harold, I remind thee of thy troth and thy plight, to cross the seas thyself, and restore the child to the mother."

"Oh, rise, rise!" exclaimed Harold, deeply moved.

"Patient hast thou been, O my mother, and now I will linger no more, nor hearken to other voice than your own. I will see the king this day, and ask his leave to cross the sea to Duke William."

Then Githa rose, and fell on the earl's breast, weeping.

CHAPTER IV.

It so chanced, while this interview took place between Githa and the earl, that Gurth, hawking in the woodlands round Hilda's house, turned aside to visit his Danish kinswoman. The prophetess was absent, but he was told that Edith was within; and Gurth, about to be united to a maiden who had long won his noble affections, cherished a brother's love for his brother's fair betrothed. He entered the gynœcium, and there still, as when we were first made present in that chamber, sat the maids, employed on a work more brilliant to the eye and more pleasing to the labour than that which had then tasked their active hands. They were broidering into a tissue of the purest gold the effigy of a fighting warrior, designed by Hilda for the banner of Earl Harold; and, removed from the awe of their mistress, as they worked, their tongues sang gayly, and it was in the midst of song and laughter that the fair young Saxon lord entered the chamber. The babble and the mirth ceased at his entrance; each voice was stilled, each eye cast down demurely. Edith was not among them; and in answer to his inquiry the eldest of the maidens pointed towards the peristyle without the house.

The winning and kindly thegn paused a few moments, to admire the tissue and commend the work, and then sought the peristyle.

Near the water-spring that gushed free and bright through the Roman fountain, he found Edith, seated in an attitude of deep thought and gloomy dejection. She started as he approached, and springing forward to meet him, exclaimed:—

"O Gurth, Heaven hath sent thee to me, I know well, though I cannot explain to thee why, for I cannot explain it to myself; but know I do, by the mysterious bodements of my own soul, that some great danger is at this moment encircling thy brother Harold. Go to him, I pray, I implore thee, forthwith; and let thy clear sense and warm heart be by his side."

"I will go instantly," said Gurth, startled. "But do not suffer, I adjure thee, sweet kinswoman, the superstition that wraps this place, as a mist wraps a marsh, to infect thy pure spirit. In my early youth I submitted to the influence of Hilda; I became man, and outgrew it. Much, secretly, has it grieved me of late, to see that our kinswoman's Danish lore has brought even the strong heart of Harold under its spell; and where once he only spoke of *duty*, I now hear him speak of *fate*."

"Alas! alas!" answered Edith, wringing her hands; "when the bird hides its head in the brake, doth it shut out the track of the hound? Can we baffle fate by refusing to heed its approaches? But we waste precious moments. Go, Gurth, dear Gurth! Heavier and darker, while we speak, gathers the cloud on my heart."

Gurth said no more, but hastened to remount his steed; and Edith remained alone by the Roman fountain, motionless and sad, as if the nymph of the old religion stood there to see the lessening stream well away from the shattered stone, and know that the life of the nymph was measured by the ebb of the stream.

Gurth arrived in London just as Harold was taking boat for the palace of Westminster, to seek the king; and after interchanging a hurried embrace with his mother, he accompanied Harold to the palace, and learned his errand by the way. While Harold spoke, he did not foresee any danger to be incurred by a friendly visit to the Norman court; and the interval that elapsed between Harold's communication and their entrance into the king's chamber allowed no time for mature and careful reflection.

Edward, on whom years and infirmity had increased of late with rapid ravage, heard Harold's request with a grave and deep attention, which he seldom vouchsafed to earthly affairs.

And he remained long silent after his brother-in-law had finished, — so long silent that the earl at first deemed that he was absorbed in one of those mystic and abstracted reveries in which more and more, as he grew nearer to the borders of the World Unseen, Edward so strangely indulged. But, looking more close, both he and Gurth were struck by the evident dismay on the king's face, while the collected light of Edward's cold eye showed that his mind was awake to the human world. In truth, it is probable that Edward at that moment was recalling rash hints, if not promises, to his rapacious cousin of Normandy, made during his exile; and, sensible of his own declining health and the tender years of the young Edgar, he might be musing over the terrible pretender to the English throne, whose claims his earlier indiscretion might seem to sanction. Whatever his thoughts, they were dark and sinister, as at length he said slowly, —

"Is thine oath indeed given to thy mother, and doth she keep thee to it?"

"Both, O King," answered Harold, briefly.

"Then I can gainsay thee not. And thou, Harold, art a man of this living world; thou playest here the part of a centurion; thou sayest ' Come,' and men come, — ' Go,' and men move at thy will. Therefore thou mayest well judge for thyself. I gainsay thee not, nor interfere between man and his vow. But think not," continued the king, in a more solemn voice and with increasing emotion, — "think not that I will charge my soul that I counselled or encouraged this errand. Yea, I foresee that thy journey will lead but to great evil to England, and sore grief or dire loss to thee." [1]

"How so, dear Lord and King?" said Harold, startled by Edward's unwonted earnestness, though deeming it but one of the visionary chimeras habitual to the saint. "How so? William thy cousin hath ever borne the name of one fair to friend, though fierce to foe; and foul indeed his dishonour, if he could meditate harm to a man trusting his faith and sheltered by his own roof-tree."

"Harold, Harold," said Edward, impatiently, "I know

[1] Brompton Chronicle, Knyghton, Walsingham, Hoveden, etc.

William of old. Nor is he so simple of mind that he will
cede aught for thy pleasure, or even to my will, unless it
bring some gain to himself.[1] I say no more. Thou art cau-
tioned, and I leave the rest to Heaven."

It is the misfortune of men little famous for worldly lore,
that on those few occasions when, in that sagacity caused by
their very freedom from the strife and passion of those around,
they seem almost prophetically inspired, — it is their misfortune to lack the power of conveying to others their own convic-
tions; they may divine, but they cannot reason: and Harold
could detect nothing to deter his purpose in a vague fear,
based on no other argument than as vague a perception of the
duke's general character. But Gurth, listening less to his
reason than his devoted love for his brother, took alarm, and
said, after a pause, —

"Thinkest thou, good my King, that the same danger were
incurred if Gurth, instead of Harold, crossed the seas to demand the hostages?"

"No," said Edward, eagerly; "and so would I counsel.
William would not have the same objects to gain in practis-
ing his worldly guile upon thee. No; methinks *that* were the
prudent course."

"And the ignoble one for Harold," said the elder brother,
almost indignantly. "Howbeit I thank thee gratefully, dear
King, for thy affectionate heed and care. And so the saints
guard thee!"

On leaving the king, a warm discussion between the brothers
took place. But Gurth's arguments were stronger than those
of Harold, and the earl was driven to rest his persistence on
his own special pledge to Githa. As soon, however, as they
had gained their home, that plea was taken from him; for the
moment Gurth related to his mother Edward's fears and cautions, she, ever mindful of Godwin's preference for the earl,
and his last commands to her, hastened to release Harold from
his pledge, and to implore him at least to suffer Gurth to be
his substitute to the Norman court. "Listen dispassion-
ately," said Gurth; "rely upon it that Edward has reasons

---

[1] Brompton, Knyghton, etc.

for his fears, more rational than those he has given to us. He knows William from his youth upward, and hath loved him too well to hint doubts of his good faith without just foundation. Are there no reasons why danger from William should be special against thyself? While the Normans abounded in the court, there were rumours that the duke had some designs on England, which Edward's preference seemed to sanction; such designs now, in the altered state of England, were absurd, — too frantic for a prince of William's reputed wisdom to entertain. Yet he may not unnaturally seek to regain the former Norman influence in these realms. He knows that in you he receives the most powerful man in England; that your detention alone would convulse the country from one end of it to the other, and enable him, perhaps, to extort from Edward some measures dishonourable to us all. But against me he can harbour no ill design, — my detention would avail him nothing. And, in truth, if Harold be safe in England, Gurth must be safe in Rouen. Thy presence here at the head of our armies guarantees me from wrong. But reverse the case, and with Gurth in England, is Harold safe in Rouen? I, but a simple soldier and homely lord, with slight influence over Edward, no command in the country, and little practised of speech in the stormy Witan, — I am just so great that William dare not harm me, but not so great that he should even wish to harm me."

"He detains our kinsmen, why not thee?" said Harold.

"Because with our kinsmen he has at least the pretext that they were pledged as hostages; because I go simply as guest and envoy. No, to me danger cannot come. Be ruled, dear Harold."

"Be ruled, O my son," cried Githa, clasping the earl's knees, "and do not let me dread in the depth of the night to see the shade of Godwin, and hear his voice say, ' Woman, where is Harold?' "

It was impossible for the earl's strong understanding to resist the arguments addressed to it; and, to say truth, he had been more disturbed than he liked to confess by Edward's sinister forewarnings. Yet, on the other hand, there were reasons against his acquiescence in Gurth's proposal. The primary, and, to do him justice, the strongest, was in his native courage and his generous pride. Should he for the first time in his life shrink from a peril in the discharge of his duty, — a peril, too, so uncertain and vague? Should he suffer Gurth to fulfil the pledge he himself had taken? And granting even that Gurth were safe from whatever danger he individually might incur, did it become him to accept the proxy? Would Gurth's voice, too, be as potent as his own in effecting the return of the hostages?

The next reasons that swayed him were those he could not avow. In clearing his way to the English throne, it would be of no mean importance to secure the friendship of the Norman Duke, and the Norman acquiescence in his pretensions; it would be of infinite service to remove those prepossessions against his House, which were still rife with the Normans, who retained a bitter remembrance of their countrymen deci-mated,[1] it was said, with the concurrence if not at the order of Godwin, when they accompanied the ill-fated Alfred to the English shore, and who were yet sore with their old expulsion from the English court at the return of his father and himself.

Though it could not enter into his head that William, possessing no party whatever in England, could himself aspire to the English crown, yet at Edward's death there might be pretenders whom the Norman arms could find ready excuse to sanction. There was the boy Atheling on the one side, there was the valiant Norwegian King Hardrada on the other, who might revive the claims of his predecessor Magnus as heir to the rights of Canute. So near and so formidable a neighbour as the Count of the Normans, every object of policy led him to propitiate; and Gurth, with his unbending hate of all that was Norman, was not, at least, the most politic envoy he could select for that end. Add to this, that despite their

---

[1] The word "decimated" is the one generally applied by the historians to the massacre in question; and it is therefore retained here. But it is not correctly applied; for that butchery was perpetrated not upon one out of ten, but nine out of ten.

present reconciliation Harold could never long count upon amity with Tostig; and Tostig's connection with William, through their marriages into the House of Baldwin, was full of danger to a new throne, to which Tostig would probably be the most turbulent subject: the influence of this connection how desirable to counteract![1]

Nor could Harold, who, as patriot and statesman, felt deeply the necessity of reform and regeneration in the decayed edifice of the English monarchy, willingly lose an occasion to witness all that William had done to raise so high in renown and civilization, in martial fame and commercial prosperity, that petty duchy which he had placed on a level with the kingdoms of the Teuton and the Frank. Lastly, the Normans were the special darlings of the Roman Church. William had obtained the dispensation to his own marriage with Matilda; and might not the Norman influence, duly conciliated, back the prayer which Harold trusted one day to address to the pontiff, and secure to him the hallowed blessing, without which ambition lost its charm, and even a throne its splendour?

All these considerations, therefore, urged the earl to persist in his original purpose; but a warning voice in his heart, more powerful than all, sided with the prayer of Githa and the arguments of Gurth. In this state of irresolution Gurth said seasonably, —

"Bethink thee, Harold, if menaced but with peril to thyself, thou wouldst have a brave man's right to resist us; but it was of 'great evil to England' that Edward spoke, and thy reflection must tell thee that in this crisis of our country danger to thee is evil to England, — evil to England thou hast no right to incur."

"Dear mother, and generous Gurth," said Harold, then joining the two in one embrace, "ye have well-nigh conquered. Give me but two days to ponder well, and be assured

---

[1] The *above* reasons for Harold's memorable expedition are sketched at this length, because they suggest the most probable motives which induced it, and furnish, in no rash and inconsiderate policy, that key to his visit which is not to be found in chronicler or historian.

that I will not decide from the rash promptings of an ill-considered judgment."

Further than this they could not then move the earl; but Gurth was pleased shortly afterwards to see him depart to Edith, whose fears, from whatever source they sprang, would, he was certain, come in aid of his own pleadings.

But as the earl rode alone towards the once stately home of the perished Roman, and entered at twilight the darkening forest-land, his thoughts were less on Edith than on the Vala, with whom his ambition had more and more connected his soul. Perplexed by his doubts, and left dim in the waning lights of human reason, never more involuntarily did he fly to some guide to interpret the future and decide his path.

As if fate itself responded to the cry of his heart, he suddenly came in sight of Hilda herself, gathering leaves from elm and ash amidst the woodland. He sprang from his horse and approached her.

"Hilda," said he, in a low but firm voice, "thou hast often told me that the dead can advise the living. Raise thou the Scin-læca of the hero of old, — raise the Ghost, which mine eye or my fancy beheld before, vast and dim, by the silent bautastein, and I will stand by thy side. Fain would I know if thou hast deceived me and thyself; or if, in truth, to man's guidance Heaven doth vouchsafe saga and rede from those who have passed into the secret shores of Eternity."

"The dead," answered Hilda, "will not reveal themselves to eyes uninitiate save at their own will, uncompelled by charm and rune. To me their forms can appear distinct through the airy flame, — to me, duly prepared by spells that purge the eye of the spirit and loosen the walls of the flesh. I cannot say that what I see in the trance and the travail of my soul thou also wilt behold; for even when the vision hath passed from my sight, and the voice from my ear, only memories, confused and dim, of what I saw and heard, remain to guide the waking and common life. But thou shalt stand by my side while I invoke the phantom, and hear and interpret the words which rush from my lips, and the runes that take meaning from the sparks of the charmed fire. I knew ere thou camest, by the darkness and trouble of Edith's soul, that some shade from the Ash-tree of Life had fallen upon thine."

Then Harold related what had passed, and placed before Hilda the doubts that beset him.

The prophetess listened with earnest attention; but her mind, when not under its more mystic influences, being strongly biassed by its natural courage and ambition, she saw at a glance all the advantages towards securing the throne predestined to Harold, which might be effected by his visit to the Norman court, and she held in too great disdain both the worldly sense and the mystic reveries of the monkish king (for the believer in Odin was naturally incredulous of the visitation of the Christian saints) to attach much weight to his dreary predictions.

The short reply she made was therefore not calculated to deter Harold from the expedition in dispute; but she deferred till the following night, and to wisdom more dread than her own, the counsels that should sway his decision.

With a strange satisfaction at the thought that he should at least test personally the reality of those assumptions of preternatural power which had of late coloured his resolves and oppressed his heart, Harold then took leave of the Vala, who returned mechanically to her employment; and leading his horse by the rein, slowly continued his musing way towards the green knoll and its heathen ruins. But ere he gained the hillock, and while his thoughtful eyes were bent on the ground, he felt his arm seized tenderly, — turned, and beheld Edith's face full of unutterable and anxious love.

With that love, indeed, there was blended so much wistfulness, so much fear, that Harold exclaimed, —

"Soul of my soul, what hath chanced; what affects thee thus?"

"Hath no danger befallen thee?" asked Edith, falteringly, and gazing on his face with wistful, searching eyes.

"Danger! none, sweet trembler," answered the earl, evasively.

Edith dropped her eager looks, and clinging to his arm,

drew him on silently into the forest-land.   She paused at last where the old fantastic trees shut out the view of the ancient ruins; and when, looking round, she saw not those gray gigantic shafts which mortal hand seemed never to have piled together, she breathed more freely.

"Speak to me," then said Harold, bending his face to hers; "why this silence?"

"Ah, Harold!" answered his betrothed, "thou knowest that ever since we have loved one another, my existence hath been but a shadow of thine; by some weird and strange mystery, which Hilda would explain by the stars or the fates, that have made me a part of thee, I know by the lightness or gloom of my own spirit when good or ill shall befall thee.   How often, in thine absence, hath a joy suddenly broke upon me; and I felt by that joy, as by the smile of a good angel, that thou hast passed safe through some peril or triumphed over some foe!   And now thou askest me why I am so sad; I can only answer thee by saying that the sadness is cast upon me by some thunder-gloom on thine own destiny."

Harold had sought Edith to speak of his meditated journey, but seeing her dejection, he did not dare; so he drew her to his breast, and chid her soothingly for her vain apprehensions.   But Edith would not be comforted; there seemed something weighing on her mind and struggling to her lips, not accounted for merely by sympathetic forebodings; and at length, as he pressed her to tell all, she gathered courage and spoke: —

"Do not mock me," she said; "but what secret, whether of vain folly or of meaning fate, should I hold from thee?   All this day I struggled in vain against the heaviness of my forebodings.   How I hailed the sight of Gurth thy brother!   I besought him to seek thee, — thou hast seen him?"

"I have," said Harold.   "But thou wert about to tell me of something more than this dejection."

"Well," resumed Edith, "after Gurth left me, my feet sought involuntarily the hill on which we have met so often. I sat down near the old tomb, a strange weariness crept on my eyes, and a sleep that seemed not wholly sleep fell over me. I struggled against it, as if conscious of some coming terror; and as I struggled, and ere I slept, Harold, — yes, ere I slept, — I saw distinctly a pale and glimmering figure rise from the Saxon's grave. I saw — I see it still! Oh, that livid front, those glassy eyes!"

"The figure of a warrior?" said Harold, startled.

"Of a warrior, armed as in the ancient days, armed like the warrior that Hilda's maids are working for thy banner. I saw it; and in one hand it held a spear, and in the other a crown."

"A crown! — Say on, say on."

"I saw no more; sleep, in spite of myself, fell on me, — a sleep full of confused and painful, rapid and shapeless, images, till at last this dream rose clear. I beheld a bright and starry shape, that seemed as a spirit, yet wore thine aspect, standing on a rock; and an angry torrent rolled between the rock and the dry safe land. The waves began to invade the rock, and the spirit unfurled its wings as to flee. And then foul things climbed up from the slime of the rock, and descended from the mists of the troubled skies, and they coiled round the wings and clogged them. Then a voice cried in my ear, 'Seest thou not on the perilous rock the Soul of Harold the Brave? Seest thou not that the waters engulf it, if the wings fail to flee? Up, Truth, whose strength is in purity, whose image is woman, and aid the soul of the brave!' I sought to spring to thy side; but I was powerless, and behold, close beside me, through my sleep as through a veil, appeared the shafts of the ruined temple in which I lay reclined. And, me-thought, I saw Hilda sitting alone by the Saxon's grave, and pouring from a crystal vessel black drops into a human heart which she held in her hands; and out of that heart grew a child, and out of that child a youth, with dark mournful brow. And the youth stood by thy side and whispered to thee; and from his lips there came a reeking smoke, and in that smoke as in a blight the wings withered up. And I heard the Voice say, 'Hilda, it is thou that hast destroyed the good angel, and reared from the poisoned heart the loathsome tempter!' And I cried aloud, but it was too late; the waves swept over thee, and above the waves there floated an iron helmet, and on the helmet was a golden crown, — the crown I had seen in the hand of the spectre!"

"But this is no evil dream, my Edith," said Harold, gayly.

Edith, unheeding him, continued: "I started from my sleep. The sun was still high, the air lulled and windless. Then through the shafts and down the hill there glided, in that clear waking daylight, a grisly shape like that which I have heard our maidens say the witch-hags, sometimes seen in the forest, assume; yet in truth, it seemed neither of man nor woman. It turned its face once towards me, and on that hideous face were the glee and hate of a triumphant fiend. Oh, Harold, what should all this portend?"

"Hast thou not asked thy kinswoman, the diviner of dreams?"

"I asked Hilda, and she, like thee, only murmured, 'The Saxon crown!' But if there be faith in those airy children of the night, surely, O adored one, the vision forebodes danger, not to life, but to soul; and the words I heard seemed to say that thy wings were thy valour, and the Fylgia thou hadst lost was — No, *that* were impossible — "

"That my Fylgia was TRUTH, which losing, I were indeed lost to thee. Thou dost well," said Harold, loftily, "to hold *that* among the lies of the fancy. All else may perchance desert me, but never mine own free soul. Self-reliant hath Hilda called me in mine earlier days; and wherever fate casts me, in my truth and my love and my dauntless heart I dare both man and the fiend."

Edith gazed a moment in devout admiration on the mien of her hero-lover; then she drew closer and closer to his breast, consoled and believing.

CHAPTER V.

WITH all her persuasion of her own powers in penetrating the future, we have seen that Hilda had never consulted her oracles on the fate of Harold without a dark and awful sense of the ambiguity of their responses. That fate, involving the mightiest interests of a great race, and connected with events operating on the farthest times and the remotest lands, lost itself to her prophetic ken amidst omens the most contradictory, shadows and lights the most conflicting, meshes the most entangled. Her human heart, devotedly attached to the earl through her love for Edith; her pride, obstinately bent on securing to the last daughter of her princely race that throne which all her vaticinations, even when most gloomy, assured her was destined to the man with whom Edith's doom was interwoven, — combined to induce her to the most favourable interpretation of all that seemed sinister and doubtful. But according to the tenets of that peculiar form of magic cultivated by Hilda, the comprehension became obscured by whatever partook of human sympathy. It was a magic wholly distinct from the malignant witchcraft more popularly known to us, and which was equally common to the Germanic and Scandinavian heathens.

The magic of Hilda was rather akin to the old Cimbrian Alirones, or sacred prophetesses; and, as with them, it demanded the *priestess*, — that is, the person without human ties or emotions, a spirit clear as a mirror, upon which the great images of destiny might be cast untroubled.

However the natural gifts and native character of Hilda might be perverted by the visionary and delusive studies habitual to her, there was in her very infirmities a grandeur not without its pathos. In this position which she had assumed between the earth and the heaven, she stood so solitary and in such chilling air; all the doubts that beset

her lonely and daring soul came in such gigantic forms of
terror and menace! On the verge of the mighty Heathenesse
sinking fast into the night of ages, she towered amidst the
shades, a shade herself; and round her gathered the last
demons of the Dire Belief, defying the march of their luminous foe, and concentring round their mortal priestess the
wrecks of their horrent empire over a world redeemed.

All the night that succeeded her last brief conference with
Harold, the Vala wandered through the wild forest-land, seeking haunts or employed in collecting herbs hallowed to her
dubious yet solemn lore; and the last stars were receding into
the cold gray skies, when, returning homeward, she beheld
within the circle of the Druid temple a motionless object,
stretched on the ground near the Teuton's grave. She approached, and perceived what seemed a corpse, it was so still
and stiff in its repose, and the face upturned to the stars was
so haggard and death-like, — a face horrible to behold. The
evidence of extreme age was written on the shrivelled livid
skin and the deep furrows, but the expression retained that
intense malignity which belongs to a power of life that extreme age rarely knows. The garb, which was that of a
remote fashion, was foul and ragged, and neither by the garb
nor by the face was it easy to guess what was the sex of this
seeming corpse. But by a strange and peculiar odour that
rose from the form,[1] and a certain glistening on the face
and the lean folded hands, Hilda knew that the creature was
one of those witches, esteemed of all the most deadly and
abhorred, who by the application of certain ointments were
supposed to possess the art of separating soul from body, and,
leaving the last as dead, to dismiss the first to the dismal
orgies of the *Sabbat*. It was a frequent custom to select for
the place of such trances heathen temples and ancient graves;
and Hilda seated herself beside the witch to await the waking. The cock crowed thrice, heavy mists began to arise
from the glades, covering the gnarled roots of the forest-
trees, when the dread face on which Hilda calmly gazed
showed symptoms of returning life. A strong convulsion

---

[1] See note N.

shook the vague indefinite form under its huddled garments; the eyes opened, closed, opened again; and what had a few moments before seemed a dead thing, sat up and looked round.

"Wicca," said the Danish prophetess, with an accent between contempt and curiosity, "for what mischief to beast or man hast thou followed the noiseless path of the Dreams through the airs of Night?"

The creature gazed hard upon the questioner from its bleared but fiery eyes, and replied slowly, —

"Hail, Hilda, the Morthwyrtha! Why art thou not of us, why comest thou not to our revels? Gay sport have we had to-night with Faul and Zabulus;[1] but gayer far shall our sport be in the wassail hall of Senlac, when thy grandchild shall come in the torchlight to the bridal bed of her lord. A buxom bride is Edith the Fair, and fair looked her face in her sleep on yester noon, when I sat by her side, and breathed on her brow, and murmured the verse that blackens the dream; but fairer still shall she look in her sleep by her lord. Ha, ha! Ho! we shall be there, with Zabulus and Faul; we shall be there!"

"How," said Hilda, thrilled to learn that the secret ambition she cherished was known to this loathed sister in the art, — "how dost thou pretend to that mystery of the future, which is dim and clouded even to me? Canst thou tell when and where the daughter of the Norse kings shall sleep on the breast of her lord?"

A sound that partook of laughter, but was so unearthly in its malignant glee that it seemed not to come from a human lip, answered the Vala; and as the laugh died, the witch rose and said, —

"Go and question thy dead, O Morthwyrtha! Thou deemest thyself wiser than we are, — we wretched hags, whom the ceorl seeks when his herd has the murrain, or the girl when her false love forsakes her, — we, who have no dwelling known to man, but are found at need in the wold or the

---

[1] Faul was an evil spirit much dreaded by the Saxons. Zabulus and Diabolus (the devil) seem to have been the same.

cave, or the side of dull slimy streams where the murderess-mother hath drowned her babe. Askest thou, O Hilda, the rich and the learned, — askest thou counsel and lore from the daughter of Faul?"

"No," answered the Vala, haughtily; "not to such as thou do the great Nornas unfold the future. What knowest thou of the runes of old, whispered by the trunkless skull to the mighty Odin, — runes that control the elements, and conjure up the Shining Shadows of the grave? Not with thee will the stars confer; and thy dreams are foul with revelries obscene, not solemn and haunted with the bodements of things to come! Only I marvelled, while I beheld thee on the Saxon's grave, what joy such as thou can find in that life above life which draws upward the soul of the true Vala."

"The joy," replied the witch, — "the joy which comes from wisdom and power, higher than you ever won with your spells from the rune or the star. Wrath gives the venom to the slaver of the dog, and death to the curse of the witch. When wilt thou be as wise as the hag thou despisest? When will all the clouds that beset thee roll away from thy ken? When thy hopes are all crushed, when thy passions lie dead, when thy pride is abased, when thou art but a wreck, like the shafts of this temple, through which the starlight can shine, — *then* only, thy soul will see clearly the sense of the runes, and then thou and I will meet on the verge of the Black Shoreless Sea!"

So, despite all her haughtiness and disdain, did these words startle the lofty prophetess, that she remained gazing into space long after that fearful apparition had vanished, and up from the grass, which those obscene steps had profaned, sprang the lark, carolling.

But ere the sun had dispelled the dews on the forest sward, Hilda had recovered her wonted calm, and, locked within her own secret chamber, prepared the seid and the runes for the invocation of the dead.

CHAPTER VI.

RESOLVING, should the auguries consulted permit him to depart, to entrust Gurth with the charge of informing Edith, Harold parted from his betrothed without hint of his suspended designs; and he passed the day in making all preparations for his absence and his journey, promising Gurth to give his final answer on the morrow, when either himself or his brother should depart for Rouen. But more and more impressed with the arguments of Gurth and his own sober reason, and somewhat perhaps influenced by the forebodings of Edith (for that mind, once so constitutionally firm, had become tremulously alive to such airy influences), he had almost predetermined to assent to his brother's prayer, when he departed to keep his dismal appointment with the Morthwyrtha. The night was dim, but not dark; no moon shone, but the stars, wan though frequent, gleamed pale, as from the farthest deeps of the heaven; clouds gray and fleecy rolled slowly across the welkin, veiling and disclosing by turns the melancholy orbs.

The Morthwyrtha, in her dark dress, stood within the circle of stones. She had already kindled a fire at the foot of the bautastein, and its glare shone redly on the gray shafts, playing through their forlorn gaps upon the sward. By her side was a vessel, seemingly of pure water, filled from the old Roman fountain, and its clear surface flashed blood-red in the beams. Behind them, in a circle round both fire and water, were fragments of bark, cut in a peculiar form, like the head of an arrow, and inscribed with the mystic letters; nine were the fragments, and on each fragment were graved the runes. In her right hand the Morthwyrtha held her seid staff, her feet were bare, and her loins girt by the Hunnish belt inscribed with mystic letters; from the belt hung a pouch, or gipsire, of bearskin, with plates of silver. Her face, as

Harold entered the circle, had lost its usual calm; it was
wild and troubled.

She seemed unconscious of Harold's presence, and her eye,
fixed and rigid, was as that of one in a trance. Slowly, as
if constrained by some power not her own, she began to move
round the ring with a measured pace; and at last her voice
broke, low, hollow, and internal, into a rugged chant, which
may be thus imperfectly translated : —

> " By the **Urdar-fount** dwelling,
>   Day by day from the rill,
> The Nornas besprinkle
>   The ash Ygg-drassill ; [1]
> The hart bites the buds,
>   And the snake gnaws the root,
> But the eagle all-seeing
>   Keeps watch on the fruit.

> " These drops on thy tomb
>   From the fountain I pour ;
> With the rune I invoke thee,
>   With flame I restore.
> Dread Father of men,
>   In the land of thy grave,
> Give voice to the Vala,
>   And light to the Brave."

As she thus chanted, the Morthwyrtha now sprinkled the
drops from the vessel over the bautastein, now, one by one,
cast the fragments of bark scrawled with runes on the fire.
Then, whether or not some glutinous or other chemical material had been mingled in the water, a pale gleam broke from
the gravestone thus besprinkled, and the whole tomb glistened in the light of the leaping fire. From this light a mist
or thin smoke gradually rose, and took, though vaguely, the
outline of a vast human form. But so indefinite was the outline to Harold's eye, that, gazing on it steadily, and stilling
with strong effort his loud heart, he knew not whether it was
a phantom or a vapour that he beheld.

The Vala paused, leaning on her staff, and gazing in awe

[1] The mystic Ash-tree of Life, or symbol of the earth, watered by the
Fates. See Note O.

on the glowing stone; while the earl, with his arms folded on his broad breast, stood hushed and motionless. The sorceress recommenced: —

" Mighty dead, I revere thee,
    Dim-shaped from the cloud,
With the light of thy deeds
    For the web of thy shroud !

" As Odin consulted
    Mimir's skull hollow-eyed,[1]
Odin's heir comes to seek
    In the Phantom a guide."

As the Morthwyrtha ceased, the fire crackled loud, and from its flame flew one of the fragments of bark to the feet of the sorceress, the runic letters all indented with sparks.

The sorceress uttered a loud cry, which, despite his courage and his natural strong sense, thrilled through the earl's heart to his marrow and bones, so appalling was it with wrath and terror; and while she gazed aghast on the blazing letters, she burst forth: —

" No warrior art thou,
    And no child of the tomb;
I know thee and shudder,
    Great Asa of Doom.

" Thou constrainest my lips,
    And thou crushest my spell,
Bright Son of the Giant,
    Dark Father of Hell ! " [2]

The whole form of the Morthwyrtha then became convulsed and agitated, as if with the tempest of frenzy; the foam gathered to her lips, and her voice rang forth like a shriek: —

[1] Mimir, the most celebrated of the giants. The Vaner, with whom he was left as a hostage, cut off his head. Odin embalmed it by his *seid*, or magic art, pronounced over it mystic runes, and, ever after, consulted it on critical occasions.

[2] Asa-Lok or Loke (distinct from Utgard-Lok, the demon of the Infernal Regions), descended from the giants, but received among the celestial Deities; a treacherous and malignant Power, fond of assuming disguises and plotting evil, — corresponding in his attributes with our " Lucifer." One of his progeny was Hela, the Queen of Hell.

"In the Iron Wood rages
　　The Weaver of Harm,
　　The giant Blood-drinker
　　Hag-born MANAGARM.[1]

" A keel nears the shoal ;
　　From the slime and the mud
Crawl the newt and the adder,
　　The spawn of the flood.

" Thou stand'st on the rock
　　Where the dreamer beheld thee.
O soul, spread thy wings,
　　Ere the glamour hath spelled thee.

" Oh, dread is the tempter,
　　And strong the control ;
But conquered the tempter,
　　If firm be the soul ! "

The Vala paused; and though it was evident that in her frenzy she was still unconscious of Harold's presence, and seemed but to be the compelled and passive voice to some Power, real or imaginary, beyond her own existence, the proud man approached and said, —

"Firm shall be my soul; nor of the dangers which beset it would I ask the dead or the living. If plain answers to mortal sense can come from these airy shadows or these mystic charms, reply, O interpreter of fate; reply but to the questions I demand. If I go to the court of the Norman, shall I return unscathed?"

The Vala stood rigid as a shape of stone while Harold thus spoke; and her voice came so low and strange as if forced from her scarce-moving lips, —

"Thou shalt return unscathed."

"Shall the hostages of Godwin, my father, be released?"

---

[1] " A hag dwells in a wood called Janvid, the Iron Wood, the mother of many gigantic sons shaped like wolves; there is one of a race more fearful than all, named 'Managarm.' He will be filled with the blood of men who draw near their end, and will swallow up the moon, and stain the heavens and the earth with blood." (From the *Prose Edda.*) In the Scandinavian poetry Managarm is sometimes the symbol of *war*, and the " Iron Wood " a metaphor for *spears*.

"The hostages of Godwin shall be released," answered the same voice; "the hostage of Harold be retained."

"Wherefore hostage from me?"

"In pledge of alliance with the Norman."

"Ha! then the Norman and Harold shall plight friendship and troth?"

"Yes!" answered the Vala; but this time a visible shudder passed over her rigid form.

"Two questions more, and I have done. The Norman priests have the ear of the Roman Pontiff. Shall my league with William the Norman avail to win me my bride?"

"It will win thee the bride thou wouldst never have wedded but for thy league with William the Norman. Peace with thy questions, peace!" continued the voice, trembling as with some fearful struggle; "for it is the demon that forces my words, and they wither my soul to speak them."

"But one question more remains: shall I live to wear the crown of England; and if so, when shall I be a king?"

At these words the face of the prophetess kindled, the fire suddenly leaped up higher and brighter; again vivid sparks lighted the runes on the fragments of bark that were shot from the flame. Over these last the Morthwyrtha bowed her head, and then, lifting it, triumphantly burst once more into song:—

> " When the Wolf Month, [1] grim and still,
>   Heaps the snow-mass on the hill ;
>   When through white air, sharp and bitter,
>   Mocking sunbeams freeze and glitter ;
>   When the ice-gems, bright and barbed,
>   Deck the boughs the leaves had garbed,—
>   Then the measure shall be meted,
>   And the circle be completed.
>   Cerdic's race, the Thor-descended,
>   In the monk-king's tomb be ended ;
>   And no Saxon brow but thine
>   Wear the crown of Woden's line.
>
> " Where thou wendest, wend unfearing,
>   Every step thy throne is nearing.

---

[1] January.

Fraud may plot, and force assail **thee**, —
Shall the soul thou trustest fail thee ?
If it fail thee, scornful hearer,
Still the throne shines near and nearer.
Guile with guile oppose, and never
Crown and brow shall Force dissever :
Till the dead men, unforgiving,
Loose the war-steeds on the living ;
Till a sun whose race is ending
Sees the rival stars contending ;
Where the dead men, unforgiving,
Wheel the war-steeds round the living.

" Where thou wendest, wend unfearing ;
Every step thy throne is nearing.
Never shall thy House decay,
Nor thy sceptre pass away,
While the Saxon name endureth
In the land thy throne secureth ;
Saxon name and throne together,
Leaf and root, shall wax and wither ;
So the measure shall be meted,
And the circle close completed.

" Art thou answered, dauntless seeker ?
Go, thy bark shall ride the breaker,
Every billow high and higher,
Waft thee up to thy desire ;
And a force beyond thine own,
Drift and strand thee on the throne.

" When the Wolf Month, grim and still,
Piles the snow-mass on the hill,
In the white air sharp and bitter
Shall thy kingly sceptre glitter :
When the ice-gems barb the bough
Shall the jewels clasp thy brow ;
Winter-wind, the oak uprending,
With the altar-anthem blending ;
Wind shall howl, and mone shall sing,
' Hail to Harold, — HAIL THE KING ! ' "

An exultation that seemed more than human, so intense it
was and so solemn, thrilled in the voice which thus closed
predictions that seemed signally to belie the more vague and
menacing warnings with which the dreary incantation had

commenced. The Morthwyrtha stood erect and stately, still gazing on the pale blue flame that rose from the burial-stone, till slowly the flame waned and paled, and at last died with a sudden flicker, leaving the gray tomb standing forth all weather-worn and desolate, while a wind rose from the north and sighed through the roofless columns. Then as the light over the grave expired, Hilda gave a deep sigh, and fell to the ground senseless.

Harold lifted his eyes towards the stars, and murmured,—

"If it be a sin, as the priests say, to pierce the dark walls which surround us here, and read the future in the dim world beyond, why gavest thou, O Heaven, the reason, never resting, save when it explores? Why hast Thou set in the heart the mystic Law of Desire, ever toiling to the High, ever grasping at the Far?"

Heaven answered not the unquiet soul. The clouds passed to and fro in their wandering; the wind still sighed through the hollow stones; the fire shot with vain sparks towards the distant stars. In the cloud and the wind and the fire couldst thou read no answer from Heaven, unquiet soul?

The next day, with a gallant company, the falcon on his wrist,[1] the sprightly hound gambolling before his steed, blithe of heart and high in hope, Earl Harold took his way to the Norman court.

[1] Bayeux tapestry.

BOOK IX.

THE BONES OF THE DEAD.

CHAPTER I.

WILLIAM, Count of the Normans, sat in a fair chamber of his palace of Rouen; and on the large table before him were ample evidences of the various labours, as warrior, chief, thinker, and statesman, which filled the capacious breadth of that sleepless mind.

There lay a plan of the new port of Cherbourg, and beside it an open manuscript of the duke's favourite book, the Commentaries of Cæsar, from which, it is said, he borrowed some of the tactics of his own martial science; marked, and dotted, and interlined with his large bold handwriting, were the words of the great Roman. A score or so of long arrows, which had received some skilful improvement in feather or bolt, lay carelessly scattered over some architectural sketches of a new abbey church, and the proposed charter for its endowment. An open cyst, of the beautiful workmanship for which the English goldsmiths were then pre-eminently renowned, that had been among the parting gifts of Edward, contained letters from the various potentates near and far, who sought his alliance or menaced his repose.

On a perch behind him sat his favourite Norway falcon unhooded; for it had been taught the finest polish in its dainty education,—namely, "to face company undisturbed." At a kind of easel at the farther end of the hall, a dwarf, misshapen in limbs, but of a face singularly acute and intelligent, was employed in the outline of that famous action at Val des Dunes, which had been the scene of one of the most brilliant of William's feats in arms, — an outline intended to be transferred to the notable "stitchwork" of Matilda the Duchess.

Upon the floor, playing with a huge boar-hound of English breed, that seemed but ill to like the play, and every now and then snarled and showed his white teeth, was a young boy, with something of the duke's features, but with an expression more open and less sagacious; and something of the duke's broad build of chest and shoulder, but without promise of the duke's stately stature, which was needed to give grace and dignity to a strength otherwise cumbrous and graceless. And indeed, since William's visit to England, his athletic shape had lost much of its youthful symmetry, though not yet deformed by that corpulence which was a disease almost as rare in the Norman as the Spartan. Nevertheless, what is a defect in the gladiator is often but a beauty in the prince; and the duke's large proportions filled the eye with a sense both of regal majesty and physical power. His countenance, yet more than his form, showed the work of time; the short dark hair was worn into partial baldness at the temples by the habitual friction of the casque, and the constant indulgence of wily stratagem and ambitious craft had deepened the wrinkles round the plotting eye and the firm mouth: so that it was only by an effort like that of an actor, that his aspect regained the knightly and noble frankness it had once worn. The accomplished prince was no longer, in truth, what the bold warrior had been, — he was greater in state and less in soul. And already, despite all his grand qualities as a ruler, his imperious nature had betrayed signs of what he (whose constitutional sternness the Norman freemen, not without effort, curbed into the limits of justice) might become, if wider scope were afforded to his fiery passions and unsparing will.

Before the duke, who was leaning his chin on his hand, stood Mallet de Graville, speaking earnestly; and his discourse seemed both to interest and please his lord.

"Eno'!" said William, "I comprehend the nature of the land and its men, — a land that, untaught by experience, and persuaded that a peace of twenty or thirty years must last till the crack of doom, neglects all its defences, and has not one fort, save Dover, between the coast and the capital, — a land which must be won or lost by a single battle, and men " (here the duke hesitated), — "and *men*," he resumed with a sigh, "whom it will be so hard to conquer that, *pardex*, I don't wonder they neglect their fortresses. Enough, I say, of them. Let us return to Harold, — thou thinkest, then, that he is worthy of his fame?"

"He is almost the only Englishman I have seen," answered De Graville, "who hath received scholarly rearing and nurture; and all his faculties are so evenly balanced, and all accompanied by so composed a calm, that methinks, when I look at and hear him, I contemplate some artful castle, — the strength of which can never be known at the first glance, nor except by those who assail it."

"Thou art mistaken, Sire de Graville," said the duke, with a shrewd and cunning twinkle of his luminous dark eyes. "For thou tellest me that he hath no thought of my pretensions to the English throne, — that he inclines willingly to thy suggestions to come himself to my court for the hostages, — that, in a word, he is not suspicious."

"Certes, he is not suspicious," returned Mallet.

"And thinkest thou that an artful castle were worth much without warder or sentry; or a cultivated mind strong and safe without its watchman, — Suspicion?"

"Truly, my lord speaks well and wisely," said the knight, startled; "but Harold is a man thoroughly English, and the English are a *gens* the least suspecting of any created thing between an angel and a sheep."

William laughed aloud. But his laugh was checked suddenly; for at that moment a fierce yell smote his ears, and looking hastily up, he saw his hound and his son rolling together on the ground, in a grapple that seemed deadly.

William sprang to the spot; but the boy, who was then under the dog, cried out, "*Laissez aller! laissez aller!* no rescue! I will master my own foe;" and so saying, with a vigorous effort he gained his knee, and with both hands griped the hound's throat, so that the beast twisted in vain to and fro with gnashing jaws, and in another minute would have panted out its last.

"I may save my good hound now," said William, with the gay smile of his earlier days; and, though not without some exertion of his prodigious strength, he drew the dog from his son's grasp.

"That was ill done, Father," said Robert, surnamed even then the *Courthose*, "to take part with thy son's foe."

"But my son's foe is thy father's property, my *vaillant*," said the duke; "and thou must answer to me for treason in provoking quarrel and feud with my own four-footed vavasour."

"It is not thy property, Father; thou gavest the dog to me when a whelp."

"Fables, Monseigneur de Courthose; I lent it to thee but for a day, when thou hadst put out thine ankle-bone in jumping off the rampire; and all maimed as thou wert, thou hadst still malice enow in thee to worry the poor beast into a fever."

"Given or lent, it is the same thing, Father; what I have once, that will I hold, as thou didst before me, in thy cradle."

Then the great duke, who in his own house was the fondest and weakest of men, was so doltish and doting as to take the boy in his arms and kiss him; nor, with all his far-sighted sagacity, deemed he that in that kiss lay the seed of the awful curse that grew up from a father's agony, to end in a son's misery and perdition.

Even Mallet de Graville frowned at the sight of the sire's infirmity; even Turold the dwarf shook his head. At that moment an officer entered, and announced that an English nobleman, apparently in great haste (for his horse had dropped down dead as he dismounted), had arrived at the palace, and craved instant audience of the duke. William put down the boy, gave the brief order for the stranger's admission, and, punctilious in ceremonial, beckoning De Graville to follow him, passed at once into the next chamber, and seated himself on his chair of state.

In a few moments one of the seneschals of the palace ushered in a visitor whose long mustache at once proclaimed him Saxon, and in whom De Graville with surprise recognized his old friend Godrith. The young thegn, with a reverence more hasty than that to which William was accustomed, advanced to the foot of the daïs, and using the Norman language, said, in a voice thick with emotion, —

"From Harold the Earl, greeting to thee, Monseigneur. Most foul and unchristian wrong hath been done the earl by thy liegeman, Guy, Count of Ponthieu. Sailing hither in two barks from England, with intent to visit thy court, storm and wind drove the earl's vessels towards the mouth of the Somme;[1] there landing, and without fear, as in no hostile country, he and his train were seized by the count himself, and cast into prison in the castle of Belrem.[2] A dungeon fit but for malefactors holds, while I speak, the first lord of England, and brother-in-law to its king. Nay, hints of famine, torture, and death itself have been darkly thrown out by this most disloyal count, whether in earnest or with the base view of heightening ransom. At length, wearied perhaps by the earl's firmness and disdain, this traitor of Ponthieu hath permitted me in the earl's behalf to bear the message of Harold. He came to thee as to a prince and a friend; sufferest thou thy liegeman to detain him as a thief or a foe?"

"Noble Englishman," replied William, gravely, "this is a matter more out of my cognizance than thou seemest to think. It is true that Guy, Count of Ponthieu, holds fief under me, but I have no control over the laws of his realm; and by those laws he hath right of life and death over all stranded and waifed on his coast. Much grieve I for the mishap of your famous earl, and what I can do, I will; but I can only treat in this matter with Guy as prince with prince, not as lord to vassal. Meanwhile I pray you to take rest and food; and I will seek prompt counsel as to the measures to adopt."

The Saxon's face showed disappointment and dismay at this answer, so different from what he had expected; and he replied

---

[1] Roman de Rou, see part ii. 1078.
[2] The present Beaurain, near Montreuil.

with the natural honest bluntness which all his younger affection of Norman manners had never eradicated, —

"Food will I not touch, nor wine drink, till thou, Lord Count, hast decided what help, as noble to noble, Christian to Christian, man to man, thou givest to him who has come into this peril solely from his trust in thee."

"Alas!" said the grand dissimulator, "heavy is the responsibility with which thine ignorance of our land, laws, and men would charge me. If I take but one false step in this matter, woe indeed to thy lord! Guy is hot and haughty, and in his *droits;* he is capable of sending me the earl's head in reply to too dure a request for his freedom. Much treasure and broad lands will it cost me, I fear, to ransom the earl. But be cheered; half my duchy were not too high a price for thy lord's safety. Go, then, and eat with a good heart, and drink to the earl's health with a hopeful prayer."

"An it please you, my lord," said De Graville, "I know this gentle thegn, and will beg of you the grace to see to his entertainment and sustain his spirits."

"Thou shalt, but later; so noble a guest none but my chief seneschal should be the first to honour." Then turning to the officer in waiting, he bade him lead the Saxon to the chamber tenanted by William Fitzosborne (who then lodged within the palace), and committed him to that count's care.

As the Saxon sullenly withdrew, and as the door closed on him, William rose and strode to and fro the room exultingly.

"I have him! I have him!" he cried aloud; "not as free guest, but as ransomed captive. I have him, — the earl! — I have him! Go, Mallet, my friend, now seek this sour-looking Englishman; and, hark thee! fill his ear with all the tales thou canst think of as to Guy's cruelty and ire. Enforce all the difficulties that lie in my way towards the earl's delivery. Great make the danger of the earl's capture, and vast all the favour of release. Comprehendest thou?"

"I am Norman, Monseigneur," replied De Graville, with a slight smile; "and we Normans can make a short mantle cover a large space. You will not be displeased with my address."

"Go, then, — go," said William, "and send me forthwith

Lanfranc, — no, hold! — not Lanfranc, he is too scrupulous; Fitzosborne, — no, too haughty. Go, first, to my brother, Odo of Bayeux, and pray him to seek me on the instant."

The knight bowed and vanished; and William continued to pace the room, with sparkling eyes and murmuring lips.

CHAPTER II.

Not till after repeated messages, at first without talk of ransom and in high tone, affected, no doubt, by William to spin out the negotiations and augment the value of his services, did Guy of Ponthieu consent to release his illustrious captive, — the guerdon a large sum and *un bel maneir*[1] on the river Eaulne. But whether that guerdon were the fair ransom-fee or the price for concerted snare, no man now can say, and sharper than ours the wit that forms the more likely guess. These stipulations effected, Guy himself opened the doors of the dungeon; and affecting to treat the whole matter as one of law and right, now happily and fairly settled, was as courteous and debonair as he had before been dark and menacing.

He even himself, with a brilliant train, accompanied Harold to the Château d'Eu,[2] whither William journeyed to give him the meeting; and laughed with a gay grace at the earl's short and scornful replies to his compliments and excuses. At the gates of this château, not famous, in after times, for the good faith of its lords, William himself, laying aside all the pride of etiquette which he had established at his court, came to receive his visitor; and aiding him to dismount, embraced him cordially, amidst a loud fanfaron of fifes and trumpets.

The flower of that glorious nobility which a few generations had sufficed to rear out of the lawless pirates of the Baltic, had been selected to do honour alike to guest and host.

[1] Roman de Rou, part ii. 1079.
[2] William of Poitiers, "apud Aucense Castrum."

There were Hugo de Montfort and Roger de Beaumont, famous in council as in the field, and already gray with fame. There was Henri, Sire de Ferrers, whose name is supposed to have arisen from the vast forges that burned around his castle, on the anvils of which were welded the arms impenetrable in every field. There was Raoul de Tancarville, the old tutor of William, hereditary Chamberlain of the Norman Counts; and Geoffroi de Mandeville, and Tonstain the Fair, whose name still preserved, amidst the general corruption of appellations, the evidence of his Danish birth; and Hugo de Grantmesnil, lately returned from exile; and Humphrey de Bohun, whose old castle in Carcutan may yet be seen; and St. John, and Lacie, and D'Aincourt, of broad lands between the Maine and the Oise; and William de Montfichet, and Roger, nicknamed "Bigod," and Roger de Mortemer; and many more, whose fame lives in another land than that of Neustria! There, too, were the chief prelates and abbots of a church that since William's accession had risen into repute with Rome and with learning, unequalled on this side the Alps; their white aubes over their gorgeous robes: Lanfranc, and the Bishop of Coutance, and the Abbot of Bec, and foremost of all in rank, but not in learning, Odo of Bayeux.

So great the assemblage of quens and prelates that there was small room in the courtyard for the lesser knights and chiefs, who yet hustled each other, with loss of Norman dignity, for a sight of the lion which guarded England; and still, amidst all those men of mark and might, Harold, simple and calm, looked as he had looked on his war-ship in the Thames, the man who could lead them all!

From those, indeed, who were fortunate enough to see him as he passed up by the side of William, as tall as the duke, and no less erect, — of far slighter bulk, but with a strength almost equal, to a practised eye, in his compacter symmetry and more supple grace, — from those who saw him thus, an admiring murmur rose; for no men in the world so valued and cultivated personal advantages as the Norman knighthood.

Conversing easily with Harold, and well watching him

while he conversed, the duke led his guest into a private chamber in the third floor[1] of the castle, and in that chamber were Haco and Wolnoth.

"This, I trust, is no surprise to you," said the duke, smiling; "and now I shall but mar your commune." So saying, he left the room; and Wolnoth rushed to his brother's arms, while Haco more timidly drew near and touched the earl's robe.

As soon as the first joy of the meeting was over, the earl said to Haco, whom he had drawn to his breast with an embrace as fond as that bestowed on Wolnoth, —

"Remembering thee a boy, I came to say to thee, ' Be my son;' but seeing thee a man, I change the prayer: ' Supply thy father's place, and be my brother!' And thou, Wolnoth, hast thou kept thy word to me? Norman is thy garb, in truth; is thy heart still English?"

"Hist!" whispered Haco; "hist! We have a proverb, that walls have ears."

"But Norman walls can hardly understand our broad Saxon of Kent, I trust," said Harold, smiling, though with a shade on his brow.

"True; continue to speak Saxon," said Haco, "and we are safe."

"Safe!" echoed Harold.

"Haco's fears are childish, my brother," said Wolnoth, "and he wrongs the duke."

"Not the duke, but the policy which surrounds him like an atmosphere," exclaimed Haco. "Oh, Harold, generous indeed wert thou to come hither for thy kinsfolk, — generous! But for England's weal, better that we had rotted out our lives in exile, ere thou, hope and prop of England, set foot in these webs of wile."

"Tut!" said Wolnoth, impatiently; "good is it for England that the Norman and Saxon should be friends."

Harold, who had lived to grow as wise in men's hearts as

[1] As soon as the rude fort of the Middle Ages admitted something of magnificence and display, the state rooms were placed in the third story of the inner court, as being the most secure.

his father, save when the natural trustfulness that lay under his calm reserve lulled his sagacity, turned his eye steadily on the faces of his two kinsmen; and he saw at the first glance that a deeper intellect and a graver temper than Wolnoth's fair face betrayed characterized the dark eye and serious brow of Haco. He therefore drew his nephew a little aside, and said to him, —

"Forewarned is forearmed. Deemest thou that this fair-spoken duke will dare aught against my life?"

"Life, no; liberty, yes."

Harold started; and those strong passions native to his breast, but usually curbed beneath his majestic will, heaved in his bosom and flashed in his eye.

"Liberty! — let him dare! Though all his troops pave the way from his court to his coasts, I would hew my way through their ranks."

"Deemest thou that I am a coward?" said Haco, simply; "yet contrary to all law and justice, and against King Edward's well-known remonstrance, hath not the count detained me years, yea, long years, in his land? Kind are his words, wily his deeds. Fear not force; fear fraud."

"I fear neither," answered Harold, drawing himself up, "nor do I repent me one moment. No! nor did I repent in the dungeon of that felon count — whom God grant me life to repay with fire and sword for his treason! — that I myself have come hither to demand my kinsmen. I come in the name of England, strong in her might, and sacred in her majesty."

Before Haco could reply, the door opened, and Raoul de Tancarville, as grand chamberlain, entered, with all Harold's Saxon train, and a goodly number of Norman squires and attendants, bearing rich vestures.

The noble bowed to the earl with his country's polished courtesy, and besought leave to lead him to the bath, while his own squires prepared his raiment for the banquet to be held in his honour; so all further conference with his young kinsmen was then suspended.

The duke, who affected a state no less regal than that of the Court of France, permitted no one, save his own family and guests, to sit at his own table. His great officers (those imperious lords) stood beside his chair; and William Fitzosborne, "the Proud Spirit," placed on the board with his own hand the dainty dishes for which the Norman cooks were renowned. And great men were those Norman cooks; and often for some "delicate," more ravishing than wont, gold chain and gem, and even *bel maneir*, fell to their guerdon.[1] It was worth being a cook in those days!

The most seductive of men was William in his fair moods; and he lavished all the witcheries at his control upon his guest. If possible, yet more gracious was Matilda the Duchess. This woman, eminent for mental culture, for personal beauty, and for a spirit and ambition no less great than her lord's, knew well how to choose such subjects of discourse as might most flatter an English ear. Her connection with Harold, through her sister's marriage with Tostig, warranted a familiarity almost caressing, which she assumed towards the comely earl; and she insisted, with a winning smile, that all the hours the duke would leave at his disposal he must spend with her.

The banquet was enlivened by the song of the great Taillefer himself, who selected a theme that artfully flattered alike the Norman and the Saxon; namely, the aid given by Rolfganger to Athelstan, and the alliance between the English King and the Norman founder. He dexterously introduced into the song praises of the English, and the value of their friendship; and the countess significantly applauded each gallant compliment to the land of the famous guest. If Harold was pleased by such poetic courtesies, he was yet more surprised by the high honour in which duke, baron, and prelate evidently held the poet; for it was among the worst signs of that sordid spirit, honouring only wealth, which had crept over the original character of the Anglo-Saxon, that the bard, or scop, with them had sunk into great disrepute, and it was

---

[1] A manor (but not, alas, in Normandy) was held by one of his cooks, on the tenure of supplying William with a dish of dillegrout.

even forbidden to ecclesiastics[1] to admit such landless va-
grants to their company.

Much, indeed, there was in that court which, even on the
first day, Harold saw to admire. That stately temperance,
so foreign to English excesses, but which, alas! the Norman
kept not long when removed to another soil; that methodical
state and noble pomp which characterized the feudal system,
linking so harmoniously prince to peer, and peer to knight;
the easy grace, the polished wit of the courtiers; the wisdom
of Lanfranc and the higher ecclesiastics, blending worldly lore
with decorous, not pedantic, regard to their sacred calling;
the enlightened love of music, letters, song, and art, which
coloured the discourse both of duke and duchess and the
younger courtiers, prone to emulate high example, whether
for ill or good, — all impressed Harold with a sense of civilization and true royalty, which at once saddened and inspired
his musing mind, — saddened him when he thought how far
behind-hand England was in much with this comparatively
petty principality, inspired him when he felt what one great
chief can do for his native land.

The unfavourable impressions made upon his thoughts by
Haco's warnings could scarcely fail to yield beneath the prodigal courtesies lavished upon him, and the frank openness
with which William laughingly excused himself for having
so long detained the hostages, "in order, my guest, to make
thee come and fetch them. And, by Saint Valery, now thou
art here, thou shalt not depart till at least thou hast lost in
gentler memories the recollection of the scurvy treatment thou
hast met from that barbarous count. Nay, never bite thy lip,
Harold, my friend; leave to me thy revenge upon Guy.
Sooner or later the very *maneir* he hath extorted from me
shall give excuse for sword and lance, and then, *pardex*, thou
shalt come and cross steel in thine own quarrel. How I
rejoice that I can show to the *beau frère* of my dear cousin
and seigneur some return for all the courtesies the English
King and kingdom bestowed upon me! To-morrow we will

---

[1] The Council of Cloveshoe forbade the clergy to harbour poets, harpers,
musicians, and buffoons.

ride to Rouen; there all knightly sports shall be held to grace thy coming; and by Saint Michael, knight-saint of the Norman, nought less will content me than to have thy great name in the list of my chosen *chevaliers*. But the night wears now, and thou sure must need sleep;" and thus talking, the duke himself led the way to Harold's chamber, and insisted on removing the *ouche* from his robe of state. As he did so, he passed his hand, as if carelessly, along the earl's right arm. "Ha!" said he, suddenly, and in his natural tone of voice, which was short and quick, "these muscles have known practice! Dost think thou couldst bend my bow?"

"Who could bend that of — Ulysses?" returned the earl, fixing his deep blue eye upon the Norman's. William unconsciously changed colour, for he felt that he was at that moment more Ulysses than Achilles.

CHAPTER III.

SIDE by side, William and Harold entered the fair city of Rouen, and there a succession of the brilliant pageants and knightly entertainments comprising those "rare feats of honour," expanded, with the following age, into the more gorgeous display of joust and tourney, was designed to dazzle the eyes and captivate the fancy of the earl. But though Harold won, even by the confession of the chronicles most in favour of the Norman, golden opinions in a court more ready to deride than admire the Saxon, — though not only the "strength of his body" and "the boldness of his spirit," as shown in exhibitions unfamiliar to Saxon warriors, but his "manners," his "eloquence, intellect, and other good qualities"[1] were loftily conspicuous amidst those knightly courtiers, — that sublimer part of his character, which was found in its simple manhood and intense nationality, kept him unmoved and serene amidst all intended to exercise that

[1] Ord. Vital.

fatal spell which Normanized most of those who came within the circle of Norman attraction.

These festivities were relieved by pompous excursions and progresses from town to town and fort to fort throughout the duchy, and, according to some authorities, even to a visit to Philip the French King at Compeigne. On the return to Rouen, Harold and the six thegns of his train were solemnly admitted into that peculiar band of warlike brothers which William had instituted, and to which, following the chronicles of the after century, we have given the name of *Knights*. The silver baldrick was belted on, and the lance, with its pointed banderol, was placed in the hand, and the seven Saxon lords became Norman knights.

The evening after this ceremonial, Harold was with the duchess and her fair daughters, — all children. The beauty of one of the girls drew from him those compliments so sweet to a mother's ear. Matilda looked up from the broidery on which she was engaged, and beckoned to her the child thus praised.

"Adeliza," she said, placing her hand on the girl's dark locks, "though we would not that thou shouldst learn too early how men's tongues can gloze and flatter, yet this noble guest hath so high a repute for truth that thou mayest at least believe him sincere when he says thy face is fair. Think of it, and with pride, my child; let it keep thee through youth proof against the homage of meaner men; and, peradventure, Saint Michael and Saint Valery may bestow on thee a mate valiant and comely as this noble lord."

The child blushed to her brow, but answered with the quickness of a spoiled infant, — unless, perhaps, she had been previously tutored so to reply, —

"Sweet mother, I will have no mate and no lord but Harold himself; and if he will not have Adeliza as his wife, she will die a nun."

"Froward child, it is not for thee to woo!" said Matilda, smiling. "Thou heardest her, noble Harold; what is thine answer?"

"That she will grow wiser," said the earl, laughing, as he

kissed the child's forehead. "Fair damsel, ere thou art ripe for the altar, time will have sown gray in these locks; and thou wouldst smile indeed in scorn, if Harold then claimed thy troth."

"Not so," said Matilda, seriously; "high-born damsels see youth not in years but in fame, — fame, which is young forever!"

Startled by the gravity with which Matilda spoke, as if to give importance to what had seemed a jest, the earl, versed in courts, felt that a snare was round him, and replied in a tone between jest and earnest, —

"Happy am I to wear on my heart a charm proof against all the beauty even of this court."

Matilda's face darkened; and William entering at that time with his usual abruptness, lord and lady exchanged glances, not unobserved by Harold.

The duke, however, drew aside the Saxon, and saying gayly, "We Normans are not naturally jealous; but then, till now we have not had Saxon gallants closeted with our wives," added more seriously, "Harold, I have a grace to pray at thy hands, — come with me."

The earl followed William into his chamber, which he found filled with chiefs, in high converse; and William then hastened to inform him that he was about to make a military expedition against the Bretons; and knowing his peculiar acquaintance with the warfare, as with the language and manners, of their kindred Welch, he besought his aid in a campaign which he promised him should be brief.

Perhaps the earl was not, in his own mind, averse from returning William's display of power by some evidence of his own military skill, and the valour of the Saxon thegns in his train. There might be prudence in such exhibition, and at all events he could not with a good grace decline the proposal. He enchanted William therefore by a simple acquiescence; and the rest of the evening, deep into night, was spent in examining charts of the fort and country intended to be attacked.

The conduct and courage of Harold and his Saxons in this

expedition are recorded by the Norman chroniclers. The earl's personal exertions saved, at the passage of Coësnon, a detachment of soldiers who would otherwise have perished in the quicksands; and even the warlike skill of William in the brief and brilliant campaign was, if not eclipsed, certainly equalled, by that of the Saxon chief.

While the campaign lasted, William and Harold had but one table and one tent. To outward appearance, the familiarity between the two was that of brothers; in reality, however, these two men, both so able, — one so deep in his guile, the other so wise in his tranquil caution, — felt that a silent war between the two for mastery was working on, under the guise of loving peace.

Already Harold was conscious that the politic motives for his mission had failed him; already he perceived, though he scarce knew why, that William the Norman was the last man to whom he could confide his ambition, or trust for aid.

One day, as during a short truce with the defenders of the place they were besieging, the Normans were diverting their leisure with martial games, in which Taillefer shone pre-eminent, while Harold and William stood without their tent, watching the animated field, the duke abruptly exclaimed to Mallet de Graville, —

"Bring me my bow. Now, Harold, let me see if thou canst bend it."

The bow was brought, and Saxon and Norman gathered round the spot.

"Fasten thy glove to yonder tree, Mallet," said the duke, taking that mighty bow in his hand, and bending its stubborn yew into the noose of the string with practised ease.

Then he drew the arc to his ear; and the tree itself seemed to shake at the shock, as the shaft, piercing the glove, lodged half-way in the trunk.

"Such are not our weapons," said the earl; "and ill would it become me, unpractised, so to peril our English honour as to strive against the arm that could bend that arc and wing that arrow. But that I may show these Norman knights that at least we have some weapon wherewith we can parry shaft and smite assailer, bring me forth, Godrith, my shield and my Danish axe."

Taking the shield and axe which the Saxon brought to him, Harold then stationed himself before the tree.

"Now, fair duke," said he, smiling, "choose thou thy longest shaft, — bid thy ten doughtiest archers take their bows; round this tree will I move, and let each shaft be aimed at whatever space in my mailless body I leave unguarded by my shield."

"No!" said William, hastily; "that were murder."

"It is but the common peril of war," said Harold, simply, and he walked to the tree.

The blood mounted to William's brow, and the lion's thirst of carnage parched his throat.

"An he will have it so," said he, beckoning to his archers, "let not Normandy be shamed. Watch well, and let every shaft go home; avoid only the head and the heart; such orgulous vaunting is best cured by blood-letting."

The archers nodded, and took their post, each at a separate quarter; and deadly indeed seemed the danger of the earl, for as he moved, though he kept his back guarded by the tree, some parts of his form the shield left exposed, and it would have been impossible, in his quick-shifting movements, for the archers so to aim as to wound, but to spare life. Yet the earl seemed to take no peculiar care to avoid the peril, — lifting his bare head fearlessly above the shield, and including in one gaze of his steadfast eye, calmly bright even at the distance, all the shafts of the archers.

At one moment five of the arrows hissed through the air, and with such wonderful quickness had the shield turned to each that three fell to the ground blunted against it, and two broke on its surface.

But William, waiting for the first discharge, and seeing full mark at Harold's shoulder as the buckler turned, now sent forth his terrible shaft. The noble Taillefer, with a poet's true sympathy, cried, "Saxon, beware!" but the watchful Saxon needed not the warning. As if in disdain, Harold met not the shaft with his shield, but swinging high the mighty axe, which with most men required both arms to wield it, he advanced a step, and clove the rushing arrow in twain.

Before William's loud oath of wrath and surprise left his lips, the five shafts of the remaining archers fell as vainly as their predecessors against the nimble shield.

Then advancing, Harold said cheerfully: "This is but defence, fair Duke; and little worth were the axe if it could not smite as well as ward. Wherefore, I pray you, place upon yonder broken stone pillar, which seems some relic of Druid heathenesse, such helm and shirt of mail as thou deemest most proof against sword and pertuizan, and judge then if our English axe can guard well our English land."

"If thy axe can cleave the helmet I wore at Bavent, when the Franks and their king fled before me," said the duke, grimly, "I shall hold Cæsar in fault not to have invented a weapon so dread."

And striding back into his pavilion, he came forth with the helm and shirt of mail, which was worn stronger and heavier by the Normans, as fighting usually on horseback, than by Dane and Saxon, who, mainly fighting on foot, could not have endured so cumbrous a burden; and if strong and dour generally with the Norman, judge what solid weight that mighty duke could endure! With his own hand William placed the mail on the ruined Druid stone, and on the mail the helm.

Harold looked long and gravely at the edge of the axe; it was so richly gilt and damaskeened, that the sharpness of its temper could not well have been divined under that holiday glitter. But this axe had come to him from Canute the Great, who himself, unlike the Danes, small and slight,[1] had supplied his deficiency of muscle by the finest dexterity and the most perfect weapons. Famous had been that axe in the delicate hand of Canute, — how much more tremendous in the ample grasp of Harold! Swinging now in both hands this weapon, with a peculiar and rapid whirl, which gave it an inconceivable impetus, the earl let fall the crushing blow. At the first stroke, cut right in the centre, rolled the helm;

---

[1] Canute made his inferior strength and stature his excuse for not meeting Edward Ironsides in single combat.

at the second, through all the woven mail (cleft asunder, as if
the slightest filigree work of the goldsmith), shore the blade,
and a great fragment of the stone itself came tumbling on the
sod.

The Normans stood aghast, and William's face was as pale
as the shattered stone. The great duke felt even his matchless dissimulation fail him; nor, unused to the special practice
and craft which the axe required, could he have pretended,
despite a physical strength superior even to Harold's, to rival
blows that seemed to him more than mortal.

"Lives there any other man in the wide world whose arm
could have wrought that feat?" exclaimed Bruse, the ancestor of the famous Scot.

"Nay," said Harold, simply, "at least thirty thousand such
men have I left at home! But this was but the stroke of an
idle vanity, and strength becomes tenfold in a good cause."

The duke heard, and fearful lest he should betray his sense
of the latent meaning couched under his guest's words, he
hastily muttered forth reluctant compliment and praise; while
Fitzosborne, De Bohun, and other chiefs more genuinely
knightly, gave way to unrestrained admiration.

Then beckoning De Graville to follow him, the duke strode
off towards the tent of his brother of Bayeux, who, though
except on extraordinary occasions he did not join in positive
conflict, usually accompanied William in his military excursions, both to bless the host, and to advise (for his martial
science was considerable) the council of war.

The bishop, who, despite the sanctimony of the court and
his own stern nature, was, though secretly and decorously,
a gallant of great success in other fields than those of Mars,[1]
sat alone in his pavilion, inditing an epistle to a certain fair
dame in Rouen, whom he had unwillingly left to follow his
brother. At the entrance of William, whose morals in such
matters were pure and rigid, he swept the letter into the chest

---

[1] Odo's licentiousness was, at a later period, one of the alleged causes of his
downfall, or rather against his release from the prison to which he had been
consigned. He had a son named John, who distinguished himself under
Henry I. — *Ord. Vital.* lib. iv.

of relics which always accompanied him, and rose, saying indifferently, —

"A treatise on the authenticity of Saint Thomas's little finger! But what ails you? You are disturbed!"

"Odo, Odo, this man baffles me, this man fools me; I make no ground with him. I have spent — Heaven knows what I have spent," — said the duke, sighing with penitent parsimony, "in banquets and ceremonies and processions, to say nothing of my *bel maneir* of Yonne, and the sum wrung from my coffers by that greedy Ponthevin. All gone, all wasted, all melted like snow! and the Saxon is as Saxon as if he had seen neither Norman splendour, nor been released from the danger by Norman treasure. But, by the splendour Divine, I were fool indeed if I suffered him to return home. Would thou hadst seen the sorcerer cleave my helmet and mail just now, as easily as if they had been willow twigs. Oh, Odo, Odo, my soul is troubled, and Saint Michael forsakes me!"

While William ran on thus distractedly, the prelate lifted his eyes inquiringly to De Graville, who now stood within the tent, and the knight briefly related the recent trial of strength.

"I see nought in this to chafe thee," said Odo; "the man once thine, the stronger the vassal, the more powerful the lord."

"But he is not mine; I have sounded him as far as I dare go. Matilda hath almost openly offered him my fairest child as his wife. Nothing dazzles, nothing moves him. Thinkest thou I care for his strong arm? Tut, no: I chafe at the proud heart that set the arm in motion; the proud meaning his words symbolled out, — 'So will English strength guard English land from the Norman; so axe and shield will defy your mail and your shafts.' But let him beware!" growled the duke, fiercely, "or —"

"May I speak," interrupted De Graville, "and suggest a counsel?"

"Speak out, in God's name!" cried the duke.

"Then I should say, with submission, that the way to tame a lion is not by gorging him, but daunting. Bold is the lion against open foes; but a lion in the toils loses his nature. Just now, my lord said that Harold should not return to his native land —"

"Nor shall he, but as my sworn man!" exclaimed the duke.

"And if you now put to him that choice, think you it will favour your views? Will he not reject your proffers, and with hot scorn?"

"Scorn! darest thou that word to me?" cried the duke. "Scorn! have I no headsman whose axe is as sharp as Harold's? — and the neck of a captive is not sheathed in my Norman mail."

"Pardon, pardon, my liege," said Mallet, with spirit; "but to save my chief from a hasty action that might bring long remorse, I spoke thus boldly. Give the earl at least fair warning: a prison, or fealty to thee, — that is the choice before him! Let him know it; let him see that thy dungeons are dark, and thy walls impassable. Threaten not his life, — brave men care not for that! Threaten thyself nought, but let others work upon him with fear of his freedom. I know well these Saxish men; I know well Harold. Freedom is their passion; they are cowards when threatened with the doom of four walls."[1]

"I conceive thee, wise son," exclaimed Odo.

"Ha!" said the duke, slowly; "and yet it was to prevent such suspicions that I took care, after the first meeting, to separate him from Haco and Wolnoth, for they must have learned much in Norman gossip ill to repeat to the Saxon."

"Wolnoth is almost wholly Norman," said the bishop, smiling; "Wolnoth is bound, *par amours*, to a certain fair Norman dame; and, I trow well, prefers her charms here to the thought of his return. But Haco, as thou knowest, is sullen and watchful."

"So much the better companion for Harold now," said De Graville.

"I am fated ever to plot and to scheme!" said the duke,

---

[1] William of Poitiers, the contemporary Norman chronicler, says of Harold, that he was a man to whom imprisonment was more odious than shipwreck.

groaning, as if he had been the simplest of men; "but, nathless, I love the stout earl, and I mean all for his own good, — that is, compatibly with my rights and claims to the heritage of Edward my cousin."

"Of course," said the bishop.

CHAPTER IV.

THE snares now spread for Harold were in pursuance of the policy thus resolved on. The camp soon afterwards broke up, and the troops took their way to Bayeux. William, without greatly altering his manner towards the earl, evaded markedly, or as markedly replied not to, Harold's plain declarations that his presence was required in England, and that he could no longer defer his departure; while, under pretence of being busied with affairs, he absented himself much from the earl's company, or refrained from seeing him alone, and suffered Mallet de Graville and Odo the bishop to supply his place with Harold. The earl's suspicions now became thoroughly aroused; and these were fed both by the hints, kindly meant, of De Graville, and the less covert discourse of the prelate. While Mallet let drop, as, in gossiping illustration of William's fierce and vindictive nature, many anecdotes of that cruelty which really stained the Norman's character, Odo more bluntly appeared to take it for granted that Harold's sojourn in the land would be long.

"You will have time," said he, one day, as they rode together, "to assist me, I trust, in learning the language of our forefathers. Danish is still spoken much at Bayeux, the sole place in Neustria [1] where the old tongue and customs still

---

[1] In the environs of Bayeux still may perhaps linger the sole remains of the Scandinavian Normans, apart from the gentry. For centuries the inhabitants of Bayeux and its vicinity were a class distinct from the Franco-Normans, or the rest of Neustria; they submitted with great reluctance to the ducal authority, and retained their old heathen cry of "Thor-aide!" instead of "Dieu-aide!"

linger; and it would serve my pastoral ministry to receive your lessons. In a year or so I might hope so to profit by them as to discourse freely with the less Frankish part of my flock."

"Surely, Lord Bishop, you jest," said Harold, seriously; "you know well that within a week, at farthest, I must sail back for England with my young kinsmen."

The prelate laughed. "I advise you, dear Count and son, to be cautious how you speak so plainly to William. I perceive that you have already ruffled him by such indiscreet remarks; and you must have seen eno' of the duke to know that when his ire is up, his answers are short, but his arms are long."

"You most grievously wrong Duke William," cried Harold, indignantly, "to suppose, merely in that playful humour, for which ye Normans are famous, that he could lay force on his confiding guest?"

"No, not a confiding guest, — a ransomed captive. Surely my brother will deem that he has purchased of Count Guy his rights over his illustrious prisoner. But courage! The Norman court is not the Ponthevin dungeon; and your chains at least are roses."

The reply of wrath and defiance that rose to Harold's lip was checked by a sign from De Graville, who raised his finger to his lip with a face expressive of caution and alarm; and some little time after, as they halted to water their horses, De Graville came up to him and said in a low voice and in Saxon, —

"Beware how you speak too frankly to Odo. What is said to him is said to William; and the duke at times so acts on the spur of the moment that — But let me not wrong him, or needlessly alarm you."

"Sire de Graville," said Harold, "this is not the first time that the prelate of Bayeux hath hinted at compulsion, nor that you (no doubt kindly) have warned me of purpose hostile or fraudful. As plain man to plain man, I ask you, on your knightly honour, to tell me if you know aught to make you believe that William the Duke will, under any pretext, detain me here a captive."

Now, though Mallet de Graville had lent himself to the service of an ignoble craft, he justified it by a better reason than complaisance to his lords; for, knowing William well, his hasty ire and his relentless ambition, he was really alarmed for Harold's safety. And, as the reader may have noted, in suggesting that policy of intimidation, the knight had designed to give the earl at least the benefit of forewarning. So, thus adjured, De Graville replied sincerely, —

"Earl Harold, on my honour as your brother in knighthood I answer your plain question. I have cause to believe and to know that William will not suffer you to depart unless fully satisfied on certain points, which he himself will doubtless ere long make clear to you."

"And if I insist on my departure, not so satisfying him?"

"Every castle on our road hath a dungeon as deep as Count Guy's; but where another William to deliver you from William?"

"Over yon seas, a prince mightier than William, and men as resolute at least as your Normans."

"*Cher et puissant,* my Lord Earl," answered De Graville, "these are brave words, but of no weight in the ear of a schemer so deep as the duke. Think you really that King Edward — pardon my bluntness — would rouse himself from his apathy to do more in your behalf than he has done in your kinsmen's, — remonstrate and preach? Are you even sure that on the representation of a man he hath so loved as William, he will not be content to rid his throne of so formidable a subject? You speak of the English people. Doubtless you are popular and beloved; but it is the habit of no people, least of all your own, to stir actively and in concert, without leaders. The duke knows the factions of England as well as you do. Remember how closely he is connected with Tostig, your ambitious brother. Have you no fear that Tostig himself, earl of the most warlike part of the kingdom, will not only do his best to check the popular feeling in your favour, but foment every intrigue to detain you here, and leave himself the first noble in the land? As for other leaders, save Gurth (who is but your own vice-earl), who is there that will not rejoice at the absence of Harold? You have made foes of the only family that approaches the power of your own, — the heirs of Leofric and Algar. Your strong hand removed from the reins of the empire, tumults and dissensions erelong will break forth that will distract men's minds from an absent captive, and centre them on the safety of their own hearths or the advancement of their own interests. You see that I know something of the state of your native land; but deem not my own observation, though not idle, sufficed to bestow that knowledge. I learn it more from William's discourses, — William, who from Flanders, from Boulogne, from England itself, by a thousand channels, hears all that passes between the cliffs of Dover and the marches of Scotland."

Harold paused long before he replied, for his mind was now thoroughly awakened to his danger; and while recognizing the wisdom and intimate acquaintance of affairs with which De Graville spoke, he was also rapidly revolving the best course for himself to pursue in such extremes. At length he said, —

"I pass by your remarks on the state of England with but one comment. You underrate Gurth, my brother, when you speak of him but as the vice-earl of Harold. You underrate one who needs but an object to excel, in arms and in council, my father Godwin himself. That object a brother's wrongs would create from a brother's love; and three hundred ships would sail up the Seine to demand your captive, manned by warriors as hardy as those who wrested Neustria from King Charles."

"Granted," said De Graville. "But William, who could cut off the hands and feet of his own subjects for an idle jest on his birth, could as easily put out the eyes of a captive foe; and of what worth are the ablest brain and the stoutest arm when the man is dependent on another for very sight?"

Harold involuntarily shuddered, but recovering himself on the instant, he replied with a smile, —

"Thou makest thy duke a butcher more fell than his ancestor Rolfganger. But thou saidst he needed but to be satisfied on certain points. What are they?"

"Ah, *that* thou must divine, or he unfold. But see, William himself approaches you."

And here the duke, who had been till then in the rear, spurred up with courteous excuses to Harold for his long defection from his side; and as they resumed their way, talked with all his former frankness and gayety.

"By the way, dear brother in arms," said he, "I have provided thee this evening with comrades more welcome, I fear, than myself, — Haco and Wolnoth. That last is a youth whom I love dearly; the first is unsocial eno', and methinks would make a better hermit than soldier. But, by Saint Valery, I forgot to tell thee that an envoy from Flanders to-day, amongst other news, brought me some that may interest thee. There is a strong commotion in thy brother Tostig's Northumbrian earldom, and the rumour runs that his fierce vassals will drive him forth and select some other lord; talk was of the sons of Algar, — so I think ye called the stout dead earl. This looks grave, for my dear cousin Edward's health is failing fast. May the saints spare him long from their rest!"

"These are indeed ill tidings," said the earl; "and I trust that they suffice to plead at once my excuse for urging my immediate departure. Grateful I am for thy most gracious hostship, and thy just and generous intercession with thy *liegeman*" (Harold dwelt emphatically on the last word) "for my release from a capture disgraceful to all Christendom. The ransom so nobly paid for me I will not insult thee, dear my lord, by affecting to repay; but such gifts as our cheapmen hold most rare, perchance thy lady and thy fair children will deign to receive at my hands. Of these hereafter. Now may I ask but a vessel from thy nearest port."

"We will talk of this, dear guest and brother knight, on some later occasion. Lo, yon castle, — ye have no such in England. See its vawmures and fosses!"

"A noble pile," answered Harold. "But pardon me that I press for —"

"Ye have no such strongholds, I say, in England?" interrupted the duke, petulantly.

"Nay," replied the Englishman, "we have two strongholds
far larger than that, — Salisbury Plain and Newmarket
Heath,[1] — strongholds that will contain fifty thousand men
who need no walls but their shields. Count William, England's ramparts are her men, and her strongest castles are her
widest plains."

"Ah!" said the duke, biting his lip, "ah, so be it, — but
to return: in that castle, mark it well, the Dukes of Normandy hold their prisoners of state;" and then he added
with a laugh, "But we hold you, noble captive, in a prison
more strong, — our love and our heart."

As he spoke, he turned his eye full upon Harold, and the
gaze of the two encountered: that of the duke was brilliant,
but stern and sinister; that of Harold, steadfast and reproach-
ful. As if by a spell, the eye of each rested long on that of
the other, — as the eyes of two lords of the forest, ere the
rush and the spring.

William was the first to withdraw his gaze; and as he did
so, his lip quivered and his brow knit. Then waving his hand
for some of the lords behind to join him and the earl, he
spurred his steed, and all further private conversation was
suspended. The train pulled not bridle before they reached
a monastery, at which they rested for the night.

CHAPTER V.

On entering the chamber set apart for him in the convent,
Harold found Haco and Wolnoth already awaiting him; and
a wound he had received in the last skirmish against the
Bretons having broken out afresh on the road, allowed him

---

[1] Similar was the answer of Goodyn the Bishop of Winchester, ambassa-
dor from Henry VIII. to the French King. To this day the English entertain the same notion of forts as Harold and Goodyn.

an excuse to spend the rest of the evening alone with his kinsmen.

On conversing with them — now at length and unrestrainedly — Harold saw everything to increase his alarm; for even Wolnoth, when closely pressed, could not but give evidence of the unscrupulous astuteness with which, despite all the boasted honour of chivalry, the duke's character was stained. For indeed, in his excuse, it must be said that from the age of eight, exposed to the snares of his own kinsmen, and more often saved by craft than by strength, William had been taught betimes to justify dissimulation, and confound wisdom with guile. Harold now bitterly recalled the parting words of Edward, and recognized their justice, though as yet he did not see all that they portended. Fevered and disquieted yet more by the news from England, and conscious that not only the power of his House and the foundations of his aspiring hopes, but the very weal and safety of the land, were daily imperilled by his continued absence, a vague and unspeakable terror for the first time in his life preyed on his bold heart, — a terror like that of superstition, for, like superstition, it was of the Unknown; there was everything to shun, yet no substance to grapple with. He, who could have smiled at the brief pangs of death, shrunk from the thought of the perpetual prison; he, whose spirit rose elastic to every storm of life, and exulted in the air of action, stood appalled at the fear of *blindness*, — blindness in the midst of a career so grand; blindness in the midst of his pathway to a throne; blindness, that curse which palsies the strong and enslaves the free, and leaves the whole man defenceless, — defenceless in an Age of Iron.

What, too, were those mysterious points on which he was to satisfy the duke? He sounded his young kinsmen: but Wolnoth evidently knew nothing; Haco's eye showed intelligence, but by his looks and gestures he seemed to signify that what he knew he would only disclose to Harold. Fatigued, not more with his emotions than with that exertion to conceal them so peculiar to the English character (proud virtue of manhood so little appreciated, and so rarely understood!), he

at length kissed Wolnoth, and dismissed him, yawning, to his
rest. Haco, lingering, closed the door, and looked long and
mournfully at the earl.

"Noble kinsman," said the young son of Sweyn, "I foresaw from the first that as our fate will be thine, — only round
thee will be wall and fosse; unless, indeed, thou wilt lay aside
thine own nature — it will give thee no armour here — and
assume that which — "

"Ho!" interrupted the earl, shaking with repressed passion, "I see already all the foul fraud and treason to guest
and noble that surround me! But if the duke dare such
shame, he shall do so in the eyes of day. I will hail the first
boat I see on his river or his seacoast; and woe to those who
lay hand on this arm to detain me!"

Haco lifted his ominous eyes to Harold's; and there was
something in their cold and unimpassioned expression which
seemed to repel all enthusiasm and to deaden all courage.

"Harold," said he, "if but for one such moment thou
obeyest the impulses of thy manly pride or thy just resentment, thou art lost forever; one show of violence, one word
of affront, and thou givest the duke the excuse he thirsts for.
Escape! It is impossible. For the last five years I have
pondered night and day the means of flight, — for I deem that
my hostageship, by right, is long since over, — and no means
have I seen or found. Spies dog my every step, as spies, no
doubt, dog thine."

"Ha! it is true," said Harold; "never once have I wandered three paces from the camp or the troop, but under some
pretext I have been followed by knight or courtier. God and
our Lady help me, if but for England's sake! But what coun-
sellest thou? Boy, teach me; thou hast been reared in this
air of wile, — to me it is strange, and I am as a wild beast
encompassed by a circle of fire."

"Then," answered Haco, "meet craft by craft, smile by
smile. Feel that thou art under compulsion, and act — as
the Church itself pardons men for acting, so compelled."

Harold started, and the blush spread red over his cheeks.

Haco continued: "Once in prison, and thou art lost evermore to the sight of men. William would not then dare to release thee, — unless, indeed, he first rendered thee powerless to avenge. Though I will not malign him, and say that he himself is capable of secret murder, yet he has ever those about him who are. He drops in his wrath some hasty word; it is seized by ready and ruthless tools. The great Count of Bretagne was in his way. William feared him as he fears thee; and in his own court and amongst his own men the great Count of Bretagne died by poison. For *thy* doom, open or secret, William, however, could find ample excuse."

"How, boy? What charge can the Norman bring against a free Englishman?"

"His kinsman Alfred," answered Haco, "was blinded, tortured, and murdered; and in the court of Rouen they say these deeds were done by Godwin, thy father. The Normans who escorted Alfred were decimated in cold blood; again, they say Godwin thy father slaughtered them."

"It is hell's own lie!" cried Harold; "and so have I proved already to the duke."

"Proved? No! The lamb does not prove the cause which is prejudged by the wolf. Often and often have I heard the Normans speak of those deeds, and cry that vengeance yet shall await them. It is but to renew the old accusation, to say Godwin's sudden death was God's proof of his crime, and even Edward himself would forgive the duke for thy bloody death. But grant the best, — grant that the more lenient doom were but the prison, grant that Edward and the English invaded Normandy to enforce thy freedom, — knowest thou what William hath ere now done with hostages? He hath put them in the van of his army, and seared out their eyes in the sight of both hosts. Deemest thou he would be more gentle to us and to thee? Such are thy dangers. Be bold and frank, and thou canst not escape them; be wary and wise, promise and feign, and they are baffled; cover thy lion heart with the fox's hide until thou art free from the toils."

"Leave me, leave me," said Harold, hastily. "Yet, hold! Thou didst seem to understand me when I hinted of — In a word, what is the object William would gain from me?"

Haco looked round, again went to the door, again opened and closed it, approached, and whispered, "The crown of England!"

The earl bounded as if shot to the heart; then again he cried: "Leave me. I must be alone,— alone now. Go! go!"

———•———

CHAPTER VI.

ONLY in solitude could that strong man give way to his emotions; and at first they rushed forth so confused and stormy, so hurtling one the other, that hours elapsed before he could serenely face the terrible crisis of his position.

The great historian of Italy has said that whenever the simple and truthful German came among the plotting and artful Italians and experienced their duplicity and craft, he straightway became more false and subtle than the Italians themselves. To his own countrymen, indeed, he continued to retain his characteristic sincerity and good faith; but, once duped and tricked by the southern schemers, as if with a fierce scorn, he rejected troth with the truthless. He exulted in mastering them in their own wily statesmanship; and if reproached for insincerity, retorted with *naïve* wonder, —

"Ye Italians, and complain of insincerity! How otherwise can one deal with you,— how be safe among you?"

Somewhat of this revolution of all the natural elements of his character took place in Harold's mind that stormy and solitary night. In the transport of his indignation, he resolved not doltishly to be thus outwitted to his ruin. The perfidious host had deprived himself of that privilege of Truth, — the large and heavenly security of man; it was but a struggle of wit against wit, snare against snare. The state and law of warfare had started up in the lap of fraudful peace; and ambush must be met by ambush, plot by plot.

Such was the nature of the self-excuses by which the Saxon defended his resolves; and they appeared to him more sanc

tioned by the stake which depended on success, — a stake
which his undying patriotism allowed to be far more vast
than his individual ambition. Nothing was more clear than
that if he were detained in a Norman prison at the time of
King Edward's death the sole obstacle to William's design
on the English throne would be removed. In the interim the
duke's intrigues would again surround the infirm king with
Norman influences; and in the absence both of any legitimate
heir to the throne capable of commanding the trust of the
people, and of his own preponderating ascendancy both in the
Witan and the armed militia of the nation, what could arrest
the designs of the grasping duke? Thus his own liberty was
indissolubly connected with that of his country; and for that
great end, the safety of England, all means grew holy.

When the next morning he joined the cavalcade, it was only
by his extreme paleness that the struggle and agony of the
past night could be traced, and he answered with correspond-
ent cheerfulness William's cordial greetings.

As they rode together, still accompanied by several knights,
and the discourse was thus general, the features of the country suggested the theme of the talk; for, now in the heart of
Normandy, but in rural districts remote from the great towns,
nothing could be more waste and neglected than the face of
the land. Miserable and sordid to the last degree were the
huts of the serfs; and when these last met them on their way,
half naked and hunger-worn, there was a wild gleam of hate
and discontent in their eyes, as they louted low to the Norman
riders, and heard the bitter and scornful taunts with which
they were addressed: for the Norman and the Frank had more
than indifference for the peasants of their land; they literally
both despised and abhorred them, as of different race from
the conquerors. The Norman settlement especially was so
recent in the land that none of that amalgamation between
class and class which centuries had created in England existed
there; though in England the theowe was wholly a slave, and
the ceorl in a political servitude to his lord, yet public opinion, more mild than law, preserved the thraldom from wanton
aggravation; and slavery was felt to be wrong and unchris-

tian. The Saxon Church — not the less, perhaps, for its very ignorance — sympathized more with the subject population, and was more associated with it, than the comparatively learned and haughty ecclesiastics of the Continent, who held aloof from the unpolished vulgar. The Saxon Church invariably set the example of freeing the theowe and emancipating the ceorl, and taught that such acts were to the salvation of the soul. The rude and homely manner in which the greater part of the Saxon thegns lived — dependent solely for their subsistence on their herds and agricultural produce, and therefore on the labour of their peasants — not only made the distinctions of rank less harsh and visible, but rendered it the interest of the lords to feed and clothe well their dependents. All our records of the customs of the Saxons prove the ample sustenance given to the poor, and a general care for their lives and rights, which, compared with the Frank laws, may be called enlightened and humane; and above all, the lowest serf ever had the great hope both of freedom and of promotion. But the beast of the field was holier, in the eyes of the Norman, than the wretched villein.[1] We have likened the Norman to the Spartan; and, most of all, he was like him in his scorn of the helot.

Thus embruted and degraded, deriving little from religion

---

[1] See Mr. Wright's very interesting article on the "Condition of the English Peasantry," etc., Archæologia, vol. xxx. pp. 205–244. I must however observe that one very important fact seems to have been generally overlooked by all inquirers, or at least not sufficiently enforced; namely, that it was the Norman's contempt for the general mass of the subject population which more, perhaps, than any other cause broke up positive slavery in England. Thus the Norman very soon lost sight of that distinction the Anglo-Saxons had made between the agricultural ceorl and the theowe; that is, between the serf of the soil and the personal slave. Hence these classes became fused in each other, and were gradually emancipated by the same circumstances. This, be it remarked, could never have taken place under the Anglo-Saxon laws, which kept constantly feeding the class of slaves by adding to it convicted felons and their children. The subject population became too necessary to the Norman barons, in their feuds with each other or their king, to be long oppressed; and in the time of Froissart, that worthy chronicler ascribes the insolence, or high spirit, of *le menu peuple* to their *grand aise, et abondance de biens.*

itself except its terrors, the general habits of the peasants on the continent of France were against the very basis of Christianity, — marriage. They lived together for the most part without that tie; and hence the common name, with which they were called by their masters, lay and clerical, was the coarsest word contempt can apply to the sons of women.

"The hounds glare at us," said Odo, as a drove of these miserable serfs passed along. "They need ever the lash to teach them to know the master. Are they thus mutinous and surly in England, Lord Harold?"

"No; but there our meanest theowes are not seen so clad, nor housed in such hovels," said the earl.

"And is it really true that a villein with you can rise to be a noble?"

"Of at least yearly occurrence. Perhaps the forefathers of one-fourth of our Anglo-Saxon thegns held the plough, or followed some craft mechanical."

Duke William politicly checked Odo's answer, and said mildly, —

"Every land its own laws; and by them alone should it be governed by a virtuous and wise ruler. But, noble Harold, I grieve that you should thus note the sore point in my realm. I grant that the condition of the peasants and the culture of the land need reform. But in my childhood there was a fierce outbreak of rebellion among the villeins, needing bloody example to check; and the memories of wrath between lord and villein must sleep before we can do justice between them, as please Saint Peter, and by Lanfranc's aid, we hope to do. Meanwhile one great portion of our villeinage in our larger towns we have much mitigated; for trade and commerce are the strength of rising States, and if our fields are barren our streets are prosperous."

Harold bowed, and rode musingly on. That civilization he had so much admired bounded itself to the noble class, and at farthest to the circle of the duke's commercial policy. Beyond it, on the outskirts of humanity, lay the mass of the people; and here no comparison in favour of the latter could be found between English and Norman civilization.

The towers of Bayeux rose dim in the distance, when William proposed a halt in a pleasant spot by the side of a small stream, overshadowed by oak and beech. A tent for himself and Harold was pitched in haste; and after an abstemious refreshment, the duke, taking Harold's arm, led him away from the train along the margin of the murmuring stream.

They were soon in a remote, pastoral, primitive spot, — a spot like those which the old menestrels loved to describe, and in which some pious hermit might, pleased, have fixed his solitary home.

Halting where a mossy bank jutted over the water, William motioned to his companion to seat himself, and reclining at his side, abstractedly took the pebbles from the margin and dropped them into the stream. They fell to the bottom with a hollow sound; the circle they made on the surface widened, and was lost; and the wave rushed and murmured on, disdainful.

"Harold," said the duke, at last, "thou hast thought, I fear, that I have trifled with thy impatience to return. But there is on my mind a matter of great moment to thee and to me, and it must out, before thou canst depart. On this very spot where we now sit, sat, in early youth, Edward thy King and William thy host. Soothed by the loneliness of the place and the music of the bell from the church tower, rising pale through yonder glade, Edward spoke of his desire for the monastic life, and of his content with his exile in the Norman land. Few then were the hopes that he should ever attain the throne of Alfred. I, more martial, and ardent for him as myself, combated the thought of the convent, and promised, that if ever occasion meet arrived, and he needed the Norman help, I would with arm and heart do a chief's best to win him his lawful crown. Heedest thou me, dear Harold?"

"Ay, my host, with heart as with ear."

"And Edward then, pressing my hand as I now press thine, while answering gratefully, promised that if he did, contrary to all human foresight, gain his heritage, he, in case I survived him, would bequeath that heritage to me. Thy hand withdraws itself from mine."

"But from surprise. Duke William, proceed."

"Now," resumed William, "when thy kinsmen were sent to me as hostages for the most powerful House in England, — the only one that could thwart the desire of my cousin, — I naturally deemed this a corroboration of his promise, and an earnest of his continued designs; and in this I was reassured by the prelate, Robert, Archbishop of Canterbury, who knew the most secret conscience of your king. Wherefore my pertinacity in retaining those hostages; wherefore my disregard to Edward's mere remonstrances, which I not unnaturally conceived to be but his meek concessions to the urgent demands of thyself and House. Since then, Fortune or Providence hath favoured the promise of the king, and my just expectations founded thereon. For one moment it seemed, indeed, that Edward regretted or reconsidered the pledge of our youth. He sent for his kinsman, the Atheling, natural heir to the throne; but the poor prince died. The son, a mere child, if I am rightly informed, the laws of thy land will set aside, should Edward die ere the child grow a man; and moreover I am assured that the young Edgar hath no power of mind or intellect to wield so weighty a sceptre as that of England. Your king also, even since your absence, hath had severe visitings of sickness, and ere another year his new Abbey may hold his tomb."

William here paused, again dropped the pebbles into the stream, and glanced furtively on the unrevealing face of the earl. He resumed, —

"Thy brother Tostig, as so nearly allied to my House, would, I am advised, back my claims; and wert thou absent from England, Tostig, I conceive, would be in thy place as the head of the great party of Godwin. But to prove how little I care for thy brother's aid compared with thine, and how implicitly I count on thee, I have openly told thee what a wilier plotter would have concealed; namely, the danger to which thy brother is menaced in his own earldom. To the point, then, I pass at once. I might, as my ransomed captive, detain thee here until without thee I had won my English throne, and I know that thou alone couldst obstruct my just claims, or interfere with the king's will, by which that appanage will be left to me. Nevertheless, I unbosom myself to thee, and would owe my crown solely to thine aid. I pass on to treat with thee, dear Harold, not as lord with vassal, but as prince with prince. On thy part thou shalt hold for me the castle of Dover, to yield to my fleet when the hour comes; thou shalt aid me in peace, and through thy National Witan, to succeed to Edward, by whose laws I will reign in all things conformably with the English rites, habits, and decrees. A stronger king to guard England from the Dane, and a more practised head to improve her prosperity, I am vain eno' to say thou wilt not find in Christendom. On my part, I offer to thee my fairest daughter, Adeliza, to whom thou shalt be straightway betrothed; thine own young unwedded sister, Thyra, thou shalt give to one of my greatest barons; all the lands, dignities, and possessions thou holdest now, thou shalt still retain; and if, as I suspect, thy brother Tostig cannot keep his vast principality north the Humber, it shall pass to thee. Whatever else thou canst demand in guarantee of my love and gratitude, or so to confirm thy power that thou shalt rule over thy countships as free and as powerful as the great Counts of Provence or Anjou reign in France over theirs, subject only to the mere form of holding in fief to the Suzerain, as I, stormy subject, hold Normandy under Philip of France, shall be given to thee. In truth, there will be two kings in England, though in name but one; and far from losing by the death of Edward, thou shalt gain by the subjection of every meaner rival, and the cordial love of thy grateful William. Splendour of God, Earl, thou keepest me long for thine answer!"

"What thou offerest," said the earl, fortifying himself with the resolution of the previous night, and compressing his lips, livid with rage, "is beyond my deserts, and all that the greatest chief under royalty could desire. But England is not Edward's to leave, nor mine to give; its throne rests with the Witan."

"And the Witan rests with thee," exclaimed William, sharply. "I ask but for possibilities, man; I ask but all thine influence on my behalf; and if it be less than I deem, mine is the loss. What dost thou resign? I will not presume to menace thee; but thou wouldst indeed despise my folly, if now, knowing my designs, I let thee forth, — not to aid, but betray them. I know thou lovest England; so do I. Thou deemest me a foreigner; true, but the Norman and Dane are of precisely the same origin. Thou, of the race of Canute, knowest how popular was the reign of that king. Why should William's be less so? Canute had no right whatsoever, save that of the sword. My right will be kinship to Edward; Edward's wish in my favour; the consent through thee of the Witan; the absence of all other worthy heir; my wife's clear descent from Alfred, which in my children restores the Saxon line, through its purest and noblest ancestry, to the throne. Think over all this, and then wilt thou tell me that I merit not this crown?"

Harold yet paused; and the fiery duke resumed, —

"Are the terms I give not tempting eno' to my captive, — to the son of the great Godwin, who, no doubt falsely, but still by the popular voice of all Europe, had power of life and death over my cousin Alfred and my Norman knights? Or dost thou thyself covet the English crown, and is it to a rival that I have opened my heart?"

"Nay," said Harold, in the crowning effort of his new and fatal lesson in simulation. "Thou hast convinced me, Duke William; let it be as thou sayest."

The duke gave way to his joy by a loud exclamation, and then recapitulated the articles of the engagement, to which Harold simply bowed his head. Amicably then the duke embraced the earl, and the two returned towards the tent.

While the steeds were brought forth, William took the opportunity to draw Odo apart; and after a short whispered conference the prelate hastened to his barb, and spurred fast to Bayeux in advance of the party. All that day and all that night and all the next morn till noon, couriers and riders went abroad, north and south, east and west, to all the more famous abbeys and churches in Normandy; and holy and awful was the spoil with which they returned for the ceremony of the next day.

CHAPTER VII.

THE stately mirth of the evening banquet seemed to Harold as the malign revel of some demoniac orgy. He thought he read in every face the exultation over the sale of England. Every light laugh in the proverbial ease of the social Normans rang on his ear like the joy of a ghastly *Sabbat*. All his senses preternaturally sharpened to that magnetic keenness in which we less hear and see than conceive and divine, the lowest murmur William breathed in the ear of Odo boomed clear to his own; the slightest interchange of glance between some dark-browed priest and large-breasted warrior flashed upon his vision. The irritation of his recent and neglected wound combined with his mental excitement to quicken, yet to confuse, his faculties. Body and soul were fevered; he floated, as it were, between a delirium and a dream.

Late in the evening he was led into the chamber where the duchess sat alone with Adeliza and her second son William, —a boy who had the red hair and florid hues of the ancestral Dane, but was not without a certain bold and strange kind of beauty, and who even in childhood, all covered with broidery and gems, betrayed the passion for that extravagant and fantastic foppery for which William the Red King, to the scandal of Church and pulpit, exchanged the decorous pomp of his father's generation. A formal presentation of Harold to the little maid was followed by a brief ceremony of words, which conveyed what to the scornful sense of the earl seemed the mockery of betrothal between infant and bearded man. Glozing congratulations buzzed around him; then there was a flash of lights on his dizzy eyes, he found himself moving through a corridor, between Odo and William. He was in his room hung with arras and strewed with rushes; before him, in niches, various images of the Virgin, the Archangel Michael, Saint Stephen, Saint Peter, Saint John, Saint Valery; and from the bells in the monastic edifice hard by tolled the third watch[1] of the night, — the narrow casement was out of reach, high in the massive wall, and the starlight was darkened by the great church tower. Harold longed for air. All his earldom had he given at that moment, to feel the cold blast of his native skies moaning round his Saxon wolds. He opened his door, and looked forth. A lantern swung on high from the groined roof of the corridor. By the lantern stood a tall sentry in arms, and its gleam fell red upon an iron grate that jealously closed the egress. The earl closed the door, and sat down on his bed, covering his face with his clenched hand. The veins throbbed in every pulse; his own touch seemed to him like fire. The prophecies of Hilda on the fatal night by the bautastein, which had decided him to reject the prayer of Gurth, the fears of Edith, and the cautions of Edward, came back to him, dark, haunting, and overmasteringly. They rose between him and his sober sense, whenever he sought to re-collect his thoughts, now to madden him with the sense of his folly in belief, now to divert his mind from the perilous present to the triumphant future they foretold; and of all the varying chants of the Vala, ever two lines seemed to burn into his memory and to knell upon his ear, as if they contained the counsel they ordained him to pursue, —

> "GUILE BY GUILE OPPOSE, and never
> Crown and brow shall Force dissever!"

So there he sat, locked and rigid, not reclining, not disrobing, till in that posture a haggard, troubled, fitful sleep came over him; nor did he wake till the hour of prime,[2] when ringing bells, and trampling feet, and the hum of prayer from the neighbouring chapel roused him into waking yet more troubled and well-nigh as dreamy. But now Godrith and Haco entered the room; and the former inquired with some surprise in his

---

[1] Twelve o'clock.   [2] Six A. M.

tone, if he had arranged with the duke to depart that day; "for," said he, "the duke's hors-thegn has just been with me, to say that the duke himself and a stately retinue are to accompany you this evening towards Harfleur, where a ship will be in readiness for our transport; and I know that the chamberlain (a courteous and pleasant man) is going round to my fellow-thegns in your train, with gifts of hawks and chains and broidered palls."

"It is so," said Haco, in answer to Harold's brightening and appealing eye.

"Go then at once, Godrith," exclaimed the earl, bounding to his feet; "have all in order to part at the first break of the trump. Never, I ween, did trump sound so cheerily as the blast that shall announce our return to England. Haste, — haste!"

As Godrith, pleased in the earl's pleasure, though himself already much fascinated by the honours he had received and the splendour he had witnessed, withdrew, Haco said, —

"Thou hast taken my counsel, noble kinsman?"

"Question me not, Haco! Out of my memory, all that hath passed here!"

"Not yet," said Haco, with that gloomy and intense seri- ousness of voice and aspect which was so at variance with his years, and which impressed all he said with an indescribable authority, — "not yet; for even while the chamberlain went his round with the parting gifts, I, standing in the angle of the wall in the yard, heard the duke's deep whisper to Roger Bigod, who has the guard of the keape: 'Have the men all armed at noon in the passage below the council-hall, to mount at the stamp of my foot; and if then I give thee a prisoner, wonder not, but lodge him — ' The duke paused; and Bigod said, 'Where, my liege?' And the duke answered fiercely, 'Where? why, where but in the *Tour noir?* — where but in the cell in which Malvoisin rotted out his last hour?' Not yet, then, let the memory of Norman wile pass away; let the lip guard the freedom still."

All the bright native soul that before Haco spoke had dawned gradually back on the earl's fair face now closed itself up, as the leaves of a poisoned flower; and the pupil of the eye receding, left to the orb that secret and strange expression which had baffled all readers of the heart in the look of his impenetrable father.

"*Guile by guile oppose!*" he muttered vaguely; then started, clenched his hand, and smiled.

In a few moments more than the usual levee of Norman nobles thronged into the room; and what with the wonted order of the morning, in the repast, the church service of tierce, and a ceremonial visit to Matilda, who confirmed the intelligence that all was in preparation for his departure, and charged him with gifts of her own needlework to his sister the queen, and various messages of gracious nature, the time waxed late into noon without his having yet seen either William or Odo.

He was still with Matilda, when the Lords Fitzosborne and Raoul de Tancarville entered in full robes of state, and with countenances unusually composed and grave, and prayed the earl to accompany them into the duke's presence.

Harold obeyed in silence, not unprepared for covert danger, by the formality of the counts, as by the warnings of Haco; but, indeed, undivining the solemnity of the appointed snare. On entering the lofty hall, he beheld William seated in state, — his sword of office in his hand, his ducal robe on his impos- ing form, and with that peculiarly erect air of the head which he assumed upon all ceremonial occasions.[1] Behind him stood Odo of Bayeux, in aube and pallium; some score of the duke's greatest vassals; and at a little distance from the throne chair was what seemed a table, or vast chest, covered all over with cloth of gold.

Small time for wonder or self-collection did the duke give the Saxon.

[1] A celebrated antiquary, in his treatise in the "Archæologia," on the au- thenticity of the Bayeux tapestry, very justly invites attention to the rude attempt of the artist to preserve individuality in his portraits; and especially to the singularly erect bearing of the duke, by which he is at once recog- nized wherever he is introduced. Less pains are taken with the portrait of Harold; but even in that a certain elegance of proportion and length of limb as well as height of stature are generally preserved.

"Approach, Harold," said he, in the full tones of that voice, so singularly effective in command; "approach, and without fear as without regret. Before the members of this noble assembly — all witnesses of thy faith, and all guarantees of mine — I summon thee to confirm by oath the promises thou madest me yesterday; namely, to aid me to obtain the kingdom of England on the death of King Edward, my cousin; to marry my daughter Adeliza; and to send thy sister hither, that I may wed her, as we agreed, to one of my worthiest and prowest counts. Advance thou, Odo my brother, and repeat to the noble earl the Norman form by which he will take the oath."

Then Odo stood forth by that mysterious receptacle covered with the cloth of gold, and said briefly, "Thou wilt swear, as far as is in thy power, to fulfil thy agreement with William, Duke of the Normans, if thou live, and God aid thee; and in witness of that oath thou wilt lay thy hand upon the reliquaire," pointing to a small box that lay on the cloth of gold.

All this was so sudden, — all flashed so rapidly upon the earl, whose natural intellect, however great, was, as we have often seen, more deliberate than prompt; so thoroughly was the bold heart, which no siege could have sapped, taken by surprise and guile; so paramount through all the whirl and tumult of his mind rose the thought of England irrevocably lost if he who alone could save her was in the Norman dungeons; so darkly did all Haco's fears and his own just suspicions quell and master him, — that mechanically, dizzily, dreamily he laid his hand on the reliquaire, and repeated with automaton lips, —

"If I live, and if God aid me to it!"

Then all the assembly repeated solemnly: "God aid him!"

And suddenly, at a sign from William, Odo and Raoul de Tancarville raised the gold cloth, and the duke's voice bade Harold look below.

As when man descends from the gilded sepulchre to the loathsome charnel, so at the lifting of that cloth all the dread ghastliness of Death was revealed. There, from abbey and

HAROLD TAKING THE OATH OF ALLEGIANCE TO DUKE WILLIAM.

from church, from cyst and from shrine, had been collected all the relics of human nothingness in which superstition adored the mementos of saints divine; there lay, pell-mell and huddled, skeleton and mummy, — the dry dark skin, the white gleaming bones of the dead, mockingly cased in gold, and decked with rubies; there grim fingers protruded through the hideous chaos, and pointed towards the living man ensnared; there the skull grinned scoff under the holy mitre; — and suddenly rushed back, luminous and searing upon Harold's memory, the dream long forgotten, or but dimly remembered in the healthful business of life, — the gibe and the wirble of the dead men's bones.

"At that sight," say the Norman chronicles, "the earl shuddered and trembled."

"Awful, indeed, thine oath, and natural thine emotion," said the duke; "for in that cyst are all those relics which religion deems the holiest in our land. The dead have heard thine oath, and the saints even now record it in the halls of heaven! Cover again the holy bones!"

NOTES.

NOTE A, PAGE 12.

THERE are various accounts in the Chroniclers as to the stature of William the First; some represent him as a giant, others as of just or middle height. Considering the vulgar inclination to attribute to a hero's stature the qualities of the mind (and putting out of all question the arguments that rest on the pretended size of the disburied bones, for which the authorities are really less respectable than those on which we are called upon to believe that the skeleton of the mythical Gawaine measured eight feet), we prefer that supposition, as to the physical proportions, which is most in harmony with the usual laws of Nature. It is rare, indeed, that a great intellect is found in the form of a giant.

NOTE B, PAGE 24.

Game Laws before the Conquest.

UNDER the Saxon kings a man might, it is true, hunt in his own grounds, but that was a privilege that could benefit few but thegns; and over cultivated ground or shireland there was not the same sport to be found as in the vast wastes called forest-land, and which mainly belonged to the kings.

Edward declares, in a law recorded in a volume of the Exchequer: "I will that *all* men do abstain from hunting in my woods, and that my will shall be obeyed under penalty of life."[1]

Edgar, the darling monarch of the monks, and indeed one of the most popular of the Anglo-Saxon kings, was so rigorous in his forest-laws that the thegns murmured as well as the lower husbandmen, who had been accustomed to use the woods for pasturage and boscage. Canute's forest-laws were meant as a liberal concession to public feeling on the subject; they are more definite than Edgar's, but terribly stringent: if a freeman killed one of the king's deer, or struck his forester, he lost

[1] Thomson's Essay on Magna Charta.

his freedom and became a penal serf (white theowe), — that is, he ranked with felons. Nevertheless, Canute allowed bishops, abbots, and thegns to hunt in his woods, — a privilege restored by Henry III. The nobility, after the Conquest, being excluded from the royal chases, petitioned to enclose parks, as early even as the reign of William I.; and by the time of his son, Henry I., parks became so common as to be at once a ridicule and a grievance.

NOTE C, PAGE 30.

Belin's Gate.

VERSTEGAN combats the Welsh antiquaries who would appropriate this gate to the British deity Bal or Beli; and says, if so, it would not have been called by a name half Saxon, half British, gate (geat) being Saxon; but rather Belinsport than Belinsgate. This is no very strong argument; for in the Norman time many compound words were half Norman, half Saxon. But, in truth, Belin was a Teuton deity, whose worship pervaded all Gaul; and the Saxons might either have continued, therefore, the name they found, or given it themselves from their own god. I am not inclined, however, to contend that any deity, Saxon or British, gave the name, or that Billing is not, after all, the right orthography. Billing, like all words ending in *ing*, has something very Danish in its sound; and the name is quite as likely to have been given by the Danes as by the Saxons.

NOTE D, PAGE 33.

Vineyards in England.

THE question whether or not real vineyards were grown, or real wine made from them, in England has been a very vexed question among the antiquaries. But it is scarcely possible to read Pegge's dispute with Daines Barrington in the "Archæologia" without deciding both questions in the affirmative. (See Archæol. vol. iii. p. 53.) An engraving of the Saxon wine-press is given in Strutt's "Horda." Vineyards fell into disuse, either by treaty with France, or Gascony falling into the hands of the English. But vineyards were cultivated by private gentlemen as late as 1621. Our first wines from Bordeaux — the true country of Bacchus — appear to have been imported about 1154, by the marriage of Henry II. with Eleanor of Aquitaine.

NOTE E, PAGE 69.

Lanfranc, the first Anglo-Norman Archbishop of Canterbury.

LANFRANC was in all respects one of the most remarkable men of the eleventh century. He was born in Pavia, about 1105. His family was noble, — his father ranked among the magistrature of Pavia, the Lombard capital. From his earliest youth he gave himself up, with all a scholar's zeal, to the liberal arts, and the special knowledge of law, civil and ecclesiastical. He studied at Cologne, and afterwards taught and practised law in his own country. " While yet extremely young," says one of the lively chroniclers, " he triumphed over the ablest advocates, and the torrents of his eloquence confounded the sub-tlest rhetorician." His decisions were received as authorities by the Italian jurisconsults and tribunals. His mind, to judge both by his history and his peculiar reputation (for probably few, if any, students of our day can pretend to more than a partial or superficial acquaintance with his writings), was one that delighted in subtleties and casuistical re-finements; but a sense too large and commanding for those studies which amuse but never satisfy the higher intellect, became disgusted betimes with mere legal dialectics. Those grand and absorbing mysteries con-nected with the Christian faith and the Roman Church (grand and absorbing in proportion as their premises are taken by religious belief as mathematical axioms already proven) seized hold of his imagination, and tasked to the depth his inquisitive reason. The Chronicle of Knyghton cites an interesting anecdote of his life at this, its important crisis. He had retired to a solitary spot beside the Seine, to meditate on the mysterious essence of the Trinity, when he saw a boy ladling out the waters of the river that ran before him into a little well. His curiosity arrested, he asked what the boy proposed to do. The boy re-plied, " To empty yon deep into this well." " That canst thou never do," said the scholar. " Nor canst thou," answered the boy, " exhaust the deep on which thou dost meditate into the well of thy reason." Therewith the speaker vanished; and Lanfranc, resigning the hope to achieve the mighty mystery, threw himself at once into the arms of faith, and took his refuge in the monastery of Bec.

The tale may be a legend, but not an idle one. Perhaps he related it himself as a parable, and by the fiction explained the process of thought that decided his career. In the prime of his manhood, about 1042, when he was thirty-seven years old and in the zenith of his scholarly fame, he professed. The Convent of Bec had been lately foऻnded, under Herluin, the first abbot; there Lanfranc opened a school, which became one of the most famous throughout the West of Europe. Indeed, under the Lombard's influence, the then obscure Convent of Bec, to which the solitude of the site and the poverty of the endowment allured his choice, grew the Academe of the age. "It was," says Orderic, in his charming chronicle, — "it was under such a master that the Normans received their first notions of literature; from that school emerged the multitude of eloquent philosophers who adorned alike divinity and science. From France, Gascony, Bretagne, Flanders, scholars thronged to receive his lessons." [1]

At first, as superficially stated in the tale, Lanfranc had taken part against the marriage of William with Matilda of Flanders, — a marriage clearly contrary to the formal canons of the Roman Church, — and was banished by the fiery duke; though William's displeasure gave way at "the decent joke" (*jocus decens*) recorded in the text. At Rome, however, his influence, arguments, and eloquence were all enlisted on the side of William; and it was to the scholar of Pavia that the great Norman owed the ultimate sanction of his marriage, and the repeal of the interdict that excommunicated his realm. [2]

At Rome he assisted in the council held 1059 (the year wherein the ban of the Church was finally and formally taken from Normandy), at which the famous Berenger, Archdeacon of Angers (against whom he had waged a polemical controversy that did more than all else to secure his repute at the Pontifical Court), abjured "his heresies" as to the Real Presence in the sacrament of the Eucharist.

In 1062 or 1063 Duke William, against the Lombard's own will (for Lanfranc genuinely loved the liberty of letters more than vulgar power), raised him to the abbacy of St. Stephen of Caen. From that time his ascendancy over his haughty lord was absolute. The contemporary historian (William of Poitiers) says that "William respected him as a father, venerated him as a preceptor, and cherished him as a brother or son." He confided to him his own designs, and committed to him the entire superintendence of the ecclesiastical orders throughout Normandy.

---

[1] Ord. Vital. lib. 4.

[2] The date of William's marriage has been variously stated in English and Norman history, but is usually fixed in 1051-52. M. Pluquet, however, in a note to his edition of the "Roman de Rou," says that the only authority for the date of that marriage is in the Chronicle of Tours, and it is there referred to 1053. It would seem that the papal excommunication was not actually taken off till 1059, nor the formal dispensation for the marriage granted till 1063.

Eminent no less for his practical genius in affairs than for his rare piety and theological learning, Lanfranc attained indeed to the true ideal of the Scholar, — to whom, of all men, nothing that is human should be foreign; whose closet is but a hermit's cell, unless it is the microcosm that embraces the mart and the forum; who by the reflective part of his nature seizes the higher region of philosophy, by the energetic is attracted to the central focus of action. For scholarship is but the parent of ideas; and ideas are the parents of action.

After the conquest, as prelate of Canterbury, Lanfranc became the second man in the kingdom, — happy, perhaps, for England had he been the first; for all the anecdotes recorded of him show a deep and genuine sympathy with the oppressed population. But William the King of the English escaped from the control which Lanfranc had imposed on the Duke of the Normans. The scholar had strengthened the aspirer; he could only imperfectly influence the conqueror.

Lanfranc was not, it is true, a faultless character. He was a priest, a lawyer, and a man of the world, — three characters hard to amalgamate into perfection, especially in the eleventh century. But he stands in gigantic and brilliant contrast to the rest of our priesthood in his own day, both in the superiority of his virtues, and in his exemption from the ordinary vices. He regarded the cruelties of Odo of Bayeux with detestation, opposed him with firmness, and ultimately, to the joy of all England, ruined his power. He gave a great impetus to learning; he set a high example to his monks, in his freedom from the mercenary sins of their order; he laid the foundations of a powerful and splendid church, which, only because it failed in future Lanfrancs, failed in effecting the civilization of which he designed it to be the instrument. He refused to crown William Rufus, until that king had sworn to govern according to law and to right; and died, though a Norman usurper, honoured and beloved by the Saxon people.

Scholar, and morning star of light in the dark age of force and fraud, it is easier to praise thy life than to track through the length of centuries all the measureless and invisible benefits which the life of one scholar bequeaths to the world, — in the souls it awakens, in the thoughts it suggests![1]

---

[1] For authorities for the above sketch, and for many interesting details of Lanfranc's character, see Ord. Vital; Hen. de Knyghton, lib. ii.; Gervasius: and the life of Lanfranc, to be found in the collection of his Works, etc.

NOTE F, PAGE 71.

Edward the Confessor's Reply to Magnus of Denmark, who claimed his Crown.

ON rare occasions Edward was not without touches of a brave kingly nature.

Snorro Sturleson gives us a noble and spirited reply of the Confessor to Magnus, who, as heir of Canute, claimed the English crown; it concludes thus: " Now, he [Hardicanute] died, and then it was the resolution of all the people of the country to take me for the king here in England. So long as I had no kingly title I served my superiors in all respects like those who had no claims by birth to land or kingdom. Now, however, I have received the kingly title, and am consecrated king; I have established my royal dignity and authority, as my father before me; and while I live I will not renounce my title. If King Magnus comes here with an army, I will gather no army against him; but he shall only get the opportunity of taking England when he has taken my life. Tell him these words of mine." If we may consider this reply to be authentic, it is significant, as proof that Edward rests his title on the resolution of the people to take him for king; and counts as nothing, in comparison, his hereditary claims. This, together with the general tone of the reply, particularly the passage in which he implies that he trusts his defence not to his army but his people, makes it probable that Godwin dictated the answer; and, indeed, Edward himself could not have couched it either in Saxon or Danish. But the king is equally entitled to the credit of it, whether he composed it, or whether he merely approved and sanctioned its gallant tone and its princely sentiment.

NOTE G, PAGE 74.

Heralds.

So much of the " pride, pomp, and circumstance" which invest the Age of Chivalry is borrowed from these companions of princes and blazoners of noble deeds, that it may interest the reader, if I set briefly before him what our best antiquaries have said as to their first appearance in our own history.

Camden (somewhat, I fear, too rashly) says that " their reputation, honour, and name began in the time of Charlemagne." The first mention of heralds in England occurs in the reign of Edward III., a reign in which Chivalry was at its dazzling zenith. Whitlock says that " some derive the name of Herald from Hereauld," a Saxon word (old soldier, or old master), " because anciently they were chosen from veteran soldiers." Joseph Holland says : " I find that Malcolm, King of Scots, sent a herald unto William the Conqueror, to treat of a peace, when both armies were in order of battle." Agard affirms that " at the conquest there was no practice of heraldry ; " and observes truly, " that the Conqueror used a monk for his messenger to King Harold."

To this I may add that monks or priests also fulfil the office of heralds in the old French and Norman Chronicles. Thus Charles the Simple sends an archbishop to treat with Rolfganger ; Louis the De-bonair sends to Mormon, chief of the Bretons, " a sage and prudent abbot." But in the Saxon times the nuncius (a word still used in heraldic Latin) was in the regular service both of the king and the great earls. The Saxon name for such a messenger was *bode*, and when employed in hostile negotiations, he was styled *war-bode*. The messengers between Godwin and the king would seem, by the general sense of the chronicles, to have been certain thegns acting as mediators.

NOTE H, PAGE 103.

The Fylgia, or Tutelary Spirit.

THIS lovely superstition in the Scandinavian belief is the more re-markable because it does not appear in the creed of the Germanic Teutons, and is closely allied with the good angel, or guardian genius, of the Persians. It forms, therefore, one of the arguments that favour the Asiatic origin of the Norsemen.

The Fylgia (*following*, or attendant, spirit) was always represented as a female. Her influence was not uniformly favourable, though such was its general characteristic. She was capable of revenge if neglected, but had the devotion of her sex when properly treated. Mr. Grenville Pigott, in his popular work, entitled " A Manual of Scandinavian Mythology," relates an interesting legend with respect to one of these supernatural ladies : —

A Scandinavian warrior, Halfred Vandrædakald, having embraced Christianity, and being attacked by a disease which he thought mortal, was naturally anxious that a spirit who had accompanied him through his pagan career should not attend him into that other world, where her society might involve him in disagreeable consequences. The persevering Fylgia, however, in the shape of a fair maiden, walked on the waves of the sea after her viking's ship. She came thus in sight of all the crew ; and Halfred, recognizing his Fylgia, told her point blank that their connection was at an end forever. The forsaken Fylgia had a high spirit of her own, and she then asked Thorold if he would take her. Thorold ungallantly refused; but Halfred the younger said, " Maiden, I will take thee." [1]

In the various Norse Saga there are many anecdotes of these spirits, who are always charming, because with their less earthly attributes they always blend something of the woman. The poetry embodied in their existence is of a softer and more humane character than that common with the stern and vast demons of the Scandinavian mythology.

Note I, page 111.

The Origin of Earl Godwin.

SHARON TURNER quotes from the Knytlinga Saga what he calls "an explanation of Godwin's career or parentage, which no other document affords; " namely, — " that Ulf, a Danish chief, after the battle of Skorstein, between Canute and Edmund Ironsides, pursued the English fugitives into a wood, lost his way, met, in the morning, a Saxon youth driving cattle to their pasture, asked him to direct him in safety to Canute's ships, and offered him the bribe of a gold ring for his guidance. The young herdsman refused the bribe, but sheltered the Dane in the cottage of his father (who is represented as a mere peasant), and conducted him the next morning to the Danish camp ; previously to which, the youth's father represented to Ulf that his son Godwin could never, after aiding a Dane to escape, rest in safety with his countrymen, and besought him to befriend his son's fortunes with Canute." The Dane promised, and kept his word : hence Godwin's rise. Thierry, in his " History of the Norman Conquest," tells the same story, on the authority of Torfæus, Hist. Rer. Norweg. Now I need not say to any scholar in our early history, that the Norse Chronicles, abounding with romance and legend, are never to be received as authorities *counter* to our own records, though occasionally valuable to supply omissions in the latter ; and, unfortunately for this pretty story, we have *against* it the direct statements of the very best authorities we possess, namely, The Saxon Chronicle and Florence of Worcester. The Saxon

---

[1] Pigott's Scand. Mythol. p. 360. Half. Vand. Saga.

Chronicle expressly tells us that Godwin's father was Childe of Sussex (Florence calls him minister or thegn of Sussex[1]), and that Wolnoth was nephew to Edric, the all-powerful Earl or Duke of Mercia. Florence confirms this statement, and gives the pedigree, which may be deduced as follows: —

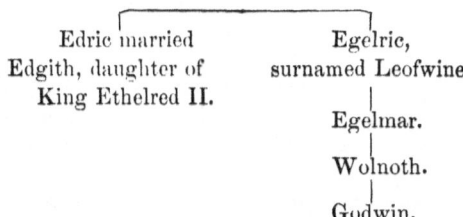

Edric married
Edgith, daughter of
King Ethelred II.

Egelric,
surnamed Leofwine

Egelmar.

Wolnoth.

Godwin.

Thus this "old peasant," as the North Chronicles call Wolnoth, was, according to our most unquestionable authorities, a thegn of one of the most important divisions in England, and a member of the most powerful family in the kingdom! Now, if our Saxon authorities needed any aid from probabilities, it is scarcely worth asking which is the more probable, — that the son of a Saxon herdsman should in a few years rise to such power as to marry the sister of the royal Danish Conqueror ; or that that honour should be conferred on the most able member of a House already allied to Saxon royalty, and which evidently retained its power after the fall of its head, the treacherous Edric Streone! Even after the Conquest, one of Streone's nephews, Edricus Sylvaticus, is mentioned (Simon. Dunelm.) as "a very powerful thegn." Upon the whole, the account given of Godwin's rise in the text of the work appears the most correct that conjectures, based on our scanty historical information, will allow.

In 1009 A. D., Wolnoth, the Childe or Thegn of Sussex, defeats the fleets of Ethelred, under his uncle Brightric, and goes therefore into rebellion. Thus when in 1014 (five years afterwards) Canute is chosen king by all the fleet, it is probable that Wolnoth and Godwin, his son, espoused his cause : and that Godwin, subsequently presented to Canute as a young noble of great promise, was favoured by that sagacious king, and ultimately honoured with the hand, first of his sister, secondly of his niece, as a mode of conciliating the Saxon thegns.

[1] "Suthsaxonum Ministrum Wolfnothem." Flor., Wig.

NOTE K, page 225.

The Want of Fortresses in England.

THE Saxons were sad destroyers. They destroyed the strongholds which the Briton had received from the Roman, and built very few others. Thus the land was left open to the Danes. Alfred, sensible of this defect, repaired the walls of London and other cities, and urgently recommended his nobles and prelates to build fortresses, but could not persuade them. His great-souled daughter, Elfleda, was the only imitator of his example. She built eight castles in three years.[1]

It was thus that in a country in which the general features do not allow of protracted warfare, the inhabitants were always at the hazard of a single pitched battle. Subsequent to the Conquest, in the reign of John, it was, in truth, the strong castle of Dover, on the siege of which Prince Louis lost so much time, that saved the realm of England from passing to a French dynasty ; and as, in later periods, strongholds fell again into decay, so it is remarkable to observe how easily the country was overrun after any signal victory of one of the contending parties. In this truth the Wars of the Roses abound with much instruction. The handful of foreign mercenaries with which Henry VII. won his crown, though the real heir, the Earl of Warwick (granting Edward IV.'s children to be illegitimate, which they clearly were according to the rites of the Church), had never lost his claim, by the defeat of Richard at Bosworth ; the march of the Pretender to Derby, the dismay it spread throughout England, and the certainty of his conquest had he proceeded ; the easy victory of William III. at a time when certainly the bulk of the nation was opposed to his cause, — are all facts pregnant with warnings, to which we are as blind as we were in the days of Alfred.

NOTE L, page 249.

The Ruins of Penmaen-mawr.

IN Camden's "Britannia" there is an account of the remarkable relics assigned, in the text, to the last refuge of Gryffyth ap Llewellyn, taken from a manuscript by Sir John Wynne in the time of Charles I. In this account are minutely described, "ruinous walls of an exceeding strong fortification, compassed with a treble wall, and within each wall

[1] Asser. de Reb. Gest. Alf. pp. 17, 18.

the foundations of at least one hundred towers, about six yards in diameter within the walls. This castle seems (while it stood) impregnable,
— there being no way to offer any assault on it; the hill being so very
high, steep, and rocky; and the walls of such strength; the way or
entrance into it ascending with many turnings, so that one hundred
men might defend themselves against a whole legion; and yet it should
seem that there were lodgings within those walls for twenty thousand
men.

" By the tradition we receive from our ancestors, this was the strongest refuge, or place of defence, that the ancient Britons had in all Snowdon; moreover, the greatness of the work shows that it was a princely
fortification, strengthened by nature and workmanship." [1]

But in the year 1771 Governor Pownall ascended Penmaen-mawr, inspected these remains, and published his account in the " Archæologia,"
vol. iii. p. 303, with a sketch both of the mount and the walls at the
summit. The governor is of opinion that it never was a fortification.
He thinks that the inward inclosure contained a carn (or arch-Druid's
sepulchre), that there is not room for any lodgment, that the walls are
not of a kind which can form a cover and give at the same time the advantage of fighting from them, — in short, that the place was one of the
Druids' consecrated high places of worship. He adds, however, that " Mr.
Pennant has gone twice over it, intends to make an actual survey, and
anticipates much from that great antiquary's knowledge and accuracy."

We turn next to Mr. Pennant, and we find him giving a flat contra-
diction to the governor. " I have more than once," [2] says he, " visited
this noted rock, to view the fortifications described by the editor of
Camden, from some notes of that sensible old baronet, Sir John Wynne,
of Gwidir, *and have found his account very just.*

" The fronts of three, if not four, walls presented themselves very
distinctly one above the other. I measured the height of one wall,
which was at the time nine feet, the thickness seven feet and a half."
(Now, Governor Pownall also measured the walls, agrees pretty well
with Pennant as to their width, but makes them only five feet high.)
" Between these walls, in all parts, were innumerable small buildings, mostly circular. These had been much higher, as is evident from
the fall of stones which lie scattered at their bottoms, and probably had
once the form of towers, as Sir John asserts. Their diameter is, in *general*, from twelve to eighteen feet (ample room here for lodgment); the
walls were in certain places intersected with others equally strong.

[1] Camden, Caernarvonshire.
[2] Pennant, Wales, vol. ii. p. 146.

This stronghold of the Britons is exactly of the same kind with those on Carn Madryn, Carn Boduan, and Tre'r Caer.

"This was most judiciously chosen to cover the passage into Anglesea, and the remoter part of their country, and must, from its *vast strength*, have been invulnerable, except by famine, being inaccessible by its natural steepness towards the sea, and on the parts fortified in the manner described." So far, Pennant *versus* Pownall! "Who shall decide when doctors disagree?" The opinion of both these antiquarians is liable to demur. Governor Pownall might probably be a better judge of military defences than Pennant; but he evidently forms his notions of defence with imperfect knowledge of the forts which would have amply sufficed for the warfare of the ancient Britons; and moreover, he was one of those led astray by Bryant's crotchets as to "high places," etc. What appears most probable is, that the place was *both* carn and fort; that the strength of the place and the convenience of stones suggested the surrounding the narrow area of the central sepulchre with walls intended for refuge and defence. As to the *circular* buildings, which seem to have puzzled these antiquaries, it is strange that they appear to have overlooked the accounts which serve best to explain them. Strabo says that "the houses of the Britons were round, with a high pointed covering;" Cæsar says that they were only lighted by the door; in the Antonine Column they are represented as *circular*, with an arched entrance, single or double. They were always small, and seem to have contained but a single room. These circular buildings were not, therefore, necessarily Druidical cells, as has been supposed; nor perhaps actual towers, as contended for by Sir John Wynne; but habitations, after the usual fashion of British houses, for the inmates or garrison of the enclosure. Taking into account the traditions of the spot mentioned by Sir John Wynne, and other traditions still existing, which mark in the immediate neighbourhood the scenes of legendary battles, it is hoped that the reader will accept the description in the text as suggesting, amidst conflicting authorities, the most probable supposition of the nature and character of these very interesting remains in the eleventh century,[1] and during the most memorable invasion of Wales (under Harold), which occurred between the time of Geraint, or Arthur, and that of Henry II.

---

[1] The ruins still extant are much diminished since the time even of Pownall or Pennant; and must be indeed inconsiderable, compared with the buildings or walls which existed at the date of my tale.

Note M, page 250.

The Idol Bel.

Monsieur Johanneau considers that Bel, or Belinus, is derived from the Greek, a surname of Apollo, and means " the Archer ; " from Belos, " a dart or arrow." [1]

I own I think this among the spurious conceits of the learned, suggested by vague affinities of name ; but it is quite as likely (if there be anything in the conjecture) that the Celt taught the Greek as that the Greek taught the Celt.

There are some very interesting questions, however, for scholars to discuss ; namely, First, *When* did the Celts first introduce idols ? Second, Can we believe the classical authorities that assure us that the Druids originally admitted no idol worship ? If so, we find the chief idols of the Druids cited by Lucan; and they therefore acquired them long before Lucan's time. From whom would they acquire them ? Not from the Romans; for the Roman gods are not the least similar to the Celtic, when the last are fairly examined. Not from the Teutons, from whose deities those of the Celt equally differ. Have we not given too much faith to the classic writers, who assert the original simplicity of the Druid worship ? And will not their popular idols be found to be as ancient as the remotest traces of the Celtic existence ? Would not the Cimmerii have transported them from the period of their first traditional immigration from the East ? And is not their Bel identical with the Babylonian deity ?

Note N, page 288.

Unguents used by Witches.

Lord Bacon, speaking of the ointments used by the witches, supposes that they really did produce illusions by stopping the vapours and sending them to the head. It seems that all witches who attended the *sabbat* used these unguents, and there is something very remarkable in the concurrence of their testimonies as to the scenes they declared themselves to have witnessed, not in the body, which they left behind, but as present in the soul; as if the same anointments and preparatives produced dreams nearly similar in kind. To the believers in mesmerism I may add that few are aware of the extraordinary degree to which somnambulism appears to be heightened by certain chemical aids ; and the

[1] Johann. ap. Acad. Celt. tom. iii. p. 151.

disbelievers in that agency, who have yet tried the experiments of some of those now neglected drugs to which the medical art of the Middle Ages attached peculiar virtues, will not be inclined to dispute the powerful and as it were systematic effect which certain drugs produce on the imagination of patients with excitable and nervous temperaments.

NOTE O, PAGE 292.

Hilda's Adjurations.

I.

" By the Urdar fount dwelling,
Day by day from the rill,
The Nornas besprinkle
The Ash Ygg-drasill."

THE ASH YGG-DRASILL. — Much learning has been employed by Scandinavian scholars in illustrating the symbols supposed to be couched under the myth of the Ygg-drasill, or the great Ash-tree. With this I shall not weary the reader, especially since large systems have been built on very small premises, and the erudition employed has been equally ingenious and unsatisfactory; I content myself with stating the simple myth.

The Ygg-drasill has three roots; two spring from the infernal regions, —- that is, from the home of the frost-giants and from Niffl-heim, " vapour-home, or hell," — one from the heavenly abode of the Asas. Its branches, says the Prose Edda, extend over the whole universe, and its stem bears up the earth. Beneath the root which stretches through Niffl-heim, and which the snake-king continually gnaws, is the fount whence flow the infernal rivers. Beneath the root which stretches in the land of the giants, is Mimir's well, wherein all wisdom is concealed; but under the root which lies in the land of the gods is the well of Urda, the Norna, — here the gods sit in judgment. Near this well is a fair building, whence issue the three maidens, Urda, Verdandi, Skulda (the Past, the Present, the Future). Daily they water the Ash-tree from Urda's well, that the branches may not perish. Four harts constantly devour the buds and branches of the Ash-tree. On its boughs sits an eagle, wise in much; and between its eyes sits a hawk. A squirrel runs up and down the tree, sowing strife between the eagle and the snake.

Such, in brief, is the account of the myth. For the various interpretations of its symbolic meaning, the general reader is referred to Mr. Blackwell's edition of Mallett's " Northern Antiquities," and Pigott's " Scandinavian Manual."

HAROLD,

THE LAST OF THE SAXON KINGS.

BOOK X.

THE SACRIFICE ON THE ALTAR.

CHAPTER I.

THE good Bishop Alred, now raised to the See of York, had been summoned from his cathedral-seat by Edward, who had indeed undergone a severe illness during the absence of Harold; and that illness had been both preceded and followed by mystical presentiments of the evil days that were to fall on England after his death. He had therefore sent for the best and the holiest prelate in his realm, to advise and counsel with.

The bishop had returned to his lodging in London (which was in a Benedictine abbey, not far from the Aldgate), late one evening, from visiting the king at his rural palace of Havering; and he was seated alone in his cell, musing over an interview with Edward, which had evidently much disturbed him, when the door was abruptly thrown open; and pushing aside in haste the monk, who was about formally to announce him, a man so travel-stained in garb, and of a mien so disordered, rushed in, that Alred gazed at first as on a stranger, and not till the intruder spoke did he recognize Harold the Earl. Even then, so wild was the earl's eye, so dark his brow, and so livid his cheek, that it rather seemed the ghost of the man than the man himself. Closing the door on the monk, the earl stood a moment on the threshold, with a breast heaving with emotions which he sought in vain to master; and, as if resigning the effort, he sprang forward, clasped the prelate's knees, bowed his head on his lap, and sobbed aloud. The good bishop, who had known all the sons of Godwin from their infancy, and to whom Harold was as dear as his own child, folding his hands over the earl's head, soothingly murmured a benediction.

"No, no," cried the earl, starting to his feet, and tossing the dishevelled hair from his eyes, "bless me not yet! Hear my tale first, and then say what comfort, what refuge, thy Church can bestow!"

Hurriedly then the earl poured forth the dark story, already known to the reader,—the prison at Belrem, the detention at William's court, the fears, the snares, the discourse by the river-side, the oath over the relics. This told, he continued, "I found myself in the open air, and knew not, till the light of the sun smote me, what might have passed into my soul. I was, before, as a corpse which a witch raises from the dead, endows with a spirit not its own,— passive to her hand, life-like, not living. Then, then it was as if a demon had passed from my body, laughing scorn at the foul things it had made the clay do. O, father, father! is there not absolution from this oath,— an oath I dare not keep? Rather perjure myself than betray my land!"

The prelate's face was as pale as Harold's, and it was some moments before he could reply.

"The Church can loose and unloose,— such is its delegated authority. But speak on; what saidst thou at the last to William?"

"I know not, remember not, aught save these words, 'Now, then, give me those for whom I placed myself in thy power; let me restore Haco to his fatherland, and Wolnoth to his mother's kiss, and wend home my way.' And, saints in heaven! what was the answer of this caitiff Norman, with his glittering eye and venomed smile? 'Haco thou shalt have, for he is an orphan, and an uncle's love is not so hot as to burn from a distance; but Wolnoth, thy mother's son, must stay with me as a hostage for thine own faith. Godwin's hostages are released; Harold's hostage I retain: it is but a form, yet these forms are the bonds of princes.'

"I looked at him, and his eye quailed. And I said, 'That is not in the compact.' And William answered, 'No, but it is the seal to it.' Then I turned from the duke, and I called my brother to my side, and I said, 'Over the seas have I come for thee. Mount thy steed and ride by my side, for I will not leave the land without thee.' And Wolnoth answered, 'Nay, Duke William tells me that he hath made treaties with thee, for which I am still to be the hostage; and Normandy has grown my home, and I love William as my lord.' Hot words followed, and Wolnoth, chafed, refused entreaty and command, and suffered me to see that his heart was not with England. O, Mother, Mother, how shall I meet thine eye! So I returned with Haco. The moment I set foot on my native England, that moment her form seemed to rise from the tall cliffs, her voice to speak in the winds! All the glamour by which I had been bound forsook me; and I sprang forward in scorn, above the fear of the dead men's bones. Miserable overcraft of the snarer! Had my simple word alone bound me, or that word been ratified after slow and deliberate thought, by the ordinary oaths that appeal to God, far stronger the bond upon my soul than the mean surprise, the covert tricks, the insult, and the mocking fraud. But as I rode on, the oath pursued me; pale spectres mounted behind me on my steed, ghastly fingers pointed from the welkin; and then suddenly, O my father — I who, sincere in my simple faith, had, as thou knowest too well, never bowed submissive conscience to priest and Church — then suddenly I felt the might of some power, surer guide than that haughty conscience which had so in the hour of need betrayed me! Then I recognized that supreme tribunal, that mediator between Heaven and man, to which I might come with the dire secret of my soul, and say, as I say now, on my bended knee, O father, father, bid me die, or absolve me from my oath!"

Then Alred rose erect, and replied, "Did I need subterfuge, O son, I would say that William himself hath released thy bond, in detaining the hostage against the spirit of the guilty compact; that in the very words themselves of the oath lies the release, — '*if God aid thee.*' God aids no child to parricide, — and thou art England's child! But all school casuistry is here a meanness. Plain is the law that oaths extorted by compulsion, through fraud and in fear, the Church hath the right to loose; plainer still the law of God and of man, that an oath to commit crime it is a deadlier sin to keep than to forfeit. Wherefore, not absolving thee from the misdeed of a vow that, if trusting more to God's providence and less to man's vain strength and dim wit, thou wouldst never have uttered even for England's sake, leaving her to the angels, — not, I say, absolving thee from that sin, but pausing yet to decide what penance and atonement to fix to its committal, I do, in the name of the Power whose priest I am, forbid thee to fulfil the oath; I do release and absolve thee from all obligation thereto. And if in this I exceed my authority as Romish priest, I do but accomplish my duties as living man. To these gray hairs I take the sponsorship. Before this holy cross, kneel, O my son, with me, and pray that a life of truth and virtue may atone the madness of an hour."

So by the crucifix knelt the warrior and the priest.

CHAPTER II.

ALL other thought had given way to Harold's impetuous yearning to throw himself upon the Church, to hear his doom from the purest and wisest of its Saxon preachers. Had the prelate deemed his vow irrefragable, he would have died the Roman's death rather than live the traitor's life; and strange indeed was the revolution created in this man's character, that he, "so self-dependent," he who had hitherto deemed himself his sole judge below of cause and action, now felt the whole life of his life committed to the word of a cloistered shaveling. All other thought had given way to that fiery impulse, — home, mother, Edith, king, power, policy, ambition! Till the weight was from his soul, he was as an outlaw in his native land. But when the next sun rose, and that awful burden was lifted from his heart and his being; when his own calm sense, returning, sanctioned the fiat of the priest; when, though with deep shame and rankling remorse at the memory of the vow, he yet felt exonerated, not from the guilt of having made, but the deadlier guilt of fulfilling it, all the objects of existence resumed their natural interest, softened and chastened, but still vivid in the heart restored to humanity. But from that time, Harold's stern philosophy and stoic ethics were shaken to the dust; re-created, as it were, by the breath of religion, he adopted its tenets even after the fashion of his age. The secret of his shame, the error of his conscience, humbled him. Those unlettered monks whom he had so despised — how had he lost the right to stand aloof from their control! how had his wisdom and his strength and his courage met unguarded the hour of temptation!

Yes, might the time come, when England could spare him from her side! when he, like Sweyn the outlaw, could pass a pilgrim to the Holy Sepulchre, and there, as the creed of the age taught, win full pardon for the single lie of his truthful life, and regain the old peace of his stainless conscience!

There are sometimes event and season in the life of man the hardest and most rational, when he is driven perforce to faith the most implicit and submissive, — as the storm drives the wings of the petrel over a measureless sea, till it falls tame, and rejoicing at refuge, on the sails of some lonely ship, — seasons when difficulties, against which reason seems stricken into palsy, leave him bewildered in dismay; when darkness, which experience cannot pierce, wraps the conscience, as sudden night wraps the traveller in the desert; when error entangles his feet in its inextricable web; when, still desirous of the right, he sees before him but a choice of evil; and the Angel of the Past, with a flaming sword, closes

on him the gates of the Future. Then, Faith flashes on him,
with a light from the cloud; then, he clings to Prayer as a
drowning wretch to the plank; then, that solemn authority
which clothes the Priest, as the interpreter between the soul
and the Divinity, seizes on the heart that trembles with terror
and joy; then, that mysterious recognition of Atonement, of
sacrifice, of purifying lustration (mystery which lies hid in
the core of all religions), smooths the frown on the Past, re-
moves the flaming sword from the Future. The Orestes escapes from the hounding Furies, and follows the oracle to the
spot where the cleansing dews shall descend on the expiated
guilt.

He who hath never known in himself, nor marked in another, such strange crisis in human fate, cannot judge of the
strength and the weakness it bestows. But till he can so
judge, the spiritual part of all history is to him a blank
scroll, a sealed volume. He cannot comprehend what drove
the fierce Heathen, cowering and humbled, into the fold of
the Church; what peopled Egypt with eremites; what lined
the roads of Europe and Asia with pilgrim homicides; what,
in the elder world, while Jove yet reigned on Olympus, is
couched in the dim traditions of the expiation of Apollo, the
joy-god, descending into Hades; or why the sinner went
blithe and light-hearted from the healing lustrations of
Eleusis. In all these solemn riddles of the Jove world and
the Christ's is involved the imperious necessity that man
hath of repentance and atonement; through their clouds, as
a rainbow, shines the covenant that reconciles the God and
the man.

Now Life with strong arms plucked the reviving Harold to
itself. Already the news of his return had spread through
the city, and his chamber soon swarmed with joyous welcomes
and anxious friends. But the first congratulations over, each
had tidings, that claimed his instant attention, to relate. His
absence had sufficed to loosen half the links of that ill-woven
empire.

All the North was in arms. Northumbria had revolted as
one man from the tyrannous cruelty of Tostig; the insurgents

had marched upon York; Tostig had fled in dismay, none as yet knew whither. The sons of Algar had sallied forth from their Mercian fortresses, and were now in the ranks of the Northumbrians, who it was rumoured had selected Morcar (the elder) in the place of Tostig.

Amidst these disasters, the king's health was fast decaying; his mind seemed bewildered and distraught; dark ravings of evil portent that had escaped from his lip in his mystic reveries and visions, had spread abroad, bandied, with all natural exaggerations, from lip to lip. The country was in one state of gloomy and vague apprehension.

But all would go well, now Harold the great Earl — Harold the stout, and the wise, and the loved — had come back to his native land!

In feeling himself thus necessary to England, — all eyes, all hopes, all hearts turned to him, and to him alone, — Harold shook the evil memories from his soul, as a lion shakes the dews from his mane. His intellect, that seemed to have burned dim and through smoke in scenes unfamiliar to its exercise, rose at once equal to the occasion. His words reassured the most despondent. His orders were prompt and decisive. While, to and fro, went forth his bodes and his riders, he himself leaped on his horse, and rode fast to Havering.

At length that sweet and lovely retreat broke on his sight, as a bower through the bloom of a garden. This was Edward's favourite abode: he had built it himself for his private devotions, allured by its woody solitudes and the gloom of its copious verdure. Here it was said, that once at night, wandering through the silent glades, and musing on heaven, the loud song of the nightingales had disturbed his devotions; with vexed and impatient soul, he had prayed that the music might be stilled: and since then, never more the nightingale was heard in the shades of Havering!

Threading the woodland, melancholy yet glorious with the hues of autumn, Harold reached the low and humble gate of the timber edifice, all covered with creepers and young ivy; and in a few moments more he stood in the presence of the king.

Edward raised himself with pain from the couch on which he was reclined,[1] beneath a canopy supported by columns and surmounted by carved symbols of the bell towers of Jerusalem; and his languid face brightened at the sight of Harold. Behind the king stood a man with a Danish battle-axe in his hand, the captain of the royal house-carles, who, on a sign from the king, withdrew.

"Thou art come back, Harold," said Edward then, in a feeble voice; and the earl, drawing near, was grieved and shocked at the alteration of his face. "Thou art come back, to aid this benumbed hand, from which the earthly sceptre is about to fall. Hush! for it is so, and I rejoice." Then examining Harold's features, yet pale with recent emotions, and now saddened by sympathy with the king, he resumed: "Well, man of this world, that went forth confiding in thine own strength, and in the faith of men of the world like thee, — well, were my warnings prophetic, or art thou contented with thy mission?"

"Alas!" said Harold, mournfully; "thy wisdom was greater than mine, O King; and dread the snares laid for me and our native land, under pretext of a promise made by thee to Count William, that he should reign in England, should he be your survivor."

Edward's face grew troubled and embarrassed. "Such promise," he said falteringly, "when I knew not the laws of England, nor that a realm could not pass like house and hyde by a man's single testament, might well escape from my thoughts, never too bent upon earthly affairs. But I marvel not that my cousin's mind is more tenacious and mundane. And verily, in those vague words, and from thy visit, I see the Future dark with fate and crimson with blood."

Then Edward's eyes grew locked and set, staring into space; and even that revery, though it awed him, relieved Harold of much disquietude, for he rightly conjectured that on waking from it Edward would press him no more as to those details, and dilemmas of conscience, of which he felt that the arch-worshipper of relics was no fitting judge.

[1] Bayeux tapestry.

When the king, with a heavy sigh, evinced return from the world of vision, he stretched forth to Harold his wan, transparent hand, and said,—

"Thou seest the ring on this finger; it comes to me from above, a merciful token to prepare my soul for death. Perchance thou mayest have heard that once an aged pilgrim stopped me on my way from God's House, and asked for alms; and I, having nought else on my person to bestow, drew from my finger a ring, and gave it to him, and the old man went his way, blessing me."

"I mind me well of thy gentle charity," said the earl; "for the pilgrim bruited it abroad as he passed, and much talk was there of it."

The king smiled faintly. "Now this was years ago. It so chanced this year, that certain Englishers, on their way from the Holy Land, fell in with two pilgrims, and these last questioned them much of me. And one, with face venerable and benign, drew forth a ring, and said, 'When thou reachest England, give thou this to the king's own hand, and say, by this token, that on Twelfth-Day Eve he shall be with me. For what he gave to me, will I prepare recompense without bound; and already the saints deck for the new comer the halls where the worm never gnaws and the moth never frets.' 'And who,' asked my subjects, amazed, 'who shall we say speaketh thus to us?' And the pilgrim answered, 'He on whose breast leaned the Son of God, and my name is John!' [1] Wherewith the apparition vanished. This is the ring I gave to the pilgrim,— on the fourteenth night from thy parting miraculously returned to me. Wherefore, Harold, my time here is brief, and I rejoice that thy coming delivers me up from the cares of State to the preparation of my soul for the joyous day."

Harold, suspecting under this incredible mission some wily device of the Norman, who, by thus warning Edward (of whose precarious health he was well aware), might induce his

[1] Ailred, De Vit. Edward Confess. — Many other chroniclers mention this legend, of which the stones of Westminster Abbey itself prated, in the statues of Edward and the Pilgrim, placed over the arch in Dean's Yard.

timorous conscience to take steps for the completion of the
old promise,— Harold, we say, thus suspecting, in vain endeavoured to combat the king's presentiments; but Edward
interrupted him, with displeased firmness of look and tone,—

"Come not thou, with thy human reasonings, between my
soul and the messenger divine; but rather nerve and prepare
thyself for the dire calamities that lie greeding in the days
to come! Be thine things temporal. All the land is in rebellion. Anlaf, whom thy coming dismissed, hath just wearied
me with sad tales of bloodshed and ravage. Go and hear him,
— go hear the bodes of thy brother Tostig, who wait without
in our hall; go, take axe, and take shield, and the men of
earth's war, and do justice and right; and on thy return thou
shalt see with what rapture sublime a Christian king can soar
aloft from his throne! Go!"

More moved, and more softened, than in the former day he
had been with Edward's sincere, if fanatical piety, Harold,
turning aside to conceal his face, said,—

"Would, O royal Edward, that my heart, amidst worldly
cares, were as pure and serene as thine! But, at least, what
erring mortal may do to guard this realm, and face the evils
thou foreseest in the Far, that will I do; and perchance then,
in my dying hour, God's pardon and peace may descend on
me!" He spoke, and went.

The accounts he received from Anlaf (a veteran Anglo-
Dane) were indeed more alarming than he had yet heard.
Morcar, the bold son of Algar, was already proclaimed, by
the rebels, Earl of Northumbria; the shires of Nottingham,
Derby, and Lincoln had poured forth their hardy Dane populations on his behalf. All Mercia was in arms under his
brother Edwin; and many of the Cymrian chiefs had already
joined the ally of the butchered Gryffyth.

Not a moment did the earl lose in proclaiming the Herr-
ban; sheaves of arrows were splintered, and the fragments,
as announcing the War-Fyrd, were sent from thegn to thegn,
and town to town. Fresh messengers were despatched to
Gurth to collect the whole force of his own earldom, and
haste by quick marches to London; and, these preparations

made, Harold returned to the metropolis, and with a heavy heart sought his mother, as his next care.

Githa was already prepared for his news; for Haco had of his own accord gone to break the first shock of disappointment. There was in this youth a noiseless sagacity that seemed ever provident for Harold. With his sombre, smileless cheek, and gloom of beauty, bowed as if beneath the weight of some invisible doom, he had already become linked indissolubly with the earl's fate, as its angel,— but as its angel of darkness!

To Harold's intense relief, Githa stretched forth her hands as he entered, and said, "Thou hast failed me, but against thy will! Grieve not; I am content!"

"Now our Lady be blessed, Mother —"

"I have told her," said Haco, who was standing, with arms folded, by the fire, the blaze of which reddened fitfully his hueless countenance with its raven hair,— "I have told thy mother that Wolnoth loves his captivity, and enjoys the cage. And the lady hath had comfort in my words."

"Not in thine only, son of Sweyn, but in those of fate; for before thy coming, I prayed against the long blind yearning of my heart, prayed that Wolnoth might *not* cross the sea with his kinsmen."

"How!" exclaimed the earl, astonished.

Githa took his arm, and led him to the farther end of the ample chamber, as if out of the hearing of Haco, who turned his face towards the fire, and gazed into the fierce blaze with musing, unwinking eyes.

"Couldst thou think, Harold, that in thy journey, that on the errand of so great fear and hope, I could sit brooding in my chair, and count the stitches on the tremulous hangings? No; day by day have I sought the lore of Hilda, and at night I have watched with her by the fount and the elm and the tomb: and I know that thou hast gone through dire peril, — the prison, the war, and the snare; and I know also, that his Fylgia hath saved the life of my Wolnoth; for had he returned to his native land, he had returned but to a bloody grave!"

"Says Hilda this?" said the earl, thoughtfully.

"So say the Vala, the rune, and the Scin-læca! and such is the doom that now darkens the brow of Haco! Seest thou not that the hand of death is in the hush of the smileless lip, and the glance of the unjoyous eye?"

"Nay, it is but the thought born to captive youth, and nurtured in solitary dreams. Thou hast seen Hilda? — and Edith, my mother, — Edith is — "

"Well," said Githa, kindly, for she sympathized with that love which Godwin would have condemned; "though she grieved deeply after thy departure, and would sit for hours gazing into space, and moaning. But even ere Hilda divined thy safe return, Edith knew it; I was beside her at the time; she started up, and cried, 'Harold is in England!' 'How? Why thinkest thou so?' said I. And Edith answered, 'I feel it by the touch of the earth, by the breath of the air.' This is more than love, Harold. I knew two twins who had the same instinct of each other's comings and goings, and were present each to each even when absent: Edith is twin to thy soul. Thou goest to her now, Harold; thou wilt find there thy sister Thyra. The child hath drooped of late, and I besought Hilda to revive her, with herb and charm. Thou wilt come back, ere thou departest to aid Tostig, thy brother, and tell me how Hilda hath prospered with my ailing child?"

"I will, my mother. Be cheered! — Hilda is a skilful nurse. And now bless thee, that thou hast not reproached me that my mission failed to fulfil my promise. Welcome even our kinswoman's sayings, sith they comfort thee for the loss of thy darling!"

Then Harold left the room, mounted his steed, and rode through the town towards the bridge. He was compelled to ride slowly through the streets, for he was recognized; and cheapman and mechanic rushed from house and from stall to hail the Man of the Land and the Time.

"All is safe now in England, for Harold is come back!" They seemed joyous as the children of the mariner, when, with wet garments, he struggles to shore through the storm.

And kind and loving were Harold's looks and brief words, as he rode with veiled bonnet through the swarming streets.

At length he cleared the town and the bridge; and the yellowing boughs of the orchards drooped over the road towards the Roman home, when, as he spurred his steed, he heard behind him hoofs as in pursuit, looked back, and beheld Haco. He drew rein. "What wantest thou, my nephew?"

"Thee!" answered Haco, briefly, as he gained his side. "Thy companionship."

"Thanks, Haco; but I pray thee to stay in my mother's house, for I would fain ride alone."

"Spurn me not from thee, Harold! This England is to me the land of the stranger; in thy mother's house I feel but the more the orphan. Henceforth I have devoted to thee my life! And my life my dead and dread father hath left to thee, as a doom or a blessing; wherefore cleave I to thy side, — cleave we in life and in death to each other!"

An undefined and cheerless thrill shot through the earl's heart as the youth spoke thus; and the remembrance that Haco's counsel had first induced him to abandon his natural hardy and gallant manhood, meet wile by wile, and thus suddenly entangle him in his own meshes, had already mingled an inexpressible bitterness with his pity and affection for his brother's son. But, struggling against that uneasy sentiment, as unjust towards one to whose counsel — however sinister, and now repented — he probably owed, at least, his safety and deliverance, he replied gently, —

"I accept thy trust and thy love, Haco! Ride with me, then; but pardon a dull comrade, for when the soul communes with itself the lip is silent."

"True," said Haco, "and I am no babbler. Three things are ever silent, — Thought, Destiny, and the Grave."

Each then, pursuing his own fancies, rode on fast, and side by side, — the long shadows of declining day struggling with a sky of unusual brightness, and thrown from the dim forest trees and the distant hillocks. Alternately through shade and through light rode they on; the bulls gazing on them from holt and glade, and the boom of the bittern sounding in its peculiar mournfulness of tone as it rose from the dank pools that glistened in the western sun.

It was always by the rear of the house, where stood the ruined temple so associated with the romance of his life, that Harold approached the home of the Vala; and as now the hillock, with its melancholy diadem of stones, came in view, Haco for the first time broke the silence.

"Again — as in a dream!" he said abruptly. "Hill, ruin, grave-mound — but where the tall image of the mighty one?"

"Hast thou then seen this spot before?" asked the earl.

"Yea, as an infant here was I led by my father Sweyn; here too, from thy house yonder, dim seen through the fading leaves, on the eve before I left this land for the Norman, here did I wander alone; and there, by that altar, did the great Vala of the North chant her runes for my future."

"Alas! thou too!" murmured Harold; and then he asked aloud, "What said she?"

"That thy life and mine crossed each other in the skein; that I should save thee from a great peril, and share with thee a greater."

"Ah, youth," answered Harold, bitterly, "these vain prophecies of human wit guard the soul from no danger. They mislead us by riddles which our hot hearts interpret according to their own desires. Keep thou fast to youth's simple wisdom, and trust only to the pure spirit and the watchful God."

He suppressed a groan as he spoke, and springing from his steed, which he left loose, advanced up the hill. When he had gained the height, he halted, and made sign to Haco, who had also dismounted, to do the same. Halfway down the side of the slope which faced the ruined peristyle, Haco beheld a maiden, still young, and of beauty surpassing all that the court of Normandy boasted of female loveliness. She was seated on the sward; while a girl younger, and scarcely indeed grown into womanhood, reclined at her feet, and leaning her cheek upon her hand, seemed hushed in listening attention. In the face of the younger girl Haco recognized Thyra, the last-born of Githa, though he had but once seen her before, — the day ere he left England for the Norman court,— for the face of the girl was but little changed, save that the eye was more mournful, and the cheek was paler.

And Harold's betrothed was singing, in the still autumn air, to Harold's sister. The song chosen was on that subject the most popular with the Saxon poets, the mystic life, death, and resurrection of the fabled Phœnix, and this rhymeless song, in its old native flow, may yet find some grace in the modern ear.

THE LAY OF THE PHŒNIX. [1]

Shineth far hence — so
　Sing the wise elders —
Far to the fire-east
　The fairest of lands.

Daintily dight is that
　Dearest of joy fields;
Breezes all balm-y-filled
　Glide through its groves.

There to the blest, ope
　The high doors of heaven,
Sweetly sweep earthward
　Their wavelets of song.

Frost robes the sward not,
　Rusheth no hail-steel;
Wind-cloud ne'er wanders,
　Ne'er falleth the rain.

Warding the wood-holt,
　Girt with gay wonder,
Sheen with the plumy shine,
　Phœnix abides.

---

[1] This ancient Saxon lay, apparently of the date of the tenth or eleventh century, may be found, admirably translated by Mr. George Stephens, in the "Archæologia," vol. xxx. p. 259. In the text the poem is much abridged, reduced into rhythm, and in some stanzas wholly altered from the original. But it is, nevertheless, greatly indebted to Mr. Stephens's translation, from which several lines are borrowed verbatim. The more careful reader will note the great aid given to a rhymeless metre by *alliteration*. I am not sure that this old Saxon mode of verse might not be profitably restored to our national muse.

Lord of the Lleod,[1]
  Whose home is the **air,**
Winters a thousand
  Abideth the bird.

Hapless and heavy then
  Waxeth the hazy wing;
Year-worn and old in the
  Whirl of the earth.

Then the high holt-top,
  Mounting, the bird soars;
There, where the winds sleep,
  He buildeth a nest;

Gums the most precious, and
  Balms of the sweetest,
Spices and odours, he
  Weaves in the nest.

There, in that sun-ark, lo,
  Waiteth he wistful;
Summer comes smiling, lo,
  Rays smite the pile !

Burdened with eld-years, and
  Weary with slow time,
Slow in his odour nest
  Burneth the bird.

Up from those ashes, then,
  Springeth a rare fruit;
Deep in the rare fruit
  There coileth a worm.

Weaving bliss-meshes
  Around and around it,
Silent and blissful, the
  Worm worketh on.

Lo, from the airy web,
  Blooming and brightsome,
Young and exulting, the
  Phœnix breaks forth.

---

[1] People.

Round him the birds troop,
  Singing and hailing;
Wings of all glories
  Engarland the king.

Hymning and hailing,
  Through forest and sun-air
Hymning and hailing,
  And speaking him " King."

High flies the phœnix;
  Escaped from the worm-web
He soars in the sunlight,
  He bathes in the dew.

He visits his old haunts,
  The holt and the sun-hill,
The founts of his youth, and
  The fields of his love.

The stars in the welkin,
  The blooms on the earth,
Are glad in his gladness,
  Are young in his youth.

While round him the birds trôop, the
  Hosts of the Himmel,[1]
Blisses of music, and
  Glories of wings,

Hymning and hailing,
  And filling the sun-air
With music, and glory,
  And praise of the King.

As the lay ceased, Thyra said,—

"Ah, Edith, who would not brave the funeral pyre to live again like the phœnix!"

"Sweet sister mine," answered Edith, "the singer doth mean to image out in the phœnix the rising of our Lord, in whom we all live again."

And Thyra said mournfully,—

"But the phœnix sees once more the haunts of his youth,—

[1] Heaven.

the things and places dear to him in his life before. Shall we do the same, O Edith?"

"It is the persons we love that make beautiful the haunts we have known," answered the betrothed. "Those persons at least we shall behold again, and wherever *they* are — there is heaven."

Harold could restrain himself no longer. With one bound he was at Edith's side, and with one wild cry of joy he clasped her to his heart.

"I knew that thou wouldst come to-night, — I knew it, Harold," murmured the betrothed.

CHAPTER III.

WHILE, full of themselves, Harold and Edith wandered, hand in hand, through the neighbouring glades; while into that breast which had forestalled, at least, in this pure and sublime union, the wife's privilege to soothe and console, the troubled man poured out the tale of the sole trial from which he had passed with defeat and shame, — Haco drew near to Thyra, and sat down by her side. Each was strangely attracted towards the other; there was something congenial in the gloom which they shared in common, — though in the girl the sadness was soft and resigned, in the youth it was stern and solemn. They conversed in whispers, and their talk was strange for companions so young; for, whether suggested by Edith's song, or the neighbourhood of the Saxon grave-stone, which gleamed on their eyes, gray and wan through the crommell, the theme they selected was of death. As if fascinated, as children often are, by the terrors of the Dark King, they dwelt on those images with which the northern fancy has associated the eternal rest, — on the shroud and the worm, and the mouldering bones, on the gibbering ghost, and the sorcerer's spell that could call the spectre from the grave. They talked of the pain of the parting soul, parting while earth was yet fair, youth fresh, and joy not yet ripened from the blossom; of the wistful lingering look which glazing eyes would give to the latest sunlight it should behold on earth; and then pictured the shivering and naked soul, forced from the reluctant clay, wandering through cheerless space to the intermediate tortures, which the Church taught that none were so pure as not for a while to undergo, and hearing, as it wandered, the knell of the muffled bells and the burst of unavailing prayer. At length Haco paused abruptly and said,—

"But thou, cousin, hast before thee love and sweet life, and these discourses are not for thee."

Thyra shook her head mournfully,—

"Not so, Haco; for when Hilda consulted the runes, while, last night, she mingled the herbs for my pain, which rests ever hot and sharp here," and the girl laid her hand on her breast, "I saw that her face grew dark and overcast; and I felt, as I looked, that my doom was set. And when thou didst come so noiselessly to my side, with thy sad, cold eyes, O Haco, methought I saw the Messenger of Death. But thou art strong, Haco, and life will be long for thee; let us talk of life."

Haco stooped down and pressed his lips upon the girl's pale forehead.

"Kiss me too, Thyra."

The child kissed him, and they sat silent and close by each other, while the sun set.

And as the stars rose, Harold and Edith joined them. Harold's face was serene in the starlight, for the pure soul of his betrothed had breathed peace into his own; and, in his willing superstition, he felt as if, now restored to his guardian angel, the dead men's bones had released their unhallowed hold.

But suddenly Edith's hand trembled in his, and her form shuddered. Her eyes were fixed upon those of Haco.

"Forgive me, young kinsman, that I forget thee so long," said the earl. "This is my brother's son, Edith; thou hast not, that I remember, seen him before?"

"Yes, yes;" said Edith, falteringly.

"When, and where?"

Edith's soul answered the question, "*In a dream;*" but her lips were silent.

And Haco, rising, took her by the hand, while the earl turned to his sister,—that sister whom he was pledged to send to the Norman court; and Thyra said plaintively,—

"Take me in thine arms, Harold, and wrap thy mantle round me, for the air is cold."

The earl lifted the child to his breast, and gazed on her cheek long and wistfully; then questioning her tenderly, he took her within the house; and Edith followed with Haco.

"Is Hilda within?" asked the son of Sweyn.

"Nay, she hath been in the forest since noon," answered Edith with an effort, for she could not recover her awe of his presence.

"Then," said Haco, halting at the threshold, "I will go across the woodland to your house, Harold, and prepare your ceorls for your coming."

"I shall tarry here till Hilda returns," answered Harold, "and it may be late in the night ere I reach home; but Sexwolf already hath my orders. At sunrise we return to London, and thence we march on the insurgents."

"All shall be ready. Farewell, noble Edith; and thou, Thyra my cousin, one kiss more to our meeting again."

The child fondly held out her arms to him, and as she kissed his cheek whispered,—

"In the grave, Haco!"

The young man drew his mantle around him, and moved away. But he did not mount his steed, which still grazed by the road, while Harold's, more familiar with the place, had found its way to the stall; nor did he take his path through the glades to the house of his kinsman. Entering the Druid temple, he stood musing by the Teuton tomb.

The night grew deeper and deeper, the stars more luminous, and the air more hushed, when a voice close at his side said, clear and abrupt,—

"What does Youth the restless by Death the still?"

It was the peculiarity of Haco that nothing ever seemed to startle or surprise him. In that brooding boyhood, the solemn, quiet, and sad experience, all fore-armed, of age, had something in it terrible and preternatural; so without lifting his eyes from the stone, he answered, —

"How sayest thou, O Hilda, that the dead are still?"

Hilda placed her hand on his shoulder, and stooped to look into his face.

"Thy rebuke is just, son of Sweyn. In Time and in the Universe there is no stillness! Through all eternity the state impossible to the soul is repose! — So again thou art in thy native land?"

"And for what end, Prophetess? I remember, when but an infant, who till then had enjoyed the common air and the daily sun, thou didst rob me evermore of childhood and youth. For thou didst say to my father, that 'dark was the woof of my fate, and that its most glorious hour should be its last!'"

"But thou wert surely too childlike (I see thee now as thou wert then, stretched on the grass, and playing with thy father's falcon!) — too childlike to heed my words."

"Does the new ground reject the germs of the sower, or the young heart the first lessons of wonder and awe? Since then, Prophetess, Night hath been my comrade and Death my familiar. Rememberest thou again the hour when stealing, a boy, from Harold's house in his absence — the night ere I left my land — I stood on this mound by thy side? Then did I tell thee that the sole soft thought that relieved the bitterness of my soul, when all the rest of my kinsfolk seemed to behold in me but the heir of Sweyn, the outlaw and homicide, was the love that I bore to Harold; but that that love itself was mournful and bodeful as the hwata [1] of distant sorrow. And thou didst take me, O Prophetess, to thy bosom, and thy cold kiss touched my lips and my brow; and there, beside this altar and grave-mound, by leaf and by water, by staff and by song, thou didst bid me take comfort; for that as the mouse gnawed the toils of the lion, so the exile obscure

---

[1] Omen.

should deliver from peril the pride and the prince of my House,—that from that hour with the skein of his fate should mine be entwined; and his fate was that of kings and of kingdoms. And then, when the joy flushed my cheek, and methought youth came back in warmth to the night of my soul,—then, Hilda, I asked thee if my life would be spared till I had redeemed the name of my father. Thy seid-staff passed over the leaves that, burning with fire-sparks, symbolled the life of the man, and from the third leaf the flame leaped up and died; and again a voice from thy breast, hollow, as if borne from a hill-top afar, made answer, 'At thine entrance to manhood life bursts into blaze, and shrivels up into ashes.' So I knew that the doom of the infant still weighed unannealed on the years of the man; and I come here to my native land as to glory and the grave. But," said the young man, with a wild enthusiasm, "still with mine links the fate which is loftiest in England; and the rill and the river shall rush in one to the Terrible Sea."

"I know not that," answered Hilda, pale, as if in awe of herself: "for never yet hath the rune or the fount or the tomb revealed to me clear and distinct the close of the great course of Harold; only know I through his own stars his glory and greatness; and where glory is dim, and greatness is menaced, I know it but from the stars of others, the rays of whose influence blend with his own. So long, at least, as the fair and the pure one keeps watch in the still House of Life, the dark and the troubled one cannot wholly prevail. For Edith is given to Harold as the Fylgia, that noiselessly blesses and saves; and thou — " Hilda checked herself, and lowered her hood over her face, so that it suddenly became invisible.

"And I?" asked Haco, moving near to her side.

"Away, son of Sweyn; thy feet trample the grave of the mighty dead!"

Then Hilda lingered no longer, but took her way towards the house. Haco's eye followed her in silence. The cattle, grazing in the great space of the crumbling peristyle, looked up as she passed; the watch-dogs, wandering through the star-lit columns, came snorting round their mistress. And when she had vanished within the house, Haco turned to his steed.

"What matters," he murmured, "the answer which the Vala cannot or dare not give? To me is not destined the love of woman, nor the ambition of life. All I know of human affection binds me to Harold; all I know of human ambition is to share in his fate. This love is strong as hate, and terrible as doom,—it is jealous, it admits no rival. As the shell and the seaweed interlaced together, we are dashed on the rushing surge; whither? oh, whither?"

CHAPTER IV.

"I TELL thee, Hilda," said the earl, impatiently,—"I tell thee that I renounce henceforth all faith save in Him whose ways are concealed from our eyes. Thy seid and thy galdra have not guarded me against peril, nor armed me against sin. Nay, perchance — but peace; I will no more tempt the dark art, I will no more seek to disentangle the awful truth from the juggling lie. All so foretold me I will seek to forget, —hope from no prophecy, fear from no warning. Let the soul go to the future under the shadow of God!"

"Pass on thy way as thou wilt, its goal is the same, whether seen or unmarked. Peradventure thou art wise," said the Vala, gloomily.

"For my country's sake — Heaven be my witness! — not my own," resumed the earl, "I have blotted my conscience and sullied my truth. My country alone can redeem me, by taking my life as a thing hallowed evermore to her service. Selfish ambition do I lay aside, selfish power shall tempt me no more; lost is the charm that I beheld in a throne, and, save for Edith —"

"No! not even for Edith," cried the betrothed, advancing,
— "not even for Edith shalt thou listen to other voice than
that of thy country and thy soul."

The earl turned round abruptly, and his eyes were moist.

"O Hilda," he cried, "see henceforth my only Vala; let
that noble heart alone interpret to us the oracles of the
future."

The next day Harold returned with Haco and a numerous
train of his house-carles to the city.   Their ride was as silent
as that of the day before; but on reaching Southwark, Harold
turned away from the bridge towards the left, gained the
river-side, and dismounted at the house of one of his lithsmen (a franklin, or freed ceorl).   Leaving there his horse,
he summoned a boat, and, with Haco, was rowed over towards
the fortified palace which then rose towards the west of London, jutting into the Thames, and which seems to have formed
the outwork of the old Roman city.   The palace, of remotest
antiquity, and blending all work and architecture, Roman,
Saxon, and Danish, had been repaired by Canute; and from
a high window in the upper story, where were the royal
apartments, the body of the traitor Edric Streone (the founder
of the House of Godwin) had been thrown into the river.

"Whither go we, Harold?" asked the son of Sweyn.

"We go to visit the young Atheling, the natural heir to the
Saxon throne," replied Harold, in a firm voice.   "He lodges
in the old palace of our kings."

"They say in Normandy that the boy is imbecile."

"That is not true," returned Harold.   "I will present thee
to him, — judge."

Haco mused a moment and said, —

"Methinks I divine thy purpose; is it not formed on the
sudden, Harold?"

"It was the counsel of Edith," answered Harold, with evident emotion.   "And yet, if that counsel prevail, I may lose
the power to soften the Church and to call her mine."

"So thou wouldest sacrifice even Edith for thy country?"

"Since I have sinned, methinks I could," said the proud
man, humbly.

The boat shot into a little creek, or rather canal, which then ran inland, beside the black and rotting walls of the fort.   The two Earl-born leaped ashore, passed under a Roman arch, entered a court, the interior of which was rudely filled up by early Saxon habitations of rough timber work, already, since the time of Canute, falling into decay (as all things did which came under the care of Edward), and mounting a stair that ran along the outside of the house, gained a low narrow door, which stood open.   In the passage within were one or two of the king's house-carles who had been assigned to the young Atheling, with liveries of blue, and Danish axes, and some four or five German servitors, who had attended his father from the emperor's court.   One of these last ushered the noble Saxons into a low, forlorn ante-hall; and there, to Harold's surprise, he found Alred the Archbishop of York, and three thegns of high rank, and of lineage ancient and purely Saxon.

Alred approached Harold with a faint smile on his benign face.

"Methinks, and may I think aright! — thou comest hither with the same purpose as myself, and yon noble thegns."

"And that purpose?"

"Is to see and to judge calmly if, despite his years, we may find in the descendant of the Ironsides such a prince as we may commend to our decaying king as his heir, and to the Witan as a chief fit to defend the land."

"Thou speakest the cause of my own coming.   With your ears will I hear, with your eyes will I see; as ye judge, will judge I," said Harold, drawing the prelate towards the thegns, so that they might hear his answer.

The chiefs, who belonged to a party that had often opposed Godwin's House, had exchanged looks of fear and trouble when Harold entered; but at his words their frank faces showed equal surprise and pleasure.

Harold presented to them his nephew, with whose grave dignity of bearing beyond his years they were favourably impressed, though the good bishop sighed when he saw in his face the sombre beauty of the guilty sire.   The group then conversed anxiously on the declining health of the king, the disturbed state of the realm, and the expediency, if possible, of uniting all suffrages in favour of the fittest successor. And in Harold's voice and manner, as in Harold's heart, there was nought that seemed conscious of his own mighty stake and just hopes in that election. But as time wore, the faces of the thegns grew overcast; proud men and great satraps [1] were they, and they liked it ill that the boy-prince kept them so long in the dismal anteroom.

At length the German officer, who had gone to announce their coming, returned; and in words, intelligible indeed from the affinity between Saxon and German, but still disagreeably foreign to English ears, requested them to follow him into the presence of the Atheling.

In a room yet retaining the rude splendour with which it had been invested by Canute, a handsome boy, about the age of thirteen or fourteen, but seeming much younger, was engaged in the construction of a stuffed bird, a lure for a young hawk that stood blindfold on its perch. The employment made so habitual a part of the serious education of youth, that the thegns smoothed their brows at the sight, and deemed the boy worthily occupied. At another end of the room, a grave Norman priest was seated at a table on which were books and writing-implements; he was the tutor commissioned by Edward to teach Norman tongue and saintly lore to the Atheling. A profusion of toys strewed the floor, and some children of Edgar's own age were playing with them. His little sister Margaret [2] was seated seriously, apart from all the other children, and employed in needlework.

When Alred approached the Atheling, with a blending of reverent obeisance and paternal cordiality, the boy carelessly cried, in a barbarous jargon, half German, half Norman-French,—

[1] The Eastern word Satraps (*Satrapes*) made one of the ordinary and most inappropriate titles (borrowed, no doubt, from the Byzantine Court), by which the Saxons, in their Latinity, honoured their simple nobles.

[2] Afterwards married to Malcolm of Scotland, through whom, by the female line, the present royal dynasty of England assumes descent from the Anglo-Saxon kings.

"There, come not too near, you scare my hawk. What are you doing? You trample my toys, which the good Norman bishop William sent me as a gift from the duke. Art thou blind, man?"

"My son," said the prelate, kindly, "these are the things of childhood; childhood ends sooner with princes than with common men. Leave thy lure and thy toys, and welcome these noble thegns, and address them, so please you, in our own Saxon tongue."

"Saxon tongue! — language of villeins! not I. Little do I know of it, save to scold a ceorl or a nurse. King Edward did not tell me to learn Saxon, but Norman! and Godfroi yonder says that if I know Norman well, Duke William will make me his knight. But I don't desire to learn anything more to-day." And the child turned peevishly from thegn and prelate.

The three Saxon lords interchanged looks of profound displeasure and proud disgust. But Harold, with an effort over himself, approached, and said winningly, —

"Edgar the Atheling, thou art not so young but thou knowest already that the great live for others. Wilt thou not be proud to live for this fair country and these noble men, and to speak the language of Alfred the Great?"

"Alfred the Great! they always weary me with Alfred the Great," said the boy, pouting. "Alfred the Great, — he is the plague of my life! If I am Atheling, men are to live for me, not I for them; and if you tease me any more, I will run away to Duke William in Rouen; Godfroi says I shall never be teased there!"

So saying, already tired of hawk and lure, the child threw himself on the floor with the other children, and snatched the toys from their hands.

The serious Margaret then rose quietly, and went to her brother, and said, in good Saxon, —

"Fie! if you behave thus, I shall call you NIDDERING!"

At the threat of that word, the vilest in the language, — that word which the lowest ceorl would forfeit life rather than endure, — a threat applied to the Atheling of England,

the descendant of Saxon heroes,— the three thegns drew close
and watched the boy, hoping to see that he would start to his
feet with wrath and in shame.

"Call me what you will, silly sister," said the child, indifferently; "I am not so Saxon as to care for your ceorlish
Saxon names."

"Enow," cried the proudest and greatest of the thegns, his
very mustache curling with ire. "He who can be called niddering shall never be crowned king!"

"I don't want to be crowned king, rude man, with your
laidly mustache: I want to be made knight, and have a banderol and baldric. Go away!"

"We go, son," said Alred, mournfully.

And with slow and tottering step he moved to the door,
there he halted, turned back,— and the child was pointing at
him in mimicry, while Godfroi, the Norman tutor, smiled
as in pleasure. The prelate shook his head, and the group
gained again the ante-hall.

"Fit leader of bearded men! fit king for the Saxon land!"
cried a thegn. "No more of your Atheling, Alred my
father!"

"No more of him, indeed!" said the prelate, mournfully.

"It is but the fault of his nurture and rearing,— a neglected
childhood, a Norman tutor, German hirelings. We may re-
mould yet the pliant clay," said Harold.

"Nay," returned Alred, "no leisure for such hopes, no time
to undo what is done by circumstance, and, I fear, by nature.
Ere the year is out the throne will stand empty in our halls."

"Who then," said Haco, abruptly, "who then (pardon the
ignorance of youth wasted in captivity abroad!) — who then,
failing the Atheling, will save this realm from the Norman
Duke, who, I know well, counts on it as the reaper on the
harvest ripening to his sickle?"

"Alas, who then?" murmured Alred.

"Who then?" cried the three thegns, with one voice; "why,
the worthiest, the wisest, the bravest! Stand forth, Harold
the Earl, Thou art the man!" And without awaiting his answer, they strode from the hall.

CHAPTER V.

AROUND Northampton lay the forces of Morcar, the choice of the Anglo-Dane men of Northumbria. Suddenly there was a shout as to arms from the encampment; and Morcar, the young earl, clad in his link mail save his helmet, came forth, and cried,—

"My men are fools to look that way for a foe; yonder lies Mercia, behind it the hills of Wales. The troops that come hitherward are those which Edwin my brother brings to our aid."

Morcar's words were carried into the host by his captains and war-bodes, and the shout changed from alarm into joy. As the cloud of dust through which gleamed the spears of the coming force rolled away, and lay lagging behind the march of the host, there rode forth from the van two riders. Fast and far from the rest they rode, and behind them, fast as they could, spurred two others, who bore on high, one the pennon of Mercia, one the red lion of North Wales. Right to the embankment and palisade which begirt Morcar's camp rode the riders; and the head of the foremost was bare, and the guards knew the face of Edwin the Comely, Morcar's brother. Morcar stepped down from the mound on which he stood, and the brothers embraced amidst the halloos of the forces.

"And welcome, I pray thee," said Morcar, "our kinsman Caradoc, son of Gryffyth [1] the bold."

So Morcar reached his hand to Caradoc, stepson to his sister Aldyth, and kissed him on the brow, as was the wont of our fathers. The young and crownless prince was scarce out of boyhood, but already his name was sung by the bards, and circled in the halls of Gwynedd with the Hirlas horn; for he had harried the Saxon borders, and given to fire and sword even the fortress of Harold himself.

---

[1] By his first wife; Aldyth was his second.

But while these three interchanged salutations, and ere yet
the mixed Mercians and Welch had gained the encampment,
from a curve in the opposite road, towards Towcester and
Dunstable, broke the flash of mail like a river of light;
trumpets and fifes were heard in the distance; and all in
Morcar's host stood hushed but stern, gazing anxious and
afar, as the coming armament swept on. And from the
midst were seen the Martlets and Cross of England's king,
and the Tiger heads of Harold,— banners which, seen together, had planted victory on every tower, on every field,
towards which they had rushed on the winds.

Retiring, then, to the central mound, the chiefs of the insurgent force held their brief council.

The two young earls, whatever their ancestral renown,
being yet new themselves to fame and to power, were submissive to the Anglo-Dane chiefs, by whom Morcar had been
elected. And these, on recognizing the standard of Harold,
were unanimous in advice to send a peaceful deputation, setting forth their wrongs under Tostig, and the justice of their
cause. "For the earl," said Gamel Beorn (the head and
front of that revolution), "is a just man, and one who would
shed his own blood rather than that of any other free-born
dweller in England; and he will do us right."

"What, against his own brother?" cried Edwin.

"Against his own brother, if we convince but his reason,"
returned the Anglo-Dane.

And the other chiefs nodded assent. Caradoc's fierce eyes
flashed fire; but he played with his torque, and spoke not.

Meanwhile, the vanguard of the king's force had defiled
under the very walls of Northampton, between the town and
the insurgents; and some of the light-armed scouts who went
forth from Morcar's camp to gaze on the procession, with
that singular fearlessness which characterized, at that period,
the rival parties in civil war, returned to say that they had
seen Harold himself in the foremost line, and that he was not
in mail.

This circumstance the insurgent thegns received as a good
omen; and having already agreed on the deputation, about a

score of the principal thegns of the North went sedately towards the hostile lines.

By the side of Harold — armed in mail, with his face concealed by the strange Sicilian nose-piece used then by most of the Northern nations — had ridden Tostig, who had joined the earl on his march, with a scanty band of some fifty or sixty of his Danish house-carles. All the men throughout broad England that he could command or bribe to his cause, were those fifty or sixty hireling Danes. And it seemed that already there was dispute between the brothers, for Harold's face was flushed, and his voice stern, as he said, "Rate me as thou wilt, brother, but I cannot advance at once to the destruction of my fellow Englishmen without summons and attempt at treaty,— as has ever been the custom of our ancient heroes and our own House."

"By all the fiends of the North!" exclaimed Tostig, "it is foul shame to talk of treaty and summons to robbers and rebels. For what art thou here but for chastisement and revenge?"

"For justice and right, Tostig."

"Ha! thou comest not, then, to aid thy brother?"

"Yes, if justice and right are, as I trust, with him."

Before Tostig could reply, a line was suddenly cleared through the armed men; and with bare heads, and a monk lifting the rood on high, amidst the procession advanced the Northumbrian Danes.

"By the red sword of Saint Olave!" cried Tostig, "yonder come the traitors, Gamel Beorn and Gloneion! You will not hear them? If so, I will not stay to listen. I have but my axe for my answer to such knaves."

"Brother, brother, those men are the most valiant and famous chiefs in thine earldom. Go, Tostig, thou art not now in the mood to hear reason. Retire into the city; summon its gates to open to the king's flag. I will hear the men."

"Beware how thou judge, save in thy brother's favour!" growled the fierce warrior; and, tossing his arm on high with a contemptuous gesture, he spurred away towards the gates.

Then Harold, dismounting, stood on the ground, under the standard of his king, and round him came several of the Saxon chiefs, who had kept aloof during the conference with Tostig.

The Northumbrians approached, and saluted the earl with grave courtesy.

Then Gamel Beorn began. But much as Harold had feared and foreboded as to the causes of complaint which Tostig had given to the Northumbrians, all fear, all foreboding, fell short of the horrors now deliberately unfolded; not only extortion of tribute the most rapacious and illegal, but murder the fiercest and most foul. Thegns of high birth, without offence or suspicion, but who had either excited Tostig's jealousy, or resisted his exactions, had been snared under peaceful pretexts into his castle,[1] and butchered in cold blood by his house-carles. The cruelties of the old heathen Danes seemed revived in the bloody and barbarous tale.

"And now," said the thegn, in conclusion, "canst thou condemn us that we rose? — no partial rising, — rose all Northumbria! At first but two hundred thegns, strong in our course, we swelled into the might of a people. Our wrongs found sympathy beyond our province, for liberty spreads over human hearts as fire over a heath. Wherever we march, friends gather round us. Thou warrest not on a handful of rebels, — half England is with us!"

"And ye, thegns," answered Harold, "ye have ceased to war against Tostig your earl. Ye war now against the King and the Law. Come with your complaints to your Prince and your Witan, and, if they are just, ye are stronger than in yonder palisades and streets of steel."

"And so," said Gamel Beorn, with marked emphasis, "now *thou* art in England, O noble Earl, — so are we willing to come. But when thou wert absent from the land, justice seemed to abandon it to force and the battle-axe."

"I would thank you for your trust," answered Harold, deeply moved. "But justice in England rests not on the presence and life of a single man. And your speech I must

[1] Flor., Wig.

not accept as a grace, for it wrongs both my King and his Council. These charges ye have made, but ye have not proved them.
Armed men are not proofs; and granting that hot blood and
mortal infirmity of judgment have caused Tostig to err against
you and the right, think still of his qualities to reign over
men whose lands and whose rivers lie ever exposed to the
dread Northern sea-kings. Where will ye find a chief with
arm as strong, and heart as dauntless? By his mother's side
he is allied to your own lineage. And for the rest, if ye receive him back to his earldom, not only do I, Harold in whom
you profess to trust, pledge full oblivion of the past, but I will
undertake, in his name, that he shall rule you well for the
future, according to the laws of King Canute."

"That will we not hear," cried the thegns, with one voice;
while the tones of Gamel Beorn, rough with the rattling
Danish burr, rose above all, "for we were born free. A proud
and bad chief is by us not to be endured; we have learned
from our ancestors to live free or die!"

A murmur, not of condemnation, at these words, was heard
amongst the Saxon chiefs round Harold; and beloved and revered as he was, he felt that, had he the heart, he had scarce
the power, to have coerced those warriors to march at once on
their countrymen in such a cause. But foreseeing great evil
in the surrender of his brother's interests, whether by lowering the king's dignity to the demands of armed force, or
sending abroad in all his fierce passions a man so highly
connected with Norman and Dane, so vindictive and so grasping, as Tostig, the earl shunned further parley at that time
and place. He appointed a meeting in the town with the
chiefs; and requested them, meanwhile, to reconsider their demands, and at least shape them so that they could be transmitted to the king, who was then on his way to Oxford.

It is in vain to describe the rage of Tostig, when his brother
gravely repeated to him the accusations against him, and asked
for his justification. Justification he could give not. His
idea of law was but force, and by force alone he demanded
now to be defended. Harold, then, wishing not alone to be
judge in his brother's cause, referred further discussion to

the chiefs of the various towns and shires, whose troops had swelled the War-Fyrd; and to them he bade Tostig plead his cause.

Vain as a woman, while fierce as a tiger, Tostig assented, and in that assembly he rose, his gonna all blazing with crimson and gold, his hair all curled and perfumed as for a banquet; and such, in a half-barbarous day, the effect of person, especially when backed by warlike renown, that the Proceres were half disposed to forget, in admiration of the earl's surpassing beauty of form, the dark tales of his hideous guilt. But his passions hurrying him away ere he had gained the middle of his discourse, so did his own relation condemn himself, so clear became his own tyrannous misdeeds, that the Englishmen murmured aloud their disgust, and their impatience would not suffer him to close.

"Enough," cried Vebba, the blunt thegn from Saxon Kent; "it is plain that neither king nor Witan can replace thee in thine earldom. Tell us not further of these atrocities; or by 'r Lady, if the Northumbrians had chased thee not, we would."

"Take treasure and ship, and go to Baldwin in Flanders," said Thorold, a great Anglo-Dane from Lincolnshire, "for even Harold's name can scarce save thee from outlawry."

Tostig glared round on the assembly, and met but one common expression in the face of all.

"These are thy henchmen, Harold!" he said through his gnashing teeth; and, without vouchsafing further word, strode from the council-hall.

That evening he left the town and hurried to tell to Edward the tale that had so miscarried with the chiefs. The next day, the Northumbrian delegates were heard; and they made the customary proposition in those cases of civil differences, to refer all matters to the king and the Witan, each party remaining under arms meanwhile.

This was finally acceded to. Harold repaired to Oxford, where the king (persuaded to the journey by Alred, foreseeing what would come to pass) had just arrived.

CHAPTER VI.

THE Witan was summoned in haste. Thither came the young earls Morcar and Edwin; but Caradoc, chafing at the thought of peace, retired into Wales with his wild band.

Now, all the great chiefs, spiritual and temporal, assembled in Oxford for the decree of that Witan on which depended the peace of England. The imminence of the time made the concourse of members entitled to vote in the assembly even larger than that which had met for the inlawry of Godwin. There was but one thought uppermost in the minds of men, to which the adjustment of an earldom, however mighty, was comparatively insignificant, — namely, the succession of the kingdom. That thought turned instinctively and irresistibly to Harold.

The evident and rapid decay of the king; the utter failure of all male heir in the House of Cerdic, save only the boy Edgar, — whose character (which throughout life remained puerile and frivolous) made the minority which excluded him from the throne seem cause rather for rejoicing than grief, and whose rights, even by birth, were not acknowledged by the general tenor of the Saxon laws, which did not recognize as heir to the crown the son of a father who had not himself been crowned;[1] — forebodings of coming evil and danger, originating in Edward's perturbed visions; revivals of obscure and till then forgotten prophecies, ancient as the days of Merlin; rumours, industriously fomented into certainty by Haco, whose whole soul seemed devoted to Harold's cause, of

[1] This truth has been overlooked by writers, who have maintained the Atheling's right as if incontestable. " An opinion prevailed," says Palgrave ("English Commonwealth," pp. 559, 560), "that if the Atheling was born before his father and mother were ordained to the royal dignity, the crown did not descend to the child of uncrowned ancestors." Our great legal historian quotes Eadmer, " De Vit. Sanct. Dunstan," p. 220, for the objection made to the succession of Edward the Martyr, on this score.

the intended claim of the Norman Count to the throne,— all concurred to make the election of a man matured in camp and council doubly necessary to the safety of the realm.

Warm favourers, naturally, of Harold were the genuine Saxon population, and a large part of the Anglo-Danish,— all the thegns in his vast earldom of Wessex, reaching to the southern and western coasts, from Sandwich and the mouth of the Thames to the Land's End in Cornwall; and including the free men of Kent, whose inhabitants even from the days of Cæsar had been considered in advance of the rest of the British population, and from the days of Hengist had exercised an influence that nothing save the warlike might of the Anglo-Danes counterbalanced. With Harold, too, were many of the thegns from his earlier earldom of East Anglia, comprising the county of Essex, great part of Hertfordshire, and so, reaching into Cambridge, Huntingdon, Norfolk, and Ely. With him were all the wealth, intelligence, and power of London, and most of the trading towns; with him all the veterans of the armies he had led; with him too, generally throughout the empire, was the force, less distinctly demarked, of public and national feeling.

Even the priests, save those immediately about the court, forgot, in the exigency of the time, their ancient and deep-rooted dislike to Godwin's House; they remembered, at least, that Harold had never, in foray or feud, plundered a single convent, or in peace, and through plot, appropriated to himself a single hyde of Church land; and that was more than could have been said of any other earl of the age,— even of Leofric the Holy. They caught — as a Church must do, when so intimately, even in its illiterate errors, allied with the people as the old Saxon Church was — the popular enthusiasm. Abbot combined with thegn in zeal for Earl Harold.

The only party that stood aloof was the one that espoused the claims of the young sons of Algar. But this party was indeed most formidable; it united all the old friends of the virtuous Leofric, of the famous Siward; it had a numerous party even in East Anglia (in which earldom Algar had succeeded Harold); it comprised nearly all the thegns in Mercia (the heart of the country) and the population of Northumbria; and it involved in its wide range the terrible Welch on the one hand, and the Scottish domain of the sub-king Malcolm, himself a Cumbrian, on the other, despite Malcolm's personal predilections for Tostig, to whom he was strongly attached. But then the chiefs of this party, while at present they stood aloof, were all, with the exception perhaps of the young earls themselves, disposed, on the slightest encouragement, to blend their suffrage with the friends of Harold; and his praise was as loud on their lips as on those of the Saxons from Kent, or the burghers from London. All factions, in short, were willing, in this momentous crisis, to lay aside old dissensions; it depended upon the conciliation of the Northumbrians, upon a fusion between the friends of Harold and the supporters of the young sons of Algar, to form such a concurrence of interests as must inevitably bear Harold to the throne of the empire.

Meanwhile, the earl himself wisely and patriotically deemed it right to remain neuter in the approaching decision between Tostig and the young earls. He could not be so unjust and so mad as to urge to the utmost (and risk in the urging) his party influence on the side of oppression and injustice, solely for the sake of his brother; nor, on the other, was it decorous or natural to take part himself against Tostig; nor could he, as a statesman, contemplate without anxiety and alarm the transfer of so large a portion of the realm to the vice-kingship of the sons of his old foe, — rivals to his power, at the very time when, even for the sake of England alone, that power should be the most solid and compact.

But the final greatness of a fortunate man is rarely made by any violent effort of his own. He has sown the seeds in the time foregone, and the ripe time brings up the harvest. His fate seems taken out of his own control: greatness seems thrust upon him. He has made himself, as it were, a *want* to the nation, a thing necessary to it; he has identified himself with his age, and in the wreath or the crown on his brow, the age itself seems to put forth its flower.

Tostig, lodging apart from Harold in a fort near the gate of

Oxford, took slight pains to conciliate foes or make friends,—
trusting rather to his representations to Edward (who was
wroth with the rebellious House of Algar) of the danger of
compromising the royal dignity by concessions to armed
insurgents.

It was but three days before that for which the Witan was
summoned; most of its members had already assembled in
the city; and Harold, from the window of the monastery in
which he lodged, was gazing thoughtfully into the streets below, where, with the gay dresses of the thegns and cnehts,
blended the grave robes of ecclesiastic and youthful scholar,
— for to that illustrious University (pillaged and persecuted
by the sons of Canute), Edward had, to his honour, restored
the schools,— when Haco entered, and announced to him that
a numerous body of thegns and prelates, headed by Alred,
Archbishop of York, craved an audience.

"Knowest thou the cause, Haco?"

The youth's cheek was yet more pale than usual, as he
answered slowly,—

"Hilda's prophecies are ripening into truths."

The earl started, and his old ambition reviving, flushed on
his brow, and sparkled from his eye; he checked the joyous
emotion, and bade Haco briefly admit the visitors.

They came in, two by two,— a body so numerous that they
filled the ample chamber; and Harold, as he greeted each,
beheld the most powerful lords of the land, the highest dignitaries of the Church, and, oft and frequent, came old foe
by the side of trusty friend. They all paused at the foot of
the narrow daïs on which Harold stood, and Alred repelled
by a gesture his invitation to the foremost to mount the
platform.

Then Alred began a harangue, simple and earnest. He
described briefly the condition of the country; touched with
grief and with feeling on the health of the king, and the
failure of Cerdic's line. He stated honestly his own strong
wish, if possible, to have concentrated the popular suffrages
on the young Atheling; and under the emergence of the case,
to have waived the objection to his immature years. But as

distinctly and emphatically he stated, that that hope and intent he had now formally abandoned, and that there was but one sentiment on the subject with all the chiefs and dignitaries of the realm.

"Wherefore," continued he, "after anxious consultations with each other, those whom you see around have come to you: yea, to you, Earl Harold, we offer our hands and hearts to do our best to prepare for you the throne on the demise of Edward, and to seat you thereon as firmly as ever sat King of England and son of Cerdic,— knowing that in you, and in you alone, we find the man who reigns already in the English heart; to whose strong arm we can trust the defence of our land; to whose just thoughts, our laws. As I speak, so think we all!"

With downcast eyes, Harold heard; and but by a slight heaving of his breast under his crimson robe could his emotion be seen. But as soon as the approving murmur, that succeeded the prelate's speech, had closed, he lifted his head, and answered,—

"Holy father, and you, Right Worthy my fellow-thegns, if ye could read my heart at this moment, believe that you would not find there the vain joy of aspiring man, when the greatest of earthly prizes is placed within his reach. There you would see, with deep and wordless gratitude for your trust and your love, grave and solemn solicitude, earnest desire to divest my decision of all mean thought of self, and judge only whether indeed, as king or as subject, I can best guard the weal of England. Pardon me, then, if I answer you not as ambition alone would answer; neither deem me insensible to the glorious lot of presiding, under heaven, and by the light of our laws, over the destinies of the English realm,— if I pause to weigh well the responsibilities incurred, and the obstacles to be surmounted. There is that on my mind that I would fain unbosom, not of a nature to discuss in an assembly so numerous, but which I would rather submit to a chosen few whom you yourselves may select to hear me, in whose cool wisdom, apart from personal love to me, ye may best confide,— your most veteran thegns, your most

honoured prelates: To them will I speak, to them make clean
my bosom; and to their answer, their counsels, will I in all
things defer,— whether with loyal heart to serve another,
whom, hearing me, they may decide to choose; or to fit my
soul to bear, not unworthily, the weight of a kingly crown."

Alred lifted his mild eyes to Harold, and there were both
pity and approval in his gaze, for he divined the earl.

"Thou hast chosen the right course, my son; and we will
retire at once, and elect those with whom thou mayst freely
confer, and by whose judgment thou mayst righteously abide."

The prelate turned, and with him went the conclave.

Left alone with Haco, the last said abruptly,—

"Thou wilt not be so indiscreet, O Harold, as to confess
thy compelled oath to the fraudful Norman?"

"That is my design," replied Harold, coldly.

The son of Sweyn began to remonstrate, but the earl cut
him short.

"If the Norman say that he has been deceived in Harold,
never so shall say the men of England. Leave me. I know
not why, Haco, but in thy presence, at times, there is a
glamour as strong as in the spells of Hilda. Go, dear boy;
the fault is not in thee, but in the superstitious infirmities of
a man who hath once lowered, or, it may be, too highly
strained, his reason to the things of a haggard fancy. Go!
and send to me my brother Gurth. I would have him alone
of my House present at this solemn crisis of its fate."

Haco bowed his head, and went.

In a few moments more, Gurth came in. To this pure and
spotless spirit Harold had already related the events of his
unhappy visit to the Norman; and he felt, as the young chief
pressed his hand, and looked on him with his clear and loving
eyes, as if Honour made palpable stood by his side.

Six of the ecclesiastics, most eminent for Church learning,— small as was that which they could boast, compared
with the scholars of Normandy and the Papal States, but at
least more intelligent and more free from mere formal monas-
ticism than most of their Saxon contemporaries,— and six of
the chiefs most renowned for experience in war or council,

selected under the sagacious promptings of Alred, accompanied that prelate to the presence of the earl.

"Close, thou! close! close! Gurth," whispered Harold; "for this is a confession against man's pride, and sorely doth it shame,— so that I would have thy bold sinless heart beating near to mine."

Then, leaning his arm upon his brother's shoulder, and in a voice, the first tones of which, as betraying earnest emotion, irresistibly chained and affected his noble audience, Harold began his tale.

Various were the emotions, though all more akin to terror than repugnance, with which the listeners heard the earl's plain and candid recital.

Among the lay-chiefs the impression made by the compelled oath was comparatively slight: for it was the worst vice of the Saxon laws, to entangle all charges, from the smallest to the greatest, in a reckless multiplicity of oaths,[1] to the grievous loosening of the bonds of truth; and oaths then had become almost as much mere matter of legal form, as certain oaths — bad relic of those times! — still existing in our parliamentary and collegiate proceedings, are deemed by men, not otherwise dishonourable, even now. And to no kind of oath was more latitude given than to such as related to fealty to a chief; for these, in the constant rebellions which happened year after year, were openly violated, and without reproach. Not a sub-king in Wales who harried the border, not an earl who raised banner against the Basileus of Britain, but infringed his oath to be good man and true to the lord paramount; and even William the Norman himself never found his oath of fealty stand in his way, whenever he deemed it right and expedient to take arms against his suzerain of France.

On the churchmen the impression was stronger and more serious: not that made by the oath itself, but by the relics on which the hand had been laid. They looked at each other,

---

[1] See the judicious remarks of Henry, " History of Britain," on this head. From the lavish abuse of oaths, perjury had come to be reckoned one of the national vices of the Saxon.

doubtful and appalled, when the earl ceased his tale; while only among the laymen circled a murmur of mingled wrath at William's bold design on their native land, and of scorn at the thought that an oath, surprised and compelled, should be made the instrument of treason to a whole people.

"Thus," said Harold, after a pause, "thus have I made clear to you my conscience, and revealed to you the only obstacle between your offers and my choice. From the keeping of an oath so extorted, and so deadly to England, this venerable prelate and mine own soul have freed me. Whether as king or as subject, I shall alike revere the living and their long posterity more than the dead men's bones, and, with sword and with battle-axe, hew out against the invader my best atonement for the lip's weakness and the heart's desertion. But whether, knowing what hath passed, ye may not deem it safer for the land to elect another king, — this it is which, free and fore-thoughtful of every chance, ye should now decide."

With these words he stepped from the daïs, and retired into the oratory that adjoined the chamber, followed by Gurth. The eyes of the priests then turned to Alred, and to them the prelate spoke as he had done before to Harold; he distinguished between the oath and its fulfilment, between the lesser sin and the greater, — the one which the Church could absolve, the one which no Church had the right to exact, and which, if fulfilled, no penance could expiate. He owned frankly, nevertheless, that it was the difficulties so created that had made him incline to the Atheling; but, convinced of that prince's incapacity, even in the most ordinary times, to rule England, he shrunk yet more from such a choice, when the swords of the Norman were already sharpening for contest. Finally he said, "If a man as fit to defend us as Harold can be found, let us prefer him; if not — "

"There is no other man!" cried the thegns with one voice. "And," said a wise old chief, "had Harold sought to play a trick to secure the throne, he could not have devised one more sure than the tale he hath now told us. What! just when we are most assured that the doughtiest and deadliest foe that

our land can brave waits but for Edward's death to enforce
on us a stranger's yoke — what! shall we for that very reason
deprive ourselves of the only man able to resist him? Harold
hath taken an oath! God wot, who among us have not taken
some oath at law for which they have deemed it meet afterwards to do a penance, or endow a convent? The wisest means
to strengthen Harold against that oath is to show the moral
impossibility of fulfilling it, by placing him on the throne.
The best proof we can give to this insolent Norman that England is not for prince to leave, or subject to barter, is to choose
solemnly in our Witan the very chief whom his frauds prove
to us that he fears the most. Why, William would laugh in
his own sleeve to summon a king to descend from his throne
to do him the homage which that king, in the different capacity of subject, had (we will grant, even willingly) promised
to render."

This speech spoke all the thoughts of the laymen, and,
with Alred's previous remarks, reassured all the ecclesiastics.
They were easily induced to believe that the usual Church
penances, and ample Church gifts, would suffice for the insult offered to the relics: and — if they in so grave a case out-
stripped, in absolution, an authority amply sufficing for all
ordinary matters — Harold, as king, might easily gain from
the Pope himself that full pardon and shrift, which as mere
earl, against the Prince of the Normans, he would fail of
obtaining.

These or similar reflections soon terminated the suspense
of the select council; and Alred sought the earl in the oratory, to summon him back to the conclave. The two brothers
were kneeling side by side before the little altar; and there
was something inexpressibly touching in their humble atti-
tudes, their clasped supplicating hands, in that moment when
the crown of England rested above their House.

The brothers rose, and at Alred's sign followed the prelate
into the council-room. Alred briefly communicated the result of the conference; and with an aspect, and in a tone,
free alike from triumph and indecision, Harold replied:—

"As ye will, so will I. Place me only where I can most

serve the common cause. Remain you now, knowing my secret, a chosen and standing council: too great is my personal
stake in this matter to allow my mind to be unbiassed; judge
ye, then, and decide for me in all things: your minds should
be calmer and wiser than mine; in all things I will abide
by your counsel; and thus I accept the trust of a nation's
freedom."

Each thegn then put his hand into Harold's, and called
himself Harold's man.

"Now, more than ever," said the wise old thegn who had
before spoken, "will it be needful to heal all dissension in
the kingdom,— to reconcile with us Mercia and Northumbria,
and make the kingdom one against the foe. You, as Tostig's
brother, have done well to abstain from active interference;
you do well to leave it to us to negotiate the necessary alliance between all brave and good men."

"And to that end, as imperative for the public weal, you
consent," said Alred, thoughtfully, "to abide by our advice,
whatever it be?"

"Whatever it be, so that it serve England," answered the
earl.

A smile, somewhat sad, flitted over the prelate's pale lips,
and Harold was once more alone with Gurth.

CHAPTER VII.

THE soul of all council and cabal on behalf of Harold,
which had led to the determination of the principal chiefs,
and which now succeeded it,— was Haco.

His rank as son of Sweyn, the first-born of Godwin's House,
— a rank which might have authorized some pretensions on his
own part, — gave him all field for the exercise of an intellect
singularly keen and profound. Accustomed to an atmosphere
of practical state-craft in the Norman court, with faculties

sharpened from boyhood by vigilance and meditation, he exercised an extraordinary influence over the simple understandings of the homely clergy and the uncultured thegns. Impressed with the conviction of his early doom, he felt no interest in the objects of others; but equally believing that whatever of bright and brave and glorious in his brief, condemned career was to be reflected on him from the light of Harold's destiny, the sole desire of a nature, which, under other auspices, would have been intensely daring and ambitious, was to administer to Harold's greatness. No prejudice, no principle, stood in the way of this dreary enthusiasm. As a father, himself on the brink of the grave, schemes for the worldly grandeur of the son, in whom he confounds and melts his own life, so this sombre and predestined man, dead to earth and to joy and the emotions of the heart, looked beyond his own tomb, to that existence in which he transferred and carried on his ambition.

If the leading agencies of Harold's memorable career might be, as it were, symbolized and allegorized by the living beings with which it was connected,— as Edith was the representative of stainless Truth, as Gurth was the type of dauntless Duty, as Hilda embodied aspiring Imagination,— so Haco seemed the personator of Worldly Wisdom. And cold in that worldly wisdom Haco laboured on, now conferring with Alred and the partisans of Harold; now closeted with Edwin and Morcar; now gliding from the chamber of the sick king. That wisdom foresaw all obstacles, smoothed all difficulties; ever calm, never resting; marshalling and harmonizing the things to be, like the ruthless hand of a tranquil fate. But there was one with whom Haco was more often than with all others,— one whom the presence of Harold had allured to that anxious scene of intrigue, and whose heart leaped high at the hopes whispered from the smileless lips of Haco.

CHAPTER VIII.

It was the second day after that which assured him the allegiance of the thegns that a message was brought to Harold from the Lady Aldyth. She was in Oxford, at a convent, with her young daughter by the Welch King; she prayed him to visit her. The earl, whose active mind, abstaining from the intrigues around him, was delivered up to the thoughts, restless and feverish, which haunt the repose of all active minds, was not unwilling to escape awhile from himself. He went to Aldyth. The royal widow had laid by the signs of mourning; she was dressed with the usual stately and loose-robed splendour of Saxon matrons, and all the proud beauty of her youth was restored to her cheek. At her feet was that daughter who afterwards married the Fleance so familiar to us in Shakspeare, and became the ancestral mother of those Scottish kings who had passed, in pale shadows, across the eyes of Macbeth;[1] by the side of that child, Harold to his surprise saw the ever ominous face of Haco.

But proud as was Aldyth, all pride seemed humbled into woman's sweeter emotions at the sight of the earl, and she was at first unable to command words to answer his greeting.

Gradually, however, she warmed into cordial confidence. She touched lightly on her past sorrows; she permitted it to be seen that her lot with the fierce Gryffyth had been one not more of public calamity than of domestic grief, and that in the natural awe and horror which the murder of her lord had caused, she felt rather for the ill-starred king than the beloved spouse. She then passed to the differences still existing between her House and Harold's, and spoke well and wisely of the desire of the young earls to conciliate his grace and favour.

[1] And so, from Gryffyth, beheaded by his subjects, descended **Charles Stuart.**

While thus speaking, Morcar and Edwin, as if accidentally, entered, and their salutations of Harold were such as became their relative positions: reserved, not distant, — respectful, not servile. With the delicacy of high natures, they avoided touching on the cause before the Witan (fixed for the morrow), on which depended their earldoms or their exile.

Harold was pleased by their bearing, and attracted towards them by the memory of the affectionate words that had passed between him and Leofric, their illustrious grandsire, over his father's corpse. He thought then of his own prayer: "Let there be peace between thine and mine!" and looking at their fair and stately youth and noble carriage, he could not but feel that the men of Northumbria and of Mercia had chosen well. The discourse, however, was naturally brief, since thus made general; the visit soon ceased, and the brothers attended Harold to the door, with the courtesy of the times. Then Haco said, with that faint movement of the lips which was his only approach to a smile, —

"Will ye not, noble thegns, give your hands to my kinsman?"

"Surely," said Edwin, the handsomer and more gentle of the two, and who, having a poet's nature, felt a poet's enthusiasm for the gallant deeds even of a rival, — "surely, if the earl will accept the hands of those who trust never to be compelled to draw sword against England's hero."

Harold stretched forth his hand in reply, and that cordial and immemorial pledge of our national friendships was interchanged.

Gaining the street, Harold said to his nephew, —

"Standing as I do towards the young earls, that appeal of thine had been better omitted."

"Nay," answered Haco; "their cause is already prejudged in their favour. And thou must ally thyself with the heirs of Leofric, and the successors of Siward."

Harold made no answer. There was something in the positive tone of this beardless youth that displeased him; but he remembered that Haco was the son of Sweyn, Godwin's first-born, and that, but for Sweyn's crimes, Haco might have held the place in England he held himself, and looked to the same august destinies beyond.

In the evening a messenger from the Roman house arrived, with two letters for Harold; one from Hilda, that contained but these words: "Again peril menaces thee, but in the shape of good. Beware! and, above all, of the evil that wears the form of wisdom."

The other letter was from Edith; it was long for the letters of that age, and every sentence spoke a heart wrapped in his.

Reading the last, Hilda's warnings were forgotten. The picture of Edith — the prospect of a power that might at last effect their union, and reward her long devotion — rose before him, to the exclusion of wilder fancies and loftier hopes; and his sleep that night was full of youthful and happy dreams.

The next day the Witan met. The meeting was less stormy than had been expected; for the minds of most men were made up, and so far as Tostig was interested, the facts were too evident and notorious, the witnesses too numerous, to leave any option to the judges. Edward, on whom alone Tostig had relied, had already, with his ordinary vacillation, been swayed towards a right decision, partly by the counsels of Alred and his other prelates, and especially by the representations of Haco, whose grave bearing and profound dissimulation had gained a singular influence over the formal and melancholy king.

By some previous compact or understanding between the opposing parties, there was no attempt, however, to push matters against the offending Tostig to vindictive extremes. There was no suggestion of outlawry, or punishment, beyond the simple deprivation of the earldom he had abused. And in return for this moderation on the one side, the other agreed to support and ratify the new election of the Northumbrians. Morcar was thus formally invested with the vice-kingship of that great realm, while Edwin was confirmed in the earldom of the principal part of Mercia.

On the announcement of these decrees, which were received with loud applause by all the crowd assembled to hear them, Tostig, rallying round him his house-carles, left the town.

He went first to Githa, with whom his wife had sought refuge; and, after a long conference with his mother, he and his haughty countess journeyed to the seacoast, and took ship for Flanders.

CHAPTER IX.

GURTH and Harold were seated in close commune in the earl's chamber, at an hour long after the complin (or second vespers), when Alred entered unexpectedly. The old man's face was unusually grave, and Harold's penetrating eye saw that he was gloomy with some matters of great moment.

"Harold," said the prelate, seating himself, "the hour has come to test thy truth, when thou saidst that thou wert ready to make all sacrifice to thy land, and further, that thou wouldst abide by the counsel of those free from thy passions, and looking on thee only as the instrument of England's weal."

"Speak on, father," said Harold, turning somewhat pale at the solemnity of the address; "I am ready, if the council so desire, to remain a subject, and aid in the choice of a worthier king."

"Thou divinest me ill," answered Alred; "I do not call on thee to lay aside the crown, but to crucify the heart. The decree of the Witan assigns Mercia and Northumbria to the sons of Algar. The old demarcations of the Heptarchy, as thou knowest, are scarce worn out; it is even now less one monarchy than various States retaining their own laws, and inhabited by different races, who under the sub-kings, called earls, acknowledge a supreme head in the Basileus of Britain. Mercia hath its March law and its prince; Northumbria its Dane law and its leader. To elect a king without civil war, these realms, for so they are, must unite with and sanction the Witans elsewhere held. Only thus can the kingdom be firm against foes without and anarchy within; and the more so, from the alliance between the new earls of those great

provinces and the House of Gryffyth, which still lives in
Caradoc his son. What if at Edward's death Mercia and
Northumbria refuse to sanction thy accession? What if, when
all our force were needed against the Norman, the Welch
broke loose from their hills, and the Scots from their moors?
Malcolm of Cumbria, now King of Scotland, is Tostig's dearest friend, while his people side with Morcar. Verily these
are dangers enow for a new king, even if William's sword
slept in its sheath."

"Thou speakest the words of wisdom," said Harold; "but
I knew beforehand that he who wears a crown must abjure
repose."

"Not so; there is one way, and but one, to reconcile all England to thy dominion, — to win to thee not the cold neutrality
but the eager zeal of Mercia and Northumbria; to make the
first guard thee from the Welch, the last be thy rampart against
the Scot. In a word, thou must ally thyself with the blood of
these young earls; thou must wed with Aldyth their sister."

The earl sprang to his feet, aghast.

"No! no!" he exclaimed; "not that! any sacrifice but that!
rather forfeit the throne than resign the heart that leans on
mine! Thou knowest my pledge to Edith, my cousin, —
pledge hallowed by the faith of long years. No! no! have
mercy, — human mercy; I can wed no other! Any sacrifice
but that!"

The good prelate, though not unprepared for this burst, was
much moved by its genuine anguish; but, steadfast to his purpose, he resumed: —

"Alas, my son, so say we all in the hour of trial, — any
sacrifice but that which duty and Heaven ordain. Resign the
throne thou canst not, or thou leavest the land without a
ruler, distracted by rival claims and ambitions, an easy prey
to the Norman. Resign thy human affections thou canst and
must; and the more, O Harold, that even if duty compelled
not this new alliance, the old tie is one of sin, which, as king,
and as high example in high place to all men, thy conscience
within, and the Church without, summon thee to break. How
purify the erring lives of the churchmen, if thyself a rebel to

the Church? And if thou hast thought that thy power as king might prevail on the Roman Pontiff to grant dispensation for wedlock within the degrees, and that so thou mightest legally confirm thy now illegal troth, bethink thee well, thou hast a more dread and urgent boon now to ask, — in absolution from thine oath to William. Both prayers, surely, our Roman father will not grant. Wilt thou choose that which absolves from sin, or that which consults but thy carnal affections?"

Harold covered his face with his hands, and groaned aloud in his strong agony.

"Aid me, Gurth," cried Alred, "thou, sinless and spotless; thou, in whose voice a brother's love can blend with a Christian's zeal; aid me, Gurth, to melt the stubborn, but to comfort the human, heart."

Then Gurth, with a strong effort over himself, knelt by Harold's side, and in strong simple language, backed the representations of the priest. In truth, all arguments drawn from reason, whether in the state of the land, or the new duties to which Harold was committed, were on the one side, and unanswerable; on the other was but that mighty resistance which love opposes ever to reason. And Harold continued to murmur, while his hands concealed his face, —

"Impossible! — she who trusted, who trusts, who so loves, — she whose whole youth hath been consumed in patient faith in me! Resign her? — and for another! I cannot! I cannot! Take from me the throne! O vain heart of man, that so long desired its own curse! Crown the Atheling; my manhood shall defend his youth. But not this offering! No, no! I will not!"

It were tedious to relate the rest of that prolonged and agitated conference. All that night, till the last stars waned, and the bells of prime were heard from church and convent, did the priest and the brother alternately plead and remonstrate, chide and soothe; and still Harold's heart clung to Edith's, with its bleeding roots. At length they, perhaps not unwisely, left him to himself; and as, whispering low their hopes and their fears of the result of the self-conflict, they went forth from the convent, Haco joined them in the courtyard, and while his cold mournful eye scanned the faces of priest and brother, he asked them "how they had sped."

Alred shook his head and answered, —

"Man's heart is more strong in the flesh than true to the spirit."

"Pardon me, father," said Haco, "if I suggest that your most eloquent and persuasive ally in this were Edith herself. Start not so incredulously; it is because she loves the earl more than her own life, that — once show her that the earl's safety, greatness, honour, duty, lie in release from his troth to her — that nought save his erring love resists your counsels and his country's claims — and Edith's voice will have more power than yours."

The virtuous prelate, more acquainted with man's selfishness than woman's devotion, only replied by an impatient gesture. But Gurth, lately wedded to a woman worthy of him, said gravely, —

"Haco speaks well, my father; and methinks it is due to both that Edith should not, unconsulted, be abandoned by him for whom she has abjured all others; to whom she has been as devoted in heart as if sworn wife already. Leave we awhile my brother, never the slave of passion, and with whom England must at last prevail over all selfish thought; and ride we at once to tell to Edith what we have told to him; or rather — woman can best in such a case speak to woman — let us tell all to our Lady — Edward's wife, Harold's sister, and Edith's holy godmother — and abide by her counsel. On the third day we shall return."

"Go we so charged, noble Gurth," said Haco, observing the prelate's reluctant countenance, "and leave we our reverend father to watch over the earl's sharp struggle."

"Thou speakest well, my son," said the prelate, "and thy mission suits the young and the layman better than the old and the priest."

"Let us go, Haco," said Gurth, briefly. "Deep, sore, and lasting is the wound I inflict on the brother of my love, and my own heart bleeds in his; but he himself hath taught me to hold England as a Roman held Rome."

CHAPTER X.

IT is the nature of that happiness which we derive from our affections to be calm; its immense influence upon our outward life is not known till it is troubled or withdrawn. By placing his heart at peace, man leaves vent to his energies and passions, and permits their current to flow towards the aims and objects which interest labour or arouse ambition. Thus absorbed in the occupation without, he is lulled into a certain forgetfulness of the value of that internal repose which gives health and vigour to the faculties he employs abroad. But once mar this scarce felt, almost invisible harmony, and the discord extends to the remotest chords of our active being. Say to the busiest man whom thou seest in mart, camp, or senate, who seems to thee all intent upon his worldly schemes, "Thy home is reft from thee; thy household gods are shattered; that sweet noiseless content in the regular mechanism of the springs, which set the large wheels of thy soul into movement, is thine nevermore!"—and straightway all exertion seems robbed of its object, all aim of its alluring charm. "Othello's occupation is gone!" With a start, that man will awaken from the sunlit visions of noontide ambition, and exclaim in his desolate anguish, "What are all the rewards to my labour, now thou hast robbed me of repose? How little are all the gains wrung from strife, in a world of rivals and foes, compared to the smile whose sweetness I knew not till it was lost; and the sense of security from mortal ill which I took from the trust and sympathy of love?"

Thus was it with Harold in that bitter and terrible crisis of his fate. This rare and spiritual love, which had existed on hope, which had never known fruition, had become the subtlest, the most exquisite part of his being; this love, to the full and holy possession of which every step in his career seemed to advance him — was it now to be evermore reft from his heart, his existence, at the very moment when he had deemed himself most secure of its rewards, when he most needed its consolations? Hitherto, in that love he had lived in the future; he had silenced the voice of the turbulent human passion by the whisper of the patient angel, "A little while yet, and thy bride sits beside thy throne!" Now what was that future? how joyless! how desolate! The splendour vanished from Ambition, the glow from the face of Fame, the sense of Duty remained alone to counteract the pleadings of Affection; but Duty, no longer dressed in all the gorgeous colourings it took before from glory and power, — Duty stern and harsh and terrible, as the iron frown of a Grecian Destiny.

And thus, front to front with that Duty, he sat alone one evening, while his lips murmured, "Oh, fatal voyage! oh, lying truth in the hell-born prophecy! this, then, this was the wife my league with the Norman was to win to my arms!" In the streets below were heard the tramp of busy feet hurrying homeward, and the confused uproar of joyous wassail from the various resorts of entertainment crowded by careless revellers. And the tread of steps mounted the stairs without his door, and there paused; and there was the murmur of two voices without, — one the clear voice of Gurth, one softer and more troubled. The earl lifted his head from his bosom, and his heart beat quick at the faint and scarce heard sound of that last voice. The door opened gently, gently; a form entered, and halted on the shadow of the threshold; the door closed again by a hand from without. The earl rose to his feet, tremulously, and the next moment Edith was at his knees; her hood thrown back, her face upturned to his, bright with unfaded beauty, serene with the grandeur of self-martyrdom.

"O Harold!" she exclaimed, "dost thou remember that in the old time I said, ' Edith had loved thee less, if thou hadst not loved England more than Edith '? Recall, recall those words! And deemest thou now that I, who have gazed for years into thy clear soul, and learned there to sun my woman's heart in the light of all glories native to noblest man, — deemest thou, O Harold, that I am weaker now than then, when I scarce knew what England and glory were?"

"Edith, Edith, what wouldst thou say? What knowest thou? Who hath told thee? What led thee hither, to take part against thyself?"

"It matters not who told me; I know all. What led me? Mine own soul, and mine own love!" Springing to her feet, and clasping his hand in both hers, while she looked into his face, she resumed: "I do not say to thee, 'Grieve not to part;' for I know too well thy faith, thy tenderness, thy heart, so grand and so soft. But I do say, 'Soar above thy grief, and be more than man for the sake of men!' Yes, Harold, for this last time I behold thee. I clasp thy hand, I lean on thy heart, I hear its beating, and I shall go hence without a tear."

"It cannot, it shall not be!" exclaimed Harold, passionately. "Thou deceivest thyself in the divine passion of the hour; thou canst not foresee the utterness of the desolation to which thou wouldst doom thy life. We were betrothed to each other by ties strong as those of the Church, — over the grave of the dead, under the vault of heaven, in the form of ancestral faith! The bond cannot be broken. If England demands me, let England take me with the ties it were unholy, even for her sake, to rend!"

"Alas, alas!" faltered Edith, while the flush on her cheek sank into mournful paleness. "It is not as thou sayest. So has thy love sheltered me from the world, so utter was my youth's ignorance or my heart's oblivion of the stern laws of man, that when it pleased thee that we should love each other, I could not believe that that love was sin; and that it was sin hitherto I will not think, — *now* it hath become one."

"No, no!" cried Harold; all the eloquence on which thousands had hung, thrilled and spell-bound, deserting him in that hour of need, and leaving to him only broken exclamations, — fragments, in each of which his heart itself seemed shivered; "no, no! not sin!— sin only to forsake thee. Hush! hush! This is a dream, — wait till we wake! True heart! noble soul! I will not part from thee!"

"But I from thee! And rather than thou shouldst be lost for my sake — the sake of woman — to honour and conscience, and all for which thy sublime life sprang from the hands of Nature, if not the cloister, may I find the grave! Harold, to the last let me be worthy of thee; and feel, at least, that if not thy wife — that bright, that blessed fate not mine! — still, remembering Edith, just men may say, ' She would not have dishonoured the hearth of Harold!'"

"Dost thou know," said the earl, striving to speak calmly, "dost thou know that it is not only to resign thee that they demand, — that it is to resign thee, and for another?"

"I know it," said Edith; and two burning tears, despite her strong and preternatural self-exaltation, swelled from the dark fringe, and rolled slowly down the colourless cheek, as she added, with proud voice, "I know it; but that other is not Aldyth, it is England! In her, in Aldyth, behold the dear cause of thy native land; with her enweave the love which thy native land should command. So thinking, thou art reconciled, and I consoled. It is not for woman that thou desertest Edith."

"Hear, and take from those lips the strength and the valour that belong to the name of Hero!" said a deep and clear voice behind; and Gurth — who, whether distrusting the result of an interview so prolonged, or tenderly desirous to terminate its pain, had entered unobserved — approached, and wound his arm caressingly round his brother. "O Harold!" he said, "dear to me as the drops in my heart is my young bride, newly wed; but if for one tithe of the claims that now call thee to the torture and trial, — yea, if but for one hour of good service to freedom and law, — I would consent without a groan to behold her no more. And if men asked me how I could so conquer man's affections, I would point to thee, and say, ' So Harold taught my youth by his lessons, and my manhood by his life.' Before thee, visible, stand Happiness and Love, but with them, Shame; before thee, invisible, stands Woe, but with Woe are England and eternal Glory! Choose between them."

"He hath chosen," said Edith, as Harold turned to the wall,

and leaned against it, hiding his face; then, approaching softly, she knelt, lifted to her lips the hem of his robe, and kissed it with devout passion.

Harold turned suddenly, and opened his arms. Edith resisted not that mute appeal; she rose, and fell on his breast, sobbing.

Wild and speechless was that last embrace. The moon, which had witnessed their union by the heathen grave, now rose above the tower of the Christian church, and looked wan and cold upon their parting.

Solemn and clear paused the orb, — a cloud passed over the disk, — and Edith was gone. The cloud rolled away, and again the moon shone forth; and where had knelt the fair form and looked the last look of Edith, stood the motionless image, and gazed the solemn eye, of the dark son of Sweyn. But Harold leaned on the breast of Gurth, and saw not who had supplanted the soft and loving Fylgia of his life, — saw nought in the universe but the blank of desolation!

BOOK XI.

THE NORMAN SCHEMER, AND THE NORWEGIAN SEA-KING.

CHAPTER I.

It was the eve of the 5th of January,— the eve of the day announced to King Edward as that of his deliverance from earth; and whether or not the prediction had wrought its own fulfilment on the fragile frame and susceptible nerves of the king, the last of the line of Cerdic was fast passing into the solemn shades of eternity.

Without the walls of the palace, through the whole city of London, the excitement was indescribable. All the river before the palace was crowded with boats; all the broad space on the Isle of Thorney itself thronged with anxious groups. But a few days before, the new-built Abbey had been solemnly consecrated; with the completion of that holy edifice, Edward's life itself seemed done. Like the kings of Egypt, he had built his tomb,

Within the palace, if possible, still greater was the agitation, more dread the suspense. Lobbies, halls, corridors, stairs, ante-rooms, were filled with churchmen and thegns. Nor was it alone for news of the king's state that their brows were so knit, that their breath came and went so short. It is not when a great chief is dying that men compose their minds to deplore a loss. That comes long after, when the worm is at its work, and comparison between the dead and the living often rights the one to wrong the other. But while the breath is struggling, and the eye glazing, life, busy in the bystanders, murmurs, "Who shall be the heir?" And, in this instance, never had suspense been so keenly wrought up into hope and terror. For the news of Duke William's designs had now spread far and near; and awful was the doubt, whether the abhorred Norman should receive his sole sanction to so arrogant a claim from the parting assent of Edward. Although, as we have seen, the crown was not absolutely within the bequests of a dying king but at the will of the Witan, still, in circumstances so unparalleled, — the utter failure of all natural heirs, save a boy feeble in mind as body, and half foreign by birth and rearing; the love borne by Edward to the Church; and the sentiments, half of pity half of reverence, with which he was regarded throughout the land, — his dying word would go far to influence the council and select the successor. Some whispering to each other, with pale lips, all the dire predictions then current in men's mouths and breasts, some in moody silence, all lifted eager eyes, as, from time to time, a gloomy Benedictine passed in the direction to or fro the king's chamber.

In that chamber, traversing the past of eight centuries, enter we with hushed and noiseless feet, — a room known to us in many a later scene and legend of England's troubled history as "THE PAINTED CHAMBER," long called "THE CONFESSOR'S." At the farthest end of that long and lofty space, raised upon a regal platform, and roofed with regal canopy, was the bed of death.

At the foot stood Harold; on one side knelt Edith, the king's lady; at the other Alred; while Stigand stood near — the holy rood in his hand — and the abbot of the new monastery of Westminster by Stigand's side; and all the greatest thegns, including Morcar and Edwin, Gurth and Leofwine, all the more illustrious prelates and abbots, stood also on the daïs.

In the lower end of the hall, the king's physician was warming a cordial over the brazier, and some of the subordinate officers of the household were standing in the niches of the deep-set windows; and they — not great eno' for other emotions than those of human love for their kindly lord — *they* wept.

The king, who had already undergone the last holy offices of the Church, was lying quite quiet, his eyes half closed, breathing low but regularly. He had been speechless the two preceding days; on this he had uttered a few words, which showed returning consciousness. His hand, reclined on the coverlid, was clasped in his wife's, who was praying fervently. Something in the touch of her hand, or the sound of her murmur, stirred the king from the growing lethargy, and his eyes opening, fixed on the kneeling lady.

"Ah?" said he, faintly, "ever good, ever meek! Think not I did not love thee; hearts will be read yonder; we shall have our guerdon."

The lady looked up through her streaming tears. Edward released his hand, and laid it on her head as in benediction. Then motioning to the abbot of Westminster, he drew from his finger the ring which the palmers had brought to him,[1] and murmured scarce audibly, —

"Be this kept in the House of St. Peter in memory of me!"

"He is alive now to us; speak — " whispered more than one thegn, one abbot, to Alred and to Stigand. And Stigand, as the harder and more worldly man of the two, moved up, and bending over the pillow, between Alred and the king, said, —

"O royal son, about to win the crown to which that of earth is but an idiot's wreath of withered leaves, not yet may thy soul forsake us. Whom commendest thou to us as shepherd to thy bereaven flock; whom shall we admonish to tread in those traces thy footsteps leave below?"

The king made a slight gesture of impatience; and the queen, forgetful of all but her womanly sorrow, raised her eye and finger in reproof that the dying was thus disturbed. But the stake was too weighty, the suspense too keen, for that reverent delicacy in those around; and the thegns pressed on each other, and a murmur rose, which murmured the name of Harold.

"Bethink thee, my son," said Alred, in a tender voice,

[1] Brompton Chronicle.

The Death-Bed of Edward the Confessor.

tremulous with emotion; "the young Atheling is too much an infant yet for these anxious times."

Edward signed his head in assent.

"Then," said the Norman bishop of London, who till that moment had stood in the rear, almost forgotten amongst the crowd of Saxon prelates, but who himself had been all eyes and ears,— "then," said Bishop William, advancing, "if thine own royal line so fail, who so near to thy love, who so worthy to succeed, as William thy cousin, the Count of the Normans?"

Dark was the scowl on the brow of every thegn, and a muttered "No, no: never the Norman!" was heard distinctly. Harold's face flushed, and his hand was on the hilt of his ateghar; but no other sign gave he of his interest in the question.

The king lay for some moments silent, but evidently striving to re-collect his thoughts. Meanwhile the two arch-prelates bent over him,— Stigand eagerly, Alred fondly.

Then raising himself on one arm, while with the other he pointed to Harold at the foot of the bed, the king said,—

"Your hearts, I see, are with Harold the Earl: so be it."

At those words he fell back on his pillow; a loud shriek burst from his wife's lips; all crowded around; he lay as the dead.

At the cry, and the indescribable movement of the throng, the physician came quick from the lower part of the hall. He made his way abruptly to the bedside, and said chidingly, "Air,— give him air." The throng parted, the leech moistened the king's pale lips with the cordial, but no breath seemed to come forth, no pulse seemed to beat; and while the two prelates knelt before the human body and by the blessed rood, the rest descended the daïs, and hastened to depart. Harold only remained; but he had passed from the foot to the head of the bed.

The crowd had gained the centre of the hall, when a sound that startled them as if it had come from the grave, chained every footstep,— the sound of the king's voice, loud, terribly distinct, and full, as with the vigour of youth restored. All turned their eyes, appalled; all stood spell-bound.

There sat the king upright on the bed, his face seen above the kneeling prelates, and his eyes bright and shining down the Hall.

"Yea," he said deliberately, "yea, as this shall be a real vision or a false illusion, grant me, Almighty One, the power of speech to tell it."

He paused a moment, and thus resumed: —

"It was on the banks of the frozen Seine, this day thirty-and-one winters ago, that two holy monks, to whom the gift of prophecy was vouchsafed, told me of direful woes that should fall on England; 'For God,' said they, 'after thy death, has delivered England into the hand of the enemy, and fiends shall wander over the land.' Then I asked in my sorrow, 'Can nought avert the doom; and may not my people free themselves by repentance, like the Ninevites of old?' And the Prophets answered, 'Nay, nor shall the calamity cease, and the curse be completed, till a green tree be sundered in twain, and the part cut off be carried away; yet move, of itself, to the ancient trunk, unite to the stem, bud out with the blossom, and stretch forth its fruit.' So said the monks, and even now, ere I spoke, I saw them again, there, standing mute, and with the paleness of dead men, by the side of my bed!"

These words were said so calmly, and as it were so rationally, that their import became doubly awful from the cold precision of the tone. A shudder passed through the assembly, and each man shrunk from the king's eye, which seemed to each man to dwell on himself. Suddenly that eye altered in its cold beam; suddenly the voice changed its deliberate accent; the gray hairs seemed to bristle erect, the whole face to work with horror; the arms stretched forth, the form writhed on the couch; distorted fragments from the older Testament rushed from the lips: "*Sanguelac! Sanguelac!* — the Lake of Blood," shrieked forth the dying king, "the Lord hath bent his bow, — the Lord hath bared his sword. He comes down as a warrior to war, and his wrath is in the steel and the flame. He boweth the mountains, and comes down, and darkness is under his feet!"

As if revived but for these tremendous denunciations, while the last word left his lips the frame collapsed, the eyes set, and the king fell a corpse in the arms of Harold.

But one smile of the sceptic or the world-man was seen on the paling lips of those present: that smile was not on the lips of warriors and men of mail. It distorted the sharpened features of Stigand, the world-man and the miser, as, passing down, and amidst the group, he said, "Tremble ye at the dreams of a sick old man?" [1]

CHAPTER II.

THE time of year customary for the National Assembly; the recent consecration of Westminster, for which Edward had convened all his chief spiritual lords; the anxiety felt for the infirm state of the king, and the interest as to the impending succession,— all concurred to permit the instantaneous meeting of a Witan worthy, from rank and numbers, to meet the emergency of the time, and proceed to the most momentous election ever yet known in England. The thegns and prelates met in haste. Harold's marriage with Aldyth, which had taken place but a few weeks before, had united all parties with his own; not a claim counter to the great earl's was advanced; the choice was unanimous. The necessity of terminating at such a crisis all suspense throughout the kingdom, and extinguishing the danger of all counter intrigues, forbade to men thus united any delay in solemnizing their decision; and the august obsequies of Edward were followed on the same day by the coronation of Harold.

It was in the body of the mighty Abbey Church, not indeed as we see it now, after successive restorations and remodellings, but simple in its long rows of Saxon arch and massive column, blending the first Teuton with the last Roman ma-

---

[1] See Note P.

sonries, that the crowd of the Saxon freemen assembled to honour the monarch of their choice,— first Saxon king, since England had been one monarchy, selected not from the single House of Cerdic; first Saxon king not led to the throne by the pale shades of fabled ancestors tracing their descent from the Father-God of the Teuton, but by the spirits that never know a grave, the arch-eternal givers of crowns, and founders of dynasties,— Valour and Fame.

Alred and Stigand, the two great prelates of the realm, had conducted Harold to the church,[1] and up the aisle to the altar, followed by the chiefs of the Witan in their long robes; and the clergy with their abbots and bishops sung the anthems, "Fermetur manus tua," and "Gloria Patri."

And now the music ceased; Harold prostrated himself before the altar, and the sacred melody burst forth with the great hymn, "Te Deum."

As it ceased, prelate and thegn raised their chief from the floor, and in imitation of the old custom of Teuton and Northman — when the lord of their armaments was borne on shoulder and shield — Harold mounted a platform, and rose in full view of the crowd.

"Thus," said the arch-prelate, "we choose Harold son of Godwin for lord and for king." And the thegns drew round, and placed hand on Harold's knee, and cried aloud, "We choose thee, O Harold, for lord and for king." And row by row, line by line, all the multitude shouted forth, "We choose thee, O Harold, for lord and king." So there he stood with

---

[1] It seems by the coronation service of Ethelred II., still extant, that two bishops officiated in the crowning of the king; and hence, perhaps, the discrepancy in the chroniclers, some contending that Harold was crowned by Alred, others, by Stigand. It is noticeable, however, that it is the apologists of the Normans who assign that office to Stigand, who was in disgrace with the Pope, and deemed no lawful bishop. Thus in the Bayeux tapestry the label "Stigand" is significantly affixed to the officiating prelate, as if to convey insinuation that Harold was not lawfully crowned. Florence, by far the best authority, says distinctly that Harold was crowned by Alred. The ceremonial of the coronation described in the text is for the most part given on the authority of the "Cotton Manuscript" quoted by Sharon Turner, vol. iii. p. 151.

his calm brow, facing all, Monarch of England, and Basileus of Britain.

Now unheeded amidst the throng, and leaning against a column in the arches of the aisle, was a woman with her veil round her face; and she lifted the veil for a moment to gaze on that lofty brow, and the tears were streaming fast down her cheek, but her face was not sad.

"Let the vulgar not see, to pity or scorn thee, daughter of kings as great as he who abandons and forsakes thee!" murmured a voice in her ear; and the form of Hilda, needing no support from column or wall, rose erect by the side of Edith. Edith bowed her head and lowered the veil, as the king descended the platform and stood again by the altar, while clear through the hushed assembly rang the words of his triple promise to his people: —

"Peace to his Church and the Christian flock;

"Interdict of rapacity and injustice;

"Equity and mercy in his judgments, as God the gracious and just might show mercy to him."

And deep from the hearts of thousands came the low "Amen."

Then after a short prayer, which each prelate repeated, the crowd saw afar the glitter of the crown held over the head of the king. The voice of the consecrator was heard, low till it came to the words, "So potently and royally may he rule, against all visible and invisible foes, that the royal throne of the Angles and Saxons may not desert his sceptre."

As the prayer ceased, came the symbolical rite of anointment. Then pealed the sonorous organ,[1] and solemn along the aisles rose the anthem that closed with the chorus, which the voice of the multitude swelled, "May the king live forever!" Then the crown that had gleamed in the trembling hand of the prelate rested firm in its splendour on the front of the king; and the sceptre of rule, and the rod of justice, "to soothe the pious and terrify the bad," were placed in the royal hands. And the prayer and the blessings were renewed,— till the close, "Bless, Lord, the courage of this

[1] Introduced into our churches in the ninth century.

Prince, and prosper the works of his hand. With his horn, as the horn of the rhinoceros, may he blow the waters to the extremities of the earth; and may He who has ascended to the skies be his aid forever! "

Then Hilda stretched forth her hand to lead Edith from the place. But Edith shook her head and murmured,—

"But once again, but once!" and with involuntary step moved on.

Suddenly, close where she paused, the crowd parted, and down the narrow lane so formed amidst the wedged and breathless crowd came the august procession. Prelate and thegn swept on from the Church to the palace; and alone, with firm and measured step, the diadem on his brow, the sceptre in his hand, came the king Edith checked the rushing impulse at her heart, but she bent forward, with veil half drawn aside, and so gazed on that face and form of more than royal majesty fondly, proudly. The king swept on and saw her not; love lived no more for him.

———◆———

CHAPTER III.

THE boat shot over the royal Thames. Borne along the waters, the shouts and the hymns of swarming thousands from the land shook like a blast the gelid air of the Wolf-month. All space seemed filled and noisy with the name of Harold the King. Fast rowed the rowers, on shot the boat; and Hilda's face, stern and ominous, turned to the still towers of the palace, gleaming wide and white in the wintry sun. Suddenly Edith lifted her hand from her bosom, and said passionately, —

"Oh! mother of my mother, I cannot live again in the house where the very walls speak to me of him; all things chain my soul to the earth; and my soul should be in heaven, that its prayers may be heard by the heedful angels. The aay that the holy Lady of England predicted hath come to pass, and the silver cord is loosed at last. Ah why, why did I not believe her then? Why did I then reject the cloister? Yet no, I will not repent; at least I have been loved! But now I will go to the nunnery of Waltham, and kneel at the altars *he* hath hallowed to the mone and the monechyn."

"Edith," said the Vala, "thou wilt not bury thy life yet young in the living grave! And, despite all that now severs you,—yea, despite Harold's new and loveless ties, — still clearer than ever it is written in the heavens that a day *shall* come, in which you are to be evermore united. Many of the shapes I have seen, many of the sounds I have heard, in the trance and the dream, fade in the troubled memory of waking life; but never yet hath grown doubtful or dim the prophecy that the truth pledged by the grave shall be fulfilled."

"Oh, tempt not! Oh, delude not!" cried Edith, while the blood rushed over her brow. "Thou knowest this cannot be. Another's! he is another's! and in the words thou hast uttered there is deadly sin."

"There is no sin in the resolves of a fate that rules us in spite of ourselves. Tarry only till the year bring round the birthday of Harold; for my sayings shall be ripe with the grape, and when the feet of the vineherd are red in the Month of the Vine,[1] the Nornas shall knit ye together again!"

Edith clasped her hands mutely, and looked hard into the face of Hilda, — looked and shuddered, she knew not why.

The boat landed on the eastern shore of the river, beyond the walls of the city, and then Edith bent her way to the holy walls of Waltham. The frost was sharp in the glitter of the unwarming sun; upon leafless boughs hung the barbed ice-gems; and the crown was on the brow of Harold! And at night, within the walls of the convent, Edith heard the hymns of the kneeling monks; and the blasts howled, and the storm arose, and the voices of destroying hurricanes were blent with the swell of the choral hymns.

[1] The Wyn-month: October.

CHAPTER IV.

TOSTIG sat in the halls of Bruges, and with him sat Judith, his haughty wife. The earl and his countess were playing at chess (or the game resembling it, which amused the idlesse of that age), and the countess had put her lord's game into mortal disorder, when Tostig swept his hand over the board, and .the pieces rolled on the floor.

"That is one way to prevent defeat," said Judith, with a half smile and half frown.

"It is the way of the bold and the wise, wife mine," answered Tostig, rising; "let all be destruction where thou thyself canst win not! Peace to these trifles! I cannot keep my mind to the mock fight; it flies to the real. Our last news sours the taste of the wine, and steals the sleep from my couch. It says that Edward cannot live through the winter, and that all men bruit abroad there can be no king save Harold, my brother."

"And will thy brother as king give to thee again thy domain as earl?"

"He must!" answered Tostig, "and, despite all our breaches, with soft message he will. For Harold has the heart of the Saxon, to which the sons of one father are dear; and Githa, my mother, when we first fled, controlled the voice of my revenge, and bade me wait patient, and hope yet."

Scarce had these words fallen from Tostig's lips, when the chief of his Danish house-carles came in, and announced the arrival of a bode from England.

"His news? his news?" cried the earl; "with his own lips let him speak his news."

The house-carle withdrew but to usher in the messenger, an Anglo-Dane.

"The weight on thy brow shows the load on thy heart," cried Tostig. "Speak, and be brief."

"Edward is dead."

"Ha! and who reigns?"

"Thy brother is chosen and crowned."

The face of the earl grew red and pale in a breath, and successive emotions of envy and old rivalship, humbled pride and fierce discontent, passed across his turbulent heart. But these died away as the predominant thought of self-interest, and somewhat of that admiration for success which often seems like magnanimity in grasping minds, and something too of haughty exultation, that he stood a king's brother in the halls of his exile, came to chase away the more hostile and menacing feelings. Then Judith approached with joy on her brow, and said, —

"We shall no more eat the bread of dependence even at the hand of a father; and since Harold hath no dame to proclaim to the Church, and to place on the dais, thy wife, O my Tostig, will have state in fair England little less than her sister in Rouen."

"Methinks so will it be," said Tostig. "How now, nuncius? Why lookest thou so grim, and why shakest thou thy head?"

"Small chance for thy dame to keep state in the halls of the king; small hope for thyself to win back thy broad earldom. But a few weeks ere thy brother won the crown, he won also a bride in the house of thy spoiler and foe. Aldyth, the sister of Edwin and Morcar, is Lady of England; and that union shuts thee out from Northumbria forever."

At these words, as if stricken by some deadly and inexpressible insult, the earl recoiled, and stood a moment mute with rage and amaze. His singular beauty became distorted into the lineaments of a fiend. He stamped with his foot, as he thundered a terrible curse. Then haughtily waving his hand to the bode, in sign of dismissal, he strode to and fro the room in gloomy perturbation.

Judith, like her sister Matilda, a woman fierce and vindictive, continued, by that sharp venom that lies in the tongue of the sex, to incite still more the intense resentment of her lord. Perhaps some female jealousies of Aldyth might contribute to increase her own indignation. But without such frivolous addition to anger, there was cause eno' in this marriage thoroughly to complete the alienation between the king and his brother. It was impossible that one so revengeful as Tostig should not cherish the deepest animosity, not only against the people that had rejected, but the new earl that had succeeded him. In wedding the sister of this fortunate rival and despoiler, Harold could not, therefore, but gall him in his most sensitive sores of soul. The king thus formally approved and sanctioned his ejection, solemnly took part with his foe, robbed him of all legal chance of recovering his dominions, and, in the words of the bode, "shut him out from Northumbria forever." Nor was this even all. Grant his return to England; grant a reconciliation with Harold; still those abhorred and more fortunate enemies, necessarily made now the most intimate part of the king's family, must be most in his confidence, would curb and chafe and encounter Tostig in every scheme for his personal aggrandizement. His foes, in a word, were in the camp of his brother.

While gnashing his teeth with a wrath the more deadly because he saw not yet his way to retribution, Judith, pursuing the separate thread of her own cogitations, said, —

"And if my sister's lord, the Count of the Normans, had, as rightly he ought to have, succeeded his cousin the monk-king, then I should have a sister on the throne, and thou in her husband a brother more tender than Harold, — one who supports his barons with sword and mail, and gives the villeins rebelling against them but the brand and the cord."

"Ho!" cried Tostig, stopping suddenly in his disordered strides, "kiss me, wife, for those words! They have helped thee to power, and lit me to revenge. If thou wouldst send love to thy sister, take graphium and parchment, and write fast as a scribe. Ere the sun is an hour older, I am on my road to Count William."

CHAPTER V.

THE duke of the Normans was in the forest, or park-land, of Rouvray, and his quens and his knights stood around him, expecting some new proof of his strength and his skill with the bow. For the duke was trying some arrows, a weapon he was ever employed in seeking to improve; sometimes shortening, sometimes lengthening, the shaft; and suiting the wing of the feather, and the weight of the point, to the nicest refinement in the law of mechanics. Gay and debonair, in the brisk fresh air of the frosty winter, the great count jested and laughed as the squires fastened a live bird by the string to a stake in the distant sward; and, "*Pardex,*" said Duke William, "Conan of Bretagne and Philip of France leave us now so unkindly in peace, that I trow we shall never again have larger butt for our arrows than the breast of yon poor plumed trembler."

As the duke spoke and laughed, all the sere boughs behind him rattled and cranched, and a horse at full speed came rushing over the hard rime of the sward. The duke's smile vanished in the frown of his pride. "Bold rider and graceless," quoth he, "who thus comes in the presence of counts and princes?"

Right up to Duke William spurred the rider, and then leaped from his steed,— vest and mantle, yet more rich than the duke's, all tattered and soiled. No knee bent the rider, no cap did he doff; but seizing the startled Norman with the gripe of a hand as strong as his own, he led him aside from the courtiers, and said, —

"Thou knowest me, William?—though not thus alone should I come to thy court, if I did not bring thee a crown."

"Welcome, brave Tostig!" said the duke, marvelling. "What meanest thou? Nought but good, by thy words and thy smile."

"Edward sleeps with the dead!—and Harold is King of all England!"

"King! England! King!" faltered William, stammering in his agitation. "Edward dead!—Saints rest him! England then is *mine!* King!—*I* am the King! Harold hath sworn it; my quens and prelates heard him; the bones of the saints attest the oath!"

"Somewhat of this have I vaguely learned from our *beau-père* Count Baldwin; more will I learn at thy leisure; but take, meanwhile, my word as *Miles* and *Saxon*, —never, while there is breath on his lips, or one beat in his heart, will my brother, Lord Harold, give an inch of English land to the Norman."

William turned pale and faint with emotion, and leaned for support against a leafless oak.

Busy were the rumours, and anxious the watch, of the quens and knights, as their prince stood long in the distant glade, conferring with the rider, whom one or two of them had recognized as Tostig, the spouse of Matilda's sister.

At length, side by side, still talking earnestly, they regained the group; and William, summoning the Lord of Tancarville, bade him conduct Tostig to Rouen, the towers of which rose through the forest trees. "Rest and refresh thee, noble kinsman," said the duke; "see and talk with Matilda. I will join thee anon."

The earl remounted his steed, and saluting the company with a wild and hasty grace, soon vanished amidst the groves.

Then William, seating himself on the sward, mechanically unstrung his bow, sighing oft, and oft frowning; and without vouchsafing other word to his lords than "No further sport to-day!" rose slowly, and went alone through the thickest parts of the forest. But his faithful Fitzosborne marked his gloom, and fondly followed him. The duke arrived at the borders of the Seine, where his galley waited him. He entered, sat down on the bench, and took no notice of Fitzosborne, who quietly stepped in after his lord, and placed himself on another bench.

The little voyage to Rouen was performed in silence; and as soon as he had gained his palace, without seeking either Tostig or Matilda, the duke turned into the vast hall, in which he was wont to hold council with his barons, and walked to and fro, "often," say the chroniclers, "changing posture and attitude, and oft loosening and tightening, and drawing into knots, the strings of his mantle."

Fitzosborne, meanwhile, had sought the ex-earl, who was closeted with Matilda; and now returning, he went boldly up to the duke, whom no one else dared approach, and said, —

"Why, my liege, seek to conceal what is already known, — what ere the eve will be in the mouths of all? You are troubled that Edward is dead, and that Harold, violating his oath, has seized the English realm."

"Truly," said the duke, mildly, and with the tone of a meek man much injured, "my dear cousin's death, and the wrongs I have received from Harold, touch me nearly."

Then said Fitzosborne, with that philosophy, half grave as became the Scandinavian, half gay as became the Frank: "No man should grieve for what he can help, — still less for what he cannot help. For Edward's death, I trow, remedy there is none; but for Harold's treason, yea! Have you not a noble host of knights and warriors? What want you to destroy the Saxon and seize his realm, — what but a bold heart? A great deed once well begun, is half done. Begin, Count of the Normans, and we will complete the rest."

Starting from his sorely tasked dissimulation, for all William needed, and all of which he doubted, was the aid of his haughty barons, the duke raised his head, and his eyes shone out.

"Ha, sayest thou so? then, by the Splendour of God, we will do this deed. Haste thou! rouse hearts, nerve hands! promise, menace, win! Broad are the lands of England, and generous a conqueror's hand. Go and prepare all my faithful lords for a council, nobler than ever yet stirred the hearts and strung the hands of the sons of Rou."

CHAPTER VI.

BRIEF was the sojourn of Tostig at the court of Rouen; speedily made the contract between the grasping duke and the revengeful traitor. All that had been promised to Harold was now pledged to Tostig,— if the last would assist the Norman to the English throne.

At heart, however, Tostig was ill satisfied. His chance conversations with the principal barons, who seemed to look upon the conquest of England as the dream of a madman, showed him how doubtful it was that William could induce his quens to a service, to which the tenure of their fiefs did not appear to compel them; and at all events, Tostig prognosticated delays that little suited his fiery impatience. He accepted the offer of some two or three ships, which William put at his disposal, under pretence to reconnoitre the Northumbrian coasts, and there attempt a rising in his own favour. But his discontent was increased by the smallness of the aid afforded him; for William, ever suspicious, distrusted both his faith and his power. Tostig, with all his vices, was a poor dissimulator, and his sullen spirit betrayed itself when he took leave of his host.

"Chance what may," said the fierce Saxon, "no stranger shall seize the English crown without my aid. I offer it first to thee. But thou must come to take it in time, or — "

"Or what? " asked the duke, gnawing his lip.

"Or the Father race of Rou will be before thee! My horse paws without. Farewell to thee, Norman; sharpen thy swords, hew out thy vessels, and goad thy slow barons."

Scarce had Tostig departed, ere William began to repent that he had so let him depart; but seeking counsel of Lanfranc, that wise minister reassured him.

"Fear no rival, son and lord," said he. "The bones of the dead are on thy side, and little thou knowest, as yet, how mighty their fleshless arms! All Tostig can do is to distract the forces of Harold. Leave him to work out his worst; nor then be in haste. Much hath yet to be done, — cloud must gather and fire must form, ere the bolt can be launched. Send to Harold mildly, and gently remind him of oath and of relics, of treaty and pledge. Put right on thy side, and then" —

"Ah, what then?"

"Rome shall curse the forsworn. Rome shall hallow thy banner; this be no strife of force against force, but a war of religion; and thou shalt have on thy side the conscience of man and the arm of the Church."

Meanwhile, Tostig embarked at Harfleur; but instead of sailing to the northern coasts of England, he made for one of the Flemish ports: and there, under various pretences, new manned the Norman vessels with Flemings, Fins, and Northmen. His meditations during his voyage had decided him not to trust to William; and he now bent his course, with fair wind and favouring weather, to the shores of his maternal uncle, King Sweyn of Denmark.

In truth, to all probable calculation, his change of purpose was politic. The fleets of England were numerous, and her seamen renowned. The Normans had neither experience nor fame in naval fights; their navy itself was scarcely formed. Thus even William's landing in England was an enterprise arduous and dubious. Moreover, even granting the amplest success, would not this Norman Prince, so profound and ambitious, be a more troublesome lord to Earl Tostig than his own uncle Sweyn?

So, forgetful of the compact at Rouen, no sooner had the Saxon lord come in presence of the King of the Danes than he urged on his kinsman the glory of winning again the sceptre of Canute.

A brave, but a cautious and wily veteran was King Sweyn; and a few days before Tostig arrived, he had received letters from his sister Githa, who, true to Godwin's command, had held all that Harold did and counselled, as between himself and his brother, wise and just. These letters had placed the

Dane on his guard, and shown him the true state of affairs in England. So King Sweyn, smiling, thus answered his nephew Tostig: —

"A great man was Canute, a small man am I: scarce can I keep my Danish dominion from the gripe of the Norwegian, while Canute took Norway without slash and blow;[1] but great as he was, England cost him hard fighting to win, and sore peril to keep. Wherefore, best for the small man to rule by the light of his own little sense, nor venture to count on the luck of great Canute, — for luck but goes with the great."

"Thine answer," said Tostig, with a bitter sneer, "is not what I expected from an uncle and warrior. But other chiefs may be found less afraid of the luck of high deeds."

"So," saith the Norwegian chronicler, "not just the best friends, the earl left the king," and went on in haste to Harold Hardrada of Norway.

True Hero of the North, true darling of War and of Song, was Harold Hardrada! At the terrible battle of Stiklestad, at which his brother, Saint Olave, had fallen, he was but fifteen years of age, but his body was covered with the wounds of a veteran. Escaping from the field, he lay concealed in the house of a Bonder peasant, remote in deep forests, till his wounds were healed. Thence, chanting by the way (for a poet's soul burned bright in Hardrada), "that a day would come when his name would be great in the land he now left," he went on into Sweden, thence into Russia, and after wild adventures in the East, joined, with the bold troop he had collected around him, that famous body-guard of the Greek emperors,[2] called the Væringers, and of these he became the chief. Jealousies between himself and the Greek General of

---

[1] "Snorro Sturleson." Laing.

[2] The Væringers, or Varangi, mostly Northmen; this redoubtable force, the Janizaries of the Byzantine empire, afforded brilliant field, both of fortune and war, to the discontented spirits or outlawed heroes of the North. It was joined afterwards by many of the bravest and best born of the Saxon nobles, refusing to dwell under the yoke of the Norman. Scott, in "Count Robert of Paris," which, if not one of his best romances, is yet full of truth and beauty, has described this renowned band with much poetical vigour and historical fidelity.

the Imperial forces (whom the Norwegian chronicler calls Gyrger) ended in Harold's retirement with his Væringers into the Saracen land of Africa. Eighty castles stormed and taken, vast plunder in gold and in jewels, and nobler meed in the song of the Scald and the praise of the brave, attested the prowess of the great Scandinavian. New laurels, blood-stained, new treasures, sword-won, awaited him in Sicily; and thence, rough foretype of the coming crusader, he passed on to Jerusalem. His sword swept before him Moslem and robber. He bathed in Jordan, and knelt at the Holy Cross.

Returned to Constantinople, the desire for his northern home seized Hardrada. There he heard that his nephew Magnus, the illegitimate son of Saint Olave, had become King of Norway,—and he himself aspired to a throne. So he gave up his command under Zoe the empress; but, if Scald be believed, Zoe the empress loved the bold chief, whose heart was set on Maria her niece. To detain Hardrada, a charge of mal-appropriation, whether of pay or of booty, was brought against him. He was cast into prison. But when the brave are in danger, the saints send the fair to their help! Moved by a holy dream, a Greek lady lowered ropes from the roof of the tower to the dungeon wherein Hardrada was cast. He escaped from the prison, he aroused his Væringers, they flocked round their chief; he went to the house of his lady Maria, bore her off to the galley, put out into the Black Sea, reached Novgorod (at the friendly court of whose king he had safely lodged his vast spoils), sailed home to the North; and after such feats as became sea-king of old, received half of Norway from Magnus, and on the death of his nephew the whole of that kingdom passed to his sway. A king so wise and so wealthy, so bold and so dread, had never yet been known in the North. And this was the king to whom came Tostig the Earl, with the offer of England's crown.

It was one of the glorious nights of the North, and winter had already begun to melt into early spring, when two men sat under a kind of rustic porch of rough pine-logs, not very unlike those seen now in Switzerland and the Tyrol. This porch was constructed before a private door, to the rear of a long, low, irregular building of wood which enclosed two or more courtyards, and covering an immense space of ground. This private door seemed placed for the purpose of immediate descent to the sea, for the ledge of the rock over which the log-porch spread its rude roof jutted over the ocean; and from it a rugged stair, cut through the crag, descended to the beach. The shore, with bold, strange, grotesque slab, and peak, and splinter, curved into a large creek; and close under the cliff were moored seven war-ships, high and tall, with prows and sterns all gorgeous with gilding in the light of the splendid moon. And that rude timber house, which seemed but a chain of barbarian huts linked into one, was a land palace of Hardrada of Norway; but the true halls of his royalty, the true seats of his empire, were the decks of those lofty war-ships.

Through the small lattice-work of the windows of the log-house lights blazed; from the roof-top smoke curled; from the hall on the other side of the dwelling came the din of tumultuous wassail: but the intense stillness of the outer air, hushed in frost, and luminous with stars, contrasted and seemed to rebuke the gross sounds of human revel. And that northern night seemed almost as bright as (but how much more augustly calm, than) the noon of the golden South!

On a table within the ample porch was an immense bowl of birchwood, mounted in silver, and filled with potent drink, and two huge horns, of size suiting the mighty wassailers of the age. The two men seemed to care nought for the stern air of the cold night — true that they were wrapped in furs reft from the Polar bear; but each had hot thoughts within, that gave greater warmth to the veins than the bowl or the bearskin.

They were host and guest; and as if with the restlessness of his thoughts, the host arose from his seat, and passed through the porch and stood on the bleak rock under the light of the moon; and so seen, he seemed scarcely human, but some war-chief of the farthest time, — yea, of a time ere the deluge had shivered those rocks, and left beds on the land for the realm of that icy sea. For Harold Hardrada was in height above all the children of modern men. Five ells of Norway made the height of Harold Hardrada.[1] Nor was this stature accompanied by any of those imperfections in symmetry, nor by that heaviness of aspect, which generally render any remarkable excess above human stature and strength rather monstrous than commanding. On the contrary, his proportions were just, his appearance noble; and the sole defect that the chronicler remarks in his shape, was "that his hands and feet were large, but these were well made." [2]

His face had all the fair beauty of the Norseman; his hair, parted in locks of gold over a brow that bespoke the daring of the warrior and the genius of the bard, fell in glittering profusion to his shoulders; a short beard and long mustache of the same colour as the hair, carefully trimmed, added to the grand and masculine beauty of the countenance, in which the only blemish was the peculiarity of one eyebrow being somewhat higher than the other,[3] which gave something more sinister to his frown, something more arch to his smile. For, quick of impulse, the Poet-Titan smiled and frowned often.

Harold Hardrada stood in the light of the moon, and gazing thoughtfully on the luminous sea. Tostig marked him for some moments where he sat in the porch, and then rose and joined him.

"Why should my words so disturb thee, O King of the Norsemen?"

"Is glory, then, a drug that soothes to sleep?" returned the Norwegian.

"I like thine answer," said Tostig, smiling, "and I like still more to watch thine eye gazing on the prows of thy war-

---

[1] Laing's Snorro Sturleson. — "The old Norwegian ell was less than the present ell; and Thorlasius reckons, in a note on this chapter, that Harold's stature would be about four Danish ells; namely, about eight feet." — Laing's note to the text. Allowing for the exaggeration of the chronicler, it seems probable, at least, that Hardrada exceeded seven feet, since (as Laing remarks in the same note), and as we shall see hereafter, " our English Harold offered him, according to both English and Danish authority, seven feet of land for a grave, or *as much more* as his stature, exceeding that of other men, might require."

[2] Snorro Sturleson. See Note Q.   [3] Snorro Sturleson.

ships. Strange indeed it were if thou, who hast been fighting fifteen years for the petty kingdom of Denmark, shouldst
hesitate now, when all England lies before thee to seize."

"I hesitate," replied the king, "because he whom Fortune
has befriended so long, should beware how he strain her
favours too far. Eighteen pitched battles fought I in the
Saracen land, and in every one was a victor; never, at home
or abroad, have I known shame and defeat. Doth the wind
always blow from one point; and is Fate less unstable than
the wind?"

"Now, out on thee, Harold Hardrada," said Tostig the
fierce; "the good pilot wins his way through all winds, and
the brave heart fastens fate to its flag. All men allow that
the North never had warrior like thee; and now, in the mid-
day of manhood, wilt thou consent to repose on the mere
triumph of youth?"

"Nay," said the king, who, like all true poets, had something of the deep sense of a sage, and was, indeed, regarded
as the most prudent as well as the most adventurous chief in
the Northland, — "nay, it is not by such words, which my
soul seconds too well, that thou canst entrap a ruler of men.
Thou must show me the chances of success, as thou wouldst
to a graybeard. For we should be as old men before we engage, and as youths when we wish to perform."

Then the traitor succinctly detailed all the weak points in
the rule of his brother, — a treasury exhausted by the lavish
and profitless waste of Edward; a land without castle or bulwark, even at the mouths of the rivers; a people grown inert
by long peace, and so accustomed to own lord and king in the
northern invaders, that a single successful battle might induce
half the population to insist on the Saxon coming to terms
with the foe, and yielding, as Ironsides did to Canute, one
half of the realm. He enlarged on the terror of the Norsemen that still existed throughout England, and the affinity
between the Northumbrians and East Anglians with the race
of Hardrada. That affinity would not prevent them from resisting at the first; but grant success, and it would reconcile
them to the after sway. And, finally, he aroused Hardrada's

emulation by the spur of the news that the Count of the Normans would seize the prize if he himself delayed to forestall him.

These various representations, and the remembrance of Canute's victory, decided Hardrada; and when Tostig ceased, he stretched his hand towards his slumbering war-ships and exclaimed: —

"Eno'; you have whetted the beaks of the ravens, and harnessed the steeds of the sea!"

———◆———

CHAPTER VII.

MEANWHILE, King Harold of England had made himself dear to his people, and been true to the fame he had won as Harold the Earl. From the moment of his accession, "he showed himself pious, humble, and affable,[1] and omitted no occasions to show any token of bounteous liberality, gentleness, and courteous behaviour." "The grievous customs, also, and taxes which his predecessors had raised, he either abolished or diminished; the ordinary wages of his servants and men-of-war he increased, and further showed himself very well bent to all virtue and goodness."[2]

Extracting the pith from these eulogies, it is clear that, as wise statesman no less than as good king, Harold sought to strengthen himself in the three great elements of regal power, — Conciliation of the Church, which had been opposed to his father; the popular affection, on which his sole claim to the crown reposed; and the military force of the land, which had been neglected in the reign of his peaceful predecessor.

To the young Atheling he accorded a respect not before paid to him; and, while investing the descendant of the ancient

[1] Hoveden.

[2] Holinshed. Nearly all chroniclers (even, with scarce an exception, those most favouring the Normans) concur in the abilities and merits of Harold as a king.

line with princely state, and endowing him with large
domains, his soul, too great for jealousy, sought to give
more substantial power to his own most legitimate rival, by
tender care and noble counsels, by efforts to raise a character
feeble by nature, and denationalized by foreign rearing. In
the same broad and generous policy, Harold encouraged all
the merchants from other countries who had settled in England; nor were even such Normans as had escaped the general
sentence of banishment on Godwin's return disturbed in their
possessions.   "In brief," saith the Anglo-Norman chronicler,[1]
"no man was more prudent in the land, more valiant in arms,
in the law more sagacious, in all probity more accomplished:"
and "Ever active," says more mournfully the Saxon writer,
"for the good of his country, he spared himself no fatigue by
land or by sea." [2]

From this time Harold's private life ceased.   Love and its
charms were no more.   The glow of romance had vanished.
He was not one man; he was the state, the representative, the
incarnation of Saxon England: his sway and the Saxon freedom to live or fall together!

The soul really grand is only tested in its errors.   As we
know the true might of the intellect by the rich resources and
patient strength with which it redeems a failure, so do we
prove the elevation of the soul by its courageous return into
light, its instinctive rebound into higher air, after some error
that has darkened its vision and soiled its plumes.   A spirit
less noble and pure than Harold's, once entering on the dismal
world of enchanted superstition, had habituated itself to that
nether atmosphere; once misled from hardy truth and healthful reason, it had plunged deeper and deeper into the maze.
But, unlike his contemporary, Macbeth, the Man escaped
from the lures of the Fiend.   Not as Hecate in hell, but as
Dian in heaven, did he confront the pale Goddess of Night.
Before that hour in which he had deserted the human judgment for the ghostly delusion; before that day in which the
brave heart, in its sudden desertion, had humbled his pride,
the man, in his nature, was more strong than the god.   Now,

[1] Vit. Harold. Chron. Ang. Norm. ii. 243.   [2] Hoveden.

purified by the flame that had scorched, and more nerved from the fall that had stunned, that great soul rose sublime through the wrecks of the Past, serene through the clouds of the Future, concentring in its solitude the destinies of Mankind, and strong with instinctive Eternity amidst all the terrors of Time.

King Harold came from York, — whither he had gone to cement the new power of Morcar, in Northumbria, and personally to confirm the allegiance of the Anglo-Danes, — King Harold came from York, and in the halls of Westminster he found a monk who awaited him with the messages of William the Norman.

Bare-footed and serge-garbed, the Norman envoy strode to the Saxon's chair of state. His form was worn with mortification and fast, and his face was hueless and livid, with the perpetual struggle between zeal and the flesh.

"Thus saith William, Count of the Normans," began Hugues Maigrot, the monk: "With grief and amaze hath he heard that you, O Harold, his sworn liegeman, have, contrary to oath and to fealty, assumed the crown that belongs to himself. But, confiding in thy conscience, and forgiving a moment's weakness, he summons thee, mildly and brother-like, to fulfil thy vow. Send thy sister, that he may give her in marriage to one of his quens; give him up the stronghold of Dover; march to thy coast with thine armies to aid him, — thy liege lord, — and secure him the heritage of Edward his cousin. And thou shalt reign at his right hand, his daughter thy bride, Northumbria thy fief, and the saints thy protectors."

The king's lip was firm, though pale, as he answered: —

"My young sister, alas! is no more. Seven nights after I ascended the throne, she died; her dust in the grave is all I could send to the arms of the bridegroom. I cannot wed the child of thy count; the wife of Harold sits beside him." And he pointed to the proud beauty of Aldyth, enthroned under the drapery of gold. "For the vow that I took, I deny it not. But from a vow of compulsion, menaced with unworthy captivity, extorted from my lips by the very need of the land whose freedom had been bound in my chains, — from a vow so compelled, Church and conscience absolve me. If the vow of a maiden on whom to bestow but her hand, when unknown to her parents, is judged invalid by the Church, how much more invalid the oath that would bestow on a stranger the fates of a nation,[1] against its knowledge and unconsulting its laws! This royalty of England hath ever rested on the will of the people, declared through its chiefs in their solemn assembly. They alone who could bestow it, have bestowed it on me. I have no power to resign it to another; and were I in my grave, the trust of the crown would not pass to the Norman, but return to the Saxon people."

"Is this, then, thy answer, unhappy son?" said the monk, with a sullen and gloomy aspect.

"Such is my answer."

"Then, sorrowing for thee, I utter the words of William. 'With sword and with mail will he come to punish the perjurer; and by the aid of Saint Michael, archangel of war, he will conquer his own.' Amen."

"By sea and by land, with sword and with mail, will we meet the invader," answered the king, with a flashing eye. "Thou hast said: — so depart."

The monk turned and withdrew.

"Let the priest's insolence chafe thee not, sweet lord," said Aldyth. "For the vow which thou mightest take as subject, what matters it now thou art king?"

Harold made no answer to Aldyth, but turned to his chamberlain, who stood behind his throne chair.

"Are my brothers without?"

"They are; and my lord the king's chosen council."

"Admit them. Pardon, Aldyth; affairs fit only for men claim me now."

The Lady of England took the hint, and rose.

"But the even-mete will summon thee soon," said she.

Harold, who had already descended from his chair of state, and was bending over a casket of papers on the table, replied, —

[1] Malmesbury.

"There is food *here* till the morrow; wait me not."

Aldyth sighed, and withdrew at the one door, while the thegns most in Harold's confidence entered at the other. But, once surrounded by her maidens, Aldyth forgot all, save that she was again a queen, — forgot all, even to the earlier and less gorgeous diadem which her lord's hand had shattered on the brows of the son of Pen Dragon.

Leofwine, still gay and blithe-hearted, entered first; Gurth followed; then Haco, then some half-score of the greater thegns.

They seated themselves at the table, and Gurth spoke first, —

"Tostig has been with Count William."

"I know it," said Harold.

"It is rumoured that he has passed to our uncle Sweyn."

"I foresaw it," said the king.

"And that Sweyn will aid him to reconquer England for the Dane."

"My bode reached Sweyn, with letters from Githa, before Tostig; my bode has returned this day. Sweyn has dismissed Tostig; Sweyn will send fifty ships, armed with picked men, to the aid of England."

"Brother," cried Leofwine, admiringly, "thou providest against danger ere we but surmise it."

"Tostig," continued the king, unheeding the compliment, "will be the first assailant: him we must meet. His fast friend is Malcolm of Scotland: him we must secure. Go thou, Leofwine, with these letters to Malcolm. The next fear is from the Welch. Go thou, Edwin of Mercia, to the princes of Wales. On thy way, strengthen the forts and deepen the dikes of the Marches. These tablets hold thy instructions. The Norman, as doubtless ye know, my thegns, hath sent to demand our crown, and hath announced the coming of his war. With the dawn I depart to our port at Sandwich,[1] to muster our fleets. Thou with me, Gurth."

"These preparations need much treasure," said an old thegn, "and thou hast lessened the taxes at the hour of need."

[1] Supposed to be our first port for shipbuilding. — FOSBROOKE, p. 320.

"Not yet is it the hour of need. When it comes, our people will the more readily meet it with their gold as with their iron. There was great wealth in the House of Godwin; that wealth mans the ships of England. What has thou there, Haco?"

"Thy new-issued coin: it hath on its reverse the word ' PEACE.'"[1]

Who ever saw one of those coins of the Last Saxon King, the bold simple head on the one side, that single word "Peace" on the other, and did not feel awed and touched? What pathos in that word compared with the fate which it failed to propitiate!

"Peace," said Harold: "to all that doth not render peace, slavery. Yea, may I live to leave peace to our children! Now, peace only rests on our preparation for war. You, Morcar, will return with all speed to York, and look well to the mouth of the Humber."

Then, turning to each of the thegns successively, he gave to each his post and his duty; and that done, converse grew more general. The many things needful that had been long rotting in neglect under the monk-king, and now sprung up, craving instant reform, occupied them long and anxiously; but cheered and inspirited by the vigour and foresight of Harold, whose earlier slowness of character seemed winged by the occasion into rapid decision (as is not uncommon with the Englishman), all difficulties seemed light, and hope and courage were in every breast.

CHAPTER VIII.

BACK went Hugues Maigrot, the monk, to William, and told the reply of Harold to the duke, in the presence of Lanfranc. William himself heard it in gloomy silence, for Fitz-

[1] *Pax.*

osborne as yet had been wholly unsuccessful in stirring up the Norman barons to an expedition so hazardous, in a cause so doubtful; and though prepared for the defiance of Harold, the duke was not prepared with the means to enforce his threats and make good his claim.

So great was his abstraction, that he suffered the Lombard to dismiss the monk without a word spoken by him; and he was first startled from his revery by Lanfranc's pale hand on his vast shoulder, and Lanfranc's low voice in his dreamy ear,—

"Up! Hero of Europe; for thy cause is won! Up! and write with thy bold characters, bold as if graved with the point of the sword, my credentials to Rome. Let me depart ere the sun sets; and as I go, look on the sinking orb, and behold the sun of the Saxon that sets evermore on England!"

Then briefly, that ablest statesman of the age (and forgive him, despite our modern lights, we must; for, sincere son of the Church, he regarded the violated oath of Harold as entailing the legitimate forfeiture of his realm, and, ignorant of true political freedom, looked upon Church and Learning as the only civilizers of men),—then briefly Lanfranc detailed to the listening Norman the outline of the arguments by which he intended to move the Pontifical court to the Norman side; and enlarged upon the vast accession throughout all Europe which the solemn sanction of the Church would bring to his strength. William's re-awaking and ready intellect soon seized upon the importance of the object pressed upon him. He interrupted the Lombard, drew pen and parchment towards him, and wrote rapidly. Horses were harnessed, horsemen equipped in haste, and with no unfitting retinue Lanfranc departed on the mission, the most important in its consequences that ever passed from potentate to pontiff.[1] Rebraced to its purpose by Lanfranc's cheering assurances,

---

[1] Some of the Norman chroniclers state that Robert, Archbishop of Canterbury, who had been expelled from England at Godwin's return, was Lanfranc's companion in this mission; but more trustworthy authorities assure us that Robert had been dead some years before, not long surviving his return into Normandy.

the resolute, indomitable soul of William now applied itself, night and day, to the difficult task of rousing his haughty vavasours. Yet weeks passed before he could even meet a select council composed of his own kinsmen and most trusted lords. These, however, privately won over, promised to serve him "with body and goods." But one and all they told him he must gain the consent of the whole principality in a general council. That council was convened: thither came not only lords and knights, but merchants and traders,— all the rising middle class of a thriving State.

The duke bared his wrongs, his claims, and his schemes. The assembly would not or did not discuss the matter in his presence, they would not be awed by its influence; and William retired from the hall. Various were the opinions, stormy the debate; and so great the disorder grew, that Fitzosborne, rising in the midst, exclaimed,—

"Why this dispute; why this unduteous discord? Is not William your lord? Hath he not need of you? Fail him now,— and you know him well — by God, he will remember it! Aid him, and — you know him well — large are his rewards to service and love!"

Up rose at once baron and merchant; and when at last their spokesman was chosen, that spokesman said,—

"William is our lord; is it not enough to pay to our lord his dues? No aid do we owe beyond the seas! Sore harassed and taxed are we already by his wars! Let him fail in this strange and unparalleled hazard, and our land is undone!"

Loud applause followed this speech; the majority of the council were against the duke.

"Then," said Fitzosborne, craftily, "I, who know the means of each man present, will, with your leave, represent your necessities to your count, and make such modest offer of assistance as may please ye, yet not chafe your liege."

Into the trap of this proposal the opponents fell; and Fitzosborne, at the head of the body, returned to William.

The Lord of Breteuil approached the daïs, on which William sat alone, his great sword in his hand, and thus spoke,—

"My liege, I may well say that never prince had people more leal than yours, nor that have more proved their faith and love by the burdens they have borne and the moneys they have granted."

A universal murmur of applause followed these words. "Good! good!" almost shouted the merchants especially. William's brows met, and he looked very terrible. The Lord of Breteuil gracefully waved his hand, and resumed,—

"Yea, my liege, much have they borne for your glory and need; much more will they bear."

The faces of the audience fell.

"Their service does not compel them to aid you beyond the seas."

The faces of the audience brightened.

"But now they *will* aid you, in the land of the Saxon as in that of the Frank."

"How?" cried a stray voice or two.

"Hush, O *gentilz amys*. Forward, then, O my liege, and spare them in nought. He who has hitherto supplied you with two good mounted soldiers will now grant you four; and he who — "

"No, no, no!" roared two thirds of the assembly; "we charged you with no such answer; we said not that, nor that shall it be!"

Out stepped a baron.

"Within this country, to defend it, we will serve our count; but to aid him to conquer another man's country, no!"

Out stepped a knight.

"If once we rendered this double service, beyond seas as at home, it would be held a right and a custom hereafter; and we should be as mercenary soldiers, not free-born Normans."

Out stepped a merchant.

"And we and our children would be burdened forever to feed one man's ambition, whenever he saw a king to dethrone, or a realm to seize."

And then cried a general chorus,—

"It shall not be,— it shall not!"

The assembly broke at once into knots of tens, twenties, thirties, gesticulating and speaking aloud, like freemen in anger; and ere William, with all his prompt dissimulation, could do more than smother his rage, and sit griping his sword-hilt, and setting his teeth, the assembly dispersed.

Such were the free souls of the Normans under the greatest of their chiefs; and had those souls been less free, England had not been enslaved in one age, to become free again, God grant, to the end of time!

CHAPTER IX.

THROUGH the blue skies over England there rushed the bright stranger, — a meteor, a comet, a fiery star! "such as no man before ever saw;" it appeared on the 8th, before the kalends of May; seven nights did it shine,[1] and the faces of sleepless men were pale under the angry glare.

The river of Thames rushed blood-red in the beam; the winds at play on the broad waves of the Humber broke the surge of the billows into sparkles of fire. With three streamers, sharp and long as the sting of a dragon, the foreboder of wrath rushed through the hosts of the stars. On every ruinous fort, by seacoast and march, the warder crossed his breast to behold it; on hill and in thoroughfare, crowds nightly assembled to gaze on the terrible star. Muttering hymns, monks huddled together round the altars, as if to exorcise the land of a demon. The gravestone of the Saxon father-chief was lit up, as with the coil of the lightning; and the Morthwyrtha looked from the mound, and saw in her visions of awe the Valkyrs in the train of the fiery star.

On the roof of his palace stood Harold the King, and with folded arms he looked on the Rider of Night; and up the stairs of the turret came the soft steps of Haco, and stealing near to the king, he said, —

[1] Saxon Chronicle

"Arm in haste, for the bodes have come breathless to tell thee that Tostig, thy brother, with pirate and war-ship, is wasting thy shores and slaughtering thy people!"

CHAPTER X.

Tostig, with the ships he had gained both from Norman and Norwegian, recruited by Flemish adventurers, fled fast from the banners of Harold. After plundering the Isle of Wight and the Hampshire coasts, he sailed up the Humber, where his vain heart had counted on friends yet left him in his ancient earldom; but Harold's soul of vigour was everywhere. Morcar, prepared by the king's bodes, encountered and chased the traitor, and, deserted by most of his ships, with but twelve small craft Tostig gained the shores of Scotland. There, again forestalled by the Saxon King, he failed in succour from Malcolm, and retreating to the Orkneys, waited the fleets of Hardrada.

And now Harold, thus at freedom for defence against a foe more formidable and less unnatural, hastened to make secure both the sea and the coast against William the Norman. "So great a ship force, so great a land force, no king in the land had before." All the summer, his fleets swept the channel; his forces "lay everywhere by the sea."

But alas! now came the time when the improvident waste of Edward began to be felt. Provisions and pay for the armaments failed.[1] On the defective resources at Harold's disposal, no modern historian hath sufficiently dwelt. The last Saxon king, the chosen of the people, had not those levies, and could impose not those burdens, which made his successors mighty in war; and men began now to think that, after all, there was no fear of this Norman invasion. The summer was gone; the autumn was come; was it likely that William

---

[1] "When it was the nativity of Saint Mary, then were the men's provisions gone, and no man could any longer keep them there." — *Saxon Chronicle.*

would dare to trust himself in an enemy's country as the winter drew near? The Saxons, unlike their fiercer kindred of Scandinavia, had no pleasure in war; they fought well in front of a foe, but they loathed the tedious preparations and costly sacrifices which prudence demanded for self-defence. They now revolted from a strain upon their energies, of the necessity of which they were not convinced! Joyous at the temporary defeat of Tostig, men said, "Marry, a joke indeed, that the Norman will put his shaven head into the hornets' nest! Let him come, if he dare!"

Still, with desperate effort, and at much risk of popularity, Harold held together a force sufficient to repel any *single* invader. From the time of his accession his sleepless vigilance had kept watch on the Norman, and his spies brought him news of all that passed.

And now what had passed in the councils of William? The abrupt disappointment which the Grand Assembly had occasioned him did not last very long. Made aware that he could not trust to the spirit of an assembly, William now artfully summoned merchant and knight and baron, one by one. Submitted to the eloquence, the promises, the craft, of that master intellect, and to the awe of that imposing presence; unassisted by the courage which inferiors take from numbers, one by one yielded to the will of the count, and subscribed his quota for moneys, for ships, and for men. And while this went on, Lanfranc was at work in the Vatican. At that time the Archdeacon of the Roman Church was the famous Hildebrand. This extraordinary man, fit fellow-spirit to Lanfranc, nursed one darling project, the success of which indeed founded the true temporal power of the Roman pontiffs. It was no less than that of converting the mere religious ascendancy of the Holy See into the actual sovereignty over the States of Christendom. The most immediate agents of this gigantic scheme were the Normans, who had conquered Naples by the arm of the adventurer Robert Guiscard, and under the gonfanon of Saint Peter. Most of the new Norman countships and dukedoms thus created in Italy had declared themselves fiefs of the Church; and the successor of the Apostle might well hope, by aid of the Norman priest-knights, to extend his sovereignty over Italy, and thence dictate to the kings beyond the Alps.

The aid of Hildebrand in behalf of William's claims was obtained at once by Lanfranc. The profound Archdeacon of Rome saw at a glance the immense power that would accrue to the Church by the mere act of arrogating to itself the disposition of crowns, subjecting rival princes to abide by its decision, and fixing the men of its choice on the thrones of the North. Despite all its slavish superstition, the Saxon Church was obnoxious to Rome. Even the pious Edward had offended, by withholding the old levy of Peter Pence; and simony, a crime peculiarly reprobated by the pontiff, was notorious in England. Therefore there was much to aid Hildebrand in the Assembly of the Cardinals, when he brought before them the oath of Harold, the violation of the sacred relics, and demanded that the pious Normans, true friends to the Roman Church, should be permitted to Christianize the barbarous Saxons,[1] and William be nominated as heir to a throne promised to him by Edward, and forfeited by the perjury of Harold. Nevertheless, to the honour of that assembly, and of man, there was a holy opposition to this wholesale barter of human rights, — this sanction of an armed onslaught on a Christian people. "It is infamous," said the good, "to authorize homicide." But Hildebrand was all-powerful, and prevailed.

William was at high feast with his barons when Lanfranc dismounted at his gates and entered his hall.

"Hail to thee, King of England!" he said. "I bring the bull that excommunicates Harold and his adherents; I bring to thee the gift of the Roman Church, the land and royalty of

---

[1] It is curious to notice how England was represented as a country almost heathen; its conquest was regarded quite as a pious, benevolent act of charity, — a sort of mission for converting the savages. And all this while England was under the most slavish ecclesiastical domination, and the priesthood possessed a third of its land! But the heart of England never forgave that league of the Pope with the Conqueror, and the seeds of the Reformed Religion were trampled deep into the Saxon soil by the feet of the invading Norman.

England. I bring to thee the gonfanon hallowed by the heir of the Apostle, and the very ring that contains the precious relic of the Apostle himself! Now who will shrink from thy side? Publish thy ban, not in Normandy alone, but in every region and realm where the Church is honoured. This is the first war of the CROSS."

Then indeed was it seen,—that might of the Church! Soon as were made known the sanction and gifts of the Pope, all the Continent stirred as to the blast of the trump in the Crusade, of which that war was the herald. From Maine and from Anjou, from Poitou and Bretagne, from France and from Flanders, from Aquitaine and Burgundy, flashed the spear, galloped the steed. The robber-chiefs from the castles now gray on the Rhine; the hunters and bandits from the roots of the Alps; baron and knight, varlet and vagrant, — all came to the flag of the Church, — to the pillage of England. For side by side with the Pope's holy bull was the martial ban: "Good pay and broad lands to every one who will serve Count William with spear and with sword and with cross-bow." And the duke said to Fitzosborne, as he parcelled out the fair fields of England into Norman fiefs, —

"Harold hath not the strength of mind to promise the least of those things that belong to me. But I have the right to promise that which is mine, and also that which belongs to him. He must be the victor who can give away both his own and what belongs to his foe."[1]

All on the continent of Europe regarded England's king as accursed, William's enterprise as holy; and mothers who had turned pale when their sons went forth to the boar-chase, sent their darlings to enter their names, for the weal of their souls, in the swollen muster-roll of William the Norman. Every port now in Neustria was busy with terrible life; in every wood was heard the axe felling logs for the ships; from every anvil flew the sparks from the hammer, as iron took shape into helmet and sword. All things seemed to favour

---

[1] William of Poitiers. — The naïve sagacity of this bandit argument, and the Norman's contempt for Harold's deficiency in "strength of mind," are exquisite illustrations of character.

the Church's chosen one. Conan, Count of Bretagne, sent to claim the Duchy of Normandy, as legitimate heir. A few days afterwards, Conan died, poisoned (as had died his father before him) by the mouth of his horn and the web of his gloves; and the new Count of Bretagne sent his sons to take part against Harold.

All the armament mustered at the roadstead of St. Valery, at the mouth of the Somme. But the winds were long hostile, and the rains fell in torrents.

CHAPTER XI.

AND now, while war thus hungered for England at the mouth of the Somme, the last and most renowned of the sea-kings, Harold Hardrada, entered his galley, the tallest and strongest of a fleet of three hundred sail, that peopled the seas round Solundir. And a man named Gyrdir, on board the king's ship, dreamed a dream.[1] He saw a great witch-wife standing on an isle of the Sulen, with a fork in one hand and a trough in the other.[2] He saw her pass over the whole fleet; by each of the three hundred ships he saw her; and a fowl sat on the stern of each ship, and that fowl was a raven; and he heard the witch-wife sing this song: —

> "From the East I allure him,
>   At the West I secure him;
>   In the feast I foresee
>   Rare the relics for me;
>   Red the drink, white the bones.

---

[1] Snorro Sturleson.

[2] Does any Scandinavian scholar know why the trough was so associated with the images of Scandinavian witchcraft? A witch was known, when seen behind, by a kind of trough-like shape; there must be some symbol, of very ancient mythology, in this superstition.

"The ravens sit greeding,
  And watching, and heeding;
Thoro' wind, over water,
Comes scent of the slaughter,
And ravens sit greeding
  Their share of the bones.

"Thoro' wind, thoro' weather,
  We're sailing together;
I sail with the ravens;
I watch with the ravens;
I snatch from the ravens
  My share of the bones."

There was also a man called Thord,[1] in a ship that lay near the king's; and he too dreamed a dream. He saw the fleet nearing land, and that land was England. And on the land was a battle-array twofold, and many banners were flapping on both sides. And before the army of the land-folk was riding a huge witch-wife upon a wolf; the wolf had a man's carcass in his mouth, and the blood was dripping and dropping from his jaws; and when the wolf had eaten up that carcass, the witch-wife threw another into his jaws; and so, one after another; and the wolf cranched and swallowed them all. And the witch-wife sang this song:—

"The green waving fields
  Are hidden behind,
The flash of the shields,
And the rush of the banners
  That toss in the wind.

"But Skade's eagle eyes
  Pierce the wall of the steel,
And behold from the skies
  What the earth would conceal;
O'er the rush of the banners
  She poises her wing,
And marks with a shadow
  The brow of the king.

---

[1] Snorro Sturleson.

"And, in bode of his doom,
Jaw of Wolf, be the tomb
Of the bones and the flesh,
Gore-bedabbled and fresh,
That cranch and that drip
Under fang and from lip,
As I ride in the van
Of the feasters on man,
  With the king!

"Grim wolf, sate thy maw,
  Full enow shall there be,
Hairy jaw, hungry maw,
  Both for ye and for me!

"Meaner food be the feast
Of the fowl and the beast;
But the witch, for her share,
Takes the best of the fare;
And the witch shall be fed
With the king of the dead,
When she rides in the van
Of the slayers of man,
  With the king."

And King Harold dreamed a dream. And he saw before him his brother, Saint Olave. And the dead to the Scald-King sang this song:—

"Bold as thou in the fight,
  Blithe as thou in the hall,
Shone the noon of my might,
  Ere the night of my fall!

"How humble is death,
  And how haughty is life;
And how fleeting the breath
  Between slumber and strife!

"All the earth is too narrow,
  O life, for thy tread!
Two strides o'er the barrow
  Can measure the dead.

"Yet mighty that space is
  Which seemeth so small;
The realm of all races,
  With room for them all!"

But Harold Hardrada scorned witch-wife and dream; and his fleets sailed on. Tostig joined him off the Orkney Isles, and this great armament soon came in sight of the shores of England. They landed at Cleveland,[1] and at the dread of the terrible Norsemen, the coastmen fled or submitted. With booty and plunder they sailed on to Scarborough; but there the townsfolk were brave, and the walls were strong. The Norsemen ascended a hill above the town, lit a huge pile of wood, and tossed the burning piles down on the roofs. House after house caught the flame, and through the glare and the crash rushed the men of Hardrada. Great was the slaughter, and ample the plunder; and the town, awed and depeopled, submitted to flame and to sword.

Then the fleet sailed up the Humber and Ouse, and landed at Richall, not far from York; but Morcar, the Earl of Northumbria, came out with all his forces,—all the stout men and tall of the great race of the Anglo-Dane.

Then Hardrada advanced his flag, called Land-Eyda, the "Ravager of the World," [2] and, chanting a war-stave, led his men to the onslaught.

The battle was fierce, but short. The English troops were defeated, they fled into York; and the Ravager of the World was borne in triumph to the gates of the town. An exiled chief, however tyrannous and hateful, hath ever some friends among the desperate and lawless; and success ever finds allies among the weak and the craven,— so many Northumbrians now came to the side of Tostig. Dissension and mutiny broke out amidst the garrison within; Morcar, unable to control the townsfolk, was driven forth with those still true to their country and king, and York agreed to open its gates to the conquering invader.

At the news of this foe on the north side of the land, King Harold was compelled to withdraw all the forces at watch in the south against the tardy invasion of William. It was the

---

[1] Snorro Sturleson.

[2] So Thierry translates the word : others, the Land-ravager. In Danish, the word is Land-ode, in Icelandic, Land-eydo. — Note to Thierry's " Hist. of the Conq. of England," book iii. vol. vi. p. 169 (of Hazlitt's translation).

middle of September; eight months had elapsed since the Norman had launched forth his vaunting threat. Would he now dare to come? Come or not, *that* foe was afar, and *this* was in the heart of the country!

Now, York having thus capitulated, all the land round was humbled and awed; and Hardrada and Tostig were blithe and gay; and many days, thought they, must pass ere Harold the King can come from the south to the north.

The camp of the Norsemen was at Stanford Bridge, and that day it was settled that they should formally enter York. Their ships lay in the river beyond; a large portion of the armament was with the ships. The day was warm, and the men with Hardrada had laid aside their heavy mail and were "making merry," talking of the plunder of York, jeering at Saxon valour, and gloating over thoughts of the Saxon maids, whom Saxon men had failed to protect, when suddenly between them and the town rose and rolled a great cloud of dust. High it rose, and fast it rolled, and from the heart of the cloud shone the spear and the shield.

"What army comes yonder?" said Harold Hardrada.

"Surely," answered Tostig, "it comes from the town that we are to enter as conquerors, and can be but the friendly Northumbrians who have deserted Morcar for me."

Nearer and nearer came the force, and the shine of the arms was like the glancing of ice.

"Advance the World-Ravager!" cried Harold Hardrada, "draw up, and to arms!"

Then, picking out three of his briskest youths, he despatched them to the force on the river with orders to come up quick to the aid. For already, through the cloud and amidst the spears, was seen the flag of the English King. On the previous night King Harold had entered York, unknown to the invaders, appeased the mutiny, cheered the townsfolks; and now came like a thunderbolt borne by the winds, to clear the air of England from the clouds of the North.

Both armaments drew up in haste, and Hardrada formed his array in the form of a circle, — the line long but not

deep, the wings curving round till they met,[1] shield to shield.
Those who stood in the first rank set their spear-shafts on
the ground, the points level with the breast of a horseman;
those in the second, with spears yet lower, level with the
breast of a horse; thus forming a double palisade against the
charge of cavalry. In the centre of this circle was placed
the Ravager of the World, and round it a rampart of shields.
Behind that rampart was the accustomed post at the onset
of battle for the king and his body-guard. But Tostig was
in front, with his own Northumbrian lion banner, and his
chosen men.

While this army was thus being formed, the English King
was marshalling his force in the far more formidable tactics,
which his military science had perfected from the warfare of
the Danes. That form of battalion, invincible hitherto under
his leadership, was in the manner of a wedge, or triangle,
thus $\triangle$. So that, in attack, the men marched on the foe pre-
senting the smallest possible surface to the missives, and, in
defence, all three lines faced the assailants. King Harold
cast his eye over the closing lines, and then, turning to
Gurth, who rode by his side, said,—

"Take one man from yon hostile army, and with what joy
should we charge on the Northmen!"

"I conceive thee," answered Gurth, mournfully, "and the
same thought of that one man makes my arm feel palsied."

The king mused, and drew down the nasal bar of his
helmet.

"Thegns," said he suddenly, to the score of riders who
grouped round him, "follow." And shaking the rein of his
horse, King Harold rode straight to that part of the hostile
front from which rose, above the spears, the Northumbrian
banner of Tostig. Wondering, but mute, the twenty thegns
followed him. Before the grim array, and hard by Tostig's
banner, the king checked his steed and cried,—

"Is Tostig, the son of Godwin and Githa, by the flag of the
Northumbrian earldom?"

With his helmet raised, and his Norwegian mantle flowing

---

[1] Snorro Sturleson.

over his mail, Earl Tostig rode forth at that voice, and came up to the speaker.[1]

"What wouldst thou with me, daring foe?"

The Saxon horseman paused, and his deep voice trembled tenderly, as he answered slowly, —

"Thy brother, King Harold, sends to salute thee. Let not the sons from the same womb wage unnatural war in the soil of their fathers."

"What will Harold the King give to his brother?" answered Tostig. "Northumbria already he hath bestowed on the son of his House's foe."

The Saxon hesitated, and a rider by his side took up the word.

"If the Northumbrians will receive thee again, Northumbria shalt thou have, and the king will bestow his late earldom of Wessex on Morcar; if the Northumbrians reject thee, thou shalt have all the lordships which King Harold hath promised to Gurth."

"This is well," answered Tostig; and he seemed to pause as in doubt, — when, made aware of this parley, King Harold Hardrada, on his coal-black steed, with his helm all shining with gold, rode from the lines, and came into hearing.

"Ha!" said Tostig, then turning round, as the giant form of the Norse King threw its vast shadow over the ground. "And if I take the offer, what will Harold son of Godwin give to my friend and ally Hardrada of Norway?"

The Saxon rider reared his head at these words, and gazed on the large front of Hardrada, as he answered, loud and distinct, —

"Seven feet of land for a grave, or, seeing that he is taller than other men, as much more as his corse may demand!"

"Then go back, and tell Harold my brother to get ready for battle; for never shall the Scalds and the warriors of Norway say that Tostig lured their king in his cause, to be-

---

[1] See Snorro Sturleson for this parley between Harold in *person* and Tostig. The account differs from the Saxon chroniclers, but in this particular instance is likely to be as accurate.

tray him to his foe. Here did he come, and here came I, to win as the brave win, or die as the brave die! "

A rider of younger and slighter form than the rest here whispered the Saxon king,—

"Delay no more, or thy men's hearts will fear treason."

"The tie is rent from my heart, O Haco," answered the king, "and the heart flies back to our England."

He waved his hand, turned his steed, and rode off. The eye of Hardrada followed the horseman.

"And who," he asked calmly, "is that man who spoke so well? " [1]

"King Harold! " answered Tostig, briefly.

"How! " cried the Norseman, reddening, "how was not that made known to me before? Never should he have gone back,— never told hereafter the doom of this day! "

With all his ferocity, his envy, his grudge to Harold, and his treason to England, some rude notions of honour still lay confused in the breast of the Saxon; and he answered stoutly,—

"Imprudent was Harold's coming, and great his danger; but he came to offer me peace and dominion. Had I betrayed him, I had not been his foe, but his murderer! "

The Norse King smiled approvingly, and, turning to his chiefs, said dryly,—

"That man was shorter than some of us, but he rode firm in his stirrups."

And then this extraordinary person, who united in himself all the types of an age that vanished forever in his grave, and who is the more interesting, as in him we see the race from which the Norman sprang, began, in the rich full voice that pealed deep as an organ, to chant his impromptu war-song. He halted in the midst, and with great composure said,—

"That verse is but ill-tuned: I must try a better." [1]

He passed his hand over his brow, mused an instant, and then, with his fair face all illumined, he burst forth as inspired.

This time, air, rhythm, words, all so chimed in with his

[1] Snorro Sturleson.

own enthusiasm and that of his men, that the effect was inexpressible. It was, indeed, like the charm of those runes which are said to have maddened the Berserker with the frenzy of war.

Meanwhile the Saxon phalanx came on, slow and firm, and in a few minutes the battle began. It commenced first with the charge of the English cavalry (never numerous), led by Leofwine and Haco, but the double palisade of the Norsemen's spears formed an impassable barrier; and the horsemen, recoiling from the frieze, rode round the iron circle without other damage than the spear and javelin could effect. Meanwhile, King Harold, who had dismounted, marched, as was his wont, with the body of footmen. He kept his post in the hollow of the triangular wedge, whence he could best issue his orders. Avoiding the side over which Tostig presided, he halted his array in full centre of the enemy, where the Ravager of the World, streaming high above the inner rampart of shields, showed the presence of the giant Hardrada.

The air was now literally darkened with the flights of arrows and spears; and in a war of missiles, the Saxons were less skilled than the Norsemen. Still King Harold restrained the ardour of his men, who, sore harassed by the darts, yearned to close on the foe. He himself, standing on a little eminence, more exposed than his meanest soldier, deliberately eyed the sallies of the horse, and watched the moment he foresaw, when, encouraged by his own suspense and the feeble attacks of the cavalry, the Norsemen would lift their spears from the ground, and advance themselves to the assault. That moment came; unable to withhold their own fiery zeal, stimulated by the tromp and the clash, and the war hymns of their king and his choral Scalds, the Norsemen broke ground and came on.

"To your axes, and charge!" cried Harold; and passing at once from the centre to the front, he led on the array.

The impetus of that artful phalanx was tremendous; it pierced through the ring of the Norwegians; it clove into the rampart of shields; and King Harold's battle-axe was the first that shivered that wall of steel; his step the first that strode into the innermost circle that guarded the Ravager of the World.

Then forth, from under the shade of that great flag, came, himself also on foot, Harold Hardrada; shouting and chanting, he leaped with long strides into the thick of the onslaught. He had flung away his shield, and swaying with both hands his enormous sword, he hewed down man after man till space grew clear before him; and the English, recoiling in awe before an image of height and strength that seemed superhuman, left but one form standing firm, and in front, to oppose his way.

At that moment the whole strife seemed not to belong to an age comparatively modern,— it took a character of remotest eld; and Thor and Odin seemed to have returned to the earth. Behind this towering and Titan warrior, their wild hair streaming long under their helms, came his Scalds, all singing their hymns, drunk with the madness of battle. And the Ravager of the World tossed and flapped as it followed, so that the vast raven depicted on its folds seemed horrid with life. And calm and alone, his eye watchful, his axe lifted, his foot ready for rush or for spring — but firm as an oak against flight — stood the Last of the Saxon Kings.

Down bounded Hardrada, and down shore his sword; King Harold's shield was cloven in two, and the force of the blow brought himself to his knee. But as swift as the flash of that sword, he sprang to his feet; and while Hardrada still bowed his head, not recovered from the force of his blow, the axe of the Saxon came so full on his helmet, that the giant reeled, dropped his sword, and staggered back; his Scalds and his chiefs rushed around him. That gallant stand of King Harold saved his English from flight; and now, as they saw him almost lost in the throng, yet still cleaving his way — on, on — to the raven standard, they rallied with one heart, and shouting forth, "Out, out! Holy Crosse!" forced their way to his side, and the fight now waged hot and equal, hand to hand. Meanwhile Hardrada, borne a little apart, and relieved from his dinted helmet, recovered the shock of the weightiest blow that had ever dimmed his eye and numbed his hand. Tossing the helmet on the ground, his bright locks glittering like sunbeams, he rushed back to the *mêlée.* Again helm and mail went down before him; again through the crowd he saw the arm that had smitten him; again he sprang forwards to finish the war with a blow,— when a shaft from some distant bow pierced the throat which the casque now left bare; a sound like the wail of a death-song murmured brokenly from his lips, which then gushed out with blood, and tossing up his arms wildly, he fell to the ground, a corpse. At that sight, a yell of such terror and woe and wrath, all commingled, broke from the Norsemen, that it hushed the very war for the moment!

"On!" cried the Saxon king; "let our earth take its spoiler! On to the standard, and the day is our own!"

"On to the standard!" cried Haco, who, his horse slain under him, all bloody with wounds not his own, now came to the king's side. Grim and tall rose the standard, and the streamer shrieked and flapped in the wind as if the raven had voice, when, right before Harold, right between him and the banner, stood Tostig his brother, known by the splendour of his mail, the gold work on his mantle,— known by the fierce laugh and defying voice.

"What matters?" cried Haco; "strike, O King, for thy crown!"

Harold's hand griped Haco's arm convulsively; he lowered his axe, turned round, and passed shudderingly away.

Both armies now paused from the attack; for both were thrown into great disorder, and each gladly gave respite to the other, to re-form its own shattered array.

The Norsemen were not the soldiers to yield because their leader was slain,— rather the more resolute to fight, since revenge was now added to valour; yet, but for the daring and promptness with which Tostig had cut his way to the standard, the day had been already decided.

During the pause, Harold, summoning Gurth, said to him in great emotion, "For the sake of Nature, for the love of God, go, O Gurth,— go to Tostig; urge him, now Hardrada is dead, urge him to peace. All that we can proffer with

honour, proffer,— quarter and free retreat to every Norseman.[1] Oh, save me, save us, from a brother's blood!"

Gurth lifted his helmet, and kissed the mailed hand that
grasped his own.

"I go," said he. And so, bareheaded, and with a single
trumpeter, he went to the hostile lines.

Harold awaited him in great agitation; nor could any man
have guessed what bitter and awful thoughts lay in that
heart, from which, in the way to power, tie after tie had been
wrenched away. He did not wait long; and even before
Gurth rejoined him, he knew by a unanimous shout of fury,
to which the clash of countless shields chimed in, that the
mission had been in vain.

Tostig had refused to hear Gurth, save in presence of the
Norwegian chiefs; and when the message had been delivered,
they all cried, "We would rather fall one across the corpse of
the other [2] than leave a field in which our king was slain."

"Ye hear them," said Tostig; "as they speak, speak I."

"Not mine this guilt, *too*, O God!" said Harold, solemnly
lifting his hand on high. "Now, then, to duty!"

By this time the Norwegian reinforcements had arrived
from the ships, and this for a short time rendered the conflict
that immediately ensued uncertain and critical. But Harold's
generalship was now as consummate as his valour had been
daring. He kept his men true to their irrefragable line.
Even if fragments splintered off, each fragment threw itself
into the form of the resistless wedge. One Norwegian,
standing on the bridge of Stanford, long guarded that pass;
and no less than forty Saxons are said to have perished by
his arm. To him the English King sent a generous pledge,
not only of safety for the life, but honour for the valour.
The viking refused to surrender, and fell at last by a javelin
from the hand of Haco. As if in him had been embodied the
unyielding war-god of the Norsemen, in that death died the
last hope of the vikings. They fell literally where they
stood; many, from sheer exhaustion and the weight of their

[1] Sharon Turner's Anglo-Saxons, vol. ii. p. 396. Snorro Sturleson.
[2] Snorro Sturleson.

mail, died without a blow.[1] And in the shades of nightfall, Harold stood amidst the shattered rampart of shields, his foot on the corpse of the standard-bearer, his hand on the Ravager of the World.

"Thy brother's corpse is borne yonder," said Haco, in the ear of the king, as wiping the blood from his sword, he plunged it back into the sheath.

CHAPTER XII.

YOUNG OLAVE, the son of Hardrada, had happily escaped the slaughter. A strong detachment of the Norwegians had still remained with the vessels, and amongst them some prudent old chiefs, who, foreseeing the probable results of the day, and knowing that Hardrada would never quit, save as a conqueror or a corpse, the field on which he had planted the Ravager of the World, had detained the prince almost by force from sharing the fate of his father. But ere those vessels could put out to sea, the vigorous measures of the Saxon King had already intercepted the retreat of the vessels. And then, ranging their shields as a wall round their masts, the bold vikings at least determined to die as men. But with the morning came King Harold himself to the banks of the river, and behind him, with trailed lances, a solemn procession that bore the body of the Scald-King. They halted on the margin, and a boat was launched towards the Norwegian fleet, bearing a monk, who demanded the chiefs to send a deputation, headed by the young prince himself, to receive the corpse of their king, and hear the proposals of the Saxon.

The vikings, who had anticipated no preliminaries to the massacre they awaited, did not hesitate to accept these over-

---

[1] The quick succession of events allowed the Saxon army no time to bury the slain; and the bones of the invaders whitened the field of battle for many years afterwards.

tures. Twelve of the most famous chiefs still surviving, and Olave himself, entered the boat; and, standing between his brothers, Leofwine and Gurth, Harold thus accosted them, —

"Your king invaded a people that had given him no offence; he has paid the forfeit. We war not with the dead! Give to his remains the honours due to the brave. Without ransom or condition, we yield to you what can no longer harm us. And for thee, young prince," continued the king, with a tone of pity in his voice, as he contemplated the stately boyhood, and proud, but deep grief in the face of Olave; "for thee, wilt thou not live to learn that the wars of Odin are treason to the Faith of the Cross? We have conquered, — we dare not butcher. Take such ships as ye need for those that survive. Three-and-twenty I offer for your transport. Return to your native shores, and guard them as we have guarded ours. Are ye contented?"

Amongst those chiefs was a stern priest, — the bishop of the Orcades; he advanced and bent his knee to the king.

"O Lord of England," said he, "yesterday thou didst conquer the form, — to-day, the soul. And never more may generous Norsemen invade the coast of him who honours the dead and spares the living!"

"Amen!" cried the chiefs, and they all knelt to Harold. The young prince stood a moment irresolute, for his dead father was on the bier before him, and revenge was yet a virtue in the heart of a sea-king. But lifting his eyes to Harold's, the mild and gentle majesty of the Saxon's brow was irresistible in its benign command; and stretching his right hand to the king, he raised on high the other, and said aloud, "Faith and friendship with thee and England evermore!"

Then all the chiefs rising, they gathered round the bier, but no hand, in the sight of the conquering foe, lifted the cloth of gold that covered the corpse of the famous king. The bearers of the bier moved on slowly towards the boat; the Norwegians followed with measured funereal steps. And not till the bier was placed on board the royal galley was there heard the wail of woe; but then it came, loud and deep and dismal, and was followed by a burst of wild song from a surviving Scald.

The Norwegian preparations for departure were soon made, and the ships vouchsafed to their convoy raised anchor, and sailed down the stream. Harold's eye watched the ships from the river banks.

"And there," said he, at last, "there glide the last sails that shall ever bear the devastating raven to the shores of England."

Truly, in that field had been the most signal defeat those warriors, hitherto almost invincible, had known. On that bier lay the last son of Berserker and sea-king; and be it, O Harold, remembered in thine honour, that not by the Norman, but by thee, true-hearted Saxon, was trampled on the English soil the Ravager of the World![1]

"So be it," said Haco, "and so, methinks, will it be. But forget not the descendant of the Norsemen, the Count of Rouen!"

Harold started, and turned to his chiefs. "Sound trumpet, and fall in. To York we march. There re-settle the earldom, collect the spoil, and then back, my men, to the southern shores. Yet first kneel thou, Haco, son of my brother Sweyn: thy deeds were done in the light of Heaven, in the sight of warriors in the open field; so should thine honours find thee! Not with the vain fripperies of Norman knighthood do I deck thee, but make thee one of the elder brotherhood of Minister and Miles. I gird round thy loins mine own baldric of pure silver; I place in thy hand mine own sword of plain steel; and bid thee rise to take place in council and camps amongst the Proceres of England, — Earl of Hertford and Essex. Boy," whispered the king, as he bent over the pale cheek of his nephew, "thank not me. From me the thanks should come. On the day that saw Tostig's crime and his death,

---

[1] It may be said indeed, that, in the following reign, the Danes under Osbiorn (brother of King Sweyn), sailed up the Humber; but it was to *assist* the English, not to invade them. They were *bought off* by the Normans, — not conquered.

thou didst purify the name of my brother Sweyn! On to our city of York!"

High banquet was held in York; and, according to the customs of the Saxon monarchs, the king could not absent himself from the Victory Feast of his thegns.

He sat at the head of the board, between his brothers. Morcar, whose departure from the city had deprived him of a share in the battle, had arrived that day with his brother Edwin, whom he had gone to summon to his aid. And though the young earls envied the fame they had not shared, the envy was noble.

Gay and boisterous was the wassail; and lively song, long neglected in England, woke, as it wakes ever, at the breath of Joy and Fame. As if in the days of Alfred, the harp passed from hand to hand; martial and rough the strain beneath the touch of the Anglo-Dane, more refined and thoughtful the lay when it chimed to the voice of the Anglo-Saxon. But the memory of Tostig — all guilty though he was — a brother slain in war with a brother, lay heavy on Harold's soul. Still, so had he schooled and trained himself to live but for England — know no joy and no woe not hers — that by degrees and strong efforts he shook off his gloom. And music, and song, and wine, and blazing lights, and the proud sight of those long lines of valiant men, whose hearts had beat and whose hands had triumphed in the same cause, all aided to link his senses with the gladness of the hour.

And now, as night advanced, Leofwine, who was ever a favourite in the banquet, as Gurth in the council, rose to propose the *drink-hæl*, which carries the most characteristic of our modern social customs to an antiquity so remote, and the roar was hushed at the sight of the young earl's winsome face. With due decorum, he uncovered his head,[1] composed his countenance, and began, —

"Craving forgiveness of my lord the king, and this noble assembly," said Leofwine, "in which are so many from whom what I intend to propose would come with better grace, I would remind you that William, Count of the Normans, medi-

---

[1] The Saxons sat at meals with their heads covered.

tates a pleasure excursion, of the same nature as our late visitor, Harold Hardrada's."

A scornful laugh ran through the hall.

"And as we English are hospitable folk, and give any man who asks, meat and board for one night, so one day's welcome, methinks, will be all that the Count of the Normans will need at our English hands."

Flushed with the joyous insolence of wine, the wassailers roared applause.

"Wherefore, this *drink-hæl* to William of Rouen! And, to borrow a saying now in every man's lips, and which, I think, our good scops will take care that our children's children shall learn by heart, — since he covets our Saxon soil, ' seven feet of land' in frank pledge to him forever!"

"*Drink-hæl* to William the Norman!" shouted the revellers; and each man, with mocking formality, took off his cap, kissed his hand, and bowed.[1] "*Drink-hæl* to William the Norman!" and the shout rolled from floor to roof, — when, in the midst of the uproar, a man all bedabbled with dust and mire rushed into the hall, rushed through the rows of the banqueters, rushed to the throne-chair of Harold, and cried aloud, "William the Norman is encamped on the shores of Sussex; and with the mightiest armament ever yet seen in England, is ravaging the land far and near!"

[1] Henry.

BOOK XII.

THE BATTLE OF HASTINGS.

CHAPTER I.

In the heart of the forest-land in which Hilda's abode was situated, a gloomy pool reflected upon its stagnant waters the still shadows of the autumnal foliage. As is common in ancient forests in the neighbourhood of men's wants, the trees were dwarfed in height by repeated loppings, and the boughs sprang from the hollow, gnarled boles of pollard oaks and beeches; the trunks, vast in girth, and covered with mosses and whitening canker-stains, or wreaths of ivy, spoke of the most remote antiquity: but the boughs which their lingering and mutilated life put forth were either thin and feeble with innumerable branchlets, or were centred on some solitary distorted limb which the woodman's axe had spared. The trees thus assumed all manner of crooked, deformed, fantastic shapes, — all betokening age, and all decay; all, in despite of the noiseless solitude around, proclaiming the waste and ravages of man.

The time was that of the first watches of night, when the autumnal moon was brightest and broadest. You might see, on the opposite side of the pool, the antlers of the deer every now and then moving restlessly above the fern in which they had made their couch; and, through the nearer glades, the hares and conies stealing forth to sport or to feed; or the bat, wheeling low, in chase of the forest moth. From the thickest part of the copse came a slow human foot, and Hilda, emerging, paused by the waters of the pool. That serene and stony

calm habitual to her features was gone; sorrow and passion
had seized the soul of the Vala, in the midst of its fancied
security from the troubles it presumed to foresee for others.
The lines of the face were deep and care-worn; age had come on
with rapid strides, and the light of the eye was vague and unset-
tled, as if the lofty reason shook, terrified in its pride, at last.

"Alone, alone!" she murmured, half aloud: "yea, evermore
alone! And the grandchild I had reared to be the mother of
kings — whose fate, from the cradle, seemed linked with royalty and love; in whom, watching and hoping for, in whom,
loving and heeding, methought I lived again the sweet human
life — hath gone from my hearth, — forsaken, broken-hearted,
withering down to the grave under the shade of the barren
cloister! Is mine heart, then, all a lie? Are the gods who
led Odin from the Scythian East but the juggling fiends whom
the craven Christian abhors? Lo! the Wine Month has come;
a few nights more, and the sun which all prophecy foretold
should go down on the union of the king and the maid, shall
bring round the appointed day: yet Aldyth still lives, and
Edith still withers; and War stands side by side with the
Church, between the betrothed and the altar. Verily, verily,
my spirit hath lost its power, and leaves me bowed, in the
awe of night, a feeble, aged, hopeless, childless woman!"

Tears of human weakness rolled down the Vala's cheeks.
At that moment, a laugh came from a thing that had seemed
like the fallen trunk of a tree, or a trough in which the herdsman waters his cattle, so still and shapeless and undefined it
had lain amongst the rank weeds and nightshade and trailing
creepers on the marge of the pool. The laugh was low yet
fearful to hear.

Slowly the thing moved, and rose, and took the outline of
a human form; and the prophetess beheld the witch whose
sleep she had disturbed by the Saxon's grave.

"Where is the banner?" said the witch, laying her hand
on Hilda's arm, and looking into her face with bleared and
rheumy eyes, — "where is the banner thy handmaids were
weaving for Harold the Earl? Why didst thou lay aside that
labour of love for Harold the King? Hie thee home, and bid

thy maidens ply all night at the work; make it potent with rune and with spell, and with gums of the seid. Take the banner to Harold the King as a marriage-gift; for the day of his birth shall be still the day of his nuptials with Edith the Fair!"

Hilda gazed on the hideous form before her; and so had her soul fallen from its arrogant pride of place, that instead of the scorn with which so foul a pretender to the Great Art had before inspired the King-born Prophetess, her veins tingled with credulous awe.

"Art thou a mortal like myself," she said after a pause, "or one of those beings often seen by the shepherd in mist and rain, driving before them their shadowy flocks, — one of those of whom no man knoweth whether they are of earth or of Helheim; whether they have ever known the lot and conditions of flesh, or are but some dismal race between body and spirit, hateful alike to gods and to men?"

The dreadful hag shook her head, as if refusing to answer the question, and said, —

"Sit we down, sit we down by the dead dull pool, and if thou wouldst be wise as I am, wake up all thy wrongs, fill thyself with hate, and let thy thoughts be curses. Nothing is strong on earth but the Will; and hate to the will is as the iron in the hands of the war-man."

"Ha!" answered Hilda, "then thou art indeed one of the loathsome brood whose magic is born not of the aspiring soul but the fiendlike heart. And between us there is no union. I am of the race of those whom priests and kings reverenced and honoured as the oracles of heaven; and rather let my lore be dimmed and weakened in admitting the humanities of hope and love than be lightened by the glare of the wrath that Lok and Rana bear the children of men."

"What, art thou so base and so doting," said the hag, with fierce contempt, "as to know that another has supplanted thine Edith, that all the schemes of thy life are undone, and yet feel no hate for the man who hath wronged her and thee, — the man who had never been king if thou hadst not breathed into him the ambition of rule? Think, and curse!"

"My curse would wither the heart that is entwined within his," answered Hilda; "and," she added abruptly, as if eager to escape from her own impulses, "didst thou not tell me, even now, that the wrong would be redressed, and his betrothed yet be his bride on the appointed day?"

"Ha! home, then! — home! and weave the charmed woof of the banner, broider it with zimmes and with gold worthy the standard of a king; for I tell thee that where that banner is planted shall Edith clasp with bridal arms her adored. And the hwata thou hast read by the bautastein, and in the temple of the Briton's revengeful gods, shall be fulfilled."

"Dark daughter of Hela," said the prophetess, "whether demon or god hath inspired thee, I hear in my spirit a voice that tells me thou hast pierced to a truth that my lore could not reach. Thou art houseless and poor; I will give wealth to thine age if thou wilt stand with me by the altar of Thor, and let thy galdra unriddle the secrets that have baffled mine own. All foreshown to me hath ever come to pass, but in a sense other than that in which my soul read the rune and the dream, the leaf and the fount, the star and the Scin-læca. My husband slain in his youth; my daughter maddened with woe; her lord murdered on his hearthstone; Sweyn, whom I loved as my child," — the Vala paused, contending against her own emotions, — "I loved them all," she faltered, clasping her hands; "for them I tasked the future. The future promised fair; I lured them to their doom, and when the doom came, lo! the promise was kept! but how? And now Edith, the last of my race; Harold, the pride of my pride! — speak, thing of Horror and Night, canst thou disentangle the web in which my soul struggles, weak as the fly in the spider's mesh?"

"On the third night from this will I stand with thee by the altar of Thor, and unriddle the rede of my masters, unknown and unguessed, whom thou hast duteously served. And ere the sun rise, the greatest mystery earth knows shall be bare to thy soul!"

As the witch spoke, a cloud passed over the moon; and before the light broke forth again, the hag had vanished.

There was only seen in the dull pool the water-rat swimming through the rank sedges; only in the forest, the gray wings of the owl, fluttering heavily across the glades; only in the grass, the red eyes of the bloated toad.

Then Hilda went slowly home, and the maids worked all night at the charmed banner. All that night, too, the watch-dogs howled in the yard, through the ruined peristyle, — howled in rage and in fear. And under the lattice of the room in which the maids broidered the banner, and the prophetess muttered her charm, there couched, muttering also, a dark, shapeless thing, at which those dogs howled in rage and in fear.

CHAPTER II.

ALL within the palace of Westminster showed the confusion and dismay of the awful time, — all, at least, save the council-chamber, in which Harold, who had arrived the night before, conferred with his thegns. It was evening: the courtyards and the halls were filled with armed men, and almost with every hour came rider and bode from the Sussex shores. In the corridors the churchmen grouped and whispered, as they had whispered and grouped in the day of King Edward's death. Stigand passed among them, pale and thoughtful. The serge gowns came rustling round the arch-prelate for counsel or courage.

"Shall we go forth with the king's army?" asked a young monk, bolder than the rest, "to animate the host with prayer and hymn?"

"Fool!" said the miserly prelate, "fool! if we do so, and the Norman conquer, what become of our abbacies and convent lands? The duke wars against Harold, not England. If he slay Harold — "

"What then?"

"The Atheling is left us yet. Stay we here and guard the last prince of the House of Cerdic," whispered Stigand, and he swept on.

In the chamber in which Edward had breathed his last, his widowed queen, with Aldyth, her successor, and Githa and some other ladies, waited the decision of the council. By one of the windows stood, clasping each other by the hand, the fair young bride of Gurth and the betrothed of the gay Leofwine. Githa sat alone, bowing her face over her hands,—desolate, mourning for the fate of her traitor son; and the wounds, that the recent and holier death of Thyra had inflicted, bled afresh. And the holy lady of Edward attempted in vain, by pious adjurations, to comfort Aldyth, who, scarcely heeding her, started ever and anòn with impatient terror, muttering to herself, "Shall I lose *this* crown too?"

In the council-hall debate waxed warm,—which was the wiser, to meet William at once in the battle-field, or to delay till all the forces Harold might expect, and which he had ordered to be levied in his rapid march from York, could swell his host?

"If we retire before the enemy," said Gurth, "leaving him in a strange land, winter approaching, his forage will fail. He will scarce dare to march upon London; if he does, we shall be better prepared to encounter him. My voice is against resting all on a single battle."

"Is that thy choice?" said Vebba, indignantly. "Not so, I am sure, would have chosen thy father; not so think the Saxons of Kent. The Norman is laying waste all the lands of thy subjects, Lord Harold; living on plunder, as a robber, in the realm of King Alfred. Dost thou think that men will get better heart to fight for their country by hearing that their king shrinks from the danger?"

"Thou speakest well and wisely," said Haco; and all eyes turned to the young son of Sweyn, as to one who best knew the character of the hostile army and the skill of its chief. "We have now with us a force flushed with conquest over a foe hitherto deemed invincible. Men who have conquered the Norwegian will not shrink from the Norman. Victory depends upon ardour more than numbers. Every hour of delay damps the ardour. Are we sure that it will swell the numbers? What I dread most is not the sword of the Norman Duke,— it is his craft. Rely upon it, that if we meet him not soon, he will march straight to London. He will proclaim by the way that he comes not to seize the throne, but to punish Harold, and abide by the Witan, or, perchance, by the word of the Roman pontiff. The terror of his armament, unresisted, will spread like a panic through the land. Many will be decoyed by his false pretexts, many awed by a force that the king dare not meet. If he come in sight of the city, think you that merchants and cheapmen will not be daunted by the thought of pillage and sack? They will be the first to capitulate at the first house which is fired. The city is weak to guard against siege,— its walls long neglected; and in sieges the Normans are famous. Are we so united (the king's rule thus fresh) but what no cabals, no dissensions, will break out amongst ourselves? If the duke come, as come he will, in the name of the Church, may not the churchmen set up some new pretender to the crown,— perchance the child Edgar? And, divided against ourselves, how ingloriously should we fall! Besides, this land, though never before have the links between province and province been drawn so close, hath yet demarcations that make the people selfish. The Northumbrians, I fear, will not stir to aid London, and Mercia will hold aloof from our peril. Grant that William once seize London, all England is broken up and dispirited,— each shire, nay, each town, looking only to itself. Talk of delay as wearing out the strength of the foe! No, it would wear out our own. Little eno', I fear, is yet left in our treasury. If William seize London, that treasury is his, with all the wealth of our burgesses. How should we maintain an army, except by preying on the people, and thus discontenting them? Where guard that army? Where are our forts,— where our mountains? The war of delay suits only a land of rock and defile, or of castle and breastwork. Thegns and warriors, ye have no castles but your breasts of mail. Abandon these, and you are lost."

A general murmur of applause closed this speech of Haco, which, while wise in arguments our historians have over-looked, came home to that noblest reason of brave men, which urges prompt resistance to foul invasion.

Up then rose King Harold.

"I thank you, fellow-Englishmen, for that applause with which ye have greeted mine own thoughts on the lips of Haco. Shall it be said that your king rushed to chase his own brother from the soil of outraged England, yet shrunk from the sword of the Norman stranger? Well indeed might my brave subjects desert my banner if it floated idly over these palace walls while the armed invader pitched his camp in the heart of England. By delay, William's force, what-ever it might be, cannot grow less; his cause grows more strong in our craven fears. What his armament may be we rightly know not; the report varies with every messenger, swelling and lessening with the rumours of every hour. Have we not around us now our most stalwart veterans,—the flower of our armies, the most eager spirits, the vanquishers of Hardrada? Thou sayest, Gurth, that all should not be perilled on a single battle. True. Harold should be perilled, but wherefore England? Grant that we win the day: the quicker our despatch, the greater our fame, the more lasting that peace at home and abroad which rests ever its best foun-dation on the sense of the power which wrong cannot provoke unchastised. Grant that we lose: a loss can be made gain by a king's brave death. Why should not our example rouse and unite all who survive us? Which the nobler example, the one best fitted to protect our country,—the recreant backs of living chiefs, or the glorious dead with their fronts to the foe? Come what may, life or death, at least we will thin the Norman numbers, and heap the barriers of our corpses on the Norman march. At least, we can show to the rest of England how men should defend their native land! And if, as I believe and pray, in every English breast beats a heart like Harold's, what matters though a king should fall?—Freedom is immortal."

He spoke; and forth from his baldric he drew his sword.

Every blade, at that signal, leaped from the sheath; and, in that council-hall at least, in every breast beat the heart of Harold.

CHAPTER III.

THE chiefs dispersed to array their troops for the morrow's march; but Harold and his kinsmen entered the chamber where the women waited the decision of the council, for that, in truth, was to them the parting interview. The king had resolved, after completing all his martial preparations, to pass the night in the Abbey of Waltham; and his brothers lodged, with the troops they commanded, in the city or its suburbs. Haco alone remained with that portion of the army quartered in and around the palace.

They entered the chamber, and in a moment each heart had sought its mate; in the mixed assembly each only conscious of the other. There Gurth bowed his noble head over the weeping face of the young bride that for the last time nestled to his bosom. There, with a smiling lip, but tremulous voice, the gay Leofwine soothed and chided in a breath the maiden he had wooed as the partner for a life that his mirthful spirit made one holiday, snatching kisses from a cheek no longer coy.

But cold was the kiss which Harold pressed on the brow of Aldyth; and with something of disdain, and of bitter remembrance of a nobler love, he comforted a terror which sprang from the thought of self.

"Oh, Harold!" sobbed Aldyth, "be not rashly brave; guard thy life for my sake. Without thee, what am I? Is it even safe for me to rest here? Were it not better to fly to York, or seek refuge with Malcolm the Scot?"

"Within three days at the farthest," answered Harold, "thy brothers will be in London. Abide by their counsel; act as they advise at the news of my victory or my fall."

He paused abruptly, for he heard close beside him the broken voice of Gurth's bride, in answer to her lord.

"Think not of me, beloved; thy whole heart now be England's. And if — if " — her voice failed a moment, but resumed proudly, "why even then thy wife is safe, for she survives not her lord and her land!"

The king left his wife's side, and kissed his brother's bride.

"Noble heart!" he said; "with women like thee for our wives and mothers, England could survive the slaughter of a thousand kings."

He turned, and knelt to Githa. She threw her arms over his broad breast, and wept bitterly.

"Say — say, Harold, that I have not reproached thee for Tostig's death. I have obeyed the last commands of Godwin my lord. I have deemed thee ever right and just; now let me not lose thee, too. They go with thee, all my surviving sons, save the exile Wolnoth, — him whom now I shall never behold again. Oh, Harold! let not mine old age be childless!"

"Mother, dear, dear mother, with these arms round my neck I take new life and new heart. No! never hast thou reproached me for my brother's death, — never for aught which man's first duty enjoined. Murmur not that that duty commands us still. We are the sons, through thee, of royal heroes; through my father, of Saxon freemen. Rejoice that thou hast three sons left, whose arms thou mayest pray God and his saints to prosper, and over whose graves, if they fall, thou shalt shed no tears of shame!"

Then the widow of King Edward, who (the crucifix clasped in her hands) had listened to Harold with lips apart and marble cheeks, could keep down no longer her human woman's heart; she rushed to Harold as he still knelt to Githa, — knelt by his side, and clasped him in her arms with despairing fondness: —

"O brother, brother, whom I have so dearly loved when all other love seemed forbidden me; when he who gave me a throne refused me his heart; when, looking at thy fair promise, listening to thy tender comfort; when, remembering the days of old, in which thou wert my docile pupil, and we dreamed bright dreams together of happiness and fame to come; when, loving thee methought too well, too much as weak mothers may love a mortal son, I prayed God to detach my heart from earth! — O Harold! now forgive me all my coldness. I shudder at thy resolve. I dread that thou should meet this man, whom an oath hath bound thee to obey. Nay, frown not — I bow to thy will, my brother and my king. I know that thou hast chosen as thy conscience sanctions, as thy duty ordains. But come back, — oh, come back, — thou who, like me " (her voice whispered), "hast sacrificed the household hearth to thy country's altars, — and I will never pray to Heaven to love thee less — my brother, oh, my brother! "

In all the room were then heard but the low sounds of sobs and broken exclamations. All clustered to one spot, — Leofwine and his betrothed, Gurth and his bride, even the selfish Aldyth, ennobled by the contagion of the sublime emotion, — all clustered round Githa, the mother of the three guardians of the fated land, and all knelt before her, by the side of Harold. Suddenly, the widowed queen, the virgin wife of the last heir of Cerdic, rose, and holding on high the sacred rood over those bended heads, said, with devout passion, —

"O Lord of Hosts, We Children of Doubt and Time, trembling in the dark, dare not take to ourselves to question thine unerring will. Sorrow and death, as joy and life, are at the breath of a mercy divine, and a wisdom all-seeing; and out of the hours of evil thou drawest, in mystic circle, the eternity of Good. 'Thy will be done on earth, as it is in heaven.' If, O Disposer of events, our human prayers are not adverse to thy pre-judged decrees, protect these lives, the bulwarks of our homes and altars, sons whom the land offers as a sacrifice. May thine angel turn aside the blade, as of old from the heart of Isaac! But if, O Ruler of Nations, in whose sight the ages are as moments, and generations but as sands in the sea, these lives are doomed, may the death expiate their sins, and, shrived on the battle-field, absolve and receive the souls! "

CHAPTER IV.

By the altar of the Abbey Church of Waltham, that night, knelt Edith in prayer for Harold.

She had taken up her abode in a small convent of nuns that adjoined the more famous monastery of Waltham; but she had promised Hilda not to enter on the novitiate until the birthday of Harold had passed. She herself had no longer faith in the omens and prophecies that had deceived her youth and darkened her life; and in the more congenial air of our Holy Church, the spirit, ever so chastened, grew calm and resigned. But the tidings of the Norman's coming, and the king's victorious return to his capital, had reached even that still retreat; and love, which had blent itself with religion, led her steps to that lonely altar. And suddenly, as she there knelt, only lighted by the moon through the high casements, she was startled by the sound of approaching feet and murmuring voices. She rose in alarm; the door of the church was thrown open, torches advanced; and amongst the monks, between Osgood and Ailred, came the king. He had come, that last night before his march, to invoke the prayers of that pious brotherhood; and by the altar he had founded, to pray, himself, that his one sin of faith forfeited and oath abjured might not palsy his arm and weigh on his soul in the hour of his country's need.

Edith stifled the cry that rose to her lips, as the torches fell on the pale and hushed and melancholy face of Harold; and she crept away under the arch of the vast Saxon columns, and into the shade of abutting walls. The monks and the king, intent on their holy office, beheld not that solitary and shrinking form. They approached the altar; and there the king knelt down lowlily, and none heard the prayer. But as Osgood held the sacred rood over the bended head of the royal suppliant, the Image on the crucifix (which had been a gift from Alred the prelate, and was supposed to have belonged of old to Augustine, the first founder of the Saxon Church,— so that by the superstition of the age it was invested with miraculous virtues) bowed itself visibly. Visibly, the pale and ghastly image of the suffering God bowed over the head of the kneeling man; whether the fastenings of the rood were loosened, or from what cause soever,— in the eyes of all the brotherhood, the Image bowed.[1]

A thrill of terror froze every heart, save Edith's, too remote to perceive the portent, and save the king's, whom the omen seemed to doom, for his face was buried in his clasped hands. Heavy was his heart, nor needed it other warnings than its own gloom.

Long and silently prayed the king; and when at last he rose, and the monks, though with altered and tremulous voices, began their closing hymn, Edith passed noiselessly along the wall, and, stealing through one of the smaller doors which communicated to the nunnery annexed, gained the solitude of her own chamber. There she stood, benumbed with the strength of her emotions at the sight of Harold thus abruptly presented. How had the fond human heart leaped to meet him! Twice, thus, in the august ceremonials of Religion, secret, shrinking, unwitnessed, had she, his betrothed, she, the partner of his soul, stood aloof to behold him. She had seen him in the hour of his pomp, the crown upon his brow,— seen him in the hour of his peril and agony, that anointed head bowed to the earth. And in the pomp that she could not share, she had exulted; but, oh, now — now,— oh, now that she could have knelt beside that humbled form, and prayed with that voiceless prayer!

The torches flashed in the court below; the church was again deserted; the monks passed in mute procession back to their cloister; but a single man paused, turned aside, and stopped at the gate of the humbler convent; a knocking was heard at the great oaken door, and the watch-dog barked. Edith started, pressed her hand on her heart, and trembled. Steps approached her door, and the abbess, entering, sum-

[1] Palgrave, " Hist. of Anglo-Saxons."

moned her below, to hear the farewell greeting of her cousin
the king.

Harold stood in the simple hall of the cloister: a single
taper, tall and wan, burned on the oak board. The abbess
led Edith by the hand, and at a sign from the king withdrew.
So, once more upon earth, the betrothed and divided were
alone.

"Edith," said the king, in a voice in which no ear but hers
could have detected the struggle, "do not think I have come
to disturb thy holy calm, or sinfully revive the memories of
the irrevocable past; where once on my breast, in the old
fashion of our fathers, I wrote thy name, is written now the
name of the mistress that supplants thee. Into Eternity melts
the Past; but I could not depart to a field from which there is
no retreat — in which, against odds that men say are fearful,
I have resolved to set my crown and my life — without once
more beholding thee, pure guardian of my happier days! Thy
forgiveness for all the sorrow that, in the darkness which
surrounds man's hopes and dreams, I have brought on thee
(dread return for love so enduring, so generous, and divine!)
— thy forgiveness I will not ask. Thou alone perhaps on
earth knowest the soul of Harold; and if he hath wronged
thee, thou seest alike in the wronger and the wronged but
the children of iron Duty, the servants of imperial Heaven.
Not thy forgiveness I ask; but — but — Edith, holy maid!
angel soul! — thy — thy blessing!" His voice faltered, and
he inclined his lofty head as to a saint.

"Oh that I had the power to bless!" exclaimed Edith, mastering her rush of tears with a heroic effort; "and methinks
I have the power, — not from virtues of my own, but from all
that I owe to thee! The grateful have the power to bless.
For what do I not owe to thee, — owe to that very love of
which even the grief is sacred? Poor child in the house of
the heathen, thy love descended upon me, and in it, the smile
of God! In that love my spirit awoke, and was baptized;
every thought that has risen from earth, and lost itself in
heaven, was breathed into my heart by thee! Thy creature
and thy slave, hadst thou tempted me to sin, sin had seemed

hallowed by thy voice; but thou saidst 'True love is virtue,' and so I worshipped virtue in loving thee. Strengthened, purified, by thy bright companionship, from thee came the strength to resign thee; from thee the refuge under the wings of God; from thee the firm assurance that our union yet shall be,— not as our poor Hilda dreams, on the perishable earth, but there! oh, there! yonder by the celestial altars, in the land in which all spirits are filled with love. Yes, soul of Harold! there are might and holiness in the blessing the soul thou hast redeemed and reared sheds on thee!"

And so beautiful, so unlike the Beautiful of the common earth, looked the maid as she thus spoke, and laid hands, trembling with no human passion, on that royal head, that could a soul from paradise be made visible, such might be the shape it would wear to a mortal's eye! Thus for some moments both were silent; and in the silence the gloom vanished from the heart of Harold, and, through a deep and sublime serenity, it rose undaunted to front the future.

No embrace, no farewell kiss, profaned the parting of those pure and noble spirits,—parting on the threshold of the grave. It was only the spirit that clasped the spirit, looking forth from the clay into measureless eternity. Not till the air of night came once more on his brow, and the moonlight rested on the roofs and fanes of the land entrusted to his charge, was the man once more the human hero; not till she was alone in her desolate chamber, and the terrors of the coming battle-field chased the angel from her thoughts, was the maid inspired once more the weeping woman.

A little after sunrise the abbess, who was distantly akin to the House of Godwin, sought Edith, so agitated by her own fear that she did not remark the trouble of her visitor. The supposed miracle of the sacred Image bowing over the kneeling king had spread dismay through the cloisters of both nunnery and abbey; and so intense was the disquietude of the two brothers, Osgood and Ailred, in the simple and grateful affection they bore their royal benefactor, that they had obeyed the impulse of their tender, credulous hearts, and left the monastery with the dawn, intending to follow the king's march,[1] and watch and pray near the awful battle-field. Edith listened, and made no reply; the terrors of the abbess infected her; the example of the two monks woke the sole thought which stirred through the nightmare-dream that suspended reason itself; and when, at noon, the abbess again sought the chamber, Edith was gone,— gone, and alone — none knew wherefore, none guessed whither.

All the pomp of the English army burst upon, Harold's view, as, in the rising sun, he approached the bridge of the capital. Over that bridge came the stately march,— battle-axe and spear and banner glittering in the ray. And as he drew aside, and the forces defiled before him, the cry of "God save King Harold!" rose with loud acclaim and lusty joy, borne over the waves of the river, startling the echoes in the ruined keape of the Roman, heard in the halls restored by Canute, and chiming, like a chorus, with the chants of the monks by the tomb of Sebba in St. Paul's,— by the tomb of Edward at St. Peter's.

With a brightened face and a kindling eye, the king saluted his lines, and then fell into the ranks towards the rear, where, among the burghers of London and the lithsmen of Middlesex, the immemorial custom of Saxon monarchs placed the kingly banner. And, looking up, he beheld, not his old standard with the Tiger heads and the Cross, but a banner both strange and gorgeous. On a field of gold was the effigies ot a Fighting Warrior; and the arms were bedecked in orient pearls, and the borders blazed in the rising sun, with ruby, amethyst, and emerald. While he gazed, wondering, on this dazzling ensign, Haco, who rode beside the standard-bearer, advanced, and gave him a letter.

"Last night," said he, "after thou hadst left the palace, many recruits, chiefly from Hertfordshire and Essex, came in; but the most gallant and stalwart of all, in arms and in stature, were the lithsmen of Hilda. With them came this banner, on which she has lavished the gems that have passed to her hand through long lines of northern ancestors, from Odin, the founder of all northern thrones. So, at least, said the bode of our kinswoman."

[1] Palgrave, "Hist. of Anglo-Saxons."

Harold had already cut the silk round the letter, and was reading its contents. They ran thus: —

"King of England, I forgive thee the broken heart of my grandchild. They whom the land feeds should defend the land. I send to thee, in tribute, the best fruits that grow in the field and the forest, round the house which my husband took from the bounty of Canute, — stout hearts and strong hands! Descending alike, as do Hilda and Harold (through Githa thy mother) from the Warrior God of the North, whose race never shall fail, take, O defender of the Saxon children of Odin, the banner I have broidered with the gems that the Chief of the Asas bore from the East. Firm as love be thy foot, strong as death be thy hand, under the shade which the banner of Hilda, — under the gleam which the jewels of Odin, — cast on the brows of the King! So Hilda, the daughter of monarchs, greets Harold the leader of men."

Harold looked up from the letter, and Haco resumed: —

"Thou canst guess not the cheering effect which this banner, supposed to be charmed, and which the name of Odin alone would suffice to make holy, at least with thy fierce Anglo-Danes, hath already produced through the army."

"It is well, Haco," said Harold, with a smile. "Let priest add his blessing to Hilda's charm, and Heaven will pardon any magic that makes more brave the hearts that defend its altars. Now fall we back, for the army must pass beside the hill with the crommell and gravestone; there, be sure, Hilda will be at watch for our march, and we will linger a few moments to thank her somewhat for her banner, yet more justly, methinks, for her men. Are not yon stout fellows all in mail, so tall and so orderly, in advance of the London burghers, Hilda's aid to our Fyrd?"

"They are," answered Haco.

The king backed his steed to accost them with his kingly greeting; and then, with Haco, falling yet farther to the rear, seemed engaged in inspecting the numerous wains, bearing missiles and forage, that always accompanied the march of a Saxon army, and served to strengthen its encampment. But when they came in sight of the hillock by which the great body of the army had preceded them, the king and the son of Sweyn dismounted, and on foot entered the large circle of the Celtic ruin.

By the side of the Teuton altar they beheld two forms, both perfectly motionless: but one was extended on the ground as in sleep or in death; the other sat beside it, as if watching the corpse, or guarding the slumber. The face of the last was not visible, propped upon the arms which rested on the knees, and hidden by the hands. But in the face of the other, as the two men drew near, they recognized the Danish Prophetess. Death in its dreadest characters was written on that ghastly face; woe and terror, beyond all words to describe, spoke in the haggard brow, the distorted lips, and the wild glazed stare of the open eyes. At the startled cry of the intruders on that dreary silence, the living form moved; and though still leaning its face on its hands, it raised its head; and never countenance of Northern Vampire, cowering by the rifled grave, was more fiendlike and appalling.

"Who and what art thou?" said the king; "and how, thus unhonoured in the air of heaven, lies the corpse of the noble Hilda? Is this the hand of Nature? Haco, Haco, so look the eyes, so set the features, of those whom the horror of ruthless murder slays even before the steel strikes. Speak, hag, art thou dumb?"

"Search the body," answered the witch, "there is no wound! Look to the throat,— no mark of the deadly gripe! I have seen such in my day. There are none on this corpse, I trow; yet thou sayest rightly, horror slew her! Ha, ha! she would know, and she hath known; she would raise the dead and the demon, — she hath raised them; she would read the riddle,— she hath read it. Pale King and dark youth, would ye learn what Hilda saw, eh? eh? Ask her in the Shadow-World where she awaits ye! Ha! ye too would be wise in the future; ye too would climb to heaven through the mysteries of hell. Worms! worms! crawl back to the clay,— to the earth! One such night as the hag ye despise enjoys as her sport and her glee would freeze your veins, and seal the life in your eyeballs, and leave your corpses to terror and wonder, like the carcass that lies at your feet!"

"Ho!" cried the king, stamping his foot. "Hence, Haco; rouse the household; summon hither the handmaids; call henchman and ceorl to guard this foul raven."

Haco obeyed; but when he returned with the shuddering and amazed attendants, the witch was gone, and the king was leaning against the altar with downcast eyes, and a face troubled and dark with thought.

The body of the Vala was borne into the house; and the king, waking from his revery, bade them send for the priests, and ordered masses for the parted soul. Then kneeling, with pious hand he closed the eyes and smoothed the features, and left his mournful kiss on the icy brow. These offices fulfilled, he took Haco's arm, and leaning on it, returned to the spot on which they had left their steeds. Not evincing surprise or awe,—emotions that seemed unknown to his gloomy, settled, impassible nature,—Haco said calmly, as they descended the knoll,—

"What evil did the hag predict to thee?"

"Haco," answered the king, "yonder, by the shores of Sussex, lies all the future which our eyes now should scan, and our hearts should be firm to meet. These omens and apparitions are but the ghosts of a dead Religion,—spectres sent from the grave of the fearful Heathenesse; they may appall,—but to lure us from our duty. Lo, as we gaze around—the ruins of all the creeds that have made the hearts of men quake with unsubstantial awe—lo, the temple of the Briton! lo, the fane of the Roman! lo, the mouldering altar of our ancestral Thor! Ages past lie wrecked around us in these shattered symbols. A new age hath risen, and a new creed. Keep we to the broad truths before us,—duty here; knowledge comes alone in the Hereafter."

"That Hereafter—is it not near?" murmured Haco.

They mounted in silence; and ere they regained the army paused, by a common impulse, and looked behind. Awful in their desolation rose the temple and the altar! And in Hilda's mysterious death it seemed that their last and lingering Genius—the Genius of the dark and fierce, the warlike and the wizard North—had expired forever. Yet, on the outskirt of the forest, dusk and shapeless, that witch without a name stood in the shadow, pointing towards them, with outstretched arm, in vague and denouncing menace,— as if, come what may, all change of creed,— be the faith ever so simple, the truth ever so bright and clear,—there *is* a SUPERSTITION native to that Border-land between the Visible and the Unseen, which will find its priest and its votaries, till the full and crowning splendour of Heaven shall melt every shadow from the world!

CHAPTER V.

ON the broad plain between Pevensey and Hastings, Duke William had arrayed his armaments. In the rear he had built a castle of wood, all the framework of which he had brought with him, and which was to serve as a refuge in case of retreat. His ships he had run into deep water, and scuttled; so that the thought of return, without victory, might be banished from his miscellaneous and multitudinous force. His outposts stretched for miles, keeping watch night and day against surprise. The ground chosen was adapted for all the manœuvres of a cavalry never before paralleled in England, nor perhaps in the world, — almost every horseman a knight, almost every knight fit to be a chief. And on this space William reviewed his army, and there planned and schemed, rehearsed and re-formed, all the stratagems the great day might call forth. But most careful and laborious and minute was he in the manœuvre of a feigned retreat. Not ere the acting of some modern play does the anxious manager more elaborately marshal each man, each look, each gesture, that are to form a picture on which the curtain shall fall amidst deafening plaudits than did the laborious captain appoint each man, and each movement, in his lure to a valiant foe: the attack of the foot, their recoil, their affected panic, their broken exclamations of despair; their retreat, first partial and reluctant, next seemingly hurried and complete, — flying, but in flight *carefully* confused; then the settled watchword, the lightning rally, the rush of the cavalry from the ambush; the sweep and hem round the pursuing foe, the detachment of levelled spears to cut off the Saxon return to the main force, and the lost ground, — were all directed by the most consummate mastership in the stage play, or *upokrisis*, of war, and seized by the adroitness of practised veterans.

Not now, O Harold! hast thou to contend against the rude heroes of the Norse, with their ancestral strategy unimproved! The civilization of Battle meets thee now! — and all the craft of the Roman guides the manhood of the North.

It was in the midst of such lessons to his foot and his horsemen — spears gleaming, pennons tossing, lines re-forming, steeds backing, wheeling, flying, circling — that William's eye blazed, and his deep voice thundered the thrilling word; when Mallet de Graville, who was in command at one of the outposts, rode up to him at full speed, and said in gasps, as he drew breath, —

"King Harold and his army are advancing furiously. Their object is clearly to come on us unawares."

"Hold!" said the duke, lifting his hand; and the knights around him halted in their perfect discipline; then after a few brief but distinct orders to Odo, Fitzosborne, and some other of his leading chiefs, he headed a numerous cavalcade of his knights, and rode fast to the outpost which Mallet had left, — to catch sight of the coming foe.

The horsemen cleared the plain, — passed through a wood, mournfully fading into autumnal hues; and, on emerging, they saw the gleam of the Saxon spears rising on the brows of the gentle hills beyond. But even the time, short as it was, that had sufficed to bring William in view of the enemy, had sufficed also, under the orders of his generals, to give to the wide plain of his encampment all the order of a host prepared. And William, having now mounted on a rising ground, turned from the spears on the hill-tops to his own fast forming lines on the plain, and said with a stern smile, —

"Methinks the Saxon usurper, if he be among those on the height of yon hills, will vouchsafe us time to breathe! Saint

Michael gives his crown to our hands, and his corpse to the crow, if he dare to descend."

And so indeed, as the duke with a soldier's eye foresaw from a soldier's skill, — so it proved. The spears rested on the summits. It soon became evident that the English general perceived that here there was no Hardrada to surprise; that the news brought to his ear had exaggerated neither the numbers, nor the arms, nor the discipline of the Norman; and that the battle was not to the bold but to the wary.

"He doth right," said William, musingly; "nor think, O my quens, that we shall find a fool's hot brain under Harold's helmet of iron. How is this broken ground of hillock and valley named in our chart? It is strange that we should have overlooked its strength, and suffered it thus to fall into the hands of the foe. How is it named? Can any of ye remember?"

"A Saxon peasant," said De Graville, "told me that the ground was called Senlac,[1] or Sanglac, or some such name, in their musicless jargon."

"Grammercy!" quoth Grantmesnil, "methinks the name will be familiar eno' hereafter; no jargon seemeth the sound to my ear, — a significant name and ominous, — Sanglac, Sanguelac, — the Lake of Blood."

"Sanguelac!" said the duke, startled; "where have I heard that name before? It must have been between sleeping and waking. Sanguelac, Sanguelac! — truly sayest thou, through a lake of blood we must wade indeed!"

"Yet," said De Graville, "thine astrologer foretold that thou wouldst win the realm without a battle."

"Poor astrologer!" said William, "the ship he sailed in was lost. Ass indeed is he who pretends to warn others, nor sees an inch before his eyes what his own fate will be! Battle shall we have, but not yet. Hark thee, Guillaume, thou hast been guest with this usurper; thou hast seemed to me to have some love for him, — a love natural since thou didst once fight by his side; wilt thou go from me to the Saxon host with

---

[1] The battle-field of Hastings seems to have been called Senlac before the Conquest, Sanguelac after it.

Hugues Maigrot, the monk, and back the message I shall send?"

The proud and punctilious Norman thrice crossed himself ere he answered, —

"There was a time, Count William, when I should have deemed it honour to hold parley with Harold the brave Earl; but now, with the crown on his head, I hold it shame and disgrace to barter words with a knight unleal and a man forsworn."

"Nathless, thou shalt do me this favour," said William, "for" (and he took the knight somewhat aside) "I cannot disguise from thee that I look anxiously on the chance of battle. Yon men are flushed with new triumph over the greatest warrior Norway ever knew; they will fight on their own soil, and under a chief whom I have studied and read with more care than the comments of Cæsar, and in whom the guilt of perjury cannot blind me to the wit of a great general. If we can yet get our end without battle, large shall be my thanks to thee, and I will hold thine astrologer a man wise, though unhappy."

"Certes," said De Graville, gravely, "it were discourteous to the memory of the star-seer not to make some effort to prove his science a just one. And the Chaldeans — "

"Plague seize the Chaldeans!" muttered the duke. "Ride with me back to the camp, that I may give thee my message, and instruct also the monk."

"De Graville," resumed the duke, as they rode towards the lines, "my meaning is briefly this. I do not think that Harold will accept my offers and resign his crown, but I design to spread dismay, and perhaps revolt, amongst his captains; I wish that they may know that the Church lays its Curse on those who fight against my consecrated banner. I do not ask thee, therefore, to demean thy knighthood by seeking to cajole the usurper; no, — but rather boldly to denounce his perjury and startle his liegemen. Perchance they may compel him to terms, perchance they may desert his banner; at the worst they shall be daunted with full sense of the guilt of his cause."

"Ha, now I comprehend thee, noble Count; and trust me I will speak as Norman and knight should speak."

Meanwhile, Harold, seeing the utter hopelessness of all sudden assault, had seized a general's advantage of the ground he had gained. Occupying the line of hills, he began forthwith to entrench himself behind deep ditches and artful palisades. It is impossible now to stand on that spot, without recognizing the military skill with which the Saxon had taken his post, and formed his precautions. He surrounded the main body of his troops with a perfect breastwork against the charge of the horse. Stakes and strong hurdles interwoven with osier plaits, and protected by deep dikes, served at once to neutralize the effect of that arm in which William was most powerful, and in which Harold almost entirely failed; while the possession of the ground must compel the foe to march, and to charge up hill against all the missiles which the Saxons could pour down from their entrenchments. Aiding, animating, cheering, directing all, while the dikes were fast hollowed, and the breastworks fast rose, the King of England rode his palfrey from line to line, and work to work, when, looking up, he saw Haco leading towards him, up the slopes, a monk, and a warrior whom, by the banderol on his spear and the cross on his shield, he knew to be one of the Norman knighthood.

At that moment Gurth and Leofwine, and those thegns who commanded counties, were thronging round their chief for instructions. The king dismounted, and beckoning them to follow, strode towards the spot on which had just been planted his royal standard. There halting, he said with a grave smile, —

"I perceive that the Norman Count hath sent us his bodes; it is meet that with me, you, the defenders of England, should hear what the Norman saith."

"If he saith aught but prayer for his men to return to Rouen, needless his message, and short our answer," said Vebba, the bluff thegn of Kent.

Meanwhile the monk and the Norman knight drew near, and paused at some short distance, while Haco, advancing, said briefly, —

"These men I found at our outposts; they demand to speak with the king."

"Under his standard the king will hear the Norman invader," replied Harold; "bid them speak."

The same sallow, mournful, ominous countenance, which Harold had before seen in the halls of Westminster, rising deathlike above the serge garb of the Benedict of Caen, now presented itself, and the monk thus spoke, —

"In the name of William, Duke of the Normans in the field, Count of Rouen in the hall, Claimant of all the realms of Anglia, Scotland, and the Walloons, held under Edward his cousin, I come to thee, Harold his liege and earl."

"Change thy titles, or depart," said Harold, fiercely, his brow no longer mild in its majesty, but dark as midnight. "What says William, the Count of the Foreigners, to Harold, King of the Angles, and Basileus of Britain?"

"Protesting against thy assumption, I answer thee thus," said Hugues Maigrot. "First, again he offers thee all Northumbria, up to the realm of the Scottish sub-king, if thou wilt fulfil thy vow, and cede him the crown."

"Already have I answered, — the crown is not mine to give; and my people stand round me in arms to defend the king of their choice. What next?"

"Next, offers William to withdraw his troops from the land, if thou and thy council and chiefs will submit to the arbitrement of our most holy Pontiff, Alexander the Second, and abide by his decision whether thou or my liege have the best right to the throne."

"This, as churchman," said the Abbot of the great Convent of Peterboro' (who, with the Abbot of Hide, had joined the march of Harold, deeming as one the cause of altar and throne), "this as churchman, may *I* take leave to answer. Never yet hath it been heard in England that the spiritual suzerain of Rome should give us our kings."

"And," said Harold, with a bitter smile, "the Pope hath already summoned me to this trial, as if the laws of England were kept in the rolls of the Vatican! Already, if rightly informed, the Pope hath been pleased to decide that **our**

Saxon land is the Norman's. I reject a judge without a right to decide; and I mock at a sentence that profanes Heaven in its insult to men. Is this all?"

"One last offer yet remains," replied the monk, sternly. "This knight shall deliver its import. But ere I depart, and thou and thine are rendered up to Vengeance Divine, I speak the words of a mightier chief than William of Rouen. Thus saith his Holiness, with whom rests the power to bind and to loose, to bless and to curse: 'Harold the Perjurer, thou art accursed! On thee and on all who lift hand in thy cause, rests the interdict of the Church. Thou art excommunicated from the family of Christ. On thy land, with its peers and its people, yea, to the beast in the field and the bird in the air, to the seed as the sower, the harvest as the reaper, rests God's anathema! The bull of the Vatican is in the tent of the Norman; the gonfanon of Saint Peter hallows yon armies to the service of Heaven. March on, then: ye march as the Assyrian; and the angel of the Lord awaits ye on the way!'"

At these words, which for the first time apprised the English leaders that their king and kingdom were under the awful ban of excommunication, the thegns and abbots gazed on each other aghast. A visible shudder passed over the whole warlike conclave, save only three, Harold and Gurth and Haco.

The king himself was so moved by indignation at the insolence of the monk, and by scorn at the fulmen, which, resting not alone on his own head, presumed to blast the liberties of a nation, that he strode towards the speaker, and it is even said of him by the Norman chroniclers, that he raised his hand as if to strike the denouncer to the earth.

But Gurth interposed, and with his clear eye serenely shining with virtuous passion, he stood betwixt monk and king.

"O thou," he exclaimed, "with the words of religion on thy lips, and the devices of fraud in thy heart, hide thy front in thy cowl, and slink back to thy master. Heard ye not, thegns and abbots, — heard ye not this bad, false man offer, as if for peace, and as with the desire of justice, that the Pope should arbitrate between your king and the Norman? Yet all the

while the monk knew that the Pope had already predetermined the cause; and had ye fallen into the wile, ye would
but have cowered under the verdict of a judgment that has
presumed, even before it invoked ye to the trial, to dispose
of a free people and an ancient kingdom!"

"It is true, it is true!" cried the thegns, rallying from their
first superstitious terror, and, with their plain English sense
of justice, revolted at the perfidy which the priest's overtures
had concealed. "We will hear no more; away with the
Swikebode!"[1]

The pale cheek of the monk turned yet paler, he seemed
abashed by the storm of resentment he had provoked; and in
some fear, perhaps, at the dark faces bent on him, he slunk
behind his comrade the knight, who as yet had said nothing,
but, his face concealed by his helmet, stood motionless like a
steel statue. And, in fact, these two ambassadors, the one in
his monk garb, the other in his iron array, were types and
representatives of the two forces now brought to bear upon
Harold and England, — Chivalry and the Church.

At the momentary discomfiture of the Priest, now stood
forth the Warrior; and, throwing back his helmet, so that
the whole steel cap rested on the nape of the neck, leaving
the haughty face and half-shaven head bare, Mallet de Graville thus spoke: —

"The ban of the Church is against ye, warriors and chiefs
of England, but for the crime of one man! Remove it from
yourselves: on his single head be the curse and the conse-
quence. Harold, called King of England, failing the two
milder offers of my comrade, thus saith from the lips of his
knight (once thy guest, thy admirer, and friend), — thus saith
William the Norman: ' Though sixty thousand warriors under
the banner of the Apostle wait at his beck (and from what I
see of thy force, thou canst marshal to thy guilty side scarce
a third of the number), yet will Count William lay aside all
advantage, save what dwells in strong arm and good cause;
and here, in presence of thy thegns, I challenge thee in his
name to decide the sway of this realm by single battle. On

---

[1] Traitor-messenger.

horse and in mail, with sword and with spear, knight to knight, man to man, wilt thou meet William the Norman?'"

Before Harold could reply, and listen to the first impulse of a valour which his worst Norman maligner, in the after day of triumphant calumny, never so lied as to impugn, the thegns themselves, almost with one voice, took up the reply.

"No strife between a man and a man shall decide the liberties of thousands!"

"Never!" exclaimed Gurth. "It were an insult to the whole people to regard this as a strife between two chiefs which should wear a crown. When the invader is in our land, the war is with a nation, not a king. And, by the very offer, this Norman Count (who cannot even speak our tongue) shows how little he knows of the laws by which, under our native kings, we have all as great an interest as a king himself in our Fatherland."

"Thou hast heard the answer of England from those lips, Sire de Graville," said Harold; "mine but repeat and sanction it. I will not give the crown to William in lieu for disgrace and an earldom. I will not abide by the arbitrement of a Pope who has dared to affix a curse upon freedom. I will not so violate the principle which in these realms knits king and people, as to arrogate to my single arm the right to dispose of the birthright of the living, and their races unborn; nor will I deprive the meanest soldier under my banner of the joy and the glory to fight for his native land. If William seek me, he shall find me where war is the fiercest, where the corpses of his men lie the thickest on the plains, defending this standard, or rushing on his own. And so, not Monk and Pope, but God in his wisdom, adjudge between us!"

"So be it," said Mallet de Graville, solemnly, and his helmet re-closed over his face. "Look to it, recreant knight, perjured Christian, and usurping King! The bones of the Dead fight against thee."

"And the fleshless hands of the Saints marshal the hosts of the living," said the monk.

And so the messengers turned, without obeisance or salute, and strode silently away.

CHAPTER VI.

THE rest of that day, and the whole of the next, were consumed by both armaments in the completion of their preparations.

William was willing to delay the engagement as long as he could, for he was not without hope that Harold might abandon his formidable position, and become the assailing party; and, moreover, he wished to have full time for his prelates and priests to inflame to the utmost, by their representations of William's moderation in his embassy, and Harold's presumptuous guilt in rejection, the fiery fanaticism of all enlisted under the gonfanon of the Church.

On the other hand, every delay was of advantage to Harold, in giving him leisure to render his entrenchments yet more effectual, and to allow time for such reinforcements as his orders had enjoined, or the patriotism of the country might arouse; but, alas! those reinforcements were scanty and insignificant; a few stragglers in the immediate neighbourhood arrived, but no aid came from London, no indignant country poured forth a swarming population. In fact, the very fame of Harold, and the good fortune that had hitherto attended his arms, contributed to the stupid lethargy of the people. That he who had just subdued the terrible Norsemen, with the mighty Hardrada at their head, should succumb to those dainty "Frenchmen," as they chose to call the Normans, of whom, in their insular ignorance of the Continent, they knew but little, and whom they had seen flying in all directions at the return of Godwin, was a preposterous demand on the imagination.

Nor was this all: in London there had already formed a cabal in favour of the Atheling. The claims of birth can never be so wholly set aside, but what, even for the most unworthy heir of an ancient line, some adherents will be

found. The prudent traders thought it best not to engage
actively on behalf of the reigning king, in his present combat
with the Norman pretender; a large number of would-be
statesmen thought it best for the country to remain for the
present neutral. Grant the worst, — grant that Harold were
defeated or slain; would it not be wise to reserve their
strength to support the Atheling? William might have
some personal cause of quarrel against Harold, but he could
have none against Edgar; he might depose the son of Godwin,
but could he dare to depose the descendant of Cerdic, the
natural heir of Edward? There is reason to think that Stigand, and a large party of the Saxon Churchmen, headed this
faction.

But the main causes for defection were not in adherence to
one chief or to another. They were to be found in selfish
inertness, in stubborn conceit, in the long peace, and the ener-
vate superstition which had relaxed the sinews of the old
Saxon manhood; in that indifference to things ancient, which
contempt for old names and races engendered; that timorous
spirit of calculation, which the over-regard for wealth had
fostered; which made men averse to leave trade and farm for
the perils of the field, and jeopardize their possessions if the
foreigner should prevail.

Accustomed already to kings of a foreign race, and having
fared well under Canute, there were many who said, "What
matters who sits on the throne? the king must be equally
bound by our laws." Then too was heard the favourite argument of all slothful minds: "Time enough yet! one battle lost
is not England won. Marry, we shall turn out fast eno' if
Harold be beaten."

Add to all these causes for apathy and desertion, the haughty
jealousies of the several populations not yet wholly fused into
one empire. The Northumbrian Danes, untaught even by their
recent escape from the Norwegian, regarded with ungrateful
coldness a war limited at present to the southern coasts; and
the vast territory under Mercia was, with more excuse, equally
supine; while their two young earls, too new in their command to have much sway with their subject populations, had

they been in their capitals, had now arrived in London, and there lingered, making head, doubtless, against the intrigues in favour of the Atheling, — so little had Harold's marriage with Aldyth brought him, at the hour of his dreadest need, the power for which happiness had been resigned!

Nor must we put out of account, in summing the causes which at this awful crisis weakened the arm of England, the curse of slavery amongst the theowes, which left the lowest part of the population wholly without interest in the defence of the land. Too late — too late for all but unavailing slaughter, the spirit of the country rose amidst the violated pledges, but under the iron heel, of the Norman Master! Had that spirit put forth all its might for one day with Harold, where had been the centuries of bondage! Oh, shame to the absent — all blessed those present! There was no hope for England out of the scanty lines of the immortal army encamped on the field of Hastings. There, long on earth, and vain vaunts of poor pride, shall be kept the roll of the robber-invaders. In what roll are *your* names, holy Heroes of the Soil? Yes, may the prayer of the Virgin Queen be registered on high; and assoiled of all sin, O ghosts of the glorious Dead, may ye rise from your graves at the trump of the angel; and your names, lost on earth, shine radiant and stainless amidst the Hierarchy of Heaven!

Dull came the shades of evening, and pale through the rolling clouds glimmered the rising stars, when — all prepared, all arrayed — Harold sat with Haco and Gurth, in his tent; and before them stood a man, half French by origin, who had just returned from the Norman camp.

"So thou didst mingle with the men undiscovered?" said the king.

"No, not undiscovered, my lord. I fell in with a knight, whose name I have since heard as that of Mallet de Graville, who wilily seemed to believe in what I stated, and who gave me meat and drink, with debonair courtesy. Then said he abruptly: 'Spy from Harold, thou hast come to see the strength of the Norman. Thou shalt have thy will, — follow me.' Therewith he led me, all startled I own, through the lines; and, O King, I should deem them indeed countless as the sands, and resistless as the waves, but that, strange as it may seem to thee, I saw more monks than warriors."

"How! thou jestest!" said Gurth, surprised.

"No; for thousands by thousands, they were praying and kneeling; and their heads were all shaven with the tonsure of priests."

"Priests are they not," cried Harold, with his calm smile, "but doughty warriors and dauntless knights."

Then he continued his questions to the spy; and his smile vanished at the accounts, not only of the numbers of the force, but their vast provision of missiles, and the almost incredible proportion of their cavalry.

As soon as the spy had been dismissed, the king turned to his kinsmen.

"What think you?" he said; "shall we judge ourselves of the foe? The night will be dark anon; our steeds are fleet, and not shod with iron like the Normans; the sward noiseless. What think you?"

"A merry conceit," cried the blithe Leofwine. "I should like much to see the boar in his den, ere he taste of my spear-point."

"And I," said Gurth, "do feel so restless a fever in my veins, that I would fain cool it by the night air. Let us go: I know all the ways of the country; for hither have I come often with hawk and hound. But let us wait yet till the night is more hushed and deep."

The clouds had gathered over the whole surface of the skies, and there hung sullen; and the mists were cold and gray on the lower grounds, when the four Saxon chiefs set forth on their secret and perilous enterprise.

> " Knights and riders took they none,
> Squires and varlets of foot not one ;
> All unarmed of weapon and weed,
> Save the shield and spear and the sword at need."[1]

[1] Ne meinent od els chevalier,
Varlet à pie ne eskuier ;
Ne nul d'els n'a armes portée,
Forz sol escu, lance, et espée.
Roman de Rou, Part ii., v. 12, 126.

Passing their own sentinels, they entered a wood, Gurth leading the way, and catching glimpses, through the irregular path, of the blazing lights, that shone red over the pause of the Norman war.

William had moved on his army to within about two miles from the farthest outpost of the Saxon, and contracted his lines into compact space; the reconnoiterers were thus enabled, by the light of the links and watchfires, to form no inaccurate notion of the formidable foe whom the morrow was to meet. The ground[1] on which they stood was high, and in the deep shadow of the wood; with one of the large dikes common to the Saxon boundaries in front, so that, even if discovered, a barrier not easily passed lay between them and the foe.

In regular lines and streets extended huts of branches for the meaner soldiers, leading up, in serried rows but broad vistas, to the tents of the knights, and the gaudier pavilions of the counts and prelates. There were to be seen the flags of Bretagne and Anjou, of Burgundy, of Flanders, even the ensign of France, which the volunteers from that country had assumed; and right in the midst of this Capital of War, the gorgeous pavilion of William himself, with a dragon of gold before it, surmounting the staff, from which blazed the Papal gonfanon. In every division they heard the anvils of the armourers, the measured tread of the sentries, the neigh and snort of innumerable steeds. And along the lines, between hut and tent, they saw tall shapes passing to and from the forge and smithy, bearing mail and swords and shafts. No sound of revel, no laugh of wassail, was heard in the consecrated camp; all was astir, but with the grave and earnest preparations of thoughtful men. As the four Saxons halted silent, each might have heard, through the remoter din, the other's painful breathing.

[1] Ke d'une angarde [1] u ils 'estuient,
Cels de l'ost virent, ki pres furent.

Roman de Rou, Part ii., v. 12, 126.

---

[1] Eminence.

At length, from two tents, placed to the right and left of the duke's pavilion, there came a sweet tinkling sound, as of deep silver bells. At that note there was an evident and universal commotion throughout the armament. The roar of the hammers ceased, and from every green hut and every gray tent swarmed the host. Now, rows of living men lined the camp-streets, leaving still a free, though narrow passage in the midst. And, by the blaze of more than a thousand torches, the Saxons saw processions of priests, in their robes and aubes, with censer and rood, coming down the various avenues. As the priests paused, the warriors knelt; and there was a low murmur as if of confession, and the sign of lifted hands, as if in absolution and blessing. Suddenly, from the outskirts of the camp, and full in sight, emerged, from one of the cross lanes, Odo of Bayeux himself, in his white surplice, and the cross in his right hand. Yea, even to the meanest and lowliest soldiers of the armament, whether taken from honest craft and peaceful calling, or the outpourings of Europe's sinks and sewers, catamarans from the Alps, and cut-throats from the Rhine, — yea, even among the vilest and the meanest, came the anointed brother of the great duke, the haughtiest prelate in Christendom, whose heart even then was fixed on the Pontiff's throne, — there he came, to absolve and to shrive and to bless. And the red watchfires streamed on his proud face and spotless robes, as the Children of Wrath knelt around the Delegate of Peace.

Harold's hand clenched firm on the arm of Gurth, and his old scorn of the monk broke forth in his bitter smile and his muttered words. But Gurth's face was sad and awed.

And now, as the huts and the canvas thus gave up the living, they could indeed behold the enormous disparity of numbers with which it was their doom to contend; and, over those numbers, that dread intensity of zeal, that sublimity of fanaticism, which from one end of that war-town to the other consecrated injustice, gave the heroism of the martyr to ambition, and blended the whisper of lusting avarice with the self-applauses of the saint!

Not a word said the four Saxons. But as the priestly

procession glided to the farther quarters of the armament, as the soldiers in their neighbourhood disappeared within their lodgments, and the torches moved from them to the more distant vistas of the camp, like lines of retreating stars, Gurth heaved a heavy sigh, and turned his horse's head from the scene.

But scarce had they gained the centre of the wood, than there rose, as from the heart of the armament, a swell of solemn voices. For the night had now come to the third watch,[1] in which, according to the belief of the age, angel and fiend were alike astir, and that church-division of time was marked and hallowed by a monastic hymn.

Inexpressibly grave, solemn, and mournful came the strain through the drooping boughs, and the heavy darkness of the air; and it continued to thrill in the ears of the riders till they had passed the wood, and the cheerful watchfires from their own heights broke upon them to guide their way. They rode rapidly, but still in silence, past their sentries; and, ascending the slopes, where the force lay thick, how different were the sounds that smote them! Round the large fires the men grouped in great circles, with the ale-horns and flagons passing merrily from hand to hand; shouts of drink-hæl and was-hæl, bursts of gay laughter, snatches of old songs, old as the days of Athelstan, — varying, where the Anglo-Danes lay, into the far more animated and kindling poetry of the Pirate North, — still spoke of the heathen time when War was a joy, and Valhalla was the heaven.

"By my faith," said Leofwine, brightening, "these are sounds and sights that do a man's heart good, after those doleful ditties, and the long faces of the shavelings. I vow by Saint Alban, that I felt my veins curdling into ice-bolts, when that dirge came through the wood-holt. Hollo, Sexwolf, my tall man, lift us up that full horn of thine, and keep thyself within the pins, Master Wassailer; we must have steady feet and cool heads to-morrow."

Sexwolf, who, with a band of Harold's veterans, was at full

---

[1] Midnight.

carousal, started up at the young earl's greetings, and looked lovingly into his smiling face as he reached him the horn.

"Heed what my brother bids thee, Sexwolf," said Harold, severely; "the hands that draw shafts against us to-morrow will not tremble with the night's wassail."

"Nor ours either, my lord the King," said Sexwolf, boldly; "our heads can bear both drink and blows, — and " — sinking his voice into a whisper — "the rumour runs that the odds are so against us, that I would not, for all thy fair brother's earl-doms, have our men other than blithe to-night."

Harold answered not, but moved on; and coming then within full sight of the bold Saxons of Kent, the unmixed sons of the Saxon soil, and the special favourers of the House of Godwin, so affectionate, hearty, and cordial was their joy-ous shout of his name, that he felt his kingly heart leap within him. Dismounting, he entered the circle, and with the august frankness of a noble chief, nobly popular, gave to all cheering smile and animating word. That done, he said more gravely: "In less than an hour, all wassail must cease, — my bodes will come round; and then sound sleep, my brave merry men, and lusty rising with the lark!"

"As you will, as you will, dear our King," cried Vebba, as spokesman for the soldiers. "Fear us not! Life and death, we are yours."

"Life and death yours, and freedom's," cried the Kent men.

Coming now towards the royal tent beside the standard, the discipline was more perfect, and the hush decorous. For round that standard were both the special body-guard of the king, and the volunteers from London and Middlesex, — men more intelligent than the bulk of the army, and more gravely aware, therefore, of the might of the Norman sword.

Harold entered his tent, and threw himself on his couch, in deep revery; his brothers and Haco watched him silently. At length Gurth approached; and, with a reverence rare in the familiar intercourse between the two, knelt at his brother's side, and taking Harold's hand in his, looked him full in the face, his eyes moist with tears, and said thus: —

"Oh, Harold! never prayer have I asked of thee that thou hast not granted: grant me this! sorest of all, it may be, to grant, but most fitting of all for me to press. Think not, O beloved brother, O honoured King, think not that it is with slighting reverence that I lay rough hand on the wound deepest at thy heart. But, however surprised or compelled, sure it is that thou didst make oath to William, and upon the relics of saints; avoid this battle, — for I see that thought is now within thy soul; that thought haunted thee in the words of the monk to-day; in the sight of that awful camp to-night, — avoid this battle, and do not thyself stand in arms against the man to whom the oath was pledged!"

"Gurth, Gurth!" exclaimed Harold, pale and writhing.

"We," continued his brother, "we at least have taken no oath, no perjury is charged against us; vainly the thunders of the Vatican are launched on our heads. Our war is just: we but defend our country. Leave us, then, to fight to-morrow; thou retire towards London and raise fresh armies; if we win, the danger is past; if we lose, thou wilt avenge us. And England is not lost while thou survivest."

"Gurth, Gurth!" again exclaimed Harold, in a voice piercing in its pathos of reproach.

"Gurth counsels well," said Haco, abruptly; "there can be no doubt of the wisdom of his words. Let the king's kinsmen lead the troops; let the king himself with his guard hasten to London and ravage and lay waste the country as he retreats by the way;[1] so that even if William beat us, all supplies will fail him; he will be in a land without forage, and victory here will aid him nought, for you, my liege, will have a force equal to his own, ere he can march to the gates of London."

"Faith and troth, the young Haco speaks like a graybeard; he hath not lived in Rouen for nought," quoth Leofwine. "Hear him, my Harold, and leave us to shave the Normans yet more closely than the barber hath already shorn."

---

[1] This counsel the Norman chronicler ascribes to Gurth, but it is so at variance with the character of that hero, that it is here assigned to the unscrupulous intellect of Haco.

Harold turned ear and eye to each of the speakers, and, as Leofwine closed, he smiled.

"Ye have chid me well, kinsmen, for a thought that had entered into my mind ere ye spake —"

Gurth interrupted the king, and said anxiously, —

"To retreat with the whole army upon London, and refuse to meet the Norman till with numbers more fairly matched?"

"That had been my thought," said Harold, surprised.

"Such for a moment, too, was mine," said Gurth, sadly; "but it is too late. Such a measure, now, would have all the disgrace of flight, and bring none of the profits of retreat. The ban of the Church would get wind; our priests, awed and alarmed, might wield it against us; the whole population would be damped and disheartened; rivals to the crown might start up; the realm be divided. No, it is impossible!"

"Impossible," said Harold, calmly. "And if the army cannot retreat, of all men to stand firm, surely it is the captain and the king. *I*, Gurth, leave others to dare the fate from which I fly! *I* give weight to the impious curse of the Pope, by shrinking from its idle blast! *I* confirm and ratify the oath, from which all law must absolve me, by forsaking the cause of the land which I purify myself when I guard! *I* leave to others the agony of the martyrdom or the glory of the conquest! Gurth, thou art more cruel than the Norman! And I, son of Sweyn, *I* ravage the land committed to my charge, and despoil the fields which I cannot keep! Oh, Haco, that indeed were to be the traitor and the recreant! No, whatever the sin of my oath, never will I believe that Heaven can punish millions for the error of one man. Let the bones of the dead war against us; in life, they were men like ourselves, and no saints in the calendar so holy as the freemen who fight for their hearths and their altars. Nor do I see aught to alarm us even in these grave human odds. We have but to keep fast these entrenchments, — preserve, man by man, our invincible line, — and the waves will but split on our rock: ere the sun set to-morrow, we shall see the tide ebb, leaving, as waifs, but the dead of the baffled invader.

"Fare ye well, loving kinsmen; kiss me, my brothers; kiss

me on the cheek, my Haco. Go now to your tents. Sleep in peace, and wake with the trumpet to the gladness of noble war!"

Slowly the earls left the king, — slowest of all the lingering Gurth; and when all were gone, and Harold was alone, he threw round a rapid, troubled glance, and then, hurrying to the simple imageless crucifix that stood on its pedestal at the farther end of the tent, he fell on his knees, and faltered out, while his breast heaved, and his frame shook with the travail of his passion, —

"If my sin be beyond a pardon, my oath without recall, on me, on me, O Lord of Hosts, on me alone the doom. Not on them, not on them, — not on England!"

CHAPTER VII.

On the 14th of October, 1066, the day of Saint Calixtus, the Norman force was drawn out in battle array. Mass had been said; Odo and the Bishop of Coutance had blessed the troops, and received their vow never more to eat flesh on the anniversary of that day. And Odo had mounted his snow-white charger, and already drawn up the cavalry against the coming of his brother the duke. The army was mar- shalled in three great divisions.

Roger de Montgommeri and William Fitzosborne led the first, and with them were the forces from Picardy and the countship of Boulogne, and the fiery Franks, Geoffric Martel and the German Hugues (a prince of fame); Aimeri, Lord of Thouars, and the sons of Alain Fergant, Duke of Bretagne, led the second, which comprised the main bulk of the allies from Bretagne and Maine and Poitou. But both these divi- sions were intermixed with Normans, under their own special Norman chiefs.

The third section embraced the flower of martial Europe, the most renowned of the Norman race; whether those knights bore the French titles into which their ancestral Scandinavian names had been transformed,— Sires of Beaufou and Harcourt, Abbeville, and De Molun, Montfichet, Grantmesnil, Lacie, D'Aincourt, and D'Asnieres,— or whether, still preserving, amidst their daintier titles, the old names that had scattered dismay through the seas of the Baltic,— Osborne and Tonstain, Mallet and Bulver, Brand and Bruse.[1] And over this division presided Duke William. Here was the main body of the matchless cavalry, to which, however, orders were given to support either of the other sections, as need might demand. And with this body were also the reserve; for it is curious to notice, that William's strategy resembled in much that of the last great Invader of Nations,— relying first upon the effect of the charge; secondly, upon a vast reserve brought to bear at the exact moment on the weakest point of the foe.

All the horsemen were in complete link or net mail,[2] armed with spears and strong swords, and long, pear-shaped shields, with the device either of a cross or a dragon.[3] The archers, on whom William greatly relied, were numerous in all three of the corps,[4] were armed more lightly,— helms on their heads, but with leather or quilted breastplates, and "panels," or gaiters, for the lower limbs.

But before the chiefs and captains rode to their several posts, they assembled round William, whom Fitzosborne had

---

[1] Osborne (Asbiorn), one of the most common of Danish and Norwegian names; Tonstain, Toustain, or Tostain, the same as Tosti, or Tostig, — Danish (Harold's brother is called Tostain or Toustain, in the Norman chronicles); Brand, a name common to Dane or Norwegian. Bulmer is a Norwegian name, and so is Bulver, or Bolvär, — which is, indeed, so purely Scandinavian that it is one of the warlike names given to Odin himself by the Norse Scalds. Bulverhithe still commemorates the landing of a Norwegian son of the war-god. Bruce, the ancestor of the deathless Scot, also bears in that name, more illustrious than all, the proof of his Scandinavian birth.

[2] This mail appears in that age to have been sewn upon linen or cloth. In the later age of the Crusaders, it was more artful, and the links supported each other, without being attached to any other material.

[3] Bayeux tapestry.

[4] The cross-bow is not to be seen in the Bayeux tapestry; the Norman bows are not long.

called betimes, and who had not yet endued his heavy mail, that all men might see suspended from his throat certain relics chosen out of those on which Harold had pledged his fatal oath. Standing on an eminence in front of all his lines, the consecrated banner behind him, and Bayard, his Spanish *destrier*, held by his squires at his side, the duke conversed cheerily with his barons, often pointing to the relics. Then, in sight of all, he put on his mail, and, by the haste of his squires, the back-piece was presented to him first. The superstitious Normans recoiled as at an evil omen.

"Tut!" said the ready chief; "not in omens and divinations, but in God, trust I! Yet, good omen indeed is this, and one that may give heart to the most doubtful; for it betokens that the last shall be first, — the dukedom a kingdom, the count a king! Ho there, Rou de Terni, as Hereditary Standard-bearer take thy right, and hold fast to yon holy gonfanon."

" *Grant merci,*" said De Terni, "not to-day shall a standard ·be borne by me, for I shall have need of my right arm for my sword, and my left for my charger's rein and my trusty shield."

"Thou sayest right, and we can ill spare such a warrior. Gautier Giffart, Sire de Longueville, to thee is the gonfanon."

" *Beau Sire,*" answered Gautier, " *par Dex, Merci.* But my head is gray and my arm weak; and the little strength left me I would spend in smiting the English at the head of my men."

" *Per la resplendar Dé,*" cried William, frowning, "do ye think, my proud vavasours, to fail me in this great need?"

"Nay," said Gautier; "but I have a great host of chevaliers and paid soldiers, and without the old man at their head will they fight as well?"

"Then approach thou, Tonstain le Blanc, son of Rou," said William; "and be thine the charge of a standard that shall wave ere nightfall over the brows of thy — *King!*" A young knight, tall and strong as his Danish ancestor, stepped forth, and laid gripe on the banner.

Then William, now completely armed save his helmet,

sprang at one bound on his steed. A shout of admiration rang from the quens and knights.

"Saw ye ever such *beau rei?*"[1] said the Vicomte de Thouars.

The shout was caught by the lines, and echoed far, wide, and deep through the armament, as in all his singular majesty of brow and mien, William rode forth: lifting his hand, the shout hushed, and thus he spoke, "loud as a trumpet with a silver sound": —

"Normans and soldiers, long renowned in the lips of men, and now hallowed by the blessing of the Church! I have not brought you over the wide seas for my cause alone, — what I gain, ye gain. If I take the land, you will share it. Fight your best, and spare not; no retreat, and no quarter! I am not come here for my cause alone, but to avenge our whole nation for the felonies of yonder English. They butchered our kinsmen the Danes, on the night of Saint Brice; they murdered Alfred, the brother of their last king, and decimated the Normans who were with him. Yonder they stand, — malefactors that await their doom! and ye the doomsmen! Never, even in a good cause, were yon English illustrious for warlike temper and martial glory.[2] Remember how easily the Danes subdued them! Are ye less than Danes, or I than Canute? By victory ye obtain vengeance, glory, honours, lands, spoil, — ay, spoil beyond your wildest dreams. By defeat, — yea, even but by loss of ground, ye are given up to the sword! Escape there is not, for the ships are useless. Before you the foe, behind you the ocean. Normans, remember the feats of your countrymen in Sicily! Behold a Sicily more rich! Lordships and lands to the living, — glory and salvation to those who die under the gonfanon of the Church! On, to the cry of the Norman warrior, — the cry before which have fled so often the prowest Paladins of Burgundy and France, — 'Notre Dame et Dex aide!'"[3]

Meanwhile, no less vigilant, and in his own strategy no less skilful, Harold had marshalled his men. He formed two divisions, — those in front of the entrenchments, those within

[1] Roman de Rou.　　[2] William of Poitiers.　　[3] *Dieu nous aide.*

it. At the first, the men of Kent, as from time immemorial, claimed the honour of the van, under "the Pale Charger,"— famous banner of Hengist. This force was drawn up in the form of the Anglo-Danish wedge; the foremost lines in the triangle all in heavy mail, armed with their great axes, and covered by their immense shields. Behind these lines, in the interior of the wedge, were the archers, protected by the front rows of the heavy armed; while the few horsemen— few indeed compared with the Norman cavalry— were artfully disposed where they could best harass and distract the formidable chivalry with which they were instructed to skirmish, and not peril actual encounter. Other bodies of the light armed, slingers, javelin-throwers, and archers, were planted in spots carefully selected, according as they were protected by trees, bushwood, and dikes. The Northumbrians (that is, all the warlike population north the Humber, including Yorkshire, Westmoreland, Cumberland, etc.) were, for their present shame and future ruin, absent from that field, save, indeed, a few who had joined Harold in his march to London; but there were the mixed races of Hertfordshire and Essex, with the pure Saxons of Sussex and Surrey, and a large body of the sturdy Anglo-Danes from Lincolnshire, Ely, and Norfolk. Men, too, there were, half of old British blood, from Dorset, Somerset, and Gloucester.

And all were marshalled according to those touching and pathetic tactics which speak of a nation more accustomed to defend than to aggrieve. To that field the head of each family led his sons and kinsfolk; every ten families (or tything) were united under their own chosen captain. Every ten of these tythings had, again, some loftier chief, dear to the populace in peace; and so on the holy circle spread from household, hamlet, town,— till, all combined as one county under one earl, the warriors fought under the eyes of their own kinsfolk, friends, neighbours, chosen chiefs! What wonder that they were brave!

The second division comprised Harold's house-carles, or body-guard, the veterans especially attached to his family, the companions of his successful wars, a select band of the martial East-Anglians, the soldiers supplied by London and Middlesex, and who, both in arms, discipline, martial temper, and athletic habits, ranked high among the most stalwart of the troops, mixed, as their descent was, from the warlike Dane and the sturdy Saxon. In this division, too, was comprised the reserve. And it was all encompassed by the palisades and breastworks, to which were but three sorties, whence the defenders might sally, or through which at need the vanguard might secure a retreat. All the heavy armed had mail and shields similar to the Normans, though somewhat less heavy; the light armed had, some tunics of quilted linen, some of hide; helmets of the last material, spears, javelins, swords, and clubs. But the main arm of the host was in the great shield, and the great axe wielded by men larger in stature and stronger of muscle than the majority of the Normans, whose physical race had deteriorated, partly by inter-marriage with the more delicate Frank, partly by the haughty disdain of foot exercise.

Mounting a swift and light steed, intended not for encounter (for it was the custom of English kings to fight on foot, in token that where they fought there was no retreat), but to bear the rider rapidly from line to line,[1] King Harold rode to the front of the vanguard, his brothers by his side. His head, like his great foe's, was bare; nor could there be a more striking contrast than that of the broad unwrinkled brow of the Saxon, with his fair locks, the sign of royalty and freedom, parted and falling over the collar of mail, the clear and steadfast eye of blue, the cheek somewhat hollowed by kingly cares, but flushed now with manly pride, the form stalwart and erect, but spare in its graceful symmetry, and void of all that theatric pomp of bearing which was assumed by William, — no greater contrast could there be than that which the simple earnest Hero-king presented, to the brow furrowed with harsh ire and politic wile, the shaven hair of monastic affectation, the dark, sparkling tiger eye, and the vast proportions that awed the gaze in the port and form of

[1] Thus, when at the battle of Barnet Earl Warwick, the king-maker, slew his horse and fought on foot, he followed the old traditional custom of Saxon chiefs.

the imperious Norman. Deep and loud and hearty as the shout with which his armaments had welcomed William was that which now greeted the king of the English host; and clear and full, and practised in the storm of popular assemblies, went his voice down the listening lines.

"This day, O friends and Englishmen, sons of our common land, — this day ye fight for liberty. The Count of the Normans hath, I know, a mighty army; I disguise not its strength. That army he hath collected together, by promising to each man a share in the spoils of England. Already, in his court and his camp, he hath parcelled out the lands of this kingdom; and fierce are the robbers who fight for the hope of plunder! But he cannot offer to his greatest chief boons nobler than those I offer to my meanest freeman, — liberty and right and law in the soil of his fathers! Ye have heard of the miseries endured in the old time under the Dane, but they were slight indeed to those which ye may expect from the Norman. The Dane was kindred to us in language and in law, and who now can tell Saxon from Dane? But yon men would rule ye in a language ye know not, by a law that claims the crown as the right of the sword, and divides the land among the hirelings of an army. We baptized the Dane, and the Church tamed his fierce soul into peace; but yon men make the Church itself their ally, and march to carnage under the banner profaned to the foulest of human wrongs! Outscourings of all nations, they come against you. Ye fight as brothers under the eyes of your fathers and chosen chiefs; ye fight for the women ye would save from the ravisher; ye fight for the children ye would guard from eternal bondage; ye fight for the altars which yon banner now darkens! Foreign priest is a tyrant as ruthless and stern as ye shall find foreign baron and king! Let no man dream of retreat; every inch of ground that ye yield is the soil of your native land. For me, on this field I peril all. Think that mine eye is upon you wherever ye are. If a line waver or shrink, ye shall hear in the midst the voice of your king. Hold fast to your ranks; remember, such amongst you as fought with me against Hardrada, — remember that it was not till the Norsemen lost, by rash sallies, their serried array, that our arms prevailed against them. Be warned by their fatal error, break not the form of the battle; and I tell you, on the faith of a soldier who never yet hath left field without victory, that ye cannot be beaten. While I speak, the winds swell the sails of the Norse ships, bearing home the corpse of Hardrada. Accomplish this day the last triumph of England; add to these hills a new mount of the conquered dead! And when, in far times and strange lands, scald and scop shall praise the brave man for some valiant deed wrought in some holy cause, they shall say, 'He was brave as those who fought by the side of Harold, and swept from the sward of England the hosts of the haughty Norman.'"

Scarcely had the rapturous hurrahs of the Saxons closed on this speech, when full in sight, northwest of Hastings, came the first division of the Invader.

Harold remained gazing at them, and not seeing the other sections in movement, said to Gurth, "If these are all that they venture out, the day is ours."

"Look yonder!" said the sombre Haco, and he pointed to the long array that now gleamed from the wood through which the Saxon kinsmen had passed the night before; and scarcely were these cohorts in view, than lo! from a third quarter advanced the glittering knighthood under the duke. All three divisions came on in simultaneous assault, two on either wing of the Saxon vanguard, the third (the Norman) towards the entrenchments.

In the midst of the duke's cohort was the sacred gonfanon, and in front of it and of the whole line, rode a strange warrior of gigantic height. And as he rode, the warrior sang,—

> " Chanting loud the lusty strain
> Of Roland and of Charlemain,
> And the dead who, deathless all,
> Fell at famous Roncesval." [1]

---

[1] Devant li Dus alout cantant
De Karlemaine è de Rollant,
Ed 'Olever e des Vassalls,
Ki morurent en Ronchevals.
Roman de Rou, Part ii. l. 13, 151.

Much research has been made by French antiquaries to discover the old Chant de Ronald, but in vain.

And the knights, no longer singing hymn and litany, swelled, hoarse through their helmets, the martial chorus. This warrior, in front of the duke and the horsemen, seemed beside himself with the joy of battle. As he rode, and as he chanted, he threw up his sword in the air like a gleeman, catching it nimbly as it fell,[1] and flourishing it wildly, till, as if unable to restrain his fierce exhilaration, he fairly put spurs to his horse, and, dashing forward to the very front of a detachment of Saxon riders, shouted, —

"A Taillefer! a Taillefer!" and by voice and gesture challenged forth some one to single combat.

A fiery young thegn, who knew the Romance tongue, started forth and crossed swords with the poet; but by what seemed rather a juggler's sleight of hand than a knight's fair fence, Taillefer, again throwing up and catching his sword with incredible rapidity, shore the unhappy Saxon from the helm to the chine, and riding over his corpse, shouting and laughing, he again renewed his challenge. A second rode forth and shared the same fate. The rest of the English horsemen stared at each other aghast; the shouting, singing, juggling giant seemed to them not knight, but demon; and that single incident, preliminary to all other battle, in sight of the whole field, might have sufficed to damp the ardour of the English, had not Leofwine, who had been despatched by the king with a message to the entrenchments, come in front of the detachment; and his gay spirit, roused and stung by the insolence of the Norman, and the evident dismay of the Saxon riders, without thought of his graver duties, he spurred his light half-mailed steed to the Norman giant; and, not even drawing his sword, but with his spear raised over his head, and his form covered by his shield, he cried in Romance tongue, "Go and chant to the foul fiend, O croaking minstrel!" Taillefer rushed forward, his sword shivered on the Saxon shield, and in the same moment he fell a corpse under the hoofs of his steed, transfixed by the Saxon spear.

A cry of woe, in which even William (who, proud of his poet's achievements, had pressed to the foremost line to see

[1] W. Pict., Chron. de Nor.

TAILLEFER, THE GIGANTIC NORMAN, CHALLENGING THE SAXONS.

this new encounter) joined his deep voice, wailed through the Norman ranks; while Leofwine rode deliberately towards them, halted a moment, and then flung his spear in the midst with so deadly an aim, that a young knight, within two of William, reeled on his saddle, groaned, and fell.

"How like ye, O Normans, the Saxon gleemen!" said Leofwine, as he turned slowly, regained the detachment, and bade them heed carefully the orders they had received,—namely, to avoid the direct charge of the Norman horse, but to take every occasion to harass and divert the stragglers; and then blithely singing a Saxon stave, as if inspired by Norman minstrelsy, he rode into the entrenchments.

CHAPTER VIII.

THE two brethren of Waltham, Osgood and Ailred, had arrived a little after daybreak at the spot in which, about half a mile to the rear of Harold's palisades, the beasts of burden that had borne the heavy arms, missiles, luggage, and forage of the Saxon march, were placed in and about the fenced yards of a farm. And many human beings, of both sexes and various ranks, were there assembled, some in breathless expectation, some in careless talk, some in fervent prayer.

The master of the farm, his sons, and the able-bodied ceorls in his employ, had joined the forces of the king, under Gurth, as earl of the county.[1] But many aged theowes, past military service, and young children, grouped around: the first, stolid and indifferent,—the last, prattling, curious, lively, gay. There, too, were the wives of some of the soldiers, who, as common in Saxon expeditions, had followed their husbands

---

[1] For, as Sir F. Palgrave shrewdly conjectures, upon the dismemberment of the vast earldom of Wessex, on Harold's accession to the throne, that portion of it comprising Sussex (the old government of his grandfather Wolnoth) seems to have been assigned to Gurth.

to the field; and there, too, were the ladies of many a Hlaford in the neighbouring district, who, no less true to their mates than the wives of humbler men, were drawn by their English hearts to the fatal spot. A small wooden chapel, half decayed, stood a little behind, with its doors wide open, a sanctuary in case of need; and the interior was thronged with kneeling suppliants.

The two monks joined, with pious gladness, some of their sacred calling, who were leaning over the low wall, and straining their eyes towards the bristling field. A little apart from them, and from all, stood a female,— the hood drawn over her face, silent in her unknown thoughts.

By and by, as the march of the Norman multitude sounded hollow, and the trumps and the fifes and the shouts rolled on through the air in many a stormy peal, the two abbots in the Saxon camp, with their attendant monks, came riding towards the farm from the entrenchments.

The groups gathered round these new comers in haste and eagerness.

"The battle hath begun," said the Abbot of Hide, gravely. "Pray God for England, for never was its people in peril so great from man."

The female started and shuddered at those words.

"And the king, the king," she cried, in a sudden and thrilling voice; "where is he,— the king?"

"Daughter," said the abbot, "the king's post is by his standard; but I left him in the van of his troops. Where he may be now I know not,— wherever the foe presses sorest."

Then dismounting, the abbots entered the yard, to be accosted instantly by all the wives, who deemed, poor souls, that the holy men must, throughout all the field, have seen *their* lords; for each felt as if God's world hung but on the single life in which each pale trembler lived.

With all their faults of ignorance and superstition, the Saxon churchmen loved their flocks; and the good abbots gave what comfort was in their power, and then passed into the chapel, where all who could find room followed them.

The war now raged.

The two divisions of the invading army that included the auxiliaries had sought in vain to surround the English vanguard, and take it in the rear: that noble phalanx had no rear. Deepest an l strongest at the base of the triangle, everywhere a front opposed the foe; shields formed a rampart against the dart, spears a palisade against the horse. While that vanguard maintained its ground, William could not pierce to the entrenchments, the strength of which, however, he was enabled to perceive. He now changed his tactics, joined his knighthood to the other sections, threw his hosts rapidly into many wings, and leaving broad spaces between his archers, — who continued their fiery hail, — ordered his heavy-armed foot to advance on all sides upon the wedge, and break its ranks for the awaiting charge of his horse.

Harold, still in the centre of the vanguard, amidst the men of Kent, continued to animate them all with voice and hand; and, as the Normans now closed in, he flung himself from his steed, and strode on foot, with his mighty battle-axe, to the spot where the rush was dreadest.

Now came the shock, the fight hand-to-hand: spear and lance were thrown aside, axe and sword rose and shore. But before the close-serried lines of the English, with their physical strength, and veteran practice in their own special arm, the Norman foot were mowed as by the scythe. In vain, in the intervals, thundered the repeated charges of the fiery knights; in vain, throughout all, came the shaft and the bolt.

Animated by the presence of their king, fighting amongst them as a simple soldier, but with his eye ever quick to foresee, his voice ever prompt to warn, the men of Kent swerved not a foot from their indomitable ranks. The Norman infantry wavered and gave way; on, step by step, still unbroken in array, pressed the English. And their cry, "Out! out! Holy Crosse!" rose high above the flagging sound of "Ha Rou! Ha Rou! Notre Dame!"

"*Per la resplendar Dé!*" cried William. "Our soldiers are but women in the garb of Normans. Ho, spears to the rescue! With me to the charge, Sires D'Aumale and De Littain! with

me, gallant Bruse, and De Mortain! with me, De Graville and
Grantmesnil! Dex aide! Notre Dame!" And heading his
prowest knights, William came, as a thunderbolt, on the bills
and shields. Harold, who scarce a minute before had been
in a remoter rank, was already at the brunt of that charge.
At his word down knelt the foremost line, leaving nought but
their shields and their spear-points against the horse; while
behind them, the axe in both hands, bent forward the soldiery
in the second rank, to smite and to crush; and, from the core
of the wedge, poured the shafts of the archers. Down rolled
in the dust half the charge of those knights. Bruse reeled on
his saddle; the dread right hand of D'Aumale fell lopped by
the axe; De Graville, hurled from his horse, rolled at the
feet of Harold; and William, borne by his great steed and
his colossal strength into the third rank, there dealt, right
and left, the fierce strokes of his iron club, till he felt his
horse sinking under him, and had scarcely time to back from
the foe, scarcely time to get beyond reach of their weapons,
ere the Spanish *destrier*, frightfully gashed through its strong
mail, fell dead on the plain. His knights swept round him.
Twenty barons leaped from selle to yield him their chargers.
He chose the one nearest to hand, sprang to foot and to stirrup, and rode back to his lines. Meanwhile De Graville's
casque, its strings broken by the shock, had fallen off, and as
Harold was about to strike, he recognized his guest.

Holding up his hand to keep off the press of his men, the
generous king said briefly, "Rise and retreat! — no time on
this field for captor and captive. He whom thou hast called
recreant knight has been Saxon host. Thou hast fought by
his side, thou shalt not die by his hand! — Go."

Not a word spoke De Graville; but his dark eye dwelt one
minute with mingled pity and reverence on the king; then
rising, he turned away; and slowly, as if he disdained to fly,
strode back over the corpses of his countrymen.

"Stay, all hands!" cried the king to his archers; "yon
man hath tasted our salt, and done us good service of old.
He hath paid his weregeld."

Not a shaft was discharged.

Meanwhile, the Norman infantry, who had been before re-coiling, no sooner saw their duke (whom they recognized by his steed and equipment) fall on the ground, than, setting up a shout, "The duke is dead!" they fairly turned round, and fled fast in disorder.

The fortune of the day was now well nigh turned in favour of the Saxons; and the confusion of the Normans, as the cry of "The duke is dead!" reached and circled round the host, would have been irrecoverable, had Harold possessed a cavalry fit to press the advantage gained, or had not William himself rushed into the midst of the fugitives, throwing his helmet back on his neck, showing his face, all animated with fierce valour and disdainful wrath, while he cried aloud,—

"I live, ye varlets! Behold the face of a chief who never yet forgave coward! Ay, tremble more at me than at yon English, doomed and accursed as they be! Ye Normans, ye! I blush for you!" and striking the foremost in the retreat with the flat of his sword, chiding, stimulating, threatening, promising in a breath, he succeeded in staying the flight, re-forming the lines, and dispelling the general panic. Then, as he joined his own chosen knights, and surveyed the field, he beheld an opening which the advanced position of the Saxon vanguard had left, and by which his knights might gain the entrenchments. He mused a moment, his face still bare, and brightening, as he mused. Looking round him, he saw Mallet de Graville, who had remounted, and said, shortly,—

"*Pardex*, dear knight, we thought you already with Saint Michael!—joy, that you live yet to be an English earl. Look you, ride to Fitzosborne with the signal-word, 'Li Hardiz passent avant!' Off, and quick."

De Graville bowed, and darted across the plain.

"Now, my quens and chevaliers," said William, gayly, as he closed his helmet, and took from his squire another spear, —"now, I shall give ye the day's great pastime. Pass the word, Sire de Tancarville, to every horseman — 'Charge! — to the Standard!'"

The word passed, the steeds bounded, and the whole force of William's knighthood, scouring the plain to the rear of the Saxon vanguard, made for the entrenchments.

At that sight, Harold, divining the object, and seeing this new and more urgent demand on his presence, halted the battalions over which he had presided, and, yielding the command to Leofwine, once more briefly but strenuously enjoined the troops to heed well their leaders, and on no account to break the wedge, in the form of which lay their whole strength, both against the cavalry and the greater number of the foe. Then mounting his horse, and attended only by Haco, he spurred across the plain, in the opposite direction to that taken by the Normans. In doing so, he was forced to make a considerable circuit towards the rear of the entrenchment, and the farm, with its watchful groups, came in sight. He distinguished the garbs of the women, and Haco said to him,—

"There wait the wives, to welcome the living victors."

"Or search their lords among the dead!" answered Harold. "Who, Haco, if we fall, will search for us?"

As the word left his lips, he saw, under a lonely thorn-tree, and scarce out of bowshot from the entrenchments, a woman seated. The king looked hard at the bended, hooded form.

"Poor wretch!" he murmured, "her heart is in the battle!" And he shouted aloud, "Farther off! farther off! The war rushes hitherward!"

At the sound of that voice the woman rose, stretched her arms, and sprang forward. But the Saxon chiefs had already turned their faces towards the neighbouring ingress into the ramparts, and beheld not her movement, while the tramp of rushing chargers, the shout and the roar of clashing war, drowned the wail of her feeble cry.

"I have heard him again, again!" murmured the woman, "God be praised!" and she re-seated herself quietly under the lonely thorn.

As Harold and Haco sprang to their feet within the entrenchments, the shout of "the king! the king! Holy Crosse!" came in time to rally the force at the farther end, now undergoing the full storm of the Norman chivalry.

The willow ramparts were already rent and hewed beneath the hoofs of horses and the clash of swords; and the sharp

points on the frontals of the Norman *destriers* were already
gleaming within the entrenchments, when Harold arrived at
the brunt of action. The tide was then turned; not one of
those rash riders left the entrenchments they had gained;
steel and horse alike went down beneath the ponderous battle-
axes; and William, again foiled and baffled, drew off his cavalry with the reluctant conviction that those breastworks,
so manned, were not to be won by horse. Slowly the knights
retreated down the slope of the hillock, and the English, animated by that sight, would have left their stronghold to pursue, but for the warning cry of Harold. The interval in the
strife thus gained was promptly and vigorously employed in
repairing the palisades. And this done, Harold, turning to
Haco and the thegns round him, said joyously, —

"By Heaven's help we shall yet win this day. And know
you not that it is my fortunate day, — the day on which,
hitherto, all hath prospered with me, in peace and in war, —
the day of my birth?"

"Of your birth!" echoed Haco in surprise.

"Ay; did you not know it?"

"Nay! strange! It is also the birthday of Duke William!
What would astrologers say to the meeting of such stars?"[1]

Harold's cheek paled, but his helmet concealed the paleness; his arm drooped. The strange dream of his youth again
came distinct before him, as it had come in the hall of the
Norman at the sight of the ghastly relics; again he saw the
shadowy hand from the cloud; again heard the voice murmuring, "Lo, the star that shone on the birth of the victor!"
again he heard the words of Hilda interpreting the dream;
again the chant which the dead or the fiend had poured from
the rigid lips of the Vala. It boomed on his ear; hollow as a
death bell it knelled through the roar of battle, —

> "Never
> Crown and brow shall Force dissever,
> Till the dead men, unforgiving,
> Loose the war-steeds on the living;

---

[1] Harold's birthday was certainly the 14th of October. According to Mr.
Roscoe, in his "Life of William the Conqueror," William was born also on
the 14th of October.

Till a sun whose race is ending
Sees the rival stars contending,
Where the dead men, unforgiving,
Wheel their war-steeds round the living ! "

Faded the vision, and died the chant, as a breath that
dims, and vanishes from, the mirror of steel. The breath
was gone,— the firm steel was bright once more; and suddenly the king was recalled to the sense of the present hour,
by shouts and cries, in which the yell of Norman triumph
predominated, at the further end of the field. The signal
words to Fitzosborne had conveyed to that chief the order for
the mock charge on the Saxon vanguard, to be followed by
the feigned flight; and so artfully had this stratagem been
practised, that despite all the solemn orders of Harold, despite even the warning cry of Leofwine, who, rash and gay-
hearted though he was, had yet a captain's skill,— the bold
English, their blood heated by long contest and seeming victory, could not resist pursuit. They rushed forward im-
petuously, breaking the order of their hitherto indomitable
phalanx, and the more eagerly because the Normans had un-
wittingly taken their way towards a part of the ground con-
cealing dikes and ditches, into which the English trusted to
precipitate the foe. It was as William's knights retreated
from the breastworks that this fatal error was committed;
and pointing towards the disordered Saxons with a wild laugh
of revengeful joy, William set spurs to his horse, and, followed by all his chivalry, joined the cavalry of Poitou and
Boulogne in their swoop upon the scattered array. Already
the Norman infantry had turned round; already the horses,
that lay in ambush amongst the brushwood near the dikes,
had thundered forth. The whole of the late impregnable
vanguard was broken up, divided corps from corps,— hemmed
in; horse after horse charging to the rear, to the front, to the
flank, to the right, to the left.

Gurth, with the men of Surrey and Sussex, had alone kept
their ground; but they were now compelled to advance to the
aid of their scattered comrades, and coming up in close order,
they not only awhile stayed the slaughter, but again half

turned the day. Knowing the country thoroughly, Gurth lured the foe into the ditches concealed within a hundred yards of their own ambush; and there the havoc of the foreigners was so great, that the hollows are said to have been literally made level with the plain by their corpses. Yet this combat, however fierce, and however skill might seek to repair the former error, could not be long maintained against such disparity of numbers. And meanwhile, the whole of the division under Geoffroi Martel and his co-captains had by a fresh order of William's occupied the space between the entrenchments and the more distant engagement; thus when Harold looked up, he saw the foot of the hillocks so lined with steel, as to render it hopeless that he himself could win to the aid of his vanguard. He set his teeth firmly, looked on, and only by gesture and smothered exclamations showed his emotions of hope and fear. At length he cried,—

"Gallant Gurth! brave Leofwine, look to their pennons! right, right; well fought, sturdy Vebba! Ha! they are moving this way. The wedge cleaves on,— it cuts its path through the heart of the foe." And indeed, the chiefs now drawing off the shattered remains of their countrymen, still disunited, but still each section shaping itself wedge-like,— on came the English, with their shields over their head, through the tempest of missiles, against the rush of the steeds, here and there, through the plains, up the slopes, towards the entrenchment, in the teeth of the formidable array of Martel, and harassed behind by hosts that seemed numberless. The king could restrain himself no longer. He selected five hundred of his bravest and most practised veterans, yet comparatively fresh, and commanding the rest to stay firm, descended the hills, and charged unexpectedly into the rear of the mingled Normans and Bretons.

This sortie, well-timed though desperate, served to cover and favour the retreat of the straggling Saxons. Many indeed were cut off, but Gurth, Leofwine, and Vebba hewed the way for their followers to the side of Harold, and entered the entrenchments, close followed by the nearer foe, who were again repulsed amidst the shouts of the English.

But, alas! small indeed the band thus saved, and hopeless the thought that the small detachments of English still surviving and scattered over the plain would ever win to their aid.

Yet in those scattered remnants were, perhaps, almost the only men who, availing themselves of their acquaintance with the country, and despairing of victory, escaped by flight from the Field of SANGUELAC. Nevertheless, within the entrenchments not a man had lost heart; the day was already far advanced, no impression had been yet made on the outworks, the position seemed as impregnable as a fortress of stone; and, truth to say, even the bravest Normans were disheartened, when they looked to that eminence which had foiled the charge of William himself. The duke, in the recent *mêlée*, had received more than one wound, his third horse that day had been slain under him. The slaughter among the knights and nobles had been immense, for they had exposed their persons with the most desperate valour. And William, after surveying the rout of nearly one half of the English army, heard everywhere, to his wrath and his shame, murmurs of discontent and dismay at the prospect of scaling the heights, in which the gallant remnant had found their refuge. At this critical juncture, Odo of Bayeux, who had hitherto remained in the rear,[1] with the crowds of monks that accompanied the armament, rode into the full field, where all the hosts were re-forming their lines. He was in complete mail, but a white surplice was drawn over the steel, his head was bare, and in his right hand he bore the crozier. A formidable club swung by a leathern noose from his wrist, to be used only for self-defence: the canons forbade the priest to strike merely in assault.

Behind the milk-white steed of Odo came the whole body of reserve, fresh and unbreathed, free from the terrors of their comrades, and stung into proud wrath at the delay of the Norman conquest.

"How now! how now!" cried the prelate; "do ye flag; do ye falter when the sheaves are down, and ye have but to

---

[1] William Pict.

gather up the harvest? How now, sons of the Church! warriors of the Cross! avengers of the Saints! Desert your count, if ye please; but shrink not back from a Lord mightier than man. Lo, I come forth, to ride side by side with my brother, bare-headed, the crozier in my hand. He who fails his liege is but a coward, — he who fails the Church is apostate! "

The fierce shout of the reserve closed this harangue, and the words of the prelate, as well as the physical aid he brought to back them, renerved the army. And now the whole of William's mighty host, covering the field, till its lines seemed to blend with the gray horizon, came on serried, steadied, orderly, to all sides of the entrenchment. Aware of the inutility of his horse till the breastworks were cleared, William placed in the van all his heavy armed foot, spearmen, and archers, to open the way through the palisades, the sorties from which had now been carefully closed.

As they came up the hills, Harold turned to Haco and said, "Where is thy battle-axe? "

"Harold," answered Haco, with more than his usual tone of sombre sadness, "I desire now to be thy shield-bearer, for thou must use thine axe with both hands while the day lasts, and thy shield is useless. Wherefore thou strike, and I will shield thee."

"Thou lovest me, then, son of Sweyn; I have sometimes doubted it."

"I love thee as the best part of my life, and with thy life ceases mine: it is my heart that my shield guards when it covers the breast of Harold."

"I would bid thee live, poor youth," whispered Harold; "but what were life if this day were lost? Happy, then, will be those who die! "

Scarce had the words left his lips ere he sprang to the breastworks, and with a sudden sweep of his axe, down dropped a helm that peered above them. But helm after helm succeeds. Now they come on, swarm upon swarm, as wolves on a traveller, as bears round a bark. Countless, amidst their carnage, on they come! The arrows of the Norman blacken the air: with deadly precision, to each arm, each limb, each front exposed above the bulwarks, whirs the shaft. They clamber the palisades, the foremost fall dead under the Saxon axe; new thousands rush on: vain is the might of Harold, vain had been a Harold's might in every Saxon there! The first row of breastworks is forced, — it is trampled, hewed, crushed down, cumbered with the dead. "Ha Rou! Ha Rou! Notre Dame! Notre Dame!" sounds joyous and shrill; the chargers snort and leap, and charge into the circle. High wheels in air the great mace of William; bright by the slaughterers flashes the crozier of the Church.

"On, Normans! — Earldom and land!" cries the duke.

"On, sons of the Church! Salvation and heaven!" shouts the voice of Odo.

The first breastwork down, the Saxons, yielding inch by inch, foot by foot, are pressed, crushed back, into the second enclosure. The same rush, and swarm, and fight, and cry, and roar: the second enclosure gives way. And now in the centre of the third — lo, before the eyes of the Normans towers proudly aloft, and shines in the rays of the westering sun, broidered with gold and blazing with mystic gems, the standard of England's King! And there are gathered the reserve of the English host; there the heroes who had never yet known defeat, — unwearied they by the battle, vigorous, high-hearted still; and round them the breastworks were thicker and stronger and higher, and fastened by chains to pillars of wood and staves of iron, with the wagons and carts of the baggage, and piled logs of timber, — barricades at which even William paused aghast, and Odo stifled an exclamation that became not a priestly lip.

Before that standard, in the front of the men, stood Gurth and Leofwine, and Haco and Harold, the last leaning for rest upon his axe, for he was sorely wounded in many places, and the blood oozed through the links of his mail.

Live, Harold; live yet, and Saxon England shall not die!

The English archers had at no time been numerous; most of them had served with the vanguard, and the shafts of those within the ramparts were spent; so that the foe had

time to pause and to breathe. The Norman arrows meanwhile flew fast and thick, but William noted to his grief that
they struck against the tall breastworks and barricades, and
so failed in the slaughter they should inflict.

He mused a moment, and sent one of his knights to call to
him three of the chiefs of the archers. They were soon at
the side of his *destrier*.

"See ye not, *maladroits*," said the duke, "that your shafts
and bolts fall harmless on those ozier walls? Shoot in the
air; let the arrow fall perpendicular on those within,— fall
as the vengeance of the saints falls, direct from heaven! Give
me thy bow, Archer,— thus." He drew the bow as he sat
on his steed; the arrow flashed up, and descended in the
heart of the reserve, within a few feet of the standard.

"So; that standard be your mark," said the duke, giving
back the bow.

The archers withdrew. The order circulated through their
bands, and in a few moments more down came the iron rain.
It took the English host as by surprise, piercing hide cap,
and even iron helm; and in the very surprise that made them
instinctively look up, death came.

A dull groan as from many hearts boomed from the entrenchments on the Norman ear.

"Now," said William, "they must either use their shields
to guard their heads,— and their axes are useless,— or while
they smite with the axe they fall by the shaft. On now to
the ramparts! I see my crown already resting on yonder
standard!"

Yet despite all, the English bear up; the thickness of the
palisades, the comparative smallness of the last enclosure,
more easily therefore manned and maintained by the small
force of the survivors, defy other weapons than those of the
bow. Every Norman who attempts to scale the breastwork
is slain on the instant, and his body cast forth under the
hoofs of the baffled steeds. The sun sinks near and nearer
towards the red horizon.

"Courage!" cries the voice of Harold, "hold but till night·
fall, and ye are saved. Courage and freedom!"

"Harold and Holy Crosse!" is the answer.

Still foiled, William again resolves to hazard his fatal stratagem. He marked that quarter of the enclosure which was most remote from the chief point of attack,—most remote from the provident watch of Harold, whose cheering voice, ever and anon, he recognized amidst the hurtling clamour. In this quarter the palisades were the weakest, and the ground the least elevated; but it was guarded by men on whose skill with axe and shield Harold placed the firmest reliance,—the Anglo-Danes of his old East-Anglian earldom. Thither, then, the duke advanced a chosen column of his heavy-armed foot, tutored especially by himself in the rehearsals of his favourite *ruse*, and accompanied by a band of archers; while at the same time, he himself, with his brother Odo, headed a considerable company of knights under the son of the great Roger de Beaumont, to gain the contiguous level heights on which now stretches the little town of "Battle," — there to watch and to aid the manœuvre. The foot column advanced to the appointed spot, and after a short, close, and terrible conflict succeeded in making a wide breach in the breastworks. But that temporary success only animates yet more the exertions of the beleagured defenders; and swarming round the breach, and pouring through it, line after line of the foe drop beneath their axes. The column of the heavy-armed Normans fell back down the slopes; they give way, they turn in disorder, they retreat, they fly; but the archers stand firm, midway on the descent; those archers seem an easy prey to the English,—the temptation is irresistible. Long galled and harassed and maddened by the shafts, the Anglo-Danes rush forth at the heels of the Norman swordsmen, and sweeping down to exterminate the archers, the breach that they leave gapes wide.

"Forward!" cried William, and he gallops towards the breach.

"Forward!" cries Odo, "I see the hands of the holy saints in the air! Forward! it is the Dead that wheel our war-steeds round the living!"

On rush the Norman knights. But Harold is already in

the breach, rallying around him hearts eager to replace the shattered breastworks.

"Close shields! Hold fast!" shouts his kingly voice.

Before him were the steeds of Bruse and Grantmesnil, at his breast their spears; Haco holds over the breast the shield. Swinging aloft with both hands his axe, the spear of Grantmesnil is shivered in twain by the king's stroke. Cloven to the skull rolls the steed of Bruse. Knight and steed roll on the bloody sward.

But a blow from the sword of De Lacie has broken down the guardian shield of Haco. The son of Sweyn is stricken to his knee. With lifted blades and whirling maces the Norman knights charge through the breach.

"Look up, look up, and guard thy head," cries the fatal voice of Haco to the king.

At that cry the king raises his flashing eyes. Why halts his stride? Why drops the axe from his hand? As he raised his head, down came the hissing death-shaft. It smote the lifted face; it crushed into the dauntless eyeball. He reeled, he staggered, he fell back several yards, at the foot of his gorgeous standard. With desperate hand he broke the head of the shaft and left the barb, quivering in the anguish.

Gurth knelt over him.

"Fight on," gasped the king, "conceal my death! Holy Crosse! England to the rescue! woe! woe!"

Rallying himself a moment, he sprang to his feet, clenched his right hand, and fell once more, — a corpse.

At the same moment a simultaneous rush of horsemen towards the standard bore back a line of Saxons, and covered the body of the king with heaps of the slain.

His helmet cloven in two, his face all streaming with blood, but still calm in its ghastly hues, amidst the foremost of those slain, fell the fated Haco. He fell with his head on the breast of Harold, kissed the bloody cheek with bloody lips, groaned, and died.

Inspired by despair with superhuman strength, Gurth, striding over the corpses of his kinsmen, opposed himself singly to the knights; and the entire strength of the English remnant, coming round him at the menaced danger to the standard, once more drove off the assailants.

But now all the enclosure was filled with the foe, the whole space seemed gay, in the darkening air, with banderols and banners. High, through all, rose the club of the Conqueror; high, through all, shone the crozier of the Churchman. Not one Englishman fled; all now centring round the standard, they fell, slaughtering if slaughtered. Man by man, under the charmed banner, fell the lithsmen of Hilda. Then died the faithful Sexwolf; then died the gallant Godrith, redeeming, by the death of many a Norman, his young fantastic love of the Norman manners; then died, last of such of the Kentmen as had won retreat from their scattered vanguard into the circle of closing slaughter, the English-hearted Vebba.

Even still in that age, when the Teuton had yet in his veins the blood of Odin, the demi-god,— even still one man could delay the might of numbers. Through the crowd, the Normans beheld with admiring awe,— here, in the front of their horse, a single warrior, before whose axe spear shivered, helm drooped; there, close by the standard, standing breast-high among the slain, one still more formidable, and even amidst ruin unvanquished. The first fell at length under the mace of Roger de Montgommeri. So, unknown to the Norman poet (who hath preserved in his verse the deeds but not the name), fell, laughing in death, young Leofwine! Still by the enchanted standard towers the other; still the enchanted standard waves aloft, with its brave ensign of the solitary "Fighting Man" girded by the gems that had flashed in the crown of Odin.

"Thine be the honour of lowering that haughty flag," cried William, turning to one of his favourite and most famous knights, Robert de Tessin.

Overjoyed, the knight rushed forth, to fall by the axe of that stubborn defender.

"Sorcery," cried Fitzosborne, "sorcery! This is no man, but fiend."

"Spare him, spare the brave," cried in a breath Bruse, D'Aincourt, and De Graville.

William turned round in wrath at the cry of mercy, and spurring over all the corpses, with the sacred banner borne by Tonstain close behind him, so that it shadowed his helmet, he came to the foot of the standard, and for one moment there was single battle between the Knight-Duke and the Saxon hero. Nor, even then, conquered by the Norman sword, but exhausted by a hundred wounds, that brave chief fell,[1] and the falchion vainly pierced him, falling. So, last man at the standard, died Gurth.

The sun had set, the first star was in heaven, the "Fighting Man" was laid low; and on that spot where now, all forlorn and shattered, amidst stagnant water, stands the altarstone of Battle Abbey, rose the glittering dragon that surmounted the consecrated banner of the Norman victor.

CHAPTER IX.

CLOSE by his banner, amidst the piles of the dead, William the Conqueror pitched his pavilion, and sat at meat. And over all the plain, far and near, torches were moving like meteors on a marsh; for the duke had permitted the Saxon women to search for the bodies of their lords. And as he sat and talked and laughed, there entered the tent two humble monks, — their lowly mien, their dejected faces, their homely serge, in mournful contrast to the joy and the splendour of the Victory-Feast.

They came to the Conqueror, and knelt.

"Rise up, sons of the Church," said William, mildly, "for sons of the Church are *we!* Deem not that we shall invade

---

[1] Thus Wace,—

> "Guert (Gurth) vit Engleiz amenuisier,
> Vi K'il n'i ont nul recovrier," etc.

"Gurth saw the English diminish, and that there was no hope to retrieve the day ; the duke pushed forth with such force that he reached him, and struck him with great violence (*par grant air*). I know not if he died by the stroke, but it is said that it laid him low."

the rights of the religion which we have come to avenge. Nay, on this spot we have already sworn to build an abbey that shall be the proudest in the land, and where masses shall be sung evermore for the repose of the brave Normans who fell in this field, and for mine and my consort's soul."

"Doubtless," said Odo, sneering, "the holy men have heard already of this pious intent, and come to pray for cells in the future abbey."

"Not so," said Osgood, mournfully, and in barbarous Norman; "we have our own beloved convent at Waltham, endowed by the prince whom thine arms have defeated. We come to ask but to bury in our sacred cloisters the corpse of him so lately king over all England, — our benefactor, Harold."

The duke's brow fell.

"And see," said Ailred, eagerly, as he drew out a leathern pouch, "we have brought with us all the gold that our poor crypts contained, for we misdoubted this day," and he poured out the glittering pieces at the Conqueror's feet.

"No!" said William, fiercely, "we take no gold for a traitor's body; no, not if Githa, the usurper's mother, offered us its weight in the shining metal; unburied be the Accursed of the Church, and let the birds of prey feed their young with his carcass!"

Two murmurs, distinct in tone and in meaning, were heard in that assembly, — the one of approval from fierce mercenaries, insolent with triumph; the other of generous discontent and indignant amaze, from the large majority of Norman nobles.

But William's brow was still dark, and his eye still stern; for his policy confirmed his passions; and it was only by stigmatizing, as dishonoured and accursed, the memory and cause of the dead king, that he could justify the sweeping spoliation of those who had fought against himself, and confiscate the lands to which his own quens and warriors looked for their reward.

The murmurs had just died into a thrilling hush, when a woman, who had followed the monks unperceived and u heeded, passed with a swift and noiseless step to the duke's foot-stool; and, without bending knee to the ground, said, in a voice, which, though low, was heard by all, —

"Norman, in the name of the women of England, I tell thee that thou darest not do this wrong to the hero who died in defence of their hearths and their children!"

Before she spoke she had thrown back her hood; her hair, dishevelled, fell over her shoulders, glittering like gold, in the blaze of the banquet-lights; and that wondrous beauty, without parallel amidst the dames of England, shone like the vision of an accusing angel, on the eyes of the startled duke and the breathless knights. But twice in her life Edith beheld that awful man, — once, when roused from her revery of innocent love by the holiday pomp of his trumps and banners, the childlike maid stood at the foot of the grassy knoll; and once again, when in the hour of his triumph, and amidst the wrecks of England on the field of Sanguelac, with a soul surviving the crushed and broken heart, the faith of the lofty woman defended the Hero Dead.

There, with knee unbent and form unquailing, with marble cheek and haughty eye, she faced the Conqueror; and, as she ceased, his noble barons broke into bold applause.

"Who art thou?" said William, if not daunted, at least amazed. "Methinks I have seen thy face before; thou art not Harold's wife or sister?"

"Dread lord," said Osgood, "she was the betrothed of Harold; but, as within the degrees of kin, the Church forbade their union, and they obeyed the Church."

Out from the banquet-throng stepped Mallet de Graville. "O my liege," said he, "thou hast promised me lands and earldom; instead of these gifts undeserved, bestow on me the right to bury and to honour the remains of Harold; to-day I took from him my life, let me give all I can in return, — a grave!"

William paused; but the sentiment of the assembly, so clearly pronounced, and, it may be, his own better nature, which, ere polluted by plotting craft and hardened by despotic ire, was magnanimous and heroic, moved and won him.

"Lady," said he, gently, "thou appealest not in vain to Norman knighthood: thy rebuke was just, and I repent me of a hasty impulse. Mallet de Graville, thy prayer is granted; to thy choice be consigned the place of burial, to thy care the funeral rites of him whose soul hath passed out of human judgment."

The feast was over; William the Conqueror slept on his couch, and round him slumbered his Norman knights, dreaming of baronies to come; and still the torches moved dismally to and fro the waste of death, and through the hush of night was heard near and far the wail of women.

Accompanied by the brothers of Waltham, and attended by link-bearers, Mallet de Graville was yet engaged in the search for the royal dead — and the search was vain. Deeper and stiller the autumnal moon rose to its melancholy noon, and lent its ghastly aid to the glare of the redder lights. But on leaving the pavilion, they had missed Edith; she had gone from them alone, and was lost in that dreadful wilderness. And Ailred said despondingly, —

"Perchance we may already have seen the corpse we search for, and not recognized it; for the face may be mutilated with wounds. And therefore it is that Saxon wives and mothers haunt our battle-fields, discovering those they search by signs not known without the household." [1]

"Ay," said the Norman, "I comprehend thee, — by the letter or device, in which, according to your customs, your warriors impress on their own forms some token of affection, or some fancied charm against ill."

"It is so," answered the monk; "wherefore I grieve that we have lost the guidance of the maid."

While thus conversing, they had retraced their steps, almost in despair, towards the duke's pavilion.

"See," said De Graville, "how near yon lonely woman hath

---

[1] The suggestion implied in the text will probably be admitted as correct, when we read in the Saxon annals of the recognition of the dead by peculiar marks on their bodies ; the obvious, or at least the most natural explanation of those signs, is to be found in the habit of puncturing the skin, mentioned by the Malmesbury chronicler.

come to the tent of the duke, — yea, to the foot of the holy
gonfanon, which supplanted 'the Fighting Man'! *Pardex*,
my heart bleeds to see her striving to lift up the heavy
dead!"

The monks neared the spot, and Osgood exclaimed in a
voice almost joyful, —

"It is Edith the Fair! This way, the torches! hither,
quick!"

The corpses had been flung in irreverent haste from either
side of the gonfanon, to make room for the banner of the conquest and the pavilion of the feast. Huddled together, they
lay in that holy bed. And the woman silently, and by the
help of no light save the moon, was intent on her search. She
waved her hand impatiently as they approached, as if jealous of
the dead: but as she had not sought, so neither did she oppose,
their aid. Moaning low to herself, she desisted from her task,
and knelt watching them, and shaking her head mournfully,
as they removed helm after helm, and lowered the torches
upon stern and livid brows. At length the lights fell red and
full on the ghastly face of Haco, — proud and sad as in life.

De Graville uttered an exclamation: "The king's nephew:
be sure the king is near!"

A shudder went over the woman's form, and the moaning
ceased.

They unhelmed another corpse; and the monks and the
knight, after one glance, turned away sickened and awe-
stricken at the sight: for the face was all defeatured and
mangled with wounds, and nought could they recognize save
the ravaged majesty of what had been man. But at the sight
of that face a wild shriek broke from Edith's heart.

She started to her feet, — put aside the monks with a wild
and angry gesture, and bending over the face, sought with her
long hair to wipe from it the clotted blood; then with convulsive fingers she strove to loosen the buckler of the breast-
mail. The knight knelt to assist her. "No, no," she gasped
out. "He is mine, — mine now!"

Her hands bled as the mail gave way to her efforts; the
tunic beneath was all dabbled with blood. She rent the folds,

and on the breast, just above the silenced heart, were punctured in the old Saxon letters the word "EDITH;" and just below, in characters more fresh, the word "ENGLAND."

"See, see!" she cried, in piercing accents; and clasping the dead in her arms, she kissed the lips, and called aloud, in words of the tenderest endearments, as if she addressed the living. All there knew then that the search was ended; all knew that the eyes of love had recognized the dead.

"Wed, wed," murmured the betrothed; "wed at last! O Harold, Harold! the words of the Vala were true — and Heaven is kind!" and laying her head gently on the breast of the dead, she smiled and died.

At the east end of the choir in the Abbey of Waltham was long shown the tomb of the Last Saxon King, inscribed with the touching words, "Harold Infelix." But not under that stone, according to the chronicler who should best know the truth,[1] mouldered the dust of him in whose grave was buried an epoch in human annals.

"Let his corpse," said William the Norman, "let his corpse guard the coasts which his life madly defended. Let the seas wail his dirge, and girdle his grave; and his spirit protect the land which hath passed to the Norman's sway."

And Mallet de Graville assented to the word of his chief, for his knightly heart turned into honour the latent taunt; and well he knew that Harold could have chosen no burial-spot so worthy his English spirit and his Roman end.

The tomb at Waltham would have excluded the faithful ashes of the betrothed, whose heart had broken on the bosom she had found; more gentle was the grave in the temple of heaven, and hallowed by the bridal death-dirge of the everlasting sea.

So, in that sentiment of poetry and love, which made half the religion of a Norman knight, Mallet de Graville suffered death to unite those whom life had divided. In the holy burial-ground that encircled a small Saxon chapel, on the shore, and near the spot on which William had leaped to

---

[1] The contemporary Norman chronicler, William of Poitiers. See Note R.

land, one grave received the betrothed; and the tomb of Waltham only honoured an empty name.[1]

Eight centuries have rolled away, and where is the Norman now, — or where is not the Saxon? The little urn that sufficed for the mighty lord[2] is despoiled of his very dust; but the tombless shade of the kingly freeman still guards the coasts, and rests upon the seas. In many a noiseless field, with Thoughts for Armies, your relics, O Saxon Heroes, have won back the victory from the bones of the Norman saints; and whenever, with fairer fates, Freedom opposes Force, and Justice, redeeming the old defeat, smites down the armed Frauds that would consecrate the wrong, — smile, O soul of our Saxon Harold, smile, appeased, on the Saxon's land!

[1] See Note R.

[2] " Rex magnus parva jacet hic Gulielmus in urna —
Sufficit et magno parva Domus Domino."

From William the Conqueror's epitaph (ap-Gemiticen). His bones are said to have been disinterred some centuries after his death.

NOTES.

NOTE P, PAGE 63.

Harold's Accession.

THERE are, as is well known, two accounts as to Edward the Confessor's death-bed disposition of the English crown. The Norman chroniclers affirm, first, that Edward promised William the crown during his exile in Normandy; secondly, that Siward, Earl of North umbria, Godwin, and Leofric had taken oath, "serment de la main," to receive him as Seigneur after Edward's death, and that the hostages Wolnoth and Haco were given to the duke in pledge of that oath;[1] thirdly, that Edward left him the crown by will.

Let us see what probability there is of truth in these three assertions. First, Edward promised William the crown when in Normandy.

This seems probable enough, and it is corroborated indirectly by the Saxon chroniclers, when they unite in relating Edward's warnings to Harold against his visit to the Norman court. Edward might well be aware of William's designs on the crown (though in those warnings he refrains from mentioning them), — might remember the authority given to those designs by his own early promise, and know the secret pur· pose for which the hostages were retained by William, and the advantages he would seek to gain from having Harold himself in his power. But this promise in itself was clearly not binding on the English people, nor on any one but Edward, who, without the sanction of the Witan, could not fulfil it. And that William himself could not have attached great importance to it during Edward's life is clear, because if he had, the time to urge it was when Edward sent into Germany for the Atheling, as the heir presumptive of the throne. This was a virtual annihilation of the promise; but William took no step to urge it, made no complaint and no remonstrance.

Secondly, That Godwin, Siward, and Leofric had **taken** oaths of fealty to William.

This appears a fable wholly without foundation. When could those oaths have been pledged? Certainly not after Harold's visit to William,

---

[1] William of Poitiers.

for they were then all dead. At the accession of Edward? This is obviously contradicted by the stipulation which Godwin and the other chiefs of the Witan exacted, that Edward should not come accompanied by Norman supporters; by the evident jealousy of the Normans entertained by those chiefs, as by the whole English people, who regarded the alliance of Ethelred with the Norman Emma as the cause of the greatest calamities; and by the marriage of Edward himself with Godwin's daughter, — a marriage which that earl might naturally presume would give legitimate heirs to the throne. In the interval between Edward's accession and Godwin's outlawry? No; for all the English chroniclers, and, indeed, the Norman, concur in representing the ill-will borne by Godwin and his House to the Norman favourites, whom, if they could have anticipated William's accession, or were in any way bound to William, they would have naturally conciliated. But Godwin's outlawry is the result of the breach between him and the foreigners. In William's visit to Edward? No; for that took place when Godwin was an exile; and even the writers who assert Edward's early promise to William declare that nothing was then said as to the succession to the throne. To Godwin's return from outlawry the Norman chroniclers seem to refer the date of this pretended oath, by the assertion that the hostages were given in pledge of it. This is the most monstrous supposition of all; for Godwin's return is followed by the banishment of the Norman favourites, by the utter downfall of the Norman party in England, by the decree of the Witan that all the troubles in England had come from the Normans, by the triumphant ascendancy of Godwin's House. And is it creditable for a moment, that the great English Earl could then have agreed to a pledge to transfer the kingdom to the very party he had expelled, and expose himself and his party to the vengeance of a foe he had thoroughly crushed for the time, and whom, without any motive or object, he himself agreed to restore to power for his own probable perdition? When examined, this assertion falls to the ground from other causes. It is not among the arguments that William uses in his embassies to Harold; it rests mainly upon the authority of William of Poitiers, who, though a contemporary, and a good authority on some points purely Norman, is grossly ignorant as to the most accredited and acknowledged facts in all that relate to the English. Even with regard to the hostages, he makes the most extraordinary blunders. He says they were sent by Edward, with the consent of his nobles, accompanied by Robert, Archbishop of Canterbury. Now Robert, Archbishop of Canterbury, had fled from England as fast as he could fly on the return of Godwin; and arrived in Normandy, half drowned, before the hostages were sent, or even before the Witan which reconciled Edward and Godwin had assembled. He says that William restored to Harold "his young brother;" whereas it was Haco, the nephew, who was restored; we know, by Norman as well as Saxon Chroniclers, that Wolnoth, the brother, was not released till after the Conqueror's death (he was re-imprisoned by Rufus); and his partiality may be judged by the assertions, first, that "William gave nothing to a Norman that was unjustly taken from an Englishman;" and secondly, that Odo, whose horrible oppressions revolted even William himself, "never had an equal for justice, and that all the English obeyed him willingly."

We may, therefore, dismiss this assertion as utterly groundless, on its own merits, without directly citing against it the Saxon authorities.

Thirdly, That Edward left William the crown by will.

On this assertion alone, of the three, the Norman Conqueror himself seems to have rested a positive claim.[1] But if so, where was the will? Why was it never produced or producible? If destroyed, where were the witnesses; why were they not cited? The testamentary dispositions of an Anglo-Saxon king were always respected, and went far towards the succession; but it was absolutely necessary to prove them before the Witan.[2] An oral act of this kind, in the words of the dying Sovereign, would be legal, but they must be confirmed by those who heard them. Why, when William was master of England, and acknowledged by a National Assembly convened in London, and when all who heard the dying king would have been naturally disposed to give every evidence in William's favour, not only to flatter the new sovereign, but to soothe the national pride, and justify the Norman succession by a more popular plea than conquest, — why were no witnesses summoned to prove the bequest? Alred, Stigand, and the Abbot of Westminster must have been present at the death-bed of the king, and these priests concurred in submission to William. If they had any testimony as to

---

[1] He is considered to refer to such bequest in one of his charters : "Devicto Haroldo rege cum suis complicibus qui michi regnum prudentia Domini destinatum, et beneficio concessionis Domini et cognati mei gloriosi regis Edwardi concessum conati sunt auferre." — FORESTINA, A. 3.

But William's word is certainly not to be taken, for he never scrupled to break it ; and even in these words he does not state that it was left him by Edward's will, but destined and given to him, — words founded, perhaps, solely on the promise referred to, before Edward came to the throne, corroborated by some messages in the earlier years of his reign, through the Norman Archbishop of Canterbury, who seems to have been a notable intriguer to that end.

[2] Palgrave, Commonwealth, 560.

Edward's bequest in his favour, would they not have been too glad to give it, in justification of themselves, in compliment to William, in duty to the people, in vindication of law against force? But no such attempt at proof was ventured upon.

Against these, the mere assertion of William, and the authority of Normans who could know nothing of the truth of the matter, while they had every interest to misrepresent the facts, we have the positive assurances of the best possible authorities. The Saxon Chronicle (worth all the other annalists put together) says expressly that Edward left the crown to Harold: —

> " The sage, ne'ertheless,
> The realm committed
> To a highly-born man, —
> Harold's self,
> The noble Earl.
> He in all time
> Obeyed faithfully
> His rightful lord,
> By words and deeds;
> Nor aught neglected
> Which needful was
> To his sovereign king."

Florence of Worcester, the next best authority (valuable from supplying omissions in the Anglo-Saxon Chronicle), says expressly that the king chose Harold for his successor before his decease,[1] that he was elected by the chief men of all England, and consecrated by Alred. Hoveden, Simon (Dunelm.), the Beverley chronicler, confirm these authorities as to Edward's choice of Harold as his successor. William of Malmesbury, who is not partial to Harold, writing in the reign of Henry the First, has doubts himself as to Edward's bequest (though grounded on a very bad argument, — namely, "the improbability that Edward would leave his crown to a man of whose power he had always been jealous." There is no proof that Edward had been jealous of *Harold's* power, — he had been of *Godwin's*); but Malmesbury gives a more valuable authority than his own, in the concurrent opinion of his time, for he deposes that "*the English say* " the diadem was granted him (Harold) by the king.

These evidences are, to say the least, infinitely more worthy of his-

---

[1] Quo tumulato, subregulus Haroldus Godwin Ducis filius, quem rex ante suam decessionem regni successorem elegerat, a totius Angliæ primatibus, ad regale culmen electus, die eodem ab Aldredo Eboracensi Archiepiscopo in regem est honorifice consecratus. — FLOR. *Wig.*

torical credence than the one or two English chroniclers, of little comparative estimation (such as Wike), and the prejudiced and ignorant Norman chroniclers,[1] who depose on behalf of William. I assume, therefore, that Edward left the crown to Harold; of Harold's better claim in the election of the Witan there is no doubt. But Sir F. Palgrave starts the notion that, " admitting that the prelates, earls, aldermen, and thanes of Wessex and East Anglia had sanctioned the accession of Harold, their decision could not have been obligatory on the other kingdoms (provinces) ; and the very short time elapsing between the death of Edward and the recognition of Harold utterly precludes the supposition that their consent was even asked." This great writer must permit me, with all reverence, to suggest that he has, I think, forgotten the fact that, just prior to Edward's death, an assembly, fully as numerous as ever met in any national Witan, had been convened to attend the consecration of the new abbey and church of Westminster, which Edward considered the great work of his life; that assembly would certainly not have dispersed during a period so short and anxious as the mortal illness of the king, which appears to have prevented his attending the ceremony in person, and which ended in his death a very few days after the consecration. So that during the interval, which appears to have been at most about a week, between Edward's death and Harold's coronation,[2] the unusually large concourse of prelates and nobles from all parts of the kingdom assembled in London and Westminster would have furnished the numbers requisite to give weight and sanction to the Witan. And had it not been so, the Saxon chroniclers, and still more the Norman, would scarcely have omitted some remark in qualification of the election. But not a word is said as to any inadequate number in the Witan. And as for the two great principalities of Northumbria and Mercia, Harold's recent marriage with the sister of their earls might naturally tend to secure their allegiance.

[1] Some of these Norman chroniclers tell an absurd story of Harold's seizing the crown from the hand of the bishop, and putting it himself on his head. The Bayeux Tapestry, which is William's most connected apology for his claim, shows no such violence; but Harold is represented as crowned very peaceably. With more art (as I have observed elsewhere), the **Tapestry** represents Stigand as crowning him instead of Alred, — Stigand being at that time under the Pope's interdict.

[2] Edward died January 5th. Harold's coronation is said to have taken place January the 12th ; but there is no very satisfactory evidence as to the precise day ; indeed some writers would imply that he was crowned the day after Edward's death, which is scarcely possible.

Nor is it to be forgotten that a very numerous Witan had assembled at Oxford a few months before, to adjudge the rival claims of Tostig and Morcar; the decision of the Witan proves the alliance between Harold's party and that of the young earl's, — ratified by the marriage with Aldyth. And he who has practically engaged in the contests and cabals of party will allow the probability, adopted as fact in the romance, that, considering Edward's years and infirm health, and the urgent necessity of determining beforehand the claims to the succession, some actual, if secret, understanding was then come to by the leading chiefs. It is a common error in history to regard as sudden that which in the nature of affairs never can be sudden. All that paved Harold's way to the throne must have been silently settled long before the day in which the Witan elected him *unanimi omnium consensu.*[1]

With the views to which my examination of the records of the time have led me in favour of Harold, I cannot but think that Sir F. Palgrave, in his admirable History of Anglo-Saxon England, does scanty justice to the Last of its kings; and that his peculiar political and constitutional theories, and his attachment to the principle of hereditary succession, which make him consider that Harold " had no clear title to the crown anyway," tincture with something like the prejudice of party his estimate of Harold's character and pretensions. My profound admiration for Sir F. Palgrave's learning and judgment would not permit me to make this remark without carefully considering and reweighing all the contending authorities on which he himself relies. And I own that, of all modern historians, Thierry seems to me to have given the most just idea of the great actors in the tragedy of the Norman invasion, though I incline to believe that he has overrated the oppressive influence of the Norman dynasty in which the tragedy closed.

Note Q, page 79.

Physical Peculiarities of the Scandinavians.

" It is a singular circumstance, that in almost all the swords of those ages to be found in the collection of weapons in the Antiquarian Museum at Copenhagen, the handles indicate a size of hand very much smaller than the hands of modern people of any class or rank. No modern dandy, with the most delicate hands, would find room for

[1] Vit. Harold. Chron. Ang. Norm.

his hand to grasp or wield with ease some of the swords of these Northmen." [1]

This peculiarity is by some scholars adduced, not without reason, as an argument for the Eastern origin of the Scandinavian. Nor was it uncommon for the Asiatic Scythians, and indeed many of the early warlike tribes fluctuating between the east and west of Europe, to be distinguished by the blue eyes and yellow hair of the north. The physical attributes of a deity or a hero are usually to be regarded as those of the race to which he belongs. The golden locks of Apollo and Achilles are the sign of a similar characteristic in the nations of which they are the types; and the blue eye of Minerva belies the absurd doctrine that would identify her with the Egyptian Naith.

The Norman retained perhaps longer than the Scandinavian, from whom he sprang, the somewhat effeminate peculiarity of small hands and feet; and hence, as throughout all the nobility of Europe the Norman was the model for imitation, and the ruling families in many lands sought to trace from him their descents, so that characteristic is, even to our day, ridiculously regarded as a sign of noble race. The Norman probably retained that peculiarity longer than the Dane, because his habits, as a conqueror, made him disdain all manual labour; and it was below his knightly dignity to walk, as long as a horse could be found for him to ride. But the Anglo-Norman (the noblest specimen of the great conquering family) became so blent with the Saxon, both in blood and in habits, that such physical distinctions vanished with the age of chivalry. The Saxon blood in our highest aristocracy now predominates greatly over the Norman; and it would be as vain a task to identify the sons of Hastings and Rollo by the foot and hand of the old Asiatic Scythian, as by the reddish auburn hair and the high features which were no less ordinarily their type. Here and there such peculiarities may all be seen amongst plain country gentlemen, settled from time immemorial in the counties peopled by the Anglo-Danes, and intermarrying generally in their own provinces; but amongst the far more mixed breed of the larger landed proprietors comprehended in the Peerage, the Saxon attributes of race are strikingly conspicuous, and, amongst them, the large hand and foot common with all the Germanic tribes.

[1] Laing's Note to Snorro Sturleson, vol. iii. p. 101.

NOTE R, PAGE 181.

The Interment of Harold.

HERE we are met by evidences of the most contradictory character. According to most of the English writers, the body of Harold was given by William to Githa, without ransom, and buried at Waltham. There is even a story told of the generosity of the Conqueror, in cashiering a soldier who gashed the corpse of the dead hero. This last, however, seems to apply to some other Saxon, and not to Harold. But William of Poitiers, who was the duke's own chaplain, and whose narration of the battle appears to contain more internal evidence of accuracy than the rest of his chronicle, expressly says that William refused Githa's offer of its weight in gold for the supposed corpse of Harold, and ordered it to be buried on the beach, with the taunt quoted in the text of this work, " Let him guard the coast which he madly occupied ; " and on the pretext that one whose cupidity and avarice had been the cause that so many men were slaughtered and lay unsepultured was not worthy himself of a tomb. Orderic confirms this account, and says the body was given to William Mallet, for that purpose.[1]

Certainly William de Poitiers ought to have known best ; and the probability of his story is to a certain degree borne out by the uncertainty as to Harold's positive interment, which long prevailed, and which even gave rise to a story related by Giraldus Cambrensis (and to be found also in the Harleian Manuscripts), that Harold survived the battle, became a monk in Chester, and before he died had a long and secret interview with Henry the First. Such a legend, however absurd, could scarcely have gained any credit if (as the usual story runs) Harold had been formally buried, in the presence of many of the Norman barons, in Waltham Abbey ; but would very easily creep into belief, if his body had been carelessly consigned to a Norman knight, to be buried privately by the seashore.

---

[1] This William Mallet was the father of Robert Mallet, founder of the Priory of Eye, in Suffolk (a branch of the House of Mallet de Graville). — PLUQUET. He was also the ancestor of the great William Mallet (or Malet, as the old Scandinavian name was now corruptly spelled), one of the illustrious twenty-five " conservators " of Magna Charta. The family is still ex-. tant ; and I have to apologize to Sir Alexander Malet, Bart. (Her Majesty's Minister at Stutgard), Lieut.-Col. Charles St. Lo Malet, the Rev. William Windham Malet (Vicar of Ardley), and other members of that ancient House, for the liberty taken with the name of their gallant forefather

The story of Osgood and Ailred, the childemaister (schoolmaster in the monastery), as related by Palgrave, and used in this romance, is recorded in a Manuscript of Waltham Abbey, and was written somewhere about fifty or sixty years after the event, — say at the beginning of the twelfth century. These two monks followed Harold to the field, placed themselves so as to watch its results, offered ten marks for the body, obtained permission for the search, and could not recognize the mutilated corpse until Osgood sought and returned with Edith. In point of fact, according to this authority, it must have been two or three days after the battle before the discovery was made.

THE END.

www.ingramcontent.com/pod-product-compliance
Lightning Source LLC
Chambersburg PA
CBHW030741030726
47497CB00001B/86